D0931403

Library of America, a nonprofit organization,
champions our nation's cultural heritage
by publishing America's greatest writing in
authoritative new editions and providing resources
for readers to explore this rich, living legacy.

JOHN O'HARA

John O'Hara

STORIES

Charles McGrath, *editor*

THE LIBRARY OF AMERICA

Contents

On His Hands. 1

Early Afternoon. 4

It Must Have Been Spring. 8

Over the River and Through the Wood. 11

The Doctor's Son 18

Price's Always Open. 48

Are We Leaving Tomorrow? 55

The Cold House 60

Trouble in 1949 64

Do You Like It Here? 73

Too Young 78

Bread Alone 82

The King of the Desert 86

Summer's Day 91

Graven Image 96

The Next-to-Last Dance of the Season 101

The Pretty Daughters 106

Common Sense Should Tell You 113

Ellie 119

The Moccasins. 124

A Phase of Life 130

Time to Go 138

Encounter: 1943. 142

The Heart of Lee W. Lee. 147

The War 154

The Time Element 158

Family Evening 166

Requiescat 170

Imagine Kissing Pete 178

Call Me, Call Me 238

Mrs. Stratton of Oak Knoll 245

You Can Always Tell Newark 301

In the Silence 316

Winter Dance 337

Appearances 344

Your Fah Neefah Neeface 353

Justice 363

The Lesson 389

Pat Collins 403

Agatha 460

Exterior: with Figure 473

The Flatted Saxophone 489

The Man on the Tractor 494

At the Window 506

The Answer Depends 516

Can I Stay Here? 524

I Spend My Days in Longing 534

I Can't Thank You Enough 547

In the Mist 557

Afternoon Waltz 570

The Assistant 598

Fatimas and Kisses.................................612

Natica Jackson....................................633

How Old, How Young 709

The Farmer.......................................718

We'll Have Fun....................................727

The Sun Room 742

A Man To Be Trusted..............................762

The Journey to Mount Clemens 784

Christmas Poem 795

Editor's Note 809

Chronology.......................................813

Note on the Texts 833

Notes..837

On His Hands

SLOANE slouched back in his chair and regarded his demitasse, the while he paused in his narrative. He was pensive. He bit his lower lip and slowly shook his head.

"So I think the poor kid liked me pretty much," said Sloane.

His companion was impressed and sympathetic. "It certainly sounds that way, Tod," said Blakely. "I think I know how you feel. I know I—"

Sloane disregarded Blakely's comment. "She said she'd resign from college and marry me right away," Sloane went on. "She told me that when I had her down for the Navy game. Yep. Even then she wanted to quit college. Which, of course, would have meant my quitting too. But I'm not the kind of a guy to wreck two lives that way. I mean to say, what would we have lived on? If the family stopped my allowance now, why, I wouldn't have a cent till I'm twenty-one, see?"

"Yeah," said Blakely, "that's the hell of it. I know I practically had—"

"So I didn't want to get off on the wrong foot about this thing and wreck two lives. This love-in-a-cottage stuff is swell—if you have the cottage. But for God's sake, I owe Wetzel four hundred dollars, and around college I owe another four hundred dollars or five hundred dollars. See, it wouldn't have been fair to myself, and it wouldn't have been fair to this poor kid. I couldn't earn my living right off the bat. There wasn't any use making us both unhappy on account of money. So I figured out, why not take a look at her family? Get the dope on what kind of people she comes from. Then if they looked O.K., why, I could talk to my Old Man and maybe they'd let us get married and give us something to start on."

"That was sensible," said Blakely.

"Uh-huh," conceded Sloane. "So at Christmas I told the Old Man I was going out to Chicago to visit the Tuckers."

"Oh, yes. Elinor Tucker. Sure, I know Elinor. Swell girl."

Sloane glared. "Well, yes. Not only Elinor, though. The whole family. My Old Man and Mr. Tucker went to college together, and I went to prep school with Brick Tucker. So I said I was going out there and I wired Brick all about what I was going to do, so he wouldn't spill the beans, and off I went to Dayton, Ohio." Sloane smiled reminiscently and shook his head.

"Well, she met me at the station, in a 1921 Pierce limousine. That was a pretty good start, because no damn *nouveau-riche* family has a 1921 Pierce limousine. They'd have a brand-new shiny wagon, all brass. So that old Pierce was a good sign. But still there was that unfortunate name. You couldn't tell if she was one of the real old German families or just a pork-packer's daughter.

"Anyhow, it was about three in the afternoon, and we drove out to the country club, instead of going right to her house. We had quite a scene. Poor kid.

"Then we went to her house to dress for some party. The little I saw of the house was O.K. Nice furniture and nice magazines lying around and so on. But I didn't see anybody but her father. Her mother was at a bridge and her kid sister was at dancing school. Which didn't prove anything, because out there every respectable kid in town gets invited to dancing school. But her father was the guy that had me guessing.

"I met him just as I came downstairs. The babe was still dressing, so when I went in the library her father was there. He looked up and smiled and reached out his paw and said, 'Hello there, my boy. You're the Tod Sloane I've been hearing so much about.' So he told me to sit down and asked me if I wanted a drink or a butt. Made me feel at home. We talked about nothing particular, but he kept up that 'my boy' stuff. Why, my Old Man never called me 'my boy' in his whole life. Gauss calls me 'my boy' when he's on the verge of firing me the hell out of college. But I couldn't dope this guy. I thought maybe the babe maybe dropped a hint that we were going to get married, but I couldn't be sure.

"Well, I didn't find out much more. The babe's father went to M.I.T., which might make him a Cabot or an ironworker, and I didn't have the nerve to ask where he went to prep school. Then the kid herself appeared and we went to this party.

"The party didn't prove anything either. It was a swell party. Good food, and champagne—which I never touch—and a good band. Saw a couple people from Princeton but nobody I really knew. The right kind of people were nice to the kid and she was cut in on all the time, but that only proved something I know, namely, that she is a damned attractive babe. Why else would I bother with her?

"I stayed in dear old Dayton, Ohio, two days, and if you must know, didn't learn a god-damn thing. Of course, then I had to go to Chicago because that's where I told the family I was going.

"Don't let anybody kid you about Chicago. It's a swell Princeton town, Chicago. Naturally I played around with Elinor Tucker while I was there. Then I came back to New York until college opened, meanwhile writing to the babe in Dayton and she writing to me. We planned to meet in New York either in January, if she could make it, or February.

"Well, one thing and another came up and we didn't get to see each other in New York. I think the poor kid sort of suspected that I wasn't so sure about her family. In any case, the whole affair just dwindled away to nothing. I haven't laid eyes on her since I was in Dayton. And who do you think I've been seeing every time I get up to New York? . . . Elinor Tucker! Absolutely. She's going to a Miss Comstock's music school. Just an excuse to be in New York, of course."

"Elinor's in New York, eh?" Blakely asked. "Say, tell me. How's Elinor?"

Sloane looked intently, kindly at Blakely, and smiled. "Well, to tell you the truth, Blake, the first thing I know I'll have *her* on my hands!"

Early Afternoon

"GOOD AFTERNOON, Mr. Grant. Home early." Mike, the doorman, smiled as usual. "Mrs. Grant left about an hour or so ago."

"Did she?" said Grant, casually. He got into the elevator and was aware that he was glad she had gone. He could have a little peace before telling her that he had been fired. God knows he would have no peace today anyhow, even if he had not been fired. He had behaved pretty badly last night, and in a way, being tight was no excuse. Or at least people always said it was no excuse: the people who got tight and did awful things always said that. "I'm sorry about last night," they always said. "I was tight, but I know that's no excuse." Why wasn't it? Because you were supposed to be able to hold your liquor like a gentleman, and not fight, or not kiss someone else's girl, or not sing loudly? What about the hearty stories of the gentlemen in, say, Washington's time, or when knighthood was in flower? If you could believe the stories they certainly were more gentlemen than men are today, and yet if you could believe all of the stories, those gentlemen certainly misbehaved. They fought just as quickly and with worse results than people do today. And if they didn't kiss any oftener, they did kiss as often. Oh, well; what the hell?

Grant entered the apartment and called: "Are you home, kid?" and then remembered that Mike said she had gone out. He threw his hat across the room; a bad shot; it knocked an ash tray off an end-table. He let his hat and the ash tray lie, and went to the bedroom.

He took off his coat and vest, tie and shoes. He opened the collar of his shirt and let down his suspenders. He unbuttoned the top button of his trunks and lay back with his hands under his head. He stretched, and deliciously was drained of tiredness for the moment. It made him more awake, made him feel less like sleeping than he had felt all day, and he frowned mentally, because he wanted to sleep. Pretty soon he was asleep. . . . He awoke. He did not know why; then was about to ascribe it to a stiff arm, when he blinked his eyes. The sun was shining in on the bed, and while he was lying down it got him in the eyes. He looked at his watch, and it was only a quarter of three. Asleep hardly more than half an hour. He shouldn't have eaten so much lunch. Well, what to do now? Read? No. Go to the club? No, not at this hour; it would mean meeting the mid-afternoon crowd, which implicitly meant a bender. He could have a drink here instead.

He went to the kitchen and made a highball, then a second, and that finished the ginger ale, so he had a straight rye with water for a chaser. He took the bottle and a glass of water and the measuring glass and returned to the living-room and sat down in "his" chair. He was sorry about last night. In the first place, Bliss Hansen was too nice a girl to make passes at when you were tight, especially if you didn't make them when you were sober, and he hadn't made any passes at Bliss, drunk or sober, since she had been a sophomore at Northampton and he a freshman at Hanover. Bliss was a really swell girl. She didn't like Nancy, but she made a good bluff of liking her. He was sorry, too, because he had made Nancy sore. He was exactly as sorry for having annoyed Nancy as he was for being so damned casual with Bliss. He got a sudden picture of Bliss. She had gray, gray eyes, and almost-black hair. Between the inside ends of her eyebrows and the beginning of her nose there was a sort of dark triangle that made her look as though she were frown-ing, or quizzical, or something. The fact was that she wasn't frowning, but was nearly always ready to break into a smile.

It might be—it *was*—a very good idea to call Bliss. Not to tell her he was sorry; she would know that. But, by God, to go over and see her. And kiss her while he was sober. That would make everything all right, would prove to her that he was just as eager to kiss her now as when he was tight. It would, after all, do no one any harm, and he and Bliss could have a drink together. She would meet him at the door, with one hand on the door, and say: "Oh, the Fuller Brush man?" or something like that. No reference to last night, and no strong feeling that there ought to be any reference to last night. She would be surprised, undoubtedly, but she would not make both of them bother about bantering excuses for his coming to see her, or make them feel that they were avoiding an explanation. He picked up the phone.

He heard the dit-dit signal when the operator repeated the number, and he heard the mechanical buzz as the number was being rung. And rung. And rung. He must have waited minutes, but there was no answer. It was less than passing strange that Bliss should not answer, but it was far from pleasing. "Nuts," he said, to the telephone.

He went back to his bed and lit a cigarette. . . . He could go to the club and instead of going to the bar, why, play backgammon or bridge. Yes, he could. Like hell he could. He was out of a job. He could imagine Nancy if he got home at about six, having lost twenty bucks, and he would have to tell her he had been fired. . . . "Oh, fine," she would say. "You lost your job, so I suppose you thought you would play backgammon and make us a lot of money." She was, more's the pity, right. Or would be. He never won.

"Yes," he said aloud. "That's the way she'd say it." He wished she weren't always so right about things like that, so perfectly justified. He wished his father would give him some more money. He would do anything in the world to be able to give Nancy a nice pile of dough and let her go. After two years and five–six months it was a bust. "Oh, I know it's my fault," he said, again aloud. He lay back and dinched the cigarette in an ash tray on the night table that stood between his and Nancy's beds. He looked around idly, blankly, at the pictures on the wall. He was waiting, he realized, with the casualness of one who is waiting for someone who will be along in ten or fifteen minutes.

There was, presently, the sound of a key in the lock. Nancy. It seemed a rather long time that Nancy was holding the door, but at last he heard the click-and-thump sound that modern apartment doors make.

"Hello," he called. He spun himself to a sitting position, and began to fix himself up.

"Hello," she answered, from the living-room.

"What have you been up to?"

"Nothing much," she said. "Muddy Rhodes called up and wanted me to go to lunch with him; but I wasn't so hungry so he took me to Twenty-One for a drink."

She came in the bedroom, a cigarette in her hand. With her free hand she took off her hat and ruffled her hair evenly. She leaned close to a mirror and looked at her clenched teeth, then she sat down on the window-seat and smoked, swinging her very pretty legs. "Why are you home? Were you fired?"

He looked up quickly. "Yes. How'd you know?"

"Why else would you be home? Are you going to get tight? I see you've been making a dent in my rye."

"Listen, kid. I'm terribly sorry about last night. I really am. I don't blame you for going out with Muddy. I deserved it."

"Deserved it? What on earth are you talking about? Deserved what? Lord God, can't I go to a speakeasy with one of your best friends without your saying you had it coming to you, as though I were punishing you? Have some sense."

He got up and put on his tie and vest and coat. There was complete silence while he dressed. Then she said: "Listen, Buzz, if they fired you they must have given you a couple of weeks' pay, so give me a hundred dollars before you go out and spend it all, will you please? We'll need it."

He smiled broadly and went to her and kissed her. "Oh, I do love you, kid. You love me, don't you, really?"

"Look out for my cigarette," she said.

It Must Have Been Spring

IT MUST have been one of the very first days of spring. I was wearing my boots and my new corduroy habit, and carrying my spurs in my pocket. I always carried my spurs on the way to the stable, because it was eight squares from home to the stable, and I usually had to pass a group of newsboys on the way, and when I wore the spurs they would yell at me, even my friends among them. The spurs seemed to make a difference. The newsboys were used to seeing me in riding breeches and boots or leather puttees, but when I wore the spurs they always seemed to notice it, and they would yell "Cowboy-crazy!", and once I got in a fight about it and got a tooth knocked out. It was not only because I hated what they called me. I hated their ignorance; I could not stop and explain to them that I was not cowboy-crazy, that I rode an English saddle and posted to the trot. I could not explain to a bunch of newsboys that Julia was a five-gaited mare, a full sister to Golden Firefly, and that she herself could have been shown if she hadn't had a blanket scald.

This day that I remember, which must have been one of the very first days of spring, becomes clearer in my memory. I remember the sounds: the woop-woop of my new breeches each time I took a step, and the clop sound of the draught horses' hooves in the thawed ground of the streets. The draught horses were pulling wagon-loads of coal from the near-by mines up the hill, and when they got halfway up the driver would give them a rest; there would be a ratchety noise as he pulled on the brake, and then the sound of the breast chains and trace chains loosening up while the horses rested. Then presently the loud slap of the brake handle against the iron guard, and the driver yelling "Gee opp!", and then the clop sound again as the horses' hooves sank into the sloppy roadway.

My father's office was on the way to the stable, and we must have been at peace that day. Oh, I know we were, because I remember it was the first time I wore the new breeches and jacket. They had come from Philadelphia that day. At school, which was across the street from our house, I had looked out the window and there was Wanamaker's truck in front of our house, and I knew that The Things had come. Probably crates and burlap rolls containing furniture and rugs and other things that did not concern me; but also a box in which I knew would be my breeches and jacket. I went home for dinner, at noon, but there was no time for me to try on the new things until after school. Then I did hurry home and changed, because I thought I might find my father in his office if I hurried, although it would be after office hours, and I wanted him to see me in the new things.

Now, I guess my mother had telephoned him to wait, but then I only knew that when I got within two squares of the office, he came out and stood on the porch. He was standing with his legs spread apart, with his hands dug deep in his hip pockets and the skirt of his tweed coat stuck out behind like a sparrow's tail. He was wearing a gray soft hat with a black ribbon and with white piping around the edge of the brim. He was talking across the street to Mr. George McRoberts, the lawyer, and his teeth gleamed under his black mustache. He glanced in my direction and saw me and nodded, and put one foot up on the porch seat and went on talking until I got there.

I moved toward him, as always, with my eyes cast down, and I felt my riding crop getting sticky in my hand and I changed my grip on it and held the bone handle. I never could tell anything by my father's nod, whether he was pleased with me or otherwise. As I approached him, I had no way of telling whether he was pleased with me for something or annoyed because someone might have told him they had seen me smoking. I had a package of Melachrinos in my pocket, and I wanted to throw them in the Johnstons' garden, but it was too late now; I was in plain sight. He would wait until I got there, even though he might only nod again when I did, as he sometimes did.

I stood at the foot of the porch. "Hello," I said.

He did not answer me for a few seconds. Then he said, "Come up here till I have a look at you."

I went up on the porch. He looked at my boots. "Well," he said. "Did you polish them?"

"No. I had Mike do it. I charged it. It was a quarter, but you said—"

"I know. Well, you look all right. How are the breeches?

You don't want to get them too tight across the knee or they'll hurt you."

I raised my knees to show him that the breeches felt all right.

"Mm-hmm," he said. And then, "Good Lord!" He took off his hat and laid it on the porch seat, and then began to tie my stock over again. I never did learn to tie it the way he wanted it, the way it should have been. Now I was terribly afraid, because he could always smell smoke—he didn't smoke himself—and I remembered I had had a cigarette at recess. But he finished tying the stock and then drew away and commenced to smile.

He called across the street to Mr. McRoberts. "Well, George. How does he look?"

"Like a million, Doctor. Regular English country squire, eh?"

"English, hell!"

"Going horseback riding?" said Mr. McRoberts to me.

"Yes," I said.

"Wonderful exercise. How about you, Doctor? You ought to be going, too."

"Me? I'm a working man. I'm going to trephine a man at four-thirty. No, this is the horseman in my family. Best horseman in Eastern Pennsylvania," said my father. He turned to me. "Where to this afternoon? See that the mare's hooves are clean and see if that nigger is bedding her the way I told him. Give her a good five-mile exercise out to Indian Run and then back the Old Road. All right."

I started to go. I went down the porch steps and we both said goodbye, and then, when I was a few steps away, he called to me to wait.

"You look fine," he said. "You really look like something. Here." He gave me a five-dollar bill. "Save it. Give it to your mother to put in the bank for you."

"Thank you," I said, and turned away, because suddenly I was crying. I went up the street to the stable with my head bent down, because I could let the tears roll right out of my eyes and down to the ground without putting my hand up to my face. I knew he was still looking.

Over the River and Through the Wood

M R. WINFIELD'S hat and coat and bag were in the hall of his flat, and when the man downstairs phoned to tell him the car was waiting, he was all ready. He went downstairs and said hello to Robert, the giant Negro chauffeur, and handed Robert the bag, and followed him out to the car. For the first time he knew that he and his granddaughter were not to make the trip alone, for there were two girls with Sheila, and she introduced them: "Grandfather, I'd like to have you meet my friends. This is Helen Wales, and this is Kay Farnsworth. My grandfather, Mr. Winfield." The names meant nothing to Mr. Winfield. What did mean something was that he was going to have to sit on the strapontin, or else sit outside with Robert, which was no good. Not that Robert wasn't all right, as chauffeurs go, but Robert was wearing a raccoon coat, and Mr. Winfield had no raccoon coat. So it was sit outside and freeze or sit on the little seat inside.

Apparently it made no difference to Sheila. He got inside, and when he closed the door behind him, she said, "I wonder what's keeping Robert?"

"He's strapping my bag on that thing in the back," said Mr. Winfield. Sheila obviously was not pleased by the delay, but in a minute or two they got under way, and Mr. Winfield rather admired the way Sheila carried on her conversation with her two friends and at the same time routed and rerouted Robert so that they were out of the city in no time. To Mr. Winfield it was pleasant and a little like old times to have the direction and the driving done for you. Not that he ever drove himself any more, but when he hired a car, he always had to tell the driver just where to turn and where to go straight. Sheila knew.

The girls were of an age, and the people they talked about were referred to by first names only. Ted, Bob, Gwen, Jean, Mary, Liz. Listening with some care, Mr. Winfield discovered that school acquaintances and boys whom they knew slightly were mentioned by their last names.

Sitting where he was, he could not watch the girls' faces, but he formed his opinions of the Misses Wales and Farnsworth.

Miss Wales supplied every other word when Sheila was talking. She was smallest of the three girls, and the peppy kind. Miss Farnsworth looked out of the window most of the time, and said hardly anything. Mr. Winfield could see more of her face, and he found himself asking, "I wonder if that child really likes anybody." Well, that was one way to be. Make the world show *you*. You could get away with it, too, if you were as attractive as Miss Farnsworth. The miles streamed by and the weather got colder, and Mr. Winfield listened and soon understood that he was not expected to contribute to the conversation.

"We stop here," said Sheila. It was Danbury, and they came to a halt in front of the old hotel. "Wouldn't you like to stop here, Grandfather?" He understood then that his daughter had told Sheila to stop here; obediently and with no dignity he got out. When he returned to the car, the three girls were finishing their cigarettes, and as he climbed back in the car, he noticed how Miss Farnsworth had been looking at him and continued to look at him, almost as though she were making a point of not helping him—although he wanted no help. He wasn't really an *old* man, an *old man*. Sixty-five.

The interior of the car was filled with cigarette smoke, and Miss Farnsworth asked Mr. Winfield if he'd mind opening a window. He opened it. Then Sheila said one window didn't make any difference; open both windows, just long enough to let the smoke get out. "My! That air feels good," said Miss Wales. Then: "But what about you, Mr. Winfield? You're in a terrible draught there." He replied, for the first use of his voice thus far, that he did not mind. And at that moment the girls thought they saw a car belonging to a boy they knew, and they were in Sheffield, just over the Massachusetts line, before Miss Farnsworth realized that the windows were open and creating a terrible draught. She realized it when the robe slipped off her leg, and she asked Mr. Winfield if he would mind closing the window. But he was unable to get the crank started; his hands were so cold there was no strength in them. "We'll be there soon," said Sheila. Nevertheless, she closed the windows, not even acknowledging Mr. Winfield's shamed apologies.

He had to be first out of the car when they arrived at the house in Lenox, and it was then that he regretted having chosen the strapontin. He started to get out of the car, but when his feet touched the ground, the hard-packed frozen cinders of the driveway flew up at him. His knees had no strength in them, and he stayed there on the ground for a second or two, trying to smile it off. Helpful Robert—almost too helpful; Mr. Winfield wasn't that old—jumped out of the car and put his hands in Mr. Winfield's armpits. The girls were frightened, but it seemed to Mr. Winfield that they kept looking toward the library window, as though they were afraid Sheila's mother would be there and blaming them for his fall. If they only knew . . .

"You go on in, Grandfather, if you're sure you're all right," said Sheila. "I have to tell Robert about the bags."

"I'm all right," said Mr. Winfield. He went in, and hung up his coat and hat in the clothes closet under the stairs. A telephone was there, and in front of the telephone a yellow card of numbers frequently called. Mr. Winfield recognized only a few of the names, but he guessed there was an altogether different crowd of people coming up here these days. Fifteen years make a difference, even in a place like Lenox. Yes, it was fifteen years since he had been up here in the summertime. These trips, these annual trips for Thanksgiving, you couldn't tell anything about the character of the place from these trips. You never saw anybody but your own family and, like today, their guests.

He went out to the darkened hall and Ula, the maid, jumped in fright. "Ugh. Oh. It's you, Mr. Winfield. You like to scare me."

"Hello, Ula. Glad to see you're still holding the fort. Where's Mrs. Day?"

"Upstairs, I think . . . Here she is now," said Ula.

His daughter came down the steps; her hand on the banister was all he could see at first. "Is that you, Father? I thought I heard the car."

"Hello, Mary," he said. At the foot of the stairs they went through the travesty of a kiss that both knew so well. He leaned forward so that his head was above her shoulder. To Ula, a good Catholic, it must have looked like the kiss of peace. "*Pax tibi*," Mr. Winfield felt like saying, but he said, "Where have you—"

"Father! You're freezing!" Mrs. Day tried very hard to keep the vexation out of her tone.

"It was a cold ride," he said. "This time of year. We had snow flurries between Danbury and Sheffield, but the girls enjoyed it."

"You go right upstairs and have a bath, and I'll send up—what would you like? Tea? Chocolate? Coffee?"

He was amused. The obvious thing would be to offer him a drink, and it was so apparent that she was talking fast to avoid that. "I think cocoa would be fine, but you'd better have a real drink for Sheila and her friends."

"Now, why do you take that tone, Father? You could have a drink if you wanted it, but you're on the wagon, aren't you?"

"Still on it. Up there with the driver."

"Well, and besides, liquor doesn't warm you up the same way something hot does. I'll send up some chocolate. I've put you in your old room, of course. You'll have to share the bathroom with one of Sheila's friends, but that's the best I could do. Sheila wasn't even sure she was coming till the very last minute."

"I'll be all right. It sounds like—I didn't bring evening clothes."

"We're not dressing."

He went upstairs. His room, the room itself, was just about the same; but the furniture was rearranged, his favorite chair not where he liked it best, but it was a good house; you could tell it was being lived in, *this year*, today, tomorrow. Little touches, ashtrays, flowers. It seemed young and white, cool with a warm breath, comfortable—and absolutely strange to him and, more especially, he to it. Whatever of the past this house had held, it was gone now. He sat in the chair and lit a cigarette. In a wave, in a lump, in a gust, the old thoughts came to him. Most of the year they were in the back of his mind, but up here Mr. Winfield held a sort of annual review of far-off, but never-out-of-sight regrets. This house, it used to be his until Mary's husband bought it. A good price, and in 1921 he certainly needed the money. He needed everything, and today he had an income from the money he got for this house, and that was about all. He remembered the day Mary's husband came to him and said, "Mr. Winfield, I hate to have to be the one to do this, but Mary—Mary doesn't—well, she thinks you weren't very nice to Mrs. Winfield. I don't know anything about it myself, of course, but that's what Mary thinks. I expected, naturally, I thought you'd come and live with us now that Mrs. Winfield has died, but—well, the point is, I know you've lost a lot of money, and also I happen to know about Mrs. Winfield's will. So I'm prepared to make you a pretty good offer, strictly legitimate based on current values, for the house in Lenox. I'll pay the delinquent taxes myself and give you a hundred and fifty thousand dollars for the house and grounds. That ought to be enough to pay off your debts and give you a fairly decent income. And, uh, I happen to have a friend who knows Mr. Harding quite well. Fact, he sees the President informally one night a week, and I know he'd be only too glad, if you were interested . . ."

He remembered how that had tempted him. Harding might have fixed it so he could go to London, where Enid Walter was. But even then it was too late. Enid had gone back to London because he didn't have the guts to divorce his wife, and the reason he wouldn't divorce his wife was that he wanted to "protect" Mary, and Mary's standing, and Mary's husband's standing, and Mary's little daughter's standing; and now he was "protecting" them all over again, by selling his house so that he would not become a family charge—protecting the very same people from the embarrassment of a poor relation. "You can have the house," he told Day. "It's worth that much, but no more, and I'm grateful to you for not offering me more. About a political job, I think I might like to go to California this winter. I have some friends out there I haven't seen in years." He had known that that was exactly what Mary and her husband wanted, so he'd gone.

There was a knock on the door. It was Ula with a tray. "Why two cups, Ula?" he said.

"Oh. Di put two cups? So I did. I'm just so used to putting two cups." She had left the door open behind her, and as she arranged the things on the marble-topped table he saw Sheila and the two girls, standing and moving in the hall.

"This is your room, Farnie," said Sheila. "You're down this way, Helen. Remember what I told you, Farnie. Come on, Helen."

"Thank you, Ula," he said. She went out and closed the door, and he stood for a moment, contemplating the chocolate, then poured out a cup and drank it. It made him a little thirsty, but it was good and warming, and Mary was right; it was better than a drink. He poured out another cup and nibbled on a biscuit. He had an idea: Miss Farnsworth might like some. He admired that girl. She had spunk. He bet she knew what she wanted, or seemed to, and no matter how unimportant were the things she wanted, they were the things she wanted, and not someone else. She could damn well thank the Lord, too, that she was young enough to have a whack at whatever she wanted, and not have to wait the way he had. That girl would make up her mind about a man or a fortune or a career, and by God she would attain whatever it was. If she found, as she surely would find, that nothing ever was enough, she'd at least find it out in time; and early disillusionment carried a compensatory philosophical attitude, which in a hard girl like this one would take nothing from her charm. Mr. Winfield felt her charm, and began regarding her as the most interesting person he had met in many dull years. It would be fun to talk to her, to sound her out and see how far she had progressed toward, say, ambition or disillusionment. It would be fun to do, and it would be just plain nice of him, as former master of this house, to invite her to have a cup of cocoa with him. Good cocoa.

He made his choice between going out in the hall and knocking on her door, and knocking on her door to the bathroom. He decided on the second procedure because he didn't want anyone to see him knocking on her door. So he entered the bathroom and tapped on the door that led to her room. "In a minute," he thought he heard her say. But then he knew he must have been wrong. It sounded more like "Come in." He hated people who knocked on doors and had to be told two or three times to come in, and it would make a bad impression if he started the friendship that way.

He opened the door, and immediately he saw how right he had been in thinking she had said "In a minute." For Miss Farnsworth was standing in the middle of the room, standing there all but nude. Mr. Winfield instantly knew that this was the end of any worthwhile life he had left. There was cold murder in the girl's eyes, and loathing and contempt and the promise of the thought his name forever would evoke. She spoke to him: "Get out of here, you dirty old man."

He returned to his room and his chair. Slowly he took a cigarette out of his case, and did not light it. He did everything slowly. There was all the time in the world, too much of it, for him. He knew it would be hours before he would begin to hate himself. For a while he would just sit there and plan his own terror.

The Doctor's Son

M Y FATHER came home at four o'clock one morning in the fall of 1918, and plumped down on a couch in the living-room. He did not get awake until he heard the noise of us getting breakfast and getting ready to go to school, which had not yet closed down. When he got awake he went out front and shut off the engine of the car, which had been running while he slept, and then he went to bed and stayed, sleeping for nearly two days. Up to that morning he had been going for nearly three days with no more than two hours' sleep at a stretch.

There were two ways to get sleep. At first he would get it by going to his office, locking the rear office door, and stretching out on the floor or on the operating table. He would put a re-volver on the floor beside him or in the tray that was bracketed to the operating table. He had to have the revolver, because here and there among the people who would come to his office, there would be a wild man or woman, threatening him, shouting that they would not leave until he left with them, and that if their baby died they would come back and kill him. The revolver, lying on the desk, kept the more violent patients from becoming too violent, but it really did no good so far as my father's sleep was concerned; not even a doctor who had kept going for days on coffee and quinine would use a revolver on an Italian who had just come from a bedroom where the last of five children was being strangled by influenza. So my father, with a great deal of profanity, would make it plain to the Italian that he was not being intimidated, but would go, and go without sleep.

There was one other way of getting sleep. We owned the building in which he had his office, so my father made an ar-rangement with one of the tenants, a painter and paperhanger, so he could sleep in the room where the man stored rolls of wallpaper. This was a good arrangement, but by the time he had thought of it, my father's strength temporarily gave out and he had to come home and go to bed.

Meanwhile there was his practice, which normally was about

forty patients a day, including office calls and operations, but which he had lost count of since the epidemic had become really bad. Ordinarily if he had been ill his practice would have been taken over by one of the young physicians; but now every young doctor was as busy as the older men. Italians who knew me would even ask me to prescribe for their children, simply because I was the son of Mister Doctor Malloy. Young general practitioners who would have had to depend upon friends of their families and fraternal orders and accidents and gonorrhea for their start, were seeing—hardly more than seeing—more patients in a day than in normal times they could have hoped to see in a month.

The mines closed down almost with the first whiff of influenza. Men who for years had been drilling rock and had chronic miner's asthma never had a chance against the mysterious new disease; and even younger men were keeling over, so the coal companies had to shut down the mines, leaving only maintenance men, such as pump men, in charge. Then the Commonwealth of Pennsylvania closed down the schools and churches, and forbade all congregating. If you wanted an ice cream soda you had to have it put in a cardboard container; you couldn't have it at the fountain in a glass. We were glad when school closed, because it meant a holiday, and the epidemic had touched very few of us. We lived in Gibbsville; it was in the tiny mining villages—"patches"—that the epidemic was felt immediately.

The State stepped in, and when a doctor got sick or exhausted so he literally couldn't hold his head up any longer, they would send a young man from the graduating class of one of the Philadelphia medical schools to take over the older man's practice. This was how Doctor Myers came to our town. I was looking at the pictures of the war in the *Review of Reviews*, my father's favorite magazine, when the doorbell rang and I answered it. The young man looked like the young men who came to our door during the summer selling magazines. He was wearing a short coat with a sheepskin collar, which I recognized as an S. A. T. C. issue coat.

"Is this Doctor Malloy's residence?" he said.

"Yes."

"Well, I'm Mr. Myers from the University."

"Oh," I said. "My father's expecting you." I told my father, and he said: "Well, why didn't you bring him right up?"

Doctor Myers went to my father's bedroom and they talked, and then the maid told me my father wanted to speak to me. When I went to the bedroom I could see my father and Doctor Myers were getting along nicely. That was natural: my father and Doctor Myers were University men, which meant the University of Pennsylvania; and University men shared a contempt for men who had studied at Hahnemann or Jefferson or Medico-Chi. Myers was not an M.D., but my father called him Doctor, and as I had been brought up to tip my hat to a doctor as I did to a priest, I called him Doctor too, although Doctor Myers made me feel like a lumberjack; I was so much bigger and obviously stronger than he. I was fifteen years old.

"Doctor Myers, this is my boy James," my father said, and without waiting for either of us to acknowledge the introduction, he went on: "Doctor Myers will be taking over my practice for the time being and you're to help him. Take him down to Hendricks' drug store and introduce him to Mr. Hendricks. Go over the names of our patients and help him arrange some kind of a schedule. Doctor Myers doesn't drive a car, you'll drive for him. Now your mother and I think the rest of the children ought to be on the farm, so you take them there in the big Buick and then bring it back and have it overhauled. Leave the little Buick where it is, and you use the Ford. You'll understand, Doctor, when you see our roads. If you want any money your mother'll give it to you. And no cigarettes, d'you understand?" Then he handed Doctor Myers a batch of prescription blanks, upon which were lists of patients to be seen, and said goodbye and lay back on his pillow for more sleep.

Doctor Myers was almost tiny, and that was the reason I could forgive him for not being in the Army. His hair was so light that you could hardly see his little moustache. In conversation between sentences his nostrils would twitch and like all doctors he had acquired a posed gesture which was becoming habitual. His was to stroke the skin in front of his right ear with his forefinger. He did that now downstairs in the hall. "Well . . . I'll just take a walk back to the hotel and wait till you get back from the farm. That suit you, James?" It did, and he left and I performed the various chores my father had ordered, and then I went to the hotel in the Ford and picked up Doctor Myers.

He was catlike and dignified when he jumped in the car. "Well, here's a list of names. Where do you think we ought to go first? Here's a couple of prescription blanks with only four names apiece. Let's clean them up first."

"Well, I don't know about that, Doctor. Each one of those names means at least twenty patients. For instance Kelly's. That's a saloon, and there'll be a lot of people waiting. They all meet there and wait for my father. Maybe we'd better go to some single calls first."

"O.K., James. Here's a list." He handed it to me. "Oh, your father said something about going to Collieryville to see a family named Evans."

I laughed. "Which Evans? There's seventy-five thousand Evanses in Collieryville. Evan Evans. William W. Evans. Davis W. Evans. Davis W. Evans, Junior. David Evans?"

"David Evans sounds like it. The way your father spoke they were particular friends of his."

"David Evans," I said. "Well—he didn't say who's sick there, did he?"

"No. I don't think anybody. He just suggested we drop in to see if they're all well."

I was relieved, because I was in love with Edith Evans. She was nearly two years older than I, but I liked girls a little older. I looked at his list and said: "I think the best idea is to go there first and then go around and see some of the single cases in Collieryville." He was ready to do anything I suggested. He was affable and trying to make me feel that we were pals, but I could tell he was nervous, and I had sense enough to know that he had better look at some flu before tackling one of those groups at the saloons.

We drove to Collieryville to the David Evans home. Mr. Evans was district superintendent of one of the largest mining corporations, and therefore Collieryville's third citizen. He would not be there all the time, because he was a good man and due for promotion to a bigger district, but so long as he was there he was ranked with the leading doctor and the leading lawyer. After him came the Irish priest, the cashier of the larger bank (of which the doctor or the lawyer or the superintendent of the mines is president), the brewer, and the leading merchant. David Evans had been born in Collieryville, the son of a superintendent, and was popular, a thirty-second degree Mason, a graduate of Lehigh, and a friend of my father's. They would see each other less than ten times a year, but they would go hunting rabbit and quail and pheasant together every autumn and always exchanged expensive Christmas gifts. When my mother had large parties she would invite Mrs. Evans, but the two women were not close friends. Mrs. Evans was a Collieryville girl, half Polish, and my mother had gone to an expensive school and spoke French, and played bridge long before Mrs. Evans had learned to play "500." The Evanses had two children: Edith, my girl, and Rebecca, who was about five.

The Evans Cadillac, which was owned by the coal company, was standing in front of the Evans house, which also was owned by the coal company. I called to the driver, who was sitting behind the steering wheel, hunched up in a sheepskin coat and with a checkered cap pulled down over his eyes. "What's the matter, Pete?" I called. "Can't the company get rid of that old Caddy?"

"Go on wid you," said Pete. "What's the wrong wid the doctorin' business? I notice Mike Malloy ain't got nothin' better than Buicks."

"I'll have you fired, you round-headed son of a bitch," I said. "Where's the big lad?"

"Up Mike's. Where'd you t'ink he is?"

I parked the Ford and Doctor Myers and I went to the door and were let in by the pretty Polish maid. Mr. Evans came out of his den, wearing a raccoon coat and carrying his hat. I introduced Doctor Myers. "How do you do, sir," he said. "Doctor Malloy just asked me to stop in and see if everything was all right with your family."

"Oh, fine," said Mr. Evans. "Tell the dad that was very thoughtful, James, and thank you too, Doctor. We're all O.K. here, thank the Lord, but while you're here I'd like to have you meet Mrs. Evans. Adele!"

Mrs. Evans called from upstairs that she would be right down. While we waited in the den Mr. Evans offered Doctor Myers a cigar, which was declined. Doctor Myers, I could see, preferred to sit, because Mr. Evans was so large that he had to look up to him. While Mr. Evans questioned him about his knowledge of the anthracite region, Doctor Myers spoke with a barely discernible pleasant hostility which was lost on Mr. Evans, the simplest of men. Mrs. Evans appeared in a house dress. She looked at me shyly, as she always did. She always embarrassed me, because when I went in a room where she was sitting she would rise to shake hands, and I would feel like telling her to sit down. She was in her middle thirties and still pretty, with rosy cheeks and pale blue eyes and nothing "foreign" looking about her except her high cheek bones and the lines of her eyebrows, which looked as though they had been drawn with crayon. She shook hands with Doctor Myers and then clasped her hands in front of her and looked at Mr. Evans when he spoke, and then at Doctor Myers and then at me, smiling and hanging on Mr. Evans' words. He was used to that. He gave her a half smile without looking at her and suggested we come back for dinner, which in Collieryville was at noon. Doctor Myers asked me if we would be in Collieryville at that time, and I said we would, so we accepted his invitation. Mr. Evans said: "That's fine. Sorry I won't be here, but I have to go to Wilkes-Barre right away." He looked at his watch. "By George! By now I ought to be half way there." He grabbed his hat and kissed his wife and left.

When he had gone Mrs. Evans glanced at me and smiled and then said: "Edith will be glad to see you, James."

"Oh, I'll bet she will," I said. "Where's she been keeping herself anyway?"

"Oh, around the house. She's my eldest," she said to Doctor Myers. "Seventeen."

"Seventeen?" he repeated. "You have a daughter seventeen? I can hardly believe it, Mrs. Evans. Nobody would ever think you had a daughter seventeen." His voice was a polite protest, but there was nothing protesting in what he saw in Mrs. Evans. I looked at her myself now, thinking of her for the first time as someone besides Edith's mother. . . . No, I couldn't see her. We left to make some calls, promising to be back at twelve-thirty.

Our first call was on a family named Loughran, who lived in a neat two-story house near the Collieryville railroad station. Doctor Myers went in. He came out in less than two minutes, followed by Mr. Loughran. Loughran walked over to me. "You," he said. "Ain't we good enough for your dad no more? What for kind of a thing is this he does be sending us?"

"My father is sick in bed, just like everybody else, Mr. Loughran. This is the doctor that is taking all his calls till he gets better."

"It is, is it? So that's what we get, and doctorin' with Mike Malloy sincet he come from college, and always paid the day after payday. Well, young man, take this back to Mike Malloy. You tell him for me if my woman pulls through it'll be no thanks to him. And if she don't pull through, and dies, I'll come right down to your old man's office and kill him wid a rock. Now you and this one get the hell outa here before I lose me patience."

We drove away. The other calls we made were less difficult, although I noticed that when he was leaving one or two houses the people, who were accustomed to my father's quick, brusque calls, would stare at Doctor Myers' back. He stayed too long, and probably was too sympathetic. We returned to the Evans home.

Mrs. Evans had changed her dress to one that I thought was a little too dressy for the occasion. She asked us if we wanted "a little wine," which we didn't, and Doctor Myers was walking around with his hands in his trousers pockets, telling Mrs. Evans what a comfortable place this was, when Edith appeared. I loved Edith, but the only times I ever saw her were at dancing school, to which she would come every Saturday afternoon. She was quite small, but long since her legs had begun to take shape and she had breasts. It was her father, I guess, who would not let her put her hair up; she often told me he was very strict and I knew that he was making her stay in Collieryville High School a year longer than was necessary because he thought her too young to go away. Edith called me Jimmy—one of the few who did. When we danced together at dancing school she scarcely spoke at all. I suspected her of regarding me as very young. All the little kids at dancing school called me James, and the oldest girls called me sarcastic. "James Malloy," they would say, "you think you're sarcastic. You think you're clever, but you're not. I consider the source of that remark." The remark might be that I had heard that Wallace Reid was waiting for that girl to grow up—and so was I. But I never said things like that to Edith. I would say: "How's everything out in the metropolis of Collieryville?" and she would say they were all right. It was no use trying to be sarcastic or clever with Edith, and no use trying to be romantic. One time I offered her the carnation that we had to wear at dancing school, and she refused it because the pin might tear her dress. It was useless to try to be dirty with her; there was no novelty in it for a girl who had gone to Collieryville High. I told her one story, and she said her grandmother fell out of the cradle laughing at that one.

When Edith came in she took a quick look at Doctor Myers which made me slightly jealous. He turned and smiled at her, and his nostrils began to twitch. Mrs. Evans rubbed her hands together nervously, and it was plain to see that she was not sure how to introduce Doctor Myers. Before she had a chance to make any mistakes I shook hands with Edith and she said, "Oh, hello, Jimmy," in a very offhand way, and I said: "Edith, this is Doctor Myers."

"How do you do?" said Edith.

"How are you?" said the doctor.

"Oh, very well, thank you," Edith said, and realized that it wasn't quite the thing to say.

"Well," said Mrs. Evans. "I don't know if you gentlemen want to wash up. Jimmy, you know where the bathroom is." It was the first time she had called me Jimmy. I glanced at her curiously and then the doctor and I went to wash our hands. Upstairs he said: "That your girl, James?"

"Oh, no," I said. "We're good friends. She isn't that kind."

"What kind? I didn't mean anything." He was amused.

"Well, I didn't know what you meant."

"Edith certainly looks like her mother," he said.

"Oh, I don't think so," I said, not really giving it a thought, but I was annoyed by the idea of talking about Edith in the bathroom. We came downstairs.

Dinner was a typical meal of that part of the country: sauerkraut and pork and some stuff called nep, which was nothing but dough, and mashed potatoes and lima beans, coffee, tea, and two kinds of pie, and you were expected to take both kinds. It was a meal I liked, and I ate a lot. Mrs. Evans got some courage from somewhere and was now talkative, now quiet, addressing most of her remarks to Doctor Myers and then turning to me. Edith kept looking at her and then turning to the doctor. She paid no attention to me except when I had something to say. Rebecca, whose table manners were being neglected, had nothing to contribute except to stick out her plate and say: "More mash potatoes with butter on."

"Say please," said Edith, but Rebecca only looked at her with the scornful blankness of five.

After dinner we went to the den and Doctor Myers and I smoked. I noticed he did not sit down; he was actually a little taller than Edith, and just about the same height as her mother. He walked around the room, standing in front of enlarged snapshots of long-deceased setter dogs, one of which my father had given Mr. Evans. Edith watched him and her mother and said nothing, but just before we were getting ready to leave Mrs. Evans caught Edith staring at her and they exchanged mysterious glances. Edith looked defiant and Mrs. Evans seemed puzzled and somehow alarmed. I could not figure it out.

II

In the afternoon Doctor Myers decided he would like to go to one of the patches where the practice of medicine was wholesale, so I suggested Kelly's. Kelly's was the only saloon in a patch of about one hundred families, mostly Irish, and all except one family were Catholics. In the spring they have processions in honor of the Blessed Virgin at Kelly's patch, and a priest carries the Blessed Sacrament the length of the patch, in the open air, to the public school grounds, where they hold Benediction. The houses are older and stauncher than in most patches, and they look like pictures of Ireland, except that there are no thatched roofs. Most patches were simply unbroken rows of company houses, made of slatty wood, but Kelly's had more ground between the houses and grass for the goats and cows to feed on, and the houses had plastered walls. Kelly's saloon was frequented by the whole patch because it was the postoffice substation, and it had a good reputation. For many years it had the only telephone in the patch.

Mr. Kelly was standing on the stoop in front of the saloon when I swung the Ford around. He took his pipe out of his mouth when he recognized the Ford, and then frowned slightly when he saw that my father was not with me. He came to my side of the car. "Where's the dad? Does he be down wid it now himself?"

"No," I said. "He's just all tired out and is getting some sleep. This is Doctor Myers that's taking his place till he gets better."

Mr. Kelly spat some tobacco juice on the ground and took a wad of tobacco out of his mouth. He was a white-haired, sickly man of middle age. "I'm glad to make your acquaintance," he said.

"How do you do, sir?" said Doctor Myers.

"I guess James here told you what to be expecting?"

"Well, more or less," said Doctor Myers. "Nice country out here. This is the nicest I've seen."

"Yes, all right I guess, but there does be a lot of sickness now. I guess you better wait a minute here till I have a few words with them inside there. I have to keep them orderly, y'understand."

He went in and we could hear his loud voice: ". . . young Malloy said his dad is seriously ill . . . great expense out of his own pocket secured a famous young specialist from Phil-adelphee so as to not have the people of the patch without a medical man . . . And any lug of a lunkhead that don't stay in line will have me to answer to . . ." Mr. Kelly then made the people line up and he came to the door and asked Doctor Myers to step in.

There were about thirty women in the saloon as Mr. Kelly guided Doctor Myers to an oilcloth-covered table. One Irish-man took a contemptuous look at Doctor Myers and said: "Jesus, Mary and Joseph," and walked out, sneering at me before he closed the door. The others probably doubted that the doctor was a famous specialist, but they had not had a doctor in two or three days. Two others left quietly but the rest remained. "I guess we're ready, Mr. Kelly," said Doctor Myers.

Most of the people were Irish, but there were a few Hunkies in the patch, although not enough to warrant Mr. Kelly's learning any of their languages as the Irish had had to do in certain other patches. It was easy enough to deal with the Irish: a woman would come to the table and describe for Doctor Myers the symptoms of her sick man and kids in language that was painfully polite. My father had trained them to use terms like "bowel movement" instead of those that came more quickly to mind. After a few such encounters and wasting a lot of time, Doctor Myers more or less got the swing of pre-scribing for absent patients. I stood leaning against the bar, taking down the names of patients I didn't know by sight, and wishing I could have a cigarette, but that was out of the question because Mr. Kelly did not approve of cigarettes and might have told my father. I was standing there when the first of the Hunkie women had her turn. She was a worried-looking woman who even I could see was pregnant and had been many times before, judging by her breasts. She had on a white knit-ted cap and a black silk shirtwaist—nothing underneath—and a nondescript skirt. She was wearing a man's overcoat and a pair of Pacs, which are short rubber boots that men wear in the mines. When Doctor Myers spoke to her she became voluble in her own tongue. Mr. Kelly interrupted: "Wait a minute, wait a minute," he said. "You sick?"

"No, no. No me sick. Man sick." She lapsed again into her own language.

"She has a kid can speak English," said Mr. Kelly. "Hey, you. Leetle girl Mary, you daughter, her sick?" He made so-high with his hand. The woman caught on.

"Mary. Sick. Yah, Mary sick." She beamed.

Mr. Kelly looked at the line of patients and spoke to a woman. "Mame," he said. "You live near this lady. How many has she got sick?"

Mame said: "Well, there's the man for one. Dyin' from the way they was carryin' on yesterday and the day before. I ain't seen none of the kids. There's four little girls and they ain't been out of the house for a couple of days. And no wonder they're sick, runnin' around wild widout no—"

"Never mind about that, now," said Mr. Kelly. "I guess, Doctor, the only thing for you to do is go to this woman's house and take a look at them."

The woman Mame said: "To be sure, and ain't that nice? Dya hear that, everybody? Payin' a personal visit to the likes of that but the decent people take what they get. A fine how-do-ya-do."

"You'll take what you get in the shape of a puck in the nose," said Mr. Kelly. "A fine way you do be talkin' wid the poor dumb

Hunkie not knowing how to talk good enough to say what's the matter wid her gang. So keep your two cents out of this, Mame Brannigan, and get back into line."

Mame made a noise with her mouth, but she got back into line. Doctor Myers got through the rest pretty well, except for another Hunkie who spoke some English but knew no euphemisms. Mr. Kelly finally told her to use monosyllables, which embarrassed Doctor Myers because there were some Irishwomen still in line. But "We can't be wasting no time on politeness," said Mr. Kelly. "This here's a doctor's office now." Finally all the patients except the Hunkie woman were seen to.

Mr. Kelly said: "Well, Doctor, bein's this is your first visit here you gotta take a little something on the house. Would you care for a brandy?"

"Why, yes, that'd be fine," said the doctor.

"James, what about you? A sass?"

"Yes, thank you," I said. A sass was a sarsaparilla.

Mr. Kelly opened a closet at the back of the bar and brought out a bottle. He set it on the bar and told the doctor to help himself. The doctor poured himself a drink and Mr. Kelly poured one and handed it to the Hunkie woman. "There y'are, Mary," he said. "Put hair on your chest." He winked at the doctor.

"Not joining us, Mr. Kelly?" said the doctor.

Mr. Kelly smiled. "Ask James there. No, I never drink a drop. Handle too much of it. Why, if I took a short beer every time I was asked to, I'd be drunk three quarters of the time. And another advantage is when this here Pro'bition goes into effect I won't miss it. Except financially. Well, I'll take a bottle of temperance just to be sociable." He opened a bottle of ginger ale and took half a glassful. The Hunkie woman raised her glass and said something that sounded more like a prayer than a toast, and put her whole mouth around the mouth of the glass and drank. She was happy and grateful. Doctor Myers wanted to buy another round, but Mr. Kelly said his money was no good there that day; if he wanted another drink he was to help himself. The doctor did not want another, but he said he would like to buy one for the Hunkie woman, and Mr. Kelly permitted him to pay for it, then we said goodbye to Mr. Kelly and departed, the Hunkie woman getting in the car timidly, but once in the car her bottom was so large that the doctor had to stand on the running board until we reached her house.

A herd of goats in various stages of parturition gave us the razz when we stopped at the house. The ground around the house had a goaty odor because the wire which was supposed to keep them out was torn in several places. The yard was full of old wash boilers and rubber boots, tin cans and the framework of an abandoned baby carriage. The house was a one and a half story building. We walked around to the back door, as the front door is reserved for the use of the priest when he comes on sick calls. The Hunkie woman seemed happier and encouraged, and prattled away as we followed her into the house, the doctor carefully picking his way through stuff in the yard.

The woman hung up her coat and hat on a couple of pegs on the kitchen wall, from which also hung a lunch can and a tin coffee bottle, the can suspended on a thick black strap, and the bottle on a braided black cord. A miner's cap with a safety lamp and a dozen buttons of the United Mine Workers of America was on another peg, and in a pile on the floor were dirty overalls and jumper and shirt. The woman sat down on a backless kitchen chair and hurriedly removed her boots, which left her barefoot. There was an awful stink of cabbage and dirty feet in the house, and I began to feel nauseated as I watched the woman flopping around, putting a kettle on the stove and starting the fire, which she indicated she wanted to do before going to look at the sick. Her breasts swung to and fro and her large hips jounced up and down, and the doctor smirked at these things, knowing that I was watching, but not knowing that I was trying to think of the skinniest girl I knew, and in the presence of so much woman I was sorry for all past thoughts or desires. Finally the woman led the way to the front of the house. In one of the two front rooms was an old-fashioned bed. The windows were curtained, but when our eyes became accustomed to the darkness we could see four children lying on the bed. The youngest and oldest were lying together. The oldest, a girl about five years old, was only half covered by the torn quilt that covered the others. The baby coughed as we came in. The other two were sound asleep. The half-covered little girl got awake, or opened her eyes and looked at the ceiling. She had a half-sneering look about her nose and mouth, and her eyes were expressionless. Doctor Myers leaned over her and so did her mother, speaking to the girl, but the girl apparently made no sense even in the Hunkie language. She sounded as though she were trying to clear her throat of phlegm. The doctor turned to me and said dramatically: "James, take this woman out and get her to boil more water, and go out to the car and get your father's instrument case." I grabbed the woman's arm and pulled her to the kitchen and made signs for her to boil the water, then I went out to the Ford and wrestled with the lid of the rear compartment, wondering what the hell Myers wanted with the instrument case, wondering whether he himself knew what he wanted with it. At last I yanked the lid open and was walking back with the leather case in my hand when I heard a loud scream. It sounded more deliberate than wild, it started so low and suddenly went so high. I hurried back to the bedroom and saw Doctor Myers trying to pull the heavy woman away from her daughter. He was not strong enough for her, but he kept pulling and there were tears in his eyes: "Come away, God damn it! Come away from her, you God damn fool!" He turned to me for help and said: "Oh, Jesus, James, this is awful. The little girl just died. Keep away from her. She had diphtheria!"

"I couldn't open the back of the car," I said.

"Oh, it wasn't your fault. Even a tracheotomy wouldn't have saved her, the poor little thing. But we've got to do something for these others. The baby has plenty of spots, and I haven't even looked at the other two." The other two had been awakened by their mother's screams and were sitting up and crying, not very loud. The woman had the dead girl in her arms. She did not need the English language to know that the child was dead. She was rocking her back and forth and kissing her and looking up at us with fat streams of tears running from her eyes. She would stop crying for a second, but would start again, crying with her mouth open and the tears, unheeded, sliding in over her upper lip.

Doctor Myers took some coins from his pocket and tried to make friends with the in-between kids, but they did not know what money was, so I left him to go in to see how the man was. I walked across the hall to the other bedroom and pulled up the curtains. The man was lying in his underwear; gaunt, bearded, and dead.

I knew he was dead, but I said: "Hyuh, John, hyuh." The sound of my voice made me feel silly, then sacrilegious, and then I had to vomit. I had seen men brought in from railroad wrecks and mine explosions and other violent-accident cases, but I had been prepared for them if only by the sound of an ambulance bell. This was different. Doctor Myers heard me being sick and came in. I was crying. He took a few seconds to see that the man was dead and then he took me by the arm and said: "That's all right, kid. Come out in the air." He led me outside into the cold afternoon and I felt better and hungry.

He let go of my arm. "Listen," he said. "As soon as you feel well enough, take the car and go to the hospital. The first thing you do there is get them to give you twenty thousand units of antitoxin, and while you're doing that tell them to send an ambulance out here right away. Don't go near anybody if you can help it except a doctor." He paused. "You'd better find out about an undertaker."

"You'll need more than twenty thousand units of antitoxin," I said. I had had that much in my own back when I was eight years old.

"Oh, no. You didn't understand me. The antitoxin's for you. You tell whoever's in charge at the hospital how many are sick out here, and they'll know what to send."

"What about you?"

"Oh, I'll stay here and go back in the ambulance. Don't worry about me. I want to stay here and do what I can for these kids." I suddenly had a lot of respect for him. I got into the Ford and drove away. Doctors' cars carried cardboard signs which said By Order State Department of Health, which gave them the right to break speed laws, and I broke them on my way to the hospital. I pulled in at the porte-cochère and met Doctor Kleiber, a friend of my father's, and told him everything. He gave me antitoxin. He smiled when I mentioned getting an undertaker. "Lucky if they get a wooden rough box, even, James. These people aren't patients of Daddy's, are they, James?"

"No."

"Well then, I guess maybe we have to send an Army doctor. I'm full up so I haven't a minute except for Daddy's patients. Now go home and I'll take care of everything. You'll be stiff in the back and you want to rest. Goodbye now." So I drove home and went to bed.

III

I was stiff the next morning from the antitoxin, but it had not been so bad as the other time I had taken it, and I was able to pick up Doctor Myers at the hotel. "I feel pretty damn useless, not being able to drive a car," he said. "But I never had much chance to learn. My mother never had enough money to get one. You know that joke: we can't afford a Ford."

"Oh, well," I said, "in Philadelphia you don't need one. They're a nuisance in the city."

"All the same I'd like to have one. I guess I'll have to when I start practicing. Well, where to first?" We outlined a schedule, and for the next couple of days we were on the go almost continually. We hardly noticed how the character of the region was changed. There was little traffic in the streets, but the few cars tore madly. Most of them were Cadillacs: black, company-owned Cadillacs which were at the disposal of young men like Doctor Myers and the two drunken Gibbsville doctors who did not own cars; and gray Cadillacs from the USAAC base in Allentown, which took officers of the Army Medical Corps around to the emergency hospitals. At night the officers would use the cars for their fun, and there were a few scandals. One of my friends, a Boy Scout who was acting as errand boy—"courier," he called himself—at one of the hospitals, swore he witnessed an entire assignation between an Army major and a local girl who was a clerk in the hospital office. One officer was rumored to be homosexual and had to be sent elsewhere. Opinion among us boys was divided: some said he was taken away and shot, some said he was sent to Leavenworth, others said he was dishonorably discharged. The ambulances were being driven by members of the militia, who wore uniforms resembling those of the marine corps. The militia was made up of young men who were exempt from active service. They had to make one ambulance driver give up his job, because he would drive as fast as the ambulance would go even when he was only going to a drug store for a carton of soap. Another volunteer driver made so much noise with the ambulance bell that the sick persons inside would be worse off than if they had walked. The women of wealth who could drive their own cars drove them, fetching and carrying blankets and cots, towels and cotton, but their husbands made some of the women stop because of the dangers of influenza and Army medical officers. Mrs. Barlow, the leader of society, did not stop, and her husband knew better than to try to insist. She was charming and stylish and looked very English in her Red Cross canteen division uniform. She assumed charge of the emergency hospital in the armory and bossed the Catholic sisters and the graduate nurses around and made them like it. Her husband gave money and continued to ride a sorrel hunter about the countryside. The rector of the Second Presbyterian Church appeared before the Board of Health and demanded that the nuns be taken out of the hospitals on the ground that they were baptizing men and women who were about to die, without ascertaining whether they were Catholics or Protestants. The *Standard* had a story on the front page which accused unnamed undertakers of profiteering on "rough boxes," charging as much for pine board boxes as they had for mahogany caskets before the epidemic.

Doctor Myers at first wore a mask over his nose and mouth when making calls, and so did I, but the gauze stuck to my lips and I stopped wearing it and so did the doctor. It was too much of a nuisance to put them on and take them off every time we would go to a place like Kelly's, and also it was rather insulting to walk in on a group of people with a mask on your face when nobody in the group was wearing one. I was very healthy and was always glad to go in with the doctor because it gave me something to do. Of course I could have cleaned spark plugs or shot some air into the tires while waiting for the doctor, but I hated to monkey around the car almost as much as I liked to drive it.

In a few days Doctor Myers had begun to acquire some standing among the patients, and he became more confident. One time after coming from my father's bedroom he got in the car with some prescriptions in his hand and we started out.

To himself he said, looking up from a prescription: "Digitalis . . . now I wonder?" I turned suddenly, because it was the first time in my life I had heard anyone criticize a prescription of my father's. "Oh, I'm sorry, Jimmy," he said.

"You better not ever let him hear you say anything about his prescriptions."

"Yes, I know. He doesn't want anyone to argue with him. He doesn't think I'm seeing as many people as I should."

"What does he expect?" I said.

"Oh, he isn't unreasonable, but he doesn't want his patients to think he's neglecting them. By the way, he wants us to stop in at the Evanses in Collieryville. The David Evanses. Mrs. Evans phoned and said their maid is sick."

"That's O.K. with me," I said.

"I thought it would be," he said.

Collieryville seemed strange with the streets so deserted as on some new kind of holiday. The mines did not work on holydays of obligation, and the miners would get dressed and stand around in front of poolrooms and saloons, but now they were not standing around, and there was none of the activity of a working day, when coal wagons and trucks rumble through the town, and ten-horse teams, guided by the shouted "gee" and "haw" of the driver, would pull loads of timber through the streets on the way to the mines. Collieryville, a town of about four thousand persons, was quiet as though the people were afraid to come out in the cold November gray.

We were driving along the main street when I saw Edith. She was coming out of the P. O. S. of A. Hall, which was a poolroom on the first floor and had lodge rooms on the two upper stories. It was being used as an emergency hospital. I pulled up at the curb and called to Edith. "Come on, I'll give you a ride home," I said.

"Can't. I have to get some things at the drug store," she said.

"Well, we're going to your house anyway. I'll see you there," I said.

We drove to the Evans house and I told the doctor I would wait outside until Edith came. She appeared in about five minutes and I told her to sit in the car and talk to me. She said she would.

"Well, I'm a nurse, Jimmy," she said.

"Yes, you are," I said scornfully. "That's probably how your maid got sick."

"What!"

"Why, you hanging around at the P. O. S. of A. Hall is probably the way your maid got sick. You probably brought home the flu—"

"Oh, my God!" she said. She was nervous and pale. She suddenly jumped out of the car and I followed her. She swung open the front door and ran towards the kitchen, and I was glad she did; for although I followed her to the kitchen, I caught a glimpse of Mrs. Evans and Doctor Myers in Mr. Evans' den. Through the half-closed doors I could see they were kissing.

I didn't stop, I know, although I felt that I had slowed up. I followed Edith into the kitchen and saw that she was half crying, shaking her hands up and down. I couldn't tell whether she had seen what I had seen, but something was wrong that she knew about. I blurted out, "Don't go in your father's den," and was immediately sorry I had said it; but then I saw that she had guessed. She looked weak and took hold of my arms; not looking at me, not even speaking to me, she said: "Oh, my God, now it's him. Oh, why didn't I come home with you? Sarah isn't sick at all. That was just an excuse to get that Myers to come here." She bit her lip and squeezed my arms. "Jimmy, you mustn't ever let on. Promise me."

"I give you my word of honor," I said. "God can strike me dead if I ever say anything."

Edith kissed me, then she called out: "Hey, where is every-body?" She whispered to me: "Pretend you're chasing me like as if I pulled your necktie."

"Let go!" I yelled, as loud as I could. Then we left the kitchen, and Edith would pull my necktie at every step.

Mrs. Evans came out of the den. "Here, what's going on here?"

"I'm after your daughter for pulling my tie," I said.

"Now, Edith, be a good girl and don't fight with James. I don't understand what's the matter with you two. You usedn't to ever fight, and now you fight like cats and dogs. You oughtn't to. It's not nice."

"Oh—" Edith said, and then she burst into tears and went upstairs.

I was genuinely surprised, and said: "I'm sorry, Mrs. Evans, we were only fooling."

"Oh, it's not your fault, James. She feels nervous anyhow and I guess the running was too much for her." She looked at the doctor as if to imply that it was something he would understand.

"I guess I'll go out and sit in the car," I said.

"I'll be right out," said the doctor.

I sat in the car and smoked, now and then looking at the second floor window where I knew Edith's room was, but Edith did not come to the window and in about twenty minutes the doctor came out.

"The maid wasn't sick after all," he said. "It was Mrs. Evans. She has a slight cold but she didn't want to worry your father. I guess she thought if she said she was sick, your father'd come out himself."

"Uh-huh," I said. "Where to now?"

"Oh, that Polish saloon out near the big coal banks."

"You mean Wisniewski's," I said.

IV

Doctor Myers must have known I suspected him, and he might even have suspected that I had *seen* him kissing Mrs. Evans. I was not very good at hiding my likes and dislikes, and I began to dislike him, but I tried not to show it. I didn't care, for he might have told my father I was unsatisfactory, and my father would have given me hell. Or if I had told my father what I'd seen, he'd have given Doctor Myers a terrible beating. My father never drank or smoked, and he was a good, savage amateur boxer, with no scruples against punching anyone smaller than himself. Less than a year before all this took place my father had been stopped by a traffic policeman while he was hurrying to an "OBS." The policeman knew my father's car, and could have guessed why he was in a hurry, but he stopped him. My father got out of the car, walked to the front of it, and in the middle of a fairly busy intersection he took a crack at the policeman and broke his jaw. Then he got back and drove around the unconscious policeman and on to the confinement case. It cost my father nearly a thousand dollars, and the policeman's friends and my father's enemies said: "God damn Mike Malloy, he ought to be put in jail." But my father was a staunch Republican and he got away with it.

I thought of this now and I thought of what my father would have done to Doctor Myers if he found out. Not only would he have beaten him up, but I am sure he would have used his influence at the University to keep Myers from getting his degree.

So I hid, as well as I could, my dislike for Doctor Myers, and the next day, when we stopped at my home, I was glad I did. My father had invented a signal system to save time. Whenever there was a white slip stuck in the window at home or at the office, that meant he was to stop and pick up a message. This day the message in the window read: "Mrs. David Evans, Collieryville."

Doctor Myers looked at it and showed it to me. "Well, on to Collieryville," he said.

"O.K., but would you mind waiting a second? I want to see my mother."

He was slightly suspicious. "You don't need any money, do you? I have some."

"No, I just wanted to see if she would get my father to let me have the car tonight." So I went in and telephoned to the Evanses. I got Edith on the phone and told her that her mother had sent for Doctor Myers.

"I know," she said. "I knew she would. She didn't get up this morning, and she's faking sick."

"Well, when we get there you go upstairs with the doctor, and if he wants you to leave the bedroom, you'll have to leave, but tell your mother you'll be right outside, see?"

"O.K.," said Edith.

I returned to the car. "How'd you make out?" said Doctor Myers.

"She thinks she can get him to let me have it," I said, meaning that my father would let me have the car.

When we arrived at the Evans house I had an inspiration. I didn't want him to suspect that we had any plan in regard to him, so I told him I was going in with him to apologize to Edith for our fight of the day before. There was the chance that Edith would fail to follow my advice and would come downstairs, but there was the equally good chance that she would stay upstairs.

The plan worked. In some respects Edith was dumb, but not in this. Doctor Myers stayed upstairs scarcely five minutes, but it was another five before Edith came down. Doctor Myers had gone out to wait in the Ford.

Edith appeared. "Oh, Jimmy, you're so nice to me, and I'm often mean to you. Why is that?"

"Because I love you." I kissed her and she kissed me.

"Listen, if my dad ever finds this out he'll kill her. It's funny, you and me. I mean if you ever told me a dirty story, like about *you* know—people—"

"I did once."

"Did you? I mustn't have been listening. Anyhow it's funny to think of you and me, and I'm older than you, but we know something that fellows and girls our age, they only guess at."

"Oh, I've known about it a long time, ever since I went to sisters' school."

"And I guess from your father's doctor books. But this isn't the same when it's your own mother, and I bet this isn't the first time. My dad must have suspicions, because why didn't he send me away to boarding school this year? I graduated from high last year. I bet he wanted me to be here to keep an eye on her."

"Who was the other man?"

"Oh, I can't tell you. Nobody you know. Anyhow, I'm not sure, so I wouldn't tell you. Listen, Jimmy, promise to telephone me every time before he comes here. If I'm not here I'll be at the Bordelmans' or at the Haltensteins', or if not there, the Callaways'. I'll stay home as much as I can, though. How long is he going to be around here, that doctor?"

"Lord knows," I said.

"Oh, I hope he goes. Now give me a goodbye kiss, Jimmy, and then you have to go." I kissed her. "I'm worse than she is," she said.

"No, you're not," I said. "You're the most darling girl there is. Goodbye, Ede," I said.

Doctor Myers was rubbing the skin in front of his ear when I came out. "Well, did you kiss and make up?"

"Oh, we don't go in for that mushy stuff," I said.

"Well, you will," he said. "Well . . . on to Wizziski's."

"It's a good thing you're not going to be around here long," I said.

"Why? Why do you say that?"

"Because you couldn't be in business or practice medicine without learning Hunkie names. If you stayed around here you'd have to be able to pronounce them and spell them." I started the car. I was glad to talk. "But I tell you where you'd have trouble. That's in the patches where they're all Irish with twenty or thirty cousins living in the same patch and all with the same name."

"Oh, come on."

"Well, it isn't as bad as it used to be," I said. "But my father told me about one time he went to Mass at Forganville, about fifteen miles from here, where they used to be all Irish. Now it's half Polack. Anyhow my father said the priest read the list of those that gave to the monthly collection, and the list was like this: John J. Coyle, $5; Jack Coyle, $2; Johnny Coyle, $2; J. J. Coyle, $5; Big John Coyle, $5; Mrs. John Coyle the saloonkeeper's widow, $10; the Widow Coyle, $2. And then a lot of other Coyles."

He did not quite believe this, but he thought it was a good story, and we talked about college—my father had told me I could go to Oxford or Trinity College, Dublin, if I promised to study medicine—until we reached Wisniewski's.

This was a saloon in a newer patch than Kelly's. It was entirely surrounded by mine shafts and breakers and railroads and mule yards, a flat area broken only by culm banks until half a mile away there was a steep, partly wooded hill which was not safe to walk on because it was all undermined and cave-ins occurred so frequently that they did not bother to build fences around them. The houses were the same height as in Kelly's Patch, but they were built in blocks of four and six houses each. Technically Wisniewski's saloon was not in the Patch; that is, it was not on company ground, but at a crossroads at one end of the rows of houses. It was an old stone house which had been a tavern in the days of the King's Highway. Now it was a beery smelling place with a tall bar and no tables or chairs. It was crowded, but still it had a deserted appearance. The reason was that there was no one behind the bar, and no cigars or cartons of chewing tobacco on the back bar. The only decorations were a calendar from which the October leaf had not been torn, depicting a voluptuous woman stretched out on a divan, and an Old Overholt sign, hanging askew on the toilet door.

The men and women recognized Doctor Myers and me, and made a lane for us to pass through. Wisniewski himself was sick in bed, and everybody understood that the doctor would see him first, before prescribing for the mob in the barroom.

Doctor Myers and I went to Wisniewski's room, which was on the first floor. Wisniewski was an affable man, between forty and fifty, with a Teutonic haircut that never needed brushing. His body under the covers made big lumps. He was shaking hands with another Polack whose name was Stiney. He said to us: "Oh, hyuh, Cheem, hyuh, Cheem. Hyuh, Doc."

"Hyuh, Steve," I said. "Yoksheemosh?"

"Oh, fine dandy. How's yaself? How's Poppa? You tell Poppa what he needs is lay off this here booze." He roared at this joke. "Ya, you tell him I said so, lay off this booze." He looked around at the others in the room, and they all laughed, because my father used to pretend that he was going to have Steve's saloon closed by the County. "You wanna drink, Cheem?" he asked, and reached under the bed and pulled out a bottle. I reached for it, and he pulled the bottle away. "Na na na na na. Poppa close up my place wit' the County, I give you a drink. Ya know, miners drink here, but no minors under eighteen, hey?" He passed the bottle around, and all the other men in the room took swigs.

Doctor Myers was horrified. "You oughtn't to do that. You'll give the others the flu."

"Too late now, Doc," he said. "T'ree bottle now already."

"You'll lose all your customers, Steve," I said.

"How ya figure dat out?" said Steve. "Dis flu make me die, dis bottle make dem die. Fwit! Me and my customers all togeder in hell, so I open a place in hell. Fwit!"

"Well, anyhow, how are you feeling?" said the doctor. He placed a thermometer under Steve's arm. The others and Steve were silent until the temperature had been taken. "Hm," said Doctor Myers. He frowned at the thermometer.

"'M gonna die, huh, Doc?" said Steve.

"Well, maybe not, but you—" he stopped talking. The door opened and there was a blast of sweaty air from the barroom, and Mr. Evans stood in the doorway, his hand on the knob. I felt weak.

"Doctor Myers, I'd like to see you a minute please," said Mr. Evans.

"Hyuh, Meester Ivvins," called Steve. Evans is one name which is consistently pronounced the same by the Irish, Slavs, Germans, and even the Portuguese and Negroes in the anthracite.

"Hello, Steve, I see you're drunk," said Mr. Evans.

"Not yet, Meester Ivvins. Wanna drink?"

"No, thanks. Doctor, will you step outside with me?"

Doctor Myers stalled. "I haven't prescribed for this man, Mr. Evans. If you'll wait?"

"My God, man! I can't wait. It's about my wife. I want to know about her."

"What about her?" asked the doctor.

"For God's sake," cried Mr. Evans. "She's sick, isn't she? Aren't you attending her, or don't you remember your patients?"

I sighed, and Doctor Myers sighed louder. "Oh," he said. "You certainly—frightened me, Mr. Evans. I was afraid something had happened. Why, you have no need to worry, sir. She has hardly any temperature. A very slight cold, and she did just the sensible thing by going to bed. Probably be up in a day or two."

"Well, why didn't you say so?" Mr. Evans sat down. "Go ahead, then, finish with Steve. I'll wait till you get through. I'm sorry if I seemed rude, but I was worried. You see I just heard from my timber boss that he saw Doctor Malloy's car in front of my house, and I called up and found out that Mrs. Evans was sick in bed, and my daughter sounded so excited I thought it must be serious. I'll take a drink now, Steve."

"Better not drink out of that bottle, Mr. Evans," said the doctor, who was sitting on the edge of the bed, writing a prescription.

"Oh, hell, it won't hurt me. So anyhow, where was I? Oh, yes. Well, I went home and found Mrs. Evans in bed and she seemed very pale, so I wanted to be sure it wasn't flu. I found out you were headed this way so I came right out to ask if you wouldn't come back and take another look. That's good liquor, Steve. I'll buy a case of that." He raised the bottle to his lips again.

"I give you a case, Meester Ivvins. Glad to give you a case any time," said Steve.

"All right, we'll call it a Christmas present," said Mr. Evans. "Thanks very much." He was sweating, and he opened his raccoon coat. He took another drink, then he handed the bottle to Stiney. "Well, James, I hear you and Edith were at it again."

"Oh, it was just in fun. You know. Pulling my tie," I said.

"Well, don't let her get fresh with you," he said. "You have to keep these women in their place." He punched me playfully. "Doctor, I wonder if you could come to the house now and make sure everything's all right."

"I would gladly, Mr. Evans, but there's all that crowd in the barroom, and frankly, Mrs. Evans isn't what you'd call a sick woman, so my duty as a—physician is right here. I'll be only too glad to come if you'd like to wait."

The Hunkies, hearing the Super talked to in this manner, probably expected Meester Ivvins to get up and belt the doctor across the face, but he only said: "Well, if you're sure an hour couldn't make any difference."

"Couldn't possibly, Mr. Evans," said Doctor Myers.

He finished with Steve and told him to stop drinking and take his medicine, then he turned to leave. Steve reached under his pillow and drew out a bundle of money. He peeled off a fifty-dollar bill and handed it to the doctor.

"Oh, no, thanks," said Doctor Myers. "Doctor Malloy will send you a bill."

"Aw, don't worry about him, eh, Cheem? I always pay him firs' the mont', eh, Cheem? Naw, Doc, dis for you. Go have a good time. Get twenty-five woman, maybe get drunk wit' boilo." I could imagine Doctor Myers drinking boilo, which is hot moonshine. I nudged him, and he took the money and we went to the barroom.

I carried the chair and table and set them in place, and the Hunkies lined up docilely. Mr. Evans waited in Steve's room, taking a swig out of the bottle now and then until Doctor Myers had finished with the crowd. It was the same as usual. It was impractical to get detailed descriptions from each patient, so the flu doctor would ask each person three or four questions and then pretend to prescribe for each case individually. Actually they gave the same prescription to almost all of the patients, not only to save time, but because drug supplies in the village and city pharmacies were inadequate, and it was physically impossible for druggists to meet the demand. They would make up large batches of each doctor's standard prescription and dole out boxes and bottles as the patrons presented the prescriptions.

It took about two hours to dispose of the crowd at Steve's. Mr. Evans told Doctor Myers to come in the Cadillac because it was faster than the Ford—which I denied. I followed in the Ford and got to the Evans house about three minutes after the Cadillac. Edith met me at the door. "Oh, what a scare!" she said.

"If you think you were scared, what about me?" I said. I told her how I had felt when her father appeared at Steve's.

"Your father phoned and wants you to take that Myers home," she said, when I had finished.

"Did he say why?" I asked.

"No, he just said you weren't to make any more calls this afternoon."

"I wonder why."

"I hope it hasn't got anything to do with him and my mother," she said.

"How could it? Only four people know about it. He couldn't guess it, and nobody would tell him. Maybe he's got up and wants me to drive for him."

"Maybe . . . I can't think. I'm afraid of them up there. Oh, I hope he goes away." I kissed her, and she pushed me away. "You're a bad actor, James Malloy. You're bad enough now, but wait till you grow up."

"What do you mean grow up? I'm almost six feet."

"But you're only a kid. I'm seventeen, and you're only fifteen."

"I'll be in my seventeenth year soon." We heard footsteps on the stairs, and Doctor Myers' voice: ". . . absolutely nothing to worry about. I'll come in again tomorrow. Goodbye, Mr. Evans. Goodbye, Edith. Ready, Jim?"

I gave him my father's message and we drove home fast. When we got there one of the Buicks was in front of the house, and we went in the living-room.

"Well, Doctor Myers," my father said. "Back in harness again. Fit as a fiddle, and I want to thank you for the splendid attention you've given my practice. I don't know what my patients would have done without you."

"Oh, it's been a privilege, Doctor. I'd like to be able to tell you how much I've appreciated working for you. I wouldn't have missed it for the world. I think I'd like to serve my internship in a place like this."

"Well, I'm glad to hear it. I'm chief of staff at our hospital, and I'm sorry I can't offer you anything here, but you ought to try some place like Scranton General. Get the benefit of these mining cases. God damn interesting fractures, by the way. I trephined a man, forty-eight years old—all right, James, I'll call you when I need you." I left the room and they talked for half an hour, and then my father called me. "Doctor Myers wants to say goodbye."

"I couldn't leave without saying goodbye to my partner," said the doctor. "And by the way, Doctor Malloy, I think I ought to give part of this cheque to James. He did half the work."

"If he did I'll see that he gets his share. James knows that. He wants one of these God damn raccoon coats. When I was a boy the only people that wore them drove hearses. Well—" My father indicated that it was time for the doctor and me to shake hands.

"Quite a grip James has," said the doctor.

"Perfect hands for a surgeon. Wasted, though," my father said. "Probably send him to some God damn agricultural school and make a farmer out of him. I want him to go to Dublin, then Vienna. That's where the surgeons are. Dublin and Vienna. Well, if you ever meet Doctor Deaver tell him I won't be able to come down for the Wednesday clinics till this damn thing is over. Good luck, Doctor."

"Thank you, many thanks, Doctor Malloy."

"James will drive you to the hotel."

I took him to the hotel and we shook hands. "If you ever

want a place to stay in Philadelphia you're always welcome at my house." He gave me the address of a fraternity house. "Say goodbye to the Evanses for me, will you, Jim?"

"Sure," I said, and left.

My father was standing on the porch, waiting impatiently. "We'll use the Buick," he said. "That Ford probably isn't worth the powder to blow it to hell after you've been using it. Do you really want one of those livery stable coats?"

"Sure I do."

"All right. Now, ah, drive to Kelly's." We drove to Kelly's, where there was an ovation, not too loud, because there were one or two in the crowd on whom my father was liable to turn and say: "You, ya son of a bitch, you haven't paid me a cent since last February. What are you cheering for?" We paid a few personal visits in the Patch. At one of them my father slapped a pretty Irish girl's bottom; at another he gave a little boy a dollar and told him to stop picking his nose; at another he sent me for the priest, and when I came back he had gone on foot to two other houses, and was waiting for me at the second. "What the hell kept you? Go to Terry Loughran's, unless the skunk got another doctor."

"He probably did," I said jovially. "He probably got Lucas."

"*Doctor* Lucas. Doctor Lucashinsky. Ivan the Terrible. Well; if he got Lucas it serves him right. Go to Hartenstein's."

We drove until one o'clock the next morning, taking coffee now and then, and once we stopped for a fried-egg sandwich. Twice I very nearly fell asleep while driving. The second time I awoke to hear my father saying: ". . . And my God! To think that a son of mine would rather rot in a dirty stinking newspaper office than do this. Why, I do more good and make more money in twenty minutes in the operating room than you'll be able to make the first three years you're out of college. If you *go* to college. Don't drive so fast!"

It was like that for the next two days. I slept when he allowed me to. We were out late at night and out again early in the morning. We drove fast, and a couple of times I bounded along corduroy roads with tanks of oxygen (my father was one of the first, if not the first, to use oxygen in pneumonia) ready to blow me to hell. I developed a fine cigarette cough, but my father kept quiet about it, because I was not taking quinine, and he was. We got on each other's nerves and had one terrible scene. He became angered by my driving and punched me on the shoulder. I stopped the car and took a tire iron from the floor of the car.

"Now just try that again," I said.

He did not move from the back seat. "Get back in this car." And I got back. But that night we got home fairly early and the next morning, when he had to go out at four o'clock, he drove the car himself and let me sleep. I was beginning to miss Doctor Myers. It was about eight o'clock when I came down for breakfast, and I saw my father sitting in the living-room, looking very tired, staring straight ahead, his arms lying on the arms of the chair. I said hello, but he did not answer.

My mother brought me my breakfast. "Did you speak to your father?"

"Oh, I said hello, but he's in a stupor or something. I'm getting sick of all this."

"Hold your tongue. Your father has good reason to be unhappy this morning. He just lost one of the dearest friends he had in the world. Mr. Evans."

"Mr. Evans!" I said. "When'd he die?"

"At about four o'clock this morning. They called your father but he died before he got there. Poor Mrs. Evans—"

"What he die of? The flu?"

"Yes." I thought of the bottle that he had shared with Steve and the other Hunkies, and Mrs. Evans' illness, and Doctor Myers. It was all mixed up in my mind. "Now you be careful how you behave with your father today," my mother said.

I called up Edith, but she would not come to the phone. I wrote her a note, and drove to Collieryville with some flowers, but she would not see me.

Even after the epidemic died down and the schools were reopened she would not see me. Then she went away to school and did not come home for the Easter holidays, and in May or June I fell in love with another girl and was surprised, but only surprised, when Edith eloped. Now I never can remember her married name.

Price's Always Open

THE PLACE where everybody would end up before going home was Price's. This was the second summer for Price's. Before that it had been a diner and an eyesore. The last man to run the diner had blown town owing everybody, and somehow or other that had put a curse on the place. No one, not even the creditors, wanted to open up again, and time and the weather got at the diner and for two years it had stood there, the windows all smashed by passing schoolboys, the paint gone, and the diner itself sagging in the middle like an old work horse. Then last summer Mr. Price got his bonus and he went into the all-night-restaurant business.

The first thing he did was to get permission to tear down the diner and put up his own place. It was a corner plot, and he built his place twice as wide as the diner had been. The Village Fathers were only too glad to have Mr. Price build. In other times they never would have let the place go the way the diner had. The neatness of the village was always commented upon by new summer people and bragged about by those who had been coming there for generations. But things being the way they were . . . So Mr. Price built a sort of rustic place, which, while not in keeping with the rest of the village architecture, was clean and attractive in its way. All the signboards were simulated shingles, and the lettering has been described as quaint. Mr. Price frankly admitted he got his idea from a chain of places in New York. There was one neon sign that stayed on all night, and it said, simply, "PRICE'S." Nothing about what Price's was; everyone knew.

Mr. Price had one leg, having left the other somewhere in a dressing station back of Château-Thierry. He was not a cook but a house painter, and he had had to employ a couple of short-order cooks from New York and Boston. But Mr. Price was always there. Not that anyone ever wondered about it, but it might have been interesting to find out just when he slept. He was at his position near the cash register all night, and he certainly was there at noon when the chauffeurs and a few summer-hotel clerks and people like that would come in for lunch. As a matter of fact, he did not need much sleep. No day passed without his leg bothering him, and seeing people took his mind off his leg. Best of all, he liked late at night.

Saturday night there was always a dance at the yacht club. That was a very late crowd. The dances were supposed to stop at one, but if the stricter older members had gone home, the young people would keep the orchestra for another hour or two, and even after that they would hang around while one of the boys played the piano. The boy who played the piano was Jackie Girard.

They were a nice bunch of kids, practically all of them, and Mr. Price had known their fathers and mothers for years, or many of them. Sometimes the wife's family had been coming to this island for years and years; then she married the husband, a stranger, and the husband and wife would start coming here and keep coming. Sometimes it was the husband who was old summer people. Most of the present younger crowd had been coming here every summer for fifteen, twenty years. One or two of them had been born here. But Jackie Girard was Mr. Price's favorite. He was born here, and unlike the others, he lived here all year round.

Jackie had a strange life with the summer people, and it probably was that that made Mr. Price feel closer to him than to the others. The others were nice and respectful, and they always said *Mister* Price, just as Jackie did. But they were summer people, and the winters were long. Not that Jackie was here in the winter any more, but at least he came home several times in the winter. Jackie was at college at Holy Cross, and naturally his holidays were spent here.

The strange life that Jackie had apparently did not seem strange to him. He was not a member of the yacht club, naturally. Jackie's father was a carpenter, the best in the village; the best out of three, it's true, but head and shoulders above the other two. Henry Girard was a French Canuck and had been in the Twenty-sixth Division with Mr. Price, but never an intimate of Mr. Price's. Jackie had three sisters; one older, two younger. Jackie's mother played the organ in the Catholic church. The older sister was married and lived in Worcester, and the younger ones were in high school. Anyway, Jackie was not a member of the yacht club, but he was almost always sure of being invited to one of the dinners before the regular Saturday-night dance. He was one of the clerks at the hotel, and that, plus an occasional five or ten from his sister in Worcester, gave him just enough money to pay for gas and his incidental expenses. He could hold his end up. The only trouble was, except for Saturday and Sunday, he did not have much end to hold up.

There were gatherings, if not parties, practically every night of the week. Every Thursday, for instance, the large group of young people would split up into smaller groups, sometimes three, four, five, and after dinner they would go to the boxing matches. Jackie was not invited to these small dinner parties. He had been invited two or three times, but his mother had told him he had better not go. For herself, she wished he could have gone, but his father would not have approved. After Jackie had regretted the few invitations he got, the summer people figured it out that all he cared about was the yacht-club dances. He was the only town boy who was invited to yacht-club dances, and they figured that that was all he wanted. It did not take them long to decide that this was as it should be all around. They decided that Jackie would feel embarrassed at the smaller parties, but that he did not need to feel embarrassed at the club dances, because in a sense he was earning his way by playing such perfectly marvelous piano. But this was not the way Mr. Price saw it.

Almost every night but Saturday Jackie would drop in. Two nights a week he had been to the movies, which changed twice a week, but Mr. Price at first wondered what Jackie would do to kill time the other nights. Jackie would show up around eleven-thirty and sit at the counter until some of the summer crowd began to arrive. They would yell at him, "Hi, Jackie! Hi, keed! How's it, Jackie?" And Jackie would swing around on his stool, and they would yell at him to come on over and sit at a table with them. And he would sit at the table with whichever group arrived first. In the early part of the summer that did not mean any special group, because when the other groups would arrive, they would put all the tables together and form one party. Then there would be some bickering about the bill, and more than once Mr. Price saw Jackie grab the check for the whole party. It was not exactly a big check; you could not eat much more than forty cents' worth at Mr. Price's without making a pig of yourself, and the usual order was a cereal, half-milk-half-cream, and a cup of coffee; total, twenty cents. But you take fourteen of those orders and you have a day's pay for Jackie.

As the summer passed, however, the large group did break into well-defined smaller groups; one of six, several of four. By August there would be the same foursomes every night, and of these one included the Leech girl.

The Leeches were not old people in the sense that some of them were. The Leeches belonged to the newcomers who first summered in this place in 1930 and 1931. They had come from one of the more famous resorts. Louise Leech was about twelve when her family first began to come to this place. But now she was eighteen or nineteen. She had a Buick convertible coupé. She was a New York girl, whereas most of the other boys and girls were not New Yorkers; they all went to the same schools and colleges, but they did not come from the same home towns. Some came from as far west as Denver, as Mr. Price knew from cashing their checks. And even what few New York girls did come to this place were not New York friends of the Leeches. Mr. Leech was here only on week-ends and his wife was away most of the time, visiting friends who had not had to give up Narragansett. Louise herself was away a good deal of the time.

It was easy to see, the first summer Louise was grown up, that she was discontented. She did not quite fit in with the rest of the crowd, and she not only knew it but she was content not to make the best of it. Mr. Price could hear the others, the first summer he was in business, making remarks about Louise and her thinking she was too good for this place. And they had been saying something like it the early part of this summer, too. But after the Fourth of July, somewhere around there, they began to say better things about her. Mostly they said she really wasn't so bad when you got to know her. To which a few of the girls said, "Who wants to?" And others said, "She doesn't like us any better. We're still not good enough for her. But Sandy is." Which did explain a lot.

Sandy—Sandy Hall—was from Chicago, but what with prep school and college and this place and vacation trips, he probably had not spent a hundred days in Chicago in the last seven years. In a bathing suit he was almost skinny, except for his shoulders; he looked cold, he was so thin. But Mr. Price had seen him in action one night when one of the Portuguese fishermen came in drunk and got profane in a different way from the way the summer people did. Sandy had got up and let the Portuguese have two fast hard punches in the face, and the fisherman went down and stayed down. Sandy looked at the man on the floor—it was hard to tell how long he looked at him—and suddenly he kicked him. The man was already out, and so there was no need to kick him, but the kick had several results. One was that Mr. Price brought a blackjack to work the next night. The other result was something Mr. Price noticed on Louise's face.

He had not had much time to take it all in, as he had had to leave the cash register to help the night counterman drag the fisherman out of the place. But he remembered the expression on the girl's face. It began to appear when the fisherman went down from the punches, and when Sandy kicked the man, it was all there. Mr. Price, standing where he did, was the only one who caught it. He thought of it later as the way a girl would look the first time she saw Babe Ruth hit a home run, provided she cared about home runs. Or the way she would look if someone gave her a bucketful of diamonds. And other ways, that would come with experiences that Mr. Price was sure Louise never had had.

Sandy had not come with Louise that night, but Mr. Price noticed she went home with him. And after that night they were always together. They were part of a foursome of whom the other two were the dullest young people in the crowd. It took Mr. Price some time to determine why this was, but eventually he did figure it. The foursome would come into Price's, and Louise and Sandy would watch the others while they ordered; then Sandy would say he and Louise wanted the same, and from then on neither Sandy nor Louise would pay any attention to the other two. Stooges.

Another thing that Mr. Price noticed was that Jackie could not keep his eyes off Louise.

Along about the latter part of August, it was so obvious that one night Mr. Price kidded Jackie about it. It was one of the nights Jackie dropped in by himself, and Mr. Price said, "Well, she isn't here yet."

"Who isn't here?"

"The Leech girl."

"Oh," said Jackie. "Why, did anybody say anything to you? Is that how you knew I liked her?"

"No. Figured it out for myself. I have eyes."

"You're a regular Walter Winchell. But don't say anything, Mr. Price."

"What the hell would I say, and who to?"

"I'll be back," said Jackie. He was gone for more than an hour, and when he returned the crowd was there. They all yelled as usual, but this time one of the girls added, "Jackie's tight." He was, rather. He had a somewhat silly grin on his face, and his nice teeth made a line from ear to ear. Several tables wanted him to join them and they were friendly about it. But he went to the table where sat Louise and Sandy and the others.

"Do you mind if I sit down?" he said.

"Do you mind?" said Sandy.

"No," said Louise.

"Thank you. Thank you," said Jackie. "Go fights?"

"Mm-hmm," said Sandy.

"Any good? Who won?"

"The nigger from New Bedford beat the townie," said Sandy. "Kicked the Jesus out of him."

"Oh, uh townie. You mean Bobbie Lawless. He's nice guy. Za friend of mine. I used to go to high school—"

"He's yellow," said Sandy.

"Certainly was," said Louise.

"Nope. Not yellow. Not Bobbie. I used to go to high school with Bobbie. Plain same football team."

"Where do you go to school now?" said Sandy.

"Holy Cross. We're gonna beat you this year."

"What is Holy Cross?" said Louise.

Sandy laughed. Jackie looked at her with tired eyes.

"No, really, what is it?"

"'Tsa college. It's where I go to college. Dint you ever hear of Holy Cross? Give another hoya and a choo-choo rah rah—"

"O.K.," said Sandy.

"I'll sing if I wanta. I'll sing one of your songs. Oh, hit the line for Harvard, for Harvard wins today—"

"Oh, go away," said Sandy.

"Yes, for God's *sake*," said Louise.

"Oh, very well, Miss Leech. Very well." Jackie put his hands on the table to steady himself as he got to his feet, but he stared down into her eyes and for two seconds he was sober.

"Come on, Jackie, you're stewed." Mr. Price had come around from the cash register and had taken Jackie by the right arm. At that moment Sandy lashed out with a right-hand punch, and Jackie fell down. But he had hardly reached the floor before Mr. Price snapped his blackjack from his pocket and slapped it down on the front of Sandy's head. Sandy went down and there was blood.

"Anybody else?" said Mr. Price. By this time the night counterman had swung himself over the counter, and in his hand was a baseball bat, all nicked where it had been used for tamping down ice around milk cans. None of the summer crowd made a move; then Mr. Price spoke to two of the young men. "Get your friend outa here, and get out, the whole goddam bunch of you." He stood where he was, he and the counterman, and watched the girls picking up their wraps.

"Aren't you going to do anything?" Louise screamed. "Chuck! Ted! All of you!"

"You get out or I'll throw you out," said Mr. Price. She left.

There were murmurs as well as the sounds of the cars starting. Thinking it over, Mr. Price agreed with himself that those would be the last sounds he ever expected to hear from the summer crowd.

Are We Leaving Tomorrow?

I~T WAS~ cool, quite cool, the way the weather is likely to beat an in-between resort when the Florida season is over but the Northern summer season has not yet begun. Every morning the tall young man and his young wife would come down the steps of the porch and go for their walk. They would go to the mounting block where the riders would start for the trails. The tall young man and his wife would stand not too close to the block, not speaking to anyone; just watching. But there might have been a little in his attitude, in his manner, of a man who felt that he was starting the riders, as though his presence there made their start official. He would stand there, hatless and tan, chin down almost to his chest, his hands dug deep in the pockets of his handsome tweed topcoat. His wife would stand beside him with her arm in his, and when she would speak to him she would put her face in front of him and look up. Almost always his answer would be a smile and a nod, or perhaps a single word that expressed all he wanted to put into words. They would watch the riders for a while, and then they would stroll over to the first tee of the men's golf course to watch the golfers start off. There it would be the same: not much talk, and the slightly superior manner or attitude. After they had watched their quota of golfers they would go back to the porch and she would go up to their rooms and a Negro bellboy would bring him his papers, the *Montreal Star* and the *New York Times*. He would sit there lazily looking at the papers, never so interested in a news item that he would not look up at every person who came in or went out of the hotel, or passed his chair on the porch. He watched every car come up the short, winding drive, watched the people get in and out, watched the car drive away; then when there was no human activity he would return to his paper, holding it rather far away, and on his face and in his eyes behind the gold-rimmed spectacles there was always the same suspicion of a smile.

He would go to his room before lunch, and they would come down together. After lunch, like most everyone else, they would retire, apparently for a nap, not to appear until the cocktail hour. They would be the first, usually, in the small, cheery bar, and until it was time to change for dinner he would have a highball glass, constantly refilled, in his hand. He drank slowly, sipping teaspoonfuls at a time. In that time she might drink two light highballs while he was drinking eight. She always seemed to have one of the magazines of large format in her lap, but at these times it was she who would look up, while he hardly turned his head.

Not long after they came she began to speak to people; to bow and pass the time of day. She was a pleasant, friendly little woman, not yet thirty. Her eyes were too pretty for the rest of her face; in sleep she must have been very plain indeed, and her skin was sensitive to the sun. She had good bones—lovely hands and feet—and when she was in sweater and skirt her figure always got a second look from the golfers and riders.

Their name was Campbell—Douglas Campbell, and Sheila. They were the youngest people over fifteen in the hotel. There were a few children, but most of the guests were forty or thereabouts. One afternoon the Campbells were in the bar and a woman came in and after hesitating at the entrance she said, "Good afternoon, Mrs. Campbell. You didn't happen to see my husband?"

"No, I didn't," said Mrs. Campbell.

The woman came closer slowly and put her hand on the back of a chair near them. "I was afraid I'd missed him," she said to no one; then suddenly she said, "Do you mind if I sit with you while he comes?"

"No, not at all," said Mrs. Campbell.

"Please do," said Campbell. He got to his feet and stood very erect. He set his glass on the little table and put his hands behind his back.

"I'm sorry I don't remember your name," said Mrs. Campbell.

"Mrs. Loomis."

Mrs. Campbell introduced her husband, who said, "Wouldn't you like a cocktail meanwhile?"

Mrs. Loomis thought a moment and said she would—a dry Daiquiri. Then Campbell sat down, picking up his drink and beginning to sip.

"I think we were the first here, as usual," said Mrs. Campbell, "so we couldn't have missed Mr. Loomis."

"Oh, it's all right. One of us is always late, but it isn't important. That's why I like it here. The general air of informality." She smiled. "I've never seen you here before. Is this your first year?"

"Our first year," said Mrs. Campbell.

"From New York?"

"Montreal," said Mrs. Campbell.

"Oh, Canadians. I met some awfully nice Canadians in Palm Beach this winter," said Mrs. Loomis. She named them off, and Mrs. Campbell said they knew them, and he smiled and nodded. Then Mrs. Loomis tried to remember the names of some other people she knew in Montreal (they turned out to have been Toronto people), and Mr. Loomis arrived.

A white-haired man, a trifle heavy and about fifty, Mr. Loomis wore young men's clothes. He was brown and heavy lidded. He had good manners. It was he who corrected his wife about the people from Montreal who actually were from Toronto. That was the first time the Loomises and the Campbells had done more than speak in passing, and Mrs. Campbell was almost gay that afternoon.

The Campbells did not come down to dinner that evening, but they were out for their stroll the next morning. Mr. Loomis waved to them at the first tee, and they waved—*she* waved, Campbell nodded. They did not appear for cocktails that afternoon. For the next few days they took their stroll, but they had their meals in their room. The next time they came to the cocktail lounge they took a small table at the side of the bar, where there was room only for the table and two chairs. No one spoke to them, but that night was one of the nights when the hotel showed movies in the ballroom, and after the movie the Loomises fell in with them and insisted on buying them a drink, just a nightcap. That was the way it was.

Mr. Loomis brought out his cigar case and offered Mr. Campbell a cigar, which was declined, and gave the orders for drinks, "Scotch, Scotch, Scotch, and a Cuba Libre." Mrs. Loomis was having the Cuba Libre. As the waiter took the order Mr. Campbell said, "And bring the bottle."

There was a fraction of a second's incredulity in Mr. Loomis's face; incredulity, or more likely doubt that he had heard his own ears. But he said, "Yes, bring the bottle." Then they talked about the picture. It had been a terrible picture, they all agreed. The Loomises said it was too bad, too, because they had crossed with the star two years ago and she had seemed awfully nice, not at all what you'd expect a movie star to be like. They all agreed that the Mickey Mouse was good, although Mr. Loomis said he was getting a little tired of Mickey Mouse. Their drinks came, and Mrs. Loomis was somewhat apologetic about her drink, but ever since she had been in Cuba she'd developed a taste for rum, always rum. "And before that gin," said Mr. Loomis. Mr. Campbell's glass was empty and he called the waiter to bring some more ice and another Cuba Libre, and he replenished the highball glasses from the bottle of Scotch on the table.

"Now this was my idea," said Mr. Loomis.

"Only the first one," said Mr. Campbell. They let it go at that, and the ladies returned to the subject of the star of the picture, and soon Mr. Loomis joined in. They got all mixed up in the star's matrimonial record, which inevitably brought up the names of other movie stars and *their* matrimonial records. Mr. and Mrs. Loomis provided the statistics, and Mrs. Campbell would say yes or no as the statement or opinion required. Mr. Campbell sipped his drink wordlessly until the Loomises, who had been married a long time, became simultaneously aware of Mr. Campbell's silence, and they began directing their remarks at him. The Loomises were not satisfied with Mrs. Campbell's ready assents. They would address the first few words of a remark to the young wife, because she had been such a polite listener, but then they would turn to Mr. Campbell and most of what they had to say was said to him.

For a while he would smile and murmur "Mm-hmm," more or less into his glass. Then it seemed after a few minutes that he could hardly wait for them to end an item or an anecdote. He began to nod before it was time to nod, and he would keep nodding, and he would say, "Yes, yes, yes," very rapidly. Presently, in the middle of an anecdote, his eyes, which had been growing brighter, became very bright. He put down his drink and leaned forward, one hand clasping and unclasping the other. "And—yes—and—yes," he kept saying, until Mrs. Loomis had finished her story. Then he leaned farther forward and stared at Mrs. Loomis, with that bright smile and with his breathing become short and fast.

"Can I tell you a story?" he said.

Mrs. Loomis beamed. "Why, of course."

Then Campbell told a story. It had in it a priest, female anatomy, improbable situations, a cuckold, unprintable words, and no point.

Long before Campbell finished his story Loomis was frowning, glancing at his wife and at Campbell's wife, seeming to listen to Campbell but always glancing at the two women. Mrs. Loomis could not look away; Campbell was telling her the story, and he looked at no one else. While Mrs. Campbell, the moment the story was begun, picked up her drink, took a sip, and put the glass on the table and kept her eyes on it until Campbell signaled by his chuckling that the story was at an end.

He kept chuckling and looking at Mrs. Loomis after he had finished, and then he smiled at Loomis. "Huh," came from Loomis, and on his face a muscular smile. "Well, dear," he said. "Think it's about time—"

"Yes," said Mrs. Loomis. "Thank you so much. Good night, Mrs. Campbell, and good night." Campbell stood up, erect, bowing.

When they were entirely out of the room he sat down and crossed his legs. He lit a cigarette and resumed his drinking and stared at the opposite wall. She watched him. His eyes did not even move when he raised his glass to his mouth.

"Oh," she said suddenly. "I wonder if the man is still there at the travel desk. I forgot all about the tickets for tomorrow."

"Tomorrow? Are we leaving tomorrow?"

"Yes."

He stood up and pulled the table out of her way, and when she had left he sat down to wait for her.

The Cold House

T HE HOUSE in the country was cold, and Mrs. Carnavon sat with her hat on, her sealskin coat open, her bag in her lap, her left hand lying flat on the bag. The slight exertion—but not slight to her—of getting out of the car, stepping down, walking up the three steps of the porte-cochère, had left her breathing heavily, and the thumb of her right hand was beating against the forefinger. She had had a long nap in the car, coming up from New York. Driscoll drove so you could sleep. He had to; that was his job. She knew Driscoll, and how he would look in the mirror to see if she was asleep before he would increase his speed. Driscoll was so thoroughly trained in moderate speed that she often had had to feign sleep in order to get some place in a hurry. But today she had not had to feign sleep. Up at six-thirty, away at seven-thirty, and now it was almost time for lunch. But first a rest, a little rest. The house was very cold. Mrs. Carnavon rang for the maid.

"I didn't expect you till late afternoon," said the maid. "I'll build you a fire."

"Never mind, Anna."

"But it'll only *take* a *minute*, Ma'am. I kin—"

"No, never *mind*."

"Well, but of course if you—"

"I won't change my mind. Is the phone connected? I mean here in the house."

"No, only over the garage, where we are."

"Then will you go out and telephone the Inn and tell Mr. McCall—ask him if I could have a chop and a baked potato. Or anything. Nothing much. Cup of tea."

"I could fix you something."

"Too much trouble to start a fire. No, just tell Mr. McCall, and find out how soon he can have it."

"Of course he'll more than likely have to go out and buy it, and—"

"All right. He can go out and buy it." Mrs. Carnavon hated to be short with Anna, but Anna had the hide of an elephant. She knew that Anna would not be hurt; she watched Anna leave the room and knew that Anna was thinking: "The poor woman is all upset."

She looked out of the window and saw Anna, with a very ugly shawl over her head and shoulders, looking rather pathetic, hurrying to the garage to telephone Mr. McCall. Mrs. Carnavon lit a cigarette. It steadied her a little. It steadied her body, her hands; there was no unsteadiness to the lump in her heart, the thing in her mind. She held the cigarette as high as her face, taking regular, deep inhales. She idly opened a china cigarette box on the table beside her, just tilting the lid. There were four cigarettes in the box. She took one out and it was as crisp as a twig. She broke it with her fingers. It was from last summer. A cigarette that her son could have smoked. She looked at it and saw that it was a cigarette that Harry would *not* have smoked; it was a brand he never had liked. But still, when he had had a few drinks she had seen him smoking just that brand without noticing any difference. "Mom, why do you have those things in the house? Everybody passes them up. They're really vile. They are. They're vile. I hate to tell you what they remind me of." One time he had emptied all the available boxes of that brand. But she noticed that when some friends of his were at the house, they would ask Anna if there didn't happen to be some of that brand—"on the premises," one boy had said. She didn't remember much about the boy, but she remembered that strange expression.

Now that she was here—"I came up here for something," she said aloud. Well, what? The cracked windowpane that she had noticed the first time one morning after Harry and his friends had been to a dance. Two decks of cards on the desk. The copy of *Life* magazine on the rack. The summer *Social Register*, with its warped cover curling up. She heard a screen door slam, an odd sound in this kind of weather, when the flies had died. It was Anna, of course. Anna's hands were cold; Mrs. Carnavon noticed them when Anna reached up to take off her shawl.

"He said he'd be glad to serve you in about three-quarters of an hour," said Anna. "I was right. He does have to go out and buy the chops. About three-quarters of an hour, he said. I think what he's doing, I think he wants to warm up the dining-room a little, too. You know, it was awful this winter for Mr. McCall. I don't believe he had more than two or three people there a week. A couple regulars, like salesmen, passing through, but overnight I don't believe he had more than two or three people. Just for lunch, the regulars. I don't think it paid him to keep open."

"Anna, will you go upstairs in Mr. Harry's room, there's a picture in a silver frame—"

"Of Dr. Carnavon. I have it out in our room."

"How dare you!"

"I'm sorry, Ma'am, I only meant to do the right thing. I didn't want anybody to steal—"

"You had no right to touch anything in that room. Go bring it to me!"

The tears came and Anna fled, and Mrs. Carnavon was weary of herself, flaring up at this miserable soul, who had no way of knowing that that room was not to be disturbed. No order had been given. Indeed, Mrs. Carnavon admitted that until now she had not thought of leaving that room the way it was, the way it had been all winter. It was part of her confusion, trying to find some reason for making this trip. Trying to find some excuse, she admitted, that would explain the trip to the servants, to Anna. And then, finally, finding the worst excuse of all: Anna would know she had not driven all this distance merely to take home a picture of a husband long dead. Weary, wearily, Mrs. Carnavon climbed the stairs to her son's room.

On the wall the same diamond-shaped plaque, with the clasped hands and the Greek letters; another wooden diamond, with the head of a wolf; a photograph of a baseball team, with names badly printed in white ink under the picture; a large bare spot where there had been a reproduction which he had liked well enough to take back to town. A magazine that he may have read. She opened it: ". . . and it will become increasingly apparent that the forces of Fascism are laboring night and day . . . choice may have to be made sooner than you expect; but no matter when it comes, when it does come it will be sooner than you like. . . ." A young friend, an *old* friend, of Harry's had written that. An intense young man had come to see her a month or so ago; he had been abroad, he had just learned, he couldn't *believe* it. Why, he and Harry, for eight years . . . Eight years? What about twenty-four years? What was *eight* years?

Well, for one thing, it was eight years during which he had seen Harry a great deal more than she had, like it or not.

Everything in this room would have to go. Those things, those shields, those pictures, all that would have to go. She would send them to the right people. Everything would have to go. She now saw that in the back of her mind, as she was climbing the stairs, had been some vague plan to lock this room and leave everything as she found it; but now when she saw this she felt chilled and disgusted. Let him be dead, but let him be dead! Let him be what he was, and let it have ended with no awful sanctuary or crypt of useless things. Oh, how useless were these things! "I do not even know what Upsilon means," she whispered. "Those baseball players. Do I want to see *them*?" She recoiled from the nearness of a danger, the danger of keeping this room the way it was, and the lone, secret visits she would have paid it, looking at things that had no meaning to her. She could see clearly, like watching a motion picture of herself, what she would have done, what she had been in terrible danger of doing: next August, next September, a year from next August and a year from next July, she would have come up here, unlocked the door, come in this room and stood. She saw herself, a woman in white, trying to squeeze out a tear at the sight of these things of wood and brass and paper and glass—and all the while distracted by the sounds of passing cars, the children next door, the telephone downstairs, the whirring vacuum cleaner. And she even knew the end of this motion picture: she would end by hating a memory that she only knew how to love.

She walked out, leaving the door open, and went downstairs. Anna was standing in the hall, with fear in her eyes. Mrs. Carnavon looked at her watch. "Tell Driscoll to bring the car around."

"He's having a bite with us," said Anna.

"Tell him to bring that *car* around!" said Mrs. Carnavon. "I'm going back by train."

The train was quicker.

Trouble in 1949

B ARRY CAME out of the local skyscraper and stood on the sidewalk and took a long look at his watch, just as the Midwestern heat hit him in the face. Rutland, in his air-conditioned office, had kept him just long enough so that to make the last good New York plane he would have to hurry and sweat— and then probably miss it. He walked to the hotel and took a shower, not hot and not cold, which made him feel better if not cooler. He sent downstairs for the largest Tom Collins they could provide, and he sat in a pongee dressing gown, sipping his drink and glancing at a picture magazine and smoking a cigarette. He sent down for another Tom Collins, and stood at the window, trying to test his memory. That building was new; and that one. That one that looked like the roof of a movie house, he wasn't sure whether that was new. It had been a long time. Eleven years, almost.

"Before he knew what he was doing, he had the phone book in his hand," he said to himself, of himself, and added: "And what a liar you are, Barry." He had been lying to himself for three days, ever since he knew he was coming out here. He had lied to Rutland, who had said: "Listen, Barry, what's the use of trying to catch that plane? Why don't you wait here a few minutes and we can go over to the H-Y-P Club and have a couple of snorts. They have an air-conditioned bar. Then we can drive out to the country club and have a swim. There'll be a lot of pretty girls out there. All the young kids. Then we can either have dinner there or go to my house. Let me call my wife and tell her you're coming." But he had told Rutland that he couldn't possibly. He *had* to be back in New York first thing in the morning.

That was a lie. He wanted to go to the H-Y-P Club; there would be guys there he knew and had not seen. He wanted to go for a swim. But he knew that country club, and he knew who might be there.

He found her name in the phone book, or rather her husband's name. He called the number: "May I speak to Mrs. Nelson?"

"Yessuh, Mistah Nelson. Just one minute."

Then: "Hello, Karl?"

"No, this isn't Karl. This is Jock Barry."

A silence that made him begin to think he was cut off, and then: "Jock? What are you doing in these parts?" And before he could answer she added: "Or are you in these parts?"

"Yes, I'm at the Deshler."

"Well, then you're not in these parts. The Deshler is in Columbus, Ohio."

"Well, whatever the name of it is."

"The Imperial, most likely," she said. "How long are you going to be here?"

He noticed that the invitation to dinner which he had been expecting was slow in coming, if it was coming. "I'm going back to New York tomorrow."

"Well, in that case you must come out for dinner. Karl won't be here for dinner, I'm afraid, but he'll be back later."

"Oh, that's too bad."

"What's too bad?" she said.

"I leave that to you," he said. "Look, why don't you have dinner with me?"

"At the Imperial? I wouldn't think of it. Drive four miles to sit in—oh, no, thanks."

"I didn't say it had to be the Imperial. There must be some place in the country. There used to be lots of places."

"There still are, but when I go to them I go with Karl."

"I see," he said, and deliberately waited.

"How is Connie?" she asked.

"She's fine. She's in Maine. Shall I give her your love?"

Now it was she who waited. "I'll be there in about an hour. Meet me at the State Street entrance. It's a light blue convertible coupé. More's the pity," she said.

"We can put it in a garage and hire a drive-yourself," he said, but she had hung up.

He took a small steel mirror out of his shaving kit and went to the window, examining his beard and trying to give it the benefit of a doubt; but it was no go, and so he shaved. The waiter arrived with the second Tom Collins and Barry told him to see about having his other suit pressed. In half an hour he inspected himself in the full-length mirror. Not really so bad.

If he pulled his chin back it doubled a little, and there was the beginning of a faint suspicion of a tiny bulge over his collar; but when he held his chin up the double and the bulge disappeared. "Chin up, mahst dress," he quoted from Bert Lahr. He buttoned the three buttons on his coat, made an unnecessary rearrangement of his tie, put on his straw hat at an angle, and with a Maurice Chevalier tap of the crown he made a face at himself: "Eef da nighteengales cood sing glike yoo, dey'd sing motch sweedah dan dey do." He went downstairs, to the State Street entrance of the Imperial Hotel. He almost wished he had a bamboo walking stick.

At ten minutes past the hour of seven a medium-sized blue convertible coupé turned into State Street, half a block away. He darted between the battling taxicabs and jumped to the running board. "Hello," she said, and looked at him only once, as though she had not seen him since lunch, and not a very romantic lunch either. He got in. He leaned forward and very exaggeratedly pretended to be dazzled. "Now don't be silly," she said. "And don't tell me I haven't changed. You have. You better get out of this town before the meat packers see you."

"Oh, now really, Mrs. Nelson. You don't have to work so hard at it."

"At what, pray?"

"At being the happily wed Mrs. Nelson, Mrs. Nelson." He pretended to quote: "Mrs. Karl J. Nelson—"

"Karl W."

"Mrs. Karl Q. Nelson, one of our most attractive young matrons, who is chairman of the bird-bath committee of the Junior League, pictured with her twelve interesting children at her home on Ridgewood Place. Mrs. Nelson is the former, uh, the former, uh. Now what was the name? What—was—that—name? Everyone seems to have forgotten it, including Mrs. Nelson. Excepting Mr. J. J. Barry, of New York. He remembers when Mrs. Nelson was a Miss Judy Hayes. Does he remember!"

"Well, forget it. She's Mrs. Nelson now, all evening, too. We can go to a place called the Château, where they have a waiter that used to be at 21, if that'll make you homesick. I understand they have excellent wines, and I know the food is good. I don't imagine wine interests you any more than it ever did."

"Or did you."

"Or did me. They have a four-piece band, not bad. We can have dinner, dance once or twice around, and be home in plenty of time for the historic meeting between you and Karl. He hates you."

"I'd be pretty sore if he didn't."

"Do you want to drive?" she asked.

"Yes."

"As soon as we get out of this traffic," she said. They changed seats, and at that there was a subtler change. He felt more in control of the situation when he had his hands on the wheel and the responsibility of the car; and apparently some change had affected her. "Bear right. Left at the next light. The cops are always hanging around this gas station." That was all she said for the first few minutes, then: "It's funny I never ran into you somewhere."

"You never tried," he said.

"No, but I never tried not to," she said. He turned, but she was staring straight ahead, and he knew she expected him to turn, and then when his eyes were back on the road he knew she was smiling at him.

"Hello, Judy," he said.

"Hello, Jock," she said, and as he reached his hand toward her she came closer.

"Don't some people named McAllister live out this way?"

"McPherson."

"They have a herd of cattle," he said.

"Champion Jerseys," she said.

"I thought so," he said.

The Château was not near. It turned out to be a good twenty miles from the hotel, but it was a good twenty miles. Barry held her hand, and they had only one more conversation before they arrived at the roadhouse. She began it: "Are you confused, Jock?"

"Yes, darling. I'm confused. Why?"

"I am. It's no use pretending we're the same, because we're not. I weigh a hundred and twenty-seven, and you must weigh—I don't know men's weights very well. I'm three years younger than you are, so that makes you thirty-four, doesn't it?"

"Yep. That makes you thirty-one. You thirty-one!"

"Yes, and you thirty-four."

"Yes, but you thirty-one! You thirty-anything, Judy. Why are you confused?"

"I'm not actually, all of a sudden. Time marches on, and I have two children. You have two children. You have a wife, and I have a husband. But I feel only very slightly disloyal to all that. To them. And you? What about you?"

"Only very slightly."

"Because I loved you when I didn't know anything except that I loved you. So let's have a good time tonight? Let's accept it that you aren't twenty-three and I'm not twenty. We'll accept it and forget it."

"Yes, that's what I want." And with the effect of that agreement still on them they arrived at the Château, so-called no doubt for the reason that it resembled no château in the world. He stopped the car to let her out. She put a hand on the door and then she turned and put her arms around his neck and kissed him.

"That's all for now, darling. I'll meet you in the bar." She got out and he waited until she was inside. For a second he found himself not liking, not caring about the girl of eleven years ago; but very much in love with this woman in the brown-and-white sport shoes and white gabardine dress. He admired the way her beautiful legs took her up the porch steps. There was even something about the way she opened the screen door. Or maybe it was only that it was she who was opening the screen door. He parked the car and found the bar.

It was a pleasant bar. One look at the saintly white-haired Irish bartender and he knew that it was a good bar, an efficient bartender. Probably one of those bachelor bartenders who spend their time going from Florida to New York to Saratoga, going on two or three benders a year, winning a little on the races, losing a little, and then taking jobs at places like the Château to recoup their losses. It was the kind of bar which would be a good place for a small group, or an equally good place to drink alone, for the entire back bar was stocked with bottles—labels to read.

There was one other couple at the bar. A man about Barry's age; a woman about Judy's age.

"Good evening, sir," said the bartender.

"Good evening. I think I'll wait just a minute."

"Yes, sir." The bartender brought him a glass of ice water and Judy came in from Mesdames.

"Hello, Judy," said the man.

"Oh, hello, Paul," she said. The two women did not speak.

"What are you going to drink?" said Barry.

They decided on Martinis, and the bartender sent for the waiter. They ordered: melon, chicken Château (chicken hash, ham, and grapes). And champagne. Be ready as soon as they cared to sit down. They ordered a second cocktail to be sent to the table, and when they sat down she said: "Paul, the man at the bar, in case you're interested, is my brother-in-law. Karl's brother."

"Well, isn't that nice? But I don't think that's his wife."

"No, it isn't. Nobody blames Paul, though. At least I don't. His wife is racketing around with a football player from the University. His wife has the money."

"What about your husband? Wouldn't he help him?"

"No. Karl says he's lost respect for him. They don't get along very well. You know, I'm rather hungry."

The food, what there was of it, was good, and the wine was acceptable. The owner of the place came to their table and asked if everything was satisfactory, and they said it was, but where was the orchestra. The Basque shrugged his shoulders and apologetically explained that he could only afford the band on weekends this summer. When the man had bowed himself away Paul Nelson succeeded him. He bowed to Barry and said, "Excuse me, Judy—"

"It's all right. Paul, this is Mr. Barry, from New York. My brother-in-law, Mr. Nelson."

They shook hands and Barry asked him to sit down. Nelson said he would and then, addressing Barry: "Do you mind if I speak frankly?"

"Notta tall, if you're asking me," said Barry.

"What is it, Paul?"

"Judy," said Nelson, "if I were you, I mean, I think it would be a good idea if you finished your drinks and got out of here. Karl's coming here with a crowd of men."

"How do you know?" said Judy.

Paul smiled. "Because Luigi gave me the same tip. When I first got here he told me, 'Ah, Mr. Nelson. Early,' and I asked him what he meant, and then he explained. He thought I was meeting my brother here. They're all coming from the plant and Karl's secretary phoned and ordered dinner. Then when you and this gentleman got here Luigi called me aside and asked if you weren't Karl's wife. So, there it is." He looked at his watch. "They ought to be here fairly soon, and you know Karl. Arriving here with his big business pals and finding his wife with a stranger. I take it you don't know Karl?"

"No, I've never met him. But thanks. I think it would be better if we ducked, Judy."

"Yes—but it's too late now. Look at those cars."

"It isn't too late," said Paul. "You can go through the bar and out the other end of the porch."

"No. I have my car."

"Oh, God," said Paul. "No, it isn't too late. You can be here with me. Mr. . . . Barry can go over and sit with the lady with me. Her name is Mrs. Jewett. She knows all this."

"I guess that's the best thing, Jock," said Judy.

Barry joined Mrs. Jewett. "How do you do?" she said. "This ought to be innaresting. That's Paul's brother. He just spotted Paul and Mrs. Nelson." It was innaresting. First, Karl the hearty host, giving the impression of having his arms on the shoulders of seven men, all at once; taking their orders at the bar, memorizing them instantly, and repeating them to the bartender. Then turning around and spotting his brother and his wife. (Apparently he had not recognized the blue car.) He walked to their table, and Barry could see restrained anger in the set of Karl's shoulders. He could not see Karl's face, but he could see Judy's, and he could guess what she was saying. Something like: "If you don't trust me, you ought to trust your own brother," et cetera. Then Judy and Paul rose and left.

"Have you got a car?" said Barry to Mrs. Jewett.

"We came in Paul's. It's that little black sedan."

He got the check and paid it. They got in Paul's car and started in the direction of the city. Half a mile ahead the blue coupé was parked. Barry pulled up and got out, and Paul got out of the coupé. Barry put out his hand. "Thanks very much, Nelson," he said.

"Thanks for what? I wasn't doing it for you."

"O.K.," said Barry. "But I wasn't thanking you for myself. Get that straight."

"Go on back to New York and leave her alone," said Paul, and left him.

Barry drove slowly; he was looking for a certain road. When he came to that road he turned off the main highway, and crawled along the road for a mile or so. They had been silent all the while. He well remembered that you drove for a while past a long white fence until you reached an arch of trees. That was where he stopped, under the arch of trees. "Cigarette?" he said.

"Yes," she said. "What did Paul say to you?"

"You're sure he said something, aren't you?"

"I know he was going to. I didn't listen," she said.

"Well," Barry began, and before continuing he took a long, long inhale of his cigarette. "I'll tell you what he said, in effect. He said, 'Barry, don't you realize you're not twenty-three? You're thirty-four,' he said. He said, 'You have a wife and two children.'"

"And then I imagine he said, 'And Judy is thirty-one, and she has a husband and two children.'"

"Something like that," said Barry. "Something like that. He didn't say anything about being in love with you himself, and I didn't ask him. I didn't have to."

"Well?" she said.

"Well, what?"

"Well, aren't you going to ask me if I'm in love with him?"

"I wasn't going to, but now I guess I don't have to," he said. He looked at her, and there was something besides tears in her eyes. It wasn't one thing; it was a lot of things. There was something he had seen a long time ago, when he had said he would be good to her. But now there was something else, and he thought he knew what it was; it was the need of someone to tell, someone to tell. Then her face was on his chest, and his kiss was in her hair; and she was twenty-one again, and he was a hundred.

"He doesn't know I love him," she said. "It's all so damn much trouble, Jock." She stopped crying, and he gave her a handkerchief. "How did you happen to pick this road?" she said.

"Don't you know?"

She smiled and kissed his cheek. "I think I do, but we passed that road. It's about a mile back."

"It's about eleven years back," he said.

"Well, just so you remember this one in—1949," she said.

The next day, on the plane, he thought of the answer to that. "But I won't remember," he should have said. "It'll be too damn much trouble."

Do You Like It Here?

THE DOOR was open. The door had to be kept open during study period, so there was no knock, and Roberts was startled when a voice he knew and hated said, "Hey, Roberts. Wanted in Van Ness's office." The voice was Hughes'.

"What for?" said Roberts.

"Why don't you go and find out what for, Dopey?" said Hughes.

"Phooey on you," said Roberts.

"Phooey on *you*," said Hughes, and left.

Roberts got up from the desk. He took off his eyeshade and put on a tie and coat. He left the light burning.

Van Ness's office, which was *en suite* with his bedroom, was on the ground floor of the dormitory, and on the way down Roberts wondered what he had done. It got so after a while, after going to so many schools, that you recognized the difference between being "wanted in Somebody's office" and "Somebody wants to see you." If a master wanted to see you on some minor matter, it didn't always mean that you had to go to his office; but if it was serious, they always said, "You're wanted in Somebody's office." That meant Somebody would be in his office, waiting for you, waiting specially for you. Roberts didn't know why this difference existed, but it did, all right. Well, all he could think of was that he had been smoking in the shower room, but Van Ness never paid much attention to that. Everybody smoked in the shower room, and Van Ness never did anything about it unless he just happened to catch you.

For minor offenses Van Ness would speak to you when he made his rounds of the rooms during study period. He would walk slowly down the corridor, looking in at each room to see that the proper occupant, and no one else, was there; and when he had something to bawl you out about, something unimportant, he would consult a list he carried, and he would stop in and bawl you out about it and tell you what punishment went with it. That was another detail that made the summons to the office a little scary.

Roberts knocked on Van Ness's half-open door and a voice said, "Come in."

Van Ness was sitting at his typewriter, which was on a small desk beside the large desk. He was in a swivel chair and when he saw Roberts he swung around, putting himself behind the large desk, like a damn judge.

He had his pipe in his mouth and he seemed to look over the steel rims of his spectacles. The light caught his Phi Beta Kappa key, which momentarily gleamed as though it had diamonds in it.

"Hughes said you wanted me to report here," said Roberts.

"I did," said Van Ness. He took his pipe out of his mouth and began slowly to knock the bowl empty as he repeated, "I did." He finished emptying his pipe before he again spoke. He took a long time about it, and Roberts, from his years of experience, recognized that as torture tactics. They always made you wait to scare you. It was sort of like the third degree. The horrible damn thing was that it always did scare you a little, even when you were used to it.

Van Ness leaned back in his chair and stared through his glasses at Roberts. He cleared his throat. "You can sit down," he said.

"Yes, sir," said Roberts. He sat down and again Van Ness made him wait.

"Roberts, you've been here now how long—five weeks?"

"A little over. About six."

"About six weeks," said Van Ness. "Since the seventh of January. Six weeks. Strange. Strange. Six weeks, and I really don't know a thing about you. Not much, at any rate. Roberts, tell me a little about yourself."

"How do you mean, Mister?"

"How do I mean? Well—about your life, before you decided to honor us with your presence. Where you came from, what you did, why you went to so many schools, so on."

"Well, I don't know."

"Oh, now. Now, Roberts. Don't let your natural modesty overcome the autobiographical urge. Shut the door."

Roberts got up and closed the door.

"Good," said Van Ness. "Now, proceed with this—uh

—dossier. Give me the—huh—huh—*lowdown* on Roberts, Humphrey, Second Form, McAllister Memorial Hall, et cetera."

Roberts, Humphrey, sat down and felt the knot of his tie. "Well, I don't know. I was born at West Point, New York. My father was a first lieutenant then and he's a major now. My father and mother and I lived in a lot of places because he was in the Army and they transferred him. Is that the kind of stuff you want, Mister?"

"Proceed, proceed. I'll tell you when I want you to—uh—halt." Van Ness seemed to think that was funny, that "halt."

"Well, I didn't go to a regular school till I was ten. My mother got a divorce from my father and I went to school in San Francisco. I only stayed there a year because my mother got married again and we moved to Chicago, Illinois."

"Chicago, Illinois! Well, a little geography thrown in, eh, Roberts? Gratuitously. Thank you. Proceed."

"Well, so then we stayed there about two years and then we moved back East, and my stepfather is a certified public accountant and we moved around a lot."

"Peripatetic, eh, Roberts?"

"I guess so. I don't exactly know what that means." Roberts paused.

"Go on, go on."

"Well, so I just went to a lot of schools, some day and some boarding. All that's written down on my application blank here. I had to put it all down on account of my credits."

"Correct. A very imposing list it is, too, Roberts, a very imposing list. Ah, to travel as you have. Switzerland. How I've regretted not having gone to school in Switzerland. Did you like it there?"

"I was only there about three months. I liked it all right, I guess."

"And do you like it here, Roberts?"

"Sure."

"You do? You're sure of that? You wouldn't want to change anything?"

"Oh, I wouldn't say that, not about any school."

"Indeed," said Van Ness. "With your vast experience,

naturally you would be quite an authority on matters educational. I suppose you have many theories as to the strength and weaknesses inherent in the modern educational systems."

"I don't know. I just—I don't know. Some schools are better than others. At least I like some better than others."

"Of course. Of course." Van Ness seemed to be thinking about something. He leaned back in his swivel chair and gazed at the ceiling. He put his hands in his pants pockets and then suddenly he leaned forward. The chair came down and Van Ness's belly was hard against the desk and his arm was stretched out on the desk, full length, fist closed.

"Roberts! Did you ever see this before? Answer me!" Van Ness's voice was hard. He opened his fist, and in it was a wristwatch.

Roberts looked down at the watch. "No, I don't think so," he said. He was glad to be able to say it truthfully.

Van Ness continued to hold out his hand, with the wristwatch lying in the palm. He held out his hand a long time, fifteen seconds at least, without saying anything. Then he turned his hand over and allowed the watch to slip onto the desk. He resumed his normal position in the chair. He picked up his pipe, slowly filled it, and lit it. He shook the match back and forth long after the flame had gone. He swung around a little in his chair and looked at the wall, away from Roberts. "As a boy I spent six years at this school. My brothers, my two brothers, went to this school. My *father* went to this school. I have a deep and abiding and lasting affection for this school. I have been a member of the faculty of this school for more than a decade. I like to think that I am part of this school, that in some small measure I have assisted in its progress. I like to think of it as more than a mere stepping-stone to higher education. At this very moment there are in this school the sons of men who were my classmates. I have not been without my opportunities to take a post at this and that college or university, but I choose to remain here. Why? Why? Because I love this place. I love this place, Roberts. I cherish its traditions. I cherish its good name." He paused, and turned to Roberts. "Roberts, there is no room here for a thief!"

Roberts did not speak.

"There is no room here for a thief, I said!"

"Yes, sir."

Van Ness picked up the watch without looking at it. He held it a few inches above the desk. "This miserable watch was stolen last Friday afternoon, more than likely during the basketball game. As soon as the theft was reported to me I immediately instituted a search for it. My search was unsuccessful. Sometime Monday afternoon the watch was put here, here in my rooms. When I returned here after classes Monday afternoon, this watch was lying on my desk. Why? Because the contemptible rat who stole it knew that I had instituted the search, and like the rat he is, he turned yellow and returned the watch to me. Whoever it is, he kept an entire dormitory under a loathsome suspicion. I say to you, I do not know who stole this watch or who returned it to my rooms. But by God, Roberts, I'm going to find out, if it's the last thing I do. If it's the last thing I do. That's all, Roberts. You may go." Van Ness sat back, almost breathless.

Roberts stood up. "I give you my word of honor, I—"

"I said you may go!" said Van Ness.

Roberts was not sure whether to leave the door open or to close it, but he did not ask. He left it open.

He went up the stairs to his room. He went in and took off his coat and tie, and sat on the bed. Over and over again, first violently, then weakly, he said it, "The bastard, the dirty bastard."

Too Young

IT WAS the time of year when once again Bud was made to feel very young. It had happened last year, and it had happened the year before; it seemed as though it had been happening a great many more years than that. It *always* seemed that the Tuesday after Labor Day was around again; Father would be staying at the apartment in town, planning to come out for two or three weekends but not making it. The fathers of the other kids the same way. It just seemed that there were no older men at the beach club, giving you black looks or even coming right out and telling you if you did not get the heck off the tennis courts when they wanted to play their stiff and creaky mixed doubles. Through the summer, being with your own bunch, you did not think much about being young or old or anything. But when the fathers started to go back to town, and the young married people, only the mothers and the young boys and girls were left, and it made you remember that you were young.

Much too young to be in love with Kathy Mallet.

This had been the first summer Bud had come right out and called her Kathy. "Hyuh, Kathy," he often would say.

"Hello, Bud," she would say. "When are we going to have that match?"

"Any time you say," he would say.

She had started it. Watching him play one day in June, she had sat there and had seen him just *cream* Ned Work. He *creamed* him: 6–4, 6–2. It had been exciting knowing that Kathy was taking the trouble to wait and watch him before she went on to play. It was the best compliment he ever had from anybody. Then she had said, "Will you play me sometime, Bud?" And he had told her any time. They were always talking about it, but all summer they never got around to it, and now Bud was a little glad, because he could have beaten Kathy. He didn't want to do that, and yet he couldn't have played her and insulted her by easing up on her.

In ten years he would be twenty-five and Kathy would be twenty-nine. That wasn't so bad. Both in their late twenties.

And by that time she no longer would be a little tall for him. He had heard a thousand times that on his mother's side they were all six-footers and all got their height in their teens, just sprouted up suddenly.

In no time he would be back at school, and naturally Kathy, back in college, would be going to New Haven and Princeton and New York all the time, because they had an awful lot of liberty where Kathy went to college and were in New York half the time. He would be very lucky to see her before next June. He wished he could do something or give her something that would make her just think of him once in a while during the school year. Well, there was one thing: he could beat her at tennis. That would make her remember him. He could make it up to her years from now. Someday in the future he would say to her, offhand, "Darling, I remember when I was just a kid—oh, back in thirty-nine—and I decided the only way to make you remember me that year was to beat you straight sets. Remember that time I practically forced you to play me?"

The hall clock said twenty after three, and he remembered that there was a touch-football game at three, so there wouldn't be many guys on the tennis courts and most of the girls of his own crowd would be watching the silly game. It seemed like an ideal day to challenge Kathy, if she happened to show up at the club, which she usually did every afternoon anyway. He put on white flannels and went out and took his mother's car and drove to the club. He noticed that Kathy's tan Ford convertible sedan was parked at the Mallets' porte-cochère. That meant she was home. Good. On his way to the club he had a bad moment when he saw Martin standing beside his motorcycle. Martin was tough. Watkins, the other cop, wasn't so bad, but some of the guys said that Martin never gave anybody a break. If you didn't have a license, that was just too bad. Some of the guys said Martin actually carried a list of the kids that had licenses, and Bud had no license. But today Martin did not even notice Bud. Bud looked in the mirror to make sure, but Martin was already looking in the opposite direction.

At the club, Bud parked the car just inside the parking space, behind the high hedge, but on second thought he decided not to get out. He would stretch out and seem casual, and then when Kathy arrived he would sit up and say, "Oh, you wouldn't like a little tennis, would you, Kathy? We haven't much time left before college opens." No, it would be better to say when *school* opens; some people said school when they meant college, whereas if he said college, she would think he was being silly to talk about college when everybody knew he had three more years before he would get to college.

He stretched out, sure that he was looking casual enough. He stayed there quite a while and one or two cars came and went, and the casual attitude was becoming uncomfortable when he heard a car coming pretty fast, and then, faster, a motorcycle.

The motorcycle caught up to the car only a few yards away from the club entrance. Without looking, he knew who was on the motorcycle: Martin. He raised his head and sure enough, the car was Kathy's tan Ford.

Bud sank down in the seat, so that Martin would not see him, and he heard Martin start out the regular cop's line: "Well, baby, you *were* in a hurry."

He could not hear what Kathy said, but he hoped she said something that would put Martin in his place for calling her baby. The next thing Bud heard was unexpected. Martin said, "*You* can't duck *me* this way. Why weren't you there yesterday? I waited till seven o'clock."

"I told you I wouldn't be there," said Kathy.

"Oh, I *know* you *told* me. But *I* told *you* to *be* there, and you weren't. What is this, the brusheroo?"

"I told you I was never going there again. And I'm not," said Kathy.

"What's the matter with you? Why don't you stop this? All summer—you're the one, half the time you were the one that wanted to meet *me*."

"I know, I know. But it's over."

"No, get that out of your head. It isn't over."

"I'm not going to meet you again. I don't *want* to meet you again."

"Yes, but I want to meet you. You'll meet me. You be there at six o'clock."

"No, I won't, so don't wait for me," said Kathy.

"Listen, you little bitch, you *be* there," said Martin.

"No," said Kathy.

There was a moment's silence, then, "Are you gonna be there?"

"No," said Kathy. Then, "All right."

"O.K. I didn't hurt your arm. I'll be there at six o'clock," said Martin. The motorcycle spat a couple of times and went away.

Bud heard Kathy's Ford come into the parking space and heard her slam the door and the sound of her steps on the gravel. He waited until he heard the door of the bar slam to, then he got out of the car. No one must see him; he could tell his mother he had forgotten about her car. Right now he wanted to walk alone and to think thoughts that he hated and that would forever ruin his life. And the god-damn awful part was that there was nothing, nothing, nothing to do but what he was doing now. "Let me alone!" he said, to no one.

Bread Alone

I<small>T WAS</small> the eighth inning, and the Yankees had what the sportswriters call a comfortable lead. It was comfortable for them, all right. Unless a miracle happened, they had the ball game locked up and put away. They would not be coming to bat again, and Mr. Hart didn't like that any more than he was liking his thoughts, the thoughts he had been thinking ever since the fifth inning, when the Yanks had made their five runs. From the fifth inning on, Mr. Hart had been troubled with his conscience.

Mr. Hart was a car-washer, and what colored help at the Elbee Garage got paid was not much. It had to house, feed, and clothe all the Harts, which meant Mr. Hart himself; his wife, Lolly Hart; his son, Booker Hart; and his three daughters, Carrie, Linda, and the infant, Brenda Hart. The day before, Mr. Ginsburg, the bookkeeper who ran the shop pool, had come to him and said, "Well, Willie, you win the sawbuck."

"Yes sir, Mr. Ginsburg, I sure do. I was watchin' them newspapers all week," said Mr. Hart. He dried his hands with the chamois and extended the right.

"One, two, three, four, five, six, seven, eight, nine, anduh tenner. Ten bucks, Willie," said Mr. Ginsburg. "Well, what are you gonna do, with all that dough? I'll bet you don't tell your wife about it."

"Well, I don't know, Mr. Ginsburg. She don't follow the scores, so she don't know I win. I don't know what to do," said Mr. Hart. "But say, ain't I suppose to give you your cut? I understand it right, I oughta buy you a drink or a cigar or something."

"That's the custom, Willie, but thinking it over, you weren't winners all year."

"No sir, that's right," said Mr. Hart.

"So I tell you, if you win another pool, you buy me *two* drinks or *two* cigars. Are you going in this week's pool?"

"Sure am. It don't seem fair, though. Ain't much of the season left and maybe I won't win again. Sure you don't want a drink or a cigar or something?"

"That's all right, Willie," said Mr. Ginsburg.

On the way home, Mr. Hart was a troubled man. That money belonged in the sugar bowl. A lot could come out of that money: a steak, stockings, a lot of stuff. But a man was entitled to a little pleasure in this life, the only life he ever had. Mr. Hart had not been to a ball game since about fifteen or twenty years ago, and the dime with which he bought his ticket in the pool every week was his own money, carfare money. He made it up by getting rides home, or pretty near home, when a truck-driver or private chauffeur friend was going Harlem-ward; and if he got a free ride, or two free rides, to somewhere near home every week, then he certainly was entitled to use the dime for the pool. And this was the first time he had won. Then there was the other matter of who won it for him: the Yankees. He had had the Yankees and the Browns in the pool, the first time all season he had picked the Yanks, and it was they who made the runs that had made him the winner of the ten dollars. If it wasn't for those Yankees, he wouldn't have won. He owed it to them to go and buy tickets and show his gratitude. By the time he got home his mind was made up. He had the next afternoon off, and, by God, he was going to see the Yankees play.

There was, of course, only one person to take; that was Booker, the strange boy of thirteen who was Mr. Hart's only son. Booker was a quiet boy, good in school, and took after his mother, who was quite a little lighter complected than Mr. Hart. And so that night after supper he simply announced, "Tomorrow me and Booker's going over to see the New York Yankees play. A friend of mine happened to give me a choice pair of sets, so me and Booker's taking in the game." There had been a lot of talk, and naturally Booker was the most surprised of all—so surprised that Mr. Hart was not sure his son was even pleased. Booker was a very hard one to understand. Fortunately, Lolly believed right away that someone had really given Mr. Hart the tickets to the game; he had handed over his pay as usual, nothing missing, and that made her believe his story.

But that did not keep Mr. Hart from having an increasingly bad time from the fifth inning on. And Booker didn't help him to forget. Booker leaned forward and he followed the game all right but never said anything much. He seemed to know the game and to recognize the players, but never *talked*. He got up and yelled in the fifth inning when the Yanks were making their runs, but so did everybody else. Mr. Hart wished the game was over.

DiMaggio came to bat. Ball one. Strike one, called. Ball two. Mr. Hart wasn't watching with his heart in it. He had his eyes on DiMaggio, but it was the crack of the bat that made Mr. Hart realize that DiMaggio had taken a poke at one, and the ball was in the air, high in the air. Everybody around Mr. Hart stood up and tried to watch the ball. Mr. Hart stood up too. Booker sort of got up off the seat, watching the ball but not standing up. The ball hung in the air and then began to drop. Mr. Hart was judging it and could tell it was going to hit about four rows behind him. Then it did hit, falling the last few yards as though it had been thrown down from the sky, and smacko! it hit the seats four rows behind the Harts, bounced high but sort of crooked, and dropped again to the row directly behind Mr. Hart and Booker.

There was a scramble of men and kids, men hitting kids and kids darting and shoving men out of the way, trying to get the ball. Mr. Hart drew away, not wanting any trouble, and then he remembered Booker. He turned to look at Booker, and Booker was sitting hunched up, holding his arms so's to protect his head and face.

Where the hell's the ball? Where's the ball?" Men and kids were yelling and cursing, pushing and kicking each other, but nobody could find the ball. Two boys began to fight because one accused the other of pushing him when he almost had his hand on the ball. The fuss lasted until the end of the inning. Mr. Hart was nervous. He didn't want any trouble, so he concentrated on the game again. Booker had the right idea. He was concentrating on the game. They both concentrated like hell. All they could hear was a mystified murmur among the men and kids. "Well, somebody must of got the god-damn thing." In two minutes the Yanks retired the side and the ball game was over.

"Let's wait till the crowd gets started going, Pop," said Booker.

"O.K.," said Mr. Hart. He was in no hurry to get home,

with the things he had on his mind and how sore Lolly would be. He'd give her what was left of the ten bucks, but she'd be sore anyhow. He lit a cigarette and let it hang on his lip. He didn't feel so good sitting there with his elbow on his knee, his chin on his fist.

"Hey, Pop," said Booker.

"Huh?"

"Here," said Booker.

"What?" said Mr. Hart. He looked at his son. His son reached inside his shirt, looked back of him, and then from the inside of the shirt he brought out the ball. "Present for you," said Booker.

Mr. Hart looked down at it. "Lemme see that!" he said. He did not reach for it. Booker handed it to him.

"Go ahead, take it. It's a present for you," said Booker.

Suddenly Mr. Hart threw back his head and laughed. "I'll be god-damn holy son of a bitch. You got it? The ball?"

"Sure. It's for you," said Booker.

Mr. Hart threw back his head again and slapped his knees. "I'll be damn—boy, some Booker!" He put his arm around his son's shoulders and hugged him. "Boy, some Booker, huh? You givin' it to me? Some Booker!"

The King of the Desert

D AVE, BY far the biggest of the three men, gently tapped the edge of the table off the beat of the old record of "You Go to My Head" that was on the nickel-a-record phonograph. He was smiling, but not at anything, not even at himself. It was his regular smile that his face relaxed into when he was not revealing one of his emotions. Artie looked at the smile and turned and grinned at Ben.

"It must be nice to be like that," said Artie. "How is it to be like that, Dave old boy?"

"Like what, Artie?" said Dave.

"Like you. Nothing to worry about. Go-as-you-please and happy-go-lucky. Let a smile be your umbrella."

"That's where you're wrong," said Dave. "I got plenty to worry about. If I could tell you the stuff I worry about."

"You can," said Artie. "Go ahead, tell us. We're here till the station wagon comes. Make it a good story and we'll miss the bus, eh, Ben? Anything to keep from going back to that ranch. Only fooling. No, come on, Dave. What kind of thing would worry a big, rangy, easy-going feller like you?"

"Lots of things. I worry, but I'm sitting here enjoying a drink with a couple good fellers, why should I talk about my worries?" Dave smiled and then stopped smiling. "I got the ranch to worry about."

"Aah, don't give me that. The ranch? It runs itself. I could run it and I don't know a maverick from a congressman. Maverick the congressman. Skip it. No, now Dave, you can't give us that about the ranch." Artie patted his hands together several times. "Look, you got a piece of California desert. You put a house on it, dig yourself a well, put a couple horses on it, get credit. A feller like you can get credit anywhere, with that honest face."

"That's what *you* think," said Dave, grinning.

"All right, say you have a dishonest face and you can't get credit. Then you strike oil and you don't *need* credit. Not a gusher. Just enough oil to get you started running a dude ranch and a few quarts left over for the car, the windmill, the sewing machine. Will we let him have a few quarts left over, Bennie?"

"Sure. About a gallon and a half."

"Fine," said Artie. "So you have the whole setup *plus—plus*, mind you—this gallon of oil—"

"I said a gallon and a half! I let him have a gallon and a half!" screamed Bennie.

"A gallon's plenty. He wouldn't know what to do with a gallon and a half, a big boy like Dave. I decided to let him have four quarts, one gallon, and that's enough to start with. If he needs more, let him come to me and maybe I'll let him have my credit card at the filling station, good at any station in the U.S.A. It is, too. Here it is. You want to see it, Dave?" He pulled out his wallet and started to hand it to Dave, who reached for it. As he reached, Artie slapped his hand, playfully but sharply. "Take your hands off, you with your dishonest face. If you can't get credit. Anyway, you have the ranch. You advertise. Bennie and I see the ad and we get into our Super-Nooper Twin Sixteen Diesel and drive all the way from the film capital. Hollywood. One hundred fifteen miles. Between the two of us we pay you one hundred and twenty dollars a week for a room about the size of one of those shelfs they put stiffs on at the morgue. Not that I ever went there, please God, but *I* read the *Life* magazine. Anyway, for a room and seven threes, twenty-one, times two, forty-two meals that we don't eat we pay you a one, a two, a zero. That's your overhead. The profit on us takes care your overhead. For a month, if I'm any guesser."

"Two months," said Bennie.

"A gallon and a *half*!" said Artie. "Then multiply that by forta forta forta forta times sibba sibba sibba sabba, and what have you got?"

"He's got worries," said Bennie.

"Precisely," said Artie. "Precisely. Dave, you haven't a thing to worry about. Unless it's a woman. . . . *Ahhhhh.*"

Artie rolled his eyes. He stood up and shook his hips and sat down. "Ahhhh."

"Ah-ah-ah-ah-ah," said Bennie.

"Is it a woman, Dave? I'm glad you came to me instead

of one of those quacks on the next floor," said Artie. "Is it a woman, Artie? I mean Dave. My name's Artie."

"Aw, you guys're too fast for me," said Dave. He shifted in his chair and turned his head around to look at the other people in the bar. Artie kept looking at him. They sipped their drinks.

"That bus takes *long* enough," said Bennie. "How about another drink?" The waiter took their order.

Artie kept looking at Dave. "Now you've hurt Dave's feelings with your talk. Bus. *Station wagon*, you vulgarian. Dave spends frannis hundred dollars for a station wagon and you vulgarians from the film capital come down here and call it a bus. I know, though, don't I, Dave?"

"That's right, Artie," said Dave. "I think I'll put a nickel in the machine." He started to get up. Artie put his hands on his shoulders.

"I wouldn't think of it. Let me. Waiter!" said Artie. The waiter was coming with the drinks, and when he got to the table Artie gave him a quarter and told him to put five nickels in the phonograph. "You're the king of the desert but your money's no good here, Dave."

"O.K.," said Dave. "Only don't call me king of the desert. I'm not that."

"Well, prince then. What the hell," said Artie. "You know Dave, they tell me you use to play a lot of football for Southern Cal. Is there any truth in that rumor?"

"I got my letter."

"When was that, Dave? About ten years ago?"

"Just about," said Dave.

"You were a tackle, probably?"

"No, I was an end. I only weighed about one-ninety then," said Dave.

"Is that so? Now you're around two-thirty," said Artie.

"Hell, no. Two-eighteen's bad enough." He patted the heavy engraved-silver buckle of his belt.

"I see. Are you what they call a native son, Dave?"

"Well, I am, but my folks aren't Californians."

"Oh? Back East?" said Artie.

"Both sides of the family. From New England. Father's family came from Gloucester, Mass.—"

"Oh, sure. A whaling family?"

"Well, fishing. I guess some whaling," said Dave.

"And your mother's family, they from Gloucester too?" said Artie.

"Nope. All from Boston. Both my mother *and* my father's family came to this country right around the time of the *Mayflower*."

"I see. That makes you real old American stock, then."

"I guess just about as old as they come," said Dave.

"That's wonderful. I guess you can look down on these Whitneys and Vanderbilts and all these jerks that come out here during the racing season."

"Oh, I don't know. I imagine they go pretty far back. Anyway, what difference does it make?"

"What difference does it make? Why, you ought to take pride in a thing like that, oughtn't he, Ben? These days with all these un-Americanisms. Like rheumatism."

"What?"

"Now, come on, Dave, admit it. Down underneath, you having all these family ancestors and old New England stock, you feel that they're a little better than the rest of the common herd, don't you now, honest?"

"Sure I do, if it comes right down to it," said Dave.

Artie turned to Bennie. "What'd I tell you? A bit of a jerk."

He did not finish the long smile that he had begun. His face was not there. He was lying on the floor, and Dave, who had hit him sitting down, now stood up and started around the table after Bennie. Bennie was on his feet, but Dave grabbed him, raised his fist, and was about to hammer down on him, but changed his mind.

"What the hell's the idea?" said Bennie.

Dave started to laugh. "Sit down," he said, and threw Bennie back in his chair. The other people in the saloon were standing watching, but they stayed where they were.

"If you want your stuff, you can send out for it, but don't come yourself," said Dave.

"We'll fix you in Hollywood, Mister," said Bennie.

A young cop appeared. "What's the matter, Dave?"

"It's all right, Marv," said Dave. "A couple of wise guys."

"What about him?" said the cop, looking at Artie, who was out on the floor.

"His boy friend can worry about him," said Dave. "I got enough to worry about." Now he suddenly laughed.

Summer's Day

THERE WERE not very many people at the beach when Mr. and Mrs. Attrell arrived. On this particular day, a Wednesday, possibly a little more than half the morning swimming crowd had come out of the water and gone home for lunch, some on their bicycles, some on the bus which stopped almost anywhere you asked to stop, and a still rather large number driving their cars and station wagons. The comparatively few persons who stayed at the club for lunch sat about in their bathing suits in groups of anywhere from two to seven.

Mrs. Attrell got out of the car—a shiny black 1932 Buick with fairly good rubber and only about thirty thousand miles on it—at the clubhouse steps and waited while Mr. Attrell parked it at the space marked "A. T. Attrell." Mr. Attrell then joined his wife, took her by the arm, and adapted his pace to her slightly shorter steps. Together they made their way to their bench. The bench, seating six, had a sign with "A. T. Attrell" on it nailed to the back, and it was placed a few feet from the boardwalk. On this day, however, it was occupied by four young persons, and so Mr. and Mrs. Attrell altered their course and went to a bench just a bit lower on the dune than their own. Mrs. Attrell placed her blue tweed bag and her book, which was in its lending-library jacket, in her lap. She folded her hands and looked out at the sea. Mr. Attrell seated himself on her left, with his right arm resting on the back of the bench. In this way he was not sitting too close to her, but he had only to raise his hand and he could touch her shoulder. From time to time he did this, as they both looked out at the sea.

It was a beautiful, beautiful day and some of the hungry youngsters of teen age forgot about lunch and continued to swim and splash. Among them was Bryce Cartwright, twelve, grandson of Mr. and Mrs. Attrell's friend T. K. Cartwright, whose bench they now occupied.

"Bryce," said Mr. Attrell.

"Mm-hmm," said Mrs. Attrell, nodding twice.

They filled their lungs with the wonderful air and did not

speak for a little while. Then Mr. Attrell looked up the beach to his left. "Mr. O'Donnell," he said.

"Oh, yes. Mr. O'Donnell."

"Got some of his boys with him. Not all, though."

"I think the two oldest ones are at war," said Mrs. Attrell.

"Yes, I believe so. I think one's in the Army and the other's in, I *think*, the Navy."

Mr. O'Donnell was a powerfully built man who had played guard on an obscure Yale team before the last war. With him today, on parade, were his sons Gerald, Norton, Dwight, and Arthur Twining Hadley O'Donnell, who were sixteen, fourteen, twelve, and nine. Mrs. O'Donnell was at home with the baby which no one believed she was going to have until she actually had it. Mr. O'Donnell and the boys had been for a walk along the beach and now the proud father and his skinny brown sons were coming up the boardwalk on their way to lunch. A few yards away from the Cartwright bench Mr. O'Donnell began his big grin for the Attrells, looking at Mrs. Attrell, then at Mr. Attrell, then by compulsion at Mr. Attrell's hatband, that of a Yale society, which Mr. O'Donnell had nothing against, although he had not made it or any other.

"Mr. and Mrs. Attrell," he said, bowing.

"How do you do, Mr. O'Donnell?" said Mr. Attrell.

"How do you do, Mr. O'Donnell?" said Mrs. Attrell.

"You don't want to miss that ocean today, Mr. Attrell," said Mr. O'Donnell. "Magnificent." He passed on, and Mr. Attrell laughed politely. Mr. O'Donnell's greetings had, of course, done for the boys as well. They did not speak, nor did they even, like their father, slow down on their way to the bathhouse.

"He's an agreeable fellow, Henry O'Donnell," said Mr. Attrell.

"Yes, they're a nice big family," said his wife. Then she removed the rubber band which marked her page in her book and took out her spectacles. Mr. Attrell filled his pipe but made no move to light it. At that moment a vastly pregnant and pretty young woman—no one he knew—went down the boardwalk in her bathing suit. He turned to his wife, but she was already reading. He put his elbow on the back of the bench and he was about to touch his wife's shoulder again when a shadow fell across his leg.

"Hello, Mrs. Attrell, Mr. Attrell. I just came over to say hello." It was a tall young man in a white uniform with the shoulder-board stripe-and-a-half of a lieutenant junior grade.

"Why, it's Frank," said Mrs. Attrell. "How are you?"

"Why, hello," said Mr. Attrell, rising.

"Just fine," said Frank. "Please don't get up. I was on my way home and I saw your car in the parking space so I thought I'd come and say hello."

"Well, I should think so," said Mr. Attrell. "Sit down. Sit down and tell us all about yourself."

"Yes, we're using your bench. I suppose you noticed," said Mrs. Attrell.

"Father'll send you a bill for it, as you well know," said Frank. "You know Father."

They all had a good laugh on that.

"Where are you now?" said Mr. Attrell.

"I'm at a place called Quonset."

"Oh, yes," said Mrs. Attrell.

"Rhode Island," said Frank.

"Oh, I see," said Mrs. Attrell.

"Yes, I think I know where it is," said Mr. Attrell. "Then do you go on a ship?"

"I hope to. You both look extremely well," said Frank.

"Well, you know," said Mr. Attrell.

"When you get our age you have nothing much else to do," said Mrs. Attrell.

"Well, you do it beautifully. I'm sorry I've got to hurry away like this but I have some people waiting in the car, but I had to say hello. I'm going back this afternoon."

"Well, thank you for coming over. It was very nice of you. Is your wife down?" said Mrs. Attrell.

"No, she's with her family in Hyannis Port."

"Well, remember us to her when you see her," said Mrs. Attrell.

"Yes," said Mr. Attrell. They shook hands with Frank and he departed.

Mr. Attrell sat down. "Frank's a fine boy. That just shows how considerate, seeing our car. How old is Frank, about?"

"He'll be thirty-four in September," said Mrs. Attrell.

Mr. Attrell nodded slowly. "Yes, that's right," he said. He began tamping down the tobacco in his pipe. "You know, I think that water—would you mind if I had a dip?"

"No, dear, but I think you ought to do it soon, before it begins to get chilly."

"Remember we're on daylight saving, so it's an hour earlier by the sun." He stood up. "I think I'll just put on my suit and get wet, and if it's too cold I'll come right out."

"That's a good idea," she said.

In the bathhouse Mr. Attrell accepted two towels from the Negro attendant and went to his booth, which was open and marked "A. T. Attrell," to undress. From the voices there could not have been more than half a dozen persons in the men's side. At first he paid no attention to the voices, but after he had untied the double knot in his shoelaces he let the words come to him.

"And who is T. K. Cartwright?" a young voice was saying.

"He's dead," said the second young voice.

"No he isn't," said the first young voice. "That's the old buzzard that's sitting in front of us."

"And what makes you think *he* isn't dead, he and the old biddy?"

"You're both wrong," said a third young voice. "That isn't Mr. Cartwright sitting there. That's Mr. Attrell."

"So what?" said the first young voice.

"All right, so what, if you don't want to hear about them, old Attrell and his wife. They're the local tragedy. Ask your mother; she used to come here. They had a daughter or, I don't know, maybe it was a son. Anyway, whichever it was, he or she hung himself."

"Or herself," said the first young voice.

"I think it was a girl. They came home and found her hanging in the stable. It was an unfortunate love affair. I don't see why—"

"Just a minute, there." Mr. Attrell recognized the voice of Henry O'Donnell.

"Yes, sir?" asked one young voice.

"You sound to me like a pack of goddam pansies. You oughta be over on the girls' side," said Mr. O'Donnell.

"I'd like to know what business of—" a young voice said, then there was a loud smack.

"Because I made it my business. Get dressed and get outa here," said O'Donnell. "I don't give a damn whose kids you are."

Mr. Attrell heard the deep breathing of Henry O'Donnell, who waited a moment for his command to be obeyed, then walked past Mr. Attrell's booth with his head in the other direction. Mr. Attrell sat there, many minutes probably, wondering how he could ever again face Henry O'Donnell, worrying about how he could face his wife. But then of course he realized that there was really nothing to face, really nothing.

Graven Image

THE CAR turned in at the brief, crescent-shaped drive and waited until the two cabs ahead had pulled away. The car pulled up, the doorman opened the rear door, a little man got out. The little man nodded pleasantly enough to the doorman and said "Wait" to the chauffeur. "Will the Under Secretary be here long?" asked the doorman.

"Why?" said the little man.

"Because if you were going to be here, sir, only a short while, I'd let your man leave the car here, at the head of the rank."

"Leave it there *anyway*," said the Under Secretary.

"Very good, sir," said the doorman. He saluted and frowned only a little as he watched the Under Secretary enter the hotel. "Well," the doorman said to himself, "it was a long time coming. It took him longer than most, but sooner or later all of them—" He opened the door of the next car, addressed a colonel and a major by their titles, and never did anything about the Under Secretary's car, which pulled ahead and parked in the drive.

The Under Secretary was spoken to many times in his progress to the main dining room. One man said, "What's your hurry, Joe?" to which the Under Secretary smiled and nodded. He was called Mr. Secretary most often, in some cases easily, by the old Washington hands, but more frequently with that embarrassment which Americans feel in using titles. As he passed through the lobby, the Under Secretary himself addressed by their White House nicknames two gentlemen whom he had to acknowledge to be closer to The Boss. And, bustling all the while, he made his way to the dining room, which was already packed. At the entrance he stopped short and frowned. The man he was to meet, Charles Browning, was chatting, in French, very amiably with the maître d'hôtel. Browning and the Under Secretary had been at Harvard at the same time.

The Under Secretary went up to him. "Sorry if I'm a little late," he said, and held out his hand, at the same time looking at his pocket watch. "Not so very, though. How are you, Charles? Fred, you got my message?"

"Yes, sir," said the maître d'hôtel. "I put you at a nice table all the way back to the right." He meanwhile had wigwagged a captain, who stood by to lead the Under Secretary and his guest to Table 12. "Nice to have seen you again, Mr. Browning. Hope you come see us again while you are in Washington. Always a pleasure, sir."

"Always a pleasure, Fred," said Browning. He turned to the Under Secretary. "Well, shall we?"

"Yeah, let's sit down," said the Under Secretary.

The captain led the way, followed by the Under Secretary, walking slightly sideways. Browning, making one step to two of the Under Secretary's, brought up the rear. When they were seated, the Under Secretary took the menu out of the captain's hands. "Let's order right away so I don't have to look up and talk to those two son of a bitches. I guess you know which two I mean." Browning looked from right to left, as anyone does on just sitting down in a restaurant. He nodded and said, "Yes, I think I know. You mean the senators."

"That's right," said the Under Secretary. "I'm not gonna have a cocktail, but you can. . . . I'll have the lobster. Peas. Shoestring potatoes. . . . You want a cocktail?"

"I don't think so. I'll take whatever you're having."

"O.K., waiter?" said the Under Secretary.

"Yes, sir," said the captain, and went away.

"Well, Charles, I was pretty surprised to hear from you."

"Yes," Browning said, "I should imagine so, and by the way, I want to thank you for answering my letter so promptly. I know how rushed you fellows must be, and I thought, as I said in my letter, at your convenience."

"Mm. Well, frankly, there wasn't any use in putting you off. I mean till next week or two weeks from now or anything like that. I could just as easily see you today as a month from now. Maybe easier. I don't know where I'll be likely to be a month from now. In more ways than one. I may be taking the Clipper to London, and then of course I may be out on my can! Coming to New York and asking *you* for a job. I take it that's what you wanted to see me about."

"Yes, and with hat in hand."

"Oh, no. I can't see you waiting with hat in hand, not for anybody. Not even for The Boss."

Browning laughed.

"What are you laughing at?" asked the Under Secretary.

"Well, you know how I feel about him, so I'd say least of all The Boss."

"Well, you've got plenty of company in this goddam town. But why'd you come to me, then? Why didn't you go to one of your Union League or Junior League or whatever-the-hell-it-is pals? There, that big jerk over there with the blue suit and the striped tie, for instance?"

Browning looked over at the big jerk with the blue suit and striped tie, and at that moment their eyes met and the two men nodded.

"You *know* him?" said the Under Secretary.

"Sure, I know him, but that doesn't say I *approve* of him."

"Well, at least that's something. And I notice he knows you."

"I've been to his house. I think he's been to our house when my father was alive, and naturally I've seen him around New York all my life."

"Naturally. Naturally. Then why didn't you go to *him*?"

"That's easy. I wouldn't like to ask him for anything. I don't approve of the man, at least as a politician, so I couldn't go to him and ask him a favor."

"But, on the other hand, you're not one of our team, but yet you'd ask me a favor. I don't get it."

"Oh, yes you do, Joe. You didn't get where you are by not being able to understand a simple thing like that."

Reluctantly—and quite obviously it was reluctantly—the Under Secretary grinned. "All right. I was baiting you."

"I know you were, but I expected it. I have it coming to me. I've always been against you fellows. I wasn't even for you in 1932, and that's a hell of an admission, but it's the truth. But that's water under the bridge—or isn't it?" The waiter interrupted with the food, and they did not speak until he had gone away.

"You were asking me if it isn't water under the bridge. Why should it be?"

"The obvious reason," said Browning.

"'My country, 'tis of thee'?"

"Exactly. Isn't that enough?"

"It isn't for your Racquet Club pal over there."

"You keep track of things like that?"

"Certainly," said the Under Secretary. "I know every god-dam club in this country, beginning back about twenty-three years ago. I had ample time to study them all then, you recall, objectively, from the outside. By the way, I notice you wear a wristwatch. What happens to the little animal?"

Browning put his hand in his pocket and brought out a small bunch of keys. He held the chain so that the Under Secretary could see, suspended from it, a small golden pig. "I still carry it," he said.

"They tell me a lot of you fellows put them back in your pockets about five years ago, when one of the illustrious breth-ren closed his downtown office and moved up to Ossining."

"Oh, probably," Browning said, "but quite a few fellows, I believe, that hadn't been wearing them took to wearing them again out of simple loyalty. Listen, Joe, are we talking like grown men? Are you sore at the Pork? Do you think you'd have enjoyed being a member of it? If being sore at it was even partly responsible for getting you where you are, then I think you ought to be a little grateful to it. You'd show the bastard. O.K. You showed them. Us. If you hadn't been so sore at the Porcellian so-and-so's, you might have turned into just another lawyer."

"My wife gives me that sometimes."

"There, do you see?" Browning said. "Now then, how about the job?"

The Under Secretary smiled. "There's no getting away from it, you guys have got something. O.K., what are you interested in? Of course, I make no promises and I don't even know if what you're interested in is something I can help you with."

"That's a chance I'll take. That's why I came to Washington, on just that chance, but it's my guess you can help me." Browning went on to tell the Under Secretary about the job he wanted. He told him why he thought he was qualified for it, and the Under Secretary nodded. Browning told him everything he knew about the job, and the Under Secretary continued to nod silently. By the end of Browning's recital the Under Secretary had become thoughtful. He told Browning that he thought there might be some little trouble with a certain character but that that character could be handled, because the real say-so, the green light, was controlled by a man who was a friend of the Under Secretary's, and the Under Secretary could almost say at this moment that the matter could be arranged.

At this, Browning grinned. "By God, Joe, we've got to have a drink on this. This is the best news since—" He summoned the waiter. The Under Secretary yielded and ordered a cordial. Browning ordered a Scotch. The drinks were brought. Browning said, "About the job. I'm not going to say another word but just keep my fingers crossed. But as to you, Joe, you're the best. I drink to you." The two men drank, the Under Secretary sipping at his, Browning taking half of his. Browning looked at the drink in his hand. "You know, I was a little afraid. That other stuff, the club stuff."

"Yes," said the Under Secretary.

"I don't know why fellows like you—you never would have made it in a thousand years, but"—then, without looking up, he knew everything had collapsed—"but I've said exactly the wrong thing, haven't I?"

"That's right, Browning," said the Under Secretary. "You've said exactly the wrong thing. I've got to be going." He stood up and turned and went out, all dignity.

The Next-to-Last Dance of the Season

IT WAS not the last dance of the summer. There would be one more, which was to be as much of a gala as there could be under the present circumstances. The women were marshalling and pooling their points for the dinner parties that would take place before the final dance They were saving their nicest dresses and watching their gasoline coupons so they could wait until the next Friday, the very last minute, to drive the fifteen miles—thirty for the round trip—to the nearest good hairdresser. This harassed individual was having the devil's own time trying to satisfy all her customers with appointments for that one day, and almost every request for a half hour of her time carried with it some pleading, a bribe, or both. But of course no threats of discontinued patronage. Not this year.

A good many of the husbands were not coming down to the country for this dance. They too were saving up for the final one. Some of them were going to do some extra work, and a few had no great amount of work in mind, but in either case the men who stayed in town this weekend were doing so because the final dance was a must. Sons in the armed forces knew without being reminded that they were wanted and expected next week. The younger girls were urging them to be on their good behavior and remain eligible for leaves. Servants were given extra time off against the extra work they would inevitably be asked to do the next week. The tradespeople were being handled with extraordinary care, and especially the proprietors of the three filling stations, who were rather spoiled already.

The flags and the bunting were stored in the club office. Sonny Wine had promised he would appear with an augmented orchestra. The House Committee had O.K.'d the bar order back early in August, to assure delivery in plenty of time. All things considered, the final dance of the season was being well planned, and you didn't really have to add "under the present circumstances."

And yet sometime late in the afternoon of the semi-final dance there began to be something in the air. There was the obvious fact that it threatened rain. Around three o'clock the lovely breeze from the southwest shifted to the west and north-west, but suddenly shifted back again a few minutes past five. By that time the good, browning sun had gone for the day and the swimmers were on their way home or on the tennis courts. But it was something other than the weather that affected people this particular afternoon. It may have been the simple fact that tonight's dance was going to be a relaxed sort of affair, with none of the elaborate preparations that were being made for the final shindig. Only five or six women planned to dress for tonight's dance and not a few of the men were wearing the same white ducks they had worn to the beach in the morning. At the most there were three small dinner parties planned at the club for the evening; everybody else was eating at home. Not a single sizable cocktail party had been arranged. And yet around five-thirty things began to happen.

It is manifestly impossible to determine which was the first occurrence that started the rather remarkable series of events on the evening of the next-to-last dance of the season. But, sticking to the actual facts, it is absolutely true that at exactly five twenty-eight Mary Choate said "Hello, Doris" to Doris Cantwell. Both girls were on their bicycles on their way to their respective homes. As everyone in the community knew, Mary Choate never in her life had spoken to Doris Cantwell. Mary spoke to no one who had not been summering in the community for thirteen years, or, roughly, since the Crash. The girls were of an age—thirty. They never had quarrelled, nor was there any trouble between the Cantwells and the Choates. It was just that Mary never had said a word to Doris Cantwell until this particular afternoon. Doris nearly fell off her bicycle, and Mary had pedalled away before Doris was able to return the greeting. The confusion engendered in Doris's mind may well be imagined.

A minute later, in another part of the village, Sam Ainsley, who was down to his shorts, said to his wife, Vera, who still had on the white sharkskin dress she'd been playing tennis in, "Go ahead. You take your bath first."

"What!" exclaimed Vera. This reversal of the Ainsleys' bath-ing order shattered a tradition of nineteen years' standing, or, in other words, took them back to the second summer of their marriage. Unfortunately, Vera did not take advantage of Sam's offer. Being a practical woman, she argued that Sam was ready for his bath and she was still dressed. Sam pointed out that what she had on could be taken off in less than sixty seconds, but Vera was stern. Sam warned her she might catch cold, and Vera replied that she never had before so why didn't he stop arguing. Sam yielded, went in, and was singing of D.K.E., the mother of jollity, whose children are gay and free, and thus did not hear Vera's sneeze. This served her right, as at that precise moment she was wondering if perhaps Sam wasn't getting some of his mail at the University Club.

Things were quiet in the village for the next ten minutes. Then Rouge, a three-gaited bay mare owned by some people called Scott, reared up while being rubbed down, jumped a six-foot fence, and was shot by Coast Guardsmen at one-thirty the next morning. Rouge would have been nine years old the first of the year.

At six, or thereabouts, Elton Ponsonby, who is a man in his late forties, telephoned Mrs. Hagedorn, a lady old enough to be his mother, and said, "Mizz Hagedorn, thiz Elton Ponsonby. I just heard you said I never draw a sober breath."

"Now Elton," said Mrs. Hagedorn, who had known Elton's mother very well.

"Well, come on overt our place tomorrow afternoon about three o'clock. I'm gonna draw one." He then hung up.

Sonny Wine and his regular, unaugmented band arrived on the six-five, but Artie Burns' drums had been put off the train at some earlier station. Musically, this may have been all to the good, since Artie was not exactly a Sonny Greer in percussion circles and he was more than likely, after the long intermission, to permit Elton Ponsonby or the youngest Boone kid to sit in in his place. Elton Ponsonby no more belonged at the drums in a dance band than the late E. T. Stotesbury and young Boone hadn't even entered Mercersburg yet. Still, the accident of the jettisoned drums somehow fitted in the general picture, it not having happened ever before.

The coming fact bears only the remotest relation to the preceding and those to follow, and it is germane only for obvious reasons: at twenty past six Norman Chew, one of the village policemen, missed a cross-corner shot which, if he had made it, would have equalled the high run of forty-eight balls which is the record at the Elks'. Norman had not intended to be present at the dance, as he hated the summer people, but he usually helped the late stayers with his flashlight. He was so disappointed at failing to equal the Elks' high run that he spent the rest of the evening playing pinochle. That was sad, because some people rather counted on Norman.

Not that this is important either, but Dr. Gordon Macgregor, who possessed a collection of eighty-four pipes, could not find a match in the whole goddam house. That was going on twenty of seven.

At six forty-five more than two hundred of the sporting enthusiasts (natives and summer people) tried to tune in on Stan Lomax. They all either turned off their radios or changed to some other station, so bad was the static. This proves that there may have been something in the air after all. Dressed, ready for dinner, hungry, and thwarted by the static and with at least fifteen minutes on his hands, a certain lad of fifteen made a serious pass at his mother's maid, and this time she slapped him right across the face. This was noteworthy principally because she had been threatening to for over a year, but never had.

There was no hot water at the Barbours'. This was infuriating and embarrassing to Mr. Barbour, because the hot-water system was practically brand-new (1941) and Mr. Barbour, who was a Tau Beta Pi from M. I. T., went over the whole system and couldn't find a single thing wrong with it.

A girl named Sallie Lynes, who was staying with the Stevenses, came across a dozen pairs of nylons while looking around her room for a safety pin. So delighted was Augusta Stevens that she shared this wonderful find with her honorable guest. Augusta couldn't remember ever having bought them and absolutely insisted that Sallie take half a dozen pairs.

The preceding two items are placed at roughly seven o'clock. At three minutes past seven—1903, as time is indicated in the services—the burglar alarm at the bank went off by accident. This was quite a coincidence, as Wayne Buffington, assistant cashier at the bank, was born in 1903 and has a son in the Navy who will be nineteen next March (third month of the year). Wayne, as is the local custom, was married very young. He fits into the picture because he is one of the few natives who are members of the club and as a matter of fact was planning to attend the dance. Wayne has always gotten along very well with the summer people and has won several cups with his knockabout in competition with the club members. He decided not to go to the dance at the last minute, as he only lives down the street from the bank and he thought, after the alarm went off, that he ought to stick around in case there was anything to it. The Buffingtons are an interesting old family and sometime it might be worth someone's while to go into their history.

Practically everyone sat down to dinner shortly after seven and apparently no one had any adventures worth repeating, or if they did, perhaps they were not *fit* to repeat. A few of the young kids turned up at the dance a little before nine o'clock, at which time the music began. By ten-thirty the floor was about half full. At ten past eleven three couples came and stood on the porch for a while but decided the party didn't look too tempting, so they went home and four of them played bridge and the other two played gin rummy.

The club lost money on the dance, not even making enough to pay the orchestra, but that was more or less anticipated, with all the big plans for the final dance. Nevertheless, as almost everybody remarked the next day, many remarkable things occurred on what most people thought was going to be the dullest Saturday of the season.

The Pretty Daughters

THE MAJOR climbed in the company car and gave the driver the address. He put the attaché case beside him, stretched out his legs at an angle, and lit a cigar. At the exit gate the plant guard picked up the Major's pass and gave him a snappy non-reg salute, and the Major was on his way.

The night before and that morning there had been a heavy fall of snow. It had stopped now, but there had not been time to clear the streets, and the car's progress toward the city's residential district was slow. The Major was enjoying his cigar, the fact that soon he would be out of the Army, and the ride. It took him back to Christmas holidays twenty years ago when he would visit his classmates in cities like Hartford and Buffalo and Harrisburg. Once you got out of the built-up districts and into the sections where the houses were larger and had more ground around them, each anonymous house would hold a promise of fun. White house. Redbrick house. French type. Georgian type. Dutch Colonial type. Old Manse type. You didn't know who lived in any of them, but maybe in one of them, as you went from the station to the home of the people you were visiting, there would be a girl, a pretty daughter. Maybe at the very moment you passed her house she was out skiing or tobogganing, or maybe she was right there, taking a nap so she would look her best for the dance that night, the dances that occurred every night of your visit to these towns—Columbus, Reading, Binghamton. You never got to know much about the towns. If you did happen to drive a borrowed car, you were told where to go and how to get there, and "there" meant someone's house or the country club or the city club or the big hotel. You never stayed long enough to find your way about the town, and anyhow most of the driving was done at night, in a Packard or a Jordan or a Marmon or a Ford, with the side curtains flopping and the tire chains banging.

In the daytime if you went anywhere it usually was to some-one's house three or four doors away, and you walked. You wore your coonskin coat and no hat and galoshes. You would time your arrival so that you would get there after the athletic ones who had been sliding down some hill. Everybody would drink a lot of tea and eat a great many watercress sandwiches. The girls would kick off their ski boots, which they wore whether they had been skiing or sitting around the country-club fireplace. The mother of the hostess of the moment would look in and there would be introductions and then she would depart, and presently the father would come home and beam on everyone, kissing most of the girls and making a joke about taking the boys to see the moose head in his den. The daughter of the house would pretend to be irritated. "Lord and *Tay*lor, Daddy! You'll have everybody fried before the Baldwins'." The boys would go to Daddy's den and have straight whiskey or ginger-ale highballs, and Daddy would shake up Orange Blossoms and take the shaker back to the girls. He would return to the den and politely inquire about the out-of-town boys' school and family origins and then he would turn the job of barkeep over to his son, if any, or to a neighbor's son who had the run of the house, and excuse himself to get into his tux or full dress . . .

"Was that twenty-three thirty-eight, sir?" said the driver.

"I think so. Wait till I look." The Major opened his trench coat and unbuttoned the top left pocket of his blouse. He read from a slip of paper. "Twenty-three forty-eight," he said.

The driver slowed down until the car was barely moving. "I think this must be it. I don't see no number, but that last was twenty-three thirty-eight."

"I think you're probably right," said the Major. "I'll get out here."

"I'll go up and ask if it's the right house," said the driver.

"Will you? Fine. Thanks."

The driver went up to the porte-cochère, following car tracks that obviously had been made hours before and in which there were a few footprints. In a few minutes he was back. "Yes, sir, this is it. They're expecting you. Major Robb, the lady said."

"That's me," said the Major. He got out and gave the driver two dollars. "I'll get a taxi from here. You needn't wait."

He followed the driver's path and was knocking the snow off his feet when the door opened, before he had rung.

"Come in, Major Robb. I'm Jean Reeves. Mother's around the corner at a meeting and she told me to entertain you till she got here."

"That's very nice of you," he said. He put his gear on a chair in the dark hall and followed the girl into a small, panelled room, in which there was a fire. The girl was quite tall and she wore a slipover and a cardigan, a tweed skirt, moccasins, a pearl necklace. He placed her age at twenty, but knew he must be wrong—she should be younger—and he was confused by her total lack of resemblance to Nancy, who beside this girl would be short and probably, by this time, sturdy. This girl had a superb, pared-down figure.

"I'd never know you were Nancy's daughter."

"I'm not. I'm her stepdaughter. She inherited me when she married Daddy."

"Oh, that explains it. I'm sorry your father's not here. I'd like to have met him."

"He had to go to Chicago this morning. I suppose Mother told you. We'll have tea when she gets here. Meanwhile, would you like something else? We have just about everything."

"I'd love a, uh, bourbon with a piece of ice in it," he said. "No fruit, no bitters, no sugar. Can you swing that?"

"That can be arranged and it's what I want, too." She opened a panelled door to a bar. He stood by the fire until she handed him his drink, and they sat down, facing each other, in front of the fireplace.

"Well, this is mighty pleasant. I was afraid your mother wouldn't remember me when I phoned."

"Well, frankly, she was quite surprised. But pleased, I can tell you that." She smiled. For the first time he noticed she was wearing a miniature Navy cap device.

"I see the Navy has moved in," he said.

"In a manner of speaking," she said.

"In a manner of speaking? Not married."

"Not married, but spoken for, in a manner of speaking."

"The Navy has good taste," said Robb.

"Thank you. And I'm glad to hear you say it, not only because of me, but don't you get tired of hearing the Army pan the Navy and vice versa? It's pretty silly."

"It is if you're fighting the kind of war I'm fighting. It doesn't make a hell of a lot of difference what color suit I wear. You can see by the absence of any ribbons that I haven't been using up much plasma."

"Well, you're a major, though."

"Even that's fairly recent, and I'm getting out pretty soon. I'm doing just about what I've always done, except I'm doing it for slightly less money. In civil life I'm a lawyer. I read contracts. In the Army I'm a lawyer, reading contracts. What about you, Jean? What did you do before the war? Paint, for instance?"

"Why did you happen to pick on that?"

"I used to know a girl in New York that looked a little like you. She was an artist's model and she painted."

"Oh, that's a relief. The kind of painting I've done wouldn't justify my looking artistic."

"Don't let it worry you. Even if I hadn't known the other girl painted, I would have guessed that you'd done some posing."

"I have a little, for Mother."

"Does she paint, too? I didn't know that. Of course, I haven't seen her in fifteen years or more, so in that time she could have turned into a—a rodeo rider."

"That sounds a little disrespectful, but I'll let it pass."

"It isn't a bit disrespectful. I once knew a damned attractive rodeo rider. Very pretty, very intelligent, went to the University of Wyoming."

The girl nodded. "Mother did say you—you got around a lot."

"What did she *actually* say?" He smiled.

She hesitated. "Well, she said that if the term had been used in her day, you'd probably have been called a wolf."

"*Dear* Nancy. That's quite a build-up, isn't it?" He was annoyed.

"I think she's wrong about wolf."

"Why?"

She considered a moment. "Because wolf means predatory. I don't think Mother knows that. Wolf's a new word since her day. I think she thinks anybody that goes around with a lot of girls is a wolf. That isn't what wolf means, necessarily. A wolf—a wolf is out to make a score, just for the sake of the score. I don't think you're that."

"Thank you," he said. "You're not entirely right about me, but thank you."

"Why? Were you a wolf? Or *are* you?"

He studied his glass. "I've—I've done some howling on occasion. Put it that way. The fact is, I suppose your mother is justified. Shall I wait outside till your mother gets here?"

She did not answer, but got up and took his glass and filled it again, and her own with it.

"How old are you, Jean?"

"Twenty-three. Why?"

"I don't know," he said. He was suddenly unaccountably depressed.

She waited for him to go on, and when he did not, she addressed him rather too heartily. "What's come over you? Don't sit there making a long face."

"And don't you give me orders. Remember I'm old enough to be your father."

"And don't you pull rank on me, or age either."

"I can certainly pull age on you."

"Oh, no," she said. She put her hand over the Navy pin. "Do you think this stands for some twenty-three-year-old j.g.? How old are *you?*"

"Thirty-nine."

She laughed condescendingly. "A boy. This character is forty and a lieutenant commander."

"Maybe he's a *young* forty. I'm an old thirty-nine."

"You're both the same."

He realized that the time had passed for making jokes. "What did you mean when you said you were spoken for? I assume the gentleman is married."

"Very much married. Very *happily* married, probably, although he'd never admit it to me. Spoken for? I don't know what I did mean. I don't know why I said that, any more than I know why I wear this pin." She looked down at it and then very deliberately took it off. "I hope that will do some good."

"Maybe it will," he said, "if you want it to enough."

"Good God! If I want it to! He won't answer my phone calls. He's in San Francisco, but I know he's been East twice without looking me up or letting me know so I could go and see him. He's one of you New Yorkers. You probably know him. Nobody *here* knows him. Oh, he is *really* a bastard."

Her fury was exciting, but Robb did not know what to do next, or say. "We all are," he said.

"Yes," she said. She looked at him intently. "Why did you look up Mother after all these years?"

"In the neighborhood. Thought it'd be nice to see her again."

"No," she said.

"No?"

"No. You thought to yourself, 'Nancy lives in this town. Might be a good idea to look her up. She might not be too bad and it might be a very nice thing. A very nice thing.' That's what you thought."

He laughed. "You're exactly right. That's exactly what I did think."

"Of course it was. Well, Major Robb, you'd be disappointed, if I know you. She's completely domesticated, doing good works and not taking care of her figure. Oh, I can see your face when you get your first look at Mother. In fact, you're beginning to look that way now."

"I'll try not to any more," he said. He showed his teeth in a burlesque smile. "Is that better?"

"You have nice teeth," she said.

"Thanks. Listen, kid, do you want me to go?" When she did not answer, he went on. "You do, don't you?"

"No," she said.

"I ought to wait and say hello to your mother."

"I don't want you to go." She stood up and then seemed not to know why she had stood up. She looked at him helplessly and he got up and put his arms around her. She shut her eyes and kissed him, but there was nothing to it.

"I'm sorry, Jean," he said.

"I wanted you to kiss me."

"That isn't what I'm sorry about," he said. She looked down and away from him.

"You're sorry for me?"

"Yes."

"I'll say goodbye now," she said.

"All right," he said. She went out of the room and he heard her go upstairs, heard her moving around on the floor above, and again came that feeling of depression, but now, with it, the feeling that he was beginning to serve a sentence.

Common Sense Should Tell You

THERE WERE five in the party, and when they had been seated, the proprietor came over to their table. He nodded to the two girls and to two of the men, none of whose names he knew, although the girls spoke to him by name. Then he said to the third man, "Glad to see you in Chicago, Mr. Spring. Gonna be with us a while, I hope."

"Hello, Mike," said Mr. Spring. He shook hands without standing up. "No, I'm on my way back to the Coast. Just staying overnight."

"Whenner you gonna stay over a couple days again? Like to throw a little party for you again. Remember that one six or seven years ago? In nineteen-and-thirty-nine, I think it was."

"Indeed I do remember it. I'll never forget it. But those days are gone forever, I'm afraid."

"Not for you, Mr. Spring," said Mike. He leaned over and whispered in Spring's ear. "If you see anything in the show you like I'll be glad to fix it up for you."

"Thanks, Mike. I'll let you know. Uh, you know all these people? This is Harry Field, charge of publicity on the Coast, and this is Jake Coombs, my trainer, and I forget the young ladies' names."

"Betty Donaldson," said Betty Donaldson. "Hello, Mike."

"Audrey French," said Audrey French. "Hello, Mike."

"Oh, I've known Mike for years," said Harry Field. "I very seldom pass through Chicago without dropping in."

"That's right," said Mike. "Well, enjoy yourselves, Mr. Spring." He left them, stopping to speak to the maître-dee and at two or three tables, obviously explaining to the people at the tables that Mr. Spring was Mr. Spring, the famous Hollywood producer, an old friend, on his way back to the Coast with his press agent and trainer. The pretty girls were Chicago girls.

The floor show had not started and the relief band was at work. "You people dance if you feel like it," said Mr. Spring.

"Don't you want to, Mr. Spring?" said Field.

"Not right away," said Mr. Spring. His four companions got up and Mr. Spring was alone, practically the first time he had been alone in the two days since he had left Johns Hopkins. He took out a cigar from a case which had been given him by an ex-President of the United States. He replaced the case in the coat of a suit which he had bought from Eddie Schmidt. He snipped off the end of the cigar with a gold cigar cutter which an English actor had bought for him at Asprey's, and lit the cigar with a gold lighter-and-watch which he could not with any certainty ever have identified, since he possessed at least twenty exactly like it. He got a good light and then remembered the orders of the men at Johns Hopkins. "You'd better limit yourself to two a day, Mr. Spring," one man had said. "None at all, if you can do without them. No brandy. No golf. I don't want you to drive a car or gamble or run upstairs, and try to keep your temper and don't get in quarrels with people. No more making speeches."

"You don't leave me much. What about women?"

The doctor had smiled. "From my information, Mr. Spring, you're going to go right on doing as you please about women, but common sense should tell you . . ."

"What if I ignored everything you tell me?"

"Then one of these days you'll feel as if somebody had given you a good swift kick all over the whole left side of your body."

"How long'll that last?"

"I don't know. You might lose your eyesight, too."

"How long'll I last if I *take* your advice?" Mr. Spring had asked.

The doctor had hesitated. "As a rule, I give an evasive answer to that one, but with you I don't think I have to. Take care of yourself, and you have between five and ten years more."

"It hardly seems worth it, does it?"

The doctor had been slightly shocked and annoyed. "I don't know why not. A lot of people that come here would be glad of your chance."

"You're a Catholic, aren't you, Doctor? I never been able to understand how a Catholic can be a good doctor or a good doctor can be a Catholic. Notwithstanding a lot of them are."

"Well, we haven't got time to go into that now, Mr. Spring. I have other patients waiting."

"I beg pardon, Doctor." It was not often that Mr. Spring was put in his place.

He let the cigar go out, resting the lighted end in the ashtray. He watched the dancers with no interest and hummed with the music. When his companions returned he put his right hand on the back of the chair to his right, then put his left hand on the back of the chair to his left. This served as a substitute for standing up for the young ladies. Betty and Audrey looked at him, waiting for him to say something.

"Enjoy your dance?" he said.

They said they had, and he nodded with solemn approval, putting across the further idea that he didn't feel like talking, whereupon Harry and Jake reopened their conversations with the girls. Almost immediately the floor show started.

It was awful. It hadn't been good to begin with, but tonight everyone played with the knowledge that Mr. Spring was at Table 12. In case anyone didn't know the location of Table 12, it was the table behind which stood a captain and two waiters, and if people to the rear could not see through the captain and waiters, that was too bad.

The chorus came out, bumping into each other and generally lousing up the routine in their eagerness to smile for Mr. Spring. The master of ceremonies trotted out to the microphone and tried hard not to look in Mr. Spring's direction, but before he was halfway through his song he was looking nowhere else. Zita and Leonardo, the society dancers, kept to Mr. Spring's side of the floor, and Leonardo almost dropped Zita during a spin. The chorus and the showgirls came out again and got in each other's way; Patsy Whitney, who did imitations, became confused at finding herself started on a rather mean imitation of one of Mr. Spring's stars after Mike had distinctly told her to leave it out tonight; Bobby Renwick, the harmonica player, came right over and stood at the edge of the floor and played Gershwin, Grieg, Arlen, Brahms, and Ravel for a table two removed from Mr. Spring's, an error attributable to Bobby's nearsightedness. It all came to some kind of climax during the finale, when one chorus girl was sent into such a bad fall that the other girls had to dance around her while she was getting to her feet. The other girls grinned, but the one little girl cried, got out of the line, and ran off.

"Harry," said Mr. Spring.

"Yes, Mr. Spring." Harry, Jake, Audrey, and Betty turned

to Mr. Spring, and the captain and waiters behind him leaned forward.

"Just Harry," said Mr. Spring to his companions. He whispered in Harry's ear. "Tell Mike I want to see him."

Harry got up from the table, and when he came back Mike was with him. "Here he is," said Harry.

"Yes, I know," said Mr. Spring. "Mike, who's the little girl took the spill?"

Mike leaned down and put a hand on Mr. Spring's shoulder. "Her name is Zita. Zita and Leonardo. I got them out of a hotel in Detroit."

"I don't mean her," said Mr. Spring. "She's all right, but a dime a dozen, Mike. *You* know that. I mean the chorus kid. The number they just finished."

"Oh. She's—I think her name is—" Mike halted and whispered to the captain of waiters, who whispered back. Mike nodded and continued. "Goes by the name of Hilary Kingston. You like her?"

"I might," said Mr. Spring. His companions drank their champagne and tried to pick up their talk where they had left off and to keep talking until the arrival of Hilary Kingston. In a few moments she was there. With a flat-palm gesture, like someone testing a mattress, Mr. Spring bade Harry and Jake and the girls to remain seated. He rose. He put out his hand. "Are you all right, Hilary?" he said. "Sit here next to me." She sat on the chair only just vacated by Audrey, who remained standing while a waiter brought another chair.

"Thanks," said Hilary Kingston. She folded her hands in her lap.

"Did you get hurt? I mean when you fell that time?" asked Mr. Spring.

"No, sir. Not when I fell. I think one of the kids kicked me here, but I can take it," said Hilary. She was wearing a flannel suit and she indicated a slit in the coat where a pocket might have been.

Mr. Spring sternly did not lower his eyes to the place indicated. He smiled. "I was worried for you. It reminded me of when a jockey's thrown in a horse race and I can't look at anything else only him till I see the other horses are safely past him, Hilary. Even when I have a horse running in that particular race. I always shut my eyes to everything else. That can be awful, you know."

"Yes, I know," she said.

"Do you like horse racing, Hilary?"

"Like them? Love them is more the word. This Jake. Is he your trainer?"

Mr. Spring smiled. "If you mean does he train my horses, no. He trains *me*. I have a workout with him every day, boxing, road work, massaging. No, you're thinking of Jock, not Jake. Jock Doyle. He trains my horses, Hilary. But I'm glad to see you have an interest in horse racing. That means two things we have in common. You said you can take it, and so can I. And you like horse racing."

"If I could be a boy, that's what I'd be," said Hilary.

"What?" asked Mr. Spring.

"A jockey."

"Well, just let me say I prefer you the way you are." Mr. Spring smiled.

"Thanks."

Mr. Spring smiled directly at Hilary, straight in the eye and then at the place in her coat where she had thought she might have been kicked. "Did you ever know Harry before?"

"Harry who?"

"Well, if you don't know Harry who, then you didn't. Mr. Field, the handsome gentleman in the blue suit."

"Oh, I don't think he's so handsome," said Hilary.

"You don't? He's considered a very good-looking man, I've always heard."

"Oh, I have nothing against him."

"Very nice fellow to be with and a very good host," said Mr. Spring.

"I thought he worked for you."

"He works for the same company, but when we're out like this, it isn't any question of working for me. All I can say is I'm glad he brought me here. You can see I'm not *with* anybody, Hilary. At least not till you so kindly joined us. Harry's having a party a little later. Would you like to go with me? I'm sure it'll be all right with Mike. I've known Mike since probably before you were born."

"I was born in 1927."

"Oh, is that so?" said Mr. Spring. He leaned forward and spoke to Harry. "Harry, I have a new recruit for your party back at the suite."

"What's that, Mr. Spring?" said Harry.

"I said I persuaded Miss Kingston to join your little party back at the suite," said Mr. Spring. He turned back to Hilary. "If you think there'll be any trouble about you doing another show, I can speak to Mike."

"That's all right, Mr. Spring. That was the last show. We don't do any more."

"Well, that's fine. Then we can go to Harry's party. Harry, whenever you're ready, we are."

"Right," said Harry, signalling to the captain.

Mr. Spring was smiling. He leaned toward Hilary. "We don't have to all go in the same car if you prefer," he said.

"I don't care," said Hilary.

Mr. Spring raised his head. "Harry, Miss Kingston and I will go in the black car and meet you there, if that's all right."

"Right," said Harry.

Mr. Spring smiled, took out a special Upmann cigar from the ex-President's case, snipped off the end with the English actor's Asprey cutter, and put the cigar in his mouth. Then the smiling corners of his mouth turned down for the lighting of the cigar, and he remembered who had given him the cigar case and the cigar cutter and, more clearly, he remembered the words of the doctor in Baltimore. He snapped the lighter shut and turned to Hilary.

"Maybe you don't want to go on this party," he said. He hoped she would say no, but he knew she would say yes.

Ellie

ALTHOUGH MY sister and I were born in Texas, we have lived most of our lives in the North, from the time our father and mother were killed in a railroad accident, about twenty-five years ago. We were brought up by an aunt and uncle who lived in Westchester. I was eleven and Caroline was seven when Father and Mother died, and I never went back to Texas except briefly, on business. Our aunt and uncle sent me to camp in New Hampshire in the summer, and I went to boarding school when I was fourteen. Caroline, however, did go back to Texas several times and kept up a few friendships there. She was always lavishly entertained, and, naturally, when her Texan friends came to New York, she did her best to show them the town. This was simple enough; it usually involved one big evening of dinner at "21," the theatre, and supper at Larue's. Caroline lives her own life and I live mine, in apartments in different parts of town. Her job is in the midtown district, and I work downtown. For a sister and brother who are quite fond of each other, we are together infrequently, and it is unusual for her even to ask me in for a cocktail when she has some Texans to entertain.

When she telephoned me that Ham and Ellie Glendon were in town, I had to ask who they were. "He's a lawyer in Dallas, and they've never been to New York before," said Caroline. "They're about my age, a year or two younger, but they were awfully nice to me the last two or three times I was down there."

"Uh-huh," I said, waiting.

"She's very pretty and quiet. He's—well—more Texan. He likes to get tight, and I thought—well—you know more places than I do. They'll want to go to '21,' but that won't be all. I mean he will . . . You're *not* being very helpful."

I laughed. "I get it. Colonel Glendon wants to raise a little hell. O.K. Does he carry a gun?"

"Probably," said Caroline. "They all do."

"Well, tell him to check the gun and I'll take you around. What did you have in mind?"

"Nothing in particular, but I just know he'll want to go someplace where I don't know the proprietor. Night-club kind of place. And it's my treat. You don't have to spend any money. I just want you to sort of steer us around. Black tie. My place at seven."

Ham Glendon was a rather large man with red hair and a red face, the kind that does not tan. In Caroline's hall, I saw one of those cream-colored hats with a half-inch band and I heard his voice, soft and for the moment not unpleasant but likely to become tiresome. He was wearing a double-breasted dinner coat and new patent-leather shoes and diamond-and-onyx studs. He called me Jim right off the bat, when he introduced me to his wife. She was something.

She was standing when I entered, Caroline having gone to the kitchen. As I shook hands with her, I was surprised that I so quickly had to change my first impression of her height. She was not nearly as tall as I'd thought when I came into the room. She held her head back, but the top of it did not reach my chin. "I'm happy to know you," she said, and turned and sat down. Her figure was beautiful, and Neiman-Marcus had done their best by it—or probably had been delighted to clothe it, as much of it as was clothed. When she was turning to sit down, I caught her taking a quick look at me; she was trying to see what effect she had had on me, and when she found out, she dropped her eyes and reached for a cigarette.

We went to "21" and to "Oklahoma!," which Caroline and I had seen three times. At dinner, Ham and Caroline did most of the talking, about Texas friends whom I barely remembered or did not know. Ham would ask Ellie to fill in details on some of the people, and that was about all of her contribution to the conversation. I contributed even less, but I knew I wasn't bored and I was sure Ellie wasn't, because every once in a while she would look at me and smile. I remembered that Caroline had said she was quiet, and she didn't seem to expect much talk from me or to want to converse with me herself. In fact, she seemed to be quite happy just knowing that she had had an effect on me. At the restaurant and at the theatre other men looked at her too, and their admiration was something she breathed in.

When we came out of the theatre, Caroline suggested going back to "21" for a drink while we decided where we wanted to go. I wanted to go someplace where we could dance; there were some things I wanted to say to Ellie. But when we got to "21" Ham fixed that. "Jim, I raickon from here on we're in *your* hands." He laughed and I laughed.

"A pleasure," I said. "What kind of a place did you have in mind?"

"Well, more or less leave that up to you, Jim," said Ham.

"No, be frank, Ham," said Caroline. "My ne'er-do-well brother knows them all."

"Yes," I said.

"Well, *Harlem* is one place. We heard a lot about that Dorchester Ballroom."

"Oh, sure," I said, and thought of the way we were dressed. "You'll see some of the best dancing up there you'll ever see in your life. Of course, the smaller places don't begin to open up for quite a while, and if we wanted to go to one of them, I think we ought to change our clothes."

"Tell you the truth, Jim, we more or less had our hearts set on the Dorchester. You asked me to be *frank*."

"By all means," I said. I had the waiter bring a telephone to the table, and I called the manager of the Dorchester, a white man, whom I had known for many years. I was very careful to emphasize that I was with my *sister* and *some friends from Texas*. Max, my manager friend, was not obtuse and he promised he would save a box for us.

More than that, when we arrived at the Dorchester, he was waiting for us on the curb, and I was grateful, for there was a long queue of Negro boys and girls at the box office. Max took over and led us past the box office, and when we were inside, we were accompanied by Al Spode, the old-time Negro heavyweight who was head bouncer at the Dorchester, another old friend of mine.

They usually don't serve hard liquor at the Dorchester, but Max put a couple of coke bottles filled with bourbon on the table, and I thanked him and he went on about his business.

Ham turned out to like jazz and Caroline is a minor authority, so they were entertained by the two good bands. Our box, which was on the level of the dance floor and quite near the bandstand, was conveniently situated for me, or so I thought; the noise of the bands and the dancers would cover up the questions I was going to ask Ellie once we got settled. For the time being, we watched the superb dancing and drank our drinks. It was that way until one band finished a set. The dancers stood where they had stopped, waiting for the other band to start, and when it did, and the noise began again, I spoke to Ellie: "You know, if I'd had my way, we'd be where we could be dancing without being conspicuous, which we certainly are now." And she knew I meant the way we were dressed.

"Would we?" She half sneered and raised her eyes and let them indicate the dancers.

"Maybe Ham and Caroline will get bored soon and we can go someplace else. I don't think you're having too good a time."

"Oh, don't mind me."

"But I want you to have a good time. Do you like to dance? Because if you do, there are a few places where there's tea dancing. Now, for instance, if you were going to be free Saturday afternoon." I came down heavy on "free," so she would be sure I meant her, alone, without Ham.

"Saturday I was planning to have lunch with an old school friend I went to Randolph-Macon with." She paused and shifted in her seat. "But who ever heard of two girls just sitting around all afternoon in New York City? I imagine we'll have said all we have to say to each other by three, and after that I'll just saunter down Park Avenue in the direction of the Vanderbilt, and if I happened to meet somebody . . ."

"That's exactly the vicinity I was going to be in," I said. "Walking up Park Avenue around three."

I poured her a drink and one for myself, and I had that moment of peace when you know everything is settled and nothing much has been said. For all I know, Ham had been conversing in like manner with Caroline. Presently the set ended and the bands were changing again. The dancers slowed down, then stopped while the outgoing musicians left the bandstand and the incoming group took their places.

A boy and girl whom I had been half observing came over to the railing near our table. The girl leaned against the railing, her back toward us. The boy, who was very black, was facing in our direction. They had the confidence of artistry; they were surely the best dancers in the ballroom, and it may be that I myself showed applause by my facial expression. It doesn't much matter.

"Ham," said Ellie.

"Yes, honey," said Ham.

"Ham, that niggah's *lookin'* at me," said Ellie.

I looked at her and at her husband. "Now, wait a minute," I said.

"Which one, honey?" said Ham.

"Oh, God," said my sister, appealing to me.

I rose. "Up! Up, everybody! Come on!" I put a bill on the table and took Ellie's wrist. "We're getting out of here now, this minute."

"Not before I—" said Ham.

"Listen, you silly son of a bitch," I said. I pulled Ellie along with me, counting on Caroline to grab hold of Ham, which she did. We got out fast and stepped right into a taxi.

The ride downtown through the Park was a silent one until we were among the buildings south of Fifty-ninth Street. "Jim," said Ham, "you hadn't oughta called me a son of a bitch."

"I know," I said. "I'm sorry."

"Well, that's all right, then, if you apologize." He grinned. "Now wuddia say we all go over to the El Morocco club?"

"I don't think so," I said.

"*It's* all right, Jim," said Ham. "All's forgiven. I take into consideration you been living with Yankees too long."

"That may be," I said.

They dropped Caroline and then me. I went to bed with my mind made up that that was the last I'd ever see of Missy Ellie, but when Saturday came, I got out my car and at three o'clock I was cruising along lower Park Avenue, excited as a kid. But when I saw her, actually saw her, walking down Park, keeping her date with me, I grew old and cautious, and I drove away from her and trouble, her kind of trouble.

The Moccasins

ABOUT TWENTY people were sitting in the half darkness of the living room and the even darker screened-in porch, but the people were in twos and fours, conversing quietly or not at all, so it did not seem like a party. The gathering lacked the unity of noise that often goes with a much smaller group. It did have something else, which could have been an air of unified expectancy, or simple languorousness, or the two combined. Mary thought she sensed both, as though the people were just sitting around, lying around, waiting for something, but nothing in particular, to happen. It was late at night. The people were all—except for one woman—deeply tanned, and half of them could have got their tan from sports, which would account for their being tired. None of the men got up when Mary and her brother followed the Negro houseman into the living room. A portly man in an unbuttoned Hawaiian printed shirt was playing drums, using the wire brushes softly and expertly to the recorded music of the Dorsey brothers on the radio-phonograph. He was one of the brownest of all, down his chest to the khaki shorts and then again down his legs to his short socks. He flashed a smile and waved a wire brush in greeting, but went on playing without interruption, more interested in the tune, "Blue Lou," than in the arrival of Mary and her brother.

A stout, golden-haired woman, the only person not burned by the sun, came up to greet Mary and Jack. Her smile was quick and polite and no more, implying that that would be all until the visitors identified themselves—and that if the identification were not satisfactory, the newcomers would be thrown right out.

"Mrs. Fothergill, I'm Jack Tracy, and this is my sister Mary."

The smile immediately warmed. "Oh, yes. Why, yes! I'm very *pleased*. Carl *Shepherd*."

"That's right," said Jack. He looked around, but in the dim light he could not recognize anyone. "He here?"

"No, he isn't. He isn't here *yet*, but he phoned from Hobe

Sound. He's coming all right, and we're expecting you—my husband and I. Doc!" she called to the man at the drums.

He nodded in time with the music and spoke on the beat: "Com-eeng, Moth-thurr." The record ended and he joined the three. He moved quickly and with power that would not be good to run up against, but his gait was feminine. He waddled. Then immediately there was another contradiction—his hands were large and his grip was strong. He probably had been a capable guard in the late Hugo Bezdek or early Rockne era. His thin gray hair was parted in the middle and he looked as though he ought to be wearing a fraternity pin. His wife introduced the Tracys, and he put one hand on Jack's shoulder and the other on Mary's, which was bare.

"Carl'll be scooting in here any minute, but what's to keep us from a little libation? You name it, and we have it," he said. "There's a little thing of mine own called a Crusher." He grinned.

"Now, Doc," said Mrs. Fothergill.

"What's a Crusher?" Mary asked.

"You wouldn't want to try it and see, would you?"

"Maybe I'd just better have a Scotch," said Mary.

"Aw, no clients?" said Doc.

"Well . . ." said Mary.

"That's more like it," said Doc. "How about you, Mr. Tracy?"

"I think I'd better stick to bourbon-and-soda, sir," said Jack.

"Maybe you're right, if you've been drinking bourbon," said Doc. He chuckled. "I thought you were starting from scratch."

"*I* am," said Mary.

"Then, you come right along with Dr. Fothergill and learn how to make a Crusher. Mr. Tracy, you go along with *Mother-gill* and give the ladies a treat." He put his arm around Mary and took her to a bar, which was on the porch.

"Fothergill and Mothergill, that's cute," said Mary.

He laughed. "I don't know who thought that up—at least, not in this generation. It's an old family joke, of course, back in West Virginia, where I come from, but they started calling us that, when we got married, in New York, too. Cannes. California. Down here. Whenever we meet a new crowd, sooner or later somebody'll get the idea of calling us Fothergill and Mothergill. Shanghai. India. Nairobi."

"You've lived everywhere," said Mary.

"Pretty near. Just about approximately everywhere—everywhere they'll have us," he said. He automatically but precisely mixed the drink during his chatter.

"This is a darling house," said Mary.

"It is that, all right. Frank and Hazel *really* know how to live."

"Who?"

"Oh, don't you know Frank and Hazel—the Blaylocks? You don't suppose this house belongs to us! No, child. We happen to know these friends of ours, and Hazel Blaylock broke her leg skiing up in the Laurentians, so they asked Mothergill and I to come down and open it for them, hold the fort till—now a little dash of Pernod. There. Yes, we keep it open for them till Hazel's leg heals, and, of course, much as we adore Hazel and much as I admire a pretty leg—well, we hope she takes good care of that leg for another month. Up north. That'll bring us right up to when we want to go to Palm Springs. There, take a sip of that and hold on to the top of your head."

Mary tasted the drink, putting a hand on her head. She smiled. "No effect so far."

"Of course not. I exaggerate a little, but it does have a wallop. Now your brother's, and one for Dr. Fothergill, and then you come over and sit with me." He made two highballs. As he was about finished, a man and a woman who had been talking earnestly in a far corner of the porch started for the door, which opened, Mary now could see, out onto a boat landing. A speedboat was tied up there.

"Hey, Buzz, don't go out there without a flashlight," Doc said.

"We know our way around," said the woman.

"Around each other," said Doc. "No, seriously—take a flashlight."

"Why?" said Buzz.

"Moccasins," said Doc. He reached under the bar.

The man looked at the woman and frowned. She shrugged, whereupon the man took the torch from Doc and they went out to the speedboat.

"If she feels that way about it, it must be love," said Doc. "Come on."

"Love could never get me to go out there," said Mary.

"Not at your age," said Doc.

Doc paused to give one of the highballs to Jack, who was sitting with Mrs. Fothergill and a couple—a young girl whom Mary had seen in New York and a second-rate movie actor, whom she had not noticed before. Then she and Doc went on inside to chairs near the drums.

"If you want to play, go ahead," said Mary.

"I will later. Just now I'd rather fan the breeze with you."

"All right," said Mary. "What did you mean about not at my age?"

They lit cigarettes before he answered. "At your age, love comes to *you*, and plenty of it, I imagine. You don't have to walk through moccasins for it."

"No?"

He studied her, then shook his head. "No." He waited a moment and then decided not to say what he might have been going to say. He swallowed half his highball before going on, and when he did, he returned to the chit-chat form. "Where do you usually go for the winter?"

"I've usually been in school."

"Good Lord, I knew you were young, but not that young. You probably came out this year."

"Last summer," she said.

"Last summer. Are you from Long Island?"

"Yes," she said.

"I smell money," he said. "Oh, sure. Your father is probably Herman Tracy."

"Yes," she said.

"Well, you've got nothing to worry about, except taxes, your head on a pikestaff, and stuff. Where does Carl Shepherd fit in? If I'm asking too many questions, it's because I always do. You're not related to Carl?"

"No," she said.

"That answers a *lot* of questions," he said.

"Does it? That's good," she said.

He smiled. "Don't be haughty with old Doc Fothergill. If I

have your age right, I knew Carl before you were born, and if I haven't got it right, I'm only wrong by a year or so."

"Really?"

"Really," he said. "Now, I don't figure where your brother comes in." He looked out to the porch. "Well, now, maybe I do. In just this short space of time, he seems to be moving in on little Emily. Got that hambo from Hollywood talking to himself. I hope your brother can handle a sneak punch."

"How do you mean?"

"Well, our actor friend was doing all right with Emily before your brother got here," he said. "That's what I meant by a sneak punch. Mr. Hollywood's a bad actor, and I can say that again."

"Jack's a good fighter."

"Then that's settled. Maybe he belongs here," said Doc.

"Well, I should hope so."

"No, you shouldn't hope so," said Doc. The houseman took Doc's empty glass and Mary shook her head. Somebody got up and turned on the phonograph, which filled in the silence between Mary and Doc. She turned and saw that he was watching her. He smiled.

"Just beautiful, that's all."

"Thank you," she said.

"Not quite all. There's a lot of other things I'd like to know about you."

"Ask," she said.

"No. The things I want to know, you don't ask. You find out, but you don't ask. And it wouldn't do me any good to know anyway."

"No?"

The houseman handed Doc his drink. "No," said Doc. He drank deeply again, and looked slowly around the room and out to the porch. Two couples were dancing, the partners holding close to each other, and the conversations in the two rooms remained as subdued as when Mary had arrived at the party. Doc leaned forward and turned his head so that he faced Mary.

"Well?" she said.

"I'd give a year of my life to kiss you. Not a future year, mind you. One of the good ones."

"Would you?" she said.

"However, that's out of the question, for sixteen thousand reasons, so will you do me another favor?"

"I won't kiss you," she said.

"I have another favor. Will you please go home? Will you do me a favor and do yourself a favor and get out of here?"

"All right," she said, and started to rise. He reached out and touched her hand, but she pulled it away and went out to her brother. It took a minute to persuade him to leave, and Doc could not hear what words she used in doing it. When they came to the living room, Doc got up.

"I'll show you the way," he said.

"Thanks, we can find it," Mary said.

He walked with them to their car. "Tracy, I'd like to say one thing to your sister."

"My guess is you've said too much already. I probably ought to punch you in the nose, if I knew what this was all about."

"You don't, and anyway don't try it," said Doc. He spoke to Mary. "Just remember one thing. You don't have to walk through moccasins for it."

"What's he talking about?" said Jack.

"Oh, who cares?" said Mary.

A Phase of Life

THE RADIO was tuned in to an all-night recorded program, and the man at the good upright piano was playing the tunes that were being broadcast. He was not very original, but he knew all the tunes and the recordings, and he was having a pleasant time. He was wearing a striped pajama top which looked not only as though he had slept in it, but had lived in it for some days as well. His gray flannel slacks were wrinkled, spotted, and stained and were held up not with a belt but by being turned over all around at the waist, narrowing the circumference. On the rug in back of him, lined up, were a partly filled tall glass, a couple of bottles of beer, and a bottle of rye, far enough away from the vibration of the piano so they would not be spilled. He had the appearance of a man who had been affable and chunky and had lost considerable weight. His eyes were large and with the fixed brightness of a man who had had a permanent scare.

The woman on the davenport was reading a two-bit reprint of a detective story, and either she was re-reading it or it had been read by others many times before. Twice a minute she would chew the corners of her mouth, every four or five minutes she would draw up one leg and straighten out the other, and at irregular intervals she would move her hand across her breasts, inside the man's pajamas she was wearing.

The one o'clock news was announced and the woman said, "Turn it off, will you, Tom?"

He got up and turned it off. He took a cigarette from his hip pocket. "You know what the first money I get I'm gonna do with?" he asked.

She did not speak.

"Buy a car," he said. He straddled the piano bench, freshened his drink. "We coulda been up in the Catskills for the weekend, or that place in Pennsylvania."

"And tonight in one of those traffic jams. Labor Day night. Coming back to the city. And you could walk it faster than those people."

"But, Honey, we could stay till tomorrow," he said.

"I'd be in favor of that, but not you. Three nights away from the city is all you can take. You always think they're gonna close everything up and turn out all the lights if you don't get back."

"I like *Saratoga*, Honey," he said.

"Show me the difference between Broadway, Saratoga, and Broadway, New York. Peggy, Jack, Phil, Mack, Shirl, McGovern, Rapport, Little Dutchy, Stanley Walden. Even the cops aren't different. Aren't you comfortable here, Honey? If we were driving back from Saratoga tonight you'd be having a spit hemorrhage in the traffic."

"Fresh air, though," said Tom.

He kept straddling the piano bench, hitting a few treble chords with his left hand, holding his drink and his cigarette in his right hand. "Do you remember that one?" he said.

"Hmm?" She had gone back to her mystery novel.

"That was one of the numbers I used when you sent over the note. That was 'Whenever they cry about somebody else, the somebody else is me.' I was getting three leaves a week. The High Hat Box. Three hundred bucks for sittin' and drinkin'."

"Mm-hmm. And some kind of a due bill," she said.

"Uh-huh."

"And nevertheless in hock," she said.

"On the junk, though, Honey," he said.

"If you wouldn't of been taking that stuff it'd been something else."

"You're right," he said.

"Well? Don't say you aren't better off now, even without any three hundred dollars a week. At least you don't go around looking like some creep."

"Oh, I'm satisfied, Honey. I was just remarking, I used to get that three every Thursday. Remember that blue Tux?"

"Mm-hmm."

"I had two of them, and in addition I had to have two white ones. You know with the white ones, those flowers I wore in the button-hole, they were phonies. I forget what the hell they were made out of, but they fastened on with some kind of a button. They were made out of some kind of a wax preparation."

"I remember. You showed me," she said.

He put his drink on top of the upright and played a little. "Remember that one?"

"Hmm?"

He sang a little. "'When will you apologize for being sorry?' I laid out two leaves for that. I liked it. Nobody else did."

"I did. It had a twist."

"The crazy one. Do you remember the cute crazy one? 'You mean to say you never saw a basketball game?' Where was it they liked that? Indianapolis."

"Yep," she said. She laid down the mystery novel, surrendering to the reminiscent mood. "I wore that blue sequin job. And of course the white beaded. Faust! Were they ever sore at me!"

"They loved you!" he said.

"I don't mean those characters from the cow barns. I mean the company manager and them."

He laughed. "Well, Honey, all you did was walk out on their show for some lousy society entertainer." He sneaked a glance at her. "I guess you been sorry ever since."

"Put that away for the night," she said, and picked up her mystery novel.

He played choruses of a half dozen tunes she liked, and was beginning to play another when the doorbell rang. They looked at each other.

"That wasn't downstairs. That was the *doorbell*," he whispered.

"Don't you think I know it?" she said. "Are you sure we're in the clear with the cops?"

"May my mother drop dead," he said.

"Well, go see who it is."

"Who the hell would it be tonight? Labor Day," he said.

"Go to the door and find out," she said. She got up and tip-toed down the short hall. He picked up the poker from the fireplace and held it behind his back, and went to the door.

"Who is it?" he called.

"Tom? It's Francesca."

"Who?" he said.

"Francesca. Is that Tom?"

He looked down the hall and Honey nodded. "Oh, okay, Francesca," he said. He stashed the poker and undid the chain lock and held the door open. In came Francesca, and her half-brother, Cyril, and a girl and a man whom Tom never had seen before.

"Is there someone else here?" said Francesca.

"No," said Tom.

"Honey's here, I hope," said Francesca.

"Oh, yeah," said Tom. "Come in, sit down." He nodded in greeting to Cyril.

"This is Maggie, a friend of ours," said Francesca, "and Sid, also a friend of ours."

"Glad to know you," said Tom. There was no shaking of hands. "These are friends of yours," he said, studying Francesca.

"Definitely. You have nothing to worry about," said Francesca. She sat down, and her half brother lit her cigarette. She was in evening clothes, with a polo coat outside. The girl Maggie was in evening clothes under a raincoat. Both men were wearing patent-leather pumps and black trousers with grosgrain stripes down the sides, and Shetland jackets. Sid's jacket was too small for him and most likely came out of Cyril's wardrobe. Francesca and Sid looked about the same age—late thirties—and Cyril was a few years younger, and Maggie could not have been more than twenty-one.

"I know we should have called up. We drove in from the country. But we decided to take a chance." Francesca liked being haughty with Tom.

"That's all right. It's quiet tonight," said Tom.

"I was going to *ask* you if it was quiet tonight," said Francesca.

"Yeah, we were just sitting here listening to the radio. I was playing the piano," said Tom.

"Really? Have you anything in the Scotch line?" said Francesca.

"Sure," said Tom. He named two good brands.

They ordered various Scotch drinks, doubles all, and Tom told Francesca that Honey'd be right out. He opened Honey's door on the way to the kitchen and saw that she was almost dressed. "Did you hear all that?" he said.

"Yes," she said.

"What do you want?"

"Brandy, probly," she said.

He continued to the kitchen, and when he brought back the drinks Honey was sitting with the society group, very society herself with Francesca and Cyril, and breaking the ice for Maggie and Sid. Sid was holding Maggie's hand, but Tom broke it up by the way he handed those two their drinks.

"Oh, Von said to say hello," said Francesca.

"Really? What's with Von these days? We didn't see Von since early in the summer," said Honey.

"He was abroad for a while," said Francesca.

"He's thinking of getting married," said Cyril.

"God help her, whoever she is," said Honey.

Sid laughed heartily. "You're so right."

"Is that the Von we know?" said Maggie.

"Yes, but no last names here, Maggie," said Honey. "Except on checks." She laughed ladylike.

Maggie joined up with the spirit of the jest. "How do you know Von isn't marrying *me*?" she said.

"The gag still goes. If you're gonna marry Von, God help you. But my guess is you aren't," said Honey.

"I'm not, don't you worry," said Maggie.

"I'm not worried," said Honey.

"I oughta rise and defend my friend," said Sid. He was still laughing from his own comment.

"Have you *got* a friend?" said Honey.

"You're so right," said Sid, starting a new laugh.

"I understand you're moving," said Francesca.

"We were, but we had a little trouble. I'll speak to you about that, Frannie," said Honey.

"Anything I can do," said Francesca.

"Or me either," said Cyril.

"Well, it's the same thing, isn't it?" said Honey.

"Not entirely," said Cyril. "Frannie has the dough in this family."

"Ah, yes," said Francesca. "But you go to the office."

They all required more drinks and Tom renewed them. When he served the fresh ones the seatings had been changed. Honey and Francesca and Cyril were sitting on the davenport, and Maggie was sitting on the arm of Sid's chair. They sipped the new drinks and Francesca whispered to Honey and Honey nodded. "Will you excuse us?" she said, and she and Francesca and Cyril carried their drinks down the hallway. Tom went to the piano and played a chorus. He turned and asked Maggie and Sid if they wanted to hear anything.

"Not specially," said Maggie.

"No. Say, Old Boy, I understand you have some movies here," said Sid.

"Sure," said Tom. "Plenty. You ever been to Cuba?"

"*I* have. Have you, Maggie?"

"No. Why?"

"Well, then, let's go easy the first few, hah?" said Sid.

"Sit over here and I'll set everything up. I have to get the screen and the projection machine. By the way, if you ever want to buy any of these—"

"I'll let you know," said Sid.

Sid and Maggie moved to the davenport and crossed their legs while Tom set up the entertainment devices. "You want me to freshen your drinks before I start?" he said.

"That's a thought," said Sid.

Tom got the drinks and handed them over. "You know I have to turn out the lights, and some people prefer it if I keep the lights out between pictures. That's why I said did you want another drink now."

"Very damn considerate," said Sid. "When do we get to see the movies? Eh, Maggie?"

"I'm ready," she said.

The lights were turned off and the sound of the 16 mm. machine was something like the sound of locusts. The man and the girl on the davenport smoked their cigarettes and once in a while there was so much smoke that it made a shadow on the portable screen. Sid tried a few witty comments until Maggie told him, "Darling, don't speak."

In about fifteen minutes Tom spoke. "Do you want me to go ahead with the others?" he said.

"What about it, Kid? Can you take the others, or shall we look at those again, or what?" said Sid.

The girl whispered to him. He turned around. "Old Boy, have you got some place where we can go?"

"Sure," said Tom. "Room down the hall."

"Right," said Sid.

"I'll see if it's ready. I think it is, but I'll make sure."

He came back in a minute or so and stood in the lighted doorway of the hall and nodded. "Third door," he said.

"Thanks, Old Boy," said Sid. He put one of his ham-hands on Maggie's shoulder and they went to the third door.

Tom put the movie equipment away, and now that the lights were up he had nothing to do but wait.

The waiting never had been easy. As the years, then the months went on, it showed no sign of getting easier. The rye and beer did less and less for him, and the only time Honey got tough was if he played piano at moments exactly like this. He was not allowed to play piano, he *could* have a drink to pass the hour, but he could not leave the apartment because his clothes were in one room, and the little tin aspirin box that Honey did not know about was in another room. He was glad for that. He had fought that box for damn near a year, and lost not more than twice.

One of these days the thing to do was call up Francesca and get five palms out of her, just for the asking. Not spend it all on a Cadillac. A Buick, and wherever the horses were running at the time go there. What if Honey *did* get sore? What about giving up three leaves a week for her? And she'd always get along. What about tonight? Wasn't he ready to swing that poker for her? Where would Honey be if he let fly with that poker? Stepping over the body and on her way to Harrisburg, and leaving him to argue it out under the cold water with the Blues.

"What are *you* thinking about?"

It was Francesca.

"Me? I was just thinking," said Tom.

"Mm. A reverie," said Francesca. "What do I owe you?"

"Leave that up to you," said Tom.

"I don't mean Honey. I mean you," said Francesca.

"Oh," said Tom. "Including—"

"Including my friends," she said.

"Five thousand?" said Tom.

Francesca laughed. "Okay. Five thousand. Here's thirty, forty, forty-five on account. Forty-five from five thousand is five, four from nine leaves five. Forty-nine fifty-five. Tom, I never knew you had a sense of humor." She lowered her voice.

"Tell Sid he owes you a hundred dollars. That'll make him scream."

"Sure."

"He has it, so make him pay," said Francesca. "He has something like two hundred dollars. Shall we wait for them, Cyril?"

"Oh, we have to," said Cyril.

"Here they are," said Francesca.

"Hundred dollars, Sid," said Tom.

"A what?" said Sid.

"Pay up or you'll never be asked again," said Francesca.

"A *hun*-dred *bucks*!" said Sid. "I haven't got that much."

"Pay up, Sid," said Francesca.

Maggie giggled. "I hope it was worth it," she said.

"Oh, by all means, but—am I giving the party?" said Sid.

"If you are you owe me plenty," said Francesca.

"I've some money," said Maggie.

"You know what that makes *you*, Sid," said Francesca. "Oh, Tom, I beg your pardon." She curtsied.

"Don't pay it then. Von never squawks," said Tom.

Sid took out his billfold and tossed Tom a hundred and twenty dollars and another ten. "Well, let's get the hell out of here," he said.

They all said good night to Tom and he to them. He counted the money and was recounting it when Honey came in.

"We got any more beer in the icebox?" she said.

"Three or four," said Tom.

"I see one fifty, two twenties, and a lot of tens. It's all yours sweetie. For not going away to the country." She sank down in a chair. "You had a funny expression on your face when I came in. What were you thinking of?"

"Francesca."

She laughed a little. "Well, anyway I don't have to be jealous of that bum. The beer, Tommy, the beer."

He went to get the beer gladly. From now on the waiting would not be so bad.

Time to Go

THE WEATHER was fine, and that was the only thing Sam Derr could not have bought with money. He may have bought it with prayer; almost from the day Rosie announced her engagement, and certainly from the day she picked the date of her wedding, he had been saying, "God, I hope she has nice weather. Friday and Saturday, anyway." His prayer had been more than answered; it had been complied with. She had had nice weather all week, for all the parties, and the day of her wedding was all her father could have asked. The tennis court had been boarded over for dancing and there were large and small tables for the wedding party and the guests, and a tent for the buffet, open at the sides, and another for the bar, and the June afternoon was neither too warm for dancing nor too cool for sitting.

Sam wandered among the guests and he was not uncomfortable in his cutaway. He remembered names of many persons whom he never had seen until two or three days before and that made them think he was wonderful and made him think he was pretty remarkable too: school friends of Rosie's and of Frank's, and Frank's relatives. Fourteen ushers and the best man. Six bridesmaids and a matron of honor for Rosie. Sam remembered almost all their names. He stopped at a table here and a table there carrying a Delmonico glass to sip from at the mention of how darling Rosie looked. He chatted with the leader of the orchestra, who had played for Rosie's coming-out party, and with the caterer, making a mental note to give them both surprise tips. He watched Rosie on the dance floor. It was her wedding day, to be sure, but she seemed even more popular than all the other brides he had seen. She would get scarcely a half dozen steps before someone would cut in. For instance, Sam saw her dancing with one of the ushers. He turned away to pick up a bottle to freshen the Delmonico glass, and when he looked again Rosie was dancing with young Jimmy Hayes, and Sam looked away long enough to put the champagne back on the table and she was dancing with Ben Gilbert. Ben was one of the very few natives who belonged to the yacht club, but he never danced. That was something, when Ben Gilbert danced. In sixteen years that the Derrs had been coming to this community he never had seen Ben Gilbert on the dance floor.

Ben moved along all right, too, the few steps he got. He was allowed to remain with Rosie a little longer than some of the others, because naturally he was older and was being treated with a certain amount of respect, and none of the ushers knew him. But for the time he was permitted with Rosie he moved along all right. When someone cut in he left the dance floor and went to the bar tent. Sam followed him.

He put his hand on Ben's shoulder, although Ben was a few inches taller. "I know where a fella could get some drinkin' whiskey instead of champagne," said Sam. "They pour champagne, no matter what you ask for."

"Well, I'm easily persuaded," said Ben. Sam took his arm and they went inside the house, to Sam's den.

"Now of course if you feel like champagne I have plenty of it here, on ice, but all the years I've known you I never heard you order it deliberately."

"No, I guess not," said Ben.

"Now I didn't mean anything by that, Ben. I just happened to think I never saw you drink anything but whiskey."

"I know what you mean, Sam."

Sam poured two stiff highballs in oversize glasses from a set of two dozen, each glass bearing a different etching of several breeds of duck. Sam handed Ben his glass.

"To Rosie," said Ben.

"To our girl."

"Well, hardly my girl, Sam," said Ben, laughing.

"In a way. You were the one taught her to sail a boat, which was more than I could do. Crabbing. Things like that. She always had a genuine fondness for you."

"Yes, I guess you're right. We always hit it off."

Sam sat down and pointed to a chair for Ben. "Let's see," said Sam. "Rosie was about eight years old the first year we came down here. That'd put you around—you'd have been about—"

"How long ago was it?"

"Sixteen years ago."

"I was twenty-six," said Ben.

"Oh, no, you must of been younger than that, Ben."

"I'm forty-two now, so I was twenty-six then."

"I thought you were younger than that. You looked younger. Seemed younger. You do now. Never put on a pot belly and you never seem to lose your sunburn."

"Well, you know how it is," said Ben. "Being in the real-estate business in a place like this, it just about runs itself. Either things are slack and you can't force people to do business with you, so there's no use trying, or else like the past few years when they're begging you to rent or sell. Either way you don't need to spend much time in an office. No sense in sitting in an office when nobody'll be in to see you, and no sense sitting in the office when everybody's coming in to see you. So—why not go fishing?"

"Yes, I suppose that's why you Islanders all live to be a hundred. You have the right philosophy, but it'd never work for me."

"Why not, Sam? You have enough."

"Maybe I will, now," said Sam.

" 'Now'? You mean with Rosie married."

"That's right. I'd like to go away some place—I don't know where the hell to. California, maybe. Mildred and I. Play a little golf if we felt like it. Or Honolulu. Anywhere Mildred wants to go. She's entitled to a trip. You know she isn't Rosie's mother. Rosie's mother died twenty years ago."

"Yes, I knew that."

"Oh, sure you did. I guess Rosie told you just about everything."

"We used to have long talks," said Ben.

"Yes, she had great confidence in your judgment. 'Ben said this, Ben said that.' Mildred and I often commented on it, how Rosie'd prefer your company instead of the young fellows more her own age."

"Well, I guess I knew things that Rosie wanted to know, and it was easy to teach her." Ben spoke slowly and squirmed in the leather club chair. A silence came between the two men, and when Sam broke it, it was as though he were talking to himself.

"I looked at that little girl out there today, and earlier at the church, and I know what I did. I did what I've done all my life, from when she was just a tiny baby. Maybe I'm doing it now. At the office, or traveling, I'd find myself thinking of her, and then suddenly I'd stop thinking of her, but even though I'd stopped thinking of her there'd still be a smile on my face. I used to laugh about it. My partners caught on early. 'Sam's thinking of Rosie,' they'd say. People on trains, strangers, they must of thought I was an imbecile. I remember Willkie said to me, 'Listen, Derr, you're paying me a hell of a lot of *money* for what I've been telling you the last five minutes, but you haven't paid any *attention* at *all*.' So I had to tell Wendell L. Willkie about Rosie Derr.

"I guess I ought to be out there, but she'll be leaving soon." He looked at his watch. "Few minutes. I don't know where they're going for their honeymoon. I know in a general way. Canada. I don't want to know. Well, yes I do, but I wouldn't have wanted my father or mother telephoning me on my honeymoon." He stood up and took Ben's nearly empty glass out of his hand and poured two highballs. "To our girl, Ben."

"To Rosie," said Ben.

Sam smiled. "You don't have to be so careful, Ben. I know about you and Rosie."

"What *about* me and Rosie?" said Ben, angrily. "There *isn't* anything about me and Rosie."

"I know. That's *what* I know. But I've seen you look at her." Sam put his hand on Ben's shoulder, then looked again at his watch. "Time to go. But I wish you'd stick around and get drunk with me."

Ben stretched out his long legs. "I will," he said.

Encounter: 1943

ALLEN WAS standing near the curb, waiting with the other people to cross Forty-sixth. He was glad he wore his muffler and he wished he knew where his gloves were. The last cheating taxi whizzed past and the cops' whistles blew and Allen was ready to move when he got the little punch in the ribs. It wasn't a hard punch, feeling it, but it must have started as a pretty hard punch to feel as much of it as he did through his overcoat, and without looking he knew who it was all right.

"Hey," she said, and he looked down and around, and it was Mildred all right. She was grinning.

"Hyuh," he said.

"Didn't they get you yet?" she said.

"Didn't who?" he asked, then, "Oh. No, I'm too smart for them."

"Yeah, I'll bet," she said. Somebody bumped her. "Which way you going, I'll walk along with you."

"Just uptown," he said. "I'm not headed anywhere in particular."

"Well! Then we could go some place and have a beer or something. I'd like to *talk* to you."

They were walking slowly uptown. "What about?"

"What about?" she said. "Anything. Mutual acquaintances. Or maybe you do' wanna sit and talk and have a drink with me."

"I do' wanna sit and have a *fight* with you," he said.

"Why do we *have* to fight? We don't have to fight if you control your temper and so forth. Let's go down the street to Eddie Spellman's."

"All right," he said. They turned at Forty-seventh.

"Now *don't* do me any *favors*," she said. "If you rather not go, say so now but don't act disagreeable when we get there."

"They'll think I'm Victor Mature," he said.

"Yeah? *They* will, but *I* won't. Oh, you mean *polite*. Victor Mature isn't polite. He's a blabber-mouth."

"I jist mentioned the first name of an actor that came into my head," he said.

"Well pick one that's polite if that's what you mean. Herbert

Marshall. Ronnie Colman. But don't pick Victor Mature if you're picking a person for their politeness. My God! Victor Mature polite! Anybody as dumb as you I'm surprised you had the sense enough to wear an overcoat if you're that dumb. You'd be more typical if you came out in a bathing suit."

"All right," he said. They turned in at Spellman's and went straight back to a booth. A bald-headed Irishman came to them before they had sat down.

"Well, here's a couple of strangers for you," he said.

"Hello, Eddie," they said.

"But don't go start getting ideas," said Mildred.

"Now I wasn't getting no ideas, Mrs. Allen. I only made the statement that it was a pleasure to see a couple of old customers."

"That's all right, Eddie," said Allen. To her: "A rye?"

"No," she said. "Why do I have to have a rye? Because it's cheaper? I think I'll have a Ballantine's and soda and with some lemon peel in it."

"I'll have a rye," said Allen.

"Right," said Eddie, and went away.

"That Mick will have us in bed by five o'clock," said Mildred.

"You never liked him," said Allen.

"He never liked me, so why should I like *him*?"

"You're crazy. Eddie likes everybody," said Allen.

"All right, he likes everybody, then I don't want to be everybody and be liked by Mr. Spellman."

"Well, only—you suggested going here," said Allen.

"Because I assure you only because I ran into you. I assure you I didn't give him or his lousy joint a thought since the last time we were here together two years ago, and I never would of given it another thought for another two years if it wasn't that I ran into you."

"How are conditions at the 21 and the El Morocco?" said Allen.

"If that was intended for sarcasm it just shows how wrong you are. I was at Elmer's twice last week if you want some information."

"Who said anything about Elmer's?"

"See? That's how much you and your sarcasm. Elmer's is what they call the El Morocco."

"Don't get me wrong. I believe you go to them places. Once in a while I read the papers."

"When somebody leaves them on a subway train," she said.

"When somebody leaves them on a table at the Automat," he said. A waiter, not Eddie, served their drinks. They drank. She drank about half of hers and looked at him, at his face, his hair, his tie, both shoulders.

"Did I ever sleep with you? I can't believe it," she said.

"No, it was two other fellows," he said. "Or twenty."

"I'll hit you right across the mouth with this bag, you talk like that to me. You started it, you with that little bum off the streets from Harrisburg."

"All right, I apologize. Only I don't know what you expect me to do. Sit here and take it while you look at me like I was a ghost and then come out with 'Did I ever sleep with you?'"

"I shouldn't allow myself to even get mad at you."

"Then why do you?"

"Oh, it isn't because I'm still in love with you. Don't think that, for God's sake. I *don't* even get mad at you. I get mad at myself. My God, seventeen years old . . . Say, I *voted*."

"Yeah? Who for?"

"None of your business. I don't have to tell who I voted for. I didn't tell—anybody else. A lot of people asked me to vote for certain people because they knew it was my first vote and they all said to get started right, then when 1944 came along I'd know which way."

"I get it," he said.

"You get what?"

"It's easy. The gang I see your name in the paper with, they were all for Dewey."

"Very clever, aren't you? Well, I'm not admitting anything, see? Oh, what about you?"

"Who did I vote for? Al Smith. That's the last person I voted for."

"I didn't mean that. I mean, where are you in the draft?"

"Where do *you* think?" he said, sipping his drink.

"I don't *know*. You could put your mother down for a dependent, and are you all right again?"

"Go on," he said.

"That's right," she said. "I guess you're over age too."

"I'm surprised I didn't see you in some Waac uniform or something."

"Is that a crack?"

"No. You mean a corny crack about wacky? Give me credit for better than that."

"Well, I never can tell with you," she said. "Do you think I have time for another drink?"

He laughed. "How should I know?"

"My date," she said. "Oh, that's right, I didn't tell you what time I had the date for." She looked at the bar clock. "No, I guess not. I'm going to a cocktail party but I have to meet somebody before I go."

"You're right up there, aren't you?" he said.

"What do you mean?"

"Cocktail parties. Elmer's. All that big stuff."

"Well, why not?"

"Sure. Why not? You're young, and you're a dish."

"You think so, Harry?"

"I still got eyes," he said.

"Well, thanks for the compliment," she said. "I apologize for what I said when we came in. About rye being cheap. You were always all right with money when we had it. It wasn't money that was your trouble—*our* trouble."

"Thanks, kid," he said. "I guess you better blow now or you'll be late."

"Don't you want me to stay for another? We aren't fighting now."

"No, but maybe in two minutes we would be," he said.

"Maybe you're right," she said. She stood up. "Well, I guess I better say goodbye. I'd like to see you sometime, Harry."

"Why?"

"Didn't we get along all right just now? We had a little scrap but we ended up all right. Here—" She reached in her purse and tore the back off a pack of matches. "That's where I live. Give me a call."

"All right," he said.

"Don't forget," she said. "G'bye." She smiled and left.

From his corner of the booth Allen called out to Eddie, who came back and stood at the table. "Yes, Harry," he said.

"Could you let me have a quart?"

Eddie rubbed his hand over his smooth bald head. "I don't know, Harry. That tab is gettin' pretty big and you oughtn'ta be drinking so's it is." He turned his head, looked in the direction in which the girl had gone, then he looked at his diamond ring. "All right, Harry. I'll wrap it for you."

The Heart of Lee W. Lee

I LAINT a little more about Lee W. Lee a while ago. You remember me telling you maybe a year ago, maybe two years ago I told you. This group come into the Copa and Joe Lopez like he knew them, he gave them a table, desirable table one back of ringside, but not ringside, and the faist thing I got fascinated was by his size, this one guy. Enormous in size. He could of easly tipped the scales at three-ten if not more and his heightth was in proportionate. You know what I mean on him it looked good? Take off like a ceytain amount of the weight and you easly could end up with one of them Southwest Kentucky State Teacher College centers. On the other hand, take off a ceytain amount of the heightth and you have on the order of Tony Galento. Well, that night I faist saw the party in question I took particular interest in studding how he ate from the standpoint of quantity. It was all right. To scale. All he did, he sat down at that table and put away more food than any white man—white or colored, I don't care which—that I ever saw, and you know doorn my brief but long enough sojourn with the Army I saw some great eaters. Just now reminds me of a cute little yarn I heard a while ago about this guy is a songwriter out on the Coast. Hollywood songwriter. I don't remember what his name was but call him Harry Jones. Harry was a big man, too, but fat, because all he lived for was to eat. Eat, eat, eat, eat, eat. Diamonds Brady, whatever they called him, the old-timer back for God's sake at the tain of the century? Diamonds wasn't in it with this guy. This Harry. Harry? Harry? I know the name because it's a common name like Jones, but not Jones. No, not Jones. But call him Harry. In any case Harry took the greatest *pride*, you know, in how much he could *eat*. You know what I mean? He was *proud* of it. The *amount*. How some people take pride in accomplishing one thing? And some another? *That's* the way it was with Harry and what he took pride in was how much he could eat.

Well, Al Hitchcock, the great English director boasting like with Madelon Carroll that picture. "The Steps." A number of steps. Thaity-nine! That's right. Al boasted that one and countless other psychological and thrillers. You haid of Al Hitchcock. But he had another propensity similar to Harry the songwriter's. He loved to eat, too. So when Al signed for Hollywood somebody mention to Harry. "Harry," they said. "You know this Al Hitchcock that they recently signed. They tell me he's quite an eater. Quite a knife-and-fork man." "Yeah?" says Harry. "I tell you what I'll do. I'll eat everything Hitchcock eats, and *then*," Harry says, "*and then I'll eat Hitchcock*!" Cute story don't you think, if you never haid it before? Nothing to do with Lee W. Lee but it just happened to occur to me, and we're not doing anything more important.

I'd still like to tell you about Lee W. Lee, though. After the faist night I watched him eat he must of come to the city to stay, becuss I bunked into him numerous places here and there at the various spots. I didn't get to meet him at faist but I inquired who he was. Lee W. Lee, they said. That meant little or nothing to me. To tell the truth I never haid the name before. A while I figured him for one of the black markets or other, but then they went passé so I figured him for a fix man in like football, basketball, and them. But the trouble was, one night he'd be around stashing away a few steaks with the sports mob and the next night he'd be chumming with Garsong, you know the tubercular Frenchman making the deals for sending cars to his native France. Then the next night he'd be buying the wine for little Mildrene Shalimar, the little song stylist on the radio. Then the next night after that he'd be sitting there alone at a small table for two and the other chair he'd have tilted against the table, vaitually the equivalent of putting a sign "No Visitors" up. Always a bundle, mind you! Oho! Brother! You know what he was? You haid of Bill Gorman the sport writer being a fast man with the lettuce. Well, I never happened to witness Lee W. Lee reaching for a check for the simple reason there *was* no check. Not that he was cuffing anything. He paid. Always paid. I inquired from the various waiters in this spot and that spot and I was assured he wasn't running up any tabs. But when he came in the place, any place, it was the understood thing, wherever he sat down the bill at that particular location was for Lee W. Lee and nobody else. Not even if like a party of four or five'd be going for the full treatment, meats and wines—if Lee W. Lee happened to sit down for a momentary double brandy or two and then powdered out, the bill was his. And the people would never find it out till finally they asked for the check, and always the same story. The waiter: "Sorry, sir, taken care of by Mr. Lee. No, thank you, sir. Tip, too, Mr. Lee's pleasure." Always paid on the way out, you know what I mean? Never at the table. Later he told me why this was. He said he couldn't entertain in his modest quarters these lovely people but he didn't like to flash a bundle out in a public restaurant, so he made it a habit of remunerating without any ostentation, you know what I mean. Of course as a side remark I might hazard the thought that if I was carrying around a stack of bills this here thick laid out flat I wouldn't remunerate with any ostentation eyether myself, and physically I'm a much smaller man than Lee W. Lee.

In that connection was how I happened to meet him finally. I was standing chatting with Ben the doorman at Eywin's Chop House and Lee W. Lee came out. One of his nights alone. He had his usual heater in his kisser and Ben went over and asked him if he wanted a taxi, Mr. Lee. Mr. Lee: "I think not, Ben, thank you. A nice night for a stroll." Then all of a sudden what did he do but he pointid over at me and says, "Little man, I'd like to stroll with *you*." "Me?" I said. I never met the guy in my life before. Saw him countless *times*, you know what I mean, but never had two waids with him. *One* waid! But he was so goddam enormous, even ten feet away like he was standing, I had the feeling he could reach over and pick me up if he so desired. So I—I went over and I said to him, I asked him what was it, Mr. Lee. He didn't say anything only handed Ben a piece of money, folded up, wished Ben good night, and said, "Let's stroll." We strolled till we got to Sixth Avenue and then tained down Sixth and suddenly he stopped at some bar-and-grill gin mill. Paddy's or John J. McGillahooley's or I don't know. They're all alike to me. I never frequented them in my whole lifetime. On Sixth Avenue they can't do me any good. "Let's drop in here and chat," he said. Well, at least that proved the cat didn't get his tongue, which I thought but didn't say. It was the faist time he spoke since we left Ben.

We went to a table in the back and he ordered something

and I ordered something, I don't know what. I didn't know *then* is how I felt, waiting for him to broach whatever he wanted to broach.

Mr. Lee W. Lee: "Now, then, what's your name and what do you do for a living?" he said.

Me: "My name? My name is Milton Black and what do I do for a living? I imagine you'd call me an account executive," I said.

Him: "No, I wouldn't," he said, "becuss I don't know what the hell that is, an account executive."

So I explained to him I was account executive with an independent advertising agency where I handle the advertising for some various night spots and restaurants.

"Oh," he said, and then he thought a minute. Then he asked me a question, how much did that pay me.

Me: "Now, wait a minute, Mr. Lee," I starred to say.

Him: "*How much?*"

So I named him a figure, upped it a little in case I didn't know maybe he might be going to make me an offer, but not too much in case I didn't know maybe he was a tax man.

Him: "Married?" he asked me.

Me: "Divorced," I said.

"You pay alimony?" he said.

"I do," I said, and he asked me how much and seemed very sympathetic to the situation, till suddenly.

Him: "I want to tell you something, you—" He called me some very profane and obscene things that I liked to take the ketchup bottle off the table and give it to him right then and there, but of course he would of known that in advance and anyway I doubt if a bottle of ketchup would break on him. He ripped me up and down, but never raising his vaice, till finally what he tains out he was sore about, he didn't like the way I kept looking at him in all the spots. What develops is he had a Kodak memory for faces, and especially if they exposed any curiosity about him. Displayed. "You've been displaying a lot of curiosity about me and everywhere I go I see your—your face. I want to know why. You don't worry me. You just bother me," he said.

Well, it took me the best part of an hour and a half to tell him my life history, my likes and dislikes, who I went around with, and one thing or another. Finally I was telling him about when I was a little boy in school and people used to take advantage of my size and pick on me, and all of a sudden he made like spitting, only no saliva came out. "Finish your drink and never mind finishing your story. I feel like taking in a club."

He meant I was to go with him so we got into a hack and went over to the Copa to catch the twelve-thaity show. There was a large group of young couples outside waiting to get inside and it wasn't the regular bobby-sockers. Couples, they were. Dressed up. Then I remembered it was high-school graduation time. These young fellows and gals, they were like you make a date six months ahead of time for Commencement and you're always reminding the mouse it's you and nobody else or no Copa at Commencement, and that keeps her in line, the mouse. With me it wasn't any Copa, becuss one thing when I was in high school it was Rudy Vallee's place, not the Copa, and secondly and fifthly and tenthly, we didn't have big ideas about coming downtown to a night club when I was at Evander.

Lee W. Lee: "Look! They giving away milk or something?" he said. I explained to him and he laughed. All of a sudden he went over to the crowd and picked out two kids and said, "Come on, you're going in and be my guests."

Well, two more surprised kids you never saw. A big groan went up from the ones ahead of them that happened to be standing in line longer, but one look from Lee W. Lee and silence reigned supremely. He took the kids in and as if Joe Lopez wasn't surprised enough seeing me with Lee W. Lee, what about these two kids? But Lopez played it straight, and gave the kids a ringside table. Not for four, just for two. The kids. I and Lee W. Lee sat at another table.

Well, the kids ordered Cokes and got up and danced and had steak sandwiches and watched the show and had the time of their life, and Lee W. and I just sat there watching them. Two kids really stuck on one another, you could tell that. We didn't talk much, becuss I didn't feel like intruding my thoughts, and Lee was studding them. Then he said, "She has a nice pair of jugs, that kid." Aw-haw, I thought to myself. Here it comes. He'll put away ten or a dozen more highballs and start moving

in. But I was wrong. He kept looking at her, but he didn't
go over to the table, at least right away. Once in a while he'd
say, "A beautiful pair of jugs. Do you think he's getting any of
that?"

"I don't know," I said. "Kids nowadays."

"*I* don't think he *is*," said Lee, very sad. Then he watched
them a few minutes more and said, "He isn't, and it's a goddam
shame." Then a few minutes later he called our waiter and ordered a bottle of champagne. "Don't bring any bucket. Cool it
off outside and bring me the bottle." So when the waiter came
with the wine Lee took it and went over to the kids' table. I
stayed at our table but I could hear the whole conversation. He
pulled up a chair and sat down and held the bottle in his hand
and said, "Are you having a good time?" And they went into
rhapsodies and he said for them to drink up their Cokes and
have some of this, meaning the wine. The young fellow didn't
want to take any, but the gail did. I mean she pretended like
she didn't, but she wasn't drinking wine, she was drinking a
waid called champagne. Lee poured their glasses full of bubbly
and left it there and then came back to our table. He didn't say
anything till they got up and danced again. Lee said, "I think
he's in."

Me: "He is if he wants to be."

He tained on me. "That's a hell of a thing to say!" he said.

"Don't get me wrong, Mr. Lee," I said. "Maybe he's in
love with her and they don't want to do anything till they get
married or engaged."

He didn't say anything only snarl at me and then a little
while later the kids came over and thanked him, and one thing
I could see, the young fellow was in all right, if he wanted to
be, becuss Lee could of been, or I could of, or Joe Schmo from
Kokomo. Anybody. I guess that's a lot of champagne if you're
not used to it, what she drank. I noticed there was only like a
fingerful left in the bottle. They knocked that over fast.

They went home, or wherever they were going, and I said I
guessed I would likewise take a powder about fifteen or twenty
minutes later. All that time he sat there thinking. "All right, go
ahead," he said. "But answer me this question."

"Glad to accommodate," I said.

"I think maybe you're right," he said.

"About those kids?" I asked him.

"Yes," he agreed.

In other waids, he was considering the possibility such as I pointed out, where we have the situation of a young couple not wishing to do anything till they get married, very likely. It just shows you one thing: I happen to've come across a lot of mysterious talk about Lee W. Lee and the whereabouts of his source of income, but you must say for the man, he's got a heart. That's what I laint about Lee W. Lee, my friends.

The War

THE ELECTRIC refrigerator, in its own room off the kitchen, was of a size that could be suitably recommended for a small hotel. The young man held a quart bottle of homogenized milk in one hand, the while he inspected other contents of the refrigerator.

"Now who the hell are you?" said a deep voice.

"Sir?" said the young man.

"I just asked you who the hell you were," said the man, who was overweight and past his youth.

"Me? Why? Who are you, for that matter?"

"Somebody owns this establishment, and I could be the one."

"Nuts. You could, maybe, but you're not," said the young man.

"Listen, kid. Identify yourself. I don't like to see my friends' iceboxes being raided by some unidentified squirt."

"Go away, mister, whoever you are. I was invited here. And don't try any funny stuff or I'll crack you with this bottle."

"I see you would, too," said the man. "What's your name?"

"Oh, shut up and go away. My name is Frank Ankle. Does that suit you?"

The middle-aged man looked at the young fellow and then burst out laughing. "Frank Ankle?"

"That's good enough for you, mister."

The man put his hand over his entire face, over and over again, bending his nose, roughing up the grain of his eyebrows. "Is your name—now tell me the truth—is your name Something Wheelwright?"

The boy frowned. "Why'd you pick that name?"

"Are you a nephew of Bob Wheelwright's?"

"Yes," said the boy.

The man shook his head. "All the characteristics. All the characteristics. You are—Ed Montgomery's kid. Your mother was Ellen Wheelwright."

"Yes sir." The boy nodded.

"Frank Ankle. I haven't heard of Frank Ankle for twenty years at least. Put down the milk bottle, son. I could have taken it away from you any time. Like this." The man put his left arm in front of the boy's right arm and grabbed hold of the back of the boy's coat at the same time he gently but quickly put the heel of his right hand under the boy's chin, and gently kicked the boy's left foot, throwing him off balance. "A little respect for your elders, son. If you hadn't said Frank Ankle I was about to put you back in the icebox, you and the bottle of milk." He tapped the boy's chin a few times.

"I'm convinced," said the boy.

"One of these little taps would break your neck."

"I'm convinced," said the boy. The man released him.

"One thing," said the man. "Never *threaten* to hit a man with a milk bottle. Hit him. Now tell me about Bob Wheelwright. What's happened to him? I haven't heard anything from him for four-five years."

"Uncle Bob's dead," said the boy.

"Dead? When'd he die? I mean, Bob Wheelwright died?"

"Yes sir. He died last spring. May the twelfth, I think it was. By the way, my name is Ted Montgomery."

"My name is Joe Rutledge." He took a cigarette from an old-fashioned curved case. "Have one. Look at what it says in that case." He handed over the case and rested on a kitchen chair.

The boy read: "'To perhaps the best man. June the twenty-second, Nineteen-twenty-three.' I see."

"You know, you lose track of those things," said Rutledge. "I mean, Bob did, and I did. But I wonder where the hell I was last May? Where have I been since, that I didn't know about Robbie?"

"Uncle Bob died in a sanitarium."

"Well, I knew that. At least I knew he was off his rocker, but at least somebody should have told me and not just find it out from somebody out of the blue. That's a hell of a note. Did your Aunt Angie go to the funeral?"

"No sir. Mother and Father went, but not my grandmother. It was very private."

"Didn't they send it to the alumni paper?"

"I think they did. I'm not sure," said the boy. "I don't know. Maybe they didn't. I thought maybe Father did, but I don't know for sure. You know—Uncle Bob was given up."

"I know, but how didn't I happen to hear he was even dead? Where was he?"

"Near Poughkeepsie. But nobody could ever see him," said the boy.

"I suppose you know why, don't you? That little cigarette case, I was best man. Grosse Pointe, Michigan. That girl was not very good. She was not. No. Not a very good girl. But old Robbie was stuck on her. All those kind of people used to take advantage of your uncle, and he'd let them get away with it . . . Save the goddam world! Help every son of a bitch that breathes the breath of life, but when it comes to where you can help somebody you love, you can't tell him anything, you can't advise him, you can't do anything for him. You just sit on your prat and keep your yap shut! You can't even go to his funeral."

The boy crushed the cigarette butt in a saucer. "Mr. Rutledge, sir, I was in the Navy. I got security-conscious."

"Are you trying to tell me to keep my trap shut?"

"Yes sir."

Rutledge lighted another cigarette. "What is going on in your mind is what I said about saving the world. Right?"

"Yes sir, but that's not all."

"Oh, and the fact that last May I didn't know your uncle was dead?"

"Yes sir," said the boy.

"Well, you have a point there," said the man. "You mean I must have been in some part of the world where I wouldn't hear he was dead?"

"Yes sir," said the boy.

"What else?"

The boy stared at him accusingly. "About how you could break my neck."

"Oh, is that so? That impressed you?"

"Yes sir," said the boy. "That isn't the way we were taught."

The man nodded. "Suppose I told you I haven't been out of this country since 1940? That would deflate the hell out of you, wouldn't it?"

"Yes sir," the boy said.

"I mean and convinced you that I haven't been out of the country since 1940."

"Yes sir," said the boy.

"Oh, stop. Now you think you're talking to rank, don't you?"

"Yes sir," said the boy.

The man stood up, and walked to the icebox. "Did you happen to notice who made this?"

"No sir. These kind of iceboxes—I don't know."

"What about your girl?" said the man.

The boy grinned. "Sir, I told you I was in the Navy."

"Never mind about the Navy. I asked you a question."

"Oh. You mean seriously. I thought you were trying to trap me again. My girl's here and she's hungry. That's what I was doing when you came in. Trying to get her a sandwich. If you see any roast beef . . ."

The man sat down. He looked unhappy and as though he were trying to hear distant sounds, of music, from God, of nothing falling on nothing. Then he stood up again, and his voice was musical. "All right, Ted. You'll come and work for us, won't you?"

"Yes sir," said the boy.

"That's good," said the man.

The Time Element

A T ABOUT five minutes to three the man appeared on the little balcony beneath the annunciator, and as if he had all the time in the world, seated himself in the high-backed old chair. In a minute or two he rose and stood with his eye on the clock until fifteen seconds before three, when he set off the bell that rang until precisely three. Then it stopped, and trading on the Stock Exchange was closed for another day.

Wilson had watched the ritual from a jump seat at one of the posts in the center of the floor. He could have left the floor earlier; from experience he knew at two-thirty that business for the remaining half hour was not likely to keep him occupied. At a quarter to three he began to want a cigarette, but he did not leave the floor. For years he had been saying—without full justice to himself—that maybe he wasn't the smartest member of the Stock Exchange, but at least he was always there. It was an unfair assertion, because he was not the stupidest member either; and it was only partially accurate, because there had been days when he had been physically present on the floor, when he might more conscientiously have been elsewhere. Some-times it had been a hangover that resisted all known remedies; other times, more recently, it had been the simple mysterious thing that was going on inside him. The thing, whatever it was, was simple because it seemed to be nothing more, in its manifestations, than that he was tired, beat. It was mysterious, though, because neither medical check-ups nor introspection had disclosed any reason for the way he so often felt.

As the clanging ended Wilson looked up at the balcony and said, "And that, said John, is that." No one heard him. He said so-long to the men in his immediate vicinity and walked toward the checkroom, automatically unfastening his badge as he went. He turned in the badge, got his hat, and stepped out into Broad Street and proceeded to Wall and his firm's office. He avoided encounters with friends by assuming an interest in the vehicular traffic. In the tiny room which he shared with Ned Dell, one of his partners, he hung up his hat and seated himself at his desk.

"Pretty quiet, wasn't it?" said Ned. He stopped work, putting down his fountain pen and lighting a cigarette.

"Uh-huh," said Wilson. "Now and then you could hear a commodity drop."

"You got a new suit," said Ned.

"Every time I wear this suit you say that," said Wilson. He opened the coat and put his hand down in the inside pocket and turned out the label that gave the date the suit had been delivered. "I happen to know it's April, 1946, without reading it."

"Well, every time I say that you show me the label, so maybe we're both in a rut."

"That—is for certain," said Wilson. "Or maybe you're hinting that I *need* a new suit. Think I ought to dress up more, like Wakely or one of those guys?"

"Yeah. Wakely's just the guy. Or Fenimore. Maybe you ought to dress more like Fenimore. What this office needs is more double-breasted vests."

"All right, if we can get Fenimore's mother-in-law's business I'll wear double-breasted vests. I'll wear an uplift bra if that'll get her business." He glanced at the mail that had accumulated since his early-morning call at the office. Dell picked up his pen and bent over his desk, but did not resume working. "Say, Marge called and she wanted to make sure about Saturday. Are you coming?"

"As far as I know," said Wilson. "Phyllis made the date, and as far as I know it's all set."

"Marge wanted to be sure. She called Phyllis this morning but I think she said Phyllis was in town. But as far as you're concerned it's okay?"

"Absolutely," said Wilson.

"Because—now not like the last time, Rob."

"Oh, what are you beefing about? I apologized to Marge, and she understood," said Wilson. "I told you at the time, hell, you were better off without me that weekend. I was stewed by four o'clock in the afternoon."

"I know, but this time don't have one of those late lunches. You asked me what I'm beefing about? I'll tell you. Beef is one thing. Marge bought a twelve-pound roast just because the last time you came out to our place you said you'd like to eat nothing but roast beef for a whole weekend. Then you didn't show. You know how much Marge likes you. She wasn't sore, but you know she loves to be the hostess and so on. Why don't you come out Friday night with me?"

"I know we can't Friday," said Wilson. "I'll be there, Ned. Don't worry. Don't worry, boy. Take it easy, boy. I'll be there. I'll be there." He stood up. "I think I'll knock off. This mail can wait till morning. Does anybody want to see me about anything? If not, I think I'll shoot uptown."

"No. Unless you want to stop in Fred's office, he might have something, but not that I know of."

"He had somebody in there when I came in, so I think I'll pass him up. Goodnight, Doctor."

"Goodnight, Robert," said Ned.

The letters he was leaving behind were—some of them—just important enough to give Wilson a briefly satisfying feeling of truancy. The letters could be taken care of in the morning, but properly they should have been attended to before he left the office, and in the subway on the way uptown he enjoyed the sensation of running away. But when the train was slowing down for Grand Central that rather juvenile pleasure ceased to be. When he left the office he had intended only to go home early, but by the time the train had stopped he had decided not to take the four-ten. All he knew was that he was not going to take the four-ten, and he was not going to the Commodore Bar, the Biltmore Bar, or the Yale Club, the three places in the vicinity where he usually dropped in for a drink. He came out onto Forty-second Street and while he was making up his mind which direction to take he noticed an airline bus discharging passengers. It was not an event that he ordinarily noticed, but his attention was attracted by four men who were getting out of the "limousine." They may or may not have been traveling together, but they all were wearing those rainproof transparent covers on their hats. It was not raining on Forty-second Street, although it could have been out at the airport. Wilson had a non-violent but firm aversion to the hat covers, and he never had happened to see four of them together. The four men walked around to the back of the bus to repossess their luggage, and Wilson was about to move on, actually had taken a step, when he saw the last passenger, a woman, getting out of the bus. He knew immediately who it was, and he hurried away until he got to Lexington Avenue. He turned south on Lexington and entered the first clean-looking saloon.

He sat at a table, took off his hat and laid it on a chair.

"Yes, sir?" said the waiter, a man in his late fifties.

"I'm alone. All right if I sit at a table?"

"Sure. Suit yourself," said the waiter.

"I'm tired, but I'll be out of here before your dinner customers start coming."

"Yeah, it's a kind of a muggy day." The waiter held his napkin with both hands.

"Have you got a telephone here?"

"Yeah. There's somebody in there now, but I guess they'll be out."

"I hope so, eventually," said Wilson.

"If you're in a hurry I guess you could use the house phone," said the waiter.

"No, I was joking. Hoping whoever's in there wouldn't be there permanently."

"Oh, uh-huh?" The waiter did not like jokes. "You, uh, wanta order now?"

Wilson ordered a Scotch and soda and the waiter withdrew. He brought the full shot-glass, the highball glass, and the club soda. "Will I mix it for you?"

"Not this one," said Wilson. He drank the whiskey straight. "Another of the same, please."

"Uh-huh," said the waiter. He brought the second whiskey and said: "How do you want this one? Straight or mixed?"

"This one straight too," said Wilson.

"Okay." The waiter watched him down the second drink and held out his hand for the empty glass. "Same?"

"Same thing," said Wilson.

This time the waiter held out the replenished glass, expecting Wilson to take it and down it.

"No, I crossed you. I want to mix this one."

"Okay," said the waiter. He went back to the end of the bar, leaning against it and talking sideways to the bartender. Wilson knew they were talking about him, but what they thought or said was of so little consequence in his present frame of mind that they could have put on Hallowe'en masks and he would have ignored them. He was only waiting for time to pass.

He looked at his watch again and again, and then he went to the telephone booth and dialed the number of the Barclay. "I'd like to speak to Mrs. Dunbar."

"Mrs. Richard Dunbar?" said the operator.

He waited, and then the voice of the woman from the airline bus: "Hello?" It was a questioning, faintly surprised voice.

"Kit?" said Wilson.

"Who's that?"

"It's Rob."

"What?"

"It's Rob," he repeated.

"Who *is* that? Is this Norman?"

"No, it isn't Norman. It's Rob."

"If this is somebody trying to be funny I wish you'd stop. Who is it?"

"Rob Wilson."

She did not speak for two seconds. "Say that again," she said.

"Rob Wilson."

"So it is," she said. "What do you want?"

"I don't know."

"Why did you call me?" she said.

"I don't know that, either."

"How did you know I was in this hotel? Were you in the lobby or something?"

"No, I saw you getting off the bus," he said. "At Forty-second Street."

"And then followed me?"

"No. And this is the first hotel I called."

"Well, that's natural. What do you want?"

"Well, I'd like to see you."

"Well, of course *that's* impossible."

"Why?"

"*Why?*" she said.

"I'm not very far away. I could—"

"Oh, but you *are*. You don't *know* how far. Oh, one of those planes could go for *days* and not be as far."

"Will you come downstairs and have a drink with me?"

"No, of course not. Are you downstairs now? If you saw me at the bus you know I wasn't with my husband, but how do you know he wasn't here ahead of me?"

"I never thought of that, but now I know he isn't. Please see me for ten minutes. Downstairs."

"Ten minutes? For nine years my life's been wonderful because I didn't see you for *one* minute. Why did you call me? Why didn't you pretend to yourself it wasn't me?"

"I couldn't *do* that, Kit. And I did run away."

"You what?"

"I was quite close to you when you got out of the bus, with those four guys with the hat covers. But I beat it. I got out of that neighborhood, but here I am telephoning you. Nine years, Kit. You've been lucky if you didn't want to see me."

"*If* I didn't want to see you? You say *if*?"

"Kit! You've *got* to see me for ten *minutes*." There was more desperation in his tone than he would have permitted if he had been able to control it, but the trouble was he had not known in advance that the desperation was there to control. She was silent again, and he could almost see her at her old habit, chewing her lower lip while confronted with a problem. Then:

"All right, ten minutes. I'll be downstairs in fifteen minutes. But someone's coming to take me out to dinner, so don't think I'll be with you any longer than ten minutes."

"Yes, I know. Norman," he said.

He paid his waiter at the bar, gave him a good tip, and had luck getting a taxi. It was not far to walk, but he did not want to look tired or hurried when she saw him.

She was punctual. She was wearing her traveling suit but no hat. She was thinner than before, but that was the way he had said she would be: thinner, when she was thirty-five, and achieving her true beauty. He had been right about the beauty, too; people in the lobby made a pleasurable point of looking twice at her.

They met and she said "Hello," with no mention of his name and no handshake. "Let's sit in here, not in the bar. I don't want a drink and I'd rather you didn't too."

"All right," he said. They found two vacant chairs.

"I've given up smoking," she said.

"I suppose I ought to," he said. He smiled. "We haven't much time, so—who's Norman?"

"We won't have any time at all if you're going to ask that kind of question. I gather you're still married to Phyllis."

"Isn't that the same kind of question?" he said.

"Perhaps it is, but I can ask them, and you can't. I didn't ask to see you, you know."

"That's true. I wonder why you did?"

"Because of an overwhelming curiosity to see what you looked like," she said. "What are you now? Forty-three?"

"Yes."

"What did you do in the war?"

"I was in Washington, in the Navy."

"You didn't get overseas?"

"No."

"How many children have you?"

"Three. The same three. Two boys at South Kent and my daughter's at Westover."

"I knew where she was. I saw her name. I went there myself, you know."

"I know."

"Are you living in the city?"

"No. Stamford."

"Are you making a lot of money?"

"Not much. All right."

"Well, I guess that's all I wanted to ask you," she said. "Ask me questions if you want to, but the right kind."

"Well, I know about you."

"Do you? What? How do you know about me?"

"I have a partner in Chicago, and my wife gets the Junior League magazine. You have two kids, and your husband's a doctor."

"Yes, he's also the finest man I ever knew. And rather than have you go on with your nasty little suspicions about Norman, he's my husband's brother."

"I see."

"My husband would like to meet you sometime."

"Oh, he would?"

"Yes. To beat the hell out of you."

"Why?" he asked. "He didn't know you when I did."

"Just on principle. He thinks a married man that pretended he was single and—well, just what you did. Almost made me commit suicide. I hope you never meet him, because it wouldn't be a fair fight, now that I've seen you again. Well, our ten minutes aren't up, but I guess you're as anxious to end this as I am."

"I guess so," he said. They both got up. "Well, I guess this makes us even."

"Does it?"

"Doesn't it?" he said. "You came back in my life at just the right time. This little interview makes me want to commit suicide."

"But you won't."

"No, I don't suppose I will. But you didn't either, remember. Now you're absolutely free, and I'm stuck. You know all about me that you want to know. You've seen me—and you *used* to think I was a pretty good-looking guy. And you've certainly brought home to me that I'm not any more. And one more thing, which makes us *not* even."

"Tell me."

"I love you, and I will as long as I live. So it isn't even, is it?"

"No," she said.

"You did one good thing for me, though. Now I know what's been the matter with me."

"Really?" she said. "Well, now why don't you just go and get drunk?"

"All right. Well, goodbye, Kit."

"Goodbye," she said.

He took a taxi and returned to the saloon with the sour waiter, who, however, had liked the big tip. "Back again the same day?" said the waiter.

"Oh, sure. I couldn't desert this place, my home away from home."

The waiter laughed. "Yes, *sir*. Same thing?"

"The very same," said Wilson. But when the drink came he drank it, looked at his watch, and paid for the drink.

"Not going away mad?" said the waiter.

"Oh, nothing like that," said Wilson. He would be late for dinner, but not very late.

Family Evening

"MOTHER," SAID Rosie, "who's the fourth for dinner to-night? Are you planning some neat surprise for me, like Gregory Peck? Fat chance, end parentheses."

"It just so happens that Gregory Peck backed out at the last minute," said Mrs. James. "No, we're having Bob Martin, a friend of ours from home."

"'From home, said Rosie. "Mother, isn't this home? This is where we live, isn't it? I was born in New York City. What about Mr. Martin?"

"He's what you used to call one of the B. D.'s."

"*I* used to call the B. D.'s? I never even heard the expression. It rings no bell here."

"Well, I remember it, and so does your father," said Mrs. James.

"Then lift me out of this suspense. What does it mean?"

"Oh, a few years ago when we were all spending the weekend at Aunt Ada's we overheard you and Kenny and the rest of you talking about B. D.'s." Mrs. James waited. "You were referring to me, and your father, and Aunt Ada, and Uncle Archie, and people of our age."

"Oh, yes! The *Better Deads*. I must have been at the Brearley then," said Rosie.

"Yes, and it made me cry," said Mrs. James. "I was only thirty-five or thirty-six then. Only. I don't suppose thirty-five seems like the prime of life to you even now."

"A girl in my class quit college to marry a man thirty-*four*. That brings thirty-five much closer to me. I'm capable of mar-rying a man thirty-five. What's to stop me? You, of course, but I mean theoretically. What about Mr. Martin? Is he attractive?"

"He used to be. I haven't seen him for years."

"Well, I like that. Every Christmas vacation you make me spend one evening at home with you and Father, then you go and invite some total stranger. I call *that* consistent."

"We don't *make* you spend an evening at home. We ask you to because we want to see something of you, and Bob Martin is not a total stranger. He was an usher at our wedding and he's somebody we've known all our lives. He called up this afternoon and it's the only time we could see him. He wanted to take us to 21."

"Three good parties I passed up to be with the bosom of my family. If he's remotely presentable can't we all go to Larry's later?"

"Larry Who?"

"Larue's," said Rosie.

"Let's see how it works out," said Mrs. James.

"Maybe you're right," said Rosie. "A little caution now."

Martin turned up in evening clothes and when Libby James chided him he made the old joke about dressing for dinner in the tropics. It was neither old nor a joke to Rosie, but she noticed he wore pumps, of which she definitely approved. He was heavy but not yet fat, so that his regular features were not altogether lost in cheek and chin.

"Martinis okay for you, Robert?" said Rosie's father.

"They better be. It's what I've had a string of," said Martin. "Why don't you pour Rosie's in the cup I gave her and she can catch up with me?"

"Oh, a tragedy, Bob," said Libby James. "Your cup was lost in the fire. We had a fire when we were living on Fifty-first Street. Luckily most of our things were in storage, but the cup Bob gave you when you were born, Rosie, that was one of the things we lost. I was convinced the firemen stole it, but Norman said I was crazy. I still think I was right. Firemen are honest, they look honest, but with the thousands of them in New York City there must be one or two."

"Well, I'll give Rosie another one when she has her first baby," said Martin. "Or will you settle for a cocktail shaker now, Rosie?"

"I'll settle for a cocktail shaker," said Rosie.

"Why, Rosie!" said her mother.

"Well, Mr. Martin suggested it, and I haven't got a cocktail shaker."

"You'll have one tomorrow afternoon," said Martin.

"No such thing, Bob Martin," said Mrs. James.

"There'll be no more discussion. This young lady needs

a cocktail shaker, and it's Christmastime, and that's what middle-aged friends are for. E. R. J. I *know* somebody, so I can have it engraved right away."

"I don't use the 'E,'" said Rosie. "Too much confusion."

"Okay. R. J.," said Martin.

"Let's have dinner," said Libby. "We're letting the servants off early."

"I'll take mine in with me," said Martin.

"We all will," said Norman James.

Throughout dinner Rosie could see that Martin thoroughly approved of her and of her mother. She was less sure that she approved of him. He told the story of the time he broke his leg while skiing at the country club, and of the time Libby's father forbade her going out with him because he kept her up so late, and of the time they drove seventy miles to a dance that was not to take place until the following evening. Libby James remembered almost all of it in the same detail as Martin's. Norman James smoked a good deal and kept his champagne glass empty and full, supplying a name or a date when he was called upon, or admitting total ignorance of an entire episode. Once or twice Mr. Martin began stories with the statement that Rosie would like this item, if she wanted to know what kind of person her mother was at *her* age. The martinis and the wine, in addition to the string of martinis he had had before his arrival, had no apparent effect on Mr. Martin. This was not quite the case with Rosie's mother and father. Rosie herself did not like to drink much.

"Wanta come in here, Robert?" said Norman James.

"Why sure, if you do," said Martin.

"I do. I do indeed," said Norman James. Rosie and her mother went to Rosie's room.

"Well," said Rosie, "I'm getting a bird's-eye view of an old romance."

"How do you mean, dear?" said her mother. "Bob Martin? And I?" She laughed.

"Stop giggling. You've been giggling all through dinner. I'll bet it wasn't Father that asked him here."

"As a *matter* of *fact*, it *was*," said Libby James.

"Well then, he was just being polite."

"Oh, stop. I was thinking I might put on my new evening

dress and you could put on yours, and we could step out. Not if you're going to be disagreeable, though."

"Well, if you think I'd wear my new evening dress for this occasion, pardon me. I'm in favor of lights and music, especially if Mr. Martin wants to pay for it, but I'll wear the pink I got last summer."

"Wear what you please, my dear. Could you do something about my hair? Does it look all right?"

"Mother, Mr. Martin hasn't said anything about going out. Besides, he probably has a late date."

"You're such a child. I know he hasn't said anything, but what if he hasn't? I'll merely suggest it to your father, and if Bob Martin has a late date I'll take great pleasure in watching him wriggle out of it." She studied herself in the mirror, at first arrogantly, chin up; but then that disappeared. She looked at the mirror's reflection of Rosie's face. "How do I really look?" she said.

"You look fine," said Rosie.

"No, I don't," said her mother. She turned away from the mirror. "Do me a favor, Rosie. *You* suggest it."

"Me! . . . All right, if you stop feeling sorry for yourself all of a sudden. You and the rest of the B. D.'s."

Her mother smiled. "*Dear* Rosie. It hurt, but it worked." She got up and followed Rosie down the hall, humming "Do It Again," a danceable number of 1922.

Requiescat

I T WAS about nine-thirty in the morning when the first car passed the big white house slowly, but not too slowly, went up the street a hundred yards or more, and turned around and came back and parked under the chestnut trees, but still a respectful distance from the big white house. For a little while it was the only car. It was an old LaSalle sedan, from which the rear half of the body had been cut away and a drop-delivery-truck body substituted. On the sides was painted "Brainard's Garage, Claude Brainard Prop., Tel. 391." It had a hoist, and old headlights had been added that could be used as searchlights. The fat man behind the wheel was Claude Brainard. He stayed in the car until a Chevrolet coach passed him, went up the street, turned around, and came back and parked close behind him. Claude got out and walked back to the Chevy. As he walked, he unbuttoned his overcoat and took a pack of cigarettes out of his suit-coat pocket, and out of the pack he took one cigarette. He made a big thing of getting one cigarette to jump up from the others; by shaking the pack and squeezing it in a certain way one cigarette, and one only, was made available. He put the cigarette in the very left corner of his mouth. Lighting the cigarette was like anyone else's lighting a cigarette, except that his hands were so fat and big that the cigarette disappeared inside the globe his hands made.

The man in the Chevy got out. He was small and thin, and the leather jacket he wore had been worn by someone taller before he ever got hold of it, someone in the Army Air Forces, someone younger than he. "It don't look to me like they was anybody here before us," he said. The car doors had removable leather signs that read, "Heber Smallwood, Plumbing & Heating, Tel. 305."

"Not so far," said Claude. He put his right foot on the running board of the Chevy and fondled the door handle with his right hand. The two men looked up at the big white house. No car stood in the driveway; the shades were lowered in all the windows. The fat man took a deep, sighing breath, and the little man did likewise.

"Smoke coming out of that chimley," said Heber Smallwood.

"Uh-huh," said Claude. "This looks like Frank Duviller's truck. . . . Yes. It's Frank." Claude and Heber waved to the man in the Model A station wagon, with the lettering, "Frank Duviller, Florist, Landscaping, Tel. 333." The station wagon made the same turn that Claude and Heber had made, and parked behind the Chevy. Frank joined the others, who were somewhat younger than he. He wore a mackinaw and felt-and-rubber boots.

"Claude, Heber," he said. "Confirm anything, boys?"

"Just got here ourselves, Frank," said Heber.

Now the three of them looked up at the house, each busy with his own thoughts. Then Claude, in some ways the shrewdest of the three, looked at the others. He scraped some snow off the roof of the Chevy and made a ball, but instead of throwing it at anything he let it drop and break. "Here's the three of us," he said. "First, I come and went up about Willoughby's and turned around, then Heber come and done the same thing."

"Yeah, that's right," said Heber.

"Then along come you, Frank," said Claude.

"Correct, Claude," said Frank.

"Yeah. I got here right after you, Claude. Then Frank come," said Heber.

"Well?" said Claude, looking questioningly at one, then the other.

"Well what?" said Heber.

"I didn't ask you what you was doing here, Heber. You didn't ask me what I was doing. And nobody asked Frank what he was doing, and Frank didn't ask nobody," said Claude.

Frank nodded and smiled understandingly. He studied Heber. "Catch on to Claude's meaning, Heber?"

"I do not. If I was to say I always caught on to Claude's meaning, I'd be the biggest liar in this part the state," said Heber.

"What Claude is getting at is, here's the three of us, nobody asking any questions, nobody volunteering any information, but here we are all right, and all seem to—I don't know—take for granted why we're here," said Frank.

"Say, that's right," said Heber.

"What did you hear, Frank?" said Claude.

"Well, I guess I heard about the same thing you fellows heard," said Frank.

"What was that, Frank?" said Heber.

"Well, now you ask me a point-blank question like that, I hate to put it into words," said Frank.

The others nodded. "If you're worried because you got an idea it'd be bad luck to put it into words," said Claude, "you don't have to worry about that. I'll relieve your mind on that, Frank. What you heard's true."

Frank looked at the ground.

"I know it's true, too, Frank," said Heber. He tried to sound comforting. "What do you know about it, Claude?"

"Ada told me. My sister Ada. That has to be a Lodge secret, or Ada'd get fired for telling me. She didn't tell anybody only me, and if it ever got out she told anybody, she could never get another job with the phone company," said Claude.

"Lodge secret," said Frank.

"Lodge secret," said Heber.

"Ada handled the call to the doc and the Governor and all them, and what she heard she had to tell somebody, so she figured it was safe to tell her own brother," said Claude.

"You don't have to worry about it getting traced back to Ada, Claude," said Frank. "What I heard I probly heard before they put in any call to the Governor. I was sitting in Police Headquarters talking to Ed, on my way home from the post office. About half past eight this morning. Just passing the time of day with Ed and the phone rang. Ed answered and right away started in acting like I don't know what. Put his hand over the mouthpiece. 'Frank,' he said, 'you gotta beat it. This is a private call.' Or maybe he said official. Or secret. Anyway, he shooed me out before he'd do any more talking. Well, hell, you know that kind of thing never happened to me before. I was a deputy sheriff in the county when Ed was in short pants. On the school board a good many years. Founding member of the Village Improvement and Protective. Holy smokes, I know more official secrets and unofficial secrets about this community than Ed'll ever know, so I stood outside debating with myself what I was going to tell Ed Wheelwright to take the starch out of him. Then Ed come out himself. 'Frank,' he said,

'I'm alone here and I have to go out on an emergency call. Will you take over till I come back and keep your mouth shut about anything you hear? If anybody calls, you're a police officer. I hereby swear you in.' Well, he swore me in like that, without telling me anything more, and I said, 'Listen here, Ed, it's all right for me to be dumb like a police officer, but I don't have to be stupid like one, too.' So Ed, he asked me to be dumb and stupid till I heard from him or till he got back, and then he got into his car. Not the police car, you understand. His own car. That I considered meaningful, but I asked no questions. Went back in his office and sat down.

"I'll be honest with you. I looked at his scratch pad on his desk, thinking he'd of left some scribbling, but all was there was the name. Joe Hubbard." He tossed his head to indicate the big white house, and Claude and Heber nodded, glanced up at the house, and nodded again.

"Perhaps five minutes went by before the phone rang. 'Police Headquarters,' I said. Woman's voice. 'Mr. Wheelwright,' she started to say, and I started to tell her I wasn't Ed, but she didn't pay any attention. 'Thank goodness you're still there,' she said. 'I want to ask you a favor. Would you mind please don't wear your uniform?' It was her, up the house there."

"How'd you know that, Frank?" said Heber.

"How'd I know that? Well, I've known her since she was born. Couldn't mistake her voice. Know every tree on the place. Put in that back hedge last summer. Helped her start her first flower garden when she went there a bride twenty-some years ago. She and I worked many's the time eight, ten hours a day together. And when I heard her voice, I naturally connected up the name on the pad. I said to her this wasn't Ed Wheelwright, it was me, and she hung up. Not another word out of her, but there didn't have to be. I sat there worrying about her about a half an hour, till Ed called up and said Bob Hoffman was coming in to take over Headquarters."

"What did Ed say otherwise, Frank?" said Claude.

"Thanked me," said Frank.

"Didn't volunteer any more information?" said Heber.

"Yes, he did," said Frank. "He said there was an accident and I'd hear all about it, but for the time being that was all he could say. Well, if there was an accident, I knew it had to be Joe, what with his name on the pad and all, and I guess deep down I even knew what kind of an accident it was. When a man takes on the worries of the world . . ."

The others nodded. "He stopped for some gas at my place yesterday, late afternoon," said Claude. "'Well, Claude,' he said. I waited for him to say something, usually some joke or other. I waited a couple minutes, but like he forgot I was there. Off he drove. I said to myself, 'Joe really got something on his mind.'"

"No doubt about that," said Heber.

"What about you, Heber? What'd you hear, and how, and when?" said Frank.

"What'd I hear? I heard what you two heard. I heard Joe took and put a bullet through his head about eight o'clock this morning. When'd I hear it? How'd I hear it? Well, this don't have to be no Lodge secret. Either you two happen to have anybody working in that house?"

"Forgot about that," said Frank. "Rhoda."

"I happen to have a sister cooking in that house over fifteen years," said Heber.

"I didn't think to ask you about Rhoda," said Claude.

"The natural thing when you hear a shot go off and a couple minutes later one lady of the house lets out a scream, you do what Rhoda done. You go upstairs and see what's wrong. Call Doc Tanner. Then the natural thing, you call your closest relative, your brother. That's what Rhoda done."

"Sure," said Claude. "That's what Ada done."

"Rhoda was all upset and crying," Heber went on. "Said Joe'd shot himself. She had a look at him and he was too far gone for any Doc Tanner. But I said now was the time when Mrs. needed her the most, so get off the phone and go back to *her*. In a situation like that, you have to talk sharp to a woman or otherwise they go to pieces, so I said to Rhoda, 'You go back there where you're most needed.'"

Frank took out a pipe and tobacco, and Claude and Heber watched him as though filling a pipe were an unfamiliar operation. When the tobacco had been properly tamped down and the oilskin pouch put back in his mackinaw pocket, Frank slapped the loose grains off his hands, and Claude had a book of matches waiting for him. Frank lit the pipe, and as he was handing the matches back to Claude, a black, enclosed-drive limousine drove down the street and made the turn into the driveway. There was a liveried chauffeur on the box, and in back were a man and a woman.

"Governor's car," said Heber.

"That's him in it," said Claude. "I guess that's his wife."

"He made it quick," said Heber.

"He oughta make it quick," said Frank. "I don't give him anything for making it quick."

"You gotta give him something for making it quick," said Heber. "Joe made speeches against him, remember."

"And Joe was right. When Joe was governor, he was a better governor than this fellow," said Frank. "Hell and damnation, Joe was better than anybody."

"Granted," said Heber, "but it shows this fellow's decent to get here in this short a time. He wasn't the kind of man Joe was, but he knew a good man when he saw one."

Claude cleared his throat. "I don't give the Governor anything or I don't take anything away from him. I voted *for* this fellow, and you two know it. I don't give him anything more for coming here than I give myself. But I don't take anything away from him, either."

"Well, that's a pretty good point, Claude," said Frank.

"I never voted for Joe in my life, but that don't take away from the fact that Joe himself was the best man we ever had in this goddam state in *my* lifetime. And maybe the whole goddam *United* States." Claude was a little out of breath when he finished.

"Some more cars," said Heber. They watched two small sedans coming up the street. The group of three nodded to the drivers of the sedans. "Harry Parker," said Heber. "Representing the Legion, I guess."

"Will Gallo, representing Gallo's Pool Room," said Frank.

"That's no kind of a remark to make," said Claude. "Will Gallo, representing *me*, as far as that goes. I don't represent anything."

"Yes, you do," said Heber. "You represent the Lodge."

"The Lodge?" said Claude. "I didn't come here representing the Lodge any more than you did, or you, either, Frank. No more than Harry's representing the Legion or Will Gallo's representing the Ladies' Aid Society, for Christ's sake. Why don't you bastards face a fact when you see it? We all come here because we wanted to see if there was anything we can do, and there goddam ain't. What was I doing when I decided to come? I was putting a new set of plugs in Clarence Bond's Pontiac. 'The hell with Clarence Bond's Pontiac,' I said to myself. 'Joe Hubbard's dead.' I locked up and come out here. Did I think there was anything I could do? No. I didn't even think anything, but you couldn't of stopped me from coming, and the same with you and you and Harry and Will Gallo. Well, there's one thing I can do, I can get the hell outa here. There's gettin' too many of us, cars lining up, standing around." He turned to the newcomers. "Hello, Harry. Hello, Will. So long." He got in his car and drove away.

"Hello, Harry. Will," said Frank.

"Frank," said Harry. "Terrible thing about Joe."

"Yes," said Frank.

"Jesus," said Gallo, "it tells you what a terrible shape the world is in, a man like him knocks himself off."

"It sure does," said Harry.

"And he *knows* more than we do—I mean he knew," said Gallo. "He got to hear things we didn't get to hear, a man in his position. Think of *that*." He offered cigarettes; nobody took one, and he decided not to take one himself. "I don't think I'll stay here. I don't know why I come in the first place. So long, fellows." He left.

"What undertaker do they have, Frank?" said Harry.

"Search me. Dawson Brothers, I presume. They're the biggest in the county, although Prescott buried Joe's father and brother."

"I'll get in touch with Prescott," said Harry. "If he isn't handling it, he'll know who is. You know, the Legion'll have to provide a firing squad. Is the Lodge having a service, Frank?"

Frank and Heber looked at each other.

"Harry, you don't have to make no excuses," said Heber. "You didn't come here for the Legion."

"Yes, I did. Who else *did* I come here for if I didn't come for the Legion?"

"Claude was right—just about everything he said," said Frank, to no one.

"You heard Joe was dead and you didn't want to believe it," Heber said, "and then when you had to believe it, you *still* wouldn't believe it. So, just like me and Frank, here, Claude, Gallo, you got in your car and come out here to fight it, only there don't happen to be anything to fight."

"I guess so," said Harry.

"Here comes Prescott in the dead-wagon," said Frank. They watched the undertaker's car turning in the driveway. "There's getting too many of us," Frank said. "See you later." He went back to the station wagon and drove away.

"More cars," said Heber.

"Yes. Beginning to come on foot, too," said Harry.

"Mm-hmm."

"I guess there'll be a steady stream back and forth all day," said Harry.

"Well, there oughta be. Joe's entitled to it," said Heber.

"Poor Joe."

"Poor Joe?" Heber hesitated before getting in his car. "I don't know's I see it that way. He's out of it."

"The world, you mean?"

"Honest to God, Harry, I don't know what I mean."

Imagine Kissing Pete

To those who knew the bride and groom, the marriage of Bobbie Hammersmith and Pete McCrea was the surprise of the year. As late as April of '29 Bobbie was still engaged to a fellow who lived in Greenwich, Connecticut, and she had told friends that the wedding would take place in September. But the engagement was broken and in a matter of weeks the invitations went out for her June wedding to Pete. One of the most frequently uttered comments was that Bobbie was not giving herself much opportunity to change her mind again. The comment was doubly cruel, since it carried the implication that if she gave herself time to think, Pete McCrea would not be her ideal choice. It was not only that she was marrying Pete on the rebound; she seemed to be going out of her way to find someone who was so unlike her other beaus that the contrast was unavoidable. And it was.

I was working in New York and Pete wrote to ask me to be an usher. Pete and I had grown up together, played together as children, and gone to dancing school and to the same parties. But we had never been close friends and when Pete and I went away to our separate prep schools and, later, Pete to Princeton and I to work, we drifted into that relationship of young men who had known each other all their lives without creating anything that was enduring or warm. As a matter of fact, I had never in my life received a written communication from Pete McCrea, and his handwriting on the envelope was new to me, as mine in my reply was to him. He mentioned who the best man and the other ushers would be—all Gibbsville boys—and this somewhat pathetic commentary on his four years in prep school and four years in college made an appeal to home town and boyhood loyalty that I could not reject. I had some extra days coming to me at the office, and so I told Pete I would be honored to be one of his ushers. My next step was to talk to a Gibbsville girl who lived in New York, a friend of Bobbie Hammersmith's. I took her to dinner at an Italian speakeasy where my credit was good, and she gave me what information she had. She was to be a bridesmaid.

"Bobbie isn't saying a word," said Kitty Clark. "That is, nothing about the inner turmoil. Nothing *intime*. Whatever happened happened the last time she was in New York, four or five weeks ago. All she'd tell me was that Johnny White was impossible. Impossible. Well, he'd been very possible all last summer and fall."

"What kind of a guy was he?" I asked.

"Oh—*attractive*," she said. "Sort of wild, I guess, but not a roué. Maybe he is a roué, but I'd say more just wild. I honestly don't know a thing about it, but it wouldn't surprise me if Bobbie was ready to settle down, and he wasn't. She was probably more in love with him than he was with her."

"I doubt that. She wouldn't turn around and marry Pete if she were still in love with this White guy."

"Oh, *wouldn't* she? Oh, are you ever wrong there. If she wanted to thumb her nose at Johnny, I can't think of a better way. Poor Pete. You know *Pete*. Ichabod McCrea. Remember when Mrs. McCrea made us stop calling him Ichabod? Lord and Taylor! She went to see my mother and I guess all the other mothers and said it just had to stop. Bad enough calling her little Angus by such a common nickname as Pete. But calling a boy Ichabod. I don't suppose Pete ever knew his mother went around like that."

"Yes he did. It embarrassed him. It always embarrassed him when Mrs. McCrea did those things."

"Yes, she was uncanny. I can remember when I was going to have a party, practically before I'd made out the list Mrs. McCrea would call Mother to be sure Pete wasn't left out. Not that I ever would have left him out. We all always had the same kids to our parties. But Mrs. McCrea wasn't leaving anything to chance. I'm dying to hear what she has to say about this marriage. I'll bet she doesn't like it, but I'll bet she's in fear and trembling in case Bobbie changes her mind again. Ichabod McCrea and Bobbie Hammersmith. Beauty and the beast. And actually he's not even a beast. It would be better if he were. She's the third of our old bunch to get married, but much as I hate to say it, I'll bet she'll be the first to get a divorce. Imagine *kissing* Pete, let alone any of the rest of it."

The wedding was on a Saturday afternoon; four o'clock in Trinity Church, and the reception at the country club. It had been two years since I last saw Bobbie Hammersmith and she was now twenty-two, but she could have passed for much more than that. She was the only girl in her crowd who had not bobbed her hair, which was jet-black and which she always wore with plaited buns over the ears. Except in the summer her skin was like Chinese white and it was always easy to pick her out first in group photographs; her eyes large dark dots, quite far apart, and her lips small but prominent in the whiteness of her face beneath the two small dots of her nose. In summer, with a tan, she reminded many non-operagoers of Carmen. She was a striking beauty, although it took two years' absence from her for me to realize it. In the theatre they have an expression, "walked through the part," which means that an actress played a role without giving it much of herself. Bobbie walked through the part of bride-to-be. A great deal of social activity was concentrated in the three days—Thursday, Friday, and Saturday—up to and including the wedding reception; but Bobbie walked through the part. Today, thirty years later, it would be assumed that she had been taking tranquilizers, but this was 1929.

Barbara Hammersmith had never been anything but a pretty child; if she had ever been homely it must have been when she was a small baby, when I was not bothering to look at her. We—Pete McCrea and the other boys—were two, three, four years older than Bobbie, but when she was fifteen or sixteen she began to pass among us, from boy to boy, trying one and then another, causing several fist fights, and half promising but never delivering anything more than the "soul kisses" that were all we really expected. By the time she was eighteen she had been in and out of love with all of us with the solitary exception of Pete McCrea. When she broke off with a boy, she would also make up with the girl he had temporarily deserted for Bobbie, and all the girls came to understand that every boy in the crowd had to go through a love affair with her. Consequently Bobbie was popular; the boys remembered her kisses, the girls forgave her because the boys had been returned virtually intact. We used the word hectic a lot in those days; Kitty Clark explained the short duration of Bobbie's love affairs by observing that being in love with Bobbie was too hectic for most boys. It was also true that it was not hectic enough. The boys agreed that Bobbie was a hot little number, but none of us could claim that she was not a virgin. At eighteen Bobbie entered a personal middle age, and for the big social occasions her beaus came from out-of-town. She was also busy at the college proms and football games, as far west as Ann Arbor, as far north as Brunswick, Maine. I was working on the Gibbsville paper during some of those years, the only boy in our crowd who was not away at college, and I remember Ann Arbor because Bobbie went there wearing a Delta Tau Delta pin and came back wearing the somewhat larger Psi U. "Now don't you say anything in front of Mother," she said. "She thinks they're both the same."

We played auction bridge, the social occupation in towns like ours, and Bobbie and I were assimilated into an older crowd: the younger married set and the youngest of the couples who were in their thirties. We played for prizes—flasks, cigarette lighters, vanity cases, cartons of cigarettes—and there was a party at someone's house every week. The hostess of the evening usually asked me to stop for Bobbie, and I saw her often. Her father and mother would be reading the evening paper and sewing when I arrived to pick up Bobbie. Philip Hammersmith was not a native of Gibbsville, but he had lived there long enough to have gone to the Mexican Border in 1916 with the Gibbsville company of mounted engineers, and he had gone to France with them, returning as a first lieutenant and with the Croix de Guerre with palm. He was one of the best golfers in the club, and everyone said he was making money hand-over-fist as an independent coal operator. He wore steel-rim glasses and he had almost completely gray hair, cut short. He inspired trust and confidence. He was slow-moving, taller than six feet, and always thought before speaking. His wife, a Gibbsville girl, was related, as she said, to half the town; a lively little woman who took her husband's arm even if they were walking only two doors away. I always used to feel that whatever he may have wanted out of life, yet unattained or unattainable, she had just what she wanted: a good husband, a nice home, and a pretty daughter who would not long remain unmarried. At home in the evening, and whenever I saw him on the street, Mr. Hammersmith was wearing a dark-gray worsted suit, cut loose and with a soft roll to the lapel; black knit four-in-hand necktie; white shirt; heavy gray woolen socks, and thick-soled brogues. This costume, completely unadorned—he wore a wrist watch—was what he always wore except for formal occasions, and the year-to-year sameness of his attire constituted his only known eccentricity. He was on the board of the second most conservative bank, the trustees of Gibbsville Hospital, the armory board, the Y.M.C.A., and the Gibbsville and Lantenengo country clubs. Nevertheless I sensed that that was not all there was to Philip Hammersmith, that the care he put into the creation of the general picture of himself—hard work, quiet clothes, thoughtful manner, conventional associations—was done with a purpose that was not necessarily sinister but was extraordinarily private. It delighted me to discover, one night while waiting for Bobbie, that he knew more about what was going on than most of us suspected he would know. "Jimmy, you know Ed Charney, of course," he said.

I knew Ed Charney, the principal bootlegger in the area. "Yes, I know him pretty well," I said.

"Then do you happen to know if there's any truth to what I heard? I heard that his wife is threatening to divorce him."

"I doubt it. They're Catholics."

"Do you know her?"

"Yes. I went to Sisters' school with her."

"Oh, then maybe you can tell me something else. I've heard that she's the real brains of those two."

"She quit school after eighth grade, so I don't know about that. I don't remember her being particularly bright. She's about my age but she was two grades behind me."

"I see. And you think their religion will keep them from getting a divorce?"

"Yes, I do. I don't often see Ed at Mass, but I know he carries rosary beads. And she's at the eleven o'clock Mass every Sunday, all dolled up."

This conversation was explained when Repeal came and with it public knowledge that Ed Charney had been quietly buying bank stock, one of several moves he had made in the direction of respectability. But the chief interest to me at the time Mr. Hammersmith and I talked was in the fact that he knew anything at all about the Charneys. It was so unlike him even to mention Ed Charney's name.

To get back to the weekend of Bobbie Hammersmith's wedding: it was throughout that weekend that I first saw Bobbie have what we called that faraway look, that another generation called Cloud 90. If you happened to catch her at the right moment, you would see her smiling up at Pete in a way that must have been reassuring to Mrs. McCrea and to Mrs. Hammersmith, but I also caught her at several wrong moments and I saw something I had never seen before: a resemblance to her father that was a subtler thing than the mere duplication of such features as mouth, nose, and set of the eyes. It was almost the same thing I have mentioned in describing Philip Hammersmith; the wish yet unattained or unattainable. However, the pre-nuptial parties and the wedding and reception went off without a hitch, or so I believed until the day after the wedding.

Kitty Clark and I were on the same train going back to New York and I made some comment about the exceptional sobriety of the ushers and how everything had gone according to plan. "Amazing, considering," said Kitty.

"Considering what?"

"That there was almost no wedding at all," she said. "You must promise word of honor, Jimmy, or I won't tell you."

"I promise. Word of honor."

"Well, after Mrs. McCrea's very-dull-I-must-say luncheon, when we all left to go to Bobbie's? A little after two o'clock?"

"Yes."

"Bobbie asked me if I'd go across the street to our house and put in a long-distance call to Johnny White. I said I couldn't do that, and what on earth was she thinking of. And Bobbie said, 'You're my oldest and best friend. The least you can do is make this one last effort, to keep me from ruining my life.' So I gave in and I dashed over to our house and called Johnny. He was out and they didn't know where he could be reached or what time he was coming home. So I left my name. *My* name, not Bobbie's. Six o'clock, at the reception, I was dancing with—I was dancing with *you*."

"When the waiter said you were wanted on the phone."

"It was Johnny. He'd been sailing and just got in. I made up some story about why I'd called him, but he didn't swallow it. '*You* didn't call me,' he said. '*Bobbie* did.' Well of course I wouldn't admit that. By that time she was married, and if her life was already ruined it would be a darned sight more ruined if I let him talk to her. Which he wanted to do. Then he tried to pump me. Where were they going on their wedding trip? I said nobody knew, which was a barefaced lie. I knew they were going to Bermuda. Known it since Thursday. But I wouldn't tell Johnny . . . I don't like him a bit after yesterday. I'd thought he was attractive, and he *is*, but he's got a mean streak that I never knew before. Feature this, if you will. When he realized I wasn't going to get Bobbie to come to the phone, or give him any information, he said, 'Well, no use wasting a long-distance call. What are you doing next weekend? How about coming out here?' 'I'm not that hard up,' I said, and banged down the receiver. I hope I shattered his eardrum."

I saw Pete and Bobbie McCrea when I went home the following Christmas. They were living in a small house on Twin Oaks Road, a recent real-estate development that had been instantly successful with the sons and daughters of the big two- and three-servant mansions. They were not going to any of the holiday dances; Bobbie was expecting a baby in April or early May.

"You're not losing any time," I said.

"I don't want to lose any time," said Bobbie. "I want to have a lot of children. Pete's an only child and so am I, and we don't think it's fair, if you can afford to have more."

"If we can afford it. The way that stock market is going, we'll be lucky to pay for this one," said Pete.

"Oh, don't start on that, Pete. That's all Father talks about," said Bobbie. "My father *was* hit pretty hard, but I wish he didn't have to keep talking about it all the time. Everybody's in the same boat."

"No they're not. *We're* on a *raft*."

"I asked you, please, Pete. Jimmy didn't come here to listen to our financial woes. Do you see much of Kitty? I've owed her a letter for ages."

"No, I haven't seen her since last summer, we went out a few times," I said.

"Kitty went to New York to try to rope in a millionaire. She isn't going to waste her time on Jim."

"That's not what she went to New York for at all. And as far as wasting her time on Jim, Jim may not want to waste his time on her." She smiled. "Have you got a girl, Jim?"

"Not really."

"Wise. Very wise," said Pete McCrea.

"I don't know how wise. It's just that I have a hell of a hard time supporting myself, without trying to support a wife, too," I said.

"Why I understood you were selling articles to magazines, and going around with all the big shots."

"I've had four jobs in two years, and the jobs didn't last very long. If things get any tougher I may have to come back here. At least I'll have a place to sleep and something to eat."

"But I see your name in magazines," said Pete. "I don't always read your articles, but they must pay you well."

"They don't. At least I can't live on the magazine pieces without a steady job. Excuse me, Bobbie. Now you're getting *my* financial woes."

"She'll listen to yours. It's mine she doesn't want to hear about."

"That's because I know about ours. I'm never allowed to forget them," said Bobbie. "Are you going to all the parties?"

"Yes, stag. I have to bum rides. I haven't got a car."

"We resigned from the club," said Pete.

"Well we didn't *have* to do that," said Bobbie. "Father was going to give it to us for a Christmas present. And you have your job."

"We'll see how much longer I have it. Is that the last of the gin?"

"Yes."

Pete rose. "I'll be back."

"Don't buy any more for me," I said.

"You flatter yourself," he said. "I wasn't only getting it for you." He put on his hat and coat. "No funny business while I'm gone. I remember you two."

He kept a silly grin on his face while saying the ugly things, but the grin was not genuine and the ugly things were.

"I don't know what's the matter with him," said Bobbie. "Oh, I do, but why talk about it?"

"He's only kidding."

"You know better than that. He says worse things, much worse, and I'm only hoping they don't get back to Father. Father has enough on his mind. I thought if I had this baby right away it would—you know—give Pete confidence. But it's had just the opposite effect. He says it isn't his child. *Isn't his child!* Oh, I married him out of spite. I'm sure Kitty must have told you that. But it *is* his child, I swear it, Jim. It couldn't be anybody else's."

"I guess it's the old inferiority complex," I said.

"The first month we were married—Pete was a virgin—and I admit it, I wasn't. I stayed with two boys before I was married. But I was certainly not pregnant when I married Pete, and the first few weeks he was loving and sweet, and grateful. But then something happened to him, and he made a pass at I-won't-say-who. It was more than a pass. It was quite a serious thing. I might as well tell you. It was Phyllis. We were all at a picnic at the Dam and several people got pretty tight, Pete among them. And there's no other word for it, he tried to rape Phyllis. Tore her bathing suit and slapped her and did other things. She got away from him and ran back to the cottage without anyone seeing her. Luckily Joe didn't see her or I'm sure he'd have killed Pete. You know, Joe's strong as an ox and terribly jealous. I found out about it from Phyllis herself. She came here the next day and told me. She said she wasn't going to say anything to Joe, but that we mustn't invite her to our house and she wasn't going to invite us to hers."

"I'm certainly glad Joe didn't hear about it. He would do something drastic," I said. "But didn't he notice that you two weren't going to his house, and they to yours? It's a pretty small group."

She looked at me steadily. "We haven't been going anywhere. My excuse is that I'm pregnant, but the truth is, we're not being asked. It didn't end with Phyllis, Jim. One night at a dinner party Mary Lander just slapped his face, in front of everybody. Everybody laughed and thought Pete must have said something, but it wasn't something he'd said. He'd taken her hand and put it—you know. This is *Pete*! *Ichabod*! Did you ever know any of this about him?"

"You mean have I heard any of this? No."

"No, I didn't mean that. I meant, did he go around making passes and I never happened to hear about it?"

"No. When we'd talk dirty he'd say, 'Why don't you fellows get your minds above your belts?'"

"I wish your father were still alive. I'd go see him and try to get some advice. I wouldn't think of going to Dr. English."

"Well, you're not the one that needs a doctor. Could you get Pete to go to one? He's a patient of Dr. English's, isn't he?"

"Yes, but so is Mrs. McCrea, and Pete would never confide in Dr. English."

"Or anyone else at this stage, I guess," I said. "I'm not much help, am I?"

"Oh, I didn't expect you to have a solution. You know, Jim, I wish you would come back to Gibbsville. Other girls in our crowd have often said it was nice to have you to talk to. Of course you were a very bad boy, too, but a lot of us miss you."

"That's nice to hear, Bobbie. Thank you. I may be back, if I don't soon make a go of it in New York. I won't have any choice."

During that Christmas visit I heard other stories about Pete McCrea. In general they were told as plain gossip, but two or three times there was a hint of a lack of sympathy for Bobbie. "She knew what she was doing . . . she made her bed . . ." And while there was no lack of righteous indignation over Pete's behavior, he had changed in six months from a semi-comic figure to an unpleasant man, but a man nevertheless. In half a year he had lost most of his old friends; they all said, "You've never seen such a change come over anybody in all your life," but when they remembered to call him Ichabod it was only to emphasize the change.

Bobbie's baby was born in April, but lived only a few weeks. "She was determined to have that baby," Kitty Clark told me. "She had to prove to Pete that it was anyway *conceived* after she married him. But it must have taken all her strength to hold on to it that long. All her strength *and* the baby's. Now would be a good time for her to divorce him. She can't go on like that."

But there was no divorce, and Bobbie was pregnant again when I saw her at Christmas, 1930. They no longer lived in the Twin Oaks Road house, and her father and mother had given up their house on Lantenengo Street. The Hammersmiths were living in an apartment on Market Street, and Bobbie and Pete were living with Mrs. McCrea. "Temporarily, till Pete decides whether to take this job in Tulsa, Oklahoma," said Bobbie.

"Who do you think you're kidding?" said Pete. "It isn't a question of me deciding. It's a cousin of mine deciding if he'll take me on. And why the hell should he?"

"Well, you've had several years' banking experience," she said.

"Yes. And if I was so good, why did the bank let me go? Jim knows all this. What else have you heard about us, Jim? Did you hear Bobbie was divorcing me?"

"It doesn't look that way from here," I said.

"You mean because she's pregnant? That's elementary biology, and God knows you're acquainted with the facts of life. But if you want to be polite, all right. Pretend you didn't hear she was getting a divorce. You might as well pretend Mr. and Mrs. Hammersmith are still living on Lantenengo Street. If they were, Bobbie'd have got her divorce."

"Everybody tells me what I *was* going to do or *am* going to do," said Bobbie. "Nobody ever consults me."

"I suppose that's a crack at my mother."

"Oh, for Christ's sake, Pete, lay off, at least while I'm here," I said.

"Why? You like to think of yourself as an old friend of the family, so you might as well get a true picture. When you get married, if you ever do, I'll come and see you, and maybe your wife will cry on my shoulder." He got up and left the house.

"Well, it's just like a year ago," said Bobbie. "When you came to call on us last Christmas?"

"Where will he go now?"

"Oh, there are several places where he can charge drinks. They all think Mrs. McCrea has plenty of money, but they're due for a rude awakening. She's living on capital, but she's not going to sell any bonds to pay his liquor bills."

"Then maybe *he's* due for a rude awakening."

"Any awakening would be better than the last three months, since the bank fired him. He sits here all day long, then after Mrs. McCrea goes to bed he goes to one of his speakeasies." She sat up straighter. "He has a lady friend. Or have you heard?"

"No."

"Yes. He graduated from making passes at all my friends. He had to. We were never invited anywhere. Yes, he has a girl friend. Do you remember Muriel Nierhaus?"

"The chiropractor's wife. Sure. Big fat Muriel Minzer till she married Nierhaus, then we used to say he gave her some adjustments. Where is Nierhaus?"

"Oh, he's opened several offices. Very prosperous. He divorced her but she gets alimony. She's Pete's girl friend. Muriel Minzer is *Angus McCrea's* girl friend."

"You don't seem too displeased," I said.

"Would you be, if you were in my position?"

"I guess I know what you mean. But—well, nothing."

"But why don't I get a divorce?" She shook her head. "A spite marriage is a terrible thing to do to anybody. If I hadn't deliberately selected Pete out of all the boys I knew, he'd have gone on till Mrs. McCrea picked out somebody for him, and it would almost have had to be the female counterpart of Pete. A girl like—oh—Florence. Florence Temple."

"Florence Temple, with her cello. Exactly right."

"But I did that awful thing to Pete, and the first few weeks of marriage were just too much for him. He went haywire. I'd slept with two boys before I was married, so it wasn't as much of a shock to me. But Pete almost wore me out. And such adoration, I can't tell you. Then when we came back from Bermuda he began to see all the other girls he'd known all his life, and he'd ask me about them. It was as though he'd never seen them before, in a way. In other ways, it was as though he'd just been waiting all his life to start ripping their clothes off. He was dangerous, Jim. He really was. I could almost tell who would be next by the questions he'd ask. Before we'd go to a party, he'd say 'Who's going to be there tonight?' And I'd say I thought the usual crowd. Then he'd rattle off the list of names of our friends, and leave out one name. That was supposed to fool me, but it didn't for long. The name he left out, that girl was almost sure to be in for a bad time."

"And now it's all concentrated on Muriel Minzer?"

"As far as I know."

"Well, that's a break for you, *and* the other girls. Did you ever talk to him about the passes he made at the others?"

"Oh, how could we avoid it? Whoever it was, she was always 'that little whore.'"

"Did he ever get anywhere with any of them?"

She nodded. "One, but I won't tell you who. There was one girl that didn't stop him, and when that happened he wanted me to sleep with her husband."

"Swap, eh?"

"Yes. But I said I wasn't interested. Pete wanted to know why not? Why wouldn't I? And I almost told him. The boy was one of the two boys I'd stayed with before I was married—oh, when I was seventeen. And he never told anybody and neither have I, or ever will."

"You mean one of our old crowd actually did get somewhere with you, Bobbie?"

"One did. But don't try to guess. It won't do you any good to guess, because I'd never, never tell."

"Well, whichever one it was, he's the best liar I ever knew. And I guess the nicest guy in our whole crowd. You know, Bobbie, the whole damn bunch are going to get credit now for being as honorable as one guy."

"You were all nice, even if you all did talk too much. If it had been you, you would have lied, too."

"No, I don't think I would have."

"You lied about Kitty. Ha ha ha. You didn't know I knew about you and Kitty. I knew it the next day. The very next day. If you don't believe me, I'll tell you where it happened and how it happened, and all about it. That was the great bond we had in common. You and Kitty, and I and this other boy."

"Then Kitty's a gentleman, because she never told me a word about you."

"I kissed every boy in our crowd except Pete, and I necked, heavy-necked two, as you well know, and stayed with one."

"The question is, did you stay with the other one that you heavy-necked with?"

"You'll never know, Jim, and please don't try to find out."

"I won't, but I won't be able to stop theorizing," I said.

We knew everything, everything there was to know. We were so far removed from the technical innocence of eighteen, sixteen, nineteen. I was a man of the world, and Bobbie was indeed a woman, who had borne a child and lived with a husband who had come the most recently to the knowledge we had acquired, but was already the most intricately involved in the complications of sex. We—Bobbie and I—could discuss him and still remain outside the problems of Pete McCrea. We could almost remain outside our own problems. We knew so much, and since what we knew seemed to be all there was to know, we were shockproof. We had come to our maturity and our knowledgeability during the long decade of cynicism that was usually dismissed as "a cynical disregard of the law of the land," but that was something else, something deeper. The law had been passed with a "noble" but nevertheless cynical disregard of men's right to drink. It was a law that had been imposed on some who took pleasure in drinking by some who did not. And when the law was an instant failure, it was not admitted to be a failure by those who had imposed it. They fought to retain the law in spite of its immediate failure and its proliferating corruption, and they fought as hard as they would have for a law that had been an immediate success. They gained no recruits to their own way; they had only deserters, who were not brave deserters but furtive ones; there was no honest mutiny but only grumbling and small disobediences. And we grew up listening to the grumbling, watching the small disobediences; laughing along when the grumbling was intentionally funny, imitating the small disobediences in other ways besides the customs of drinking. It was not only a cynical disregard for a law of the land; the law was eventually changed. Prohibition, the zealots' attempt to force total abstinence on a temperate nation, made liars of a hundred million men and cheats of their children; the West Point cadets who cheated in examinations, the basketball players who connived with gamblers, the thousands of uncaught cheats in the high schools and colleges. We had grown up and away from our earlier esteem of God and country and valor, and had matured at a moment when riches were vanishing for reasons that we could not understand. We were the losing, not the lost, generation. We could not blame Pete McCrea's troubles—and Bobbie's—on the Southern Baptists and the Northern Methodists. Since we knew everything, we knew that Pete's sudden release from twenty years of frustrations had turned him loose in a world filled with women. But Bobbie and I sat there in her mother-in-law's house, breaking several laws of possession, purchase, transportation and consumption of liquor, and with great calmness discussing the destruction of two lives—one of them hers—and the loss of her father's fortune, the depletion of her mother-in-law's, the allure of a chiropractor's divorcée, and our own promiscuity. We knew everything, but we were incapable of recognizing the meaning of our complacency.

I was wearing my dinner jacket, and someone was going to pick me up and take me to a dinner dance at the club. "Who's stopping for you?" said Bobbie.

"It depends. Either Joe or Frank. Depends on whether they go in Joe's car or Frank's. I'm to be ready when they blow their horn."

"Do me a favor, Jim. Make them come in. Pretend you don't hear the horn."

"If it's Joe, he's liable to drive off without me. You know Joe if he's had a few too many."

In a few minutes there was a blast of a two-tone horn, repeated. "That's Joe's car," said Bobbie. "You'd better go." She went to the hall with me and I kissed her cheek. The front door swung open and it was Joe Whipple.

"Hello, Bobbie," he said.

"Hello, Joe. Won't you all come in? Haven't you got time for one drink?" She was trying not to sound suppliant, but Joe was not deceived.

"Just you and Jim here?" he said.

"Yes. Pete went out a little while ago."

"I'll see what the others say," said Joe. He left to speak to the three in the sedan, and obviously he was not immediately persuasive, but they came in with him. They would not let Bobbie take their coats, but they were nice to her and with the first sips of our drinks we were all six almost back in the days when Bobbie Hammersmith's house was where so many of our parties started from. Then we heard the front door thumping shut and Pete McCrea looked in.

There were sounds of hello, but he stared at us over his horn-rims and said to Bobbie: "You didn't have to invite me, but you could have told me." He turned and again the front door thumped.

"Get dressed and come with us," said Joe Whipple.

"I can't do that," said Bobbie.

"She can't, Joe," said Phyllis Whipple. "That would only make more trouble."

"What trouble? She's going to have to sit here alone till he comes home. She might as well be with us," said Joe.

"Anyway, I haven't got a dress that fits," said Bobbie. "But thanks for asking me."

"I won't have you sitting here—"

"Now don't make matters worse, Joe, for heaven's sake," said his wife.

"I could lend you a dress, Bobbie, but I think Phyllis is right," said Mary Lander. "Whatever *you* want to do."

"*Want* to do! That's not the question," said Bobbie. "Go on before I change my mind. Thanks, everybody. Frank, you haven't said a word."

"Nothing much for me to say," said Frank Lander. But as far as I was concerned he, and Bobbie herself, had said more than anyone else. I caught her looking at me quickly.

"Well, all right, then," said Joe. "I'm outnumbered. Or outpersuaded or something."

I was the last to say goodbye, and I whispered to Bobbie: "Frank, eh?"

"You're only guessing," she said. "Goodnight, Jim." Whatever they would be after we left, her eyes were brighter than they had been in years. She had very nearly gone to a party, and for a minute or two she had been part of it.

I sat in the back seat with Phyllis Whipple and Frank Lander. "If you'd had any sense you'd know there'd be a letdown," said Phyllis.

"Oh, drop it," said Joe.

"It might have been worth it, though, Phyllis," said Mary Lander. "How long is it since she's seen anybody but that old battle-ax, Mrs. McCrea? God, I hate to think what it must be like, living in that house with Mrs. McCrea."

"I'm sure it would have been a *lot* easier if Bobbie'd come with us," said Phyllis. "That would have fixed things just right with Mrs. McCrea. She's just the type that wants Bobbie to go out and have a good time. Especially without Pete. You forget how the old lady used to call up all the mothers as soon as she heard there was a party planned. What Joe did was cruel because it was so downright stupid. Thoughtless. Like getting her all excited and then leaving her hung up."

"You've had too much to drink," said Joe.

"*I* have?"

"Yes, you don't say things like that in front of a bachelor," said Joe.

"Who's—oh, Jim? It is to laugh. Did I shock you, Jim?"

"Not a bit. I didn't know what you meant. Did you say something risqué?"

"My husband thinks I did."

"Went right over my head," I said. "I'm innocent about such things."

"So's your old man," said Joe.

"Do you think she should have come with us, Frank?" I said.

"Why ask me? No. I'm with Phyllis. What's the percentage for Bobbie? You saw that son of a bitch in the doorway, and you know damn well when he gets home from Muriel Nierhaus's, he's going to raise hell with Bobbie."

"Then Bobbie had nothing to lose," said Joe. "If Pete's going to raise hell with her, anyway, she might as well have come with us."

"How does he raise hell with her?" I said.

No one said anything.

"Do you know, Phyllis?" I said.

"What?" said Phyllis.

"Oh, come on. You heard me," I said. "Mary?"

"I'm sure I don't know."

"Oh, nuts," I said.

"Go ahead, tell him," said Frank Lander.

"Nobody ever knew for sure," said Phyllis, quietly.

"That's not true. Caroline English, for one. She knew for sure."

Phyllis spoke: "A few weeks before Bobbie had her baby she rang Caroline's doorbell in the middle of the night and asked Caroline if she could stay there. Naturally Caroline said yes, and she saw that Bobbie had nothing but a coat over her nightgown and had bruises all over her arms and shoulders. Julian was away, a lucky break because he'd have gone over and had a fight with Pete. As it was, Caroline made Bobbie have Dr. English come out and have a look at her, and nothing more was said. I mean, it was kept secret from everybody, especially Mr. Hammersmith. But the story got out somehow. Not widespread, but we all heard about it."

"We don't want it to get back to Mr. Hammersmith," said Mary Lander.

"He knows," said Frank Lander.

"You keep saying that, but I don't believe he does," said Mary.

"I don't either," said Joe Whipple. "Pete wouldn't be alive today if Phil Hammersmith knew."

"That's where I think you're wrong," said Phyllis. "Mr. Hammersmith might want to kill Pete, but killing him is another matter. And what earthly good would it do? The Hammersmiths have lost every penny, so I'm told, and at least with Pete still alive, Mrs. McCrea supports Bobbie. Barely. But they have food and a roof over their heads."

"Phil Hammersmith knows the whole damn story, you can bet anything on that. And it's why he's an old man all of a sudden. Have you seen him this trip, Jim?" said Frank Lander.

"I haven't seen him since the wedding."

"Oh, well—" said Mary.

"You won't—" said Joe.

"You won't recognize him," said Frank Lander. "He's bent over—"

"They say he's had a stroke," said Phyllis Whipple.

"And on top of everything else he got a lot of people sore at him by selling his bank stock to Ed Charney," said Joe. "Well, not a lot of people, but some that could have helped him. My old man, to name one. And I don't think that was so hot. Phil Hammersmith was a carpetbagger himself, and damn lucky to be in the bank. Then to sell his stock to a lousy stinking bootlegger . . . You should hear Harry Reilly on the subject."

"I don't want to hear Harry Reilly on any subject," said Frank Lander. "Cheap Irish Mick."

"I don't like him any better than you do, Frank, but call him something else," I said.

"I'm sorry, Jim. I didn't mean that," said Frank Lander.

"No. It just slipped out," I said.

"I apologize," said Frank Lander.

"Oh, all right."

"Don't be sensitive, Jim," said Mary.

"Stay out of it, Mary," said Frank Lander.

"*Everybody* calm down," said Joe. "Everybody knows that Harry Reilly is a cheap Irish Mick, and nobody knows it better than Jim, an Irish Mick but not a cheap one. So shut the hell up, everybody."

"Another country heard from," said Phyllis.

"Now *you*, for Christ's sake," said Joe. "Who has the quart?"

"I have my quart," said Frank Lander.

"I have mine," I said.

"I asked who has mine. Phyllis?"

"When we get to the club, time enough," said Phyllis.

"Hand it over," said Joe.

"Three quarts of whiskey between five people. I'd like to know how we're going to get home tonight," said Mary Lander.

"Drunk as a monkey, if you really want to know," said Joe. "Tight as a nun's."

"Well, at least we're off the subject of Bobbie and Pete," said Phyllis.

"I'm not. I was coming back to it. Phyllis. The quart," said Joe.

"No," said Phyllis.

"Here," I said. "And remember where it came from." I handed him my bottle.

Joe took a swig in the corner of his mouth, swerving the car only slightly. "Thanks," he said, and returned the bottle. "Now, Mary, if you'll light me a cigarette like a dear little second cousin."

"Once removed," said Mary Lander.

"Once removed, and therefore related to Bobbie through her mother."

"No, *you* are but I'm not," said Mary Lander.

"Well, you're in it some way, through me. Now for the benefit of those who are not related to Bobbie or Mrs. Hammersmith, or Mary or me. Permit me to give you a little family history that will enlighten you on several points."

"Is this going to be about Mr. Hammersmith?" said Phyllis. "I don't think you'd better tell that."

"You're related only by marriage, so kindly keep your trap shut. If I want to tell it, I can."

"Everybody remember that I asked him not to," said Phyllis.

"Don't tell it, Joe, whatever it is," said Mary Lander.

"Yeah, what's the percentage?" said Frank Lander. "They have enough trouble without digging up past history."

"Oh, you're so noble, Lander," said Joe. "You fool nobody."

"If you're going to tell the story, go ahead, but stop insulting Frank," said Mary Lander.

"We'll be at the club before he gets started," said Phyllis.

"Then we'll sit there till I finish. Anyway, it doesn't take that long. So, to begin at the beginning. Phil Hammersmith. Phil Hammersmith came here before the war, just out of Lehigh."

"You're not even telling it right," said Phyllis.

"Phyllis is right. I'm screwing up my own story. Well, I'll begin again. Phil Hammersmith graduated from Lehigh, then a few years *later* he came to Gibbsville."

"That's better," said Phyllis.

"The local Lehigh contingent all knew him. He'd played lacrosse and he was a Sigma Nu around the time Mr. Chew was there. So he already had friends in Gibbsville."

"Now you're on the right track," said Phyllis.

"Thank you, love," said Joe.

"Where was he from originally?" I asked.

"Don't ask questions, Jim. It only throws me. He was from some place in New Jersey. So anyway he arrived in Gibbsville and got a job with the Coal & Iron Company. He was a civil engineer, and he had the job when he arrived. That is, he didn't come here looking for a job. He was hired before he got here."

"You've made that plain," said Phyllis.

"Well, it's important," said Joe.

"Yes, but you don't have to say the same thing over and over again," said Phyllis.

"Yes I do. Anyway, apparently the Coal & Iron people hired him on the strength of his record at Lehigh, plus asking a few questions of the local Lehigh contingent, that knew him, *plus* a very good recommendation he'd had from some firm in Bethlehem. Where he'd worked after getting out of college. But after he'd been here a while, and was getting along all right at the Coal & Iron, one day a construction engineer from New York arrived to talk business at the C. & I. Building. They took him down-cellar to the drafting-room and who should he see but Phil Hammersmith. But apparently Phil didn't see him. Well, the New York guy was a real wet smack, because he tattled on Phil.

"Old Mr. Duncan was general superintendent then and he sent for Phil. Was it true that Phil had once worked in South America, and if so, why hadn't he mentioned it when he applied for a job? Phil gave him the obvious answer. 'Because if I had, you wouldn't have hired me.' 'Not necessarily,' said Mr. Duncan. 'We might have accepted your explanation.' 'You say that now, but I tried telling the truth and I couldn't get a job.' 'Well, tell me the truth now,' said Mr. Duncan. 'All right,' said Phil. So he told Mr. Duncan what had happened.

"He was working in South America. Peru, I think. Or maybe Bolivia. In the jungle. And the one thing they didn't want the natives, the Indians, to get hold of was firearms. But one night he caught a native carrying an armful of rifles from the shanty, and when Phil yelled at him, the native ran, and Phil shot him. Killed him. The next day one of the other engineers was found with his throat cut. And the day after that the native chief came and called on the head man of the construction outfit. Either the Indians thought they'd killed the man that had killed their boy, or they didn't much care. But the chief told the white boss that the next time an Indian was killed, two white men would be killed. And not just killed. Tortured. Well, there were four or maybe five engineers, including Phil and the boss. The only white men in an area as big as Pennsylvania, and I guess they weighed their chances and being mathematicians, the odds didn't look so hot. So they quit. No hero stuff. They just quit. Except Phil. He was fired. The boss blamed Phil for everything and in his report to the New York office he put in a lot of stuff that just about fixed Phil for good. The boss, of course, was the same man that spotted Phil at the C. & I. drafting-room."

"You told it very well," said Phyllis.

"So any time you think of Phil Hammersmith killing Pete McCrea, it wouldn't be the first time," said Joe.

"And the war," I said. "He probably killed a few Germans."

"On the other hand, he never got over blaming himself for the other engineer's getting his throat cut," said Joe. "This is all the straight dope. Mr. Duncan to my old man."

We were used to engineers, their travels and adventures in far-off places, but engineers came and went and only a few became fixtures in our life. Phil Hammersmith's story was all new to Mary and Frank and me, and in the cold moonlight, as we sat in a heated automobile in a snow-covered parking area of a Pennsylvania country club, Joe Whipple had taken us to a dark South American jungle, given us a touch of fear, and in a few minutes covered Phil Hammersmith in mystery and then removed the mystery.

"Tell us more about Mr. Hammersmith," said Mary Lander.

Mary Lander. I had not had time to realize the inference that must accompany my guess that Frank Lander was the one boy in our crowd who had stayed with Bobbie. Mary Lander was the only girl who had not fought off Pete McCrea. She was the last girl I would have suspected of staying with Pete, and yet the one that surprised me the least. She had always been the girl our mothers liked us to take out, a kind of mothers' ideal for their sons, and possibly even for themselves. Mary Morgan Lander was the third generation of a family that had always been in the grocery business, the only store in the county that sold caviar and English biscuits and Sportsman's Bracer chocolate, as well as the most expensive domestic items of fruit, vegetables, and tinned goods. Her brother Llewellyn Morgan still scooped out dried prunes and operated the rotary ham slicer, but no one seriously believed that all the Morgan money came from the store. Lew Morgan taught Sunday School in the Methodist Episcopal Church and played basketball at the Y.M.C.A., but he had been to Blair Academy and Princeton, and his father had owned one of the first Pierce-Arrows in Gibbsville. Mary had been unfairly judged a teaser, in previous years. She was not a teaser, but a girl who would kiss a boy and allow him to wander all over her body so long as he did not touch bare skin. Nothing surprised me about Mary. It was in character for her to have slapped Pete McCrea at a dinner party, and then to have let him stay with her and to have discussed with him a swap of husbands and wives. No casual dirty remark ever passed unnoticed by Mary; when someone made a slip we would all turn to see how Mary was taking it, and without fail she had heard it, understood it, and taken a pious attitude. But in our crowd she was the one person most conscious of sex and scatology. She was the only one of whom I would say she had a dirty mind, but I kept that observation to myself along with my theory that she hated Frank Lander. My theory, based on no information whatever, was that marriage and Frank Lander had not been enough for her and that Pete McCrea had become attractive to her because he was so awful.

"There's no more to tell," said Joe Whipple. We got out of the car and Mary took Joe's arm, and her evening was predictable: fathers and uncles and older brothers would cut in on her, and older women would comment as they always did that Mary Lander was *such* a sensible girl, so considerate of her elders, a *wonderful* wife to Frank. And we of her own age would dance with her because under cover of the dancing crowd Mary would wrap both legs around our right legs with a promise that had fooled us for years. Quiet little Mary Lander, climbing up a boy's leg but never forgetting to smile her Dr. Lyons smile at old Mrs. Ginyan and old Mr. Heff. And yet through some mental process that I did not take time to scrutinize, I was less annoyed with Mary than I had been since we were children. I was determined not to dance with her, and I did not, but my special knowledge about her and Pete McCrea reduced her power to allure. Bobbie had married Pete McCrea and she was still attractive in spite of it; but Mary's seductiveness vanished with the revelation that she had picked Pete as her lover, if only for once, twice, or how many times. I had never laughed at Mary before, but now she was the fool, not we, not I.

I got quite plastered at the dance, and so did a lot of other people. On the way home we sang a little—"Body and Soul" was the song, but Phyllis was the only one who could sing the middle part truly—and Frank Lander tried to tell about an incident in the smoking-room, where Julian English apparently had thrown a drink in Harry Reilly's face. It did not seem worth making a fuss about, and Frank never finished his story. Mary Lander attacked me: "You never danced with me, not once," she said.

"I didn't?"

"No, you didn't, and you know you didn't," she said. "And you always do."

"Well, this time I guess I didn't."

"Well, *why* didn't you?"

"Because he didn't want to," said Frank Lander. "You're

making a fool of yourself. I should think you'd have more pride."

"Yeah, why don't you have more pride, Mary?" said Joe Whipple. "You'd think it was an honor to dance with this Malloy guy."

"It is," I said.

"That's it. You're getting so conceited," said Mary. "Well, I'm sure I didn't have to sit any out."

"Then why all the fuss?" said Frank Lander.

"Such popularity must be deserved," I said, quoting an advertising slogan.

"Whose? Mary's or yours?" said Phyllis.

"Well, I was thinking of Mary's, but now that you mention it . . ." I said.

"How many times did he dance with *you*, Phyllis?" said Joe.

"Three or four," said Phyllis.

"In that case, Frank, Jim has insulted your wife. I don't see any other way out of it. You have to at least slap his face. Shall I stop the car?"

"My little trouble-maker," said Phyllis.

"Come on, let's have a fight," said Joe. "Go ahead, Frank. Give him a punch in the nose."

"Yeah, like you did at the Dam, Frank," I said.

"Oh, God. I remember that awful night," said Phyllis. "What did you fight over?"

"Bobbie," I said.

"Bobbie was the cause of *more* fights," said Mary Lander.

"Well, we don't need her to fight over now. We have you," said Joe. "Your honor's been attacked and your husband wants to defend it. The same as I would if Malloy hadn't danced with *my* wife. It's a good thing you danced with Phyllis, Malloy, or you and I'd get out of this car and start slugging."

"Why did you fight over Bobbie? I don't remember that," said Mary.

"Because she came to the picnic with Jim and then went off necking with Frank," said Phyllis. "I remember the whole thing."

"Stop *talking* about fighting and let's *fight*," said Joe.

"All right, stop the car," I said.

"Now you're talking," said Joe.

"Don't be ridiculous," said Phyllis.

"Oh, shut up," said Joe. He pulled up on the side of the road. "I'll referee." He got out of the car, and so did Frank and I and Phyllis. "All right, put up your dukes." We did so, moved around a bit in the snow and slush. "Go on, mix it," said Joe, whereupon Frank rushed me and hit me on the left cheek. All blows were directed at the head, since all three of us were armored in coonskin coats. "That was a good one, Frank. Now go get him, Jim." I swung my right hand and caught Frank's left eye, and at that moment we were all splashed by slush, taken completely by surprise as Phyllis, whom we had forgotten, drove the car away.

"That bitch!" said Joe. He ran to the car and got hold of a door handle but she increased her speed and he fell in the snow. "God damn that bitch, I should have known she was up to something. Now what? Let's try to bum a ride." The fight, such as it was, was over, and we tried to flag down cars on their way home from the dance. We recognized many of them, but not one would stop.

"Well, thanks to you, we've got a nice three-mile walk to Swedish Haven," said Frank Lander.

"Oh, she'll be back," said Joe.

"I'll bet you five bucks she's not," I said.

"Well, I won't bet, but I'll be damned if I'm going to walk three miles. I'm just going to wait till we can bum a ride."

"If you don't keep moving you'll freeze," said Frank.

"We're nearer the club than we are Swedish Haven. Let's go back there," I said.

"And have my old man see me?" said Joe.

"Your old man went home hours ago," I said.

"Well, somebody'll see me," said Joe.

"Listen, half the club's seen you already, and they wouldn't even stop," I said.

"Who has a cigarette?" said Joe.

"Don't give him one," said Frank.

"I have no intention of giving him one," I said. "Let's go back to the club. My feet are soaking wet."

"So are mine," said Frank. We were wearing pumps, and our feet had been wet since we got out of the car.

"That damn Phyllis, she knows I just got over a cold," said Joe.

"Maybe that's why she did it," I said. "It'd serve you right if you got pneumonia."

We began to walk in the middle of the road, in the direction of the clubhouse, which we could see, warm and comfortable on top of a distant plateau. "That old place never looked so good," said Joe. "Let's spend the night there."

"The rooms are all taken. The orchestra's staying there," I said.

We walked about a mile, our feet getting sorer at every step, and the combination of exhaustion and the amount we had had to drink made even grumbling an effort. Then a Dodge touring car, becurtained, stopped about fifty yards from us and a spotlight was turned on each of our faces. A man in a short overcoat and fur-lined cap came toward us. He was a State Highway patrolman. "What happened to you fellows?" he said. "You have a wreck?"

"I married one," said Joe.

"Oh, a weisscrackah," said the patrolman, a Pennsylvania Dutchman. "Where's your car?"

"We got out to take a leak and my wife drove off with it," said Joe.

"You from the dance at the golf club?"

"Yes," said Joe. "How about giving us a lift?"

"Let me see you' driwah's license," said the cop.

Joe took out his billfold and handed over the license. "So? From Lantenengo Street yet? All right, get in. Whereabouts you want to go to?"

"The country club," said Joe.

"The hell with that," said Frank. "Let's go on to Gibbsville."

"This ain't no taxi service," said the cop. "And I ain't taking you to no Gippsfille. I'm on my way to my substation. Swedish Haven. You can phone there for a taxi. Privileged characters, you think you are. A bunch of drunks, you ask me."

I had to go back to New York on the morning train and the events of the next few days, so far as they concerned Joe and Phyllis Whipple and Frank and Mary Lander, were obscured by the suicide, a day or two later, of Julian English, the man who had thrown a drink at Harry Reilly. The domestic crisis of the Whipples and the Landers and even the McCreas seemed very unimportant. And yet when I heard about English, who had not been getting along with his wife, I wondered about my own friends, people my own age but not so very much younger than Julian and Caroline English. English had danced with Phyllis and Mary that night, and now he was dead. I knew very little about the causes of the difficulties between him and Caroline, but they could have been no worse than the problems that existed in Bobbie's marriage and that threatened the marriage of Frank and Mary Lander. I was shocked and saddened by the English suicide; he was an attractive man whose shortcomings seemed out of proportion to the magnitude of killing himself. He had not been a friend of mine, only an acquaintance with whom I had had many drinks and played some golf; but friends of mine, my closest friends in the world, boys-now-men like myself, were at the beginning of the same kind of life and doing the same kind of thing that for Julian English ended in a sealed-up garage with a motor running. I hated what I thought those next few days and weeks. There is nothing young about killing oneself, no matter when it happens, and I hated this being deprived of the sweetness of youth. And that was what it was, that was what was happening to us. I, and I think the others, had looked upon our squabbles as unpleasant incidents but belonging to our youth. Now they were plainly recognizable as symptoms of life without youth, without youth's excuses or youth's recoverability. I wanted to love someone, and during the next year or two I confused the desperate need for love with love itself. I had put a hopeless love out of my life; but that is not part of this story, except to state it and thus to show that I knew what I was looking for.

2.

When you have grown up with someone it is much easier to fill in gaps of five years, ten years, in which you do not see him, than to supply those early years in the life of a friend you meet in maturity. I do not know why this is so, unless it is a mere matter of insufficient time. With the friends of later life you may exchange boyhood stories that seem worth telling, but boyhood is not all stories. It is mostly not stories, but day-to-day, unepisodic living. And most of us are too polite to burden our later-life friends with unexciting anecdotes about people they will never meet. (Likewise we hope they will not burden us.) But it is easy to bring old friends up to date in your mental dossiers by the addition of a few vital facts. Have they stayed married? Have they had many more children? Have they made money or lost it? Usually the basic facts will do, and then you tell yourself that Joe Whipple is still Joe Whipple, plus two sons, a new house, a hundred thousand dollars, forty pounds, bifocals, fat in the neck, and a new concern for the state of the nation.

Such additions I made to my friends' dossiers as I heard about them from time to time; by letters from them, conversations with my mother, an occasional newspaper clipping. I received these facts with joy for the happy news, sorrow for the sad, and immediately went about my business, which was far removed from any business of theirs. I seldom went back to Gibbsville during the Thirties—mine and the century's—and when I did I stayed only long enough to stand at a grave, to toast a bride, to spend a few minutes beside a sickbed. In my brief encounters with my old friends I got no information about Bobbie and Pete McCrea, and only after I had returned to New York or California would I remember that I had intended to inquire about them.

There is, of course, some significance in the fact that no one volunteered information about Bobbie and Pete. It was that they had disappeared. They continued to live in Gibbsville, but in parts of the town that were out of the way for their old friends. There is no town so small that that cannot happen, and Gibbsville, a third-class city, was large enough to have all the grades of poverty and wealth and the many half grades in between, in which $10 a month in the husband's income could make a difference in the kind and location of the house in which he lived. No one had volunteered any information about Bobbie and Pete, and I had not remembered to inquire. In five years I had had no new facts about them, none whatever, and their disappearance from my ken might have continued but for a broken shoelace.

I was in Gibbsville for a funeral, and the year was 1938. I had broken a shoelace, it was evening and the stores were closed, and I was about to drive back to New York. The only place open that might have shoelaces was a poolroom that in my youth had had a two-chair bootblack stand. The poolroom was in a shabby section near the railroad stations and a couple of cheap hotels, four or five saloons, an automobile tire agency, a barber shop, and a quick-lunch counter. I opened the pool-room door, saw that the bootblack's chairs were still there, and said to the man behind the cigar counter: "Have you got any shoelaces?"

"Sorry I can't help you, Jim," said the man. He was wearing an eyeshade, but as soon as he spoke I recognized Pete McCrea.

"Pete, for God's sake," I said. We shook hands.

"I thought you might be in town for the funeral," he said. "I should have gone, too, I guess, but I decided I wouldn't. It was nice of you to make the trip."

"Well, you know. He was a friend of my father's. Do you own this place?"

"I run it. I have a silent partner, Bill Charney. You remember Ed Charney? His younger brother. I don't know where to send you to get a shoelace."

"The hell with the shoelace. How's Bobbie?"

"Oh, Bobbie's fine. *You* know. A lot of changes, but this is better than nothing. Why don't you call her up? She'd love to hear from you. We're living out on Mill Street, but we have a phone. Call her up and say hello. The number is 3385-J. If you have time maybe you could go see her. I have to stay here till I close up at one o'clock, but she's home."

"What number on Mill Street? You call her up and tell her I'm coming? Is that all right?"

"Hell, yes."

Someone thumped the butt of a cue on the floor and called out: "Rack 'em up, Pete?"

"I have to be here. You go on out and I'll call her up," he said. "Keep your shirt on," he said to the pool player, then, to me: "It's 402 Mill Street, across from the open hearth, second house from the corner. I guess I won't see you again, but I'm glad we had a minute. You're looking very well." I could not force a comment on his appearance. His nose was red and larger, his eyes watery, the dewlaps sagging, and he was wearing a blue denim work shirt with a dirty leather bow tie.

"Think I could get in the Ivy Club if I went back to Princeton?" he said. "I didn't make it the first time around, but now I'm a big shot. So long, Jim. Nice to've seen you."

The open hearth had long since gone the way of all the mill equipment; the mill itself had been inactive for years, and as a residential area the mill section was only about a grade and a half above the poorest Negro slums. But in front of most of the houses in the McCreas' row there were cared-for plots; there always had been, even when the mill was running and the air was full of smoke and acid. It was an Irish and Polish neighborhood, but knowledge of that fact did not keep me from locking all the doors of my car. The residents of the neighborhood would not have touched my father's car, but this was not his car and I was not he.

The door of Number 402 opened as soon as I closed my car door. Bobbie waited for me to lock up and when I got to the porch, she said: "*Jim.* Jim, Jim, Jim. How nice. I'm so glad to see you." She quickly closed the door behind me and then kissed me. "Give me a real kiss and a real hug. I didn't dare while the door was open." I kissed her and held her for a moment and then she said: "Hey, I guess we'd better cut this out."

"Yes," I said. "It's nice, though."

"Haven't done that since we were—God!" She stood away and looked at me. "You could lose some weight, but you're not so bad. How about a bottle of beer? Or would you rather have some cheap whiskey?"

"What are you drinking?"

"Cheap whiskey, but I'm used to it," she said.

"Let's both have some cheap whiskey," I said.

"Straight? With water? Or how?"

"Oh, a small slug of whiskey and a large slug of water in it. I'm driving back to New York tonight."

She went to the kitchen and prepared the drinks. I recognized some of the furniture from the Hammersmith and McCrea houses. "Brought together by a shoestring," she said. "Here's to it. How do I look?"

"If you want my frank and candid opinion, good enough to

go right upstairs and make up for the time we lost. Pete won't be home till one o'clock."

"If then," she said. "Don't think I wouldn't, but it's too soon after my baby. Didn't Pete tell you I finally produced a healthy son?"

"No."

"You'll hear him in a little while. We have a daughter, two years old, and now a son. Angus McCrea, Junior. Seven pounds two ounces at birth."

"Good for you," I said.

"Not so damn good for me, but it's over, and he's healthy."

"And what about your mother and father?" I said.

"Oh, poor Jim. You didn't know? Obviously you didn't, and you're going to be so sorry you asked. Daddy committed suicide two years ago. He shot himself. And Mother's in Swedish Haven." Swedish Haven was local lore for the insane asylum. "I'm sorry I had to tell you."

"God, why won't they lay off you?" I said.

"Who is they? Oh, you mean just—life?"

"Yes."

"I don't know, Jim," she said. "I've had about as much as I can stand, or so I keep telling myself. But I must be awfully tough, because there's always something else, and I go right on. Will you let me complain for just a minute, and then I'll stop? The only one of the old crowd I ever see is Phyllis. She comes out and never forgets to bring a bottle, so we get tight together. But some things we don't discuss, Phyllis and I. Pete is a closed subject."

"What's he up to?"

"Oh, he has his women. I don't even know who they are any more, and couldn't care less. Just as long as he doesn't catch a disease, I told him that, so he's been careful about it." She sat up straight. "I haven't been the soul of purity, either, but it's Pete's son. Both children are Pete's. But I haven't been withering on the vine."

"Why should you?"

"That's what *I* said. Why should I have nothing? Nothing? The children are mine, and I love them, but I need more than that, Jim. Children don't love you back. All they do is depend on you to feed them and wash them and all the rest of it. But after they're in bed for the night—I never know whether Pete will be home at two o'clock or not at all. So I've had two tawdry romances, I guess you'd call them. Not you, but Mrs. McCrea would."

"Where is dear Mrs. McCrea?"

"She's living in Jenkintown, with an old maid sister. Thank heaven they can't afford carfare, so I'm spared that."

"Who are your gentlemen friends?"

"Well, the first was when we were living on the East Side. A gentleman by the name of Bill Charney. Yes, Ed's brother and Pete's partner. I was crazy about him. Not for one single minute in love with him, but I never even thought about love with him. He wanted to marry me, too, but I was a nasty little snob. I *couldn't* marry Bill Charney, Jim. I just couldn't. So he married a nice little Irish girl and they're living on Lantenengo Street in the house that used to belong to old Mr. Duncan. And I'm holding court on Mill Street, thirty dollars a month rent."

"Do you want some money?"

"Will you give me two hundred dollars?"

"More than that, if you want it."

"No, I'd just like to have two hundred dollars to hide, to keep in case of emergency."

"In case of emergency, you can always send me a telegram in care of my publisher." I gave her $200.

"Thank you. Now I have some money. For the last five or six years I haven't had any money of my own. You don't care how I spend this, do you?"

"As long as you spend it on yourself."

"I've gotten so stingy I probably won't spend any of it. But this is wonderful. Now I can read the ads and say to myself I could have some expensive lingerie. I think I will get a permanent, next month."

"Is that when you'll be back in circulation again?"

"Good guess. Yes, about a month," she said. "But not the same man. I didn't tell you about the second one. You don't know him. He came here after you left Gibbsville. His name is McCormick and he went to Princeton with Pete. They sat next to each other in a lot of classes, McC, McC, and he was sent here to do some kind of an advertising survey and ran into Pete. They'd never been exactly what you'd call pals, but they *knew* each other and Mac took one look and sized up the situation and—well, I thought, why not? He wasn't as exciting as Mr. Charney, but at one time I would have married him. *If* he'd asked me. He doesn't live here any more."

"But you've got the next one picked out?"

"No, but I know there will be a next one. Why lie to myself? And why lie to you? I don't think I ever have."

"Do you ever see Frank?"

"Frank? Frank Lander? What made you think of him?"

"Bobbie," I said.

"Oh, of course. That was a guess of yours, a long time ago," she said. "No, I never see Frank." She was smoking a cigarette, and sitting erect with her elbow on the arm of her chair, holding the cigarette high and with style. If her next words had been "Jeeves, have the black Rolls brought round at four o'clock" she would not have been more naturally grand. But her next words were: "I haven't even thought about Frank. There was another boy, Johnny White, the one I was engaged to. *Engaged to.* That close to spending the rest of my life with him—or at least part of it. But because he wanted me to go away with him before we were married, I broke the engagement and married Pete."

"Is that all it was? That he wanted you to go away with him?"

"That's really all it was. I got huffy and said he couldn't really love me if he wanted to take that risk. Not that we hadn't been taking risks, but a pre-marital trip, that was something else again. My five men, Jim. Frank. Johnny. Bill and Mac. And Pete."

"Why didn't you and Frank ever get engaged?"

"I wonder. I *have* thought about *that*, so I was wrong when I said I never think of Frank. But Frank in the old days, not Frank now. What may have happened was that Frank was the only boy I'd gone all the way with, and then I got scared because I didn't want to give up the fun, popularity, good times. Jim, I have a confession to make. About you."

"Oh?"

"I told Frank I'd stayed with you. He wouldn't believe he

was my first and he kept harping on it, so I really got rid of Frank by telling him you were the first."

"Why me?"

"Because the first time I ever stayed with Frank, or anybody, it was at a picnic at the Dam, and I'd gone to the picnic with you. So you were the logical one."

"Did you tell him that night?"

"No. Later. Days later. But you had a fight with him that night, and the fight made it all the more convincing."

"Well, thanks, little pal," I said.

"Oh, you don't care, do you?"

"No, not really."

"You had Kitty, after all," she said. "Do you ever see Kitty?"

"No. Kitty lives in Cedarhurst and they keep to themselves, Cedarhurst people."

"What was your wife like?"

"She was nice. Pretty. Wanted to be an actress. I still see her once in a while. I like her, and always will, but if ever there were two people that shouldn't have got married . . ."

"I can name two others," said Bobbie.

"You and Pete. But you've stuck to him."

"Don't be polite. I'm stuck with him. Can you imagine what Pete would be like if I left him?"

"Well, to be brutally frank, what's he like anyway? You don't have to go on paying for a dirty trick the rest of your life."

"It wasn't just a dirty trick. It would have been a dirty trick if I'd walked out on him the day we were getting married. But I went through with it, and that made it more than a dirty trick. I *should have* walked out on him, the day we got married. I even tried. And he'd have recovered—then. Don't forget, Pete McCrea was used to dirty tricks being played on him, and he might have got over it if I'd left him at the church. But once I'd married him, he became a different person, took himself much more seriously, and so did everyone else. They began to dislike him, but that was better than being laughed at." She sipped her drink.

"Well, who did it? I did. Your little pal," she said. "How about some more cheap whiskey?"

"No thanks, but you go ahead," I said.

"The first time I ever knew there *was* a Mill Street was the day we rented this house," she said, as she poured herself a drink. "I'd never been out this way before."

"You couldn't have lived here when the mill was operating. The noise and the smoke."

"I can live anywhere," she said. "So can anyone else. And don't be too surprised if you find us back on Lantenengo. Do you know the big thing nowadays? Slot machines and the numbers racket. Pete wants to get into The Numbers, but he hasn't decided how to go about it. Bill Charney is the kingpin in the county, although not the real head. It's run by a syndicate in Jersey City."

"Don't let him do it, Bobbie," I said. "Really don't."

"Why not? He's practically in it already. He has slot machines in the poolroom, and that's where people call up to find out what number won today. He might as well be in it."

"No."

"It's the only way Pete will ever have any money, and if he ever gets his hands on some money, maybe he'll divorce me. Then I could take the children and go away somewhere. California."

"That's a different story. If you're planning it that way. But stay out of The Numbers if you ever have any idea of remaining respectable. You can't just go in for a few years and then quit."

"Respectable? Do you think my son's going to be able to get into Princeton? His father is the proprietor of a poolroom, and they're going to know that when Angus gets older. Pete will never be anything else. He's found his niche. But if I took the children to California they might have a chance. And *I* might have a chance, before it's too late. It's our only hope, Jim. Phyllis agrees with me."

I realized that I would be arguing against a hope and a dream, and if she had that much left, and only that much, I had no right to argue. She very nearly followed my thinking. "It's what I live on, Jim," she said. "That—and this." She held up her glass. "And a little admiration. A little—admiration. Phyllis wants to give me a trip to New York. Would you take us to '21' and those places?"

"Sure."

"Could you get someone for Phyllis?"

"I think so. Sure. Joe wouldn't go on this trip?"

"And give up a chance to be with Mary Lander?"

"So now it's Joe and Mary?"

"Oh, that's old hat in Gibbsville. They don't even pretend otherwise."

"And Frank? What about him?"

"Frank is the forgotten man. If there were any justice he ought to pair off with Phyllis, but they don't like each other. Phyllis calls Frank a wishy-washy namby-pamby, and Frank calls Phyllis a drunken trouble-maker. We've all grown up, Jim. Oh, haven't we just? Joe doesn't like Phyllis to visit me because Mary says all we do is gossip. Although how she'd know *what* we do . . ."

"They were all at the funeral, and I thought what a dull, stuffy little group they've become," I said.

"But that's what they are," said Bobbie. "Very stuffy and very dull. What else is there for them to do? If I were still back there with them I'd be just as bad. Maybe worse. In a way, you know, Pete McCrea has turned out to be the most interesting man in our old crowd, present company excepted. Joe was a very handsome young man and so was Frank, and their families had lots of money and all the rest of it. But you saw Joe and Frank today. I haven't seen them lately, but Joe looks like a professional wrestler and I remember how hairy he was, all over his chest and back and his arms and legs. And Frank just the opposite, skin like a girl's and slender, but now we could almost call *him* Ichabod. He looks like a cranky schoolteacher, and his glasses make him look like an owl. Mary, of course, beautifully dressed I'm sure, and not looking a day older."

"Several days older, but damn good-looking," I said.

A baby cried and Bobbie made no move. "That's my daughter. Teething. Now she'll wake up my son and you're in for a lot of howling." The son began to cry, and Bobbie excused herself. She came back in a few minutes with the infant in her arms. "It's against my rules to pick them up, but I wanted to show him to you. Isn't he an ugly little creature? The answer is yes." She took him away and returned with the daughter. "She's begun to have a face."

"Yes, I can see that. Your face, for which she can be thankful."

"Yes, I wouldn't want a girl to look like Pete. It doesn't

matter so much with a boy." She took the girl away and when she rejoined me she refilled her glass.

"Are you sorry you didn't have children?" she said.

"Not the way it turned out, I'm not," I said.

"These two haven't had much of a start in life, the poor little things. They haven't even been christened. Do you know why? There was nobody we could ask to be their godfathers." Her eyes filled with tears. "That was when I really saw what we'd come to."

"Bobbie, I've got a four-hour drive ahead of me, so I think I'd better get started."

"Four hours to New York? In that car?"

"I'm going to stop and have a sandwich halfway."

"I could give you a sandwich and make some coffee."

"I don't want it now, thanks."

We looked at each other. "I'd like to show how much I appreciate your coming out to see me," she said. "But it's probably just as well I can't. But I'll be all right in New York, Jim. That is, if I ever get there. I won't believe that, either, till I'm on the train."

If she came to New York I did not know about it, and during the war years Bobbie and her problems receded from my interest. I heard that Pete was working in a defense plant, from which I inferred that he had not made the grade in the numbers racket. Frank Lander was in the Navy, Joe Whipple in the War Production Board, and by the time the war was over I discovered that so many other people and things had taken the place of Gibbsville in my thoughts that I had almost no active curiosity about the friends of my youth. I had even had a turnover in my New York friendships. I had married again, I was working hard, and most of my social life originated with my wife's friends. I was making, for me, quite a lot of money, and I was a middle-aged man whose physician had made some honest, unequivocal remarks about my life expectancy. It took a little time and one illness to make me realize that if I wanted to see my child grow to maturity, I had to retire from night life. It was not nearly so difficult as I had always anticipated it would be.

After I became reconciled to middle age and the quieter life I made another discovery: that the sweetness of my early youth was a persistent and enduring thing, so long as I kept it at the distance of years. Moments would come back to me, of love and excitement and music and laughter that filled my breast as they had thirty years earlier. It was not nostalgia, which only means homesickness, nor was it a wish to be living that excitement again. It was a splendid contentment with the knowledge that once I had felt those things so deeply and well that the throbbing urging of George Gershwin's "Do It Again" could evoke the original sensation and the pictures that went with it: a tea dance at the club and a girl in a long black satin dress and my furious jealousy of a fellow who wore a yellow foulard tie. I wanted none of it ever again, but all I had I wanted to keep. I could remember precisely the tone in which her brother had said to her: "Are you coming or aren't you?" and the sounds of his galoshes after she said: "I'm going home with Mr. Malloy." They were the things I knew before we knew everything, and, I suppose, before we began to learn. There was always a girl, and nearly always there was music; if the Gershwin tune belonged to that girl, a Romberg tune belonged to another and "When Hearts Are Young" became a personal anthem, enduringly sweet and safe from all harm, among the protected memories. In middle age I was proud to have lived according to my emotions at the right time, and content to live that way vicariously and at a distance. I had missed almost nothing, escaped very little, and at fifty I had begun to devote my energy and time to the last, simple but big task of putting it all down as well as I knew how.

In the midst of putting it all down, as novels and short stories and plays, I would sometimes think of Bobbie McCrea and the dinginess of her history. But as the reader will presently learn, the "they"—life—that had once made me cry out in anger, were not through with her yet. (Of course "they" are never through with anyone while he still lives, and we are not concerned here with the laws of compensation that seem to test us, giving us just enough strength to carry us in another trial.) I like to think that Bobbie got enough pleasure out of a pair of nylons, a permanent wave, a bottle of Phyllis Whipple's whiskey, to recharge the brightness in her. As we again take up her story I promise the reader a happy ending, if only because I want it that way. It happens also to be the true ending. . . .

Pete McCrea did not lose his job at the end of the war. His Princeton degree helped there. He had gone into the plant, which specialized in aluminum extrusion, as a manual laborer, but his IBM card revealed that he had taken psychology courses in college, and he was transferred to Personnel. It seemed an odd choice, but it is not hard to imagine that Pete was better fitted by his experience as a poolroom proprietor than as a two-year student of psychology. At least he spoke both languages, he liked the work, and in 1945 he was not bumped by a returning veteran.

Fair Grounds, the town in which the plant was situated, was only three miles from Gibbsville. For nearly a hundred years it had been the trading center for the Pennsylvania Dutch farmers in the area, and its attractions had been Becker's general store, the Fair Grounds Bank, the freight office of the Reading Railway, the Fair Grounds Hotel, and five Protestant churches. Clerks at Becker's and at the bank and the Reading, and bartenders at the hotel and the pastors of the churches, all had to speak Pennsylvania Dutch. English was desirable but not a requirement. The town was kept scrubbed, dusted and painted, and until the erection of the aluminum plant, jobs and trades were kept in the same families. An engineman's son worked as waterboy until he was old enough to take the examinations for brakeman; a master mechanic would give his boy calipers for Christmas. There were men and women in Fair Grounds who visited Gibbsville only to serve on juries or to undergo surgery at the Gibbsville Hospital. There were some men and women who had never been to Gibbsville at all and regarded Gibbsville as some Gibbsville citizens regarded Paris, France. That was the pre-aluminum Fair Grounds.

To this town in 1941 went Pete and Bobbie McCrea. They rented a house no larger than the house on Mill Street but cleaner and in better repair. Their landlord and his wife went to live with his mother-in-law, and collected the $50 legally frozen monthly rent and $50 side payment for the use of the radio and the gas stove. But in spite of under-the-table and black-market prices Peter and Bobbie McCrea were financially better off than they had been since their marriage, and nylons at black-market prices were preferable to the no nylons she had had on Mill Street. The job, and the fact that he continued to hold it, restored some respectability to Pete, and they discussed rejoining the club. "Don't try it, I warn you," said Phyllis Whipple. "The club isn't run by your friends any more. Now it's been taken over by people that couldn't have got in ten years ago."

"Well, we'd have needed all our old friends to go to bat for us, and I guess some would think twice about it," said Pete. "So we'll do our drinking at the Tavern."

The Dan Patch Tavern, which was a new name for the renovated Fair Grounds Hotel bar, was busy all day and all night, and it was one of the places where Pete could take pleasure in his revived respectability. It was also one of the places where Bobbie could count on getting that little admiration that she needed to live on. On the day of Pearl Harbor she was only thirty-four years old and at the time of the Japanese surrender she was only thirty-eight. She was accorded admiration in abundance. Some afternoons just before the shift changed she would walk the three blocks to the Tavern and wait for Pete. The bartender on duty would say "Hi, Bobbie," and bring her currently favorite drink to her booth. Sometimes there would be four men sitting with her when Pete arrived from the plant; she was never alone for long. If one man tried to persuade her to leave, and became annoyingly insistent, the bartenders came to her rescue. The bartenders and the proprietor knew that in her way Bobbie was as profitable as the juke box. She was an attraction. She was a good-looking broad who was not a whore or a falling-down lush, and all her drinks were paid for. She was the Tavern's favorite customer, male or female, and if she had given the matter any thought she could have been declared in. All she wanted in return was a steady supply of Camels and protection from being mauled. The owner of the Tavern, Rudy Schau, was the only one who was aware that Bobbie and Pete had once lived on Lantenengo Street in Gibbsville, but far from being impressed by their background, he had a German opinion of aristocrats who had lost standing. He was actively suspicious of Bobbie in the beginning, but in time he came to accept her as a wife whose independence he could not condone and a good-looking woman whose morals he had not been able to condemn. And she was good for business. Beer business was good, but at Bobbie's table nobody drank beer, and the real profit was in the hard stuff.

In the Fair Grounds of the pre-aluminum days Bobbie would have had few women friends. No decent woman would have gone to a saloon every day—or any day. She most likely would have received warnings from the Ku Klux Klan, which was concerned with personal conduct in a town that had only a dozen Catholic families, no Negroes and no Jews. But when the aluminum plant (which was called simply The Aluminum or The Loomy) went into war production the population of Fair Grounds immediately doubled and the solid Protestant character of the town was changed in a month. Eight hundred new people came to town and they lived in apartments in a town where there were no apartments: in rooms in private houses, in garages and old stables, in rented rooms and haylofts out in the farming area. The newcomers wasted no time with complaints of double-rent, inadequate heating, holes in the roof, insufficient sanitation. The town was no longer scrubbed, dusted or painted, and thousands of man-hours were lost while a new shift waited for the old to vacate parking space in the streets of the town. Bobbie and Pete were among the lucky early ones: they had a house. That fact of itself gave Bobbie some distinction. The house had two rooms and kitchen on the first floor, three rooms and bath on the second, and it had a cellar and an attic. In the identical houses on both sides there were a total of four families and six roomers. As a member of Personnel it was one of Pete's duties to find housing for workers, but Bobbie would have no roomers. "The money wouldn't do us much good, so let's live like human beings," she said.

"You mean there's nothing to buy with the money," said Pete. "But we could save it."

"If we had it, we'd spend it. You've never saved a cent in your life and neither have I. If you're thinking of the children's education, buy some more war bonds and have it taken out of your pay. But I'm not going to share my bathroom with a lot of dirty men. I'd have to do all the extra work, not you."

"You could make a lot of money doing their laundry. Fifty cents a shirt."

"Are you serious?"

"No."

"It's a good thing you're not, because I could tell you how else I could make a lot more money."

"Yes, a lot more," said Pete.

"Well, then, keep your ideas to yourself. I won't have boarders and I won't do laundry for fifty cents a shirt. That's final."

And so Bobbie had her house, she got the admiration she needed, and she achieved a moderate popularity among the women of her neighborhood by little friendly acts that came spontaneously out of her friendly nature. There was a dinginess to the new phase: the house was not much, the men who admired her and the women who welcomed her help were the ill-advantaged, the cheap, the vulgar, and sometimes the evil. But the next step down from Mill Street would have been hopeless degradation, and the next step up, Fair Grounds, was at least up. She was envied for her dingy house, and when Pete called her the Queen of the Klondike she was not altogether displeased. There was envy in the epithet, and in the envy was the first sign of respect he had shown her in ten years. He had never suspected her of an affair with Mac McCormick, and if he had suspected her during her infatuation with Bill Charney he had been afraid to make an accusation; afraid to anticipate his own feelings in the event that Charney would give him a job in The Numbers. When Charney brought in a Pole from Detroit for the job Pete had wanted, Pete accepted $1,000 for his share of the poolroom and felt only grateful relief. Charney did not always buy out his partners, and Pete refused to wonder if the money and the easy dissolution of the partnership had been paid for by Bobbie. It was not a question he wanted to raise, and when the war in Europe created jobs at Fair Grounds he believed that his luck had begun to change.

Whatever the state of Pete's luck, the pace of his marriage had begun to change. The pace of his marriage—and not his alone—was set by the time he spent at home and what he did during that time. For ten years he had spent little more time at home than was necessary for sleeping and eating. He could not sit still in the same room with Bobbie, and even after the children were born he did not like to have her present during the times he would play with them. He would arrive in a hurry to have his supper, and in a short time he would get out of the house, to be with a girl, to go back to work at the poolroom. He was most conscious of time when he was near Bobbie; everywhere else he moved slowly, spoke deliberately, answered hesitantly. But after the move to Fair Grounds he spent more time in the house, with the children, with Bobbie. He would sit in the front room, doing paper work from the plant, while Bobbie sewed. At the Tavern he would say to Bobbie: "It's time we were getting home." He no longer darted in and out of the house and ate his meals rapidly and in silence.

He had a new girl. Martha—"Martie"—Klinger was a typist at the plant, a Fair Grounds woman whose husband was in the Coast Guard at Lewes, Delaware. She was Bobbie's age and likewise had two children. She retained a young prettiness in the now round face and her figure had not quite reached the stage of plumpness. Sometimes when she moved an arm the flesh of her breast seemed to go all the way up to her neckline, and she had been one of the inspirations for a plant memo to women employees, suggesting that tight sweaters and tight slacks were out of place in wartime industry. Pete brought her to the Tavern one day after work, and she never took her eyes off Bobbie. She looked up and down, up and down, with her mouth half open as though she were listening to Bobbie through her lips. She showed no animosity of a defensive nature and was not openly possessive of Pete, but Bobbie knew on sight that she was Pete's new girl. After several sessions at the Tavern Bobbie could tell which of the men had already slept with Martie and which of them were likely to again. It was impossible to be jealous of Martie, but it was just as impossible not to feel superior to her. Pete, the somewhat changed Pete, kept up the absurd pretense that Martie was just a girl from the plant whom he happened to bring along for a drink, and there was no unpleasantness until one evening Martie said: "Jesus, I gotta go or I won't get any supper."

"Come on back to our house and have supper with us," said Pete. "That's okay by you, isn't it, Bobbie?"

"No, it isn't," said Bobbie.

"Rudy'll give us a steak and we can cook it at home," said Pete.

"I said no," said Bobbie, and offered no explanation.

"I'll see you all tomorrow," said Martie. "Goodnight, people."

"Why wouldn't you let her come home with us? I could have got a steak from Rudy. And Martie's a hell of a good cook."

"When we can afford a cook I may hire her," said Bobbie.

"Oh, that's what it is. The old snob department."

"That's exactly what it is."

"We're not in any position—"

"*You're* not."

"*We're* not. If I can't have my friends to my house," he said, but did not know how to finish.

"It's funny that she's the first one you ever asked. Don't forget what I told you about having boarders, and fifty cents a shirt. You keep your damn Marties out of my house. If you don't, I'll get a job and you'll be just another boarder yourself."

"Oh, why are you making such a stink about Martie?"

"Come *off* it, Pete, for heaven's *sake*."

The next statement, he knew, would have to be a stupidly transparent lie or an admission, so he made no statement. If there had to be a showdown he preferred to avert it until the woman in question was someone more entertaining than Martie Klinger. And he liked the status quo.

They both liked the status quo. They had hated each other, their house, the dinginess of their existence on Mill Street. When the fire whistle blew it was within the hearing of Mill Street and of Lantenengo Street; rain from the same shower fell on Mill Street and on Lantenengo Street; Mill Street and Lantenengo Street read the same Gibbsville newspaper at the same time every evening. And the items of their proximity only made the nearness worse, the remoteness of Mill Street from Lantenengo more vexatious. But Fair Grounds was a new town, where they had gone knowing literally nobody. They had spending money, a desirable house, the respectability of a white-collar job, and the restored confidence in a superiority to their neighbors that they had not allowed themselves to feel on Mill Street. In the Dan Patch Tavern they would let things slip out that would have been meaningless on Mill Street, where their neighbors' daily concern was a loaf of bread and a bottle of milk. "Pete, did you know Jimmy Stewart, the movie actor?" "No, he was several classes behind me, but he was in my club." "Bobbie, what's it like on one of them yachts?" "I've only been on one, but it was fun while it lasted." They could talk now about past pleasures and luxuries without being contradicted by their surroundings, and their new friends at the Tavern had no knowledge of the decade of dinginess that lay between that past and this present. If their new friends also guessed that Pete McCrea was carrying on with Martie Klinger, that very fact made Bobbie more credibly and genuinely the woman who had once cruised in a yacht. They would have approved Bobbie's reason for not wanting Martie Klinger as a guest at supper, as they would have fiercely resented Pete's reference to Bobbie as the Queen of the Klondike. Unintentionally they were creating a symbol of order that they wanted in their lives as much as Bobbie needed admiration, and if the symbol and the admiration were slightly ersatz, what, in war years, was not?

There was no one among the Tavern friends whom Bobbie desired to make love with. "I'd give a week's pay to get in bed with you, Bobbie," said one of them.

"Fifty-two weeks' pay, did you say?" said Bobbie.

"No dame is worth fifty-two weeks' pay," said the man, a foreman named Dick Hartenstein.

"Oh, I don't know. In fifty-two weeks you make what?"

"A little over nine thousand. Nine gees, about."

"A lot of women can get that, Dick. I've heard of women getting a diamond necklace for just one night, and they cost a lot more than nine thousand dollars."

"Well, I tell you, Bobby, if I ever hit the crap game for nine gees I'd seriously consider it, but not a year's pay that I worked for."

"You're not romantic enough for me. Sorry."

"Supposing I did hit the crap game and put nine gees on the table in front of you? Would you and me go to bed?"

"No."

"No, I guess not. If I asked you a question would you give me a truthful answer? No. You wouldn't."

"Why should I?"

"Yeah, why should you? I was gonna ask you, what does it take to get you in bed with a guy?"

"I'm a married woman."

"I skipped all that part, Bobbie. You'd go, if it was the right guy."

"You could get to be an awful nuisance, Dick. You're not far from it right this minute."

"I apologize."

"In fact, why don't you take your drink and stand at the bar?"

"What are you sore at? You get propositioned all the time."

"Yes, but you're too persistent, and you're a bore. The others don't keep asking questions when I tell them no. Go on, now, or I'll tell Rudy to keep you out of here."

"You know what you are?"

"Rudy! Will you come here, please?" she called. "All right, Dick. What am I? Say it in front of Rudy."

Rudy Schau made his way around from the bar. "What can I do for you, Bobbie?"

"I think Dick is getting ready to call me a nasty name."

"He won't," said Rudy Schau. He had the build of a man who had handled beer kegs all his life and he was now ready to squeeze the wind out of Hartenstein. "Apolochise to Bobbie and get the hell outa my place. And don't forget you got a forty-dollar tab here. You won't get a drink nowheres else in tahn."

"I'll pay my God damn tab," said Hartenstein.

"That you owe me. Bobbie you owe an apolochy."

"I apologize," said Hartenstein. He was immediately clipped behind the ear, and sunk to the floor.

"I never like that son of a bitch," said Rudy Schau. He looked down at the unconscious Hartenstein and very deliberately kicked him in the ribs.

"Oh, *don't*, Rudy," said Bobbie. "*Please* don't."

Others in the bar, which was now half filled, stood waiting for Rudy's next kick, and some of them looked at each other and then at Rudy, and they were ready to rush him. Bobbie stood up quickly. "Don't, Rudy," she said.

"All right. I learned him. Joe, throw the son of a bitch out," said Rudy. Then suddenly he wheeled and grabbed a man by the belt and lifted him off the floor, holding him tight against his body with one hand and making a hammer of his other hand. "You, you son of a bitch, you was gonna go after me, you was, yeah? Well, go ahead. Let's see you, you son of a bitch. You son of a bitch, I break you in pieces." He let go and the man retreated out of range of Rudy's fist. "Pay your bill and don't come back. Don't ever show your face in my place again. And any other son of a bitch was gonna gang me. You gonna gang Rudy, hey? I kill any two of you." Two of the men picked Hartenstein off the floor before the bartender got to him. "Them two, they paid up, Joe?"

"In the clear, Rudy," said the bartender.

"You two. Don't come back," said Rudy.

"Don't worry. We won't," they said.

Rudy stood at Bobbie's table. "Okay if I sit down with you, Bobbie?"

"Of course," said Bobbie.

"Joe, a beer, please, hey? Bobbie, you ready?"

"Not yet, thanks," she said.

Rudy mopped his forehead with a handkerchief. "You don't have to take it from these bums," said Rudy. "Any time any them get fresh, you tell me. You're what keeps this place decent, Bobbie. I know. As soon as you go home it's a pigpen. I get sick of hearing them, some of the women as bad as the men. Draft-dotchers. Essengial industry! Draft-dotchers. A bunch of 4-F draft-dotchers. I like to hear what your Daddy would say about them."

"Did you know him, my father?"

"Know him? I was in his platoon. Second platoon, C Company. I went over with him and come back with him. Phil Hammersmith."

"I never knew that."

Rudy chuckled. "Sure. Some of these 4-F draft-dotchers from outa town, they think I'm a Nazi because I never learn to speak good English, but my Daddy didn't speak no English at all and he was born out in the Walley. My old woman says put my dischartch papers up over the back-bar. I say what for? So's to make the good impression on a bunch of draft-dotchers? Corporal Rudolph W. Schau. Your Daddy was a good man and a good soldier."

"Why didn't you ever tell me you knew him?"

"Oh, I don't know, Bobbie. I wasn't gonna tell you now, but I did. It don't pay to be a talker in my business. A listener, not a talker."

"You didn't approve of me, did you?"

"I'm a saloonkeeper. A person comes to my—"

"You didn't approve of me. Don't dodge the issue."

"Well, your Daddy wouldn't of liked you coming to a saloon that often. But times change, and you're better off here than the other joints."

"I hope you don't *mind* my coming here."

"Listen, you come here as much as you want."

"Try and stop me," she said, smiling.

Pete joined them. "What happened to Dick Hartenstein?" he said.

"The same as will happen to anybody gets fresh with your wife," said Rudy, and got up and left them.

"There could be a hell of a stink about this. Rudy could lose his license if the Company wanted to press the point."

"Well, you just see that he doesn't," said Bobbie.

"Maybe it isn't such a good idea, your coming here so often."

"Maybe. On the other hand, maybe it's a wonderful idea. I happen to think it's a wonderful idea, so I'm going to keep on coming. If *you* want to go to one of the other places, that's all right. But I like Rudy's. I like it better than ever, now."

No action was taken against Rudy Schau, and Bobbie visited the Tavern as frequently as ever. Hartenstein was an unpopular foreman and the women said he got what had been coming to him for a long time. Bobbie's friends were pleased that their new symbol had such a forthright defender. It was even said that Bobbie had saved Hartenstein from a worse beating, a rumor that added to the respect she was given by the men and the women.

The McCrea children were not being brought up according to Lantenengo Street standards. On the three or four afternoons a week that Bobbie went to the Tavern she would take her son and daughter to a neighbor's yard. On the other afternoons the neighbors' children would play in her yard. During bad weather and the worst of the winter the McCreas' house was in more frequent service as a nursery, since some of the neighbors were living in one- or two-room apartments. But none of the children, the McCreas' or the neighbors', had individual supervision. Children who had learned to walk were separated from those who were still crawling, on the proven theory that the crawling children were still defenseless against the whimsical cruelties of the older ones. Otherwise there was no distinction, and all the children were toughened early in life, as most of their parents had been. "I guess it's all right," Pete once said to Bobbie. "But I hate to think what they'll be like when they get older. Little gangsters."

"Well, that was never your trouble, God knows," said Bobbie. "And I'm no shining example of having a nannie take care of me. Do you remember my nannie?"

"Vaguely."

"'Let's go and see the horsies,' she'd say. And we'd go to Mr. Duncan's stable and I'd come home covered with scratches from the stable cat. And I guess Patrick was covered with scratches from my nannie. Affectionate scratches, of course. Do you remember Mr. Duncan's Patrick?"

"Sure."

"He must have been quite a man. Phyllis used to go there with her nannie, too. But the cat liked Phyllis."

"I'm not suggesting that we have a nannie."

"No. You're suggesting that I stay away from the Tavern."

"In the afternoon."

"The afternoon is the only time the mothers will watch each other's children, except in rare cases. Our kids are all right. I'm with them all day most of the time, and we're home every evening, seven nights a week."

"What else is there to do?"

"Well, for instance once a month we could go to a movie."

"Where? Gibbsville?"

"Yes. Two gallons of gas at the most."

"Are you getting the itch to move back to Gibbsville?"

"Not at all. Are you?"

"Hell, no."

"We could get some high school kid to watch the children. I'd just like to have a change once in a while."

"All right. The next time there's something good at the Globe."

Their first trip to the Globe was their last. They saw no one they knew in the theatre or in the bar of the John Gibb Hotel, and when they came home the high school kid was naked in bed with a man Pete recognized from the plant. "Get out of here," said Pete.

"Is she your kid, McCrea?"

"No, she's not my kid. But did you ever hear of statutory rape?"

"Rape? This kid? I had to wait downstairs, for God's sake. She took on three other guys tonight. Ten bucks a crack."

The girl put on her clothes in sullen silence. She never spoke except to say to the man: "Do you have a room some place?"

"Well," said Pete, when they had gone. "Where did you get her from? The Junior League?"

"If you'd stared at her any more you'd have had to pay ten dollars too."

"For sixteen she had quite a shape."

"She won't have it much longer."

"You got an eyeful, too, don't pretend you didn't."

"Well, at least she won't get pregnant that way. And she *will* get *rich*," said Bobbie.

Pete laughed. "It was really quite funny. Where *did* you get her?"

"If you want her name and telephone number, I have it downstairs. I got her through one of the neighbors. She certainly got the word around quickly enough, where she'd be. There's the doorbell. Another customer?"

Pete went downstairs and informed the stranger at the door that he had the wrong address.

"Another customer, and I think he had two guys with him in the car. Seventy dollars she was going to make tonight. I guess I'm supposed to report this at the plant. We have a sort of a V-D file of known prostitutes. We sic the law on them before they infect the whole outfit, and I'll bet this little character—"

"Good heavens, yes. I must burn everything. Bed linen. Towels. Why that little bitch. Now I'm getting sore." She collected the linen and took it downstairs and to the trash burner in the yard. When she returned Pete was in bed, staring at the ceiling. "I'm going to sleep in the other room," she said.

"What's the matter?"

"I didn't like that tonight. I don't want to sleep with you."

"Oh, all right then, go to hell," said Pete.

She made up one of the beds in the adjoining room. He came and sat on the edge of her bed in the dark. "Go away, Pete," she said.

"Why?"

"Oh, all right, I'll *tell* you why. Tonight made me think of the time you wanted to exchange with Mary and Frank. That's all I've been able to think of."

"That's all passed, Bobbie. I'm not like that any more."

"You would have got in bed with that girl. I saw you."

"Then I'll tell you something. You would have got in bed with that man. I saw you, too. You were excited."

"How could I help being excited, to suddenly come upon something like that. But I was disgusted, too. And still am. Please go away and let me try to get some sleep."

She did not sleep until first light, and when the alarm clock sounded she prepared his and the children's breakfasts. She was tired and nervous throughout the day. She could not go to the Tavern because it was her turn to watch neighbors' children, and Pete telephoned and said bluntly that he would not be home for supper, offering no excuse. He got home after eleven that night, slightly drunk and with lipstick on his neck.

"Who was it? Martie?" said Bobbie.

"What difference does it make who it was? I've been trying to give up other women, but you're no help."

"I have no patience with that kind of an excuse. It's easy enough to blame me. Remember, Pete, I can pick up a man just as easily as you can make a date with Martie."

"I know you can, and you probably will."

It was the last year of the war, and she had remained faithful to Pete throughout the life of their son Angus. A week later she resumed her affair with Bill Charney. "You never forgot me," he said. "I never forgot you, either, Bobbie. I heard about you and Pete living in Fair Grounds. You know a couple times I took my car and dro' past your house to see which one it was. I didn't know, maybe you'd be sitting out on the front porch and if you saw me, you know. Maybe we just say hello and pass the time of day. But I didn't think no such thing, to tell you the God's honest truth. I got nothing against my wife, only she makes me weary. The house and the kids, she got me going to Mass every Sunday, all like that. But I ain't built that way, Bobbie. I'm the next thing to a hood, and you got that side of you, too. I'll make you any price you say, the other jerks you slept with, they never saw that side of you. You know, you hear a lot about love, Bobbie, but I guess I came closer to it with you than any other woman I ever knew. I never forgot you any more than you ever forgot me. It's what they call a mutual attraction. Like you know one person has it for another person."

"I know."

"I don't see how we stood it as long as we did. Be honest, now, didn't you often wish it was me instead of some other guy?"

"Yes."

"All right, I'll be honest with you. Many's the time in bed with my wife I used to say to myself, 'Peggy, you oughta take lessons from Bobbie McCrea.' But who can give lessons, huh? If you don't have the mutual attraction, you're nothin'. How do you think I look?" He slapped his belly. "You know I weigh the same as I used to weigh? You look good. You put on a little. What? Maybe six pounds?"

"Seven or eight."

"But you got it distributed. In another year Peggy's gonna weigh a hundred and fifty pounds, and I told her, I said either she took some of that off or I'd get another girl. Her heighth, you know. She can't get away with that much weight. I eat everything, but I do a lot of walking and standing. I guess I use up a lot of excess energy. Feel them muscles. Punch me in the belly. I got no fat on me anywhere, Bobbie. For my age I'm a perfect physical specimen. I could get any amount of insurance if I got out of The Numbers. But nobody's gonna knock me off so why do I want insurance? I may even give up The Numbers one of these days. I got a couple of things lined up, strictly, strictly legitimate, and when my kids are ready to go away to school, I may just give up The Numbers. For a price, naturally."

"That brings up a point."

"You need money? How much do you want? It's yours. I *mean* like ten, fifteen gees."

"No, no money. But everybody knows you now. Where can we meet?"

"What's the matter with here? I told you, I own this hotel."

"But I can't just come and go. People know me, too. I have an idea, though."

"What?"

"Buy a motel."

"Buy a motel. You know, that thought crossed me a year ago, but you know what I found out? They don't make money. You'd think they would, but those that come out ahead, you be surprised how little they make."

"There's one near Swedish Haven. It's only about a mile from my house."

"We want a big bed, not them twin beds. I tell you what I could do. I could rent one of the units by the month and move my own furniture in. How would that suit you?"

"I'd like it better if you owned the place."

"Blackmail? Is that what you're thinking about? Who'd blackmail me, Bobbie? Or my girl? I'm still a hood in the eyes of some people."

There was no set arrangement for their meetings. Bill Charney postponed the purchase of the motel until she understood he had no intention of buying it or of making any other arrangement that implied permanence. At first she resented his procrastination, but she discovered that she preferred his way; he would telephone her, she would telephone him whenever desire became urgent, and sometimes they would be together within an hour of the telephone call. They spaced out their meetings so that each one produced novelty and excitement, and a year passed and another and Bobbie passed the afternoon of her fortieth birthday with him.

It was characteristic of their relationship that she did not tell him it was her birthday. He always spoke of his wife and children and his business enterprises, but he did not notice that she never spoke of her home life. He was a completely egocentric man, equally admiring of his star sapphire ring on his strong short-fingered hand and of her slender waist, which in his egocentricity became his possession. Inevitably, because of the nature of his businesses, he had a reputation for being close-mouthed, but alone with Bobbie he talked freely. "You know, Bobbie, I laid a friend of yours?"

"Was it fun?"

"Aren't you gonna ask me who?"

"You'll tell me."

"At least I guess she's a friend of yours. Mary Lander."

"She used to be a friend of mine. I haven't seen her in years."

"Yeah. While her husband was in the service. Frank."

"You're so busy, with all your women."

"There's seven days in the week, honey, and it don't take up too much of your time. This didn't last very long, anyway. Five, maybe six times I slept with her. I took her to New York twice, that is I met her there. The other times in her house. You know, she's a neighbor of mine."

"And very neighborly."

"Yeah, that's how it started. She come to my house to collect for something, some war drive, and Peggy said I took care of all them things so when I got home I made out a cheque and took it over to the Landers' and inside of fifteen minutes—less than that—we were necking all over the parlor. Hell, I knew the minute she opened the door—"

"One of those mutual attractions?"

"Yeah, sure. I gave her the cheque and she said, 'I don't know how to thank you,' and I said if she had a couple minutes I'd show her how. 'Oh, Mr. Charney,' but she didn't tell me to get out, so I knew I was in."

"What ever broke up this romance?"

"Her. She had some guy in Washington, D.C., she was thinking of marrying, and when I finally got it out of her who the guy was, I powdered out. Joe Whipple. I gotta do business with Joe. We got a home-loan proposition that we're ready to go with any day, and this was three years ago when Joe and I were just talking about it, what they call the talking stage."

"So you're the one that broke it off, not Mary."

"If a guy's looking at you across a desk and thinking you're laying his girl, you stand to get a screwing from that guy. Not that I don't trust Joe, because I do."

"Do you trust Mary?"

"I wondered about that, if she'd blab to Joe. A dame like Mary Lander, is she gonna tell the guy she's thinking of marrying that she's been laying a hood like me? No. By the way, she's queer. She told me she'd go for a girl."

"I'm surprised she hasn't already."

"Maybe she has. I couldn't find out. I always try to find out."

"You never asked me."

"I knew you wouldn't. But a dame like Mary, as soon as

she opened the door I knew I was in, but then the next thing is you find out what else she'll go for. In her case, the works, as long as it isn't gonna get around. I guess I always figured her right. I have to figure all angles, men *and* women. That's where my brother Ed was stupid. I used to say to him, find out what kind of a broad a guy goes for before you declare him in. Ed used to say all he had to do was play a game of cards with a guy. But according to my theory, everybody goes into a card game prepared. Both eyes open. But not a guy going after a broad. You find out more from broads, like take for instance Mary. Now I know Frank is married to a dame that is screwing his best friend, laid a hood like me, and will go for a girl. You think I'd ever depend on Frank Lander? No. And Joe Whipple. Married to a lush, and sleeping with his best friend's wife, Mary."

"Then you wouldn't depend on Joe, either?"

"Yes, I would. Women don't bother him. He don't care if his wife is a lush, he'll get his nooky from his best friend's wife, he *isn't* going to marry her because that was three-four years ago, and he's tough about everybody. His wife, his dame, his best friend, *and* the United States government. Because I tell you something, if we ever get going on the home-loan proposition, don't think Joe didn't use his job in Washington every chance he got. The partnership is gonna be me and Joe Whipple, because he's just as tough as I am. And one fine day he'll fall over dead from not taking care of himself, and I'll be the main guy. You know the only thing I don't like about you, Bobbie, is the booze. If you'd lay off the sauce for a year I'd get rid of Peggy, and you and I could get married. But booze is women's weakness like women are men's weakness."

"Men are women's weakness."

"No, you're wrong. Men don't make women talk, men don't make women lose their looks, and women can give up men for a hell of a long time, but a female lush is the worst kind of a lush."

"Am I a lush?"

"You have a couple drinks every day, don't you?"

"Yes."

"Then you're on the way. Maybe you only take three-four drinks a day now, but five years from now three or four drinks will get you stewed, so you'll be stewed every day. That's a lush. Peggy eats like a God damn pig, but if she ever started drinking, I'd kick her out. Fortunately her old man died with the D.T.'s, so she's afraid of it."

"Would you mind getting me a nice double Scotch with a little water?"

"Why should I mind?" He grinned from back molar to back molar. "When you got a little load on, you forget home and mother." He got her the drink, she took it in her right hand and slowly poured it down his furry chest. He jumped when the icy drink touched him.

"Thank you so much," she said. "Been a very pleasant afternoon, but the party's over."

"You sore at me?"

"Yes, I am. I don't like being called a lush, and I certainly don't like you to think I'd make a good substitute for Peggy."

"You *are* sore."

"Yes."

The children did not know it was her birthday, but when Pete came home he handed her two parcels. "For me?" she said.

"Not very much imagination, but I didn't have a chance to go to Gibbsville," he said.

One package contained half a dozen nylons, the other a bottle of Chanel Number 5. "Thank you. Just what I wanted. I really did."

He suddenly began to cry, and rushed out of the room.

"Why is Daddy crying?" said their daughter.

"Because it's my birthday and he did a very sweet thing."

"Why should he cry?" said their son. He was nine years old, the daughter eleven.

"Because he's sentimental," said the daughter.

"And it's a very nice thing to be," said Bobbie.

"Aren't you going to go to him?"

"Not quite yet. In a minute. Angus, will you go down to the drug store and get a quart of ice cream? Here's a dollar, and you and your sister may keep the change, divided."

"What flavor?" said the boy.

"Vanilla and strawberry, or whatever else they have."

Pete returned. "Kids gone to bed?"

"I sent them for some ice cream."

"Did they see me bawling?"

"Yes, and I think it did them good. Marjorie understood it. Angus was a little mystified. But it was good for both of them."

"Marjorie understood it? Did you?"

"She said it was because you were sentimental."

He shook his head. "I don't know if you'd call it sentimental. I just couldn't help thinking you were forty years old. Forty. You forty. Bobbie Hammersmith. And all we've been through, and what I've done to you. I know why you married me, Bobbie, but why did you stick it out?"

"Because I married you."

"Yes. Because you married Ichabod. You know, I wasn't in love with you when we were first married. You thought I was, but I wasn't. It was wonderful, being in bed with you and watching you walking around without any clothes on. Taking a bath. But it was too much for me and that's what started me making passes at everybody. And underneath it all I knew damn well why you married me and I hated you. You were making a fool of me and I kept waiting for you to say this farce was over. If you had, I'd have killed you."

"And I guess rightly."

"And all the later stuff. Running a poolroom and living on Mill Street. I blamed all of that on you. But things are better now since we moved here. Aren't they?"

"Yes, much better, as far as the way we live—"

"That's all I meant. If we didn't have Lantenengo Street and Princeton and those things to look back on, this wouldn't be a bad life for two ordinary people."

"It's not bad," she said.

"It's still pretty bad, but that's because we once had it better. Here's what I want to say. Any time you want to walk out on me, I won't make any fuss. You can have the children, and I won't fight about it. That's my birthday present to you, before it's too late. And I have no plans for myself. I'm not trying to get out of this marriage, but you're forty now and you're entitled to whatever is left."

"Thank you, Pete. I have nobody that wants to marry me."

"Well, maybe not. But you may have, sometime. I love

you now, Bobbie, and I never used to. I guess you can't love anybody else while you have no self-respect. When the war was over I was sure I'd get the bounce at the plant, but they like me there, they've kept me on, and that one promotion. We'll never be back on Lantenengo Street, but I think I can count on a job here maybe the rest of my life. In a couple of years we can move to a nicer house."

"I'd rather buy this and fix it up a little. It's a better-built house than the ones they're putting up over on Fair Grounds Heights."

"Well, I'm glad you like it too," he said. "The other thing, that we hardly ever talk about. In fact never talk about. Only fight about sometimes. I'll try, Bobbie. I've been trying."

"I know you have."

"Well—how about you trying, too?"

"I did."

"But not lately. I'm not going to ask you who or when or any of that, but why is it you're faithful to me while I'm chasing after other women, and then when I'm faithful to you, you have somebody else? You're forty now and I'm forty-four. Let's see how long we can go without cheating?"

"You don't mean put a time limit on it, or put up a trophy, like an endurance contest? That's the way it sounds. We both have bad habits, Pete."

"Yes, and I'm the worst. But break it off, Bobbie, whoever it is. Will you please? If it's somebody you're not going to marry, and that's what you said, I've—well, it's a long time since I've cheated, and I like it much better this way. Will you stop seeing this other guy?"

"All right. As a matter of fact I *have* stopped, but don't ask me how long ago."

"I won't ask you anything. And if you fall in love with some-body and want to marry him—"

"And he wants to marry me."

"And he wants to marry you, I'll bow out." He leaned down and kissed her cheek. "I know you better than you think I do, Bobbie."

"That's an irritating statement to make to any woman."

"I guess it is, but not the way I meant it."

Now that is as far as I need go in the story of Pete and Bob-bie McCrea. I promised a happy ending, which I shall come to in a moment. We have left Pete and Bobbie in 1947, on Bobbie's fortieth birthday. During the next thirteen years I saw them twice. On one occasion my wife and I spent the night with them in their house in Fair Grounds, which was painted, scrubbed and dusted like the Fair Grounds houses of old. My wife went to bed early, and Pete and Bobbie and I talked until past midnight, and then Pete retired and Bobbie and I continued our conversation until three in the morning. Twice she emptied our ash trays of cigarette butts, and we drank a drip-flask of coffee. It seemed to me that she was so thorough in her description of their life because she felt that the dinginess would vanish if she once succeeded in exposing it. But as we were leaving in the morning I was not so sure that it had vanished. My wife said to me: "Did she get it all out of her system?"

"Get what out of her system?"

"I don't know, but I don't think she did, entirely."

"That would be asking too much," I said. "But I guess she's happy."

"Content, but not happy," said my wife. "But the children are what interested me. The girl is going to be attractive in a few more years, but that boy! You didn't talk to him, but do you know about him? He's fourteen, and he's already passed his senior mathematics. He's *finished* the work that the high school seniors are supposed to be taking. The principal is trying to arrange correspondence courses for him. He's the brightest student they ever had in Fair Grounds High School, ever, and all the scientific men at the aluminum plant know about him. And he's a good-looking boy, too."

"Bobbie didn't tell me any of this."

"And I'll bet I know why. He's their future. With you she wanted to get rid of the past. She adores this boy, adores him. That part's almost terrifying."

"Not to me," I said. "It's the best thing that could have happened to her, and to Pete. The only thing that's terrifying is that they could have ruined it. And believe me, they could have."

In 1960, then, I saw Pete and Bobbie again. They invited

me, of all their old friends, to go with them to the Princeton commencement. Angus McCrea, Junior, led his class, was awarded the mathematics prize, the physics prize, the Eubank Prize for scholarship, and some other honors that I am sure are listed in the program. I could not read the program because I was crying most of the time. Pete would lean forward in his chair, listening to the things that were being said about his son, but in an attitude that would have been more suitable to a man who was listening to a pronouncement of sentence. Bobbie sat erect and smiling, but every once in a while I could hear her whisper, "Oh, God. Oh, God."

There, I guess, is our happy ending.

Call Me, Call Me

H<small>ER SHORT</small> steps, that had always called attention to her small stature, now served to conceal the fact that her walk was slower. Now, finally, there was nothing left of the youth that had lasted so long, so well into her middle age. Her hat was small and black, a cut-down modified turban that made only the difference between being hatted and hatless but called no attention to the wearer, did not with spirit of defiance or gaiety proclaim the wearer to be Joan Hamford. Her Persian lamb, a good one bought in prosperous days, was now a serviceable, sensible garment that kept her warm and nothing more. She wore shoes that she called—echoing her mother's designation—"ties." They were very comfortable and they gave her good support.

The greeting by the doorman was precisely accorded. No "good morning," but "You'll have a taxi, Miss Hamford?" If she wanted a taxi, he was there to get her a taxi; that was one of the things he was paid for; but he could expect no tip now and she gave him little enough at Christmas. She was one of the permanent guests of the hotel, those whom he classified as salary people because he was paid a salary for providing certain services. Salary people. Bread-and-butter people. Not tip people, not big-gravy, expense-account people. Salary people. Budget people. Instant-coffee-and-half-a-pint-of-cream-from-the-delicatessen people. Five-dollars-in-an-envelope-with-his-name-on-it-at-Christmas people. The hotel was coming down in another year, and the hotel that was going up in its place would have no room for salary people. Only expense-account people.

"Taxi? Yes, please, Roy. Or I'd make just as good time walking, wouldn't I?"

"I don't know, Miss Hamford. I don't know where you're going."

"It is a little far," said Joan Hamford. "Yes, a taxi. *There's one!*"

She always did that. She always spotted a taxi, so that it would seem that she had really found it herself, unaided, and really owed him nothing. He was wise to that one. He was wise to all her little tricks and dodges, her ways of saving quarters, her half pints of cream from the delicatessen. She must be on her way to a manager's office today. Most days she would not take a taxi. "Such a nice day, I think a stroll," she would say, and then stroll exactly one block to the bus stop. But today it was a taxi, because she didn't want to be worn out when she applied for a job. Yes, today was a job day; she was wearing her diamond earrings and her pearls, which were usually kept in the hotel safe.

"Six-thirty Fifth Avenue, will you tell him, please, Roy?"

"Six-thirty Fifth," he said to the taxi driver. She could have given the address herself, but this was a cheap way of queening it. He closed the door behind her and stepped back to the curb.

"Number Six Hundred and Thirty, Avenue Five," said the driver, starting the meter. "Well, you got anything to read, lady, because the traffic on Madison and Fifth, I can't promise you nothing speed-wise. You wanta try Park, we'll make better time going down Park, but I won't guarantee you going west."

"How long will it take us if we go down Fifth?"

"Fifth? You wanta go down Fifth? I give you an honest estimate of between twenty and twenty-five minutes. Them buses, you know. You ever go to the circus and take notice to the elephants, the one holds on to the-one-in-front-of-him's tail with his trunk. That's the way the buses operate. Never no less than four together at the one time, and what they do to congest up the traffic! You see they could straighten that out in two hours if they just handed out a bunch of summonses, but then the union would pull the men off the buses and the merchants would holler to the powers-that-be, City Hall. I'm getting out of this city . . . We'll try Fifth . . . It's Miss Joan Hamford, isn't it?"

"Why, yes. How nice of you."

"Oh, I rode you before. You remember when you used to live over near the River? Four-what-is-it? Four-fifty East Fifty-second?"

"Oh, heavens, that long ago?"

"Yeah, I had one of them big Paramounts, twice the size of this little crate. You don't remember Louis?"

"Louis?"

"Me. Louis Jaffee. I used to ride you four-five times a week regular, your apartment to the Henry Miller on Forty-third, east of Broadway. Fifteen-and-five in those days, but you were good for a buck every night. Well, I'm still hacking, but you been in movies and TV and now I guess you're on your way to make another big deal for TV."

"No, as a matter of fact, a play. On Broadway. I'm afraid I can't tell you just what play, but it isn't television. Still a secret, you know."

"Oh, sure. Then you was out in Hollywood all that time I remember."

"Yes, and I did a few plays in London."

"That I didn't know about. I just remember you rode out the bonnom of the depression in Hollywood. The bonnom of the depression for me, but not for you. You must of made a killing out there. What does it feel like to see some of them pictures now, on TV? You don't get any royalties on them pictures, do you?"

"No."

"Now they all go in for percentages I understand. Be nice to have a percentage of some of them oldies. Is Charles J. Hall still alive?"

"No, poor Charles passed on several years ago."

"You always heard how he was suppose to be a terrific boozer, but I seen him the other night on TV. You were his wife, where you were trying to urge him to give up the Navy and head up this big shipbuilding company."

"*Glory in Blue*."

"*Glory in Blue*, that's the one. How old was Charles J. Hall when you made that picture, do you remember?"

"How old? I should think Charles was in his early forties then."

"Christ! He'd be in his seventies."

"Yes, he would."

"I'm over the sixty mark myself, but I can't picture Charles J. Hall in his seventies."

"Well, he never quite reached them, poor dear."

"Booze, was it?"

"Oh, I don't like to say that."

"There's a lot worse you could say about some of those jerks they got out there now. Male *and* female. What they need out there is another Fatty Arbuckle case, only the trouble is the public is got so used to scandal."

"Yes, I suppose so."

"You know I was just thinking, I wonder how I missed it when Charles J. Hall passed away. Was it during the summer? I go away in the summer and I don't see a paper for two weeks."

"Yes, I think it was."

"They would have had something in."

"They didn't have very much, not as much as he deserved, considering what a really big star he was."

"But there was a long time when he wasn't in anything. That's when I understood he was hitting the booze so bad. Where was he living during that time?"

"In Hollywood. He stayed right there."

"Wouldn't take anything but big parts, I guess. That's where you were smart, Miss Hamford."

"How do you mean?"

"Well, they forgot all about Charles J. Hall. Like my daughter didn't know who the hell he was last week. But she'd know you. She'd know you right away, because from TV, when you were that lady doctor two years ago, that serial."

"Unfortunately only lasted twenty-six weeks."

"I don't care. Your face is still familiar to the new generation. I don't know what any actress fools around with Broadway for."

"Some of us love the theater."

"Sure, there's that, but I'm speaking as a member of the public. You could be in *My Fair Lady* and there wouldn't be as many people see you as if you went in one big spectacular. When I see my daughter tomorrow night, when she comes for supper, I'm gunna tell her I rode Joan Hamford. And right away she's gunna say 'Doctor McAllister? Doctor Virginia McAllister?' So they took it off after twenty-six weeks, but just think of how many million people saw you *before* they took it off. Up there in the millions. The so-called Broadway theater, that's gettin' to be for amateurs and those that, let's face it, can't get a job in TV."

"Oh, you mustn't say that."

"Well, I'm only telling you what the public thinks, basing it on my own conclusions. Here you are, Six-three-oh. Eighty-five on the clock."

"Here, Louis. I want you to have this."

"The five?"

"For old times' sake."

"Well, thanks. Thanks a lot, Miss Hamford. The best to you, but TV is where you ought to be."

She hoarded her strength during the walk to the elevator, and she smiled brightly at the receptionist in the office of Ralph Sanderson–Otto B. Kolber. "Mr. Sanderson is expecting you, Miss Hamford. Go right in."

"Good morning, Ralph," said Joan Hamford.

Sanderson rose. "Good morning, Joan. Nice of you to come down at this hour, but unfortunately it was the only absolutely only time I had. You know anything about this play?"

"Only what I've read about it."

"Well, then you probably don't know anything about the part."

"No, not really. I read the book, the novel, but I understand that's been changed."

"Oh, hell, the novel. We only kept the boy and his uncle, from the novel."

"The boy's aunt? She's not in the play? Then what is there for me, Ralph? Or would you rather have me read the play instead of you telling me?"

"No, I'd just as soon tell you. Do you remember the schoolteacher?"

"The schoolteacher? Let me think. There *was* a schoolteacher in one of the early chapters, but I don't think she had a name."

"In the novel she didn't. But she has in the play."

"You really must have changed the novel. How does the part develop?"

"Well, frankly it doesn't. We only keep the teacher for one scene in the first act."

"Oh, well, Ralph, you didn't bring me down here for that. That isn't like you. Good heavens, even if I'd never done anything else, I was Dr. Virginia McAllister to God knows how many million people, and I got twenty-two-fifty for that."

"Three years ago, Joan, and you haven't had much to do

since. That's why I thought of you for the teacher. I'd rather give it to you than someone I don't know. I'll pay three-fifty."

"What for? You can't bill me over the others, the part isn't big enough to do that."

"I couldn't anyway. The boy gets top billing, and Michael Ware is co-star. Tom Ruffo in *Illinois Sonata with* Michael Ware. But I admit you'd lead the list of featured players."

"You know how these things are, Ralph. Not a manager in town but will know I'm working for three-fifty."

"But working, and I'll take care of you publicity-wise. The theater doesn't pay movie or TV salaries; you know that."

"I understand Jackie Gleason got six thousand."

"He may have got more, but Virginia McAllister wasn't Ralph Kramden. I wish you'd think about this, Joan. It's not physically very demanding. You don't have to stand around or do any acrobatics."

"Or act, either, I suppose. No, I'm afraid not, Ralph, and I really think you were rather naughty to bring me down here."

"Joan, this is a fine play and with this boy Ruffo we're going to run ten months, and maybe a lot longer. For you it would be like a vacation with pay, and you'd be back in the theater. Stop being a stubborn bitch, and think back to times when I paid you sixty dollars a week for more work."

"In that respect you haven't changed, Ralph."

"Four hundred."

"Take-home that's still only a little over three hundred. No, I'm going right on being a stubborn bitch."

"I'll give you four hundred, and I'll release you any time after the first six months that you find a better part."

"Can you write me into the second and third acts?"

"Impossible. The locale changes, and anyway, I know the author wouldn't do it. And frankly I wouldn't ask him to. No more tinkering with this play till we open in Boston."

"Well—still friends, Ralph. You tried."

"Yes, I certainly tried."

She reached out her hand. "Give me five dollars for the taxi."

"Joan, are you that broke?"

"No, I'm not broke, but that's what it cost me to come here."

Sanderson pulled a bill from a money-clip. "If it cost you

five to get here it'll cost you another five to get home. Here's a sawbuck."

"I only wanted five, but of course I'll take the ten. In the old days you would have spent more than that on taking me to lunch."

"Considering where we usually ended up after lunch, the price wasn't high."

"I guess that's a compliment."

"You know, you have delusions of Laurette Taylor in *Menagerie*. All you senior girls have that."

"Senior girls. That sounds so Camp Fire-y."

"You're going to be sore as hell when you see who gets this part. I don't know who it'll be, but I'm going to pick somebody you hate."

"Good. Don't pick anybody I like, because I'll hate her if the play runs."

"And yourself."

"Oh—well, I hate myself already. Do you think I like going back to that hotel, feeling sure you have a hit, *hoping* you have a hit, and stuck with my own stubborn pride? But you know I can't take this job, Ralph."

"Yes, I guess I do."

"You wouldn't stretch a point and take me to lunch, would you?"

"No, I can't, Joan."

"Then—will you give me a kiss?"

"Any time." He came around from behind his desk and put his arms around her.

"On the lips," she said.

He bent down, she stood on tiptoe, and his mouth pressed on hers. "Thank you, dear," she said. "Call me, call me."

"I hope so," he said, as she went out.

Mrs. Stratton of Oak Knoll

A s WAS their nightly custom, Evan Reese and his wife Georgia finished their small chores and took their seats to watch the eleven o'clock news program on the television. Evan Reese's chore was to put the backgammon men in place for the next night's game; Georgia's was to remove the coffee tray to the kitchen. Evan Reese now lit his pipe, Georgia lit a cigarette, and they sat patiently through the preliminary commercial announcements. "And now the news," said the announcer.

"Do tell," said Georgia, stroking the head of their Airedale.

Evan Reese smiled. His wife had given up her letters of protest to the newspaper editorial pages against the length and number of commercials, but she always made some small audible comment when the man said, "And now the news."

"Quiet, please," said Evan Reese.

"A four-engine bomber on a routine training flight over the Rocky—" the announcer began. At that moment the dog growled and the Reeses' doorbell rang.

Evan Reese frowned and looked at his wife, and they said, together: "Who could that be?" and Georgia Reese added, "At this hour?"

"You pay attention to the news, I'll see who it is," said Evan Reese. He switched on the carriage lamps at the front door and the floodlight that illuminated the driveway. He peeked through the draperies and saw, in the driveway, a large black limousine. He held the dog by the collar and opened the door.

A middle-aged man in chauffeur's livery raised his hand in a semi-military salute. "Stratton residence?" he said.

"No, this isn't the Stratton residence. You have the wrong house."

"This is Ridge Road and West Branch Lane, isn't it?" said the chauffeur.

"Yes it is, but if you'll notice there's a driveway across the road, with a sign that says Oak Knoll. That's the entrance to Mrs. Stratton's place."

"Sorry, I didn't see no sign."

"It's there in plain sight," said Evan Reese.

"What the hell's the delay?" The voice came from inside the limousine, and Evan Reese could make out a man's hatless head but little more. The Airedale barked once.

"I'll leave the floodlight on and you can turn around—and you can tell your employer to mind his manners."

"I'll tell him a lot more when I get my tip," said the chauffeur. "I don't work for him, I work for the rental company. He only hired this car, and believe me, I'll never drive him again."

"Is he drunk? He sounds it."

"Drunk? He was drunk when I called for him. The Racquet Club."

"New York, or Philadelphia?"

"New York. Well, sorry to trouble you, Mister."

"That's all right. Hope you get a big tip. Goodnight."

"Goodnight, sir, and thanks again." The chauffeur saluted, and Evan Reese closed the door, watching through the draperies until the limousine was out of his driveway.

"A drunken man calling on Mrs. Stratton. Obviously with the intention of spending the night, since it's a hired car. Now we have something on her."

"I guess it must be that son."

"No, I'd rather think it was some gigolo she sent for."

"She's a little old for that. Did you get a look at him?"

"I can give you a perfect description. Black patent leather hair, waxed moustache, and a gold bracelet . . . No, I didn't really see him. Would her son belong to the Racquet Club?"

"Oh, at least. You can look him up in the Social Register."

"Where is it?"

"It's in my sewing-room, by the telephone."

"Too much trouble," said Evan Reese. "Anything in the news?"

"I wasn't listening very carefully, I was overcome with curiosity about who'd call on us at eleven o'clock at night."

"Mrs. Stratton's drunken son, I guess. Now the next time she writes us one of her neighborly notes about our dog, we can come back at her."

"Oh, Ev, that was ten years ago."

"Well, it's still the only time we ever heard from her. Ten

years and she never came to call on you. I think I *will* look up the son. By the telephone?"

"On the lower shelf of the little table."

Evan Reese obtained the book and returned to the library. "Now then," he said. "Stratton, there *she* is. Mrs. Francis, Oak Knoll, High Ridge, New Jersey. Phone number 7-1415. Ah, yes, here he is. Francis A., Junior, 640 East Eighty-third. R for Racquet, B for Brook, K for Knickerbocker, H-37. Harvard, '37. That would make him about forty-five years old. Oh, and here's one. Stratton, Mrs. Virginia C., Virginia Daniels, and under her name another Virginia, at Foxcroft, and another Francis, at St. Mark's. There we have the whole story, the whole tragic story of the drunken mama's-boy, coming home to see mama because the boys at the club were mean to him."

"It may not be that at all."

"I'll bet it's close to it. Now let's see if he's in *Who's Who*?" said Evan Reese. He took down a volume and opened it. "Nope. I didn't think he would be. I formed my impression of him when he barked at the driver of that car. Driver was a polite, decent-looking fellow. Probably very efficient, too, except for not seeing the Oak Knoll sign. *Say*, that's interesting."

"Why?"

"Wouldn't you think that Stratton would know where his mother lived? Maybe he was asleep, or so drunk—no, he wasn't that drunk. And he wasn't asleep. Maybe it isn't her son after all. But I think it is. Do you know what I think, Georgia?"

"What?"

"I think we have a mystery on our hands."

"Well, you puzzle it out, I'm retiring. I have all sorts of things to do tomorrow, and don't forget. We have Bob and Jennie for dinner tomorrow night."

"God, is tomorrow Wednesday? Well, at least they're coming here. We don't have to go out."

"If you stay up reading, don't fall asleep in your chair or your arm'll get stiff again and you won't be able to work."

This was a bit of caution she gave him about once a week. He was miserable when his arm hurt and he could not paint, especially when he was painting well, and more especially when he was finishing the last of his pictures for a one-man show in the spring. It was not only his habit of falling asleep in his chair that made his arm sore, nor was he telling the truth when he blamed the weather. He had bursitis, he knew it and she knew it, but they pretended he was in perfect health. He—they—would not admit that he was sixty years old and already a victim of the painter's occupational disease. He refused to see a doctor, to confirm what he had long suspected, to submit to treatment that was never wholly successful. "The minute I hear myself snoring, I'll come to bed," he said.

"Goodnight, dear," she said.

"Goodnight, Pussycat," he said. He put her hand to his cheek and kissed it, and she left him. The dog stretched out on the rug and dozed.

Evan Reese turned the television to a different channel and for an hour or so watched a lovely British movie that he knew by heart, having seen it at least ten times. He did not have to follow the plot, which was nothing much to begin with and concerned the refusal of some Scotsmen in a remote village to pay their taxes until the government promised them a new road. Evan Reese could share the Scotsmen's feelings toward London; he could sing "Men of Harlech" in the Welsh, although he had never been to the land of his fathers; but he knew the movie so well that he could pick up the story anywhere along the way, and there was no suspense in it for him. The charm of it was in the characters and the acting and in the verisimilitude of the exteriors and interiors—the laird had a forty-year-old Rolls-Royce station wagon instead of the 1960 Cadillac that Hollywood would have considered suitable for a laird. The house in which the laird lived was not too unlike Evan Reese's; built to last, furnished for comfort, a warm shelter whether the winds came down from Canada or from the North Sea.

The movie came to its happy ending and Evan Reese turned off the television. At the cessation of the sound, Mike, the Airedale, raised his head, expecting to be let out. "Just you hold it now till I finish my pipe," said Evan Reese. The dog wagged his tail to indicate that he knew he was being addressed, and Evan Reese reached down and scratched the animal's head. "I think you must be getting old, too," said Evan Reese. "You're not the watchdog you used to be. You never heard Mr. Stratton's car."

The dog again wagged his tail.

"Well, you're twelve years old," said Evan Reese. "And that's supposed to be the equivalent of eighty-four human years. You're a good boy."

At the words "good boy" the dog got to his feet and began to back out of the room, keeping his eyes on the master.

"All right," said Evan Reese, and opened the front door and let the dog run into the darkness. It was not his custom to turn on the floodlights for Mike, and in the moonless, starless night he noticed that Mrs. Stratton's house was lit up on two stories. The shades were drawn, but there was light behind them, and he could not recall ever having seen light in the house at such a late hour. It was past midnight. As his eyes became accustomed to the darkness he began to see smoke issuing forth from one of the chimneys on the Stratton roof, and he wondered what could be going on, what scene was taking place between the widow and her son. A happy reunion? He thought not.

Evan Reese whistled softly for his dog, which responded to the signal, and man and dog returned to the warm house. "Snow tomorrow, for sure," said Evan Reese. "I can feel it in my bones." He saw that the dog was curling up on his piece of carpet in the library, and he now retired for his own rest.

Bob and Jennie Hewitt were fourth-generation residents of High Ridge. She as an amateur painter and he as president of the local bank had been the Reeses' first acquaintances in the town and the friendship between the two couples had become a pleasant one. The men were the same age, the women were only two years apart, and when Bob Hewitt got over the first shock of discovering that he was somewhat less conservative than a man who earned a good living as a painter, the weekly dinner-and-bridge was instituted and had continued. A running score was kept, and at the end of their October-through-May season never more than $50 changed hands.

"Bob, get Evan to tell you about the visitor he had last night," said Jennie Hewitt. "Go on, Evan. He'd be interested. I think it's fascinating."

"Well, with that build-up, who was it, Ev? Brigitte Bardot?" said Bob Hewitt.

"Not quite," said Evan Reese, and related the events of the previous night.

Bob Hewitt was a good listener, and at the end of Evan's report he said: "Well, you have him pegged about right. Frank Stratton is a mama's-boy and a heavy drinker. Did you see him around today?"

"No. I looked for him, but there was no sign of him."

"The last time he did this, came home to mama, was before you moved to High Ridge. It was when his wife left him. He came home then, under almost the same circumstances. Drunk, and in a hired car. But the next day the old lady sent him packing. Banished him. She didn't want him around, or that was the story. Jennie, you tell that part."

"I'm dying to," said Jennie Hewitt. "And I'm dying to know if she lets him stay this time. What happened before was that Mrs. Stratton was furious because Frank did what everybody always said he'd do. Come home to mother at the first sign of trouble. And there *was* trouble. It even got in the papers, a little bit. You see, Frank is—well it was *in* the *papers*, so I might as well say it. Frank is a fairy."

"Well, don't say it that positively, Jennie. After all, he did marry and he had two children." Bob Hewitt spoke sardonically.

"But what was he arrested for?"

"*He* wasn't arrested. The other fellow was arrested for beating him up and stealing money and stuff. You've got it all mixed up."

"Well then you tell it," said Jennie Hewitt.

"There isn't much else to tell. He was beaten up by a young serviceman that he met in a bar, and the police found Frank's wallet and cigarette case on him. Stupid. You'd think he'd have got rid of such incriminating evidence, but as I recall it the soldier tried to sell the cigarette case in some bar on Eighth Avenue and the bartender tipped off the military police. Then the New York cops went to Frank's apartment and found him lying in a pool of blood, and that was how the story got out. You had to read between the lines—"

"Oh, Bob. Between the lines. They couldn't have been more explicit."

"No, maybe not, but there was no charge preferred against Frank. That's where you're giving the Reeses the wrong impression."

"I was trying to give them the right impression. Ev, Georgia, what would you think if you read that story in the newspapers?"

"I'd be inclined to think that Mr. Stratton was very indiscreet, not to say impulsive," said Evan Reese.

"I'd say he got what was coming to him," said Georgia Reese. "Picking up soldiers in a bar."

"And you'd be right, and his mother was furious," said Jennie Hewitt. "She told him to go right back to New York and face it out. Brazen it out, I'd call it. But she was right, as it turned out. He did go back to New York, and went right on seeing people and of course nobody could come up and say to him, point-blank, 'Were you a fairy with that soldier?' And after while people began to say well maybe the soldier *did* follow him to his apartment and try to rob him. In other words, people sort of gave him the benefit of the doubt. That was his version to the police."

"Maybe it was true," said Evan Reese. "When I was a young man living in Greenwich Village there were certain reprehensible characters who made a living by blackmailing older men. They'd see a man getting drunk in a speakeasy and they'd get in a taxi with him or follow him home, and then threaten to expose him if he didn't shell out. Some of those men were certainly guilty, or at least vulnerable, but I wonder how many were innocent. I knew a sculptor who paid blackmail for years because he got drunk with a male model and he could never actually remember whether he'd made passes at him or not. My friend, the sculptor, was of course vulnerable. He was bisexual. He said to me more than once, 'Reese, I honestly don't know. Maybe I did.'"

"What ever happened to him?" said Jennie Hewitt.

"My friend? He gave up. He became very successful, made a lot of money, and one day when the young bum came around for his cheque, my friend told him to go to hell. 'You can't blackmail me any more,' he said. 'I've stopped denying it or pretending I'm anything else, so get out.'"

"How delightful," said Jennie Hewitt.

"Not really," said Georgia Reese. "He later hanged himself.

He was genuinely in love with a girl, and she wouldn't have him."

"I guess the old Greenwich Village must have been quite a place, Ev?" said Bob Hewitt.

"It doesn't sound much different today, only worse," said Georgia.

"We had some gifted people," said Evan Reese. "Real talent. Once in a while a genius, or very close to it. Anyway, real artists. First-rate writers, some of the best. But now all I ever hear about is an occasional saxophone player. You see, we worked. We did a lot of talking, and a great deal of drinking and sleeping around, but we also worked. Now we don't hear much about work down there. Talk, yes. Drinking and sleeping around, and dope. But they don't seem to know how to paint or write."

"I never liked the Village," said Georgia. "You never did anything really good till you got out of it."

"Oh, yes, I did some good things, but I never did anything first-rate till I was past forty anyhow, so the Village did me no harm. And I did work."

"Well, this isn't very interesting to the Hewitts. We were talking about this Stratton man."

"And I wouldn't waste any pity on him," said Jennie. "Unfortunately, Bob and I weren't surprised when that happened, the beating and so on."

"No, it's one of those small-town secrets that only a few people think they're in on, but it was pretty generally known, I guess," said Bob Hewitt. "When did we first hear about it?"

"When did we first hear about it? Why, that time—"

"That time he had that friend home from college. You're right. The maid quit because Frank brought a friend home from college and—"

"Lorna. Lorna Parton."

"Lorna walked in to clean the drawing-room and there was the friend sitting at the piano, stark naked at nine o'clock in the morning. Went right on playing, too."

"Where was Stratton?" said Evan Reese.

"Oh, I don't know where he was, probably upstairs sleeping off a hangover," said Bob Hewitt. "But the friend went right on playing, even when Mrs. Stratton came in to remonstrate with him. What was it he said to her?"

"He was the boldest thing I ever heard of. He finished playing whatever it was, regardless of her saying *Mister* Jones, or whatever his name was. He came to the end of the piece and then he turned to her and said: 'Do you play?' You know, as though he expected her to join him in a duet."

"No more friends home from Harvard," said Bob Hewitt.

"What do you *mean*? No more *Frank*. She told him she didn't want him to come home at all," said Jennie Hewitt.

"That's right," said her husband. "She wouldn't have him in the house, not even at Christmas."

"Till he announced his engagement. And even then she wouldn't go to the wedding. She stayed home on some pretext or other. She never actually met Frank's wife till the first grandchild was born, and then she couldn't do enough for them. She adored the grandchildren, and they used to all four of them come visit her."

"The money," said Bob Hewitt.

"Oh, yes. She gave Frank's wife a hundred thousand dollars when each grandchild was born, *and* a trust fund for the children."

"And changed her will."

"And changed her will so that Frank gets nothing, not a penny. He gets what is it?"

"A thousand a month while she's alive. Twelve thousand a year. Then when she dies, nothing. It all goes into a trust fund for the grandchildren."

"And the ex-wife gets the income as long as she doesn't remarry. If she remarries, it all goes into the children's trusts."

"And that's our neighbor?" said Evan Reese. "I had no idea she was so rich."

"*Rich?* At one time she owned this whole mountain, or her husband did. You've never been in that house, have you?" said Bob Hewitt.

"I've never even had a good look at it from the outside. The trees and the hedges," said Evan Reese.

"Tell them about the downstairs," said Bob Hewitt.

"Tell us about the whole house," said Georgia Reese.

"Well, you knew that Frank had an older sister," said Jennie. "Bernice. She was my age."

"No, we never heard about a sister," said Georgia Reese.

"Oh, yes. Bernice, about twelve years older than Frank. I went there a lot when we were children and until Bernice eloped, at seventeen. Mrs. Stratton would send the car to my house—"

"A Rolls, needless to say," said Bob Hewitt. "Limousine when the weather was bad, and a touring car when it was good."

"I was one of the girls that Bernice was allowed to play with, but she never came to my house except to things like birthday parties. I always had to go to her house, but of course I didn't mind."

"The house, the house," said Bob Hewitt.

"But later I want to know about the daughter," said Georgia Reese.

"So do I," said her husband.

"First let her describe the house," said Bob Hewitt.

"Well, it's so long since I've been inside it that now it's almost unbelievable, although I'm told it hasn't been changed much. The main hall was two stories high, with at one end stained glass windows, imported from Italy, and they went all the way up to the second floor. On the right as you went in, a small reception room, then next to that, the drawing-room, where Frank's friend played the piano, and off that the music-room, as it was called. That was all done in white and gold and those two rooms were where we danced when they had their big parties. On the other side of the hall, the big dining room, easily room enough for, oh, sixty people. The library, lined with books all the way up to the ceiling with one of those ladders on a track like the old-time shoe stores. Two huge fireplaces. When I was little I could stand erect in the fireplaces. And a smaller room that had been Mr. Stratton's office, although they called it a study. I remember he had a stock ticker in that room, although I didn't know what it was then. They changed it after he died. On that side of the house was an enclosed porch, and on the other side, opening off the drawing-room, the conservatory. And I wouldn't attempt to describe the furniture. The dining-room chairs, high-back armchairs, brocaded, of course, and I'll bet the table weighed a ton. The paintings, you *must* have a look at them somehow, Ev. There's a Gainsborough in the main hall. A Van Dyke, a Rubens—"

"Yes, yes," said Bob Hewitt. "But don't start telling all about the paintings. Just give them the general idea. For instance, the pipe organ."

"They had a pipe organ, that was in the main hall, with the console on the first landing. They used to have an organist from Philadelphia with the wonderful name of Thunder, he'd come and give recitals once a year. Henry Thunder, a famous organist he was. And on Easter they always had a big crowd for lunch and then they'd have one of the local organists play."

"The only house in this part of the State with a pipe organ. And I'll bet no other house had something else they had. A barber chair. A real barber chair in Mr. Stratton's dressing-room."

"Sunken bathtubs?" said Georgia Reese.

"No, I guess the house was built too early for that. The tubs were iron, but had wood all around them. Encased in wood with mother-of-pearl inlaid. I remember when they added an elevator. We were absolutely forbidden to ride in it, probably because of several experiences when we got stuck in the dumbwaiter."

"Ev, this will impress you," said Bob Hewitt. "They had their own road-roller. A steam road-roller, with a little whistle. They used to lend it to the township, but it belonged to them. I suppose at one time they had around eight hundred acres. Now it's dwindled down to, oh, I think she has no more than twenty acres now, but I think I remember the figure eight hundred. This house that you're in, this used to be occupied by a cousin of Old Man Stratton's."

"Yes, I heard that when I bought it," said Evan Reese.

"They owned all these houses on Ridge Road and rented them out to relatives and retired couples for practically nothing. I don't think there was a house within a mile of the Strattons' that they didn't own. Not that there were so many houses in those days. This section wasn't started to be built up till the Thirties," said Bob Hewitt.

"Where did Stratton's money come from?" said Evan Reese.

"In two words, Wall Street. Railroad stocks, land out west, coal mines in Pennsylvania and West Virginia. He didn't make it all himself, by any means. His father was in with Jim Fisk and Dan Drew and Gould, that crowd, but not as a very big operator. Enough to leave old Frank Senior a nice fortune, and Frank had brains. He may not have been the most honest man in the world, by present-day standards, but he stayed out of trouble. He married late in life. The present Mrs. Stratton, the old lady, was about nineteen or twenty and he was in his forties when they got married. He was well in his fifties when the present Frank was born."

"Who was she?" said Georgia Reese.

"She was a High Ridge girl, born here. She was a Crowder. The Crowders weren't immensely wealthy, but they were well fixed and got around in New York society. Oh, she had plenty to offer. She was a good-looking girl."

"She was a handsome young woman," said Jennie Hewitt. "I can remember her very well. Beautiful bone structure and quite sexy-looking."

"When did he die?" said Evan Reese.

"Let me see now, in the late Twenties. He was eighty or close to it when he died," said Bob Hewitt.

"And that was when she became a recluse?" said Georgia Reese.

"Before that. Mr. Stratton was paralyzed and they practically never left Oak Knoll after that."

"Just lived there in solitary splendor?" said Evan Reese.

"Solitary splendor!" said Jennie Hewitt. "Splendor, but not solitary. They had Phillips, the majordomo. Pierre, the chauffeur. Tripp, the coachman, and a colored groom. A head gardener whose name I forget, and as many as five or six other gardeners. Mrs. Phillips, the cook. A full-time waitress. Three or four chambermaids. Mrs. Stratton's personal maid, Alice. A tweeny."

"What's a tweeny?" said Georgia Reese.

"A tweeny is a sort of a cook's helper and not quite a regular maid. In-between."

"I never heard of it," said Georgia Reese.

"It's English, and I understand that the butler has certain privileges there. *Droit du seigneur*, you know, although I don't think Phillips claimed his. How many is that?"

"About seventeen or eighteen," said Bob Hewitt. "And you didn't include the handyman-carpenter, the night watchman, or people like the old boy's secretary, O'Neill, or nurses for the children."

"Well, twenty or so. So it was splendor, Ev, but not solitary," said Jennie Hewitt.

"No, and you left out Madigan, the superintendent, and a lot of these people had husbands and wives living on the place, but not what you might call staff," said Bob Hewitt.

"Where did they put them all?" said Georgia Reese.

"Oh, some lived in the big house, some over the garage and the carriage-house," said Jennie Hewitt.

"I had no idea we were so close to such grandeur," said Evan Reese.

"Grandeur is right," said Bob Hewitt. "They even had their own buttons for the servants' livery. An oak, of course, and if you looked carefully, the letter 'S' in the foliage."

"No coat of arms?" said Georgia Reese.

"I never saw one," said Bob Hewitt. "In spite of everything we've told you, the old boy wasn't much for show. He had the very best of everything, mind you. Cars and horses, and paintings by famous artists. But when he took the train to New York, he rode in the day coach. He had a pass, of course. And when he got to Jersey City, his private car was probably sitting there on a siding. For a man as rich as he was, he lived very inconspicuously. Take for instance, living here. This was never like Tuxedo or one of your Long Island communities. Nothing fashionable about High Ridge."

"That's true," said his wife. "And they never had a yacht or a racing stable or any of those things."

"Don't disillusion me," said Evan Reese. "I was beginning to feel that some of the grandeur would rub off on me."

"I'm afraid there isn't much of it left," said Bob Hewitt. "My father told me one time how much it cost Stratton to white-wash all the post-and-rail at Oak Knoll. You know, my father was in the building supply business. Brick and lumber, cement and paint. So he knew pretty well what Stratton spent. Stratton was my Dad's best customer, year in, year out. We—my Dad, that is—supplied the trap rock for Stratton's roads. Stratton put me through college, if you want to look at it that way. But I'll tell you one thing. Madigan, the superintendent, never had any chance to knock down a little graft. You'd always see that

'S' on the upper right-hand corner of every bill, which meant that Stratton had seen it before okaying payment. If Stratton caught a man stealing or even cheating a little bit, the fellow'd be on the next train out of here, bag and baggage, with orders to never return to High Ridge."

"The result was there was very little cheating," said Jennie Hewitt. "And they all knew they had a good thing. They were well paid, and they didn't have to eat slop or live in broken-down shacks."

"Yes, the Strattons paid their help a little more than the going rate because this was such an out-of-the-way place," said Bob Hewitt. "And he was a great believer in education. For instance, Phillips's son graduated from Johns Hopkins with an M.D. degree, and practices medicine out in California somewhere. Quite a few of the kids on the place went to college with Stratton's help."

"Anybody that wanted to, if his mother or father had been with the Strattons long enough. Ten years, I think it was," said Jennie Hewitt.

"The boy that wanted to go to Harvard," said Bob Hewitt.

"Oh, yes. Pierre, the chauffeur, had a son that was the same age as Frank Stratton, and the boy decided he wanted to go to Harvard. So Pierre told Mrs. Stratton his son wanted to go to college and would she lend him—"

"Four thousand dollars," said Bob Hewitt.

"Four thousand dollars," said his wife. "Pierre didn't want to touch his savings account, and Mrs. Stratton could take the money out of his salary. 'Why of course,' she said. She'd be *glad* to help. And what college was Joseph going to? 'Harvard,' said Pierre."

"That cooked it," said Bob Hewitt.

"She said no. 'But Madame is sending her own son to Harvard,' said Pierre. 'Precisely,' said Madame. Then of course Pierre, being a Frenchman, caught on. So Joseph went to Dartmouth."

"She was no fool," said Bob Hewitt. "Frank and his naked piano-players, classmates of her chauffeur's son."

"I'm dying to know about Bernice, the sister," said Georgia Reese.

"Shall we forget about bridge tonight?" said Evan Reese.

"I'd rather hear about my neighbors. Ten years. Might as well have been living in an apartment house in New York. There you don't expect to know your neighbors."

"I'm perfectly willing, if you'd care to hear about them," said Jennie Hewitt. "You never heard of Bunnie Stratton?"

"I don't think so," said Georgia Reese.

"Madcap Bunnie Stratton? That's what she was called by the newspapers. Madcap Bunnie Stratton."

"She made up for all the publicity her father didn't get," said Bob Hewitt.

"Notoriety, you mean. Not just publicity. She was a regular F. Scott Fitzgerald heroine," said Jennie Hewitt.

"Which one?" said Evan Reese.

"Which one?" said Jennie Hewitt. "Why—I don't know which *one*."

"The reason I asked, Fitzgerald's heroines weren't madcaps," said Evan Reese.

"Well, I always thought they were," said Jennie Hewitt.

"No. Here's another example of the picture versus the printed word. People tend to think of John Held's girls when they hear Fitzgerald's name. But Fitzgerald's heroines, at least the ones I remember, were totally unlike the Held girls. Do you remember Daisy, in *The Great Gatsby*? She wasn't a Held girl. And Nicole, in *Tender Is the Night*. The very thought of John Held doing a picture of that tragic figure is repellent to me."

"Ev, I'm afraid you're a little too literal-minded. When I said an F. Scott Fitzgerald heroine I might as well admit I never read a word he wrote. And I *was* thinking of the John Held Junior drawings."

"Then call her a John Held Junior girl, but don't call her a Fitzgerald heroine. Give the artist his due, and don't distort what the author wrote."

"Oh, come on, Ev," said Bob Hewitt.

"No, now don't you protest before you think," said Evan Reese. "If I came into your bank and tried to tell you that a share of stock was a bond, you'd correct me damn quickly. Well, this happens to be something *I* know about. For years I've been hearing and reading people talking about John Held's girls and Fitzgerald's, as though they were one and the same thing. They just simply weren't. From the literary point of view, one of the worst things that ever happened to Fitzgerald was the simultaneous popularity of John Held's drawings. Those damn editorial writers were largely to blame. Who would want to take Fitzgerald seriously if all they ever knew about him was that he wrote about those John Held girls? Held was a very good satirist, and he didn't *want* his girls to be taken seriously. Of course Fitzgerald was partly to blame. He called one book *Flappers and Philosophers*, and in the public mind the flapper was the John Held girl. Actually, of course, Fitzgerald and Held and the editorial writers were all misusing the word flapper. A flapper was English slang, and it meant a society girl who had made her debut and hadn't found a husband. On the shelf, they used to say. It wasn't an eighteen-year-old girl with flopping galoshes."

"Well, according to your definition, Ev, Bernice was never a flapper, but according to mine she was," said Jennie Hewitt. "She was a sort of a John Held girl. One of the first to bob her hair and smoke in public and all the rest of it. And she didn't even make her debut."

"And *that* was a party we were looking forward to," said Bob Hewitt. "The plans."

"They started planning that party I don't know how many years ahead," said Jennie. "She was to have a New York party, but her real party was going to be here, June 1921, it was supposed to be. A thousand invitations. Mrs. Stratton hired a secretary just for that party, and she came to work over a year ahead of time. Special trains were going to leave Jersey City and Philadelphia."

"Art Hickman," said her husband.

"Art Hickman, Ted Lewis, and Markel's orchestra."

"The club," said Bob Hewitt.

"They engaged the whole club for the weekend, a year in advance, and every available hotel room for miles around. Not including families like my family and Bob's that offered to put up guests."

"Sherry. Louis Sherry."

"You can imagine the preparations Sherry's would have had to make. A thousand guests, extra servants and musicians.

Supper and breakfast. Dinner before the party and luncheon at the club the next day."

"What about liquor?" said Evan Reese. "We had Prohibition by that time."

"I don't know what they were going to do about liquor. We had Prohibition, but not much enforcement then. They wouldn't have had any trouble. The stuff was coming in from Rum Row and Canada, and you can be sure Stratton would have had the best, not just Jersey Lightning."

"What was Jersey Lightning?" said Georgia Reese.

"Applejack. What we drank instead of corn liquor. They served it over the bar in every country hotel, and it wasn't bad. It had the desired effect."

"But they never had this party?" said Georgia Reese.

"No," said Jennie Hewitt. "Bunnie eloped. Don't either of you remember that? Bunnie Stratton and Jack Boyle?"

"Oh, hell," said Evan Reese. "Of course I remember now. Jack Boyle, the baseball player. Played first base for the New York Giants, and one of the first All-Americans Fordham ever had. But I'd forgotten *her* name. How did they ever get together?"

"They weren't together very long," said Jennie Hewitt. "Less than a year. Jack was a lifeguard at Belmar."

"Belmar?" said Georgia Reese.

"Belmar-by-the-Sea. A summer resort we used to go to in those days. Bob's family went there and so did mine, and quite a few of the *nicer* Irish."

"Which didn't include Jack's family. Jack was a hell of a good athlete and a handsome son of a gun, but let's face it, they weren't the lace-curtain Irish. Jack was from Jersey City, and his father was a watch repairman for the Jersey Central. White-collar, but not lace-curtain."

"We'll come to that," said Jennie Hewitt. "Anyway, Bunnie was allowed to spend a whole week with me at Belmar, the summer of 1919. She'd never swam in the ocean before, in spite of all their money, and I can't give you any better proof of how strictly *I* was brought up than by telling you that the Strattons allowed Bunnie to visit me. And a whole *week*. Six days too long."

"She took one look at Jack Boyle," said Bob Hewitt.

"And he at her. One day was too long. Love at first sight if there ever was a case of it," said Jennie Hewitt.

"Your father," said her husband.

"My father told Jack that if he didn't stop hanging around our house he'd have him fired, and Jack told my father to go straight to hell and he *was* fired. So then he had nothing to lose, and he saw Bunnie every day and every night."

"She was sixteen then?" said Georgia Reese.

"Sixteen. Jack was about twenty-one."

"Older than that, Jennie," said Bob Hewitt. "He'd been overseas in the war. He was a good twenty-three or four."

"Well, whatever. My parents were afraid to tell Mr. and Mrs. Stratton, and hoped it would blow over, but Jack went back to Fordham and that year Bunnie was at Spence and they managed to see each other."

"Then Boyle quit Fordham and went with the Giants," said Bob Hewitt.

"Now I remember. Sure. Boyle eloped, and McGraw fired him," said Evan Reese.

"But *I* don't know any of this, so go on, Jennie," said Georgia Reese.

"Well, her family of course were outraged, but so were his. They were Catholic and Bunnie and Jack had been married by a justice of the peace, in Greenwich, Connecticut. So the Boyles wouldn't have anything to do with Jack. Wouldn't let him in the house. And the only thing Jack could do was play baseball."

"But as I remember it, he did," said Evan Reese. "He played for some team in the International League, Binghamton or one of those teams."

"It *was* Binghamton," said Bob Hewitt.

"But they didn't pay him much, and Bunnie was pregnant. Mr. Stratton sent a lawyer to talk to Bunnie, but Jack wouldn't let him see her."

"Wouldn't let him *see* her?" said Bob Hewitt. "He was arrested for giving the lawyer a punch in the nose, and he told him that was what Mr. Stratton could expect, too, if he ever came around."

"Bunnie adored her father," said Jennie Hewitt. "And he

did come to see her in Binghamton, while Jack was away, and he persuaded her to come home with him, knowing that Jack would follow her."

"*Thinking* that Jack would follow her. Mr. Stratton *wanted* Jack to follow her. I know that. And he wanted to give Jack a job. But he didn't know Jack Boyle. That fierce Irish pride, I guess. When Boyle got back to Binghamton and read Bunnie's letter, he quit baseball and Bunnie never heard from him again. Never. Not a word, not a line."

"What happened to him?" said Georgia Reese.

"He drifted around for a while, and then joined the Army. He'd been a lieutenant, but he enlisted as a private. I think you had to enlist for seven years then. Anyway, when he got out he became a bootlegger with some of his old friends in Jersey City. He's still alive. Frank Hague got him a job on the Hudson County payroll. Inspector of something or other. The last I heard he was a sort of an organizer for one of the labor unions."

"And what happened to her?" said Georgia Reese.

"Oh, plenty," said Jennie Hewitt. "She didn't have the baby. Whether she lost it or they got her an abortion, I don't know. The latter, I suspect, because after she divorced Jack and married the Englishman she had two children, one of which the Englishman refused to take the credit for."

"When you say the Englishman, you mean the first Englishman," said Bob Hewitt. "She married two Englishmen. The Army officer, and the writer."

"Yes, but the writer was an Australian, and if he was a writer, nobody ever heard of anything he wrote," said Jennie Hewitt. "Except bad cheques. I always understood that the first Englishman, the *English*man, was quite attractive and very much in love with Bunnie. He resigned from the Army to marry her, and I guess he took all he could stand."

"What happened to her two children?" said Georgia Reese.

"The first was killed in the war, North Africa. The second was a girl," said Jennie Hewitt. "I heard that she got married during the war, but what's happened to her since I have no idea."

"And where is Bunnie herself?" said Georgia Reese.

"Majorca, surrounded by pansies and Lesbians of all

nationalities. She has enough to live on and supply wine and gin for her hangers-on. She's a countess. She picked up an Italian along the way. There's some doubt about the title, or not so much about the title as her right to it. She married her Italian on a steamship, or so she says. But if she wants to call herself countess, none of her present friends are going to object. The count is over seventy and feeble-minded. I haven't seen or heard from Bunnie in over twenty years. We saw her once, briefly, in London before the war. But a friend of ours looked her up in Majorca and she said Bunnie refuses to speak English because all her little boys and girls are Italian or Spanish or French. When we saw her in London we could hardly understand her, she was so English. But not any more. She's had her face lifted a couple of times and she wears oversize sunglasses and big floppy hats, never goes out in the daylight, and her house is lit by candles. I wonder what she thinks."

"Yes," said Georgia Reese.

"You know. People like you and I, Georgia. Let's face it, we live a lot on our memories. We love our grandchildren and these two nice old things that we're stuck with—"

"Oh, thanks," said Bob Hewitt.

"But my life would be very empty without my memories, the good times we had, *and* the bad, and the old sentimental recollections. Think of what our life would be like without them. And yet I don't suppose Bunnie ever gives a thought to Jack Boyle and those days."

"Probably not," said Georgia Reese.

"Or the Englishman, or the Australian. Or the dear-knows how many lovers she had. I imagine she shuts all that out and just goes on from day to day, as though one part of her brain had been removed."

"Let me give you the other side of the coin," said Evan Reese.

"All right, Ev," said Jennie Hewitt.

"What about Mrs. Stratton, who has nothing *but* memories?"

Jennie Hewitt nodded. "Yes, that's a pretty horrible thought, too."

They were all silent for a moment, then Georgia Reese spoke. "They must suffocate her, her memories."

"Yes, who has it worse? The mother remembering everything, or the daughter remembering nothing?" said Bob Hewitt.

"Why, Robert Morris Hewitt, you're almost poetic tonight," said his wife.

"I have my moments," said Bob Hewitt. "I get in the same rut everybody gets in, and I take the old lady for granted. But every once in a while I have to talk to her on the phone, about bank business, and when she calls me Robert, I feel as though I were just starting out and she was old Queen Mary. The most personal she ever gets is to say 'Good morning, Robert,' and 'Thank you, Robert.' She never asks about Jennie or our children or grandchildren. These are business calls. But she's quite an old gal, to be able to make me feel like a fumbling assistant paying teller at my age. I don't really give a damn what Bunnie thinks, if she thinks anything. But I often wonder about the old lady in that house, the money going, the place shrinking a little every year. From eight hundred acres to twenty in a little over one generation. And the God damn futile mess that her two children have made of their lives. That was a beautiful woman once, Mrs. Stratton. I remember one time twenty-five or thirty years ago, I happened to be walking up Fifth Avenue and she was twenty or thirty feet ahead of me. She was alone. But as I followed her I couldn't help noticing how the people coming in her direction would automatically fall out of the way. Just looking at her, they'd make way for her. I never forgot that."

"I wish she hadn't written that letter about the dog," said Evan Reese. "The only communication we ever had from her."

"What did the letter say?" said Jennie Hewitt.

"Well, it was ten years ago, and I can't quote it verbatim, but to the effect that Airedales were known as one-man dogs and ours had snapped at somebody on her place."

"I know why she sent that letter," said Jennie Hewitt. "Ten years ago? Ten years ago her grandchildren used to come here a lot."

"Then why didn't she say so?" said Evan Reese.

"Oh, that wasn't her way," said Jennie Hewitt. "Nothing dramatic or appealing to your better nature. Or sentimental about children. She was simply stating the facts about

Airedales, impersonally. She wouldn't dream of mentioning her grandchildren. That would be a show of weakness on her part, inviting familiarity."

"That's true, Ev," said Bob Hewitt. "She approved of you, or you never would have got this house. She probably knew your work, and for all I know she may even own one of your paintings."

"No, I know where all my paintings are."

"In any event, you were okayed as a purchaser and a neighbor, but that's as far as she'd ever go. Like she wouldn't call on Georgia, not because she wanted to be rude to Georgia, but because she didn't want Georgia to return the call. I see her household bills, you know, and as far as I know, she hasn't had anyone for dinner in at least ten years. At least. She buys a lot of books, and she has four television sets in the house. But for instance, she hasn't bought a bottle of liquor or wine since before Pearl Harbor. She smokes a lot of cigarettes. Camels. That was the only thing she asked for during the war, was a regular supply of Camels. And I got them for her because she never cheated on gas rationing, or shoe coupons or any of those things, and it would have been easy for her to. Technically, Oak Knoll was a farm, and there was a lot of funny business by so-called farmers then."

"I'm going to have to see this woman. That's all there is to it," said Evan Reese.

"Make it accidental," said Bob Hewitt. "Don't let her see you coming up the driveway, or she'll hide in the closet."

"Not hide," said Jennie Hewitt. "She just won't be at home."

"Well, that's what I meant. Ev knows that. And it's nothing personal. I've known her all my life, and I handle a lot of her business and talk to her over the phone, but I never go to her house, even when there are papers to sign. I send my secretary, who happens to be a notary public."

"Oh, I'll make it accidental," said Evan Reese.

"And make it soon," said Jennie Hewitt. "She's over eighty."

"Yes, and *I'm* over sixty," said Evan Reese.

The Hewitts' car was covered with snow when the time came for them to depart. "I missed the weather report," said Bob Hewitt. "Was this expected?"

"Ev expected it," said Georgia Reese.

"Look at Mike," said Bob Hewitt. "He doesn't want to go out in it. Come on, Jen. Goodnight, Reeses, thanks for a pleasant evening. And I didn't lose any money."

"Have you got snow tires?" said Georgia Reese.

"We'll be all right. Bob's careful."

"I'd feel better if you'd call us when you get home," said Georgia Reese.

"All right, as soon as we get home, but don't worry. It hasn't had a chance to freeze," said Jennie Hewitt.

For a little while Evan Reese stood at the window, looking out at the new winter scene under the floodlight. "I can think of three men that I'd like to see do that. Maxfield Parrish. George Luks, and Charles Sheeler. And Salvador Dalí, that makes four. Each of them had his own special blue, and none of them would see it the way I do."

"How are you going to do it?" said his wife.

"I'm not going to attempt it. When I finish this picture I'm not going to paint anything for at least six months."

"I wasn't talking about your painting. How are you going about meeting Mrs. Stratton?"

"Is that what I was thinking about, Georgie?"

"That's my guess. Whenever you're really thinking about painting, you don't talk about it."

"It must be fun to guess. Well, you're right, this time. I'm not always thinking about something else when I talk about painting, but this time I was. With that son staying there she's not going to be very receptive, less so than usual. But then isn't that just the time to make a sortie, when she's least prepared for it?"

"Sounds mean."

"I am above meanness. However, I'm not above curiosity, and believe me, I'm damn curious. Instead of a rather dull, cranky, faceless old woman, our neighbor turns out to be— well, Jack Boyle's first mother-in-law. Boyle to me was one of the really interesting baseball players. Much more interesting really than if he'd stayed in the game and been as good as your fellow Georgian, Mr. Tyrus Raymond Cobb. And he might have been almost as good as Cobb. Potentially he was, they all said. Maybe he'd have been better. But I've always been interested in the near-misses. Understandably. I'm one myself."

"Now, now," said his wife.

"Well, you know how I feel about my work, so the hell with that. But Boyle was a near-miss, and in her way, so is Mrs. Stratton. She was never one of the famous hostesses, or mistresses, or philanthropists, and yet she could have been any of those things. Or all three. Or any two. I never even heard of her as a great beauty."

"You never heard of her husband, either."

"Yes, I did. He was a well-known millionaire, but I forgot all about him many years ago, and never connected him with the woman we bought this house from. When I was young and living in Paris and the Village, I knew the names of the millionaires. If a millionaire bought one of our pictures our prices went way up, overnight. If one of us sold a picture to Jules Bache for a thousand dollars, that was ever so much better than getting a thousand dollars from someone with less money. The inconspicuous fellow, the art-lover that happened to like your picture, and happened to have a thousand dollars—that was nice. But that kind of a sale was usually considered a lucky accident. On the other hand, if someone like Bache shelled out a thousand bucks, we never sold another picture for that little. We didn't have to. Writers have the same experience. I'm sure that William Faulkner and Ernest Hemingway got big prices for pieces that they would have sold for fifty dollars when they first wrote them. And that's as it should be. Faulkner is a great artist, and all his work is extremely valuable, whether it's his best work or his worst. The mere fact that he wrote it makes it valuable, because there is only one Faulkner. Fortunately, people believe that about painters. Look at Pablo Picasso."

"Look at Evan Reese," said his wife.

"Yes. You'll never starve, as long as you have enough of my pictures lying around," he said. "A snowscape! Tomorrow morning. I shall take my little camp stool and some of the tools of my trade, and do some sketches."

"No."

"I'll bundle up good and warm. I'll go up West Branch Road, where I can be seen from the big house. We'll *try* that anyway."

"So that's what you were thinking?" said Georgia Reese.

"Well—yes," said her husband. Bob Hewitt telephoned, and the Reeses retired for the night.

In the morning Evan Reese put on hunting socks, heavy shoes and six-buckle arctics; tweed suit and sweaters; sheepskin reefer and cap with earlaps. He carried his camp stool, large sketch pad, and a vacuum bottle of coffee, and established a vantage point in the middle of the West Branch Road, which had not yet been visited by the township snow-plow. He made several quick sketches of the valley, then paused to take a few sips of the coffee. He screwed the cap back on the bottle and resumed sketching, aware that he was about to have company.

"Do you mind if I watch?" said his visitor. Evan Reese recognized the voice from the limousine, the same harshness but now without petulance. The harshness was of the kind that is usually attributed to whiskey-drinking.

"Why, no," said Evan Reese. "If you'd like to see what effect cold weather has on fingers. My name is Reese."

"Oh, I know. My name is Frank Stratton. My mother's a neighbor of yours."

"Of course."

"I won't talk any more. Don't let me interrupt."

Evan Reese quickly finished the sketch he had begun, turned over the page and started another. "Do you know anything about this kind of work?"

"Not a thing."

"Well, then I'll explain what I'm doing. This is what I call my shorthand. My notes. As you see, I didn't try to do that barn or that farmhouse in any detail. The silo. The pigpen. I've lived here ten years and I know all that. But as I sketch—now here for instance, I'll do this clump of trees. Ten years from now, twenty years from now, if I'm alive, I'll be able to look at this sketch and remember what I don't want to forget, which is the metallic white of the snowdrifts over there to the right, as it looks at half past ten, Eastern Standard Time. There. That's enough. My fingers are getting clumsy with the cold. Would you like a spot of coffee?"

"I was going to suggest that you come back to the house and have a cup with me."

"Thank you very much, but I think I've done enough walking. I'm headed for home. But you're obviously out for exercise. Would you like to come down with me and have a cup of coffee at my house? Do you like hot cinnamon buns? That's what I'm going to have."

"I haven't had one since I was ten years old. Sure, if it's all right?"

"Of course it is. Here, you're a young fellow. I'll give you this stool to carry, and you'll feel as if you earned your cinnamon bun."

"Fine."

"I'm not going to do this again, till I get one of those electric hand-warmers. You know the ones I mean, in the Abercrombie catalog?"

"Let me send you one when I go back to New York."

"All right. I'll trade you. One of these sketches for a hand-warmer."

"Oh, no, Mr. Reese. I get much too much the best of that deal."

"I suggested it, so it's satisfactory to me."

"Well—okay. But if you're going to be generous, will you put your initials on it?"

"When we get to my house," said Evan Reese. "You know, it's God damn cold up here. That kitchen's going to feel good."

They entered the house through the kitchen door, unbuckling their arctics and leaving them inside the storm door. "Georgia, I have a customer for a hot cinnamon bun. This is Mr. Stratton, our neighbor's son. Mr. Stratton, my wife."

"How do you do, Mr. Stratton. Come in and get warm. Just put your things any old place. It's nice to have a visitor. You take coffee?"

"I'd love some coffee."

"And I dunk," said Evan Reese. "The molasses sticks to my teeth if I don't dunk. A good cold slice of butter, dunk just a little so the butter doesn't melt, and then enjoy yourself. And don't count the calories."

"I never count the calories," said Stratton. "I'm glad to see you've kept this kitchen just the way it used to be. I used to come here when I was a boy. My cousins lived in this house, and they had a cook that made apple butter."

"Apple butter," said Evan Reese. "Let's get some, Georgia?"

"All right. I'll put it down."

"Did you ever eat apple butter on fried scrapple?" said Stratton.

"Never heard of it, but I don't know why it wouldn't be delicious," said Evan Reese. "But scrapple is no good any more. We tried it, and it isn't the same. I'm a Pennsylvanian, and I got some to introduce it to my wife, but it just wasn't right."

"No, I didn't care for it," said Georgia Reese.

"It's a long time since I've had scrapple. Or fried mush with molasses."

"I had that for breakfast every morning before I went to school," said Evan Reese. "Or mush-milk. Corn meal mush in a soup dish, with milk and sugar."

"That's why children are so nervous these days. They go to school without breakfast, half the time," said Georgia Reese. "They might as well start the day with a cigarette and a Coke, the kind of breakfasts they eat nowadays. Have you got children, Mr. Stratton?"

"I have two. A boy and a girl, and I know what you mean." Stratton looked about him. "You *have* made some changes. Do you use the big range at all?"

"Hardly ever from about the first of April to November," said Georgia Reese. "But beginning around Thanksgiving I use it. I like to cook on it, and there's nothing like it for heating the kitchen."

"Please don't ever get rid of it. You have bottled gas, I suppose? Oh, now I see. You have all the new things in what used to be the laundry. Your electric icebox. This is the dishwasher? Electric iron. *That's* how you did it. You have the old kitchen, but you have the modern conveniences. You see, we didn't have bottled gas in my day, and I can remember when we had our own electricity. We had a Delco plant, for Oak Knoll and the nearest houses like this one." He got up and went to a cabinet and opened a drawer. "Oh, look. You still have it." He took from the drawer a removable hand-grip for the laundry irons. "Where are the irons? Have you still got them?"

"Where they always were. Keep looking," said Georgia Reese.

"They should be—*there* they are." On a brick ledge beside the coal range were half a dozen laundry irons. He clamped the grip on one of them. "See, I remember how it works. My sister used to love to iron. I have an older sister. She lives abroad now, but I can remember coming down here with her when I was just a small boy, and she loved to help my cousin in the kitchen. Have you ever been to Majorca, Mr. Reese?"

"No."

"That's where my sister lives. She's a good deal older than I am. But she loved this house. She was very domestic, considering. I mean she's been married a lot and lives an odd sort of life. Oh, well . . . You have all those wonderful canisters. The spices and coffee and sugar. This table used to be covered with blue-and-white checkered oilcloth. I see you like it better without the cover."

He asked to see the rest of the house, and they showed him around. He enjoyed himself in simple fashion, admiring the Reeses' possessions, exclaiming delightedly on recognizing items that had been in the house when he knew it. His delight was strange, coming from a man of middle age who carried the scars of dissipation in face and figure. His sweater and tweed jacket fitted him tightly; the jacket sleeves were a little short, indicating that he had put on weight in shoulders and arms since the jacket was made. The fat sloped down from his temples and his original features were hidden in the puffy veined cheeks. He was just under six feet tall, the same height as Evan Reese, but beside Reese he appeared chubby. Reese, mentally carving away the excess flesh, saw a sensitive man enlarded in the person Stratton had made of himself. And yet as Stratton's visit extended to an hour, Evan Reese found that he was liking the man, pitying him, and hoping that he would remain as he now saw him. No matter what his intelligence told him—which was that Frank Stratton was a committed voluptuary, beyond redemption—Evan Reese wanted to postpone the reversion, and to do so he prolonged Stratton's visit.

"I'm having an exhibition in February," said Evan Reese. "How would you like to have a preview?"

"I'd be delighted, on condition that you won't hold it against me if I say anything stupid," said Stratton. "Where do you work?"

"You remember the potting-shed your cousin used to have? I turned it into a studio. It looks small, but it has as much space as some studios I've had in New York. I'm very pleased with it. I put in skylights and a linoleum floor, and that's about all I had to do. We won't be there very long, however. The only heat is from two electric heaters, and they're so murderously expensive, I never turn them on except when I'm working. So, put your coat on."

Evan Reese put on his reefer, Stratton put on his trench coat and they went to the studio. It was a strictly utilitarian one-room house, containing canvases of various sizes in profusion; easels and paint tubes, brushes, knives and palettes and paint-stained rags; one damaged leather chair, several camp chairs and stools, and a bridge table on which lay a couple of large metal ash trays and a half-filled pipe rack. There were two naked electric bulbs hanging from the ceiling. "You see what I mean by cold," said Evan Reese. He turned one of the two spigots of a kitchen sink, and water came forth. "Not frozen," said Evan Reese. "But I'm going to have to get that snow shoveled off the skylight."

"Maybe I can do it. Have you got a ladder?"

"Thanks, but there'll be a fellow along some time today. A sort of a handy man. He'll be out to put the chains on my tires and maybe he might even clear the driveway, if he's in the mood. One of those local characters. I don't like to make suggestions to him, because he always says, 'Mr. Reese, I got it all planned out, now you just let me do it my way.' And he's usually right. He wants to make sure that I understand, you see, that he knows this property better than I do."

"Oh, I guess that's Charley Cooper."

"That's who it is, all right. But he's Mr. Cooper to me. Well, here are thirty-nine pictures, and on the big easel is the fortieth. All sizes. They're the ones I'm going to show in February. My last exhibition was six years ago, and these are all pictures I've done since about—well, since I chose the ones for my 1954 show. These aren't all I've done, of course. I often have three going at a time, and always two. Now for instance, here is a house in Rhode Island, Saunderstown. While I was painting this I was also painting—where is it, now? Here it is, this young lady. Pretty, isn't she?"

"Lovely."

"She talked a blue streak and smoked one cigarette after another. She was very stimulating company, and a very relaxing change from the job of doing that house. This is Spithead, Bermuda. This is a still life done right here in two days, actually in about six hours. But this son of a bitch, this took me three months before I got it right. Same size picture, and apparently just another still life. Same number of objects, just about. But why do you suppose this one took six hours, and this one three months?"

"Just answering for myself, you probably felt like painting when you did the quick one, and were getting fed up when you did the other."

"You've hit it on the nose. My wife and I'd been abroad and I hadn't had a brush in my hand for over two weeks, and we got home and I came right here and started painting without even taking my hat off. Literally. But this one, the one that took me three months, it wasn't because I was fed up with painting. No. You see, I'd seen a picture I didn't like, in Dublin. Had a quick glance at it and dismissed it from my mind, or so I thought. Then one day I arranged some fruit in a bowl and set a table for two. Plates, knives and forks, and began to paint. I worked on that damn thing, I thought about it, I had dreams about it. And then one morning, just before I woke up, I had a dream that I was painting this picture and someone kept getting in my way, standing in front of the table and obstructing my view. And do you know what I decided it was? It was the artist who had painted that picture in Dublin. I didn't know the artist's name or whether it was a man or a woman, but I was unconsciously plagiarizing him, or her. So I went right on and deliberately plagiarized, as much as I could remember of that ugly picture in Dublin, and when I finished it it was about as unlike the original as a picture could be. If you look on the back, I don't always give names to my pictures, but this is one called Plagiarism."

"Fascinating," said Stratton. "And they're not at all alike?"

"Yes, they are alike. A layman would say right away that the two pictures had been painted by the same man, but an expert, another painter or a first-rate dealer or an art historian, would know right away that the two pictures couldn't possibly have been painted by the same man. If I get a good price for this picture I'm going to track down the Dublin picture and buy it. It was a terrible, terrible picture, but it was that artist's masterpiece. The son of a bitch got something in there, in his picture, that offended and irritated me, and it was good. And *he* wouldn't be able to tell me what it was. He wouldn't know it was there. I'm sure of that, because he was such a bad, mediocre painter for the rest of the picture, that he couldn't possibly know what was good. Now that, of course, poses a problem in ethics."

"How so?"

"Well, I could buy his picture, pay a good price for it if he still owns it, which I don't doubt. But then what do I do? Do I tell him that I, a pretty well-known painter, have bought his picture and thereby encourage him? Or do I keep quiet? Or do I buy it and tell him the truth, that he's a bad painter and try to discourage him? Tell him to quit while he's ahead?"

"I really don't know."

"There's still another alternative. I can destroy *my* picture. But I can't, because I know it's good."

"Maybe you ought to find out all about the painter before you decide."

"That's the humanitarian approach, and I've rejected it. I don't want to know about this painter. If it's a he or a she, a dilettante, a half-taught amateur, a poor struggling bog-trotter. Art is cruel, and in this problem I represent art. This painter will never do anything good. Never."

"He did once, Mr. Reese."

Evan Reese laughed. "Damn it, Stratton, you've touched me where I'm vulnerable. I can't *be* art, with a capital A. A genius would be ruthless. A genius would do what it's only my inclination to do."

"A man that makes a mistake usually gets a second chance. I think a man that does something good ought to, too."

"Well, apparently that's what I've decided. I had all this out with myself a dozen times, and never done a thing. So I probably won't do anything."

"And the Dublin artist did inspire a good picture."

"Oh, naturally I keep telling myself that," said Evan Reese. "Hello, dear?" Georgia Reese entered the studio.

"Mr. Stratton is wanted on the telephone," said Georgia Reese.

"Wanted on the telephone?" said Stratton.

"I'll show you," said Georgia Reese. "And you come in, Ev. You've been out here long enough."

Evan and Georgia Reese waited in noncommittal silence in the kitchen while Stratton was answering the telephone in the library. He returned shortly, smiling. "That was my mother. She was afraid I might have fallen in the snow and broken my leg."

"How did she know you were here?" said Georgia Reese.

"That's funny. How did she? I never thought to ask her."

"I imagine she was going to try every house in the neighborhood before sending out a scouting expedition," said Evan Reese.

"That's probably it. Well, it's been a very interesting morning, at least for me," said Stratton. "Thank you very much for the coffee and the cinnamon buns, Mrs. Reese. And, Mr. Reese, may I remind you that we made a deal?" He obviously was about to leave.

"Here's your sketch. I'll expect the hand-warmer any day now." Evan Reese had written: "To Frank Stratton, Oak Knoll, November 1960. Faithfully, Evan Reese."

"I'll have it framed. Maybe I'll become an art collector."

"I'm all for that, if you have the money," said Evan Reese.

"That's very dubious, but many thanks. Goodbye."

"Nice to've seen you," said Evan Reese.

The Reeses watched him trudging up the hill in the snow.

"That's going to take it out of him," said Evan Reese. "He's in terrible physical condition."

"His manners aren't any too good, either," said Georgia Reese. "Not even a mention of our coming to his mother's."

"How did she seem over the phone?"

"She didn't ask for him. It was a maid with an Irish brogue."

"We'll be invited, don't think we won't," he said.

"Why are you so sure all of a sudden?"

"Why am I so sure? Because he's going to want to come back here, and he can't very well do that without inviting us to his house *sometime*."

"And why is he going to be so anxious to come back here? Were you at your most fascinating?"

"Yes, I was at my most fascinating, and you were nice to him, and he likes this house. He isn't very bright, and he isn't much of a man. But he isn't the pig I thought he was. He *has* good manners, and when I told him about the Dublin still life I liked his reactions. Decent. Honorable. Also, he isn't an art-phony. People with a bit of pansy in them are apt to be art-phonies. One thing you've got to say for the Zuleika Dobson school, they aren't art-phonies."

"That's my school."

"I know it is. Someone brought up as rich as Stratton was shouldn't have to be phony about anything, but unfortunately you get just as much bullshit about art from the rich as you do from everybody else. I wish I knew something about the ballet. I'd try this fellow out on the ballet and see if he goes phony there. Why don't *you* know something about the ballet?"

"Because for thirty-one years I've been your cook and mistress, and nursemaid and mother of your children, and haven't had time to get culture."

"Well, I'll accept that excuse. But don't let it happen again. *Telephone.* Probably Joel Channing wanting to know when he can see the pictures. Tell him I've gone skiing." He followed her slowly to the library and listened to her side of the conversation.

"Yes it is," she said. "Oh, yes . . . This afternoon? Well, I'd have to ask my husband and call you back. He's working and I can't disturb him, but he'll be in for lunch any minute . . . I hope so, too. And thank you for calling."

"The old lady?" said Evan Reese.

"Could we come in for tea this afternoon about five. So bland. You might think we'd moved here yesterday."

"Maybe from her viewpoint it *was* yesterday."

"Do you want me to say we'll go?"

"Yes, what's the use of pretending? She'd see through that," said Evan Reese. "And as Jennie pointed out, the time is getting short."

A few minutes before five that afternoon the Reeses' doorbell rang. Evan Reese recognized the man at the door, Elwood Blawen, who had a farm on West Branch Road. "Hello, Mr. Blawen. Come in."

"No thanks. I came to fetch you to Mrs. Stratton's," said Blawen. He pointed to an old jeep with a winter top.

"How did that happen?"

"How did that happen? Why, she just called me up and said I was to go fetch you at five o'clock in my jeep. Wasn't any more to it than that. But I *imagine* she figured'd take a jeep to get you there, and she's pretty near right. You'd never get up the hill in your car, 'specially without chains. No Charley Cooper, I see."

"No, he must be counting on all this to melt away."

"Charley's all right once he gets working, but I never saw such a man for putting things off. Deliberating, he always calls it. But there's other names for it, too. Good afternoon, Mizz Reese."

"Mr. Blawen. You going to be our transportation?"

"Looks that way. She's all cleaned out inside," said Blawen. "I even got a heater in there for you."

"Not just for us, I hope," said Georgia Reese.

"Oh, no. If you mean did I put it in special." He smiled. "Oh, no. Those days are gone forever. But mind you, I seen the day when the Stratton family *would* do a thing like that. Why, they tell me she used to have a man come all the way from Philadelphia just to play a few tunes on the organ." He lowered his voice. "Paid him five—hundred—dollars." They got in the jeep. "Five hundred dollars, just to play a few tunes on the pipe organ. One time they had Woodrow Wilson here for Sunday dinner. The President of the United States. And old Stratton wasn't even a Democrat. But him and Wilson were acquainted with one another outside of politics. Oh, yes, there was always something going on around here in those days. Twenty-eight people on the payroll, sometimes more."

"You don't work for Mrs. Stratton, do you?" said Evan Reese.

"Only when she has something special and I can spare the time. Like today, she knows I have my jeep, so she phoned and said would I call for you and Mizz Reese. I always try to accommodate her if I can. Never been here before, have you?"

"No, but how did you know that?" said Evan Reese.

"How did I know that? Just took a good guess. She don't have many visitors. She only got twenty acres left out of what used to be eight hundred, and I guess she feels hemmed in. Here we are."

"Thank you very much," said Evan Reese.

"Oh, I'll be here when you come out," said Blawen.

"How long will *we* be here?" said Evan Reese.

"Well, maybe that's not for me to say, but not more'n a half an hour."

Frank Stratton came out to greet them. "I heard the jeep," he said. "I'm so glad you could come."

A maid took their things and Frank Stratton showed the way to the library. Mrs. Stratton turned from gazing into the fireplace, but she did not rise. Her left hand clutched the silver mounting of a highly polished walnut walking stick. She was obviously very feeble.

"Mother, this is Mr. and Mrs. Reese."

"Good afternoon. I'm glad you could come," said Mrs. Stratton. "Did you have a nice ride in Elwood Blawen's hideous conveyance? But it does do the trick, doesn't it?"

"My first ride in a jeep," said Georgia Reese.

"And you, Mr. Reese? Your first ride in a jeep too?" said the old lady.

"Oh, no. I did some painting for the Navy during the war, and I rode in a lot of jeeps."

"What kind of painting? Camouflage?" said Mrs. Stratton.

"No. I did some pictures of the landings at Iwo Jima, in 1945."

"Photography?"

"No. Paintings."

"*Painting?*" she said. "But wouldn't photography be much more accurate? I don't understand."

"There's no lens wide enough to take in the whole scene, so we did some sketches and the painting came later."

"And weren't you frightened?"

"I was on a big ship. It was noisy, but you don't mind it so much if you have something to do."

"How far away were you?"

"Three or four miles, most of the time."

"But that's close enough to be dangerous, isn't it?"

"Yes. But not much more dangerous than it is around here during the deer season."

"Oh, come now, Mr. Reese," said the old lady. "Did you approve of this undertaking, Mrs. Reese?"

"Yes. My husband wanted to do it very much," said Georgia Reese.

"Frank, will you ring, please?" said the old lady. "And you

believe in supporting your husband in such matters? Well, I must say so do I. Division of authority only leads to confusion." She pronounced her words so slowly that they seemed to be shaking during utterance, but plainly her speech was not keeping up with her thought. "My son tells me you are preparing for an exhibition. February, did he say?"

"The last week in February," said Evan Reese.

"We'll have some tea and then Frank can show you some of my husband's purchases. They should all be in museums, but I can't bear to part with them. Not because I appreciate their merit. I don't. But I'd miss them. They're all spoken for, or I'd give one or two of them to private people. I'm not at all sure that a museum is the right place for a painting. How do you feel about that, Mr. Reese?"

"Most good pictures should be in museums," said Evan Reese.

"Then we don't agree. Do you paint to have your pictures in museums?"

"No one ever asked me that before. In fact, I never asked myself. Do I paint to have my pictures in museums? No. I paint to satisfy my need to paint, and in the hope that one person will see a picture and like it well enough to buy it. Preferably somone who can afford to pay a lot."

"I got an original Evan Reese for the price of a hand-warmer."

"What's that about a hand-warmer, my dear?"

"Mr. Reese and I made a trade. He gave me a sketch, and I'm giving him an electric hand-warmer."

"That isn't why I'm giving you the sketch, Mr. Stratton. I'm giving you the sketch because you impulsively offered to give me the hand-warmer."

"Mrs. Reese, would you with your steady young hands . . ." The old lady directed the maid with the tea things to place them in front of Georgia Reese. "Not very strong for me, please. One lump. No cream or lemon. Frank, will you take Mr. Reese on a very brief tour, but don't be gone long, as I have to leave our guests."

Evan Reese followed Stratton into the great hall and inspected the Gainsborough, the Van Dyke, and the Rubens, devoting about one minute to each picture, but making no comment. After each picture he looked at Stratton, and after the Rubens he said: "Very interesting. Now I think we ought to go back."

"Yes. You can come again and have a longer look," said Stratton.

In the library the old lady looked at Evan Reese. "Very interesting, don't you think, Mr. Reese?" she said.

"Very."

"I thought you'd find them so. Now, I'm afraid you'll have to excuse me." She got to her feet. "Thank you for coming, and now you understand why I haven't been more hospitable before. Mr. Reese, I'm sure *you* understand?"

"I do indeed, Madam," said Evan Reese. "Perfectly."

The old lady took the maid's arm and left them.

"Would you have time to see some more of the house?" said Stratton.

"Oh, I'd—" Georgia Reese began.

"Not today, thanks," said Evan Reese, quickly and emphatically. "But ask us again, will you? Or come in for a cup of coffee tomorrow. I'll have some heat in the studio, and we can have our coffee there."

The Reeses were returned to their house, and Evan Reese, taking his accustomed chair in the library, lit his pipe and stretched out his legs.

"Why did you rush us away? I wanted to see the rest of the house."

"We'll be seeing the rest of the house. And why am I sure? Well, I was sure before and I'm just as sure now. I also know why the old lady never invited us before."

"Obviously because she's so helpless and didn't want to be seen," said Georgia Reese.

Evan Reese shook his head. "You didn't get that little byplay between her and me, at the end."

"No. I thought she was being old-lady flirtatious. A byplay?"

"Yes. She and I understood each other. Do you know why we were never invited to her house? I'll tell you. Because I'm a painter. And there isn't a painter in the world over twenty-five years old that wouldn't know right away that the Rubens, the Van Dyke and the Gainsborough are all fakes. And the son doesn't know it. The Gainsborough is in Pasadena, California. The Rubens is owned by a man named Lee, in Chicago. And the Van Dyke is owned by the Spencer family, in Newport. Mrs. Stratton hasn't owned either of the originals since long before the war. I wonder if she has any jewelry that her heirs presumptive are counting on. If so, I'll bet it's all paste."

"But how do you get rid of three old masters without any publicity?"

"You do it through a dealer, who arranges a private sale, and you make sure that the picture isn't bought for a museum. You sell to people who have the money and want the pictures, but don't want the publicity. There are still a few people in this country who can pay a hundred and fifty thousand for a picture for their own private enjoyment. I imagine that a condition of the sales was that there should be no public announcement, and a reputable dealer would keep quiet."

"But Bob Hewitt knows all about her financial condition."

"No he doesn't. He talks big, but Bob only knows about her account in his bank. She probably deals with some firm like the United States Trust, in New York. Bob handles the gocery bills, but I'll bet you he's never had anything to do with her securities."

"I wonder what made her change her mind, and let you in the house?"

"Well, she knows what we're like after ten years, and I think she trusts us. But of course it also has something to do with her son's visit. We'll know when she gets ready to tell us."

"She's very feeble."

"But she's a fighter."

In the morning Evan Reese was in his studio, intent on his painting, and he was irritated when Stratton knocked on the door. "Come—in," said Evan Reese. He had his pipe in his clenched teeth and he knew he sounded fierce, but Stratton's interruption was unwelcome.

"Is it too early for a cinnamon bun?" said Stratton. "I can come back, or maybe you'd like to be left alone."

"Oh, that's all right," said Evan Reese. Stratton was almost pathetic in his desire for company. "Have a seat and I'll be with you in about two minutes."

"I'll be perfectly quiet."

"You can talk. I don't mind, if you don't mind getting delayed answers."

"You've got it nice and warm in here today."

"Yes, the electric heaters."

"With the heat on it's a very pleasant room. Cozy," said Stratton. "You must like it here."

"I do," said Evan Reese. "I can work any place, but I've done more work in this little shack than anywhere else. And I've become attached to it. Probably in more ways than one."

Stratton was silent for a moment, and Evan Reese glanced at him quickly.

"What was I thinking?" said Stratton. "I was thinking about how you can hold the pipe in your mouth and go on talking and painting. The English do that. You see them riding along on bicycles, both hands on the handlebars and never taking their pipes out of their mouths."

"But I'm not English. I'm Welsh."

"Of course. Of course," said Stratton apologetically. Then, as though to make up for his mistake, he said: "You made a great hit with my mother."

"She made a great hit with me."

"You know, Mother knows a lot more about you than you might think."

"There isn't a hell of a lot to know," said Evan Reese. "Unless you want to argue that there's a hell of a lot to know about everybody. But there's nothing very spectacular about me. I've never had much personal publicity."

"That isn't the kind of thing I meant anyway. Mother doesn't care for that sort of thing, either. But she's studied you."

"Has she? I don't see how. I never met her before yesterday."

"I'll show you how," said Stratton. He stood up and went to a window. "Would you like to see how?"

"Just one second," said Evan Reese. He pressed his thumb on the canvas, put down his brush and palette, wiped his hands with a rag, and took his pipe out of his mouth. "Okay. Through for the morning."

"Well, you see the bay window on the second floor of Mother's house?"

"Indeed I do. I've often envied her that view."

"That's where she sits. And do you know what she has there? A telescope."

"I would too, if I had that bay window. And that's how she studies me?"

Stratton nodded. "You, and Mrs. Reese, and God knows

how many others. People think of Mother as an old lady all alone in her mountain fastness. Actually she's an old busybody."

"In Pennsylvania a busybody is an arrangement of mirrors. You see them on second-story window-sills. You can see who's walking on the sidewalk to the right or left of your house, or ringing the doorbell, without opening the window."

"I've heard of them. At least I've seen them mentioned in novels without quite knowing what they were. But Mother's the other kind. The human kind."

"Oh, indeed she is. Very human. That's why I like her."

"Oh, you like her? I'm glad you like her. She's had a very tough life, at least the second half of it. My father was ill, and between me and my sister, we didn't give her much to be thankful for. I suppose you may have read about my sister, or heard about her."

"A little."

"A little is enough, and that goes for me, too, if you know anything about me, and I'm sure you do. People talk. People gossip."

"Yes. They do," said Evan Reese. "Shall we go over to the kitchen?"

"You'd rather I didn't talk about myself?"

"Oh, you're wrong. But there's coffee in the kitchen, and a place to sit."

"You don't *mind* if I talk?"

"Not a bit. I just thought we'd be more comfortable in the house."

"Oh, fine. You see, Mr. Reese, I know what people say about me, and they have every right to. But I always think that artistic people and writers take a different point of view. More tolerant, if you know what I mean."

"I don't know that they're really more tolerant, but they have to pretend to be."

"Well, that's almost as good. It's better than being avoided. I'm not going to be a pest, honestly I'm not. But I felt right away that you were someone I could talk to. I could tell that you'd heard about me. I always can. But you didn't try to get rid of me first thing, the way so many do."

"Let's have some coffee, and a cinnamon bun."

Stratton's face was transformed, from middle-aged voluptu-ary's to trusting boy's. "Yes, let's," he said.

Georgia and Evan Reese, jointly present, restrained Stratton from further candor, if that had been his inclination; but he stayed an hour and the conversation was easy and obviously enjoyable to him. "I hate to leave you two," he said. "But Mother likes me to be prompt. By the way, Mr. Reese, it's perfectly all right to tell Mrs. Reese about the telescope."

"Oh, I'd have told her without your permission."

"I know you would. I was just kidding," said Stratton. "Thank you both, I had *such* a good time."

Georgia Reese said to her husband: "Watch out, Ev. You may be taking on a responsibility that you didn't ask for."

"I've thought of that," said Evan Reese. "But the poor son of a bitch."

"Yes," said Georgia Reese. "We were lucky with ours."

"It wasn't all luck."

"No, it wasn't."

"Any more than what's happened to this fellow was all bad luck. Or what's happened to his sister. That old lady with her telescope, and her fake paintings. I must find out more about her. And the father, her husband."

"Well, you'll find out more from people like Elwood Blawen and Charley Cooper. Bob and Jennie Hewitt want us to think they knew the Strattons better than they really did."

"Frank Stratton? You mean the old man?" said Charley Cooper. "I don't know's I could tell you anything about him, beyond that he loved the almighty dollar. I ain't saying he was a stingy man, not by any manner or means. He got rid of it, but he knew where every penny went and he made sure he always got value received. Take for instance when we voted to get rid of the horses and buy motorized equipment down't the hose company. We went to Mr. Stratton and asked how much we could count on from him. And he said, and I remember because I was there, he said if we went about it the usual way, not a penny. He said he wasn't going to give any money for a fire truck, knowing that some slick salesman would arrange to take care of certain parties on the committee. Well, now how did Francis A. Stratton, a mul-tie-millionaire, know that that was the usual way? But he knew it, and that's the way it was going to be done, till he spoke up. Embarrassed hell out of the committee, and I was tickled pink, because I didn't figure to get a red cent out of it. So what Francis A. Stratton did, he bought the fire truck through one of the big corporations he was interested in. Through a regular purchasing agent. And then he *do*nated it to the borough. But he wouldn't let a few fellows have their little graft.

"Same thing with other opportunities for a bit of hanky-panky. Like one time he bought fifty dollars' worth of chances for some prize the Legion was auctioning off. By golly, the night they had the drawing, there was Francis A. Stratton, with all his stubs, in case one of his numbers won. That was kind of embarrassing, too. Because some of the Legion boys had it all arranged that one of their wives was going to get the prize. But when Francis A. Stratton showed up they had to quick dump a lot of his tickets in the bowl, and of course he won. A Victrola, I think it was. Yes. A Vic. And as soon as he won, he said he was donating it to the children's ward at the hospital. Made a certain friend of mine's wife sore as all hell. But that's the way he was, old Stratton. He you might say kept us honest. On the other hand, like donating land for a playground, he done that without the least hesitation. I guess you'd say, about honesty, he carried it to an extreme."

"Tell me about his appearance. What did he look like?"

"What did he look like? Oh-ho. If you was a stranger in town and you saw Francis A. Stratton, you'd know right away who was the big noise around these parts. If he wasn't riding in one of his Rolls-Royce English cars, if you happened to see him before he took sick, he was a regular country squire. Derby hat, checkered riding pants and polished-up boots, one of them there white collar-and-tie affairs only the tie and the collar are the same piece of cloth. They had a name for them."

"Stock."

"Stock is right. Stocks and bonds. I ought to be able to re-member that, talking about Francis A. Stratton. Well, once in a while he'd take a notion to come down to town on horseback. He usually rode a white horse, although he had every color of horse there was, and every kind of carriage and buggy. But he'd ride down and leave the horse at the livery stable and do his errands, carrying one of them riding whips. And if he didn't look like he owned the town, nobody did. Polite and all. But he was Francis A. Stratton and nobody knew it better than he did. The time he fell off his horse, he lay there because nobody had the nerve to touch him. They didn't. They stood around and looked at him lying there, unconscious, till somebody had sense enough to send for Doc Frelinghuysen."

"He fell off his horse? Was he drunk?"

"Well now that's where you won't get any two agreeing, on whether he was drunk or sober. If he was drunk, it was the only time any town people ever seen him in that condition, and some didn't believe he was a drinker. But for others it was a pretty well-known fact that Francis A. Stratton sometimes would come home from New York and more or less lock himself up with a bottle and stay out of sight for a week at a time. He had a stock ticker in his house. You know, one of those stock tickers? And he had a fellow worked for him as secretary, O'Neill, that they used to say knew as much about Stratton's business as Stratton did. And maybe more than business. Never liked that O'Neill. He was honest, but the people in town never trusted him. Everybody always shut up when O'Neill was around, for fear he'd carry tales back to Stratton. But he was faithful to Stratton, no doubt about that, and I always heard that O'Neill was a bitterly disappointed man when Stratton didn't leave him anything in his will. Must of been some reason, but I never knew what it was."

"So Stratton was a secret drinker?"

"Well, I don't know's you'd call him secret. The way he lived, as far as the town people knew, he was a secret eater. By that I mean, he didn't drink with town people, but he didn't eat with them neither."

"How old was he when he fell off the horse?"

"Along. Fifties. Maybe more. I understand he got some kind of a clot in the brain from it, but maybe that was just talk. It didn't stop him from working. Or riding horseback. He was out again in a couple months."

"He was quite a handsome man, wasn't he? Or was he?"

"Well, yes. Yes, he was handsome, for a man. Bald-headed, and he had a little black moustache. Not as big a moustache as most men wore in those days. I don't know whether you'd call him handsome or not. If you're thinking of a movie actor's looks, no. Had a nice set of teeth, I remember. In fact, you could have taken him for an Eye-talian, in the summer. Sunburned from being outdoors so much. She used to play tennis with him. They had two tennis courts, one inside and one outside, and they were the first ones around here to have a swimming pool. That was considered the height of luxury then, to have a swimming pool. But I considered the height of luxury having an inside tennis court. It's the ways they think of to spend their money that makes one rich man different than another. I used to think, who would want to play tennis in the winter? Who'd ever think of it? Would you? Maybe now you would, but not that long ago. Tennis wouldn't of been my game in the middle of the summer, let alone spend a wad of money to play it inside in the winter. But Francis A. Stratton wanted to play tennis, so he built himself a house for it, and a lot of famous players used to come there and practice."

"Who, for instance?"

"Oh, don't ask me. I never cared for tennis that much. My sport was cycling. Frank Kramer was my man, the *Iron* Man, they used to call him. I used to go over to Newark, to the Velodrome, just to watch him. If I could of been anybody else I'd have been Frank Kramer. The Iron Man."

"I don't think I ever heard of him."

"Well, that's the same way I was with your tennis players."

"To each his own, as they say."

"Yes, as far as I know, Francis A. Stratton never rode a wheel, so we didn't have much to talk about, him and I."

"What was he like, to talk to?"

"Well, as I said before, polite. There was men in town that he could buy and sell, that they wouldn't treat you as polite as Mr. Stratton. The help all liked him, too. I only ever heard of one quitting on their own accord, but she didn't quit on account of Mr. Stratton." Charley Cooper giggled. "That was a funny one, but it happened long after Francis A. Stratton passed on. You know Lorna Disney, works in the post office?"

"Know her to say hello to," said Evan Reese.

Cooper giggled again. "A fine hello she got one day. Lorna was Lorna Parton then, a hired girl working for Mrs. Stratton, and one day young Frank was home from school and had a friend visiting him. Lorna walks in to do her dusting and there sat Frank's friend in his bare skin, not a thing on him, and playing the piano. Must of been quite a shock to Lorna. She quit then and there. Did her some good, though. She got married soon after. Left an impression, you might say. Oh, there was always something to talk about going on up at the Strattons', but they had so many foreigners working for them and they didn't mix. Lorna could tell you a thing or two, but don't ask her about the piano player. She don't like to have that brought up. *I* can joke with her about it, but she wouldn't like *you* to."

"No, I guess not."

"Everybody has some story about the Strattons, everybody that was living here forty-fifty years ago, what you might call their heyday. Since then you don't hear so much about them. Young Frank—well, I don't know. And Bunnie, now that she's an Italian princess. But they're a different generation, gone to pot. And they moved away. Just as well they did move away. Young Frank, he liked the boys. And Bunnie, she liked the boys, too. If they'd of stayed around here there'd have been trouble, for certain. The old lady was right in kicking them out."

"She kicked them out?"

"As good as. Wouldn't let them hang around here. If they were gonna make damn fools of themselves and get into scrapes, she didn't want it to happen here. And don't forget, it wasn't as easy to buy their way out of trouble. Mrs. Stratton, the widow, didn't carry as much weight as Francis A. when he was alive. I doubt if she's worth a tenth as much as when Mister passed on."

"Where did it all go?"

"You tell me. A fellow like myself, an ordinary working man, I been making money and saving it all these years. But I don't know what happens to a big fortune. Taxes, but that don't explain it. I think she must of got hold of some bad advice in the stock market. I don't know *where* it went. But it's a shame and a disgrace to let a big fortune like that get all pissed away. They could of done a lot for this town if they'd of held on to it, but I'll bet you when she dies there won't be enough to pay the inheritance taxes, and nowadays you can't *give* away a house like that. They used to have thirty people working up there, but the last couple years she only has me there two days a week, and two women in the house, and Elwood Blawen helps out. You know, when she married Francis A. Stratton and got him to build that house and all, it looked like High Ridge was safe and sound. But the last twenty-five–thirty years she's been selling land, and school taxes went up four or five times and this town, I'm predicting, this town inside of another couple years will be so changed nobody will recognize it. I don't want to be living here when *that* happens, and my folks have lived here since the 1700's. No matter what you say about Francis A. Stratton, he was pretty fond of this town. And I guess when you come right down to it, we were pretty fond of him."

"That's what I wanted to hear you say."

"Well, I never would of thought to say it if it wasn't for getting started talking this way. But it's a fair statement. He didn't suck up to nobody. He wasn't natured that way. But he was polite to people, and he didn't infringe on anybody's rights. He wasn't so different from any the rest of us, except richer, and nobody minded him marching around in his riding pants. What the hell? We wouldn't of trusted a man that rich that went around wearing overhalls."

"All in all, you liked Mr. Stratton, then?" said Evan Reese.

"That's what I been trying to tell you, Mr. Reese. You wanted to know some facts, and I's willing to give them to you. You're entitled to any facts I have—"

"Why? How am I?" said Evan Reese, vaguely complimented.

"How are you entitled? Well, facts is the truth, and the truth will out, and everybody's entitled to the truth. But there's different ways of telling facts, so one person telling the same facts could give a different impression. 'S far as we know, you're a reliable man and that entitles you to the facts the way I see them."

"What if I hadn't been a reliable man, Mr. Cooper?"

Cooper smiled. "You'd be surprised how little you'd find out."

"Oh."

"Newspaper reporters been around here two-three times. Once when Bunnie run away and got married. Once when Francis A. Stratton died. And a scandal sheet when Frank

Junior got into trouble. They all went back and wrote up High Ridge people like we was afraid to talk about the Strattons. Afraid? Not afraid, Mr. Reese. One thing we never was was afraid. There was Coopers buried here two hundred years before any Stratton ever set foot in High Ridge. And plenty of Crowders in the same churchyard. She was a Crowder."

"Ah, now I see. She belongs to High Ridge, too."

"Sure does."

"So it wasn't so much that you liked Mr. Stratton that made you protect him, as much as her being a Crowder?"

"I thought you knew that, Mr. Reese."

"Well, it's a little hard to follow, unless you bear in mind that Mrs. Stratton was a Crowder."

"That's the whole thing. If she was just some stranger."

"But your real loyalty was to her, to Mrs. Stratton."

"To High Ridge, put it that way. Take Lorna Disney, for instance. Lorna wouldn't have no difficulty proving kinship to Mrs. Stratton. She might not be as close as the Coopers, but the Partons go back, and Lorna was a Parton."

"What about the Hewitts, for instance?"

Charley Cooper shook his head. "Not High Ridge. They come up from South Jersey, an altogether different breed of cat, you might say. There was some Coopers and some Hewitts got together in New York, but these weren't the same Hewitts. These here in town came from South Jersey."

"Then I take it Mrs. Stratton is a cousin of yours?"

"Yes indeed. The Crowders and the Coopers married over and over again. You take a walk through the churchyard and you'll wonder if they ever married anybody else. Didn't always draw the line at first cousins, either. Back in those days, I guess they didn't always know for sure, when it was mostly farms. Twenty miles away'd be a good strong young woman, and a young farmer had to have a wife. A young fellow tried to run a farm without a wife, he couldn't *do* it. You had to have a wife. And not only for the work, either, if you know what I mean. Come a certain age, and a young fellow had to have a *woman*."

"To go to bed with?" said Evan Reese.

"To, right, go to bed with. It was that or start buggerin' the sheep. Or one another. And when that happened it wasn't long before everybody'd know it. A farmer that didn't have a woman, first he'd go to pot. Usually he'd stink so that no-body'd want to go near him. And pretty soon the farm would go to hell."

"Was this in your lifetime?"

"Sure was in my lifetime. I remember one Crowder had a piece of land he tried to farm without a woman. Him and his brother, the two of them. Jack'd never bring the brother to town with him, just come by himself. Stink? That fellow you could smell him a hundred yards off, and he grew his hair long and a beard. He couldn't read or write and to tell the truth, his vocabulary was pretty small. Just enough to ask for what he wanted in the store, like salt, molasses, shells for his gun. Children used to yell at him and he'd throw stones at them. Hit them, too. But he never run after them. He was the slowest-moving white man I ever saw."

"And what happened to *him*?"

"The brother run away one day, and Jack shot himself with the shotgun."

"And what happened to the brother?"

"They found him living in a cave, couple of miles from the farm. They put him away, he was an idiot. And he died of some sickness a couple months after they locked him up. The sheriff accidentally on purpose set fire to the shack they lived in. He told my father no self-respecting pig would live in it. Slaughtered the stock, a couple of cows, and the court awarded the land to the next of kin. That was an uncle, and the uncle was a cousin of Mrs. Stratton's father. So you see?"

"Mm-hmm." Evan Reese nodded. He was not sure whether he was supposed to see that a farm could not be run without a wife, or that Mrs. Stratton had some odd relatives.

"We had just as bad among the Coopers, I guess. They hung a Cooper when I was a young boy, and the sheriff that sprung the trap was a Cooper. How's that for family relations?"

"Well, where I come from in Pennsylvania there were over a dozen Evan Reeses in the same town, and five Reese Evanses. Originally r, h, y, s, but pronounced Reese. And Billy Will-iamses and Tommy Thomases and Johnny Johnses."

"Then you ought to know," said Charley Cooper. "But here it's been like that for close to three hundred years."

"I guess it was a good thing Mrs. Stratton married a stranger."

"Why?"

"New blood," said Evan Reese.

"New blood? Take a look at Frank Junior. Take a look at Bunnie. If that's all new blood can do for you, you're no better off than as if you married your first cousin. You can't go by that with people."

"You have a point," said Evan Reese. "But maybe Frank's grandchildren will be all right, or Bunnie's."

"Well, I doubt if I'll be around to see it, so I don't intend to let it worry me. I got one of my own grandchildren the brightest boy in his class at Rutgers, and another, his sister, in a mental institution. They had new blood, too. You figure it out, Mr. Reese."

"All right, Mr. Cooper, and if I do I'll call you up."

Cooper smiled. "No hurry, Mr. Reese. They're gonna make babies no matter what you tell them. That we won't be able to stop. Nobody could of stopped *me* when *I* was the right age." He jabbed a thumb in Reese's rib. "Didn't wait till it was legal, either."

"I'll bet you didn't."

"There's a few extra Coopers in addition to them that have the name. Know what I mean?"

"A few extra Coopers, eh?"

"One or two, must be. And I often think to myself, I wasn't the only one after nooky. Consequently, if I's getting mine, other parties were getting theirs, and the old saying, it's a wise child that knows his own father."

"True the world over, I suppose," said Evan Reese.

"I don't know about the world over, Mr. Reese. I only know about High Ridge, but I sure know my High Ridge. An education in itself."

The conversation was taking place in Evan Reese's studio, to which Cooper had gone to report on some trees that had been overburdened in the snowfall. In cold weather it was never difficult to get Charley Cooper to talk, if the studio was warm. "Well, if you let me have your saw, I think I'll trim off some of them limbs," said Cooper, reluctantly.

"Hanging in the closet," said Evan Reese.

"Always used to rub a little ham fat on a saw," said Cooper. "As good as anything I know to keep the rust out. I never put a saw away without rubbing a little ham fat, but I guess oil's all right if it does the trick. How you coming along with your picture-painting?"

"Slow but sure," said Evan Reese.

"These here pictures, they look as good to me as some the Strattons paid thousands of dollars for."

"Thank you. They bought some very valuable paintings," said Evan Reese.

"So they did," said Cooper.

Evan Reese waited. He knew that Cooper was on the verge of saying something about the Stratton pictures.

"That puts me in mind of a question I wanted to ask you, Mr. Reese. What do they do when they *clean* a picture? Supposing you had an expensive picture. Would you send it away to have it cleaned?"

"I might, yes."

"Oh, you would?"

"Oh, yes. To have an expert job done."

"Put it in a crate and send it off to New York, eh?"

"Yes, that's done all the time, with valuable paintings. Why?"

"Costs a lot of money, I'll bet."

"It's not cheap, but it's worth it for a good picture."

"Mrs. Stratton used to do it. Anyway, she did it some years ago and I wondered why anybody'd want to go to all that trouble. She had me up there building crates for two or three pictures, oh, back before the war. That is, a fellow came from New York and told me how he wanted the crates built. That was carpentry, so I had to charge her extra, but she didn't complain. I made her a price of $15 a crate, labor and materials. Well, that's one of the ways the rich have of spending their money."

"In this case, protecting an investment."

"Very likely," said Cooper, unsatisfied. "Fifteen dollars apiece to me, and then whatever the cleaner charged. What *would* he charge?"

"That depends on the value of the painting."

"Say a painting by Van Dyke?"

"Oh, probably a thousand dollars. I don't know. Maybe more."

"Then I didn't overcharge her for my crates."

"I think that was a fair price."

"I wondered. 'S far as I know, she never sent any more away, and I wondered if she thought I overcharged her."

"The Van Dyke is the one that's hanging in the hall?" said Evan Reese.

Cooper nodded. "I wouldn't of remembered Van Dyke, except there's a whole family of Van Dykes living around here."

"Did they do a good cleaning job?"

"I don't know. I didn't unpack it for her, and I don't get in the hall very often. My work don't take me but to the cellar and the kitchen, generally speaking." He paused. "Supposing she wanted to sell a picture like that. What would she get for it?"

"Oh, Lord. Fifty, a hundred, a hundred and fifty thousand. Possibly more. The market changes, and some paintings are worth much more than others by the same man."

"What if, supposing a fellow come to you with a picture and wanted to sell it to you. Would you know right away if it was genuine?"

"That depends. If I knew the painter's work very well I think I could tell. And of course you realize that some individual paintings are famous. The Mona Lisa, for instance. Everybody knows where that is."

"I don't. I heard of it, but I don't know where it is."

"It's in the Louvre, in Paris. And to a certain extent that's true of a great many famous paintings."

"Then if you took a look at a painting by Van Dyke, you'd know right away if it was genuine?"

"If I had occasion to study it, probably. Why? Have you been wondering about Mrs. Stratton's Van Dyke?"

"Oh, I wouldn't want you to say that," said Cooper. "No, sir, I wouldn't want that at all, Mr. Reese. Don't put words in my mouth."

"I wouldn't think of doing that, Mr. Cooper."

"Hope not," said Cooper. "Well, this ain't getting my work done, much as I enjoyed talking with you."

"I enjoyed it too. Come in any time."

"And everything I said this morning—?"

"Oh, absolutely between the two of us."

"She never liked anybody talking about her. Starting with marrying a man twice her age."

"I imagine."

The expected call from Mrs. Stratton came later in the day. "I'd like your advice on something, if you have five minutes," she said. It was an invitation that unmistakably excluded Georgia Reese. "My son's gone over to Princeton for lunch, so it'll be just you and I."

Evan Reese was led by the maid to the study-office.

"Some coffee, Mr. Reese?" said Mrs. Stratton.

"No thanks."

"Do have some? It's here, and it's hot, and I always feel more like a hostess if my guests take *something*. Sugar?"

"One lump, please." He accepted the demitasse and took a chair facing hers.

"Mrs. Reese isn't going to say anything about those frauds, is she?"

"Of course not."

"No. She's a lady. I knew that. I sold the pictures quite a long while ago. It was the only way I knew to provide for my grandchildren. Even so, I didn't get a very good price for them. The dealer took a larger commission than usual. *He* said because he wasn't getting any publicity, but what he meant was that *I* wasn't getting any publicity. In other *words*, he'd keep his mouth shut for a price. Well, I had no choice but to pay him."

"I think I ought to warn you that Charley Cooper is suspicious." He reported some of his conversation with Cooper, and she listened in silence until he finished.

"Yes," she said. "Charley Cooper would like somehow to collect a little money from me for *his* silence. But first he has to have someone to back up his suspicions. He'll try you, later, when he's decided you can be trusted. Not that that will be a very high compliment, Mr. Reese."

"No, it won't be, will it?"

"I know Charley so well because he's my cousin, or has he told you that?"

"Yes, he's told me that."

"The question on Charley's mind would be whether to risk losing the few dollars I pay him fifty-two weeks a year. When he was younger he was more trustworthy. Not more honest, but more trustworthy. He was satisfied with ten or twenty dollars a week. But he's old now, and why is it that the old like money so much? Is it because that's all there is? As a young man Charley was quite dashing. The girls in High Ridge swooned over him, if that doesn't tax your imagination. He was a handsome young man, scorching about on his bicycle. My husband used to give him a lot of his clothes, and Charley cut quite a figure. But then he married and settled down. His wife made him refuse my husband's old suits, and he became very strait-laced. Always had two or three jobs at the same time and brought up his children with an iron hand. Isn't it always that way with reformed rakes? Were you a rake when you were a younger man, Mr. Reese?"

"I did some raking, but I don't think I was a rake."

"Charley was a rake, by High Bridge standards. He's supposed to have been the father of at least two children by other men's wives. Luckily for him, though, the mothers were the kind that couldn't be sure. There was more of that here than we like to admit."

"There is, no matter where you go."

"I daresay. But I didn't ask you here to discuss my cousin Charley Cooper. I want to know what you think of my son. Is there any hope for him?"

"In what way?"

"In any way. You may not think it's fair of me to ask you such a question. You don't know me very well, and I haven't been very cordial to you and Mrs. Reese. But I'm a very old woman, and we haven't got time to get acquainted by easy stages. The nice thing about being old is that I can dispense with those easy stages, dinner twice a year for ten years, tea four times a year, and so forth. You and I can make up our minds about each other much more quickly. And I knew from the way you acted after you saw those fake pictures that I could tell you anything and ask you anything. If I had known you all my life I couldn't be surer."

"Thank you."

"You're welcome. And so—what about my son? I'd hoped that when he was divorced he'd be able to face his problem squarely. In plain language, stop torturing himself with this pretense of being like other men. He never has been. He loved the girl he married, and he loves his children. But he forced that girl to marry him by convincing her that she would be his salvation. Salvation! He very nearly ruined her life as well as his own. And he knew what a dreadful thing he was doing to her, and that was what made him take to drinking. As to the children—they're exactly like dolls, animated dolls. When he speaks of them that's the way he sounds, as though he were talking about dolls. And he loved dolls when he was a little boy. But only too well I remember that for no reason at all he would smash a doll, and I sided with his wife on the question of custody of the children."

"Well, aside from his drinking, what's the matter with him now?"

"You say *aside* from his drinking? There *is* nothing *aside* from his drinking, Mr. Reese."

"But he hasn't been drinking since's he's been here."

"He doesn't drink here because I won't have it. But in New York he drinks all day long, every day."

"What do you mean when you say you won't have it? Do you lock up the whiskey supply?"

"Nothing as easy as that. He simply knows that if he takes more than a few cocktails before meals, I'll send him away. I won't have him in my house. And he understands that."

"So he complies?"

"He has no alternative," she said.

Evan Reese stood up and went to the window.

"You seem to me to want to light your pipe," said Mrs. Stratton. "Go right ahead."

"How sensitive you are. That's exactly what I want to do," said Evan Reese.

"I like the smell of pipe tobacco. I don't like the smell of pipes, but the tobacco burning is very pleasant."

"Well, I'll light up as quickly as I can," said Evan Reese. He filled his pipe and lit it, and remained standing. "Mrs. Stratton, I agree with you that we can dispense with the early stages."

"That's good."

"But even if I'd known you, we'd known each other, all our lives, that wouldn't necessarily mean that complete candor existed between us."

"No, that's true. What are you getting at, Mr. Reese?"

"This. Whether we've known each other a couple of days, or forty or fifty years, the question is how well do we know each other? In other words, what things can we say, and what things must we not say?"

"There's nothing we can't say, when I've asked you such a terribly inside-of-me, intimate question about my son. I should think that such a question would make you feel free to answer me with complete candor. In fact, Mr. Reese, as a gentleman you *have* to reply to my question with the same candor. That's the only courteous thing you can do."

"I wonder."

"Oh, don't *wonder*. It *is*. It cost me something in pride and humility to be so frank with you."

"But I don't want to be equally frank with you. It won't cost me any humility or pride, but it might cost me your friendship. I have that, haven't I?"

"You have indeed. In fact, you may be my only friend. I can't think of any other, so I guess you are."

"Madam, I *am* your friend," said Evan Reese. "Will you believe that?"

"Yes. I promise."

"Then I'll say what I think, but I hope you'll forgive me."

"Please go on."

Evan Reese emptied his pipe in the fireplace and again seated himself, facing her. "First of all, I'm what I am, a painter, and not a psychiatrist."

"I don't want a psychiatrist."

"Your son has made a failure of his marriage. He has affection and I suppose admiration for his wife. He has a great fondness for his children, his dolls. He got out of his marriage, with its heterosexual obligations. But getting out of his marriage didn't make him happy, or give him any release. You tell me that he drinks heavily all the time."

"Morning, noon and night," she said.

"*Except!* Except when he comes here, Mrs. Stratton. Except when he's here with you. The only time he's at all happy, the only time he doesn't need to drink—"

"He knows I won't have it in my house—"

"Mrs. Stratton, he doesn't drink here because he doesn't *want* to drink here. This is where he wants to be, with you."

"Do you know what you're saying?" she said.

"Of course I do. Of course I know what I'm saying."

"Then stop saying it. You know it isn't true."

"What isn't true, Mrs. Stratton?"

"What you're thinking. It was never true, never in my life."

"I believe you."

"Then why must you say these things?"

"I believe *you*, Mrs. Stratton. *You*. But I don't disbelieve what your son feels."

"He feels nothing. He's past all feeling."

"Then let him be happy, here with you."

She shook her head. "I'm too old. I don't want him here," she said.

"My dear lady, you sent him away once before. Twice before. What happens when you send him away?"

"Oh, you know these things?"

"Yes," said Evan Reese. "And now you're old, Mrs. Stratton, but even so you'll probably outlive him."

"I'm sure I will."

"Then let him stay, the more reason."

"I *am* old, you know. But he is my son. The poor, bloated, miserable boy. I hardly know him any more. Tell me, Mr. Reese, so wise and kind you are, why does *this* last?" She held her hand to her bosom.

"Something must," he said.

You Can Always Tell Newark

NOT MANY people ever see the game and not all those who see it can follow the scoring, and among those who can score it fewer still can play it, and, finally, in the entire world there are probably fewer than fifty men who play it well. It is a beautiful game to watch, requiring a quick eye, a strong wrist, and a dancer's agility of its players; but as is the case with another exciting game, high goal polo, it can become a bore. Too much skill, too much beauty, too much excitement, too much excellence, and the spectator's attention will wander, in polo, at a symphony concert, in court tennis, as in life itself.

The girl had been applauding good shots during the first set, and applauding them in a way that indicated she had some knowledge of the game. She was sitting in the first row of spectators, and from time to time one of the players, when it was his turn to serve, would address some remark to her, apparently not seeing her, but speaking her name. "How'd you like that one, Nance? Who you betting on, Nance?" he would mutter, and she would smile, and the young people sitting near her would turn and smile at her, with what they deliberately intended to be a knowing smile. There was some small joke between her and them, some special knowledge.

There were three rows of benches for the spectators, benches without backs, but the men and women in the third row could rest their backs against the wall. It was cold on the court, and not warm where the spectators sat, and at the end of the second set, when the two players stopped to sip iced soft drinks, all the spectators rose to stretch. It was then that Williams saw that the girl was pregnant, probably in her seventh month. When play resumed the girl sat down, but now she knew how tired she was, and she sat with her back against the second-row seats, and the young couple behind her, in the second row, made room for her, but it was an uncomfortable position. Williams watched her; she was tired, and once she hunched her shoulders in an involuntary reaction to the cold. Williams, from his seat in the third row, tapped her arm, and she turned and looked up at him, a stranger and an elderly stranger at that.

"Wouldn't you like to sit up here? Support your back? We can make room for you," said Williams.

"Oh, no thanks. I'm all right, thank you." She smiled with her mouth only. Now she sat up straight and lit a cigarette, and there was exasperation in the forceful blowing out of smoke and in her stiff manner of sitting. Plainly she was annoyed that a stranger had noticed her pregnancy and tiredness, and she did not look at Williams again. She wanted no help from anyone. When the match was over and the winner and loser were photographed receiving their silver bowls she did not applaud.

"What's the matter, Nance?" said one of her young companions. "Just because your man lost?"

"Oh, shut up," she said. "And stop *saying* that. Let's get out of here."

"There's free booze," said one of the young men.

"Oh, all right," said the girl. "But let's not stay forever? I'm cold."

"Have a couple of scoops and it'll warm you up," said the young man.

The picture-taking over, the player who had been speaking *sotto voce* to Nancy crossed the court to the place where she had been sitting. "Hey, Joe, where's Nancy?" he said. "Isn't she staying? She go?"

"She's staying. Hard luck, by the way."

"No, he beat me. Listen, tell her to be sure and wait, will you? I have to take a shower, I stink. But I won't be more than ten or fifteen minutes. Will you tell her?"

"Okay, Rex. See you," said Joe.

"Be sure and tell her, Joe. Now don't let her go home without my seeing her. I'll be fifteen minutes at the most," he said, then, in a lower voice: "Is Bud here?"

Joe laughed. "Bud come to see you, especially when you had a chance of winning? Get *with* it, boy."

"Well, I wanted to be sure. I have to go back to New York on the seven o'clock train."

They were all young enough so that what was overheard by someone as old as Williams did not matter. He was fifty, and they were their own world.

"Well, Ned, shall we go have some of that free booze?" said Williams's host and companion.

"Sure," said Williams. The two men smiled.

"Aren't you glad we have all that behind us?" said Smith.

"Sometimes I am," said Williams. "Who is she?"

"I'm all prepared," said Smith. "Her name is Nancy Phillips, married to Bud Phillips. They live in Chestnut Hill. Her name *was* Nancy Standish. That ought to help you."

"*Oh*. That *does* help. The daughter of Bob Standish and Evie Jeffcott."

"Uh-huh."

"No wonder I was drawn to her, so to speak."

"I was terribly amused, you know," said Smith. "I thought God damn it, here is history repeating itself right before my very eyes."

"Is that what you thought?"

"That's what I thought. Don't you think she looks a lot like Evie?"

"Well now I do, but it never occurred to me before," said Williams. "And it isn't actually that she looks so much like Evie."

"No, not terribly much, but at least you're consistent."

"Yes, I guess you could say that. So is the girl, for that matter. Her mother didn't like me the first time she saw me, either."

"She made up for it," said Smith. "We go down this way."

"Why didn't she say hello to you? Where are her manners?"

"What manners? None of them have any manners any more. No manners, no style, no ambition. They're a bunch of self-centered little pigs."

"I wonder what we were?" said Williams.

"Self-centered little pigs, no doubt, but we damn well had our manners drilled into us. These little bastards blame our generation for the state of the world. I think they're taught that in school and college. So they hate us. Really hate us, Ned. I don't think there's a God damn one of them that ever stops to think that we weren't responsible for 1929. We were the victims of it. And World War Two, we get blamed for that. What the hell did we have to do with it? We went, that's all. We had to go, so we went. But these little pricks blame us for the whole damn shooting-match. They don't even know their history. Or Social Studies, as they call it. Jesus Christ! You're lucky you have no children."

"You make me think I am."

"Well, as you know, I have four, and after they're ten years old they start taking pot-shots, and by the time they're fifteen—oh, brother. 'Daddy, you just don't *know*.' That's their stock answer for everything. I just don't know about segregation, or about war. I have one snot-nose about to go in the Army and *he*'s telling *me* how awful war is. And if I *told* him about Guadal he'd accuse me of wallowing in it, so I've never told him. I've learned to keep my mouth shut, the only way to avoid having a scene. 'Daddy, you just don't *know*.' If I'd said that to my father I'd have been clouted over the head. And if one of my sisters had said it to my father, my mother would have taken good care of her. Actually they loved my father, in a way that my daughters have never loved me. They still think he was a great and wonderful man, and all he was was an honest, decent, strict father. The whole purpose of my existence is when I get through paying for their education, to come through with an Austin-Healey for graduation. As a matter of fact I couldn't have paid for their education without help from their various grandparents. Betty and I just get by, and you know how much I make. This booze is free, so drink it up, boy. Would you like to meet Nancy?"

"Is she like the others?"

"I think so, but you can find out for yourself. She pretended not to see me before, but we'll just go right up to her. Come on. Be brave."

The men pushed through to where Nancy Phillips was leaning against a table. "Hello there, Nancy."

"Oh, hello, Mr. Smith. Have you been here all the time?" She had a drink in her hand and she smiled agreeably enough.

"Sitting right behind you. I want you to meet a friend of your mother's. *And* father's. This is Mr. Williams, Mr. Ned Williams."

"Oh, hello, Mr. Williams. *You* were there, I saw *you*. At least—weren't you the one that . . . ?"

"I'm the one that."

"Did you ever sit on anything as uncomfortable as those benches? Mr. Smith, *can't* this club afford something more *comfortable*?"

"You better take that up with your father. He's on the board. Where was he today, by the way?"

"Oh, hunting, I guess. Saturday, this time of year. Are you over from New York, Mr. Williams?"

"Just for the day."

"Just to see the match?"

"More or less. Partly business with Mr. Smith. How's your mother?"

"Mummy's fine, or I guess she is. I haven't seen her for a couple of weeks. We live in Chestnut Hill, and Mummy and Daddy are still in Ardmore. Do you know Philadelphia, Mr. Williams?"

"I used to."

"Before your mother married your father, he means," said Smith.

"Oh, you were a *beau* of Mummy's? What was she like then?"

"I don't know that she was any different then from now. I saw her about a year ago. Nowadays I seem to see her and your father at weddings, for the most part."

"I meant as a—what did they call them—flapper? Was she a flapper, my mother?"

"I wouldn't think so, would you?" Williams asked Smith.

"Definitely not. But definitely," said Smith.

"Well, you, Mr. Williams. Were you a—playboy? I guess that would be the opposite of flapper."

"George? Was I?"

"I don't know why you say 'Was I?' As far as I know, you still are."

"Oh, are you, Mr. Williams?"

"You sound incredulous. No, I was never one of the outstanding playboys. As we used to say, I got around."

"Then how did you and Mummy get together, if Mr. Smith is right." She did not wait for an answer but said, largely to herself, "Still—Bud and I."

"Well of course we *didn't* get together or you'd be my daughter instead of Bob Standish's."

"I didn't necessarily mean that close together, Mr. Williams."

"Well, now the conversation is taking a decided turn for the better," said Smith.

"It's taken a turn, all right," said the girl. "So let's turn back."

"Any direction you say," said Williams.

Now, before any more could be said, they were joined by the tennis player, whose hair was wet. "Hello, Nance," he said.

"Hello, Rex. I'd like you to know Mr. Smith, and Mr. Williams. This is Rex Ivers, who played such spec*tac*ular tennis this afternoon. Spec*tac*ular."

"Mr. Smith. Mr. Williams. Oh, hello, Mr. Williams. I've met Mr. Williams."

"I thought you played extremely well," said Williams. "Your only trouble was that you missed the easy ones."

"Four straight. But he beat me. He played better."

"Oh, you're such a good, good sport, Rex," said Nancy.

"Well, what's wrong with that? Anyway, I'm not such a good, good sport. I wish I were."

"Yes you are, that's why you missed the easy ones, as Mr. Williams said. You were playing like a good sport instead of to win, and I consider that insulting to my opponent."

"*He* doesn't feel insulted. He got the hardware, and some of my cash."

"Oh, you actually bet on yourself?" said Nancy. "You had money going on this match?"

"Yes. We bet a hundred dollars apiece. I think you put the whammy on me. Every one of those easy shots I missed, I just happened to be facing in your direction."

"Oh, of course. And I waved my handkerchief to distract you."

"I didn't say that. I meant it as a compliment, what I did say. Where's Bud?"

"He sent his regrets," said the girl.

"I think we'll leave you two," said Smith.

"Say hello to your mother, and your father," said Williams.

"I will, thank you. Nice to've seen you," said the girl.

Smith and Williams rode the elevator in silence and went to the bar, seated themselves, ordered drinks. "Well, that was a happy thought," said Smith.

"Oh, I wanted to meet her."

"I didn't mean that. I was thinking about how she could have been your daughter."

"Oh, I see. Well, is this her first child?"

"It's no excuse. At this moment she's probably raking him over the coals, and he's so much in love with her that it's coming out of his eyes."

"That's very poetic."

"Entirely accidental. Tell me about Ivers. I didn't know you knew him."

"I don't. I just see him at the club and I guess I've met him there a few times. I was surprised he remembered me. Now *he* has good manners."

"Yes, but where does it get him in his own crowd? They not only don't appreciate good manners. Did you happen to notice during the match, he'd say something to her. Nice. And those others with her, they'd all look wise, as if they knew the whole story."

"I did notice that, yes. What's her husband like?"

"He's still in medical school, out at the University. I think he has another year to go."

"Bob Standish has plenty of money."

"Oh, the Phillipses are loaded too. No money problem there. The problem is going to be when she finds out what it's like to be the wife of a doctor. It's tough enough now, of course, while Bud's in medical school, but just wait till she finds out what the first few years are going to be like."

"She seems to be having a very hard time of it."

"For God's sake, why?"

"Oh, well there you've got me."

"Hell of an attractive mother, father's a nice guy, husband working his ass off trying to be something. Plenty of money. A nice young guy in love with her, obviously. And she's having a baby. I don't know what else a young girl could want."

"Is there any chance that this baby belongs to Ivers?"

"Oh, there's always that chance, but she didn't greet him like the father of her child. Is Ivers married, do you happen to know?"

"I happen to know he's not."

"And she's a good-looking little bitch, too. Add that to the rest of her complaints. Quite a shape, when her belly's flat."

"I could see that it would be."

"Ned?"

"What?"

"She *isn't* your daughter, by any chance?"

"Well, you know, George. She could be. Evie never said so, and I was hoping you wouldn't ask, but I was just figuring it out. She could be, mathematically."

"I sort of thought so. At least as a possibility."

"As you said, there was always that chance, but you'd think Evie would have told me."

"I wouldn't think anything of the kind."

"No, I guess not. Evie was a hard one to figure sometimes."

"Why didn't you and Evie get married?"

"Before she married Bob?"

"Yes."

"Because she wasn't in love with me."

"Oh, come."

"She wasn't. She said so."

"She gave you enough proof to the contrary."

"She didn't consider that proof of anything, except of course that she considered me safe to go to bed with. But her family were against it, and God knows I wasn't very reliable in those days, and Bob had been hanging around for years."

"But then after she married Bob?"

"Well—then she discovered she was in love with me. All right, I'll give it to you straight. She wanted to divorce Bob and I was the one that prevented it. Plus the fact that I was leaving for Quantico. It was just before Pearl. Maybe I was running away from marriage, I don't know. But that's why we didn't get married. Mathematically, this girl could be the result of the summer of '41. My daughter. George, I think she is."

"I think so too."

"Something. Even before I knew her name, who she was. I felt protective. You know, when I offered her a seat with us?"

"Sure, sure."

"And it was more than her resemblance to Evie. Maybe not more. Different from. Apart from. She didn't feel anything, though."

"Yes she did."

"Yes, I guess she did."

"Something bothered her. She looked at you, and maybe she saw something without any idea of what it was. Some resemblance to herself, maybe. Not only the color of your eyes, but the shape of them."

"Maybe that's what *I* saw."

"And maybe she did too. That can be very baffling, to see resemblances to yourself in your children. Elusive. And if you didn't know of the relationship, God knows how disturbing it might be. I imagine it must be especially true for girls, who spend a lot more time looking at themselves than we do. You didn't get any feeling that she resented you because you were on the make, did you?"

"No."

"Neither did I. She was annoyed, but that wasn't what annoyed her. Well, we've got it all figured out." Smith raised his glass. "Congratulations, Papa."

"Thank you."

"Now you're one of us. The rejected generation."

"Are we rejected, George? I'd hate to think that."

"Two hours ago you didn't give a damn."

"Two hours ago I certainly didn't. But I'll never be the same as I was two hours ago."

"No, you won't. Are you going to say anything to Evie?"

"I don't know. I don't know whether she'd tell me the truth."

"Do you need to have her tell you?"

"A little bit. Yes."

"Why don't you depend on your instinct, and to hell with what Evie says or doesn't say? Don't even ask her."

"Maybe I won't. I wish I could talk to the girl again."

"That can be arranged. My daughter sees her fairly frequently. That's comparatively easy."

"Before she has her baby?"

"Ned, nobody dies in childbirth any more, if that's worrying you."

"No, but it was cold up there today."

"Nobody dies of pneumonia, either."

"Well then what the hell *do* all these people die of?"

"Worry, so stop it," said Smith. "I don't want to rush you, Ned, but if you're counting on making the seven o'clock train . . ."

The seven o'clock to New York was a train that originated in Washington and it was late, with the result that the train crew wanted no time wasted at the Thirtieth Street station. Passengers were hurried off, passengers were hurried on, and the confusion was worse than usual. An Air Force second lieutenant with a flight kit and a guitar was blocked by passengers trying to board the train, and he in turn refused to budge for them. In the disorder the train was held up for six minutes, and the delay was fortunate for Rex Ivers, who came running down the steps, taking them two or three at a leap. He had a small suitcase and an old pigskin tennis bag of a vintage that had not been manufactured in more than twenty years. He stowed the luggage on the shelf at the end of the car, and considered where to sit. There were vacant seats, but most of them had coats or hats that belonged to passengers who were in the dining-car. "Taken? Taken? Taken?" said Ivers, walking down the aisle. "Hello, Mr. Williams? Is this taken?"

"Probably, but so's the one I'm sitting in," said Williams. "They can eat or they can sit, but they can't do both."

"There'll be a row," said Ivers.

"What if there is? I'm not budging. Have a seat till they come—and I'll bet they stay in the diner till Newark."

"All right. I'm with you," said Ivers. He seemed to be a little bit tight. His hair, now dry, fell down over his forehead. His club tie was crooked, the knot somewhere under the collar. And there was lipstick on his chin.

"I see someone saw you off, affectionately," said Williams.

"Why? Oh, have I got telltale traces?"

"On your chin."

Ivers moistened his handkerchief and rubbed the lipstick off. "All gone?"

"All gone," said Williams.

"Listen, go ahead and read your paper, sir. I don't want to bother you."

"Oh, that's all right. Light's not very good. But I may doze off."

"Yes, I might too."

"I should think you would."

"I had a couple of scoops. If I'd won I'd be high, but I lost, so the only effect is to make me sleepy."

"Have you got your ticket? Give it to me and I'll give it to the conductor."

"Sir, but you want to take a nap."

"After North Philadelphia. Push that gadget and the seat goes back. Get yourself a nap."

"Well—thanks very much. Just a nap's all I want." He handed his ticket to Williams, altered the angle of the seat, stretched out and was asleep in three minutes, heavily, deeply, helplessly, rather sadly asleep.

"Teeks for North Philadelphia. North Philadelphia teeks please," said the trainman.

Williams read his *Evening Bulletin*, saw that the sleeping young man at his right—according to this edition of the newspaper—was one of the finalists in the court tennis tournament. It was strange to come upon this item after the outcome had been decided, like having a look into the future with the certainty that what one saw would take place. Williams read the item again, then turned to the Evening Chat column, which contained society news. At this moment some people he knew in Wynnewood were getting ready to receive guests for dinner. Mr. and Mrs. John Arthur Kersley will entertain at dinner this evening in honor of their daughter Willela Kersley, whose engagement, etc. What if he knew the score of that dinner party, as he now knew the score of Ivers's tennis match? What if he could call up Jack Kersley and tell him for God's sake not to let John Jones sit next to Mary Brown, that before the night was over John Jones would say something to Mary Brown that would wreck their lives? What if he could call Mary Brown and tell her not to listen to anything John Jones said? And what if he had been able to speak to Rex Ivers and persuade him to default, so that he would not have gone to Philadelphia and seen Nancy. "My daughter."

"I beg your pardon?"

"Oh—I must have dozed off," said Williams.

Young Ivers grinned. "Like somebody hit you with a croquet mallet."

"Where are we?" said Williams. He looked out the window but could not identify landmarks.

"We just passed through New Brunswick," said Ivers.

"New Brunswick? How long have you been awake?"

"Oh, I guess I only slept about ten minutes. I woke up just after North Philadelphia. Here's your paper, sir, I borrowed it. Gave me a funny feeling to read about my match before it happened. You know, when this was printed, I was on equal terms with my worthy opponent. Now I'm second banana."

"Do you know Jack Kersley?" said Williams.

"Kersley? No, I don't think so. Should I?"

"No, I just happened to think of him. Lives in Philadelphia."

"I might have met him this week. I met a lot of guys during the tournament. Oh, I did meet an older man named Kersley. Has he got a daughter, Wilhelmina or something like that?"

"Yes he has."

"Then I did meet him. What made you mention him?"

"I don't really know," said Williams. "I guess I'm still in a bit of a fog."

"Why don't you go back to sleep?"

"No, no. A nap was all I wanted."

"You know, when you said Jack Kersley, that didn't register. But the daughter is a friend of a friend of mine. In fact, my girl. My girl is going to a dinner party at the Kersleys' tonight. The girl that saw me off at the station."

"Oh, you have a girl in Philadelphia?"

"Yes. Not the way that sounds, though. A girl in Philadelphia. A girl in Boston. A girl in Chicago."

"This is the real thing? The one and only, we used to say."

"Yes. Married, though."

"Have to watch out for that," said Williams.

"Telling *me*. Do you remember my father? Was killed in World War Two?"

"Sure, I knew him. A fine man."

"That's what everybody says, without fail. But I never knew him. I was three years old when he joined the Navy, and honestly I have no recollection of him except what I hear from my mother and his friends. And I couldn't possibly live up to his reputation. Not possibly. God, at school they had his name on a tablet and every time I got into trouble, sure as hell some master would take me for a walk and steer me in the direction of the memorial. You know. Illustrating the lecture. What I'm getting at is I guess I have some kind of a guilt complex because my father was this idol, and here I am, the original mixed-up kid. It's not something you go to the head-shrinker for, and yet I don't know any minister I'd feel like talking to. That's what it is, too. More of a religious problem."

"Ethical."

"Ethical, right. This girl would marry me. She wants to divorce her husband and marry me."

"Well, if you love her. And you say she's your girl."

"It isn't all that easy. The husband hates me, and he has good reason to. He knows I was there first, she told him. But he's—he's doing something constructive. He's doing something, a line of work, that takes up all his time and energy, and it's worthwhile work. If she left him, it wouldn't only be their marriage. Well, I don't think you know the people, so I'll tell you. The husband is studying to be a doctor and they say he's brilliant. Brilliant. But I know he's dependent on her. Not financially, but for moral support. She's dependent on me—for immoral support. Or was. I hadn't seen her till today, she turned up at the tennis match with her crowd. And she came with me to the station. God, she wants me to get a job in Philadelphia, and she'll get a divorce, and we'll get married, and the hell with her husband. There's a certain reason why she wants me to be in Philadelphia now. Sort of a crisis going on."

"Well, as I see it, Rex, the thing that's holding you back is this ethical problem. Your girl's husband and his career. But where does that leave her and the child?"

"The child? Do you know who it is?"

"I think I sat two rows behind your girl at the match. The crisis is she's having a baby, isn't it?"

"Jesus, yes. Then you know who the girl is."

"Yes, I know who the girl is."

"I know you were talking to her afterward but I didn't figure you'd guess anything. Well, sir, what would you do? As an unprejudiced observer."

"Well, I have an ethical problem, too. My ethical problem is whether to advise you one way or the other. As a matter of fact, Rex, my problem is really more difficult than yours."

"Yes, I suppose it is," said Ivers. "Why should you get into the act, eh? It isn't your responsibility." The young man chewed his lip thoughtfully. "Mr. Williams, I hope you don't think I go around blabbing stuff this way all the time."

"Of course I don't, Rex."

"Well, I *don't*. If you knew me better you'd know that. I don't know whether it was because I had a couple of drinks or what. I wish I could convince you of that."

"Don't let it bother you."

"The thing is, it does bother me. I hope everything I told you is in the strictest confidence."

"It will be."

"Have I got your word on that?"

"You have my word. I promise you I won't repeat any of this conversation to anybody."

"I wish you could forget everything I told you."

"That I can't promise."

The young man was still very uneasy. "You see, Mr. Williams, this girl's had everything she ever wanted."

"Except marriage to you."

"Yes, but it wouldn't work out now. It never will work out. She thinks she wants to be married to me, but it wouldn't last a year before she was discontented. And meanwhile she'd have broken up her marriage and possibly ruined her husband's career, and the kid wouldn't have a father. In other words, this is the time for somebody to make sense, and it's up to me to be the one."

"Probably."

"So—what I'm getting at, the importance of keeping this confidential. Nancy will get over this and stay with her husband, and in two years it'll all be a thing of the past."

"And you don't think you're being tough on her."

"No tougher on her than I am on myself. She's my girl, Mr. Williams. Make no mistake about that."

"Rex, I'm going to ask you a question you may not like."

"You're entitled to ask anything you please."

"What if this baby she's having is yours?"

"If it was, I think she would have told me."

"Would that have made a difference, to you?"

The boy—for now he looked about seventeen—shook his head. "No. It would make things tougher for me, but as long as she didn't tell Bud, her husband, she and the baby are better off."

"Thank you."

"Why do you say that?"

"Oh—thank you for trusting me with your confidences."

"Hell, I ought to be thanking you. And I do. You know, her father and mother, they're your generation, but they don't seem to know what it's all about. I could never talk to them the way I've talked to you. Of course that may be Philadelphia."

"It may be Philadelphia."

"Nancy does a big production of laughing at the whole thing, but you'd never get her out of Philadelphia."

"I guess not. Well, here's Newark. I can always tell Newark, can't you?"

"Yes, you can always tell Newark."

In the Silence

THE TWO friends were having coffee together after one of their Saturday lunches. As happens in friendships, they could be silent without awkwardness, and during one such silence Charles Ellis casually picked up a small book that was lying on the coffee table. It was a club roster, bound in two colors and with the club insigne stamped on the front cover, and below the symbol a slip of paper was glued on, which in typescript read: "Not to be removed from Lounge." Ellis leafed through the book and was about to put it down when a name caught his eye. "Know anybody named Holderman?"

"No, I don't think so," said James Malloy.

"Joseph W. Holderman 2d, Eagle Summit, P-A. Joined here in 1916. I've seen that name for years and I was always going to ask you about it. If anybody'd know that name, you would."

"I do know it."

"Thought you said you didn't," said Ellis.

"Holderman alone didn't mean anything, but when you gave it the full treatment, I not only know the name. I know the man. Not only know the man, I've been to his house at Eagle Summit. What would you like to know about him?"

"Well, the only reason I'm curious about him is I've seen his name in this book all these years, and I wondered about him. I've never seen him, I've never heard anyone speak of him, and why does a man that lives in a place called Eagle Summit, Pennsylvania, keep up his membership in this club? He's been a member for forty-five years, so he isn't any chicken. Nowadays you hear men like that say they're over-clubbed. Oh, wait a second, he's a life member. Doesn't have to pay dues any more."

"I think Holderman would pay dues anyway."

"What for? So that he can wear the club tie?"

"You may think you're kidding, but that's one of the reasons."

"Sounds pretty stuffy to me," said Ellis.

"He's anything but," said Malloy. "He's no chicken, as you say. He must be in his middle seventies, but I'd like to see him again before he dies. Or *I* do. Have I aroused any more curiosity about Joseph W. Holderman 2d, of Eagle Summit, Pennsylvania?"

"Some. Give."

"I'd love to," said Malloy. . . .

First I must tell you a little about Eagle Summit (said Malloy), where it is and what kind of country it's in. There's almost no such place as Eagle Summit, it's so small. It is, or was, a post office, which was also the general store. A Protestant church, very likely Presbyterian in that part of the country. A garage that was once a blacksmith shop. Mind you, I'm talking about the way it was when I saw it in 1927. There were some private houses, a doctor lived in one and had his office there. There was a little building that was a sort of township hall, with a couple of cells in the back. The village wasn't big enough to have a bank or a movie theater. It wasn't even on the railroad, not even a branch or a spur. It was in the mountains in North Central Pennsylvania, and the nearest town of any considerable size was Williamsport. Eagle Summit was hardly more than a clearing in the woods, and the people that lived there dreaded a forest fire more than anything else in the world. The village could have been completely wiped out without anyone out-side's knowing the difference, at least for a week or so. There were only three telephones in the village itself. The town hall's, the general store's, and the doctor's, and one other about two miles away, at the Holdermans' house, but I don't want to get ahead of myself. I want to give you some more geography, et cetera.

The state highway didn't run through Eagle Summit. The village was on a county road, which was originally, I imagine, scratched out by prison labor, if they could get that many prisoners, or more likely the road was built by the loggers. Timber was the only industry in that part of the State. Thou-sands and thousands of acres of virgin timber, but so hard to get to it and to move it away that a great deal of it was left unspoiled. It was wild country. Two hundred yards away from Eagle Summit and you were a thousand years in the past, back before Columbus discovered the country. It's doubtful if there were even Indians until the Seventeenth Century, and in two minutes by car you could be transported to a time when there was only bear and elk and deer, panther, eagles, wildcats. And I assure you that if you had to spend the night on the road, if your car broke down, you'd know they were still there. If you stopped to take a leak and turned off your motor the thing that struck you most forcibly was the silence, the enormous silence. If there was no wind—that is, if you were between Eagle Summit and the actual top of the mountain—the silence would be so absolute, such a new experience, that it became spooky, and it would be actually reassuring to hear some animal cry, some bird. And then your reassurance would vanish, because almost immediately you'd get the feeling that you were being watched. And no doubt you were. I'm told that that happens when you're in the jungle. It happened to me during the war, in the Admiralties, but then there was a reason because we'd been told that there were Japs hiding out, sniping at the Seabees. At Eagle Summit it was different. It was a civilized man, me, in a place where I didn't belong. A trespasser. And I knew I was a trespasser and felt guilty about it. This place belonged to the animals and they were sending me thought waves, warnings to get the hell out of there or take the consequences. Boy, the back of my neck was awfully cold. Anyway, I guess that's enough geography. Now for the human element.

As you know, I didn't go to Groton. I went to a school in Niagara Falls that was older than Groton but considerably less fashionable. I probably never would have heard of the school if my father hadn't gone there. It's no longer in existence. But I went there for a year. It was an all-day train ride, or a sleeper jump, and I preferred the day train because I was young and fascinated by any travel. I got a kick out of taking the train to Reading, thirty-five miles away, and any trip longer than that was sheer delight, not to be wasted in sleep. In those days I never took a nap on a train. Too much to see. Well, in 1924, I was on my way back to school after Easter vacation. I was rich, must have had twenty or thirty dollars in my kick, either from bridge or a crap game, and when I changed trains and got on the Buffalo Day Express, as it was called, I bought a Pullman chair. Two of my classmates from Baltimore were on the train, but riding day coach. The hell with them, I said. I'll ride the plush. Splurge. I can see my classmates any time.

So I sat in the Pullman, really luxurious they were then,

too. Beautiful woodwork. Mother-of-pearl in the paneling. Big chairs. A brass spitoon. A polite porter who knew his job and had plenty of self-respect, instead of these characters that hate their jobs and hate you. Comfort and ease, and always the *people* that got on and off along the way. Some of them knew each other, some of them didn't.

At a place called Carter City, a station just beyond Williamsport, I looked out the car window to see who was getting on, and I noticed three people. Obviously a man and his wife saying goodbye to a third man. I'll come back to the third man in a minute, but first the man and his wife. This man was about six feet tall. He was in his middle thirties, and wearing a Norfolk suit with knickerbockers, thick-soled shoes with fringed tongues, and a cap made of the same material as the suit. A few years earlier it was collegiate to wear a Norfolk suit, but this wasn't a collegiate-type suit. This was English Country. It had four buttons, like ours, but the top button was left unbuttoned, which we never did. His wife was wearing a tweed suit, too, and a brown felt hat. She was quite short, and she and her husband were laughing very heartily at something their friend was saying. I naturally couldn't hear them through the double windows of the Pullman. Then the conductor spoke to them—they obviously knew him and he them—and the third man kissed the woman and shook hands with the man, picked up his bag, which was a beautifully banged-up but saddle-soaped kit bag, and another piece of luggage that I thought contained fishing tackle. He got on the Pullman-car platform as the train started to move, and I heard him calling out a final remark in French. I couldn't understand what he said, but there was no mistaking it for anything but French. He was holding the door open, and I heard the woman call out something in French, and then she and her husband turned and headed for their car. The car was a grey Pierce-Arrow, a Series 30, or about a 1921 or '22 model. It was a chummy roadster. That is, it seated four, with divided front seats. Also called a clover-leaf, if you recall. But it was a hell of an automobile. It had no trouble going eighty or eighty-five, and this particular job had Westinghouse shock absorbers. That model was a favorite with people who wanted a sports car but wanted the weight and size of the Pierce. There were two of them in my home town, and oddly enough one of them was painted grey, too.

The whole picture fascinated me, of course. The people, the car, and the *place*. You wouldn't have given them a second look on Long Island or the Philadelphia Main Line, but this was in the woods of North Central Pennsylvania. There were plenty of rich people in Williamsport, but this wasn't Williamsport. This was Carter City. Well, as it happened, not entirely by accident, I had lunch with the third man. He was a really big fellow. Six-four, two-thirty, and he had a beard. Also he needed a haircut, and I noticed paint stains on his back hair. I'll tell you about him some other time, but he turned out to be Rollo Fenner, the painter. The name struck a vague gong, not that I knew anything about painters, but as we made conversation in the dining-car he got on the subject of football and then I remembered. He'd been All-American at Harvard. Was with the Morgan-Harjes Unit during the war, and lived in Paris. I just didn't have the nerve to ask him what he was doing in Pennsylvania. We got along fine and he gave me his card, told me to look him up in Paris, and he was such delightful company that he really made my trip.

We now perforce skip a year or two. Or three. I got out of school and went to work on a newspaper, working my tail off, loving it, and practically unaware that I was doing grown men's work for twelve dollars a week. The cheap son of a bitch that I worked for—oh, well. Anyway, I had a car, a little four-cylinder Buick roadster, and because of it I got some assignments that you could only cover if you had a car, and on a staff of two women and five men, I was the only one that could drive. So one day the editor called me to his private office, which of course he called a sanctum sanctorum, without knowing a God damn word of Latin, and he said, "James, I have a strange hunch. Read this." He showed me a piece of U. P. copy that had come in over the Morse wire. A flyer had tried to make an emergency landing on a country road near a place called Eagle Summit. Plane caught fire, and the pilot was burned to death, before he'd had a chance to get out of the plane. "Do you know who that might be? It might be Lindbergh! The Lone Eagle!" I thought he was crazy, but he'd convinced himself that Lindbergh, who *was* flying all over the country, getting receptions, was the man that was killed. I think Lindbergh was overdue some place, too. "How long would it take you to drive up there in your car?" Well, four or five hours, I told him. So he gave me some money, swore me to secrecy, and off I went, in quest of the biggest story of the century. Naturally I was to go have a look at the dead pilot, then telephone back if I thought it was Lucky Lindy, and Gibbsville would scoop the world. Or Bob Hooker would have a scoop, not I.

But I was young, so off I went. I knew the roads for the first hundred and fifty miles, and I was convinced that all I had to do was keep the throttle down on the floor-board and I'd have a Pulitzer prize. But after I got off the state highways I began to run into trouble, and the closer I got to Eagle Summit, the more trouble I had. The Buick was developing a tappet knock, or what I hoped was a tappet knock. I much preferred a tappet knock to what I really knew it was—a loose connecting rod. I knew it would be getting dark soon, and I'd seen enough of the territory to know I didn't want to spend the night on the road. Not that road.

But the little Buick made it to Eagle Summit and I went to the town hall and introduced myself to a man there, the township supervisor. I said I was from one of the Williams-port papers and asked him if I could have a look at the pilot. "What's left of him," he said. "I got him back there in a cell." So he took me back and one look convinced me that I wasn't going to win the Pulitzer prize. Whoever he was, the poor guy, he wasn't Slim Lindbergh or Slim Anybody. His face was all burnt away, but the legs and torso belonged to a short stout man. Incidentally, the town supervisor was sore as hell at the dead man. Apparently they all hated airplanes and pilots. "He could of started a fire that would destroy this town," he said. Well, I didn't argue with him. I thanked him and got in my car, but it wouldn't start. I pushed it to the garage and asked the proprietor what he thought. He had a look and confirmed my suspicions. Connecting rod. Could he fix it? He'd have to call up and see where he could get one. It wasn't loose. It was broken. So he called up a Buick dealer in Williamsport and they had a spare, but he couldn't leave right away. I asked him where I could spend the night, and he said I could drive to Williamsport with him and go to a hotel, or I could ask the supervisor to let me sleep in a cell. There were no hotel accommodations in Eagle Summit, obviously, and obviously he didn't give a damn where I slept. While I was thinking it over I heard a Klaxon outside, and I looked and saw a grey Pierce-Arrow, pulled up at the gas tank. At first it was just another grey Pierce, but then the driver got out and it was the man I'd seen at the Carter City station three years earlier. He was even wearing the same Norfolk jacket, but instead of knickers, slacks. He came in and said hello to the garage man, and nodded to me. "Fill it up, will you please, Ed? And fix the puncture in the rear wheel spare." Ed said he wouldn't be able to fix the puncture because he had to drive to Williamsport. And so forth and so on. Leave the spare, he'd fix it the next day. Joe. He called the man Joe.

Well, I was a fresh kid. Twenty-two, and the whole scene at the railroad station came back to me, so I said to Joe, "How is Rollo Fenner?" And of course that baffled him. He tried to pretend that he really recognized me, but all the time racking his brains. Where had he met this kid? Finally it was too much for him and he said so. "I'm sorry," he said, "but I can't remember where I met you." So then I told him the whole story, and he was fascinated that I'd remember. Then I told him why I was in Eagle Summit, and he talked about the newspaper business, about which he knew absolutely nothing, and then about my car. And I told him the truth, by the way. That I was from Gibbsville, not Williamsport. The only reason I'd lied to the supervisor was that I'd learned from experience that if there's anything people dislike more than a newspaper reporter, it's a newspaper reporter from some far-off place. So Mr. Joe Holderman asked me if I knew some friends of his in Gibbsville, and I did, and gave him some details that proved that I knew them pretty well. This conversation took place while Ed was filling Holderman's gas tank, and taking off the spare tire from the carrier in the rear. He didn't have side mounts on that car, unlike most Pierces of that vintage. Anyway, he said it was ridiculous for me to go to a hotel in Williamsport or sleep in the lock-up when he had plenty of room at his house, and after a polite but not very firm protest I accepted his kind invitation. I could tell that Ed, the garage man, thought Holderman was out of his mind. But I could also see that what Ed thought made not the slightest bit of difference to Holderman, and off we went.

He lived about two miles away, in the woods, and the roads were frightful, but when you got there—what a house! It was a sort of super-shooting lodge, is the only way I can describe it. It was in a clearing, but not so much of a clearing that it wasn't protected by the trees when the wind was strong, or in a blizzard. It was a log cabin, luxury style. Two stories and a garage in the cellar, and a porch that went around three sides, and after we put the car away he showed me the view from the porch. From one side of the porch you could see, oh, probably twenty miles that looked like solid timber-land. And from all three sides you saw nothing but acres of forest. It took my breath away, literally, because I just stood and looked without saying a word. It was still daylight, and a wisp of smoke in the distance he said was Williamsport, about twenty miles away as the crow flies, but longer by road. He had a big telescope on the porch, and he gave me a look through it and I could see the fire wardens' towers on the tops of the other mountains. "I'm a sort of honorary fire warden," he said. "Let me show you something." He went to an instrument on a tripod that turned out to be a heliograph. He began working it. "My wife and I have learned the Morse Code. She's faster than I am. I'm signaling to that tower down there to the southeast. He hasn't seen me yet. There! Now he's answering. I'm telling him I just got home. I always tell him when I leave, just so that he can keep an eye on our house. It gives him something to do to break the monotony. He has field glasses but they're not as powerful as my telescope. When I get a new one I'm going to give him this one."

"Have you got a telephone here?"

"Yes, we have, and so has he. But there are times when you can't depend on it. We get some pretty terrific electrical storms in the mountains, and in the winter—you can imagine the snow."

"And at night, I suppose you can communicate with a flashlight?" I said.

"Correct. I have a little flashlight in the shape of a 25-automatic, and that's all I need. Pull the trigger for dots and dashes."

"He can see that that far away?"

"Oh, my yes. When there's no moon I can see him light his pipe. Just the light from his match. He's only about five-and-a-half miles away. Of course I can't always get him right away. He doesn't sit in the dark all night. He'd go out of his mind. And unfortunately for us, he's only there during the fire season. I mean unfortunately because he varies our routine, too. We like to talk to him."

"Do you know him?"

"Yes, we've had him here for dinner several times. Him and his wife. But frankly he's better company at this distance, and so is she. He talks better by heliograph. In fact, when he's been here he's been very economical with his words, and she's not a very stimulating conversationalist."

"Who, me?"

We turned, and there was Holderman's wife, pretty and short as I remembered her, although not quite so short, with no gigantic Rollo Fenner to make a contrast. Holderman introduced me and explained that I was spending the night and so forth, and she volunteered to show me around the house.

It was what you might imagine. Three rooms and kitchen on the first floor. The middle room was two stories high, with exposed rafters and an open stairway. A magnificent big open fireplace, and on the floor were bear rugs with heads and teeth. All around on the walls were mounted elk and deer and wildcat heads and some stuffed trout and pike. The trophies you'd expect from that part of the world, and a tiger head and a water buffalo and some others from I guess India and Africa. Big tables. Navajo rugs. Big chairs and sofas. In a room on one side of the center room Holderman had a desk and filing case and typewriter and small adding machine, obviously his office. Then on the *other* side of the big room, suddenly you're in an elegant drawing-room. Gilt furniture, light blue carpet. Small paintings, including two by Rollo Fenner. In other words, a completely feminine room. Jade ash trays, for instance. A Chippendale closet filled with bits of china. You couldn't imagine a quicker or more complete escape from the rustic, masculine atmosphere of the center room. But you didn't have to imagine it, because on the second floor, one of the bedrooms was just as feminine, with a canopied bed and a chaise-longue. I almost had to laugh, but I'm glad I didn't. There were three other bedrooms, and they were the rustic type that you'd expect, heavy furniture, sporting prints, trophies. The feminine bedroom was next door to a bedroom that you could easily tell was where they slept most of the time, but there was no connecting door between those two rooms. In her room there was one bed, not quite a double bed. In the other room, twin beds. On the other side of the second story, connected by a balcony, or a gallery, were two guest rooms, and I was given one of those. Between those two rooms there was a connecting bath, but the bathroom on the other side of the house was in the rear. It seemed like an odd arrangement to me. Her personal bedroom had the best view, south and east. It was in the front of the house, whereas their joint bedroom had only a one-elevation view. Her room was an escape from an escape, but there again I'm getting ahead of myself.

All in all, it seemed to me to be the most comfortable house I'd ever been in. Comfort, informality, and easy luxury. Because the luxury was there, too, don't think it wasn't. The center room downstairs, for instance. Polished hardwood floor. You wouldn't walk across *it* in hob-nailed boots. And the furniture didn't come from the army-and-navy store. When I said super-hunting lodge, that's what I meant, and I'm telling you so much about the house because I spent two nights there and nearly two days, and all I learned about the Holdermans was during that time.

They had a couple. I have to invent names for the couple, because I don't remember their right names. Let's say Jack and Carolyn. They had their own cabin, back of the main house and in a different clearing. They were older than the Holdermans. Jack was about fifty. Carolyn, probably in her late forties. Natives, but Joe Holderman and his wife, Violet, had taught them the little niceties. Jack was a woodsman, but he functioned as a butler, at least in some things. He wore a lumberjack shirt and no coat, but for instance he unpacked my small bag and put my things away, and he mixed and served the cocktails before dinner. But he didn't serve dinner. His wife did the cooking—or maybe he did. I don't know. But she waited on table. Not in maid's uniform, but she knew how to serve. I have to jump around a little bit. For instance, Jack ran my tub before dinner, and while I was taking my bath he pressed my suit, brushed my shoes. And later in the evening, my bed was turned down and one of Holderman's bathrobes was lying on the bed and a pair of bedroom slippers. All done by Jack and Carolyn. Dinner, by the way, was served in the big center room. There was no dining-room as such.

I was pooped. I called up my boss and told him there was no story and that I had engine trouble and wouldn't be back till late the next day. All he said was that I'd have to make it up by working some Sunday. Hell, I worked nearly every Sunday anyway. So after dinner—oh, about nine-thirty or so—Holderman suggested that I go to bed. Had a hard time keeping my eyes open. The long trip, the mountain air, cocktails and a big meal. So I went to bed and slept like an innocent child for about four hours. Then I awoke completely refreshed, turned on the light, and looked around for something to read. I could hear a big grandfather's clock strike the half hours, and I decided to go downstairs and get a magazine. They had everything. *Vanity Fair*, *The New Yorker*, *Collier's*, *Life*, *Scribner's*, *Spur*, *The Field*, *Country Life*, *Punch*. And the latest issues, at that. So I put on Holderman's bathrobe and slippers and had no trouble finding my way, because there was a light burning in the big room. Then I noticed that a light was coming from Holderman's office, although the door was closed, and on the way downstairs I heard his typewriter. I felt rather sneaky, so when I'd chosen a magazine I knocked on his door, the office door. He opened it. He was wearing pajamas and a bathrobe, and he had a pipe in his hand. I said I didn't want him to think he was imagining things, and showed him the magazine. "Oh, I heard every sound you made," he said. "Come in and have a chat, if you like." He had a Thermos of coffee and a couple of sandwiches wrapped in waxed paper. He offered me coffee, but I didn't want to get too wide awake, but I sat down and had a cigarette. "This is when I do my writing," he said. "I'm writing a history of the Holderman family, because I'm the last of my line and when I die, we disappear. We weren't very distinguished," he said, "but we did open up a lot of the country around here. I've been at it ever since my wife and I were told we couldn't have children." Naturally he didn't dwell on that, and in fact I was a little surprised that he even mentioned their inability to produce. But he gave me a few more facts, family stuff that I don't remember, but I remember what he told me about himself. He'd gone to school at Andover and that was where he'd met Rollo Fenner, and on a visit to Fenner's house in Maine he'd met Violet Fenner, Rollo's sister. He went to Cornell, but quit college to join the Morgan-Harjes Unit when Fenner did. Then he joined the American army, came home after the war, and married Violet Fenner.

Well, I began to wonder why he was lying to me, and such stupid, insane lying. He was then at least forty years old. And if he'd quit college in 1916, say at the age of twenty, he'd still only be thirty-one. But he was every bit of forty and possibly a year or two older. And yet he was telling me all this with a straight face, to no purpose as far as I could see except that he was off his rocker. And yet he seemed normal, rational, certainly well behaved. He was a polite and considerate host, and at dinner he and his wife had been conventional to the point of dullness. The only out-of-the-ordinary thing I'd noticed at all was her extra-feminine drawing-room and bedroom. And that wasn't too extraordinary. An attractive woman like that, buried in the Northern Pennsylvania woods, it would have been more remarkable if she hadn't wanted some feminine touches, some refuge from this shooting-lodge atmosphere. But I began to wonder what I'd got myself into, and frankly wished that I could get the hell out. But I was stuck, at least till morning, till I could get a ride to Williamsport.

Now this was no wild man. Everything he said was told in the belief that it would be accepted as unquestioned fact. No striving to convince me. And after about a half an hour he very politely suggested that I go back to bed and apologized for boring me with family reminiscence, et cetera. And he never had the least suspicion that I was questioning any of his statements. Nevertheless he had told me some absolutely incredible lies, and to tell you the truth, when I went up to my room, I locked the door.

Naturally I didn't go to sleep for several hours. I put out my light, and then I could look out the window and see that the light was still on in his office, and it stayed on for a couple of hours. I guess I got back to sleep sometime between four and five o'clock, and once I thought I heard people talking, but I couldn't be sure. I slept till about seven-thirty and was awakened by the grey Pierce leaving the property, with Holderman at the wheel. No more sleep for me, so I went downstairs and Carolyn was around, dusting furniture or whatever, and I ordered my breakfast. Then Mrs. Holderman, Violet, showed up. Asked me how I'd slept and so on, and said she was afraid she had bad news for me, although not for her and her husband. She said Ed had called, the garage owner, and he hadn't been able to go pick up the spare part for my car, but would do so that morning. He guessed my car might be ready late that day. So I was stuck with the Holdermans, one of them at least a congenial liar, and the other, Violet, I wasn't sure what. She had a cup of coffee and a cigarette with me, and in the most offhand way she said, "Did you and Joe have a nice chat last night?"

"Yes," I said. "He told me about the family history he's working on."

"Yes, he's been at that a long time," she said. "Sometimes I wish he wouldn't work so hard on it. But he wants to get it all down on paper. When he was in the war he saw so many men die that he developed a fatalistic attitude. The impermanence, you know. Impermanence of life. Don't count on any tomorrow."

"I guess that affected a lot of men's thinking," I said.

"Yes, and especially those that were wounded. My husband was very badly wounded at Belleau Wood," she said.

"In the Marine Corps?" I said.

"Yes. His being alive at all is a miracle, and he's had two operations since the war and is facing another. For two years after the war he was stone deaf," she said. "He hears perfectly well," she said, "but they want to operate again to correct a constant ringing noise. He has a hard time sleeping."

I said, "I hadn't realized he was in the Marines."

"Yes," she said. "He was so pleased to get in. My brother, Rollo, was quite a well-known football player at Harvard, and then he went to live in Paris to study painting, and when the war came Rollo joined the ambulance corps. Came through the war unscathed. Joe had tried out for football at Cornell, but was too light or anyway didn't do very well, and Rollo used to tease him about it. So Joe had something to crow about when he got the Distinguished Service Cross—but at what a price! I don't mean to imply that there's any hostility between them," she said. "If they were real brothers they couldn't be closer than they are." She said her brother visited them whenever he came back to the States, and the two boys, she called them, practically ignored her when Rollo was here. They'd roomed together all through Andover and had gone on a big-game hunting expedition in India the year before she married Joe. She pointed to a tiger head and skin and said that Rollo had shot it. Given it to them as a wedding present, and then gave up hunting. Joe hadn't done any hunting either, since the war. She said I might have noticed something missing in a house like theirs, and I said I couldn't think of a thing that was missing, and she said, "Well, wouldn't you expect to see a gun closet?" And it was true, there were no firearms of any kind visible. "Joe won't have them around," she said. Jack had a rifle and shotguns, but he kept them back in his own cabin.

I relaxed a bit after my conversation with Violet and I got curious about how they spent their days. Also, to be completely honest about it, although she was about forty, which was a very advanced age for me at the time, she looked very inviting in a sweater and skirt and a little pearl necklace. And as the kids say nowadays, she was sending me a message, or so I believed. Let's say the air was heavy with sex, and I wasn't sure whether she knew it or not. I would have been embarrassed to admit to any of my contemporaries that a woman of forty could make me horny, but she did. But the fact that she *was* forty kept me from making a pass at her, although I had several opportunities during the day. I had just enough doubt about what I was feeling, or suspecting, so that I was still a little afraid that if I did make an actual pass, she'd be horrified—or amused. So for the rest of the day I was in a very confused state, hoping for an opportunity to be alone with her, and then when I was alone with her, several times, I couldn't quite carry out my evil intentions. The first move had to come from her.

Well, Holderman came back from Eagle Summit, with the mail and some parcel post, and a report on my car. As to the car, he'd simply *ordered* the garage man to close up and drive to Williamsport. And he could *do* that. He didn't say so, but I inferred that he had money in the garage. But the stuff he

brought back from the Eagle Summit post office was interesting. I didn't get to see any of the letters, of course, but he
and Violet opened the packages in my presence. For her, some
special kind of expensive soap that I forget the name of but
I'd heard my aunt speak of it. It was made in France. In his
package, two pipes. He'd sent them away to have new bits put
in the bowls. I could see that Holderman and his wife got real
pleasure out of their parcel post. Like kids. And he explained
it. He said, "We live up here in the backwoods, but we don't
lose touch with the world. We get all the latest magazines, and
we're always sending away for things, little things." And he told
me that he kept up his membership in a New York club—this
one, without a doubt—although he hadn't been inside the
place more than twice since the war, and didn't know when
he'd use it again. And every four or five years he'd order a
new suit, give an old one to Jack, although the old one hadn't
been worn very much, and Jack would give the suit to his son,
who was in college somewhere, probably the only boy in the
school wearing a hundred-and-fifty-dollar suit. Holderman was
getting very close to raising the question why he or they chose
to live in the woods, and she was quick enough to anticipate
it and she changed the subject. I should mention the fact that
nothing he said or did would have aroused the least suspicion
as to his being a healthy, normal middle-aged man. Having
been alerted to it by her, I could see that he let his hair grow
in a strange way around his ear, to cover a bald spot that I
assumed was where he'd been operated on. But as far as his
conversation and behavior were concerned, he was perfectly
all right.

They had two people coming for lunch, a state senator and
his wife, who arrived in a big Cunningham phaeton driven by a
chauffeur. The wife was related to Holderman, and the senator
was just a dull politician who didn't contribute anything and
didn't try to hide the fact that he considered the visit a waste of
his valuable time. He knew my boss. All those guys knew each
other, the subsidized newspaper editors and the politicians
that were stooging for big industries in the legislature. They
were all grafters in one form or another. They'd all sold out
years ago, and they all had big cars and houses in the country
or Atlantic City, and I never knew a one of them that didn't

overestimate his influence. As long as they voted right they were in, but without the money from the big industries they couldn't have run for dogcatcher. Holderman was rich, but I don't believe he was the big stockholder in any single company of any size. When the senator and his wife left, Holderman was rather apologetic to me. He said his cousin was good company, but she always insisted on bringing her husband. Actually the senator's wife was a rather ordinary woman but at least she'd prattled away during lunch, and she seemed to amuse Violet Holderman. Violet said, "We do our entertaining, such as it is, between Easter and Thanksgiving. After that we can always expect snow, and people are afraid of being marooned up here." So once or twice a week they'd have friends for lunch, but very seldom for dinner.

In the afternoon, after the statesman and wife departed, Holderman and I went for a hike up to the top of the mountain. I was in pretty good shape from tennis and golf, and I lived in a hilly town, but I couldn't keep up with him. On the very top of the mountain he'd put up a sort of shelter. It was open on all four sides, but offered protection from the rain if the rain came straight down. He explained that it was actually a shelter from the rain and the sun. I hadn't thought of the sun. There were no chairs. Only benches, and I sat down to get my breath, and he was quite pleased that a young squirt half his age was winded and he was not. "You see, I'm used to the altitude and you're not," he said. "We're almost three thousand feet above sea level here." Not a great height, but enough to make a difference if you weren't used to it, he said. The view there was of course better than from his house, and he entertained me with a geographical and historical lecture. It was mostly all new to me, and he told it well.

We went back to the house and Violet was waiting for us. That is, she had tea for us and she liked breaking out the best stuff. Holderman commented on it. He said I ought to be complimented, and I was, although I had no way of knowing that she didn't use the silver tea service every afternoon. It would have been in character for her, or them, to use the silver set regardless of guests or no guests. There was a great deal of elegance to the way they lived, notwithstanding the tweeds and lumberjack shirts and the atmosphere of roughing it in the woods. They *weren't* roughing it in the woods. I caught on to the fact that what they were doing was living like the rich on the North Shore, or maybe more like Aiken, although I've never been to Aiken. But with the difference that they didn't belong to any colony, like Aiken people or Westbury people. Then I realized, of course, that the big difference was really the isolation from people. They had people in for meals, but they didn't say anything about going out. No mention was made of going to other people's houses. And then I began to see, with what I'd already found out, that they lived the way they wanted to live because it was the way they *had* to live.

I wasn't finding out much about how they spent their days, what they did with their time, and then within two or three minutes I got some enlightenment on that subject. Holderman finished his tea and said he thought he'd have a nap, and he left us. She said to me, "I'm so glad when he does that. Sleep is *so* important." Then she told me, just as though I'd asked her a direct question, that they never planned anything far ahead, and never had people in more than twice a week. In that way, with such an open schedule, he could go take a nap whenever he felt like it. So that was how they spent their days, waiting for sleep to overtake him. I asked her, "What do you do, Mrs. Holderman?" "What do I do?" she said. "Well, I sew. I do needlepoint." She was teaching Carolyn needlepoint. She'd tried painting, but had given it up because she'd felt that all the talent in that direction had gone to her brother. Very discouraging to look at some of the things her brother had dashed off when he visited them, and she had to work so hard to no avail. She took me to the drawing-room and had me take another look at her brother's paintings, and I dutifully admired them, although actually I was more interested in nature's handiwork—her figure. And ready for the first sign of an invitation from her. But no sign was given. However, the cosmic urge, as we used to call it, was somewhere in her thoughts, in the back of her mind. We went back to the big room and she asked me all about my marital status or engagement status. Did I have a girl? Did I have a lot of girls? Were the girls as wild as older people said they were, or was that exaggerated? Girls had so much more freedom these days, et cetera. The people who'd been there for lunch that day had a daughter that was causing them all sorts of trouble. Sent home from Wellesley, et cetera. Violet said she was glad she didn't have to bring up a daughter in 1927, and that, of course, brought us right back to the house in the woods.

A young newspaper reporter sees so much in the first few years that he begins to think he's seen it all. That makes for a very unattractive wise-guy attitude, what I call unearned cynicism. After you've lived a good many years I don't see how you can be anything but cynical, since all any of us have a right to expect is an even break, and not many get that. But I thought I knew it all, and I didn't. It took me many more years to realize that a reporter covering general news lives an abnormal life, in that he sees people every day at the highest or lowest point of their lives. Day after day after day, people in trouble with the law, having accidents, losing control of themselves—or experiencing great successes. In one month's time a district man would see enough crime and horror and selfishness to last most people the rest of their lives. I can remember a young reporter telling me, when I first went to New York, that when you've seen one electrocution you've seen them all. Well, at that stage of my career I probably would have said the same thing, if I'd thought of it and had seen any electrocutions. God knows I'd seen plenty of nasty things. But I was much too young and comparatively inexperienced to be so omniscient about the Holdermans. At about five-thirty that afternoon, after Violet and I had had our little chat, I was ready to be on my way, quite convinced that I had them ticketed. They'd been interesting enough. Unusual. A war casualty and his reasonably attractive wife, holed up in the woods in an atmosphere of quiet luxury. But they'd become what they call in the newspaper business a one-day story, and I was ready to move on.

From this distance I can be perfectly honest and admit that I was still a little bit hoping she'd make a play for me. I'd never necked or laid a woman quite as old as forty, but there was one in her thirties that used to call me up when her husband was out of town. I don't know why she counted on my keeping my mouth shut. Twenty-two-year-old boys do a lot of boasting. But anyway, Violet was *there*, and *I* was there, and we had a whole evening ahead of us, possibly just the two of us. And she was radiating sex.

Well, she went and had a bath before dinner and so did I, and when I came downstairs she said Holderman was still asleep and we'd eat without him. We did, and after dinner we listened to the radio. They had a special high-powered set, marvelous reception up there in the mountains, and I asked her if she wanted to dance. I'll never forget how she looked at me. She smiled and shook her head, and for the first time I realized that she'd been reading my mind. She didn't say a word. Just smiled and shook her head. She was nice enough not to put it into words. You know—she could have said we didn't dare. Worse yet, she could have danced with me and *then* made a big thing about loyalty to her husband. In any event, I knew right away that she was never going to make a play for me, and that I'd better not make one for her. And with that out of the way, definitely, I relaxed and had a better time. I turned off the radio and we talked. About books and authors. All along the balcony above us the walls were lined with books, and she'd read them. I read a lot then, much more than I do now, and we'd both read a lot of the same things. It wasn't often that I got a chance to pour out what I felt about writing, especially to an attractive woman, and pour it out I did. Then along about nine-thirty Holderman appeared, very apologetic about missing dinner and yet not very refreshed from his long nap. He was in a fog.

She got him something to eat but she wouldn't let him drink any coffee. She wanted him to go back to bed, but he argued with her and as a matter of fact got a little nasty. Nasty for him, that is. "I don't really need you to decide when I should sleep," he said.

"Not deciding anything, just suggesting," she said.

Well, I hung around for a little while, then I said goodnight to them and went to my room. I went to sleep and I don't know how long I slept. Past midnight. And I was awakened by a sound that I thought was some animal. A roaring sound. Not so much noisy as deep, as though the animal were saying the word roar over and over again. Roar, roar, roar, roar. I got fully awake and got up, and by this time I realized that it was not an animal but Holderman, having a nightmare in his office. I was going to go downstairs and actually had my door open, and then I saw her. She was in her nightgown, hurrying across the big room to Holderman's office, and in a minute or so they came out of the office. They had their arms around each other's waists and she was talking to him. I couldn't tell what she was saying because he was talking too. Then they went up the stairs to her room, the fancy bedroom, and she closed the door, and I closed mine.

Try and go back to sleep under those circumstances, but I did, eventually. In the morning I went down to breakfast and Holderman was there, I remember he was wearing the same old Norfolk jacket and smoking a pipe. "Your car is ready," he said. "I'll take you down to Eagle Summit as soon as you've had breakfast." He was rested and relaxed, and affable. Violet waited on me herself, and she was happy too. I was finishing breakfast and Holderman said he'd go down and get the Pierce started and I could come down when I was ready, no hurry. Soon as I finished my packing.

She lit my cigarette while I was having my second cup of coffee. "Now you understand us a little better," she said.

"A little," I said.

"Oh, you will a lot when you think about us," she said. "I saw your door open last night."

"Oh," I said, which was all I could think of to say.

Then she said, "You're going to be a nice man, you have feelings."

And I said, "Well, you're a nice woman. You have feelings."

"People aren't nice without them. *He* has them." Then she said, "Do you see anything here you'd like to take home with you? As a memento?" I looked around and God knows there were a lot of things, an embarrassment of riches, so to speak, and she obviously wanted me to take something, so I picked up an old-fashioned silver match-safe. "How about this?" I said. "It's yours," she said. "And this," and she kissed me. "Just a token," she said. And she knew what I was thinking— wondering why all the generosity. "Why?" she said. "Because I've watched your young eyes taking in everything, and your curiosity's been very complimentary," she said. "Give me your address, where I can write to you. I think you'll want to know how he comes out of this next operation, and I'd like to be able to tell you. I hardly need tell you that it won't be on his ear," she said.

Well, she never did write to me, never a line. And while I'm on the subject, I haven't the faintest idea what happened to the match box. It was very good-looking. On one side was a picture of a pack of hounds baiting a bear. I think the other side was blank.

Winter Dance

WHEN THE big Packard Twin-Six came rumbling into view it was an exciting sight to the boy. The radiator and hood had a leather cover that was streaked with ice. Strapped to the spare tires at the rear of the car was a long-handled shovel, crusted with snow. Icicles hung from the fenders, and the running-boards carried an extra thickness of frozen slush. All the side curtains were securely in place. The windshield was solid ice except for an arc, directly in front of the chauffeur, which the manually operated wiper had kept partially clear. The heavy car moved slowly as the tire chains bit into the snow. You could not see the spokes of the artillery wheels; they were hidden by a disc of ice and snow. But the big car had made it, as it nearly always made it in spite of the winter in the mountains. Now, moving slowly along South Main Street, the car made the boy think of those trains in the far West that were drawn by two and three locomotives up and through the mountain passes. There was something triumphant and majestic now in the way the big Packard eased its way along South Main. Here it was safe and sound, the dignified winner over fifteen miles of narrow, winding mountain roads and the hazards that winter could put in its way.

The boy watched the Packard until it came to a stop ten feet from the curb but as close as it could get to Winkleman, the furrier's.

"There goes your girl, Ted."

"Aw, shut up," said the boy.

"She's stopping at Winkleman's. Why don't you go in and price his coonskins? He has a coonskin in the window."

"And a card on it saying three hundred dollars," said the boy.

"Well, ask him if he's got any for less."

"In front of her?" said the boy.

"Okay. I was only trying to be helpful."

"We could take a walk down and have a *look* at the coat," said the boy.

"And wait till she comes out? She may be all day. Go on in and try it on."

"Winkleman knows I'm not in the market for a coonskin," said the boy.

"Listen, for Christ's sake, Ted. This is your best chance to talk to her. You know where she's probably going from there."

"I know."

"You want to talk to her, don't you?"

"Sure," said the boy.

"And not with the older crowd."

"Yes," said the boy.

"Well, you won't be able to get her away from the older crowd. Even if you cut in on her, they won't let you get two steps with her."

"Shall we take a walk down to Winkleman's?" said the boy.

"Give her a few seconds to get out of the car and inside of the store."

"That's a good idea. We'll wait till she gets inside," said the boy. "But then I don't know what to say."

"Just strike up a conversation."

"That's easier said than done," said the boy. "Think of something."

"Well, just casually sidle up to her and say, 'Oh, hello, Natalie. Going to the tea dance?' And she'll say, 'Yes, are you?'"

"End of conversation," said the boy.

"Not necessarily. Ask her where she's staying tonight."

"I know where she's staying, and anyway, she'll think it's kind of fresh. It's none of my business where she's staying," said the boy.

"Well, have you got some money with you?"

"Dollar and forty, forty-five cents."

"That's enough. Ask her if she wants a hot chocolate. She just had a cold ride, and I'll bet she'd welcome a hot chocolate."

"*I've* never asked her to have a hot chocolate."

"What if you haven't? You have to start sometime, you dumb bastard. I'll bet she'd give anything for a hot chocolate. That's a cold ride, believe you me. And even if she says no, at least she'll give you credit for being considerate. My sister Kit, I've heard her say a hundred times, next to a good dancer, if a boy's considerate."

"She's liable to think I'm too young to buy her a hot chocolate. She's at least twenty."

"You have a dollar and forty cents. A hot chocolate will set you back fifteen cents. She knows fifteen cents won't break you. Maybe she won't even think of that, if she *wants* a hot chocolate. She's probably half frozen."

"No. They have one of those charcoal heaters, and sixty-five robes. It's as warm in her car as Mrs. Hofman's limousine."

"How do you know?"

"Because last year she gave us all a ride home from tobogganing."

"Natalie?"

"Well, not Mrs. *Hofman*. Huh. Fancy that, Mrs. Hofman giving us a ride in her limousine. I'd like to see *that*."

"Well, she's inside. Now's your chance."

"I wish it was some other store," said the boy. "I don't like to go barging in Winkleman's. That's a woman's store."

"He has a man's raccoon coat in the window. And who else is going to buy a raccoon if we don't? Not my *father*. Not *your* father. Maybe Winkleman will think you're getting one for a Christmas present. *I* am, but not this year."

"Oh, I'm getting one, next year or the year after," said the boy.

"Well, then you have a good excuse."

"The only trouble is, Winkleman will start waiting on us, and then how do I get to strike up a conversation with *her*? 'What can I do for you, boys?' And then I barge over and ask her if she wants a hot chocolate. Boy, will she see through that. She'll know we followed her in, and she'll be sore as hell."

"She'll be so busy she won't pay any attention till you speak to her. Didn't you ever go shopping with a woman?"

"Oh, you know so much about everything, you make me sick."

"You're the one that makes me sick. What's the worst she can do? Chop off your head and put it on a pikestaff? The positively worst she can do is say, 'No thank you, Ted. I do not wish a hot chocolate.'"

"If I thought for sure she wanted a hot chocolate," said the boy. "Maybe she's not going to stay in there very long. By the time we get there maybe she'll be just leaving. Nobody gets to the tea dance before six. She's spending the night at Margery Hill's. If they all left at half past five, they'll be at the club around six. If she has to change her dress, that'll take her at least a half an hour. Five o'clock. I'm trying to dope out whether she's going to be in Winkleman's long enough. And anyway, maybe she's going some place else besides Winkleman's. I don't think Winkleman's is such a good idea. I'll bet she has other places to go. No, she wouldn't have time for a hot chocolate."

"Well, you're right. She's leaving Winkleman's. Let's see where she goes."

The girl in her six-buckle arctics came out of the fur shop, stepped into the snowbank and got in her car. The boy and his friend watched the big Packard moving slowly southward and turning west into Lantenengo Street. They did not speak until the car was out of sight.

"Well, you're fifteen cents ahead. Buy *me* a hot chocolate."

"You just had one," said the boy.

"I could polish off another."

"Oh, all right. Then what? Shall we start for the club?"

"Christ, it's only twenty after four."

"I have to pick up the kid sister. The old man wouldn't let me have the car unless I dragged her. *They* want to get there *early*. They *always* want to get there early."

"Yeah, they don't want to miss anything. What's there to miss before six o'clock? But what do *you* want to get there early for?"

"Because my damn kid sister wants to, and my old man said I had to," said the boy. "And I have to dance the first dance with her, and if she's left in the lurch I have to dance with her, and when she's ready to go home *we* have to go home. God damn it I wish I had my own car."

"I'm getting one when I graduate. I don't know whether I want a Ford or a Dodge."

"New or second-hand?"

"Brand-new."

"The Dodge costs more, but around here you need a Ford for the hills," said the boy.

"Yeah, but I wouldn't use it much around here. I'd use it mostly in the summer, and the Vineyard's practically all flat."

"I never thought of that," said the boy. "Well, I guess we ought to get started."

"Where's your car?"

"Henderson's Garage. The old man left it there to get new chains put on. Finish your hot chocolate. You'll get plenty at the club, free."

"It'll have skin on it. Christ, I hate skin on hot chocolate. It makes me puke."

"You're so delicate," said the boy.

"Well, do you like it?"

"No," said the boy. "But I have sense enough to drink tea."

The orchestra was playing "Rose of the Rio Grande," a fine fox trot with a melody that could just as easily have had a lyric about China, and the next tune *was* about Chinese—"Lime-house Blues." The band was just getting started, and trying to fill the dance floor.

"Stop trying to lead," said the boy.

"Oh, you stop being so bossy," said his sister. "Why are you so grouchy? Because your girl isn't here? Well, here she comes."

"Where?"

"In the vestibule. All the older crowd. Margery Hill has a new hat. Oh, isn't that becoming?"

"'Oh, isn't that becoming?' You sound like Mother."

"And you sound like the Terrible-Tempered Mr. Bangs. Oh, hello, Ralph. Are you cutting in on my adorable brother? Teddy, dear, will you relinquish me?"

"Thanks for the dance," said the boy. He joined the stag line and lit a cigarette.

"Got a butt?"

"Hello, Jonesy. Sure," said the boy, offering a pack.

"Your girl's here. Just got here a minute ago."

"Oh, crack wise," said the boy, and turned away. Presently the fellows from the older crowd gathered in the vestibule, waiting for the girls to come downstairs from the ladies' dressing-room.

"Hello, Teddy," said Ross Dreiber.

"Hello, Ross," said the boy.

"Why aren't you out there tripping the light fantastic? Looking them over?"

"Just looking them over."

"Any new talent? I see your sister. She fourteen?"

"Fifteen."

"Fifteen. Well, I'll be out of college by the time she's allowed to go to proms. But she certainly has sprung up since last summer."

"Sure has."

"What have you got? Two more years?"

"One more after this," said the boy.

"Then where?"

"Lafayette, I guess. Maybe Princeton."

"Well, when you get ready to go, if you decide on Lafayette, I'd be glad to write a letter to our chapter there. You know you can't go wrong with Deke, anywhere. What was your father?"

"Theta Delt."

"Well, I have nothing to say against Theta Delt. They're a keen organization. But take a look at Deke before you shake hands. And think twice about Princeton, boy. I know a lot of good eggs were awfully disappointed they went to Princeton. Take my word for it. But of course it all depends on the man."

"Yeah. Sure."

"Have you got another butt on you? . . . Omars! My brand! Deke for you, boy. You even smoke the right cigarettes."

The boy held a match to Dreiber's cigarette.

"*Hello, Teddy.*"

He turned. "Hello, Nat," he said.

"Finish your cigarette, Ross. I'll dance with Teddy. Or are you waiting for somebody?"

"No, I'm not waiting for anybody. But do you mean it?"

"Of course I do. Come on," she said.

"Probably get about two steps," said the boy.

"Well, then let's walk down to the other end of the room and start from there. Shall we?"

"Fine," said the boy.

She took his arm and they marched to the far end of the room. She greeted friends along the way, but said nothing to the boy. Then she held up her arms and said, "All right?" and they began to dance. He was good, and he had self-confidence because he was good. She was good, and she liked dancing with him. There was no need to talk, and at this end of the room people got out of their way. They got all through two choruses of "Stumbling" before the music stopped. "Oh, that was grand," she said. She applauded with him.

"Shall we sit down?" said the boy.

"Well, I think I'd better find our crowd."

"Don't do that, Nat. Please?" said the boy.

"No, Teddy. I must, really," she said. "Cut in later."

"Couldn't we just sit down a minute?"

She shook her head. "You know they'll only kid you."

"Oh, you know that?"

"Uh-huh. They kid me too, don't forget."

"They do? Who does?"

"Oh, my crowd. Same as your crowd kids you."

"You're not sore at me because they kid you?"

"Of course not. And don't you be embarrassed, either."

"You know it's all my fault, Nat," said the boy.

She hesitated. "You mean on account of the postcard?"

"I showed it to everybody. I shouldn't have."

"Well, if I felt like sending a friend of mine a postcard," she said.

"But I went around bragging about it, and showing it to everybody."

"Well, if you wanted to. I don't even remember what I said on the card."

"'You would love it here. Lots of good trout fishing. Have gone on two pack trips. See you at Christmas. Natalie.' And a picture of the ranch."

"I remember," she said. "Not very incriminating, was it? Will you take me over to their table now, Teddy?"

"And your word of honor you're not annoyed with me."

"Only if you let them embarrass you," she said.

"Nat?"

"What?"

"I don't have to say it, do I? You know, don't you? You do know?"

She nodded. "Give me your arm," she said.

Appearances

HOWARD AMBRIE stopped the car at the porte-cochère to let his wife out, then proceeded to the garage. The M-G was already there, the left-hand door was open, and the overhead lamp was burning, indicating that their daughter was home. Ambrie put the sedan in its customary place, snapped out the light, rang down the door, and walked slowly toward the house. He stopped midway and looked at the sky. The moon was high and plain, the stars were abundant.

In the kitchen his wife had poured him a glass of milk, which rested on the table with a piece of sponge cake. "I'll be able to play tomorrow after all," said Howard Ambrie. "There's hardly a cloud in the sky."

"Oh, then you've thought it over," said Lois Ambrie.

"Thought what over?"

"Jack Hill's funeral. You're not going."

"Was I thinking it over?"

"You said at dinner that you hadn't decided whether to go or not," said Lois Ambrie.

"That was only because I knew the McIvers planned to go."

"I don't understand your reasoning," she said.

"Well, then I'll explain it to you. Peter and Cathy *want* to go to the funeral. I don't. No reason why I should. But I didn't want to inflict my *not* wanting to go on their *wanting* to go. Impose, I guess, would be a better word. Influence them. Or for that matter, take away their pleasure in going to the service. I said I hadn't made up my mind, and so there was no discussion about it. If I'd said I definitely wasn't going, or if I'd definitely said I wasn't going, they would have wanted to know why."

"What would you have told them?"

"What would I have told them? I'd have told them that I'd much rather play golf tomorrow."

"Well, that would have started a discussion, all right," she said.

"I know it would," he said. "And I know what the discussion would have been. Wasn't Jack Hill one of my best friends?

344

Couldn't I play golf after the service? And so forth. But I disposed of all that by simply saying I hadn't made up my mind."

"You disposed of it as far as the McIvers were concerned, but will you tell *me* why you're not going?"

"I don't mind telling you. In the first place, I've never considered Jack Hill one of my best friends. He wasn't. He was a lifelong acquaintance, a contemporary, our families were always friends, or friendly. And if you wanted to stretch a point, we were related. All of which you know. But in a town this size, at least until just before the War, damn near everybody is related in some way or other."

"Yes, and damn near everybody will be at that funeral tomorrow," she said. "Therefore your absence will be noticed."

"Maybe it will. I thought of that. But the fact is, I never liked Jack and he never liked me. If the circumstances were reversed, I'm sure he'd be playing golf tomorrow. There won't be many more days we can play this year. I noticed driving by this afternoon, they've taken the pins out of the cups, and I wouldn't be surprised if they filled in the holes. The golf shop is boarded up for the winter. In fact, Charley closed up a week ago and went to Florida. I hope there's enough hot water for a shower. I hate to come in after playing golf in this weather and find no hot water."

"You're playing in the morning," she said.

"Playing in the morning. We're meeting at ten o'clock, playing eighteen holes. Having something to eat. Probably the usual club sandwiches. And then playing bridge. I'll be home around five, I should think."

"Who are you playing with?"

"Same three I play with every Saturday, and they won't be missed at Jack's funeral."

"No, they certainly won't be. None of Jack's old friends, and none of your old friends, either, not in that foursome."

"Lois, you talk as though the whole of Suffolk County were going to be at the church tomorrow, checking to see who stayed away. Are *you* going to the funeral?"

"Yes, I'm going. Or I was. I don't know whether I want to go without you."

"Oh, hell, call up somebody and go with *them*."

"No, if you're not going, I won't. That would make your not

going so much more noticeable. 'Where's Howard?' 'Playing golf.'"

"Listen, I'm not going, so don't try to persuade me."

"I think you ought to go," she said.

"No."

"I'll make one more try. I'm *asking* you to go," she said.

"And my answer is I think you're being God damn unreasonable about this. Jack Hill and I have known each other over fifty years, we were thrown together by age and financial circumstances. His family and my family had about the same amount of dough. But when we got older and could choose our friends, he never chose me and I never chose him. We were never enemies, but maybe if we had been we'd have found out why we didn't like each other. Then maybe we could have been friends. But we never had any serious quarrel. We never had a God damn thing."

"He was an usher at our wedding."

"I *knew* you'd bring that up. That was twenty-five years ago, and I had to have him and he had to have me because our parents were friends. It was one of those automatic things in a small town. I couldn't ask one of the clammers, and he couldn't ask one of the potato farmers, but that's *all* it was. And since you bring that up, about being ushers, Celia didn't ask me to be a pallbearer or whatever the hell she's having. Celia has more sense about this than you have."

"There aren't going to be any pallbearers, and you know it."

"All right, I do know it. And she's very sensible, Celia."

"I'm asking you again, Howard, please. Put off your golf till after lunch, and go to this funeral with me. It isn't much to ask."

"Why do you care so much whether I go or not?"

"Because I don't want Celia knowing that you stayed away."

"Oh, Christ. All right. Although why you care what Celia knows or doesn't know—you and Celia were never that good friends."

"But you will go?"

"Yes, I said I would, and I will. But you certainly screwed up my weekend."

"You can play in the afternoon and Sunday."

"Father O'Sullivan can't play Saturday afternoon, he has

to hear confessions, and he can't play Sunday at all. And Joe Bushmill is going skeet-shooting this Sunday. It's not only my schedule you loused up."

"I'm sorry about that, Howard, but I do appreciate it."

"Oh, sure. You have no idea how you complicate things. We had to get a fourth for bridge, because O'Sullivan has to be in church at three o'clock. And now they'll have to get someone to take my place at golf *and* bridge."

"I'll do something for you sometime."

"Why didn't you make your big pitch before tonight?"

"Because I took for granted that you'd be going to the funeral. I just took it for granted."

"I suppose the same way that people took for granted that Jack Hill was a friend of mine. Well, he wasn't. I'm going to bed. Oh, Amy's home. The M-G's in the garage."

"I know. Goodnight, dear."

"Goodnight," he said. He bent down and kissed her cheek.

Light showed on the floor beneath Amy's bedroom door, and he knocked gently. "Amy? You awake?" he said softly.

"Father? Come in."

She was sitting up in bed, and when he entered she took off her reading glasses. "Hi," she said.

"What are you reading?" he said.

"Detective story. Who won?"

"Oh, your mother and I took them. We always do, at their house, and they usually win when they come here." He sat on the chaise-longue. "As Mr. McCaffery says, what kind of a day's it been today?"

"Fridays are always easier than other days. The children seem to behave better on Friday. That is, their behavior is better, probably because they're in a better mood. Their schoolwork isn't as good, but you can't have everything."

"Do you like teaching?"

"Not very much, but I like the children."

"Well, it's nice having you home for a year."

"Thank you, Father. It's nice being home."

"Is it?" he said.

"Have a cigarette?" She held up a package.

"No thanks. You didn't answer my question."

"I know I didn't. Yes, it's nice being home."

"But that's as far as you'll commit yourself?" he said.

"That's as far as I want to commit myself."

"You mean you don't want to think more deeply than that?"

"Yes, I guess that's what I mean. I'm comfortable here, I have my job, my car to run around in, and I had no idea we had so many detective stories. This one was copyrighted 1924."

"There are some older than that, early Mary Roberts Rinehart," he said. "Believe I will have one of your cigarettes." He caught the pack she tossed him and lit a cigarette. "Are you making any plans for next year?"

"Not exactly. I may get married again. I may not."

"This time you ought to have children right away."

"It wouldn't be so good if I had a child now, would it?"

"It might have kept you together, Amy, a child. We had you the first year, your mother and I."

"Father, you're practically implying that if you hadn't had me—"

"I know what I'm implying," he said. "And I know you're no fool. You know it's often been touch and go with your mother and I. You've seen that."

"I guess it is with everybody. But a child wouldn't have kept Dave and me together. Nothing would."

"Well, what really separated you?"

"Well, it wasn't his fault. I fell in love with someone else."

"The man you're thinking of marrying?"

"No."

"The man you're thinking of marrying is that doctor in Greenport?"

"Yes."

"But the man you left Dave for was someone else?"

"Yes."

"And what's happened to him? He's gone out of your life?" She looked at him sharply. "Yes."

"Why? Was he married?"

"Yes."

"Where did you know him? At Cornell?"

"No, Father. And don't ask me any more questions, please. You voluntarily said you wouldn't ask me any questions, you promised that when I came home after my divorce."

"I did, but with the understanding that when you were

ready to tell us, you would. It isn't just idle curiosity, Amy. Your mother and I have a right to know those things, if only to keep you from making the same mistakes all over again."

"I won't make that mistake over again. And I'm not ready to tell you what happened to me with Dave."

"As far as I know, Dave was a hell of a nice boy."

"He was, and is, but I wasn't a hell of a nice girl. No father likes to face that fact about his daughter, but there it is."

"You're not a tart, you're not a chippy."

"No. But that's not all there is besides virgins, Father."

"Oh, I know that."

"Well, when does a girl get to be a tart in your estimation? Is it a question of how many men she sleeps with?"

"It most certainly is, yes."

"How many?"

"Yes, I walked into that one, didn't I? Well, a girl who sleeps with more than two men before she gets married, she's on her way. I can see a girl having an affair the first time she thinks she's in love. And then the second time, when she's more apt to be really in love. But the next time she'd better be damned sure, or she's going to be a pushover for everybody."

"Well—that's more or less my record. The second time was also the man I left Dave for."

"Oh, you had an affair and married Dave and continued to have this other affair?"

"Yes."

"What's going to prevent your having an affair with this same guy after you marry your doctor? . . . You had an affair with a married man before you married Dave. He sounds like a real son of a bitch."

"I guess maybe he was, although I didn't think so. I guess he was, though."

"You're not still seeing him?"

"No. I did after I divorced Dave, but not after I began dating the doctor."

"You're—to use an old-fashioned word—faithful to the doctor?"

"Oh, you're so smart, Father. You've tricked me into admitting I'm having an affair with the doctor. The answer is yes."

"Hell, I knew you were probably having an affair with the

doctor. I'm no fool, either, you know. Well, it's been a very interesting conversation between father and daughter. It's a good thing I'm not *my* father, or you'd be—well, you wouldn't be here."

"No, but we wouldn't have had this conversation, either."

"You have a point. Goodnight, dear." He kissed her cheek and she squeezed his hand. "There *is* that," he said. "We wouldn't have had this conversation. Goodnight again."

"Goodnight, Father," she said.

The girl sat in her bed, holding her glasses loosely with her right hand, her book with her left, both hands lying on the pink comforter. Her mother came in. "What was that all about?" said Lois Ambrie.

"Our conversation? Oh, mostly about Dave and me."

"He didn't say anything about Jack Hill?"

"No."

"I'll be glad when Jack is buried and out of the way."

"I know," said Amy.

"Your father is getting closer to the truth, Amy."

"I guess he is."

"I had a very difficult time persuading him to go to the funeral tomorrow."

"Why did you bother?"

"Appearances. 'Why didn't Howard Ambrie go to Jack Hill's funeral?' They'd be talking about that for a month, and somebody'd be sure to say something to Celia. And then Celia'd start asking herself questions."

"I wonder. I think Mrs. Hill stopped asking questions a long time ago. She should have. I wasn't the only one he played around with."

"You can be so casual about it. 'Played around with.' And you haven't shown the slightest feeling about him, his dying."

"I didn't show any because I haven't got any. Other than relief. I'm not grief-stricken that he died, Mother. As long as he was alive I was afraid to marry Joe. Now I think I can marry Joe and settle down in Greenport and be what I always wanted to be. But not while Jack was alive. That's the effect he had on me."

"He was no good," said Lois Ambrie. "Strange how your father knew that without knowing why."

"I know why," said Amy. "Jack was the kind of man that husbands are naturally suspicious of. Father was afraid Jack would make a play for you. Instead he made a play for me, but Father never gave that a thought."

"I suppose so. And in your father's eyes it would be just as bad for me to cover up for you as it would have been for me to have had an affair with Jack. I'll be glad when he's out of the way. Really glad when you can marry Joe."

"Did you go over and call on Mrs. Hill?"

"I went over this afternoon, but she wasn't seeing anyone. Fortunately."

"She *is* grief-stricken?"

"I don't think it's that. No, I don't think it's that. As you said a moment ago, Celia probably stopped asking questions a long time ago. I'd put it another way. That she's known for years about Jack. Now she doesn't want to see anybody because whatever she's feeling, she doesn't want anybody to see *her*. Grief, or relief. Maybe she doesn't even know yet what she feels. Fear, maybe. Whatever he was, she stuck with him all those years, and suddenly he's gone and she's fifty-two or -three. I don't know what's in Celia's mind, but I'm glad I'm not her. Did you see Joe tonight?"

"Yes, I had dinner with him. We had dinner at his sister's house in Southold. Spaghetti. She's a very good cook."

"That will be quite something, an Ambrie marrying an Italian boy. Will you have to turn Catholic?"

"I will if he wants me to. If it means that much to him. I'm not sure it does, but it would probably make a difference to his family."

"Can he marry a divorced woman? I have no idea what the Catholic church says on that."

"We haven't discussed it, so I don't know either."

"Your father's great friends with the new Catholic priest, O'Sullivan. They play golf and bridge together every Saturday."

"So I gather. When the time comes, whatever they say I'll do."

"It would be quite a feather in their cap, an Ambrie turning Catholic."

"They may not see it that way. I understand they can be very tough about some things."

"Well, I suppose it's their turn. Goodness knows I still can't get used to the idea of having one in the White House. Can I get you a glass of milk or anything?"

"No thanks, Mother."

"Then I guess I'll be off to bed."

"Mother?"

"What?"

"I'm sorry I caused you and Father so much trouble. You especially. All those lies you had to tell."

"Oh, that's all right. It's over now. And it was really harder on your father. He never knew why he didn't like that man."

"And *you* couldn't tell him, *could* you, Mother?"

"What?"

"Oh, Mother."

Lois Ambrie looked at her daughter. "Is that another detective story you're reading? You mustn't get carried away, Amy." She smiled. "Goodnight, dear," she said, and closed the door.

Your Fah Neefah Neeface

THIS WOMAN, when she was about nineteen or twenty, had a stunt that she and her brother would play, usually in a railroad station or on a train or in a hotel lobby. I saw them work the stunt under the clock at the Biltmore in the days when that meeting-place was a C-shaped arrangement of benches, and I remember it so well because it was the first time I ever saw the stunt and the first time I ever saw her or her brother. It was more than thirty years ago.

She was sitting there, quite erect, her legs crossed, smoking a cigarette and obviously, like everyone else, waiting to meet someone. She was wearing a beret sort of hat that matched her suit, and it was easy to tell by the way she smoked her cigarette that she had handled many of them in her short life. I remember thinking that I would like to hear her talk; she was so self-possessed and good-humored in her study of the young men and young women who were keeping dates at the clock. The drag she took on her cigarette was a long one; the smoke kept coming from her nostrils long after you thought it was all gone. She was terribly pretty, with a straight little nose and lively light blue eyes.

Presently a young man came up the stairs in no great hurry. He was wearing a black topcoat with a velvet collar and carrying a derby hat. He was tall, but not outstandingly so, and he had tightly curled blond hair—a 150-pound crew type, he was. He reached the meeting-place, scanned the faces of the people who were seated there, and then turned away to face the stairs. He watched the men and women coming up the stairs, but after a minute or so he turned his head and looked back at the girl, frowned as though puzzled, then again faced the incoming people. He did that several times, and I began to think that this was a young man on a blind date who had not been given a full or accurate description of his girl. She meanwhile was paying no attention to him.

Finally he went directly to the girl, and in a firm voice that everyone under the clock could hear he said, "Are you by any chance Sallie Brown?"

"I am, but what's it to you?" she said.

"Do you know who I am?" he said.

"No."

"You don't recognize me at all?"

"Never saw you in my whole life."

"Yes you did, Sallie. Look carefully," he said.

"I'm sorry, but I'm quite positive I've never seen you before."

"Asbury Park. Think a minute."

"I've been to Asbury Park, but so've a lot of people. Why should I remember you?"

"Sallie. It's Jack. I'm *Jack*."

"Jack? Jack Who? . . . No! My brother! You—you're Jack? Oh, darling, darling!" She stood up and looked at the people near her and said to them, rather helplessly, "This is my brother. My *brother*. I haven't seen him since—oh, darling. Oh, this is so wonderful." She put her arms around him and kissed him. "Oh, where have you *been*? Where have they been keeping you? Are you all right?"

"I'm all right. What about you?"

"Oh, let's go somewhere. We have so much to talk about." She smiled at all the other young men and women, then took her brother's arm and they went down the stairs and out, leaving all of us with the happy experience to think about and to tell and re-tell. The girl I was meeting arrived ten or fifteen minutes after Sallie and Jack Brown departed, and when we were in the taxi on our way to a cocktail party I related what I had seen. The girl waited until I finished the story and then said, "Was this Sallie Brown blond? About my height? And was her brother a blond too, with curly hair cut short?"

"Exactly," I said. "Do you know them?"

"Sure. The only part of the story that's true is that they are brother and sister. The rest is an act. Her name is Sallie Collins and his name is Johnny Collins. They're from Chicago. They're very good."

"Good? I'll say they're good. They fooled me and everybody else."

"They always do. People cry, and sometimes they clap as if they were at the theater. Sallie and Johnny Collins, from Chicago. Did you ever hear of the Spitbacks?"

"No. Spitbacks?"

"It's a sort of a club in Chicago. You have to be kicked out of school to be a Spitback, and Johnny's been kicked out of at least two."

"And what about her?"

"She's eligible. She was two years behind me at Farmington."

"What was she kicked out for?"

"Oh, I don't know. Smoking, I think. She wasn't there very long. Now she's going to school in Greenwich, I think. Johnny's a runner downtown."

"What other tricks do they do?"

"Whatever comes into their heads, but they're famous for the long-lost-brother-and-sister one. They have it down pat. Did she look at the other people as much as to say, 'I can't believe it, it's like a dream'?"

"Yes."

"They can't do it as much as they used to. All their friends know about it and they've told so many people. Of course it annoys some people."

"What other *kind* of thing do they do?"

"Oh—I don't know. Nothing mean. Not practical jokes, if that's what you're thinking of."

"I'd like to meet her sometime. And him. They seem like fun," I said.

I never did meet Johnny He was drowned somewhere in Northern Michigan a year or so after I was a member of their audience at the Biltmore, and when I finally met Sallie she was married and living in New Canaan; about thirty years old, still very pretty; but instinctively I refrained from immediately recalling to her the once famous long-lost-brother stunt. I do not mean to say that she seemed to be mourning Johnny after ten years. But fun was not a word that came quickly to mind when I was introduced to her. If I had never seen her before or known about her stunts I would have said that *her* idea of fun would be the winning of the Connecticut State Women's Golf Championship. Women who like golf and play it well do seem to move more deliberately than, for instance, women who play good tennis, and my guess that golf was her game was hardly brilliant, since I knew that her husband was a 4-handicap player.

"Where are you staying?" she said, at dinner.

"At the Randalls'."

"Oh, do you sail?"

"No, Tom and I grew up together in Pennsylvania."

"Well, you're going to have a lot of time to yourself this weekend, aren't you? Tom and Rebecca will be at Rye, won't they?"

"I don't mind," I said. "I brought along some work, and Rebecca's the kind of hostess that leaves you to your own devices."

"Work? What kind of work?"

"Textiles."

"Well, that must be a very profitable business these days, isn't it? Isn't the Army ordering millions of uniforms?"

"I don't know."

"You're not in that kind of textiles?"

"Yes, I am. But I'm not allowed to answer any questions about the Army."

"I would like to be a spy."

"You'd make a good one," I said.

"Do you think so? What makes you think I would?"

"Because the first time I ever saw you . . ." I then had been in her company for more than an hour, and felt better about recalling the incident at the Biltmore.

"How nice of you to remember that," she said, and smiled. "I wonder why you did?"

"Well, you were very pretty. Still are. But the whole performance was so expert. Professional. You could probably be a very good spy."

"No. That was all Johnny. All those things we used to do, Johnny thought them up. He was the brains of the team. I was the foil. Like the girl in tights that magicians always have. Anybody could have done it with Johnny masterminding . . . Would you like to come here for lunch Sunday? I happen to know that Rebecca's without a cook, so you're going to have to go to the club, otherwise. Unless of course you have another invitation."

I said I would love to come to lunch Sunday, and she thereupon engaged in conversation with the gentleman on her left. I was surprised to find on Sunday that she and I were lunching alone. We had cold soup, then were served crab flakes and some vegetables, and when the maid was gone Sallie took a piece of paper from the pocket of her blouse. "This is the clock at the Biltmore that day. This is where I was sitting. Here is where you were sitting. If I'm not mistaken, you were wearing a grey suit and you sat with your overcoat folded over your lap. You needed a haircut."

"By God, you're absolutely right."

"You had a watch on a chain, and you kept taking it out of your pocket, and putting it back."

"I don't remember that, but probably. The girl I was meeting was pretty late. Incidentally, went to Farmington with you. Laura Pratt."

"Oh, goodness. Laura. If she'd been on time you never would have seen the long-lost-brother-and-sister act. She hated me at Farmington, but I see her once in a while now. She lives in Litchfield, as I suppose you know. But have I convinced you that I remembered you as well as you remembered me?"

"It's the greatest compliment I ever had in my life."

"No. You were good-looking and still are, but what I chiefly remembered was that I was hoping you'd try to pick me up. Then I was just a little bit annoyed that you didn't try. God, that was forever ago, wasn't it?"

"Just about," I said. "How come you didn't say anything at dinner the other night?"

"I'm not sure. Selfish, I guess. That was *my* evening. I wanted you to do all the remembering, and I guess I wanted to hear you talk about Johnny."

"He drowned," I said. "In Michigan."

"Yes, but *I* didn't tell you that. How did you know?"

"I saw it in the paper at the time."

"Rebecca told me you were getting a divorce. Does that upset you? Not her telling me, but breaking up with your wife."

"It isn't the pleasantest experience in the world," I said.

"I suppose not. It never is. I was married before I married my present husband, you know."

"No, I didn't know."

"It lasted a year. He was Johnny's best friend, but other than that we had nothing in common. Not that a married couple have to have too much in common, but they ought to have something else besides loving the same person, in this case my brother. Hugh, my first husband, was what Johnny used to call one of his stooges, just like me. But somehow it isn't very attractive for a *man* to be another man's stooge. It's all right for a sister to be a stooge, but not another man, and almost the minute Johnny died I suddenly realized that without Johnny, Hugh was nothing. As a threesome we had a lot of fun together, really a lot of fun. And with Hugh I could have sex. I don't think there was any of that in my feeling for Johnny, although there may have been. If there was, I certainly managed to keep it under control and never even thought about it. I didn't know much about those things, but once or twice I vaguely suspected that if either of us had any of that feeling for Johnny, it was Hugh. But I'm sure he didn't know it either."

"So you divorced Hugh and married Tatnall."

"Divorced Hugh and married Bill Tatnall. All because you were afraid to pick me up and ditch Laura Pratt."

"But I could have become one of Johnny's stooges, too," I said. "I probably would have."

"No. Johnny's stooges all had to be people he'd known all his life, like me or Hugh, or Jim Danzig."

"Who is Jim Danzig?"

"Jim Danzig was the boy in the canoe with Johnny when it overturned. I don't like to talk about poor Jim. He blamed himself for the accident and he's become a hopeless alcoholic, at thirty-two, mind you."

"Why did he blame himself? Did he have any reason to?"

"Well—he was in the canoe, and they were both a little tight. It was at night and they'd been to a party at the Danzigs' cabin and decided to row across the lake to our cabin, instead of driving eight or nine miles. A mile across the lake, eight and a half miles by car. One of those crazy ideas you get when you're tight. Johnny would have been home in fifteen minutes by car, but they started out in the canoe, heading for the lights on our landing. I guess there was some kind of horseplay and the canoe overturned, and Jim couldn't find Johnny. He kept calling him but he didn't get any answer, and he couldn't right the canoe, although Jim was almost as good a boatman as Johnny—when sober. But they'd had an awful lot to drink, and it was pitch dark. No moon. And finally Jim floated and swam ashore and then for a while was lost in the woods. It was after Labor Day and most of the cabins were boarded up for the winter, and Jim in his bare feet, all cut and bleeding by the time he got to the Danzigs' cabin, and a little out of his head in addition to all he'd had to drink. I think they had to dynamite to recover Johnny's body. I wasn't there and I'm glad I wasn't. From the reports it must have been pretty horrible, and even now I'd rather not think about it."

"Then don't," I said.

"No, let's change the subject," she said.

"All right. Then you married Tatnall."

"Married Bill Tatnall a year and a half after Hugh and I were divorced. Two children. Betty, and Johnny, ages six and four. You haven't mentioned any children. Did you have any?"

"No."

"Children hold so many marriages together," she said.

"Yours?"

"Of course mine. I wouldn't have said that otherwise, would I? How often do you see the Randalls?"

"Oh, maybe once or twice a year."

"Did they know you were coming here for lunch?"

"No," I said. "They left very early this morning, before I was up."

"That explains it, why you don't know about Bill and me. Well, when you tell them you were here today, don't be surprised if they give you that tut-tut look. Naughty-naughty. Bill and I raise a lot of eyebrows hereabouts. Next year it'll be some other couple, but at the moment it's Bill and I."

"Who's the transgressor? You, or your husband?"

"It's the marriage, more so than Bill or I individually. In a community like this, or maybe any suburban or small-town community, they don't seem to mind adultery if they can blame one person or the other. The husband or the wife has to be the guilty party, but not both."

"I don't agree with you," I said. "I think that when a marriage is in trouble people take sides, one side or the other, and they mind a great deal."

"Yes, they want the marriage to break up and they want to be able to blame one or the other. But when the marriage doesn't break up, when people can't fix the blame on one person, they're deprived of their scandal. They feel cheated out of something, and they're outraged, horrified, that people like Bill and I go on living together. They really hate me for putting up with Bill's chasing, and they hate Bill for letting me get away with whatever I get away with. Bill and I ought to be in the divorce courts, fighting like cats and dogs. Custody fights, fights about alimony."

"But you and your husband have what is commonly called an arrangement?" I said.

"It would seem that way, although actually we haven't. At least not a spoken one. You see, we don't even care that much about each other. He just goes his way, and I go mine."

"You mean to say you never had a discussion about it? The first time he found out you were unfaithful to him, or he was unfaithful to you? You didn't have any discussion at all?"

"Why is that so incredible?" she said. "Let's have our coffee out on the porch."

I followed her out to the flagstone terrace and its iron-and-glass furniture. She poured the coffee and resumed speaking. "I guessed that Bill had another girl. It wasn't hard to guess. He left me severely alone. Then I guessed he had another, and since I hadn't made a fuss about the first one I certainly wasn't going to make a fuss about the second. Or the third."

"Then I gather you began to have gentlemen friends of your own."

"I did. And I guess Bill thought I'd been so nice about his peccadillos that he decided to be just as nice about mine."

"But without any discussion. You simply tacitly agreed not to live together as man and wife?"

"You're trying to make me say what you want me to say, that somehow we did have a discussion, a quarrel, a fight ending in an arrangement. Well, I won't say it."

"Then there's something a lot deeper that I guess I'd better not go into."

"I won't deny that, not for a minute."

"Was it sexual incompatibility?"

"You can call it that. But that isn't as deep as you seem to think it was. A lot of men and women, husbands and wives, are sexually incompatible. This was deeper, and worse. Worse because Bill is a yellow coward. He never dared come out and say what he was thinking."

"Which was?"

"He got angry with me one time and said that my brother Johnny'd been a sinister influence. That's as much as he'd actually say. That Johnny'd been a sinister influence. He didn't dare accuse me—and Johnny—of what he really meant. Why didn't he dare? Because he didn't want to admit that his wife had been guilty of incest. It wasn't really so much that incest was bad as that it had happened to his own wife. Someone, one of Bill's lady friends, had planted that little idea in his thick skull, and he believed it. Now he fully believes it, but I don't care."

"A question that naturally comes to my mind," I said, "is why are you telling me all this?"

"Because you saw us together without knowing us. You saw Johnny and me doing the long-lost-brother act. How did we seem to you?"

"I thought you were genuine. I fell for it."

"But then Laura Pratt told you it was an act. What did you think then?"

"I thought you were charming. Fun."

"That's what I hoped you thought. That's what *we* thought we were, Johnny and I. We thought we were absolutely charming—and fun. Maybe we weren't charming, but we *were* fun. And that's all we were. And now people have ruined that for us. For me, at least. Johnny never knew people thought he had a sinister influence over me. Or me over him, for that matter. But aren't people darling? Aren't they lovely? They've managed to ruin all the fun Johnny and I had together all those years. Just think, I was married twice and had two children before I began to grow up. I didn't really start to grow up till my own husband made me realize what people had been thinking, *and* saying, about Johnny and me. If that's growing up, you can have it."

"Not everybody thought that about you and Johnny."

"It's enough that anybody did. And it's foolish to think that only one or two thought it," she said. "We did so many things for fun, Johnny and I. Harmless jokes that hurt nobody and that we thought were uproariously funny. Some of them I don't ever think of any more because of the interpretation people put on them . . . We had one that was the opposite of the long-lost-brother. The newlyweds. Did you ever hear of our newlyweds?"

"No," I said.

"It came about by accident. We were driving East and had to spend the night in some little town in Pennsylvania. The car broke down and we went to the local hotel and when we went to register the clerk just took it for granted that we were husband and wife. Johnny caught on right away and he whispered to the clerk, loud enough for me to hear, that we were newlyweds but that I was shy and wanted separate rooms. So we got our separate rooms, and you should have seen the hotel people stare at us that night in the dining-room and the next morning at breakfast. We laughed for a whole day about that and then we used to do the same trick every time we had to drive anywhere overnight. Didn't hurt anybody."

"What else did you do?"

"Oh, lots of things. And not only tricks. We both adored Fred and Adele Astaire, and we copied their dancing. Not as good, of course, but everybody always guessed who we were imitating. We won a couple of prizes at parties. Johnny was really quite good. 'I lahv, yourfah, neeface. Your fah, neefah, neeface.'" She suddenly began to cry and I sat still.

That was twenty years ago. I don't believe that anything that happened to her since then made much difference to Sallie, but even if it did, that's the way I remember her and always will.

Justice

THERE WAS nothing in or about the house that had been in being more than four years, nothing that gave promise of lasting more than five. The land itself, I knew, had been bull-dozed and shoveled into its present contours to provide the setting for the house, which was split level on several levels. For the most part the house was made of glass, stained woods, and aluminum. I had heard that the house alone cost ninety-five thousand dollars, but driving up to it for the first time, seeing it from a distance, I could not help thinking that it looked like an advertisement for a trailer. Trailer advertisements have a way of looking like ads for children's playhouses, and I suppose that what made me think of trailers was that general air of imper-manence. Or maybe it was the other way around. The roof supports on the front terrace of the house were thin poles of aluminum, as though they were meant to be folded and tucked away when the trailer, or the house, moved on in the morning. The whole house, or so it seemed on my first look, could be folded according to a trailer designer's plan, and driven off to Maryland or Arizona or Florida or Oak Ridge, Tennessee.

I knew that at one time a man could have stood on the site of the house and seen General George Washington and his Continentals. The view from the house was superb: rolling country, still largely held by dairy farmers whose family names were repeated in the names of the townships and "corners" and villages of the countryside. I was sure that Harry Rupp and his wife and children had never looked out from their terrace and tried to imagine Washington and his men in the snow. But it didn't matter. Barbara Rupp, with her contact lenses, could not see that far, and from what I came to know of their children, they hated history, which they called "social studies." As for Harry, his imagination was active enough but he had trouble recalling any date prior to Pearl Harbor . . .

I parked my car, that first day, and climbed the steps to the terrace level, where Mrs. Rupp was sunning herself and Harry was standing, in Hawaiian print shirt, plaid shorts, blue ankle-length socks, and huaraches. He had a cigar in his left hand, which he held rather daintily high. "Hi, Mr. Daniels," he said. "You didn't have to come all the way out here."

I was a little out of breath.

"Steps are pretty steep," said Harry Rupp. "But they keep my legs in condition. Sit down a minute. Like you to meet my wife. Barbara, this is Mr. Daniels. He's the chairman of the hospital drive."

"No, only the special-gifts committee," I said.

"Make yourself comfortable, Mr. Daniels," said Barbara Rupp. She was wearing wrap-around sun glasses and I don't think she saw me very well. She barely raised her head from the deck chair.

"You have quite a place here, Mrs. Rupp," I said.

"Well, it's what *we* wanted," she said, closing her eyes.

"She did most of the work. I gotta be away a good deal of the time. What would you say to a little libation? Smoke a cigar?"

"Well, a Coke or something like that," I said. "I don't often drink in the daytime. And I'll have a cigarette in a minute or so."

Rupp poured a Coke and handed it to me.

"You live in the town, Mr. Daniels?" said Barbara Rupp, without opening her eyes.

"On the edge of town," I said. "Lakeside Road. It used to be called Kouwenhoven Road."

"I know where it is. How many acres do you have?"

"We have four and a half acres."

"Four and a half acres? Oh, you must live in that big old fieldstone. That's a nice property."

"Thank you."

"Is that your family home?"

"Yes, I was born there. It's been in my family a long while, though not in its present form. My grandfather added on to it. He had a large family."

"They're coming back, according to some people, but I wouldn't have more than two," she said. "If you get one of each, what else do you have to prove?"

"Yeah," said her husband. "Well, Mr. Daniels, what did you have me down for?"

I smiled. "Well, I don't know that we had you down for any

set sum. My job is to tell you what we're trying to do at the hospital, and then rely on your generosity."

"I know about that pitch, Mr. Daniels. But what did you have beside my name, in pencil? What was Harry Rupp supposed to be good for?"

"You must have had some experience in this sort of thing," I said. "Very well. We had two figures for you. One was a thousand, the other was fifteen hundred."

"You gave yourself plenty of leeway," said Rupp.

"Not really," I said. "We had you down for a thousand, but the fifteen-hundred figure was for you and Mrs. Rupp."

"Count me out," said Barbara Rupp.

"Well, I'll go for a thousand."

"That'll be fine," I said. "But what about you, Mrs. Rupp? I'd like to put you down for something. Say two-fifty?"

"I'll bet you would. No, when I said count me out, I meant count me out altogether."

"I see," I said. I stood up. "Well, Mr. Rupp. Thank you very much. You've been more than generous, and I won't take up any more of your time. I'll leave this folder with you, in case you'd care to learn about what we're doing at the hospital. And on the back page, the address and so forth. Where to send your cheque."

"Don't leave any folders, will you please?" said Barbara Rupp. "Harry can make out the cheque to the hospital and send it to you direct, can't he?"

"Of course," I said. "Well, thanks again. And nice to have seen you both."

"Well, one of us, anyway," said Barbara Rupp.

I had, of course, acted under instructions: never have an argument with a potential donor. Barbara Rupp was not exactly a potential donor, but her husband had given freely and generously, and would go down on our list as a favorable prospect in years to come. "Oh, and thanks for the Coke," I said, on my way down the steps.

Our community is not a large one, but I literally did not see Barbara Rupp again until the hospital had its drive a year later. Occasionally I would encounter Harry Rupp at our little golf club, but my friends and I had a table of our own in the smoking-room and our golf matches were made up of men from that group, all considerably older than Harry Rupp and his friends. I was sometimes in the club when Harry Rupp was there, but we did not always speak. When I was again given Harry's name for my special-gifts list I said to him, at the club: "Harry, may I come out and see you, possibly this weekend?"

"Going to cost me a thousand dollars, Norman?" he said.

"At least that, I hope."

"Tell you what I'll do. I'll send you a cheque and spare you the trip," he said.

"Well, of course if you'd prefer. But I was also hoping I could get Mrs. Rupp to change her mind."

"What the hell, you can try. I'll tell her you're coming out Sunday afternoon. Make it late, around five. I won't be there, because our kids got some other kids for Sunday lunch, and then they slop around the pool. But by five she'll be by herself."

"Oh, why don't I do it some other time?"

"Listen, either way it's gonna be a waste of time, whether you go this Sunday or a week from Thursday."

She was wearing a playsuit, and her face and body were dark brown from the sun. "Harry said you were coming," she said. "But the answer's gonna be just the same."

"Yes, he warned me. But I can't think of a better way to spend at least part of Sunday afternoon than trying to collect money for the hospital."

"Don't you go to church?"

"Yes, I do as a rule."

"Church is another one of those things like hospitals."

"How so?" I said.

"Neither one of them will ever get a nickel out of me. Harry does it because it's deductible tax-wise, but also because it looks better if you're in business."

"Is that the way you feel about all charities?"

"In other words, don't I give to charity? No."

"I should think Harry would encourage you to, if only for tax purposes."

"That's a phony. I don't want them to get my money, even if I do get a little deduction for it. If you're not related to me, or you're not some close friend of mine, I wouldn't give you five cents if you were starving. That's not personal. I mean anybody. I don't know you, so I got nothing against you. But I wouldn't give you any money whether it was for you or the hospital or your Aunt Tillie."

"Well, it's an interesting point of view."

"And you're dying to know why. Shall I tell you why you'd like to know, Mr. Daniels? Because everybody wishes they had some excuse to stop giving away money. Take away that tax deduction and the charities would starve to death inside of six months."

"There again, an interesting point of view. I don't happen to agree with you, though."

"How do you know you don't? You didn't take time to think about it. You got it ingrained in you from your parents and *their* parents, give to charity. So you give. That's all."

"Haven't you ever given to any charity?" I said.

"Are you asking for the hospital or for your own information?"

"My own information, I guess. The hospital is a losing cause, it seems to me."

"Then I'll give you the information. You want to fix me a scoop? I'll have a bourbon on the rocks and you help yourself." She lit a cigarette and seated herself in one of those things that pass for chairs and that look like a salad bowl on a tripod. "Yes, I used to give to charity. Just like everybody. The Salvation Army. The Red Cross. Somebody got married in the store—I was working in a department store—I chipped in. Or if I saw some blind man on the street, even if I was sure he was a phony. A dime. A quarter. Then I got in an automobile accident and they kept me waiting in the hall. They didn't pay a God damn bit of attention to me till I almost died on the stretcher. Then they had the nerve to charge me for blood transfusions, irregardless of my two brothers and friends of mine from the store were donating blood. I was in that hospital six weeks and when I came out I was minus the sight of one eye. I had a concussion. What they call a concussion of the brain. Nothing wrong with my brain, but my eyesight. It finally cleared up so I could see out of that eye, but the hospital ate up all my insurance and what I had saved up. So that's when I stopped giving money to charity."

"Hospital facilities—" I began.

"Sure, sure, sure. And it was right after the war. Sure, sure. Don't *you* give me that. I can recite it backwards and forwards."

"I thought you might have some philosophical reason, some principle based on objective reasons. But it isn't that, is it? It's just a very unfortunate experience. If you'd been bitten by a dog, you probably would have a prejudice against dogs. You don't deny that the hospitals do some good, Mrs. Rupp?"

"I don't deny anything, friend. Harry's got it made now, and if I have to go to a hospital, my bills get paid. But that's all they get out of me. Or any other charity. They can all go to hell."

"Well, fortunately most people don't feel that way," I said.

"You mind if I say something? You're a stuffed shirt," she said. "You're a real stuffed shirt, Daniels."

"Quite possibly," I said. "And not very good company, so I think I'll take my leave, if I may tear myself away."

"Sit down, for Christ's sake," she said. "I don't insult a person unless I like them. You know what I do? I ignore them. I'm not saying I like you as much as some people. I only saw you these two times. But there's two kinds of a stuffed shirt. Those that are stuffed shirts because that's all they are, and those that act like stuffed shirts but aren't. You're the latter."

"I see. But you'll concede, won't you, that when you tell a man's he's a stuffed shirt, he's not likely to wait around long enough to discover that there are *two* categories of stuffed shirt. Tell me why you like me. I may not like your reason for liking me, and then I *will* be a stuffed shirt."

"I think you're regular. You're all manners and politeness and all that, but get you with a load on and you'd be just like anyone else."

"Well, I can't help but feel you have a point. However, I don't often get a load on."

"Let's get stiff," she said.

"No thanks," I said. "As a matter of fact, Mrs. Rupp, I have to take my wife to a cocktail party and should leave this minute."

"What's she like, your wife? How old is she? How old are you?"

"I'm fifty-five. My wife is younger than that."

"A lot younger? Ten years younger?"

"Not ten years, but let's not get too precise."

"Do you have any children?"

"Two daughters. Both married. One in Philadelphia, one in New York." I stood up.

"You know something?" she said, getting out of her salad bowl.

"What?"

"Fifty-five's not so old."

"It's not so young, either," I said.

She moved toward me until her body was actually resting against mine. "I could get you to stay here," she said.

"Yes, if I didn't leave right this minute, you could."

"And you'd be glad you stayed," she said.

"No, there I think you're wrong. I'd be sorry, and so would you."

"You mean on account of Harry."

"Harry, in your case. My wife, in mine."

"You never cheated?"

"If I say no, you won't believe me."

"You're damn right I wouldn't," she said. "Well, go ahead go. I won't detain you, Mr. Daniels. I'll let you chicken out this time."

"You're right. That's exactly what I am doing," I said. "One question. Why me?"

"Ah, you want a little flattery, don't you?"

I laughed. "I guess so."

"Well, I tell you, honey. It's your grey hair. Will that satisfy you?"

"You know, you're quite a naughty woman," I said, smiling.

"Ho-ho. You can say that again. Why do you think Harry has me stashed away up here?"

I left her, and for a few days I seemed to have come to life again. They were disturbing days, full of disturbing thoughts, and when I attempted to treat the thing lightly, to laugh off the episode and its immediate effect on me and on the even tenor of my ways, I was only partially successful. The only thing to do *was* to laugh it off, I told myself, but in honesty I knew that I was not so invulnerable that my sense of humor could banish the thoughts that disturbed me. I felt her in her playsuit resting against my body, and that was all too real. So real that, as I have said, I came to life again. But in a week or so the routine of my life took hold once more. The disturbing thoughts became less disturbing and intruded less frequently. My business affairs, my home life, my social life, the afternoons of golf and the comradeship of my old friends, what I had done for so many years, what I had *been*, came to my rescue. Now I could look upon the episode with amused tolerance. When I was safe again I encountered Harry Rupp at the club. He apparently had been away on business. "Hi, Norman," he said. "I understand you got nowhere."

"I got absolutely nowhere at all," I said.

"She's tough," he said. He was standing naked with a towel wrapped around his middle, and his hairy chest and shoulders and arms and back and belly made me think of him as not a man alone but as a partner to her. I had never before been so close to a naked man whose wife had offered herself to me. I cannot explain what I felt; it was almost but not quite as if I were he but he was not I. His hairy body had done what I had refused to do but had been tempted to do, and my body had felt the very beginnings of what his body had felt completely and often. I was glad the towel covered his middle. I think I would have stared at him and he would think I was something I am not.

I was safely away from her, and I could calmly ask myself why I had even for a moment been so affected by her that for nearly a week she had been disturbingly in my thoughts. I had no reason to like her. Beyond a slight curiosity as to her reasons for being opposed to charities, she had not interested me. She was a woman I could have seen at the supermarket; one of many women I could have seen on the half-fare special Wednesday trains; overdressed, over-talkative, undistinguished; spending their husbands' new money in a competition among themselves. In her playsuit, with its white ruffled edges and gingham material, she was making a foolish effort to be girlish in spite of having produced two children who were in their early teens. Her figure was of the kind that I describe negatively as not bad rather than positively as good. During the war, when I was stationed in London with the Air Force, I had had two brief, meaningless affairs with women who had the same sort of figure: they looked much better in clothes than out of them, and would not take off their brassieres while the light was on.

Those women in London had faded in my memory (and in my conscience) as completely as the details of the paperwork I was then doing for the Air Force. With a strong effort I suppose I could recall an evaluation of some of our daylight bombings over Germany, and with the same effort I could recall the name of one, but not both, of the women. I knew, as a private statistic, that I had been unfaithful to my wife, but if my wife guessed it she never let on, and after the war she had no grounds for suspicion. I came home and got busy and did rather well in my real estate business, and we settled once again into the kind of life we had lived before the war. When the materials were available we repaired and improved our house, we saw our friends, I took part in the less demanding community activities, we watched our daughters through adolescence and young womanhood, and we acquired three grandchildren. We even interceded when two friends of ours talked wildly of getting a divorce, and they have been kind enough to say that Millicent and I kept them together.

With Harry Rupp at the golf club Saturday after Saturday, I cannot say that I forgot about her. Whenever I saw him, I would instantly think of her, but my mind would be occupied with the brief conversations he and I had, and that happened often enough so that I can truthfully say that the encounters with Harry had the curious effect of reminding me of her existence but reducing her to unreality. Harry seldom spoke of her, unless it was to mention her in connection with a trip he had taken with her, or some such joint activity. He rarely mentioned her by name, and I had become so sure of myself that I was able to do so. He said, one afternoon: "I see your wife's in the ladies' semi-finals."

"Yes," I said. "Never got that far before. Barbara never plays, does she?"

"Golf? The most exercise she gets is bending over to paint her toenails. Oh, maybe swim the length of the pool. But no sports. Nothing competitive, you know what I mean. She just likes to sit."

"Well, the way I played today I'd have been better off just sitting," I said.

"Yeah, but that don't happen very often. I can belt them off the tee, but Jesus I wish I had your short game."

"I didn't have it with me today," I said. "See you, Harry."

"Right, Norm. Right."

For a while after that conversation whenever I heard their names or had other reason to think of them I would get an instant mental picture of Barbara Rupp in her playsuit, sitting in the sun and bent over to paint her toenails. The picture somehow offended me: the land that had been intact for a million years, now capriciously bulldozed and gouged out to make a site for a silly house for a silly woman, who had nothing better to do than decorate herself with paint and let the sun darken her skin to falsify her age. I had not set foot inside her house, but town talk was that she had all sorts of trick lighting, and built-in loudspeakers for a high-fidelity phonograph, and the very latest electrical appliances and deep-freeze units. They of course had television antennae as complicated as the radar installations on an aircraft carrier, and I gathered that her interior furniture was of a piece with the salad-bowl chairs on the terrace. It had cost ninety-five thousand dollars to build the house; that figure was a matter of public record. How much more was spent on furniture and gadgetry was anyone's guess. Knowing Harry, and after my two interviews with her, I was sure they filled the house with items from catalogs; funny toilet paper and tricky highball glasses and that sort of thing. They had been living in our neighborhood about four years, and the wives of my close friends had yet to meet Barbara Rupp. Some of them had not even seen her, and their initial curiosity about the Rupps' house had subsided.

The men, of course, were acquainted with Harry Rupp. He was already a rich man when he came to inspect building sites; from absolutely nothing he had built up a business that fascinated me, as any simple, fabulously successful enterprise fascinated me. During the war, while working in a defense plant, he sold black market cigarettes and candy to his fellow workers, then wangled a concession to serve coffee and doughnuts in the plant, legitimately. Thereafter he never again had to lie about his source of income; he became a sort of concessionaire in small, then larger, industrial plants, supplying and managing and taking a good profit from cafeterias and executive dining-rooms. He came to our town with a top credit rating and an impressive amount of loose cash. He was a big man, direct and even blunt, according to those of my friends who had dealings with him in his early days in town. But as one of them said to me, "He's a fellow that's definitely on his way to much bigger things. You sense that after talking to him for five minutes." He was away a good deal of the time, usually arriving home on Friday afternoon. In his blunt fashion he told the right men that he and his wife had no social ambitions, but that he wanted to get his kids in the private schools and he himself wanted to play golf. "After that," he said, "you can forget about us." He almost immediately fitted into a group of men at our golf club that consisted of several retail merchants, two young doctors and a dentist, the Catholic priest, the district manager of the telephone company, and one of my younger competitors in real estate. Among them were the best golfers in the club and the hardest drinkers, and they shook dice not only for drinks but for sums of money that caused some alarm among the older members of the house committee. "Somebody's going to get hurt," the committee chairman said.

"True," I said. "But we already have rules against gambling on club property. We either enforce the rules and stop gambling entirely, or we just look the other way. Then when someone does get hurt, they may come to their senses."

As it happened, Harry Rupp, who everyone knew had plenty of money, rescued the house committee from the embarrassing predicament. "This game's getting too damn big for fun," he announced one afternoon. "I don't mind thirty or forty bucks, but when we get up around two hundred dollars on the table, I begin to take it seriously. Furthermore, we got Father Mulcahy sitting here like a bump on a log. One of these days he's gonna get in the game, and that's the day the bishop better count the Sunday collections. So wuddia say, fellows? Wuddia say we don't play for any paper money?" Rupp was the only man who could have done it, and I found out later that my friend the committee chairman had spoken to the priest, who then spoke to Rupp, and that Rupp's immediate reaction had been favorable. "Woodburn," he said, referring to the telephone company manager, "is too nice a guy to get in trouble over a lousy dice game. But I seen him turn pale last week when he dropped seventy-fi' dollars. He don't have that kind of money. I'll break it up."

That was the kind of man Harry Rupp was among men, and then as chairman of the hospital's special-gifts committee I learned a little more about him, but what I learned was really only more of the same: his quick generosity to the hospital drive was to be expected of the kind of man I had seen in the golf club smoking room. Moreover, his sort of heartily virile man's man would not necessarily be guilty of basic disrespect in calling his wife "tough" or even in speaking scornfully of her laziness. His attitude toward his wife, and toward women, had only been hinted at in Barbara's remark: "Why do you think Harry has me stashed away up here?" The remark could have more than one meaning. It might be flirtatiousness on her part; it might have been the plain truth; it might have been indicative of resentment or loneliness or boredom. But it told me almost nothing about *Harry's* attitude, and toward the end of that summer it became important for me to know just what his attitude was.

As always, there was that one day in late July or early August that Nature sends us creatures as a reminder that autumn will come. August and September can be warm, but we have been given that brief warning, although we highly intelligent human animals seldom act upon it. I took no deliberate action on it, to be sure, but I found that inexplicably I was having a recurrence of my disturbing thoughts of Barbara Rupp. I think it was because autumn could be sensed, and in the autumn I would not see her. When I had seen her it was spring or early summer, and for me she did not exist in cold weather. How can I explain to myself what happened to me? I came to life again, as I had before, but this time it was the thin chill of a distant autumn and not the recollected pressure of a real woman against me that brought me to life so desperately. I hardly even thought of *her*; I thought of myself. And then I began thinking that this new life would remain incomplete if I did not go back again to that hideous house. This new life I was feeling was hideous, too, but I had lost any sense of beauty that I had ever had. Yes, I thought, killed by an early frost, and to hell with it. One thing killed, another thing come to life; and what was gone was truly gone and better gone and useless. Only this hideous new life was not dead.

I have never been a devious man. In our business, waiting is half the game, and since Millicent and I both have small private incomes, I could always wait till I got my price before selling a piece of property. In my personal life I was equally secure: Millicent and I were completely compatible, understood each other perfectly, lived in an atmosphere of mutual respect, and were, of course, very much in love. My London episodes can be properly attributed to physical necessity and wartime strain; and since they occurred at a distance of three thousand miles and during a universal moral blackout, I did not get involved in deviousness. But now I seemed to have developed a talent for intrigue. Through the most casual questions I determined that Harry Rupp would be absent from home from Monday through Friday of the second week in August and that his two children would not yet be home from summer camp. I drove out to the Rupps' house.

To my momentary dismay Barbara Rupp was not alone. She introduced me to a young woman who was the wife of a young farmer nearby. With my new talent encouraging me I recovered quickly from my first disappointment. "I don't want to make a nuisance of myself, Mrs. Rupp," I said. "But I have a client's interested in building a house like yours. Would you mind if I just paced off a few measurements to give me some idea?"

"Help yourself," said Barbara Rupp. "You want a tape measure?"

"No thanks," I said. "I'm used to making rough estimates. You ladies forget all about me."

"I was just leaving," said the farmer's wife.

"You're not gonna leave me all alone with Mr. Daniels," said Barbara Rupp.

The farmer's wife tittered out of embarrassment for me and my decrepitude.

"I hope I'm not *quite* that harmless," I said, as stuffed-shirtedly as I could sound.

The farmer's wife went down the steps, accompanied by Barbara Rupp, while I, with pencil and paper in hand, paced off the dimensions of the terrace. Barbara Rupp returned to the terrace. "You could have got that information by phoning Harry," she said.

"I happen to know he's away."

"What is it? Just an excuse to see me?"

"Yes," I said.

"Yeah, I thought so. I saw the look on your face when you spotted Dora. You know I have two kids."

"I know they're not home from camp," I said.

"Oh, this is for real, huh?" she said. "Wuddia you, been brooding over the pass I made at you?"

"I'm here," I said.

"Well, yeah," she said. She looked at me. "Yeah."

"Can't we go inside?"

"Sure. Why not?" she said. "You want a Coke? I think you better have a *real* drink."

"So do I," I said. I fixed a bourbon on the rocks. She already had a long drink in her hand. She sat in a bright green chair and stretched her legs on the matching hassock.

"What brought this on? A little domestic quarrel with your wife?"

"Not a bit. I just wanted to see you. Had to see you."

"Yeah, that's better, because if it was only a fight with your wife it isn't worth it. A wife getting suspicious, and that's what she'd be. I don't care what you fight about, right away the wife starts getting suspicious. I got myself to think about, too."

"Does Harry trust you?"

"No, and I don't trust him either, but you picked the only time of the year when I don't have two bodyguards age fifteen and thirteen. Hell, I know Harry never passes up anything, but I have to behave myself. I used to wrap hamburgers when Harry and I were just getting started, and I'm not taking any chances of losing out on a deal where he has over eight hundred people working for him."

"You don't seem to be getting much out of the deal now."

"Who says I'm not?"

"I didn't mean financially," I said.

"Neither did I," she said.

"Oh."

"You don't think I was waiting seventeen years till you came along. I said I had to behave myself, but that's for Harry's benefit. I wouldn't give a hoot in hell for a woman that just waited around while Daddy-O was out cutting up . . . Now I got you thinking about your wife."

"It's quite true, you have."

"You want to think about her some more?"

"No."

She put down her drink. "Then why don't you try one on for size? A nice kiss."

She stood up and I took her in my arms and kissed her.

"Say, you're hungry," she said.

"Yes," I said, and we went to her room.

The strangest thing was that I was new to myself, as new as she was new to me. The self-reproach and the disgusted weariness I had expected did not occur. I did not want to leave her, and because I did not want to leave her I knew that I never would leave her entirely. She put on a pale blue kimono and walked with me to the terrace door. "Maybe in a week or so," she said. "I have ways of getting rid of my little bodyguards. And listen, don't worry about Dora. She owes *me* a few favors."

"Are you planning to tell Dora?"

"I don't have to tell her. All we ever talk about is men anyway."

"I know her father-in-law."

"So do I. A damned sight better than you ever will. So there's nothing to worry about there, either, Daniels."

"Don't call me Daniels," I said.

"I'll call you whatever comes into my head," she said. But she was not destructive. She was me, and if she had continued only to be me the affair might have had a self-destructive effect on me. But it soon became a shared experience, and one day she said, "Harry says I'm getting quieter."

"Well, are you?"

"With him I am."

"Does that mean he's getting suspicious?"

"Just about. He has an old trick he tries. Like out of the blue he'll suddenly mention some fellow's name, and watch for my reaction."

"Has he mentioned my name?"

"Not so far. But all the names of his golf friends. He had it kind of narrowed down to Woodburn there for a while. But don't you start getting careless."

"Never fear."

"Don't say never fear. Always fear. Because I'm apt to get careless. I'm smarter than Harry Rupp, but him noticing that I'm getting quieter. That was careless. But you know what the trouble is, Norman. You know why I'm getting careless."

"Why?"

"I'm the next thing to falling in love with you."

"You are, Barbara?"

"Just about. It's all I can do to fake it with that ox any more. I didn't use to mind. Enjoyed it, in fact. What's two men when the one don't mean any more than the other? Dora's father-in-law Wednesday night, Harry Saturday night. I don't hate Harry Rupp. I think the world of him, in some ways. But I never told him I loved him since we got the Schwarzberg contract, that was our first big contract. Some nights he didn't get three hours' sleep. Architect plans. Bank loans. Unions. Wholesalers. And me big as a house with Harriet. We had a semi-detached in Kew Gardens. You would of thought he had the entire responsibility for the atom bomb. Huh. Two years later he wouldn't renew with Schwarzberg. They weren't *big* enough any more. He said he was doing it for me and the kids, but not Harry. Harry's a born big shot. The only trouble is, I don't like it when he big-shots me. Him or anyone else."

I smiled. "I'll try to remember that."

"You better more than try, Norman. I could turn on you," she said.

She was now contentedly in my thoughts, where before she had been a source of disturbance. We saw each other on an average of once a week, usually at her house, but when Harry did not go away we would meet at Dora's. My real estate business is a modest operation, not requiring the services of a full-time secretary, and my office is in the second-floor rear of a two-story building on a side street. In the morning there is no one but me to answer the telephone, and it is normal for me to be seen in all parts of town and the nearby countryside, afoot or in my little car. My recently discovered talent for intrigue was being given few tests.

I say she was contentedly in my thoughts and that is true, and I am mindful of a certain ambiguity in the statement. Her confession of love for me did not come as a surprise. A man knows those things. I was able to recognize, for instance, the difference between her somewhat crude tenderness and Millicent's habitual gentleness. Millicent's behavior, her gentleness, was universal, not limited to her relations with me. Barbara, on the other hand, was learning tenderness for the first time. She loved her children, in her special way, but she sometimes would compare their childhood with her own. She had had to drop out of high school to go to work at sixteen, and the contrast between her children's private schools and summer camps and luxuries, and her struggles to earn a living, was a source of resentment. "I don't begrudge it to them," she said. "Harry has the money. But if I don't slap them down once in a while, they start correcting my grammar and all." And slap them down she did, with the result that their father's weekly homecomings were fun for him and the children, but not for their mother. For that and other reasons it was not so remarkable that she should turn to other men and finally to me.

I could not tell her that I loved her. I had never said that to anyone but Millicent, and it was the one thing of the old me that the new me withheld from Barbara. No, there was one other: she was fascinated by my affairs in London and coaxed me for all the details, and I saw no reason not to tell her as much as I remembered. She was correspondingly revealing concerning the men she had known before and since her marriage to Harry Rupp. But I refused to discuss Millicent on such terms, and my refusal infuriated Barbara. As a matter of fact my apparent loyalty to Millicent was not solely based on a question of taste; Millicent and I, as I have said, "understood" each other, but when I said that, I was speaking of the mutuality of a successful marriage. Actually there had been times in my marriage when I did *not* understand Millicent, when it seemed to me that she was taking advantage of her femininity to behave capriciously. Millicent was the last woman in the world I would call neurotic, but on several occasions she pretended that I had been neglecting her and then, with beautiful inconsistency, locked me out of our room! As for the kind of detail Barbara Rupp sought, there was nothing much to tell.

And I could not bring myself to pay Barbara the compliment that I could have done in all sincerity: that she, and not Millicent, was the woman in my life. I had every intention of staying married to Millicent as long as I lived. I would maintain the same courtesy toward her and protect her from gossip and scandal. But she would have to find her own reasons for the change that had taken place in our relationship, and I was sure she would do that. My hair was grey, my golf handicap had been raised, I needed new glasses every year, a fourth grandchild was on the way, and it was not unusual for me to go to two funerals in the same week. It was my own secret, not even shared by Barbara, that in a few days I would build up such a fierce desire for her as nothing in my old life—the early days with Millicent, the wartime days in London—had prepared me for. I had laughed, with my friends, over jokes about "the last call to the diner," and *l'age dangereux.* The jokes, though I laughed, had always seemed to be in questionable taste, possibly because I have always felt that a man's dignity is more important than his demonstrated virility, and the jokes demonstrated just the opposite at the cost of his dignity. Such jokes, however, usually concerned an aging man and a young girl, and Barbara Rupp was not a young girl. She was a woman who did not have too far to look for a dangerous age of her own. And, as she had said, fifty-five was not so old. There was this, too: that since she had fallen in love with me, we were in this thing together.

I now come to the part of this story that is the most difficult to tell. It is told by the old me, about the man whom I have called the new me; and while they are essentially separate and distinct persons, who will believe that they are not one and the same? The old me and the new me had the same name; I signed my cheques the same way, and the bank never questioned them. The new and the old occupied the same pew in church, and no one noticed when the old became the new. And the old me, now writing, can reveal the innermost thoughts of the new me without taking any so-called literary license. My insistent plea that the old me and the new be considered separately is not the whimpering of a coward: what happens to me happens to the outer me, the only me that the world can see. Nevertheless, I have the same right as anyone else to be judged fairly. I intend to write this all down and destroy it immediately, but I have come to believe that there are many things we do not fully comprehend. I believe that a man can be two men, can even have two souls, for I was two men and have had two souls. And I believe that if I put this all down, somehow the truth will get into the air, even though I destroy these pages immediately and without showing them to anyone. If I tell the truth, sparing neither myself nor anyone else, it will show in my face and in my actions, and people will at least be less positive that my punishment is completely and unquestionably just. If I can create some doubt, this painful confession will have served its purpose.

Barbara abandoned her attempts to extract information of an intimate nature on the subject of my relations with Millicent, and I was glad that we had buried that bone of contention. But without at first seeing any connection, I next had to resist her wish to *meet* Millicent. She had no desire to advance herself socially; but she was increasingly curious, to the point of obsession, about Millicent, about the woman who had been my wife for nearly thirty years. Once again I took a firm stand. "You warned *me* against getting careless," I said. "But this is simply asking for trouble. Your paths haven't crossed, so why should they now, after five years?"

"I want to meet her, and I'm going to."

"I forbid you to do any such thing," I said.

"Forbid me? Who the hell do you think you are? You sound like a God damn schoolteacher."

She wasted no time. The very next afternoon, when I got home from work, Millicent said: "You should have been here earlier. I had a caller. Mrs. Harry Rupp."

"What the devil did she want?"

"I don't know. I thought maybe you'd know. She said she wanted to talk to me about the hospital, serve on one of the committees. But she didn't impress me as the kind of woman that wanted to do any work. She had some other reason."

"Wanted to have a look inside our house," I said.

"Not from what I've heard of hers," said Millicent.

"No, and not from what I've seen of it."

"She mentioned that you'd been there twice."

"I went there to collect money, remember?"

"Oh, I remember."

"Well, are you going to try her out?"

"No," said Millicent. "She wouldn't fit in."

"I don't think she would, either," I said. "What did you tell her?"

"Well, I hope you don't mind, but I said I'd got the impression from you that she wasn't really interested in charities."

"You shouldn't have said *that*, Millicent."

"I wouldn't have, ordinarily. But I wanted to get rid of her, so I wasn't exactly polite. If she wanted a look at this house, she got it, but I don't imagine she'll pay me a second visit."

I was incensed at Barbara for her defiant disobedience, and she was furious at me for the snub Millicent had given her. She appeared in my office on the morning after her visit to Millicent, and said things that could be heard down the hall, things that, overheard, could leave no doubt about the character of our relationship. I fought back with complete silence, until she had run out of vituperation for Millicent and for me. Then I got up and opened the door and looked down the hall. No one was in the hall, and I said, "Now go, and never come here again." What I wanted most was for her to leave the building unrecognized. It was about a quarter to eleven in the morning, a busy time in the building, but there was no one in the hall or on the stairway, and she left.

My reputation, of course, was endangered. I held out no foolish hope that she had not been overheard. All I could hope was that people in the neighboring offices would not identify the woman who had been in my office. That hope was not an entirely foolish one, since it was possible for her to go downstairs and out the rear door to the parking lot, and that is what she did.

But the damage to my reputation had been done. Next door to my office was a tailor's establishment, conducted by a man who had often been behind in his rent. I had had to warn him so many times that there was no cordiality left in our daily greetings. But at noon that day he grinned and smirked. The other two rooms on my floor were rented to a milliner who was not renewing her lease but was moving to a larger store on the main street. The tailor's daughter worked for her as a saleslady, and there was no chance that the three of them would miss this opportunity to wag their tongues.

As a rule I lunched with friends of mine in the coffee shop of the hotel, and I could now tell, from day to day, the progress of the gossip about me. It was two weeks before anyone actually said anything, but if I happened to miss a day at our table, the next day I could detect uneasiness and small silences that revealed they had been discussing me in my absence. The first man to come out with it was Millicent's brother, Harvey Crimmons, who was a lifelong friend. He walked back to my office with me after lunch. "Norm, are you in any trouble?"

"You wouldn't ask me that if you didn't know I was," I said.

"It's going to get to Millicent," he said. "It's spreading like wildfire. Norm, I'm no saint, and if I can help you, say so. Is there anything *to* this talk?"

"I don't know what the talk is, by this time, but you're referring to a visitor I had in my office a couple of weeks ago?"

"Raised hell because you cut off her money or something," said Harvey. "Nobody can figure out who it is you're keeping."

"That's the story, is it?"

"I'd go to Millicent if I were you. I think I know my sister pretty well."

"Harvey, I couldn't bring myself to tell her. And yet the minute she hears anything at all, she's going to guess who the woman is."

"Then you're only postponing it. It's like the dentist. You're going to have to go sometime."

"It isn't really like the dentist, Harvey."

"No, not really, but—"

"It isn't just one tooth. It's several sets of teeth, if you want to think of it that way," I said. "And nobody's going to look very pretty when this dentist gets through."

"I still say tell Millicent before someone else does."

"I'll think about it some more, but thanks anyway," I said.

I stopped in at the tailor shop. "Why, hello there, Mr. Daniels. What can I do for you?"

"Schneider, you're going to have to find another room," I said. "I want you out of here by the first of the month."

"Where can I find a place in that short time? I gotta look,

and find some place is in my price range. Why are you kicking me out, Mr. Daniels?"

"You're not a good tenant, and you haven't lived up to the agreement. Three times in the last eleven months you've been behind, and I could have kicked you out the first time."

"You talk about good tenants, Mr. Daniels. I could talk about bad landlords. Noisy ladies cursing and swearing in the landlord's office, that's no good for business."

"That's what I wanted to make sure of, Schneider," I said. "Be out of here by the first of the month. You'll get a registered letter tomorrow."

"It wasn't only me that heard her," said Schneider.

"The first of the month, Schneider," I said. I was satisfied that he had not identified my visitor and that the milliner and her saleslady were likewise in the dark. Why was that important?

Because I wanted to be with Barbara again. For whatever time we had left, I wanted to be with her. Before Millicent learned the truth, before Harry Rupp learned the truth. I was convinced that no one knew it was Barbara who had made the stormy scene in my office. If I could see her only one more time, then it had to be that, but that it had to be. And I was not sure that it would be only one more time. Harry Rupp, for instance, might hear gossip about me, but he would not place me under suspicion. As for Millicent, if she guessed the identity of my mistress, I would lie to her, not lies of denial but lies that promised never to see Barbara again. I had no intention of giving up Barbara Rupp. Once again she was me, in my blood, and once again I was thinking of myself rather than of her. It was just like before, when I had come to life again, except that now I knew it was for the last time, whether that meant one afternoon or meetings over a period of months.

The shady character I had become dropped in at the golf club, not to play golf but to learn a few things about Harry Rupp. I must say he behaved astonishingly well. He made no mention, direct or indirect, of my new status. No one, as yet, had treated the gossip as a subject for humor in my presence, but Harry Rupp was always unpredictable, to say the least. I did not for a second doubt that he had heard the gossip; his group were as fond of gossip as a woman's sewing circle. But however much he may have joined in the gossip and jokes when he was with his cronies, he gave absolutely no indication that he had heard anything that reflected on my character. As for his suspecting that Barbara was involved, the notion was preposterous: Harry Rupp was not a man who could so convincingly hide his feelings. At all events, I ascertained that he would be absent on one of his usual Monday-to-Friday trips, and on the following Tuesday I telephoned Barbara from my office. I came right to the point. "I'll be at your house at half past one," I said.

"Are you crazy?" she said. "You know what I heard about you? You're supposed to be mixed up with a married woman!" She chose the wrong time to be funny.

"One-thirty," I said.

The autumn, that by a hint of its coming had started this thing, was now here, with colors so gorgeous that it was hard to believe there had ever been a summer or ever would be a winter. As I drove out along the country roads to that trailer-camp house I actually forgot that an unpleasant scene would occur at the end of my drive. But I was shaken back to reality by the sight of Dora's car in the driveway.

Barbara and Dora were drinking coffee in the "family room," a room so designated for no other reason that I could make out than to distinguish it from the livingroom. Both women simultaneously raised their eyelids as I entered, both expressing the same disapproval and hostility. They waited for me to speak.

"I see we're going to be chaperoned," I said. "Or were you just ready to go, Dora?"

"I'm staying," said Dora.

"Would you care to join in the fun?" I said, hoping to shock her.

"I'm here to protect Barbara," said Dora.

"What from? She hasn't needed your protection thus far."

"She sure does now," said Dora.

"Harry didn't go away," said Barbara. "He only went to Newark. He'll be back this afternoon."

"And I'm staying right here till he gets back," said Dora.

"What made him change his mind at the last minute?" I asked Barbara.

"How should I know? But that's the way it is," said Barbara.

"Was it your idea to have Dora here?"

"Partly mine, partly Dora's."

"Well, I certainly haven't got much to talk about with Dora here," I said. "I'll be in my office every morning except Thursday. Will you phone me?"

"No, she won't," said Dora.

"Dora, you're rapidly becoming a bit of a nuisance," I said. "Barbara and I have a lot of things to talk about—"

"You son of a bitch, don't you see she's scared stiff?"

"Are you scared stiff, Barbara?"

"Harry was never this way before," said Barbara. "Maybe he didn't even go to Newark. And he was suppose to go to Newport News. He was suppose to be there just about now. But he called up and cancelled his appointment, in front of me. He won't hardly talk to me."

"Well, let's see what he does tomorrow," I said.

They took that as my parting remark. They looked at me in silence, and said nothing when I left.

I never saw Barbara again, and I have no better information as to the later events of that day than has any other reader of the newspapers. No one else ever knew what happened that afternoon after Harry Rupp came home and Dora left. The driver of the school bus saw Harry Rupp, alone at the foot of the driveway. Rupp told the busman to take the Rupp daughter to Dora's house (the boy was at boarding school). That was at approximately four-ten. At five o'clock Harry telephoned the state police and told them to come and get him. Barbara, beaten and choked, was stretched out on the sofa in the family room.

I, of course, was never charged with any crime, and even when I was made to testify as a material witness the State objected so often to the defense questions that a transcript of the trial contains only a few pages of my testimony. But if ever a man was on trial, it was I. The jury found Harry Rupp not guilty, but I was convicted of an unnamed crime by my friends and fellow townsmen. I was convicted and sentenced before I ever took the stand, and the district attorney was a fool to go against the weight of public opinion. I do not know what kind of reasoning it is that blames me for the murder of Barbara Rupp, the breaking up of Harry Rupp's home and business, the disgrace to my children and grandchildren. The only person who could legitimately claim to have suffered by my infidelity was Millicent, but she and my children no longer bear my embarrassing name. For Millicent the scandal was a release, the divorce proceedings were humorously perfunctory, and she married a man who, I am told, is another Harry Rupp with fifteen years added. They live in a place called Petoskey, Michigan.

Perhaps it is too late for any real good to come of this confession. I did not expect to be judged fairly during the near-hysteria of a murder trial, with one of the New York papers referring to me as "Barbara's aging aristocratic lover." I, an aristocrat? My ancestors fought and died two centuries ago to free this land from the aristocrats, and down through the years my family have stood for justice and fair play. For that very reason I hoped, throughout my ordeal, that when the trial was ended and my fellow townsmen came to their senses, they would see this thing in its true light. I naturally released my clients from our business commitments, with the expectation that they would return to me voluntarily. Indeed, I counted on their return as the first indication of a general return of sanity after the orgy of gossip and persecution. But I have been disillusioned on that score. Younger firms, and newer firms, seized the opportunity of my temporary retirement, and timidity has overcome my former clients. My last dealings in real estate have been the sale of my house, that had been in my family for five generations, and the business property in which I had my office. I am barely able to afford my small room in the hotel, which is situated two stories above the bus terminal. I gave my golf clubs to the pro in part payment of my account with him when I resigned from the club. And Millicent extracted her pound of flesh, down to the last ounce.

I walk the streets of this old town as a convicted criminal, waiting for a word or a sign that justice is being tempered with mercy. Friends of a lifetime speak to me when they cannot avoid doing so, but they never stop to chat, although I have given them openings. It is not so much that I need their companionship; it is rather that I want to be helpful. I know that one of my lifelong friends is going to need the kind of help that I could give him; every morning and afternoon he drops in for a chat with the comely young woman who sells tickets at the bus station. If I could tell him that people have no time for compassion—but perhaps he too feels that he is coming to life again. The young woman is certainly prettier than Barbara and has a much better disposition. I go to the bus station about once a week to weigh myself. Every man over forty-five should watch his weight.

The Lesson

To the young half of the people in the little church the name Godfrey Gaines meant almost nothing. He was Mr. Gaines, father of two of their number, and a sufficiently close friend of the deceased to be selected as an usher at the service. But it had been a long time—the lifetime of the young people in the church—since Godfrey Gaines had done or been anything to attract the attention or stimulate the curiosity of anyone born after 1930. The young people were there to pay their last respects to Mr. Barton, father of the Barton twins and a man whom it was easy to call Rex. People of all ages called him Rex, and in the church that day were twenty or thirty young people who throughout their lives had called him Uncle Rex. As for Mr. Gaines, Godfrey Gaines, it so happened that none of his nieces or nephews had made the trip East to attend Rex Barton's funeral, and therefore no one present had ever called him Uncle Godfrey.

It was a little strange, or so it seemed to the young people, to see how many of the older half of the congregation greeted Mr. Gaines with warmth. The fathers, the actual uncles, all shook his hand and whispered something; the women, the mothers, the actual aunts quite obviously expected to be kissed, and were kissed. All this was strange because he was a stranger to the young people, but it was also strange because there was nothing about him now that called for any demonstration of affection or pleasurable greeting. Mr. Gaines, Godfrey Gaines, was not what you would call a distinguished-looking man, and in his blue serge suit and black four-in-hand he could easily have been mistaken for a paid pallbearer or one of Walter J. McIlhenny's assistants. The young people knew Johnny Gaines and Miriam Gaines Loomis because Johnny and Mimi had been brought up by their mother and stepfather, who lived in the neighborhood. It was known that Johnny's and Miriam's father was to be an usher at Rex Barton's funeral, and he thus escaped being identified as a paid pallbearer or an undertaker's assistant. But it was all pretty strange, to see Johnny's and

Mimi's father, whom most of them had never seen before; to see him so warmly greeted by the older people; and for him to be an usher and thereby presumably to have been an intimate friend of Rex Barton. And perhaps the strangest thing of all was that Godfrey Gaines was such an ordinary-looking man.

The young people watched him with his contemporaries, recognizing them, failing to recognize them, being recognized by them. When recognition occurred it was with a quick smile, a smile as close to elation as the circumstances would permit, and the young people, seeing the smile, had a clue to the warmth of their parents' greeting. When Godfrey Gaines smiled the fathers and mothers and uncles and aunts seemed to be remembering good times, memories that needed the appearance of Godfrey Gaines for the reawakening. A father would whisper something to Mr. Gaines and Mr. Gaines would grin and nod; the mother would kiss Godfrey Gaines, sometimes putting both hands on his shoulders as she did so. Then they would all remember where they were, the solemnity of the occasion, and the mother, the woman, would take Godfrey Gaines's arm and be led to her pew. Mr. Gaines would leave them then and come down the aisle, an ordinary-looking man who could have been mistaken for one of McIlhenny's lugubrious helpers.

The little church was known to them all. Three generations were represented on this day: Rex Barton's generation, and the preceding and succeeding generations. No one had ever seen a speck of dust on the woodwork or a smudge on the brass, and only the most faithful of the faithful noticed the difference when the floor matting was changed. Everything else was the same, year in, year out, and by some mystery of time and human association, even Godfrey Gaines began to fit into the hour. In the midst of the prayers and hymns, the friends and relations, the banks of flowers and the sacred furniture, Godfrey Gaines was one minute a stranger and the next minute a member. Everyone was extraordinarily conscious of time and the passage of it outside the church and down to the moment of entering a pew and becoming part of the congregation; but then time was suspended, minutes and fractions of hours ceased to be the measure of time. Outside, and in the past, there were years and more years or fewer, and when the service ended there would be other years, many or few, but during the ceremony a man in the pew ahead had never been anywhere else, a woman across the aisle had been there throughout eternity. And the young people had known Godfrey Gaines all their lives.

McIlhenny's six men marched beside the casket as Brendan McIlhenny, at one end, pushed it down the aisle. Mrs. Barton and the twins and their husbands darted across the transept and out a side door, and after a moment of hesitation the first pews' occupants commenced to leave. They gathered on the steps of the church and on the sidewalk. ("Are you going back to the house?" "No, nobody is. Mrs. Barton and the others are leaving right away for Manchester, Vermont. That's where he's being buried.")

Godfrey Gaines got his coat and hat out of a limousine and put them on, then went back to the gathering on the church steps. He looked for and found a group of five: his former wife, her husband; his son, his daughter and her husband.

"You're staying with Tom and Edie?" said his former wife. She was standing very close to her husband and holding the collar of her coat close to her throat.

"Staying with Tom and Edie," said Godfrey Gaines. "How are you, Bill?"

"Pretty well, thanks," said Bill Whitehill, calmly.

"Our friend here looks very well," said Godfrey Gaines.

"I wish you wouldn't refer to me as our friend," said Miriam Whitehill.

"All right," said Godfrey Gaines. "I was being polite, that's all. I thought you were going to invite me for lunch or something."

"Far from it," said Miriam Whitehill. "I only wanted to be sure where you were staying."

"So you wouldn't go there?" said Godfrey Gaines.

"Something like that," said Miriam Whitehill.

"But would it be all right if Johnny and Mimi went to Edie's for lunch?"

"I'm sorry, but I can't, Father. I have to be in New York this afternoon," said Johnny Gaines.

"Where do *you* have to be, Mimi?" said Godfrey Gaines.

"I'll go with you," said his daughter. "George is driving back to town with Johnny, but I can go to the Taylors', if that's what you want."

"That's what I do want. Very much. In fact, it's all I want. Let's go." Without another word to the others he turned and led his daughter to the limousine. "Mr. Taylor's house, please," he said to the chauffeur. "Cigarette, Mimi?"

"No thanks. I've given them up."

"Permanently?"

"I guess so. Haven't had one in four months . . . I'm having a child."

"Well, that's good news. Congratulations. What do you want?"

"I don't care. A boy, I suppose. I'm sure George would like to have a boy, and call it George the Third."

"Not if he knows his American history. When is it due?"

"Probably the second week in June."

"How does your mother feel about being a grandma?"

"She's looking forward to it. All her friends already are."

"Yes. That would be her reason."

"Oh, Father. Must you? You two, still so bitter after twenty-five years. Why don't you grow up?"

"Would you speak that way to her?"

"I have."

"In her hearing?"

"I'm not afraid of Mother, or I wouldn't be here now. I didn't ask her permission to come with you."

"No, you didn't. And she didn't like it a damn bit."

"Well, I'm not going to like it either if all you're going to do is make cracks about her."

"All right. I'll stop. But I want to point out that she's had all these years to make cracks about me. And don't tell me she didn't take advantage of that opportunity."

"I wouldn't think of trying. She's made you sound like such an awful son of a bitch that you couldn't possibly live up to it. She made you seem like Errol Flynn."

"Errol Flynn? That's reaching for one."

"No. What made me think of him was when he died, Ma said he couldn't have been any worse than you."

"A charming thing to say to a man's daughter, you have to admit that."

"She didn't exactly say it to me. To George."

"Well then it was nice of George to pass the information along to you."

"He thought it was funny. Don't criticize George."

"Did you think it was funny?"

"In a way. I only remembered Errol Flynn dressed in a pirate's costume, I think it was. And I can't picture you as a pirate."

"I have to weigh that remark. How do you picture me?"

"As you are. And every once in a while I come across a picture of you in a football suit. Did you see yourself in *Sports Illustrated* last fall?"

"Every time that picture's reprinted people send it to me. Sure, I saw it. But you never knew me when I looked like that. My Errol Flynn days, you might say."

"I can't imagine Ma falling for a football type."

"She didn't. By the time she knew me I was a golf type. Although my football reputation had preceded me."

"Lefty Gaines."

"Only because I learned to pass with my left hand. I was never lefthanded in anything else, but I spent a whole summer practicing forward passes with my left hand, and that was really how we beat Yale my sophomore year. When we played Harvard they were ready for me, in spite of the no-scouting agreement. I always used to rib Rex Barton about that. At first he maintained that Harvard hadn't broken the agreement, but I finally got him to admit that some kind alumnus had managed to convey the essential information. Well, what the hell, it was a ridiculous idea anyway. All you had to do was read the Sunday papers, the play-by-play. The New York *World* had charts of the big games."

"Were you an All-American?"

"Second. I lost out to a fellow at the University of Michigan. I'm sure Walter Camp had never seen him play, but I guess it was a fair choice."

"Only you don't really think so."

"Of course I don't, but I'm so used to saying it, I can say it in my sleep. You don't really care anything about football, do you?"

"Not very much. Sometimes people used to ask me if you were my father."

"Not very often, I'll bet. At least not people your age."

"Nobody my age, but a few years older, and of course the father of boys I went out with."

"Then why do you encourage me to talk about it? Not that I needed much encouragement. You were being nice to the old man."

"Why not?"

"Well—yes. Why not? Do you think I've had a rough time, Mimi?"

"Yes, I do."

He took his daughter's hand and looked at it, and then he put it back on her lap. "I have," he said. "But God damn few people know how rough. How did you?"

"I don't know, exactly. Stories. Not exactly stories, either. All the people around here liked you, but they talked about you as if you were dead. Uncle Rex didn't, but a lot of the others did. I knew you didn't have any money, and I heard about your divorce."

"That was in the papers."

"Yes. You married that woman to annoy Ma, didn't you?"

"Well—that may have been part of the reason. I didn't have to marry her, God knows. Nobody did. And she wasn't a bad dame. The only trouble was, she saw me with men, men that knew me as Lefty Gaines. She thought if she married me, my men friends would give her a background. Do you know what I mean? These Yale guys and Harvard guys and Princeton friends of mine, they were the big money and the social leaders of the town. But when I married Jenny my friends' wives never had us to their houses, and she began to think I was some kind of a phony. She wanted like hell to be respectable, and that's where I failed her. She took me for plenty, too, but I had no right to expect anything else. She was, let's face it, a whore."

"That was easy to guess."

"And that's what she is now. A madam. She runs a whorehouse in Kentucky. She's married again, so I don't have to pay her any more alimony. But she took me for everything I had when I walked out on her. It wasn't much by Bill Whitehill's standards, but it was all I had, and I had a hard time getting on my feet again. Your Uncle Rex helped me there. Not with money. With a job."

"I never knew Uncle Rex to be tight-fisted."

"Don't get the wrong impression. He never was tight-fisted. He'd have let me have any amount of money, within reason. But I didn't ask him for money. Him or anyone else. You know, when you get in a jam your friends will often let you have five hundred or a thousand in the hope of getting rid of you. I know. I've done it myself. But a job is a different story. So I called Uncle Rex on the phone and I put it to him straight. All he had to do was pick up the phone and I'd have a job. Rex was a director of a lot of big corporations. 'What kind of job, Lefty? What do you want to do?' And I told him, not just some stopgap kind of job. I wanted something where I could get a whole new start, and I thought the place where I'd fit in best was in some kind of personnel work. Well, to make a long story short, that's how I happened to get with Midlands Incorporated. I knew less than nothing about food processing, but all my life I had a knack of dealing with people. It's mighty interesting work, too. I make twenty thousand dollars a year. Maybe your husband makes that much, a little over half my age. But that twenty thousand represents four big raises in ten years. I started at ten. So they like me. I get results."

"That's wonderful, Father."

"I come back here and see the old crowd I used to know before you were born. Some of them probably expected to see me with my tail between my legs. Beaten. Abject. But I don't think I gave that impression, do you?"

"Not a bit."

"Were you—you weren't embarrassed or anything, were you? I can't tell about Johnny. A son takes his mother's side instinctively, and I don't know whether he had to go back to New York or not."

"He really did. I happen to know he did. He said so before the service."

"Well, I'm glad he wasn't just ducking me. I'd hate to think he didn't have any more character than that. I'm sure Bill Whitehill's been a good father to him and all that, but I know Bill, and if Johnny was only making up some excuse, Bill Whitehill wouldn't have much respect for him. You get along with Bill all right, don't you?"

"Very well."

"Bill's all right. I won't say anything against Bill. Not everybody that inherited as much money as Bill came through as well as he has. He always did everything by the book. He was in love with your mother long before I entered the picture, and when she married me instead, he took it with good grace. You *could* say he was biding his time till the roof fell in, but I never held that against him. Your mother was very lucky she had Bill to turn to. So were you, for that matter. And Johnny."

"Father?"

"What?"

"I probably shouldn't ask you this."

"If it's what I think it is, don't ask it," said Godfrey Gaines.

"How will I know we're thinking of the same thing?"

"Because there's only one question you could ask me that you'd have to soften me up first. When you say, 'I probably shouldn't ask you,' there aren't that many things that you're curious about."

"You *are* good about people," said Mimi. "Up to a point."

"Up to a point? What do you mean by that?"

"Well, you guessed the nature of what I was going to ask you, and you refused to hear the question. But where you're not good is that you don't know me."

"Not as well as I'd like to," said Godfrey Gaines.

"Thanks, but I'm not going to be diverted by compliments. Up to a point you know people, Father, but you don't know that you can't stop me from asking the question. Was it Mrs. Barton?"

"Was what Mrs. Barton?"

"Was Mrs. Barton the one that made Mother so bitter? Was Mrs. Barton your girl?"

Godfrey Gaines smiled faintly. "You have it all figured out, haven't you?"

"Yes, I think I have."

"All the wisdom of your years, all the sophistication of Long Island. You just have to know, don't you? Is that why you came along with me?"

"Not entirely, Father. But for years I've suspected that Mrs. Barton was the one that came between Mother and you. She always seemed the logical one."

"You looked over the field, and Mrs. Barton seemed the logical one."

"Yes. She must have been beautiful when she was young."

"She was indeed, and in my view she still is."

"Then I'm right. It was she?"

"No," said Godfrey Gaines.

"Is this a gentlemanly denial? Are you going by the book, too?"

"No. But I kissed Mrs. Barton once."

"Is that all?"

"That's all," said Godfrey Gaines. "I kissed her once, and then I went away."

"It doesn't sound like you at all, Father."

"No. It doesn't sound like Errol Flynn, either, I imagine." He leaned forward. "Driver, don't go to Mr. Taylor's right away. We want to drive around a while. Just take us anywhere till I tell you." Godfrey Gaines pressed the button that raised the glass division in the front seat, and looked at his daughter. "I haven't been a very good father, Mimi. I've been a lousy father. In fact, practically not a father at all. Bill Whitehill's been your father, not I, and he's a man that goes by the book. Always goes by the book. Which is all right, most of the time. But there comes a time when you have to throw the book away. I have a lesson for you, and it isn't in the book. Okay?"

"Of course."

"The first rule in the book, of course, is that a gentleman doesn't talk. Right?"

"And the rule that's broken most often."

"Right. And now your father is about to break that rule, because it's much more important for a father to teach his daughter something about life than it is for him to observe the rules."

"I'm waiting with bated breath, Father."

"All right," said Godfrey Gaines. "After you were born, and it seemed like the time had come for your mother and I to resume normal relations, she decided to go away for a while. The doctor had told me it was all right for us to sleep together, but your mother begged off. I had another talk with the doctor, and he said that while your mother was physically able to have relations with me, still it wasn't unusual for a woman after her first child to—to be reluctant. Unwilling. Indifferent. And in some cases he said the whole idea was repulsive to a wife, especially if she'd had a bad time in her pregnancy. That wasn't the case with you, at least physically. Your mother didn't have a particularly bad time having you, but then as Jerry Murphy, Doctor Murphy, said, we couldn't overlook the psychological factor. So your mother went South for four months. She was to be gone two weeks, originally, but that became a month, then two months. Then four. She'd never say she was staying another month, and several times when I said I wanted to join her, she said she'd be home the next week and there was no point in my going South. Then she'd stay another month.

"Well, I didn't suspect anything wrong, but I was young and vigorous and a couple of times I more or less picked up where I'd left off with a girl I'd known before I was married. In plain language, I slept with this girl several times while your mother was in the South, and in some way or other your mother found out about it. I don't know to this day how she found out, and it really doesn't matter. The point is, when your mother came home she accused me of being unfaithful, told me the girl's name and where she lived, and had me dead to rights. No use denying it. Her facts were too good. I asked her if she wanted a divorce, and she said she'd have to think it over. She thought it over for quite a while. She took so long, in fact, that I began seeing the girl again, and one day I realized that it had been a whole year since I'd last slept with your mother. I was never the most sensitive man in the world, but it dawned on me that this was getting to be a hell of a marriage. I was crazy about you, but you weren't the most brilliant conversationalist at that age. Goo and gah were about the extent of your conversation when you weren't yelling your head off. And it was just about that time that I realized that I wasn't in love with your mother any more. We were living in the same house and we went everywhere together and entertained a lot. But don't forget I was still kind of on trial. She was still thinking it over, whether to get a divorce or not, and finally one day I asked her what she'd decided, and she said it didn't really make all that difference unless I wanted one. That was the first inkling I had that she knew I'd been seeing the other girl again. Then, just a shot in the dark, I asked her if she was seeing anyone, and she said yes, she was. I couldn't believe it. I wasn't in love with her any more, but no man wants to feel like a chump, and believe me I did. I regret to say that I threatened to kill her and the guy. I hit her, and she ran to her room and locked the door and telephoned the Bartons. It was about eleven o'clock at night, but the Bartons came over and Rex more or less took me in hand and Mrs. Barton went in and pacified your mother. It was decided that the best thing would be if Rex and I went in town and spent the night at the club, which we did.

"Oddly enough, the quarrel seemed to be just what we both needed. I returned home next afternoon, full of remorse and apologies, and your mother said it wasn't all my fault, that I'd had provocation, and I don't remember who first suggested it, but we decided to take a trip together and see if we couldn't make a fresh start. That lasted about three weeks, or just long enough for me to bring up the subject of the other guy. She said it was part of the bargain that we weren't to talk about what had happened before, but if that was part of the bargain, I certainly didn't remember it. In fact, I didn't remember any bargain. We returned to Long Island, and shortly after that your mother announced that she was having a baby. Johnny. It should have occurred to me that she'd gone into the second-honeymoon very enthusiastically, considering that we'd been on the verge of very serious trouble. But I didn't say anything. The reason I kept quiet was because I was secretly ashamed of myself. I'd got her pregnant, but I really didn't love her. The only love in my life was you, saying goo and gah."

"Hadn't I progressed beyond goo and gah by that time?"

"Conversationally, you were in a rut."

"I was practicing up to be a good listener," she said.

"Maybe."

"All right. So you'd got Mother pregnant," she said. "Or someone had."

"Really, Mimi."

"Well, isn't that why she went away on this second honeymoon?"

"Listen, kid, I don't mind not going by the book, but you *want* me to throw the book away."

"Father, all this talk about the book, going by the book, that came from you."

"Then I guess I don't know how to talk to you," said Godfrey Gaines.

"Yes you do. I'm enjoying the conversation, but when you talk about Bill Whitehill and yourself and this nonexistent book, I wonder where you've been the last twenty-five years. You were married to a woman that runs a whorehouse. I should have thought—well, go on with your story, Father."

"I don't know how to. In my job I have to give a lot of talks, but there I know my audience. This time I don't."

"Well, try. Assume that I take it for granted that you weren't responsible for Mother's pregnancy. Who was?"

"Rex Barton," said Godfrey Gaines. He looked at her again.

"That doesn't surprise me."

"God, in your way you're as smug as I thought I was."

"But Father, I've known for *years* that Uncle Rex and Mother were a thing. Who around here doesn't know it?"

"Bill Whitehill?"

"Maybe he does and maybe he doesn't."

"Has he got somebody?"

"Well, if he hasn't it's only because he doesn't want anybody."

"What about *you*, Mimi?"

"What about me?"

"You and George?"

"Have I got somebody? No. But I happen to like George."

"Gee, that's a positive declaration," said Godfrey Gaines. "That's the old-time religion."

"Don't be sarcastic, Father. You had the old-time religion, you and Mother, and where has it got you? Twenty-five years of hating each other, not to mention a home broken up, and you marrying a whorehouse madam. That's the book you keep talking about. Well, you can have it."

"What would George do if he found out this child wasn't his?"

"What do you mean, found out? He wouldn't have to *find out*. I'd tell him."

"If you knew," said Godfrey Gaines.

"Father, ask the driver to take us to the Taylors'."

Godfrey Gaines did so, and the car wound along the roads that long ago and now once again had names that seemed so odd—Muttontown, Matinecock, Skunks Misery. Godfrey Gaines could not have found his way now, where the chopped-up estates had lost all identity.

"Father. When did you kiss Mrs. Barton?"

"Oh, you want to go back to that? Well, when I went to say goodbye to her. Your mother and Rex Barton were off somewhere together, and I decided I wouldn't be there when they got back."

"Did you know they were together, or just guess?"

He smiled. "I was like you. He seemed the logical one."

"Why?"

"Well, she'd turned down Bill Whitehill, the other logical one, and that left Rex Barton. And who did she rush to the phone to when I threatened to kill her? Oh, hell, it had to be Rex. He was all over the place anyway."

"Where was I?"

"In the nursery, where you belonged. I had no intention of taking you away, then or later. Personally I considered your mother a slut, but what did I know about raising a one-year-old daughter?"

"So you went to see Mrs. Barton."

"I told her I was leaving Miriam, and she said I was making a great mistake. I'll never forget it. 'Rex will get over it, and so will she.' That was the first I ever knew that Mrs. Barton was hep to the jive."

"Oh, Father. Not slang. Not *that* kind of slang."

"All right," said Godfrey Gaines. "She knew where they were, and she offered to make Rex come home, but I said no. Then she suddenly became very attractive to me, Mrs. Barton, and I suggested that she and I go away together. She laughed. She said she'd do a lot of traveling if she went away every time she got that kind of an offer. But she said no. 'I like you, Lefty,' she said. 'And maybe this is a good idea, your going away. But if you do go, don't ever come back. Don't *ever* come back,' she said. 'Cut them all out of your life, all of us,' she said. So that's what I did."

"And you kissed her."

"Actually it was more like she kissed me. It wasn't a pass on either side. It was affection. So I stayed away—till she sent for me, the day before yesterday. I guess most people around here wouldn't have thought of me to help give Rex Barton a send-off, but she did. And I guess she must have had her reasons. I didn't even ask. There's nothing I wouldn't do for Cyn Barton," said Godfrey Gaines.

"If you ask me, you've done quite a lot," said his daughter.

Pat Collins

Now THEY are both getting close to seventy, and when they see each other on the street Whit Hofman and Pat Collins bid each other the time of day and pass on without stopping for conversation. It may be that in Whit Hofman's greeting there is a little more hearty cordiality than in Pat Collins's greeting to him; it may be that in Pat Collins's words and smile there is a wistfulness that is all he has left of thirty years of a dwindling hope.

The town is full of young people who never knew that for about three years—1925, 1926, 1927—Whit Hofman's favorite companion was none other than Pat Collins. Not only do they not know of the once close relationship; today they would not believe it. But then it is hard to believe, with only the present evidence to go on. Today Pat Collins still has his own garage, but it is hardly more than a filling station and tire repair business on the edge of town, patronized by the people of the neighborhood and not situated on a traffic artery of any importance. He always has some young man helping out, but he does most of the work himself. Hard work it is, too. He hires young men out of high school—out of prison, sometimes—but the young men don't stay. They never stay. They like Pat Collins, and they say so, but they don't want to work at night, and Pat Collins's twenty-four-hour service is what keeps him going. Twenty-four hours, seven days a week, the only garage in town that says it and means it. A man stuck for gas, a man with a flat and no spare, a man skidded into a ditch—they all know that if they phone Pat Collins he will get there in his truck and if necessary tow them away. Some of the motorists are embarrassed: people who never patronize Pat Collins except in emergencies; people who knew him back in the days when he was Whit Hofman's favorite companion. They embarrass themselves; he does not say or do anything to embarrass them except one thing: he charges them fair prices when he could hold them up, and to some of those people who knew him long ago that is the most embarrassing thing he could do. "Twelve dollars, Pat? You could have charged me more than that."

"Twelve dollars," he says. And there were plenty of times when he could have asked fifty dollars for twelve dollars' worth of service—when the woman in the stalled car was not the wife of the driver.

Now, to the younger ones, he has become a local symbol of misfortune ("All I could do was call Pat Collins") and at the same time a symbol of dependability ("Luckily I thought of Pat Collins"). It is mean work; the interrupted sleep, the frequently bad weather, the drunks and the shocked and the guilty-minded. But it is the one service he offers that makes the difference between a profit and breaking even.

"Hello, Pat," Whit Hofman will say, when they meet on Main Street.

"Hyuh, Whit," Pat Collins will say.

Never more than that, but never less . . .

Aloysius Aquinas Collins came to town in 1923 because he had heard it was a good place to be, a rich town for its size. Big coal interests to start with, but good diversification as well: a steel mill, a couple of iron foundries, the railway car shops, shoe factories, silk mills, half a dozen breweries, four meat packing plants and, to the south, prosperous farmers. Among the rich there were two Rolls-Royces, a dozen or more Pierce-Arrows, a couple of dozen Cadillacs, and maybe a dozen each of Lincolns, Marmons, Packards. It was a spending town; the Pierce-Arrow families bought small roadsters for their children and the women were beginning to drive their own cars. The Rolls-Royces and Pierce-Arrows were in Philadelphia territory, and the franchises for the other big cars were already spoken for, but Pat Collins was willing to start as a dealer for one of the many makes in the large field between Ford-Dodge and Cadillac-Packard, one of the newer, lesser known makes. It was easy to get a franchise for one of those makes, and he decided to take his time.

Of professional experience in the automobile game he had none. He was not yet thirty, and he had behind him two years at Villanova, fifteen months as a shore duty ensign, four years as a salesman of men's hats at which he made pretty good money but from which he got nothing else but stretches of boredom between days of remorse following salesmen's parties in hotels. His wife Madge had lost her early illusions, but she loved him and partly blamed life on the road for what was happening to him. "Get into something else," she would say, "or honest to God, Pat, I'm going to take the children and pull out."

"It's easy enough to talk about getting another job," he would say.

"I don't care what it is, just as long as you're not away five days a week. Drive a taxi, if you have to."

When she happened to mention driving a taxi she touched upon the only major interest he had outside the routine of his life: from the early days of Dario Resta and the brothers Chevrolet he had been crazy about automobiles, all automobiles and everything about them. He would walk or take the "L" from home in West Philadelphia to the area near City Hall, and wander about, stopping in front of the hotels and clubs and private residences and theaters and the Academy of Music, staring at the limousines and town cars, engaging in conversation with the chauffeurs; and then he would walk up North Broad Street, Automobile Row, and because he was a nice-looking kid, the floor salesmen would sometimes let him sit in the cars on display. He collected all the manufacturers' brochures and read all the advertisements in the newspapers. Closer to home he would stand for hours, studying the sporty roadsters and phaetons outside the Penn fraternity houses; big Simplexes with searchlights on the running-boards, Fiats and Renaults and Hispanos and Blitzen-Benzes. He was nice-looking and he had nice manners, and when he would hold the door open for one of the fraternity men they would sometimes give him a nickel and say, "Will you keep your eye on my car, sonny?"

"Can I sit in it, please?"

"Well, if you promise not to blow the horn."

He passed the horn-blowing stage quickly. Sometimes the fraternity men would come out to put up the top when there was a sudden shower, and find that Aloysius Aquinas Collins had somehow done it alone. For this service he wanted no reward but a ride home, on the front seat. On his side of the room he shared with his older brother he had magazine and rotogravure pictures of fine cars pinned to the walls. The nuns at school complained that instead of paying attention, he was continually drawing pictures of auto*mo*biles, auto*mo*biles. The nuns did not know how good the drawings were; they only cared that one so bright could waste so much time, and their complaints to his parents made it impossible for Aloysius to convince Mr. and Mrs. Collins that after he got his high school diploma, he wanted to get a job on Automobile Row. The parents sent him to Villanova, and after sophomore year took him out because the priests told them they were wasting their money, but out of spite his father refused to let him take a job in the auto business. Collins got him a job in the shipyards, and when the country entered the war, Aloysius joined the Navy and eventually was commissioned. He married Madge Ruddy, became a hat salesman, and rented half of a two-family house in Upper Darby.

Gibbsville was on his sales route, and it first came to his special notice because his Gibbsville customer bought more hats in his high-priced line than any other store of comparable size. He thus discovered that it was a spending town, and that the actual population figures were deceptive; it was surrounded by a lot of much smaller towns whose citizens shopped in Gibbsville. He began to add a day to his normal visits to Gibbsville, to make a study of the automobile business there, and when he came into a small legacy from his aunt, he easily persuaded Madge to put in her own five thousand dollars, and he bought Cunningham's Garage, on Railroad Avenue, Gibbsville.

Cunningham's was badly run down and had lost money for its previous two owners, but it was the oldest garage in town. The established automobile men were not afraid of competition from the newcomer, Collins, who knew nobody to speak of and did not even have a dealer's franchise. They thought he was out of his mind when he began spending money in sprucing up the place. They also thought, and said, that he was getting pretty big for his britches in choosing to rent a house on Lantenengo Street. The proprietor of Cunningham's old garage then proceeded to outrage the established dealers by stealing Walt Michaels' best mechanic, Joe Ricci. Regardless of what the dealers might do to each other in the competition to clinch a sale, one thing you did not do was entice away a man's best mechanic. Walt Michaels, who had the Oldsmobile franchise, paid a call on the new fellow.

A. A. Collins, owner and proprietor, as his sign said, of Collins Motor Company, was in his office when he saw Michaels get out of his car. He went out to greet Michaels, his hand outstretched. "Hello, Mr. Michaels, I'm Pat Collins," he said.

"I know who you are. I just came down to tell you what I think of you."

"Not much, I guess, judging by—"

"Not much is right."

"Smoke a cigar?" said Pat Collins.

Michaels slapped at the cigar and knocked it to the ground. Pat Collins picked it up and looked at it. "I guess that's why they wrap them in tinfoil." He rubbed the dirt off the cigar and put it back in his pocket.

"Don't you want to fight?" said Michaels.

"What for? You have a right to be sore at me, in a way. But when you have a good mechanic like Joe, you ought to be willing to pay him what he's worth."

"Well, I never thought I'd see an Irishman back out of a fight. But with you I guess that's typical. A sneaky Irish son of a bitch."

"Now just a minute, Michaels. Go easy."

"I said it. A sneaky Irish son of a bitch."

"Yeah, I was right the first time," said Collins. He hit Michaels in the stomach with his left hand, and as Michaels crumpled, Collins hit him on the chin with his right hand. Michaels went down, and Collins stood over him, waiting for him to get up. Michaels started to raise himself with both hands on the ground, calling obscene names, but while his hands were still on the ground Collins stuck the foil-wrapped cigar deep in his mouth. Three or four men who stopped to look at the fight burst into laughter, and Michaels, his breath shut off, fell back on the ground.

"Change your mind about the cigar, Michaels?" said Collins.

"I'll send my son down to see you," said Michaels, getting to his feet.

"All right. What does *he* smoke?"

"He's as big as you are."

"Then I'll use a tire iron on him. Now get out of here, and quick."

Michaels, dusting himself off, saw Joe Ricci among the spectators. He pointed at him with his hat. "You, you ginny bastard, you stole tools off of me."

Ricci, who had a screwdriver in his hand, rushed at Michaels and might have stabbed him, but Collins swung him away.

"Calling me a thief, the son of a bitch, I'll kill him," said Ricci. "I'll *kill* him."

"Go on, Michaels. Beat it," said Collins.

Michaels got in his car and put it in gear, and as he was about to drive away Collins called to him: "Hey, Michaels, shall I fill her up?"

The episode, the kind that men liked to embellish in the retelling, made Pat Collins universally unpopular among the dealers, but it made him known to a wider public. It brought him an important visitor.

The Mercer phaeton pulled up at Pat Collins's gas pump and Collins, in his office, jumped up from his desk, and without putting on his coat, went out to the curb. "Can I help you?" he said.

"Fill her up, will you, please?" said the driver. He was a handsome man, about Collins's age, wearing a brown Homburg and a coonskin coat. Pat Collins knew who he was—Whit Hofman, probably the richest young man in the town—because he knew the car. He was conscious of Hofman's curiosity, but he went on pumping the gasoline. He hung up the hose and said, "You didn't need much. That'll cost you thirty-six cents, Mr. Hofman. Wouldn't you rather I sent you a bill?"

"Well, all right. But don't I get a cigar, a new customer? At least that's what I hear."

The two men laughed. "Sure, have a cigar," said Collins, handing him one. Hofman looked at it.

"Tinfoil, all right. You sure this isn't the same one you gave Walt Michaels?"

"It might be. See if it has any teeth marks on it," said Collins.

"Well, I guess Walt had it coming to him. He's a kind of a sorehead."

"You know him?"

"Of course. Known him all my life, he's always lived here. He's not a bad fellow, Mr. Collins, but you took Joe away from him, and Joe's a hell of a good mechanic. I'd be sore, too, I guess."

"Well, when you come looking for a fight, you ought to be more sure of what you're up against. Either that, or be ready to take a beating. I only hit him twice."

"When I was a boy you wouldn't have knocked him down that easily. When I was a kid, Walt Michaels was a good athlete, but he's put away a lot of beer since then." Hofman looked at Collins. "Do you like beer?"

"I like the beer you get around here. It's better than we get in Philly."

"Put on your coat and let's drink some beer," said Hofman. "Or are you busy?"

"Not that busy," said Collins.

They drove to a saloon in one of the neighboring towns, and Collins was surprised to see that no one was surprised to see the young millionaire, with his Mercer and his coonskin coat. The men drinking at the bar—workingmen taking a day off, they appeared to be—were neither cordial nor hostile to Hofman. "Hello, Paul," said Hofman. "Brought you a new customer."

"I need all I can get," said the proprietor. "Where will you want to sit? In the back room?"

"I guess so. This is Mr. Collins, just opened a new garage. Mr. Collins, Mr. Paul Unitas, sometimes called Unitas States of America."

"Pleased to meet you," said Paul, shaking hands.

"Same here," said Collins.

"How's the beer?" said Hofman.

Paul shook his head. "They're around. They stopped two truckloads this morning."

"Who stopped them? The state police?" said Hofman.

"No, this time it was enforcement agents. New ones."

Hofman laughed. "You don't have to worry about Mr. Collins. I'll vouch for him."

"Well, if you say so, Whit. What'll you have?"

"The beer's no good?"

"Slop. Have rye. It's pretty good. I cut it myself."

"Well, if you say rye, that's what we'll have. Okay, Collins?"

"Sure."

Hofman was an affable man, an interested listener and a hearty laugher. It was dark when they left the saloon; Collins had told Hofman a great deal about himself, and Hofman drove Collins home in the Mercer. "I can offer you some Canadian Club," said Collins.

"Thanks just the same, but we're going out to dinner and I have to change. Ask me again sometime. Nice to've seen you, Pat."

"Same to you, Whit. Enjoyable afternoon," said Collins.

In the house Collins kissed Madge's cheek. "Whew! Out drinking with college boys?" she said.

"I'll drink with that college boy any time. That's Whit Hofman."

"How on earth—"

She listened with increasing eagerness while he told her the events of the afternoon. "Maybe you could sell him a car, if you had a good franchise," she said.

"I'm not going to try to sell him anything but Aloysius Aquinas Collins, Esquire. And anyway, I like him."

"You can like people and still sell them a car."

"Well, I'm never going to try to make a sale there. He came to see me out of curiosity, but we hit it off right away. He's a swell fellow."

"Pat?"

"What?"

"Remember why we moved here."

"Listen, it's only ha' past six and I'm home. This guy came to see me, Madge."

"A rich fellow with nothing better to do," she said.

"Oh, for God's sake. You say remember why we moved here. To have a home. But *you* remember why I wanted to live on this street. To meet people like Whit Hofman."

"But not to spend the whole afternoon in some hunky saloon. Were there any women there?"

"A dozen of them, all walking around naked. What have you got for supper?"

"For *dinner*, we have veal cutlets. But Pat, remember what we are. We're not society people. What's she like, his wife?"

"How would I know? I wouldn't know her if I saw her. Unless she was driving that car."

They had a two weeks' wait before Whit Hofman again had the urge for Pat Collins's company. This time Hofman took him to the country club, and they sat in the smoking-room with a bottle of Scotch on the table. "Do you play squash?" said Hofman.

"Play it? I thought you ate it. No, I used to play handball."

"Well, it's kind of handball with a racquet. It's damn near the only exercise I get in the winter, at least until we go South. If you were a good handball player, you'd learn squash in no time."

"Where? At the Y.M.?"

"Here. We have a court here," said Hofman. He got up and pointed through the French window. "See that little house down there, to the right of the first fairway? That's the squash court."

"I was a caddy one summer."

"Oh, you play golf?"

"I've never had a club in my hand since then."

"How would you like to join here? I'll be glad to put you up and we'll find somebody to second you. Does your wife play tennis or golf?"

"No, she's not an athlete. How much would it cost to join?"

"Uh, family membership, you and your wife and children under twenty-one. They just raised it. Initiation, seventy-five dollars. Annual dues, thirty-five for a family membership."

"Do you think I could get in? We don't know many people that belong."

"Well, Walt Michaels doesn't belong. Can you think of anyone else that might blackball you? Because if you can't, I think I could probably get you in at the next meeting. Technically, I'm not supposed to put you up, because I'm on the admissions committee, but that's no problem."

Any hesitancy Pat Collins might have had immediately vanished at mention of the name Walt Michaels. "Well, I'd sure like to belong."

"I'll take care of it. Let's have a drink on it," said Whit Hofman.

"We're Catholics, you know."

"That's all right. We take Catholics. Not all, but some. And those we don't take wouldn't get in if they were Presbyterian or anything else."

"Jews?"

"We have two. One is a doctor, married to a Gentile. He claims he isn't a Jew, but he is. The other is the wife of a Gentile. Otherwise, no. I understand they're starting their own club, I'm not sure where it'll be."

"Well, as long as you know we're Catholics."

"I knew that, Pat," said Hofman. "But I respect you for bringing it up."

Madge Collins was upset about the country club. "It isn't only what you have to pay to get in. It's meals, and spending money on clothes. I haven't bought anything new since we moved here."

"As the Dodge people say, 'It isn't the initial cost, it's the upkeep.' But Madge, I told you before, those are the kind of people that're gonna be worth our while. I'll make a lot of connections at the country club, and in the meantime, I'll get a franchise. So far I didn't spend a nickel on advertising. Well, this is gonna be the best kind of advertising. The Cadillac dealer is the only other dealer in the country club, and I won't compete with him."

"Everything going out, very little coming in," she said.

"Stop worrying, everything's gonna be hunky-dory."

On the morning after the next meeting of the club admissions committee Whit Hofman telephoned Pat Collins. "Congratulations to the newest member of the Lantenengo Country Club. It was a cinch. You'll get a notice and a bill, and as soon as you send your cheque you and Mrs. Collins can start using the club, although there's no golf or tennis now. However, there's a dance next Friday, and we'd like you and your wife to have dinner with us. Wear your Tuck. My wife is going to phone Mrs. Collins some time today."

In her two years as stock girl and saleslady at Oppenheim, Collins—"my cousins," Pat called them—Madge had learned a thing or two about values, and she had style sense. The evening dress she bought for the Hofman dinner and club dance was severely simple, black, and Pat thought it looked too old for her. "Wait till you see it on," she said. She changed the shoulder straps and substituted thin black cord, making her shoulders, chest, and back completely bare and giving an illusion of a deeper décolletage than was actually the case. She had a good figure and a lovely complexion, and when he saw her ready to leave for the party, he was startled. "It's not too old for you any more. Maybe it's too young."

"I wish I had some jewelry," she said.

"You have. I can see them."

"Oh—oh, stop. It's not immodest. You can't see anything unless you stoop over and look down."

"Unless you happen to be over five foot five, and most men are."

"Do you want me to wear a shawl? I have a nice old shawl of Grandma's. As soon as we start making money the one thing I want is a good fur coat. That's all I want, and I can get one wholesale."

"Get one for me, while you're at it. But for now, let's get a move on. Dinner is eight-thirty and we're the guests of honor."

"Guests of honor! Just think of it, Pat. I haven't been so excited since our wedding. I hope I don't do anything wrong."

"Just watch Mrs. Hofman. I don't even know who else'll be there, but it's time we were finding out."

"Per-*fume*! I didn't put on any per*fume*. I'll be right down."

She was excited and she had youth and health, but she also had a squarish face with a strong jawline that gave her a look of maturity and dignity. Her hair was reddish brown, her eyes grey-green. It was a face full of contrasts, especially from repose to animation, and with the men—beginning with Whit Hofman—she was an instant success.

The Hofmans had invited three other couples besides the Collinses. Custom forbade having liquor bottles or cocktail shakers on the table at club dances, and Whit Hofman kept a shaker and a bottle on the floor beside him. The men were drinking straight whiskey, the women drank orange blossoms. There was no bar, and the Hofman party sat at the table and had their drinks until nine o'clock, when Hofman's wife signalled the steward to start serving. Chincoteagues were served first, and before the soup, Whit Hofman asked Madge Collins to dance. He was feeling good, and here he was king. His fortune was respected by men twice his age, and among the men and women who were more nearly his contemporaries he was genuinely well liked for a number of reasons: his unfailingly good manners, no matter how far in drink he might get; his affability, which drew upon his good manners when bores and toadies and the envious and the weak made their assaults; his emanations of strength, which were physically and tangibly demonstrated in his expertness at games as well as in the slightly more subtle self-reminders of his friends that he *was* Whit Hofman and *did have* all that money. He had a good war record, beginning with enlistment as a private in the National Guard for Mexican Border service, and including a field commission, a wound chevron, and a Croix de Guerre with palm during his A.E.F. service. He was overweight, but he could afford bespoke tailors and he cared about clothes; tonight he was wearing a dinner jacket with a white waistcoat and a satin butterfly tie. Madge Ruddy Collins had never known anyone quite like him, and her first mistake was to believe that his high spirits had something special to do with her. At this stage she had no way of knowing that later on, when he danced with his fat old second cousin, he would be just as much fun.

"Well, how do you like your club?" he said.

"My club? Oh—*this* club. Oh, it's beautiful. Pat and I certainly do thank you."

"Very glad to do it. I hope you're going to take up golf. More and more women are. Girl I just spoke to, Mrs. Dick Richards, she won the second flight this year, and she only started playing last spring."

"Does your wife play?"

"She plays pretty well, and could be a lot better. She's going to have a lot of lessons when we go South. That's the thing to do. As soon as you develop a fault, have a lesson right away, before it becomes a habit. I'm going to have Pat playing squash before we leave."

"Oh."

"He said he was a handball player, so squash ought to come easy to him. Of course it's a much more strenuous game than golf."

"It is?"

He said something in reply to a question from a man dancing by. The man laughed, and Whit Hofman laughed. "That's Johnny King," said Hofman. "You haven't met the Kings, have you?"

"No," said Madge. "She's pretty. Beautifully gowned."

"Oh, that's not his wife. She isn't here tonight. That's Mary-Louise Johnson, from Scranton. There's a whole delegation from Scranton here tonight. They all came down for Buz McKee's birthday party. That's the big table over in the corner. Well, I'm getting the high sign, I guess we'd better go back to our table. Thank you, Madge. A pleasure."

"Oh, to me, too," she said.

In due course every man in the Hofman party danced with every woman, the duty rounds. Pat Collins was the last to dance with Madge on the duty rounds. "You having a good time?" he said.

"Oh, *am* I?" she said.

"How do you like Whit?"

"He's a real gentleman, I'm crazy about him. I like him the best. Do you like her, his wife?"

"I guess so. In a way yes, and in a way no."

"Me too. She'd rather be with those people from Scranton."

"What people from Scranton?"

"At the big table. They're here to attend a birthday party for Buzzie McKee."

"Jesus, you're learning fast."

"I found that out from Whit. The blonde in the beaded white, that's Mary-Louise Johnson, dancing with Johnny King. They're dancing every dance together."

"Together is right. Take a can-opener to pry them apart."

"His wife is away," said Madge. "Where did Whit go?"

Pat turned to look at their table. "I don't know. Oh, there he is, dancing with some fat lady."

"I don't admire his taste."

"Say, you took a real shine to Whit," said Pat Collins.

"Well, he's a real gentleman, but he isn't a bit forward. Now where's he going? . . . Oh, I guess he wanted to wish Buzzie McKee a happy birthday. Well, let's sit down."

The chair at her left remained vacant while Hofman continued his visit to the McKee table. On Madge's right was a lawyer named Joe Chapin, who had something to do with the admissions committee; polite enough, but for Madge very hard to talk to. At the moment he was in conversation with the woman on his right, and Madge Collins felt completely alone. A minute passed, two minutes, and her solitude passed to uneasiness to anger. Whit Hofman made his way back to the table, and when he sat down she said, trying to keep the irritation out of her tone, "That wasn't very polite."

"I'm terribly sorry. I thought you and Joe—"

"Oh, *him*. Well, I'll forgive you if you dance this dance with me."

"Why of course," said Hofman.

They got up again, and as they danced she closed her eyes, pretending to an ecstasy she did not altogether feel. They got through eighteen bars of "Bambalina," and the music stopped. "Oh, hell," she said. "I'll let you have the next."

"Fine," he said. She took his arm, holding it so that her hand clenched his right biceps, and giving it a final squeeze as they sat down.

"Would you like some more coffee?" he said. "If not, I'm afraid we're going to have to let them take the table away."

"Why?"

"That's what they do. Ten o'clock, tables have to be cleared out, to make room for the dancing. You know, quite a few people have dinner at home, then come to the dance."

"What are they? Cheap skates?"

"Oh, I don't know about that. No, hardly that."

"But if *you* wanted to keep the table, they'd let you."

"Oh, I wouldn't do that, Madge. They really need the room."

"Then where do we go?"

"Wherever we like. Probably the smoking-room. But from now on we just sort of—circulate."

"You mean your dinner is over?"

"Yes, that's about it. We're on our own."

"I don't want to go home. I want to dance with you some more."

"Who said anything about going home? The fun is just about to begin."

"I had fun before. I'm not very good with strangers."

"You're not a stranger. You're a member of the club, duly launched. Let's go out to the smoking-room and I'll get you a drink. How would you like a Stinger?"

"What is it? Never mind telling me. I'll have one."

"If you've never had one, be careful. It could be your downfall. Very cool to the taste, but packs a wallop. Sneaks up on you."

"Good. Let's have one." She rose and quickly took his unoffered arm, and they went to the smoking-room, which was already more than half filled.

At eleven o'clock she was drunk. She would dance with no one but Whit Hofman, and when she danced with him she tried to excite him, and succeeded. "You're hot stuff, Madge," he said.

"Why what do you *mean*?"

"The question is, what do *you* mean?"

"I don't know what you're *talking* about," she said, sing-song.

"The hell you don't," he said. "Shall we go for a stroll?"

"Where to?"

"My car's around back of the caddyhouse."

"Do you think we ought to?"

"No, but either that or let's sit down."

"All right, let's sit down. I'm getting kind of woozy, anyhow."

"Don't drink any more Stingers. I told you they were dangerous. Maybe you ought to have some coffee. Maybe I ought to, too. Come on, we'll get some coffee." He led her to a corner of the smoking-room, where she could prop herself against the wall. He left her, and in the hallway to the kitchen he encountered Pat Collins on his way from the locker-room.

"Say, Pat, if I were you—well, Madge had a couple of Stingers and I don't think they agree with her."

"Is she sick?"

"No, but I'm afraid she's quite tight."

"I better take her home?"

"*You* know. Your first night here. There'll be others much worse off, but she's the one they'll talk about. The maid'll get her wrap, and you can ease her out so nobody'll notice. I'll say your goodnights for you."

"Well, gee, Whit—I'm sorry. I certainly apologize."

"Perfectly all right, Pat. No harm done, but she's ready for beddy-bye. I'll call you in a day or two."

There was no confusing suggestion with command, and Pat obeyed Hofman. He got his own coat and Madge's, and when Madge saw her coat she likewise recognized authority.

They were less than a mile from the club when she said, "I'm gonna be sick."

He stopped the car. "All right, *be* sick."

When she got back in the car she said, "Leave the windows down, I need the fresh air."

He got her to bed. His anger was so great that he did not trust himself to speak to her, and she mistook his silence for pity. She kept muttering that she was sorry, sorry, and went to sleep. Much later he fell asleep, awoke before six, dressed and left the house before he had to speak to her. He had his breakfast in an all-night restaurant, bought the morning newspapers, and opened the garage. He needed to think, and not so much about punishing Madge as about restoring himself to good standing in the eyes of the Hofmans. He had caught Kitty Hofman's cold appraisal of Madge on the dance floor; he had known, too, that he had failed to make a good impression on Kitty, who was in a sour mood for having to give up the Buz McKee dinner. He rejected his first plan to send Kitty flowers and a humorous note. Tomorrow or the next day Madge could send the flowers and a thank-you note, which he would make sure contained no reference to her getting tight or any other apologetic implication. The important thing was to repair any damage to his relationship with Whit Hofman, and after a while he concluded that aside from Madge's thank-you note to both Hofmans, the wiser course was to wait for Whit to call him.

He had a long wait.

Immediately after Christmas the Hofmans went to Florida. They returned for two weeks in late March, closed their house, and took off on a trip around the world. Consequently the Collinses did not see the Hofmans for nearly a year. It was a year that was bad for the Collins marriage, but good for the Collins Motor Company. Pat Collins got the Chrysler franchise, and the car practically sold itself. Women and the young took to it from the start, and the Collins Motor Company had trouble keeping up with the orders. The bright new car and the bright new Irishman were interchangeably associated in the minds of the citizens, and Pat and Madge Collins were getting somewhere on their own, without the suspended sponsorship of Whit Hofman. But at home Pat and Madge had never quite got back to what they had been before she jeopardized his relationship with Whit Hofman. He had counted so much on Hofman's approval that the threat of losing it had given him a big scare, and it would not be far-fetched to say that the designers of the Chrysler "70" saved the Collins marriage.

Now they were busy, Pat with his golf when he could take the time off from his work—which he did frequently; and Madge with the game of bridge, which she learned adequately well. In the absence of the Whit Hofmans the social life of the country club was left without an outstanding couple to be the leaders, although several couples tried to fill the gap. In the locker-room one afternoon, drinking gin and ginger ale with the members of his foursome, Pat Collins heard one of the men say, "You know who we all miss? Whit. The club isn't the same without him." Pat looked up as at a newly discovered truth, and for the first time he realized that he liked Whit Hofman better than any man he had ever known. It had remained for someone else to put the thought into words, and casual enough words they were to express what Pat Collins had felt from the first day in Paul Unitas's saloon. Like nearly everyone else in the club the Collinses had had a postcard or two from the Hofmans; Honolulu, Shanghai, Bangkok, St. Andrew's, St. Cloud. The Hofmans' closer friends had had letters, but the Collinses were pleased to have had a postcard, signed "Kitty and Whit"—in Whit's handwriting.

"When does he get back, does anyone know?" said Pat.

"Middle of October," said the original speaker. "You know Whit. He wouldn't miss the football season, not the meat of it anyway."

"About a month away," said Pat Collins. "Well, I can thank him for the most enjoyable summer I ever had. He got me in here, you know. I was practically a stranger."

"'A stranger in a strange land,' but not any more, Pat."

"Thank you. You fellows have been damn nice to me." He meant the sentiment, but the depth of it belonged to his affection for Whit Hofman. He had his shower and dressed, and joined Madge on the terrace. "Do you want to stay here for dinner?"

"We have nothing at home," she said.

"Then we'll eat here," he said. "Did you know the Hofmans are getting back about four weeks from now?"

"I knew it."

"Why didn't you tell me?"

"I didn't know you wanted to know, or I would have. Why, are you thinking of hiring a brass band? One postcard."

"What did you expect? As I remember, you didn't keep it any secret when we got it."

"You were the one that was more pleased than I was."

"Oh, all right. Let's go eat."

They failed to be invited to the smaller parties in honor of the returning voyagers, but they went to a Dutch Treat dinner for the Hofmans before the club dance. Two changes in the Hofmans were instantly noticeable: Whit was as brown as a Hawaiian, and Kitty was pregnant. She received the members of the dinner party sitting down. She had lost one child through miscarriage. Whit stood beside her, and when it came the Collinses' turn he greeted Pat and Madge by nickname and first name. Not so Kitty. "Oh, hel*lo*. Mrs. *Col*lins. *Nice* of you to come. Hello, Mr. Collins." Then, seeing the man next in line she called out: "Bob-bee! Bobby, where were you Tuesday? You were supposed to be at the Ogdens', you false friend. I thought you'd be at the boat."

The Collinses moved on, and Madge said, "We shouldn't have come."

"Why not? She doesn't have to like us."

"She didn't have to be so snooty, either."

"Bobby Hermann is one of their best friends."

"I'm damn sure we're not."

"Oh, for God's sake."

"Oh, for God's sake yourself," she said.

The year had done a lot for Madge in such matters as her poise and the widening of her acquaintance among club members. But it was not until eleven or so that Whit Hofman cut in on her. "How've you been?" he said.

"Lonely without you," she said.

"That's nice to hear. I wish you meant it."

"You're pretending to think I don't," she said. "But I thought of you every day. And every night. Especially every night."

"How many Stingers have you had?"

"That's a nasty thing to say. I haven't had any. I've never had one since that night. So we'll change the subject. Are you going to stay home a while?"

"Looks that way. Kitty's having the baby in January."

"Sooner than that, I thought."

"No, the doctor says January."

"Which do you want? A boy, or a girl?"

"Both, but not at the same time."

"Well, you always get what you want, so I'm told."

"That's a new one on me."

"Well, you can *have* anything you want, put it that way."

"No, not even that."

"What do you want that you haven't got?"

"A son, or a daughter."

"Well, you're getting that, one or the other. What else?"

"Right now, nothing else."

"I don't believe anybody's ever that contented."

"Well, what do *you* want, for instance?"

"You," she said.

"Why? You have a nice guy. Kids. And I hear Pat's the busiest car dealer in town."

"Those are things I have. You asked me what I wanted."

"You don't beat about the bush, do you, Madge? You get right to the point."

"I've been in love with you for almost a year."

"Madge, you haven't been in love with me at all. Maybe you're not in love with Pat, but you're certainly not in love with me. You couldn't be."

"About a month ago I heard you were coming home, and I had it all planned out how I was going to be when I saw you. But I was wrong. I couldn't feel this way for a whole year and then start pretending I didn't. You asked me how I was, and I came right out with it, the truth."

"Well, Madge, I'm not in love with you. You're damn attractive and all that, but I'm not in *love* with you."

"I know that. But answer me one question, as truthful as I am with you. Are you in love with your wife?"

"Of course I am."

"I'll tell you something, Whit. You're not. With her. With me. Or maybe with anybody."

"Now really, that *is* a nasty thing to say."

"People love you, Whit, but you don't love them back."

"I'm afraid I don't like this conversation. Shall we go back and have a drink?"

"Yes."

They moved toward the smoking-room. "Why did you say that, Madge? What makes you think it?"

"You really want me to tell you? Remember, the truth hurts, and I had a whole year to think about this."

"What the hell, tell me."

"It's not you, it's the town. There's nobody here bigger than you. They all love you, but you don't love them."

"I love this town and the people in it and everything about it. Don't you think I could live anywhere I wanted to? Why do you think I came back here? I can live anywhere in the God damn world. Jesus, you certainly have that one figured wrong. For a minute you almost had me worried."

He danced with her no more that night, and if he could avoid speaking to her or getting close to her, he did so. When she got home, past three o'clock, she gave Pat Collins a very good time; loveless but exceedingly pleasurable. Then she lay in her bed until morning, unable to understand herself, puzzled by forces that had never been mysterious to her.

The Hofman baby was born on schedule, a six-pound boy, but the reports from the mother's bedside were not especially happy. Kitty had had a long and difficult time, and one report, corroborated only by constant repetition, was that she had thrown a clock, or a flower vase, or a water tumbler, or all of them, at Whit at the start of her labor. It was said, and perfunctorily denied, that a group of nurses and orderlies stood outside her hospital room, listening fascinatedly to the obscene names she called him, names that the gossips would not utter but knew how to spell. Whatever the basis in fact, the rumors of hurled bric-a-brac and invective seemed to be partially confirmed when Kitty Hofman came home from the hospital. The infant was left in the care of a nurse, and Kitty went to every party, drinking steadily and chain-smoking, saying little and watching everything. She had a look of determination, as though she had just made up her mind about something, but the look and decision were not followed up by action. She would stay at the parties until she had had enough, then she would get her wrap and say goodnight to her hostess, without any word or sign to Whit, and it would be up to him to discover she was leaving and follow her out.

Their friends wondered how long Whit Hofman would take that kind of behavior, but no one—least of all Pat Collins—was so tactless, or bold, as to suggest to Whit that there *was* any behavior. It was Whit, finally, who talked.

He was now seeing Pat Collins nearly every day, and on some days more than once. He knew as much about automobiles as Pat Collins, and he was comfortable in Pat's office. He had made the garage one of his ports of call in his daytime rounds—his office every morning at ten, the barber's, the bank, the broker's, his lawyer, lunch at the Gibbsville Club, a game of pool after lunch, a visit with Pat Collins that sometimes continued with a couple of games of squash at the country club. On a day some six weeks after the birth of his son Whit dropped in on Pat, hung up his coat and hat, and took a chair.

"Don't let me interrupt you," he said.

"Just signing some time-sheets," said Pat Collins.

Whit lit a cigarette and put his feet up on the windowsill. "It's about time you had those windows washed," he said.

"I know. Miss Muldowney says if I'm trying to save money, that's the wrong way. Burns up more electricity. Well, there we are. Another day, another dollar. How's the stock market?"

"Stay out of it. Everything's too high."

"I'm not ready to go in it yet. Later. Little by little I'm paying back Madge, the money she put in the business."

"You ought to incorporate and give her stock."

"First I want to give her back her money, with interest."

"Speaking of Madge, Pat. Do you remember when your children were born?"

"Sure. That wasn't so long ago."

"What is Dennis, about six?"

"Dennis is six, and Peggy's four. I guess Dennis is the same in years that your boy is in weeks. How is he, Pop?"

"He's fine. At least I guess he's fine. I wouldn't know how to tell, this is all new to me."

"But you're not worried about him? You sound dubious."

"Not about him. The doctor says he's beginning to gain weight and so forth. Kitty is something else again, and that's what I want to ask you about. You knew she didn't have a very easy time of it."

"Yes, you told me that."

"How was Madge, with her children?"

"I'll have to think back," said Pat. "Let me see. With Dennis, the first, we had a couple false alarms and had the doctor come to the house one time at four o'clock in the morning. He was sore as hell. It was only gas pains, and as soon as she got rid of the gas, okay. The real time, she was in labor about three hours, I guess. About three. Dennis weighed seven and a quarter. With Peggy, she took longer. Started having pains around eight o'clock in the morning, but the baby wasn't all the way out till three-four in the afternoon. She had a much harder time with the second, although it was a smaller baby. Six and a half, I think."

"What about her, uh, mental state? Was she depressed or anything like that?"

"No, not a bit. Anything but."

"But you haven't had any more children, and I thought Catholics didn't believe in birth control."

"Well, I'll tell you, Whit, although I wouldn't tell most Protestants. I don't agree with the Church on that, and neither does Madge. If that's the criterion, we're not very good Catholics, but I can't help that. We had two children when we could only afford one, and now I don't think we'll ever have any more. Two's enough."

"But for financial reasons, not because of the effect on Madge."

"Mainly financial reasons. Even if we could afford it, though, Madge doesn't want any more. She wants to enjoy life while she's young."

"I see," said Whit Hofman. The conversation had reached a point where utter frankness or a change of the subject was inevitable, and Whit Hofman retreated from candor. It then was up to Pat Collins to break the silence.

"It's none of my business, Whit," he began. "But—"

"No, it isn't, Pat. I don't mean to be rude, but if I said any more about Kitty, I'd sound like a crybaby. Not to mention the fact that it goes against the grain. I've said too much already."

"I know how you feel. But nothing you say gets out of this office, so don't let that worry you. I don't tell Madge everything I know. Or do. She made some pretty good guesses, and we came close to busting up. When I was on the road, peddling hats and caps, I knew a sure lay in damn near every town between Philly and Binghamton, New York. Not that I got laid every night—but I didn't miss many Thursdays. Thursday nights we knew we were going home Friday, salesmen. You don't make any calls on Friday, the clients are all busy. So, somebody'd bring out a quart."

"Did you know a sure lay in this town?"

"Did I! Did you ever know a broad named Helene Holman?"

"I should say I did."

"Well, her," said Pat Collins.

"You don't see her now, though, do you?"

"Is that any of your business, Whit?"

"Touché. I wasn't really asking out of curiosity. More, uh, incredibility. *Incredulity*. In other words, I've always thought you behaved yourself here, since you've been living here."

"I have. And anyway, I understand the Holman dame is private property. At least I always see her riding around with the big bootlegger, Charney."

"Ed Charney. Yes, she's out of circulation for the present, so my friends tell me."

"Yes, and you couldn't get away with a God damn thing. You're too well known."

"So far I haven't tried to get away with anything," said Whit Hofman. "How would you feel about a little strenuous exercise?"

Pat Collins looked up at the clock. "I don't think any ripe prospect is coming in in the next twenty minutes. Two games?"

"Enough to get up a sweat."

They drove to the country club in two cars, obviating the continuance of conversation and giving each man the opportunity to think his own thoughts. They played squash for an hour or so, took long hot showers, and cooled out at the locker-room table with gin and ginger ale. "I could lie right down on that floor and go to sleep," said Whit. "You're getting better, or maybe I'm getting worse. Next year I'm not going to give you a handicap."

"I may get good enough to take you at golf, but not this game. You always know where the ball's going to be, and I have to lose time guessing." They were the only members in the locker-room. They could hear occasional sounds from the kitchen of the steward and his staff having supper, a few dozen feet and a whole generation of prosperity away. The walls of the room were lined with steel lockers, with two islands of lockers back-to-back in the center of the room, hempen matting in the passageways, a rather feeble ceiling lamp above the table where their drinks rested. It was an arcane atmosphere, like some goat-room in an odd lodge, with a lingering dankness traceable to their recent hot showers and to the dozens of golf shoes and plus-fours and last summer's shirts stored and forgotten in the lockers. Whit, in his shorts and shirt, and Pat, in his B.V.D.'s, pleasantly tired from their exercise and additionally numbed by the gin and ginger ales, were in that state of euphorious relaxation that a million men ten million times have called the best part of the game, any game. They were by no means drunk, nor were they exhausted, but once again they were back at the point of utter frankness or retreat from it that they had reached in Pat's office, only now the surrounding circumstances were different.

"Why don't you get it off your chest, Whit?"

Whit Hofman, without looking up, blew the ash off his cigarette. "Funny, I was just thinking the same thing," he said. He reached for the gin bottle and spiked Pat's and his own drinks. "I have too damn many cousins in this town. If I confided in any of them they'd call a family conference, which is the last thing I want." He scraped his cigarette against the ash tray, and with his eyes on the operation said, "Kitty hates me. She hates me, and I'm not sure why."

"Have you got a clear conscience?"

"No," said Whit. "That is, *I* haven't. When we were in Siam, on our trip, Kitty got an attack of dysentery and stayed in the hotel for a couple of days. I, uh, took advantage of that to slip off with an American newspaper fellow for some of the local nookie. So I haven't got a clear conscience, but Kitty doesn't know that. Positively. I don't think it's that. I *know* it isn't that.

It's something—I don't know where it began, or when. We didn't have any fights or anything like that. Just one day it was there, and I hadn't noticed it before."

"Pregnant."

"Oh, yes. But past the stage where she was throwing up. Taking it very easy, because she didn't want to lose this baby. But a wall between us. No, not a wall. Just a way of looking at me, as if I'd changed appearance and she was fascinated, but not fascinated because she *liked* my new appearance. 'What's this strange animal?' That kind of look. No fights, though. Not even any serious arguments. Oh, I got sore at her for trying to smuggle in a ring I bought her in Cairo. I was filling out the customs declaration and I had the damn thing all filled out and signed, then I remembered the ring. I asked her what about it, and she said she wasn't going to declare it. She was going to wear it in with the stone turned around so that it'd look like a guard for her engagement ring. So pointless. The ring wasn't *that* valuable. The duty was about a hundred and fifty dollars. An amethyst, with a kind of a scarab design. Do you know that an amethyst is supposed to sober you up?"

"I never heard that."

"Yeah. The magical power, but it doesn't work, I can tell you. Anyway, I gave her hell because if you try to pull a fast one on the customs inspectors and they catch you, they make you wait, they confiscate your luggage, and I'm told that for the rest of your life, whenever you re-enter the country, they go through everything with a fine tooth comb. And incidentally, an uncle of Jimmy Malloy's was expediting our landing, and he would have got into trouble, no doubt. Dr. Malloy's brother-in-law, has something to do with the immigration people. So I had to get new forms and fill out the whole God damn thing all over again. But that was our only quarrel of any consequence. It did make me wonder a little, why she wanted to save a hundred and fifty when it wasn't even her money."

They sipped their drinks.

"The day she went to the hospital," Whit Hofman continued, "it was very cold, and I bundled her up warm. She laughed at me and said we weren't going to the North Pole. Not a nice laugh. Then when we got to the hospital the nurse helped her change into a hospital gown, but didn't put her to bed. She sat up in a chair, and I put a blanket over her feet, asked her if she wanted anything to read. She said she did. Could I get her a history of the Hofman family? Well, there *is* one, but I knew damn well she didn't want it. She was just being disagreeable, but that was understandable under the circumstances. Then I sat down, and she told me I didn't have to wait around. I said I knew I didn't have to, but was doing it because I wanted to. Then she said, 'God damn it, don't you know when I'm trying to get rid of you?' and threw her cigarette lighter at me. Unfortunately the nurse picked that exact moment to come in the room, and the lighter hit her in the teat. I don't know what came over Kitty. 'Get that son of a bitch out of here,' and a lot more on the same order. So the nurse told me I'd better go, and I did." He paused. "Kitty had an awful time, no doubt about it. I was there when they brought the baby in to show her. She looked at it, didn't register any feeling whatsoever, and then turned her face away and shut her eyes. I have never seen her look at the baby the way you'd expect a mother to. I've never seen her pick him up out of his crib just to hold him. Naturally she's never nursed him. She probably hasn't enough milk, so I have no objection to that, but along with hating me she seems to hate the baby. Dr. English says that will pass, but I know better. She has no damn use for me *or* the child." He paused again. "The Christ-awful thing is, I don't know what the hell I *did*."

"I agree with Dr. English. It'll pass," said Pat Collins. "Women today, they aren't as simple as they used to be, fifty or a hundred years ago. They drive cars and play golf. Smoke and drink, do a lot of the same things men do."

"My mother rode horseback and played tennis. She didn't smoke that I know of, but she drank. Not to excess, but wine with dinner. She died when I was eight, so I don't really know an awful lot about her. My father died while I was still in prep school. From then on I guess you'd say I was brought up by my uncle and the housekeeper and my uncle's butler. I have an older brother in the foreign service, but he's too close to me in age to have had much to do with bringing me up. He was a freshman when our father died."

"I didn't know you had a brother."

"I saw him in Rome. He's in the embassy there. Both glad to

see each other, but he thinks I'm a country bumpkin, which I am. And since I don't speak French or Italian, and he has a little bit of an English accent, you might say we don't even speak the same language. He married a Boston girl and you should have seen her with Kitty. Every time the Italian men flocked around Kitty, Howard's wife would act as an interpreter, although the Italians all spoke English. But I don't think that has anything to do with why Kitty developed this hatred for me. Howard's wife disapproved of me just as heartily as she did Kitty. We were all pretty glad to see the last of each other. Howard's wife has twice as much money as he has, so he doesn't exactly rule the roost, but in every marriage one of the two has more money than the other. That's not what's eating Kitty." He sipped his drink. "I've been thinking if we moved away from here. Someone told me that this town is wrong for me."

"They're crazy."

"Well, it's bothered me ever since. This, uh, person said that my friends liked me but I didn't like them back."

"That *is* crap."

"As a matter of fact, the person didn't say like. She said love. Meaning that as long as I lived here, I wouldn't be able to love anybody. But I've always loved Kitty, and I certainly love this town. I don't know what more I can do to prove it."

"As far as Kitty's concerned, you're going to have to wait a while. Some women take longer than others getting their machinery back in place after a baby."

Whit Hofman shook his head. "Dr. English tells me Kitty's machinery is okay. And whatever it is, it started before the machinery got out of place. It's me, but what in the name of Christ is it? It's getting late, Pat. Would you have dinner with me here?"

"If you'll square me with Madge. It *is* late. I'm due home now."

"You want me to speak to her, now?"

"We both can."

There was a telephone in the hall off the locker-room and Pat put in the call.

"I knew that's where you'd be," said Madge. "You could just as easily called two hours ago."

"I'm going to put Whit on," said Pat, and did so.

"Madge, I take all the blame, but it'll be at least an hour before Pat could be home. We're still in our underwear. So could you spare him for dinner?"

"Your wish is our command," said Madge.

Whit turned to Pat. "She hung up. What do you do now?"

"We call Heinie and order up a couple of steaks," said Pat.

It was not only that the two men saw each other so frequently; it was Pat's availability, to share meals, to take little trips, that annoyed Madge. "You don't have to suck up to Whit Hofman," she would say. "Not any more."

"I'm glad I don't."

This colloquy in the Collins household resembled one in the Hofmans'. "Not that it matters to me, but how can you spend so much time with that Pat Collins person?" said Kitty.

"What's wrong with Pat? He's good company."

"Because your other friends refuse to yes you."

"That shows how little you know about Pat Collins," he said. "You don't seem to realize that he had hard going for a while, but he never asked me for any help of any kind."

"Saving you for something big, probably."

"No. I doubt if he'll ever ask me for anything. When he needed money to expand, he didn't even go to our bank, let alone ask me for help. And I would have been glad to put money in his business. Would have been a good investment."

"Oh, I don't care. Do as you please. I'm just amused to watch this beautiful friendship between you two. And by the way, maybe he never asked you for anything, but did he ever refuse anything you offered him? For instance, the club."

"He would have made it."

"Has he made the Gibbsville Club?"

"As far as I know, he's not interested."

"Try him."

"Hell, if I ask him, he'll say yes."

"Exactly my point. His way is so much cagier. He's always there when you want him, and naturally you're going to feel obligated to him. You'll want to pay him back for always being there, so he gets more out of you that way than if he'd asked for favors. He knows that."

"It's funny how *you* know things like that, Kitty."

She fell angrily silent. He had met her at a party just after the war, when he was still in uniform and with two or three other officers was having a lengthy celebration in New York. Whit, a first lieutenant in the 103d Engineers, 28th Division, met a first lieutenant in the 102d Engineers, 27th Division, who had with him a girl from New Rochelle. She was not a beauty, but Whit was immediately attracted to her, and she to him. "This man is only the 102d and I'm the 103d. He's only the 27th and I'm the 28th," said Whit. "Why don't you move up a grade?"

She laughed. "Why not? I *want* to get up in the world."

He made frequent trips to New York to see her. She was going to a commercial art school, living at home with her family but able to spend many nights in New York. Her father was a perfectly respectable layout man in an advertising agency, who commuted from New Rochelle and escaped from his wife by spending all the time he could in sailing small boats. His wife was a fat and disagreeable woman who had tried but failed to dominate her husband and her daughter, and regarded her husband as a nincompoop and her daughter as a wild and wilful girl who was headed for no good. One spring day Kitty and Whit drove to Greenwich, Connecticut, and were married. They then drove to New Rochelle, the first and only time Whit Hofman ever saw his wife's parents. Two days later the newly married couple sailed for Europe, and they did not put in an appearance in Gibbsville, Pennsylvania, until the autumn. It was all very unconventional and it led to considerable speculation as to the kind of person Whit Hofman had married, especially among the mothers of nubile girls. But a *fait accompli* was a *fait accompli*, and Whit Hofman was Whit Hofman, and the girls and their mothers had to make the best of it, whatever that turned out to be.

In certain respects it turned out quite well. The town, and indeed the entire nation, was ready to have some fun. There was a considerable amount of second-generation money around, and manners and customs would never revert to those of 1914. Kitty Hofman and the Lantenengo Country Club appeared almost simultaneously in Gibbsville; both were new and novel and had the backing of the Hofman family. Kitty made herself agreeable to Whit's men friends and made no effort in the direction of the young women. They had to make themselves agreeable to her, and since their alternative was self-inflicted ostracism, Kitty was established without getting entangled in social debts to any of the young women. A less determined, less independent young woman could not have achieved it, but Gibbsville was full of less determined, less independent young women whom Whit Hofman had not married. And at least Whit had not singled out one of their number to the exclusion of all the others, a mildly comforting and unifying thought. He had to marry somebody, so better this nobody with her invisible family in a New York suburb than a Gibbsville girl who would have to suffer as the object of harmonious envy.

Kitty did nothing deliberately to antagonize the young women—unless to outdress them could be so considered, and her taste in clothes was far too individualistic for her new acquaintances. She attended their ladies' luncheons, always leaving before the bridge game began. She played in the Tuesday golf tournaments. She precisely returned all invitations. And she made no close friendships. But she actively disliked Madge Collins.

From the beginning she knew, as women know better than men know, that she was not going to like that woman. Even before Madge got up to dance with Whit and made her extraordinary, possessive, off-in-dreamland impression with her closed eyes, Kitty Hofman abandoned herself to the luxury of loathing another woman. Madge's black dress was sound, so much so that Kitty accurately guessed that Madge had had some experience in women's wear. But from there on every judgment Kitty made was unfavorable. Madge's prettiness was literally natural: her good figure was natural, her amazing skin was natural, her reddish brown hair, her teeth, her bright eyes, her inviting mouth, were gifts of Nature. (Kitty used a great deal of makeup and dyed her blond hair a lighter shade of blond.) Kitty, in the first minutes of her first meeting with Madge, ticketed her as a pretty parlor-maid; when she got up to dance with Whit she ticketed her as a whore, and with no evidence to the contrary, Madge so remained. Kitty's judgments were not based on facts or influenced by considerations of fairness, then or ever, although she could be extremely realistic in her observations. (Her father, she early knew, was an ineffectual man, a coward who worked hard to protect his job and fled to the waters of Long Island Sound to avoid the occasions of quarrels with her mother.) Kitty, with her firmly middle-class background, had no trouble in imagining the background of Madge and Pat Collins, and the Collinses provided her with her first opportunity to assert herself as a Hofman. (She had not been wasting her first years in Gibbsville; her indifferent manner masked a shrewd study of individuals and their standing in the community.) Kitty, who had not been able comfortably to integrate herself into the established order, now rapidly assumed her position as Whit's wife because as Mrs. Whit Hofman she could look down on and crack down on Madge Collins. (By a closely related coincidence she also became a harsher judge of her husband at the very moment that she began to exercise the privileges of her marital status.) Kitty's obsessive hatred of the hick from West Philadelphia, as she called Madge Collins, was quick in its onset and showed every sign of being chronic. The other young women of the country club set did not fail to notice, and it amused them to get a rise out of Kitty Hofman merely by mentioning Madge Collins's name.

But the former Madge Ruddy was at least as intuitive as Kitty Hofman. Parlor-maid, whore, saleslady at Oppenheim, Collins—the real and imagined things she was or that Kitty Hofman chose to think she was—Madge was only a trifle slower in placing Kitty. Madge knew a lady when she saw one, and Kitty Hofman was not it. In the first days of her acquaintance with Kitty she would willingly enough have suspended her judgments if Kitty had been moderately friendly, but since that was not to be the case, Madge cheerfully collected her private store of evidence that Kitty Hofman was a phony. She was a phony aristocrat, a synthetic woman, from her dyed hair to her boyish hips to her no doubt tinted toenails. Madge, accustomed all her life to the West Philadelphia twang, had never waited on a lady who pronounced third *thade* and idea *ideer*. "Get a look at her little titties," Madge would say, when Kitty appeared in an evening dress that had two unjoined panels down the front. "She looks like she forgot to take her hair out of the curlers," said Madge of one of Kitty's coiffures. And, of Kitty's slow gait, "She walks like she was constipated." The animosity left Madge free to love Kitty's husband without the restraint that loyalty to a friend might have invoked. As for disloyalty to Pat Collins, he was aware of none, and did he not all but love Whit too?

Thus it was that behind the friendly relationship of Pat Collins and Whit Hofman a more intense, unfriendly relationship flourished between Madge Collins and Kitty Hofman. The extremes of feeling were not unlike an individual's range of capacity for love and hate, or, as Madge put it, "I hate her as much as you like him, and *that's* going some." Madge Collins, of course, with equal accuracy could have said: "I hate her as much as I love him, and that's going some." The two men arrived at a pact of silence where their wives were concerned, a working protocol that was slightly more to Whit's advantage, since in avoiding mention of Madge he was guarding against a slip that would incriminate Madge. He wanted no such slip to occur; he needed Pat's friendship, and he neither needed nor wanted Madge's love. Indeed, as time passed and the pact of silence grew stronger, Whit Hofman's feeling for Madge was sterilized. By the end of 1925 he would not have offered to take her out to his parked car, and when circumstances had them briefly alone together they either did not speak at all or their conversation was so commonplace that a suspicious eavesdropper would have convicted them of adultery on the theory that two such vital persons could not be so indifferent to each other's physical presence. One evening at a picnic-swimming party at someone's farm—this, in the summer of '26—Madge had had enough of the cold water in the dam and was on her way to the tent that was being used as the ladies' dressing-room. In the darkness she collided with a man on his way from the men's tent. "Who is it? I'm sorry," she said.

"Whit Hofman. Who is this?"

"Madge."

"Hello. You giving up?"

"That water's too cold for me."

"Did Pat get back?"

"From Philly? No. He's spending the night. It's funny talking and I can't really see you. Where are you?"

"I'm right here."

She reached out a hand and touched him. "I'm not going to throw myself at you, but here we are."

"Don't start anything, Madge."

"I said I wasn't going to throw myself at you. You have to make the next move. But you're human."

"I'm human, but you picked a lousy place, and time."

"Is that all that's stopping you? I'll go home now and wait for you, if you say the word. Why don't you like me?"

"I do like you."

"Prove it. I'm all alone, the children are with Pat's mother. I have my car, and I'll leave now if you say."

"No. You know all the reasons."

"Sure I do. Sure I do."

"Can you get back to the tent all right? You can see where it is, can't you? Where the kerosene lamp is, on the pole."

"I can see it all right."

"Then you'd better go, Madge, because my good resolutions are weakening."

"Are they? Let me feel. Why, you are human!"

"Cut it out," he said, and walked away from her toward the lights and people at the dam.

She changed into her dress and rejoined the throng at the dam. It was a good-sized party, somewhat disorganized among smaller groups of swimmers, drinkers, eaters of corn on the cob, and a mixed quartet accompanied by a young man on banjo-uke. Heavy clouds hid the moon, and the only light came from a couple of small bonfires. When Madge returned to the party she moved from one group to another, eventually staying longest with the singers and the banjo-uke player. "Larry, do you know 'Ukulele Lady'?"

"Sure," he said. He began playing it, and Madge sang a solo of two choruses. Her thin true voice was just right for the sad, inconclusive little song, and when she finished singing she stood shyly smiling in the momentary total silence. But then there was a spontaneous, delayed burst of applause, and she sat down. The darkness, the fires, the previously disorganized character of the party, and Madge's voice and the words—"maybe she'll find somebody else/ bye and bye"—all contributed to a minor triumph and, quite accidentally, brought the party together in a sentimental climax. "More! More! . . . I didn't know you were a singer . . . Encore! Encore!" But Madge's instinct made her refuse to sing again.

For a minute or two the party was rather quiet, and Kitty

had a whispered conversation with the ukulele player. He strummed a few introductory chords until the members of the party gave him their attention, whereupon he began to play "Yaaka hula hickey dula," and Kitty Hofman, in her bare feet and a Paisley print dress, went into the dance. It was a slow hula, done without words and with only the movements of her hips and the ritualistic language of her fingers and arms—only vaguely understood in this group—in synchronous motion with the music. The spectators put on the knowing smiles of the semi-sophisticated as Kitty moved her hips, but before the dance and the tune were halfway finished they stopped their nervous laughter and were caught by the performance. It hardly mattered that they could not understand the language of the physical gestures or that the women as much as the men were being seduced by the dance. The women could understand the movements because the movements were formal and native to themselves, but the element of seductiveness was as real for them as for the men because the men's responsiveness—taking the form of absolute quiet—was like a held breath, and throughout the group men and women felt the need to touch each other by the hand, hands reaching for the nearest hand. And apart from the physical spell produced by the circumstances and the dance, there was the comprehension by the women and by some of the men that the dance was a direct reply to Madge's small bid for popularity. As such the dance was an obliterating victory for Kitty. Madge's plaintive solo was completely forgotten. As the dance ended Kitty put her hands to her lips, kissed them and extended them to the audience as in a benediction, bowed low, and returned to the picnic bench that now became a throne. The applause was a mixture of hand clapping, of women's voices calling out "Lovely! Adorable!" and men shouting "Yowie! Some more, some more!" But Kitty, equally as well as Madge, knew when to quit. "I learned it when Whit and I were in Hawaii. Where else?" she said.

Madge Collins went to Kitty to congratulate her. "That was swell, Kitty."

"Oh, thanks. Did you think so? Of course *I* can't *sing*," said Kitty.

"You—don't—have—to—when—you—can—shake—

that—thing," said Bobby Hermann, whose hesitant enunciation became slower when he drank. "You—got—any—more—hidden—talents—like—that—one—up—your—sleeve?"

"Not up her sleeve," said Madge, and walked away.

"Hey—that's—a—good—one. Not—up—her—sleeve. Not—up—your—sleeve—eh—Kitty?"

In the continuing murmur of admiration for the dance no one—no one but Madge Collins—noticed that Whit Hofman had not added his compliments to those of the multitude. In that respect Kitty's victory was doubled, for Madge now knew that Kitty had intended the exhibition as a private gesture of contempt for Whit as well as a less subtle chastening of Madge herself. Madge sat on a circular grass-mat cushion beside Whit.

"She's a real expert," said Madge. "I didn't know she could do the hula."

"Uh-huh. Learned it in Honolulu."

"On the beach at Waikiki."

"On the beach at Waikiki," said Whit.

"Well, she didn't forget it," said Madge. "Is it hard to learn?"

"Pretty hard, I guess. It's something like the deaf-and-dumb language. One thing means the moon, another thing means home, another means lonesome, and so forth and so on."

"Maybe I could get her to teach me how to say what *I* want to say."

"What's that?" said Whit.

"Madge is going home, lonesome, and wishes Whit would be there."

"When are you leaving?"

"Just about now."

"Say in an hour or so? You're all alone?"

"Yes. What will you tell *her*?"

"Whatever I tell her, she'll guess where I am. She's a bitch, but she's not a fool."

"She's a bitch, all right. But maybe you're a fool," said Madge.

"No, Whit. Not tonight. Any other time, but not tonight."

"Whatever you say, but you have nothing to fear from her. You or Pat. Take my word for it, you haven't. She's watching us now, and she knows we're talking about her. All right, I'll tell you what's behind this exhibition tonight."

"You don't have to."

"Well I hope you don't think I'd let you risk it if I weren't positive about her."

"I did wonder, but I'm so crazy about you."

"When we were in Honolulu that time, I caught her with another guy. I'd been out playing golf, and I came back to the hotel in time to see this guy leaving our room. She didn't deny it, and I guessed right away who it was. A naval officer. I hadn't got a good look at him, but I let her think I had and she admitted it. The question was, what was I going to do about it? Did I want to divorce her, and ruin the naval officer's career? Did I want to come back here without her? That was where she knew she had me. I *didn't* want to come back here without her. This is my town, you know. We've been here ever since there was a town, and it's the only place I ever want to live. I've told you that." He paused. "Well, you don't know her, the hold she had on me, and I don't fully understand it myself. There are a lot of damn nice girls in town I might have married, and you'd think that feeling that way about the town, I'd marry a Gibbsville girl. But how was I ever to know that I was marrying the girl and not her mother, and in some cases her father? And that the girl wasn't marrying me but my father's money and my uncle's money. Kitty didn't know any of that when I asked her to marry me. She'd never heard of Gibbsville. In fact she wasn't very sure where Pennsylvania was. And I was a guy just out of the army, liked a good time, and presumably enjoying myself before I seriously began looking for a job. The first time Kitty really knew I didn't have to work for a living was when I gave her her engagement ring. I remember what she said. She looked at it and then looked at me and said, 'Is there more where this came from?' So give her her due. She didn't marry me for my money, and that was somewhat a novelty. Are you listening?"

"Sure," said Madge.

"That afternoon in the hotel she said, 'Look, you can kick me out and pay me off, but I tried to have a child for you, which I didn't want, and this is the first time I've gone to bed with another man, since we've been married.' It was a good argument, but of course the real point was that I didn't want to go home without a wife, and have everybody guessing why.

I allowed myself the great pleasure of giving her a slap in the face, and she said she guessed she had it coming to her, and then I was so God damned ashamed of myself—I'd never hit a woman before—that *I* ended up apologizing to *her*. Oh, I told her we were taking the next boat out of Honolulu, and if she was ever unfaithful to me again I'd make it very tough for her. But the fact of the matter is, her only punishment was a slap in the face, and that was with my open hand. We went to various places—Australia, Japan, the Philippines, China—and I got her pregnant."

"Yes. But what was behind this hula tonight?"

"I'd forgotten she knew how to do it. The whole subject of Honolulu, and ukuleles, hulas—we've never mentioned any of it, neither of us. But when she stood up there tonight, partly it was to do something better than you—"

"And she did."

"Well, she tried. And partly it was to insult me in a way that only I would understand. Things have been going very badly between us, we hardly ever speak a civil word when we're alone. She's convinced herself that you and I are having an affair—"

"Well, let's."

"Yes, let's. But I wish we could do it without—well, what the hell? Pat's supposed to be able to take care of himself."

"I have a few scores to settle there, too."

"Not since I've known him."

"Maybe not, but there were enough before you knew him. I used to be sick with jealousy, Monday to Friday, Monday to Friday, knowing he was probably screwing some chippy in Allentown or Wilkes-Barre. I was still jealous, even after we moved here. But not after I met you. From then on I didn't care what he did, who he screwed. Whenever I thought of him with another woman I'd think of me with you. But why isn't Kitty going to make any trouble? What have you got on her, besides the navy officer?"

"This is going to sound very cold-blooded."

"All right."

"And it's possible I could be wrong."

"Yes, but go on."

"Well—Kitty's gotten used to being Mrs. W. S. Hofman.

She likes everything about it but me—and the baby. It's got her, Madge, and she can never have it anywhere else, or with anybody else."

"I could have told you that the first time I ever laid eyes on her."

"I had to find it out for myself."

There is one law for the rich, and another law for the richer. The frequent appearances of Whit Hofman with Madge Collins were treated not so much as a scandal as the exercise of a privilege of a man who was uniquely entitled to such privileges. To mollify their sense of good order the country club set could tell themselves that Whit was with Pat as often as he was with Madge, and that the three were often together as a congenial trio. The more kindly disposed made the excuse that Whit was putting up with a great deal from Kitty, and since Pat Collins obviously did not object to Whit's hours alone with Madge, what right had anyone else to complain? The excuse made by the less kindly was that if there was anything *wrong* in the Whit-Madge friendship, Kitty Hofman would be the first to kick up a fuss; therefore there was nothing scandalous in the relationship.

The thing most wrong in the relationship was the destructive effect on Madge Collins, who had been brought up in a strict Catholic atmosphere, who in nearly thirty years had had sexual intercourse with one man, and who now was having intercourse with two, often with both in the same day. The early excitement of a sexual feast continued through three or four months and a couple of narrow escapes; but the necessary lies to Pat and the secondary status of the man she preferred became inconvenient, then annoying, then irritating. She withheld nothing from Whit, she gave only what was necessary to Pat, but when she was in the company of both men—playing golf, at a movie, at a football game—she indulged in a nervous masquerade as the contented wife and the sympathetic friend, experiencing relief only when she could be alone with one of the men. Or with neither. The shame she suffered with her Catholic conscience was no greater than the shame of another sort: to be with both men and sit in self-enforced silence while the man she loved was so easily, coolly making a fool of the man to whom she was married. The amiable, totally unsuspecting fool would have had her sympathy in different circumstances, and she would have hated the character of the lover; but Pat's complacency was more hateful to her than Whit's arrogance. The complacency, she knew, was real; and Whit's arrogance vanished in the humility of his passion as soon as she would let him make love to her. There was proficiency of a selfish kind in Pat's lovemaking; he had never been so gentle or grateful as Whit. From what she could learn of Kitty Hofman it would have been neatly suitable if Pat had become Kitty's lover, but two such similar persons were never attracted to each other. They had, emotionally, everything in common; none of the essential friction of personality. Neither was equipped with the fear of losing the other.

It was this fear that helped produce the circumstances leading to the end of Madge's affair with Whit Hofman. "Every time I see you I love you again, even though I've been loving you all along," she told Whit. Only when she was alone with him—riding in his car, playing golf, sitting with him while waiting for Pat to join them, sitting with him after Pat had left them—could she forget the increasingly insistent irritations of her position. Publicly she was, as Whit told her, "carrying it off very well," but the nagging of her Catholic conscience and the rigidity of her middle-class training were with her more than she was with Whit, and when the stimulation of the early excitement had passed, she was left with that conscience, that training, and this new fear.

The affair, in terms of hours in a bed together, was a haphazard one, too dependent on Pat's unpredictable and impulsive absences. Sometimes he would telephone her from the garage late in the afternoon, and tell her he was driving to Philadelphia and would not be home until past midnight. On such occasions, if she could not get word to Whit at his office or at one of the two clubs, the free evening would be wasted. Other times they would make love on country roads, and three times they had gone to hotels in Philadelphia. It seldom happened that Whit, in a moment of urgently wanting to be with her, could be with her within the hour, and it was on just such occasions, when she was taking a foolish chance, that they had their two narrow escapes in her own house. "You can never get away when I want you to," said Whit—which was a truth and a lie.

"Be reasonable," she said, and knew that the first excitement had progressed to complaint. Any time, anywhere, anything had been exciting in the beginning; now it was a bed in a hotel and a whole night together, with a good leisurely breakfast, that he wanted. They were in a second phase, or he was; and for her, fear had begun. It told on her disposition, so that she was sometimes snappish when alone with Whit. Now it was her turn to say they could not be together when she wanted him, and again it was a truth and a lie of exaggeration. They began to have quarrels, and to Whit this was not only an annoyance but a sign that they were getting in much deeper than he intended. For he had not deceived her as to the depth or permanence of their relationship. It was true that he had permitted her to deceive herself, but she was no child. She had had to supply her own declarations of the love she wanted him to feel; they had not been forthcoming from him, and when there were opportunities that almost demanded a declaration of his love, he was silent or noncommittal. The nature of their affair—intimacy accompanied by intrigue—was such as to require extra opportunities for candor. They were closer than if they had been free and innocent, but Whit would not use their intimacy even to make casual pretense of love. "I can't even wring it out of you," she said.

"What?"

"That you love me. You never say it."

"You can't expect to *wring* it out of anyone."

"A woman wants to hear it, once in a while."

"Well, don't try to wring it out of me."

He knew—and she knew almost as soon as he—that his refusal to put their affair on a higher, romantic love plane was quite likely to force her to put an end to the affair. And now that she was becoming demanding and disagreeable, he could deliberately provoke her into final action or let his stubbornness get the same result. It could not be said that she bored him; she was too exciting for that. But the very fact that she could be exciting added to his annoyance and irritation. He began to dislike that hold she had on him, and the day arrived when he recognized in himself the same basic weakness for Madge that he had had for Kitty. And to a lesser degree the same thing had been true of all the women he had ever known. But pursuing that thought, he recalled that Madge was the only one who had ever charged him with the inability to love. Now he had the provocation that would end the affair, and he had it more or less in the words of her accusation.

"You still won't say it," she said to him one night.

"That I love you?"

"That you love me."

"No, I won't say it, and you ought to know why."

"That's plain as day. You won't say it because you don't."

"Not *don't*. *Can't*," he said. "You told me yourself, a long time ago. That people love me and I can't love them. I'm beginning to think that's true."

"It's true all right. I was hoping I could get you to change, but you didn't."

"I used to know a guy that could take a car apart and put it together again, but he couldn't drive. He never could learn to drive."

"What's that got to do with us?"

"Don't you see? Think a minute."

"I get it."

"So when you ask me to love you, you're asking the impossible. I'm just made that way, that's all."

"This sounds like a farewell speech. You got me to go to a hotel with you, have one last thing together, and then announce that we're through. Is that it?"

"No, not as long as you don't expect something you never expected in the first place."

"That's good, that is. You'll let me go on taking all the risks, but don't ask anything in return. I guess I don't love you *that* much, Mr. Hofman." She got out of bed.

"What are you going to do?"

"I'm getting out of this dump, I promise you that. I'm going home."

"I'm sorry, Madge."

"Whit, you're not even sorry for yourself. But I can make up for it. I'm sorry for you. Do you know what I'm going to do?"

"What?"

"I'm going home and tell Pat the whole story. If he wants to kick me out, all he has to do is say so."

"Why the hell do you want to do that?"

"You wouldn't understand it."

"Is it some Catholic thing?"

"Yes! I'm surprised you guessed it. I don't have to tell him. That's not it. But I'll confess it to him instead of a priest, and whatever he wants me to do, I'll do it. Penance."

"No, I don't understand it."

"No, I guess you don't."

"You're going to take a chance of wrecking your home, your marriage?"

"I'm not very brave. I don't think it is much of a chance, but if he kicks me out, I can go back to Oppenheim, Collins. I have a charge account there now." She laughed.

"Don't do it, Madge. Don't go."

"Whit, I've been watching you and waiting for something like this to happen. I didn't know what I was going to do, but when the time came I knew right away."

"Then you really loved Pat all along, not me."

"Nope. God help me, I love you and that's the one thing I won't tell Pat. There I'll have to lie."

It was assumed, when Pat Collins began neglecting his business and spending so much time in Dick Boylan's speakeasy, that Whit Hofman would come to his rescue. But whether or not Whit had offered to help Pat Collins, nobody could long go on helping a man who refused to help himself. He lost his two salesmen and his bookkeeper, and his Chrysler franchise was taken over by Walt Michaels, who rehired Joe Ricci at decent wages. For a while Pat Collins had a fifty-dollar-a-week drawing account as a salesman at the Cadillac dealer's, but that stopped when people stopped buying Cadillacs, and Pat's next job, in charge of the hat department in a haberdashery, lasted only as long as the haberdashery. As a Cadillac salesman and head of the hat department Pat Collins paid less attention to business than to pill pool, playing a game called Harrigan from one o'clock in the afternoon till suppertime, but during those hours he was at least staying out of the speakeasy. At suppertime he would have a Western sandwich at the Greek's, then go to Dick Boylan's, a quiet back room on the second story of a business building, patronized by doctors and lawyers and merchants in the neighborhood and by recent Yale and Princeton graduates and near-graduates. It was all he saw, in those days, of his friends from the country club crowd.

Dick Boylan's speakeasy was unique in that it was the only place of its kind that sold nothing but hard liquor. When a man wanted a sandwich and beer, he had to send out for it; if he wanted beer without a sandwich, Boylan told him to go some place else for it; but such requests were made only by strangers and by them not more than once. Dick Boylan was the proprietor, and in no sense the bartender; there were tables and chairs, but no bar in his place, and Boylan wore a suit of clothes and a fedora hat at all times, and always seemed to be on the go. He would put a bottle on the table, and when the drinkers had taken what they wanted he would hold up the bottle and estimate the number of drinks that had been poured from it and announce how much was owed him. "This here table owes me eight and a half," he would say, leaving the bookkeeping to the customers. "Or I'll have one with you and make it an even nine." Sometimes he would not be around to open up for the morning customers, and they would get the key from under the stairway linoleum, unlock the door, help themselves, and leave the money where Dick would find it. They could also leave chits when they were short of cash. If a man cheated on his chits, or owed too much money, or drank badly, he was not told so in so many words; he would knock on the door, the peephole was opened, and Boylan would say, "We're closed," and the statement was intended and taken to mean that the man was forever barred, with no further discussion of the matter.

Pat Collins was at Dick Boylan's every night after Madge made her true confession. Until then he had visited the place infrequently, and then, as a rule, in the company of Whit Hofman. The shabby austerity of Dick Boylan's and Boylan's high-handed crudities did not detract from the stern respectability of the place. No woman was allowed to set foot in Boylan's, and among the brotherhood of hard drinkers it was believed—erroneously—that all conversations at Boylan's were privileged, not to be repeated outside. "What's said in here is Masonic," Boylan claimed. "I find a man blabbing what he hears—he's out." Boylan had been known to bar a customer for merely mentioning the names of fellow drinkers. "I run a san'tuary for men that need their booze," said Boylan. "If they was in that Gibbsville Club every time they needed a steam, the whole town'd know it." It was a profitable sanctuary, with almost no overhead and, because of the influence of the clientele, a minimum of police graft. Pat Collins's visits with Whit Hofman had occurred on occasions when one or the other had a hangover, and Boylan's was a quick walk from Pat's garage. At night Whit Hofman preferred to do his drinking in more elegant surroundings, and Pat Collins told himself that he was sure he would not run into Whit at Boylan's. But he lied to himself; he *wanted* to run into Whit.

At first he wanted a fight, even though he knew he would be the loser. He would be giving twenty pounds to a man who appeared soft but was in deceptively good shape, who managed to get in some physical exercise nearly every day of his life and whose eight years of prep school and college football, three years of army service, and a lifetime of good food and medical care had given him resources that would be valuable in a real fight. Pat Collins knew he did not have a quick punch that would keep Whit down; Whit Hofman was not Walt Michaels. Whit Hofman, in fact, was Whit Hofman, with more on his side than his physical strength. Although he had never seen Whit in a fight, Pat had gone with him to many football games and observed Whit's keen and knowing interest in the niceties of line play. ("Watch that son of a bitch, the right guard for Lehigh. He's spilling two men on every play.") And Whit Hofman's way of telling about a battle during one of his rare reminiscences of the War ("They were awful damn close, but I didn't lob the God damn pineapple. I *threw* it. The hell with what they taught us back in Hancock.") was evidence that he would play for keeps, and enjoy the playing. Pat admitted that if he had really wanted a fight with Whit Hofman, he could have it for the asking. Then what *did* he want? The question had a ready answer: he wanted the impossible, to confide his perplexed anger in the one man on earth who would least like to hear it. He refused to solidify his wish into words, but he tormented himself with the hope that he could be back on the same old terms of companionship with the man who was responsible for his misery. Every night he went to Dick Boylan's, and waited with a bottle on the table.

Dick Boylan was accustomed to the company of hard drinkers, and when a man suddenly became a nightly, hours-long customer, Boylan was not surprised. He had seen the same thing happen too often for his curiosity to be aroused, and sooner or later he would be given a hint of the reason for the customer's problem. At first he dismissed the notion that in Pat Collins's case the problem was money; Collins was selling cars as fast as he could get delivery. The problem, therefore, was probably a woman, and since Collins was a nightly visitor, the woman was at home—his wife. It all came down to one of two things: money, or a woman. It never occurred to Dick Boylan—or, for that matter, to Pat Collins—that Pat's problem was the loss of a friend. Consequently Dick Boylan looked for, and found, all the evidence he needed to support his theory that Collins was having wife troubles. For example, men who were having money troubles would get phone calls from their wives, telling them to get home for supper. But the men who were having wife trouble, although they sometimes got calls from women, seldom got calls from their wives. Pat Collins's wife never called him. Never. And he never called her.

It was confusing to Dick Boylan to hear that Pat Collins's business was on the rocks. Whit Hofman did not let his friends' businesses go on the rocks. And then Boylan understood it all. A long forgotten, overheard remark about Whit Hofman and Madge Collins came back to him, and it was all as plain as day. Thereafter he watched Pat Collins more carefully; the amount he drank, the cordiality of his relations with the country clubbers, the neatness of his appearance, and the state of his mind and legs when at last he would say goodnight. He had nothing against Pat Collins, but he did not like him. Dick Boylan was more comfortable with non-Irishmen; they were neither Irish-to-Irish over-friendly, nor Irish-to-Irish condescending, and when Pat Collins turned out to be so preoccupied with his problems that he failed to be over-friendly or condescending, Dick Boylan put him down for an unsociable fellow, hardly an Irishman at all, but certainly not one of the others. Pat Collins did not fit in anywhere, although he got on well enough with the rest of the customers. Indeed, the brotherhood of hard drinkers were more inclined to welcome his company than Collins was to seek theirs. Two or three men coming in together would go to Pat's table instead of starting a table of their own and inviting him to join them. It was a distinction that Dick Boylan noticed without comprehending it, possibly because as an Irishman he was immune to what the non-Irish called Irish charm.

But it was not Irish charm that made Pat Collins welcome in the brotherhood; it was their sense of kinship with a man who was slipping faster than they were slipping, and who in a manner of speaking was taking someone else's turn in the downward line, thus postponing by months or years the next man's ultimate, inevitable arrival at the bottom. They welcomed this volunteer, and they hoped he would be with them a long while. They were an odd lot, with little in common except an inability to stand success or the lack of it. There were the medical men, Brady and Williams; Brady, who one day in his early forties stopped in the middle of an operation and had to let his assistant take over, and never performed surgery again; Williams, who at thirty-two was already a better doctor than his father, but who was oppressed by his father's reputation. Lawyer Parsons, whose wife had made him run for Congress because her father had been a congressman, and who had then fallen hopelessly in love with the wife of a congressman from Montana. Lawyer Strickland, much in demand as a high school commencement speaker, but somewhat shaky on the Rules of Evidence. Jeweler Linklighter, chess player without a worthy opponent since the death of the local rabbi. Hardware Merchant Stump, Eastern Pennsylvania trapshooting champion until an overload exploded and blinded one eye. Teddy Stokes, Princeton '25, gymnast, Triangle Club heroine and solo dancer, whose father was paying blackmail to the father of an altar boy. Sterling Agnew, Yale ex-'22, Sheff, a remittance man from New York whose father owned coal lands, and who was a part-time lover of Kitty Hofman's. George W. Shuttleworth, Yale '91, well-to-do widower and gentleman author, currently at work on a biography of Nathaniel Hawthorne which was begun in

1892. Percy Keene, music teacher specializing in band instruments, and husband of a Christian Science practitioner. Lewis M. Rutledge, former captain of the Amherst golf team and assistant manager of the local branch of a New York brokerage house, who had passed on to Agnew the information that Kitty Hofman was accommodating if you caught her at the right moment. Miles Lassiter, ex–cavalry officer, ex–lieutenant of the State Constabulary, partner in the Schneider & Lassiter Detective & Protective Company, industrial patrolmen, payroll guards, private investigators, who was on his word of honor never again to bring a loaded revolver into Boylan's. Any and at some times all these gentlemen were to be found at Boylan's on any given night, and they constituted a clientele that Dick Boylan regarded as his regulars, quite apart from the daytime regulars who came in for a quick steam, drank it, paid, and quickly departed. Half a dozen of the real regulars were also daytime regulars, but Boylan said—over and over again—that in the daytime he ran a first-aid station; the sanctuary did not open till suppertime. (The sanctuary designation originated with George Shuttleworth; the first-aid station, with Dr. Calvin K. Brady, a Presbyterian and therefore excluded from Boylan's generalities regarding the Irish.)

For nearly three years these men sustained Pat Collins in his need for companionship, increasingly so as he came to know their problems. And know them he did, for in the stunned silence that followed Madge's true confession he took on the manner of the reliable listener, and little by little, bottle by bottle, the members of the brotherhood imparted their stories even as Whit Hofman had done on the afternoon of the first meeting of Whit and Pat. In exchange the members of the brotherhood helped Pat Collins with their tacit sympathy, that avoided mention of the latest indication of cumulative disaster. With a hesitant delicacy they would wait until he chose, if he chose, to speak of the loss of his business, the loss of his jobs, the changes of home address away from the western part of town to the northeastern, where the air was always a bit polluted from the steel mill, the gas house, the abattoir, and where there was always some noise, of which the worst was the squealing of hogs in the slaughterhouse.

"I hope you won't mind if I say this, Pat," said George Shuttleworth one night. "But it seems to me you take adversity very calmly, considering the first thing I ever heard about you."

"What was that, George?"

"I believe you administered a sound thrashing to Mr. Herb Michaels, shortly after you moved to town."

"Oh, that. Yes. Well, I'm laughing on the other side of my face now. I shouldn't have done that."

"But you're glad you did. I hope. Think of how you'd feel now if you hadn't. True, he owns the business you built up, but at least you have the memory of seeing him on the ground. And a cigar in his mouth, wasn't it? I always enjoyed that touch. I believe Nathaniel would have enjoyed it."

"Who?"

"Nathaniel Hawthorne. Most generally regarded as a gloomy writer, but where you find irony you'll find a sense of humor. I couldn't interest you in reading Hawthorne, could I?"

"Didn't he write *The Scarlet Letter*?"

"Indeed he did, indeed so."

"I think I read that in college."

"Oh, I hadn't realized you were a college man. Where?"

"Villanova."

"Oh, yes."

"It's a Catholic college near Philly."

"Yes, it must be on the Main Line."

"It is."

"Did you study for the priesthood?"

"No, just the regular college course. I flunked out sophomore year."

"How interesting that a Catholic college should include *The Scarlet Letter*. Did you have a good teacher? I wonder what his name was."

"Brother Callistus, I think. Maybe it was Brother Adrian."

"I must look them up. I thought I knew all the Hawthorne authorities. Callistus, and Adrian. No other names?"

"That's what they went by."

"I'm always on the lookout for new material on Nathaniel. One of these days I've just got to stop revising and pack my book off to a publisher, that's all there is to it. Stand or fall on what I've done—and then I suppose a week after I publish, along will come someone with conclusions that make me seem fearfully out of date. It's a terrifying decision for me to make after nearly thirty years. I don't see how I can face it."

"Why don't you call this Volume One?"

"Extraordinary. I thought of that very thing. In fact, in 1912 I made a new start with just that in mind, but after three years I went back to my earlier plan, a single volume. But perhaps I could publish in the next year or two, and later on bring out new editions, say every five years. Possibly ten. I'd hoped to be ready for the Hawthorne Centenary in 1904, but I got hopelessly bogged down in the allegories and I didn't dare rush into print with what I had then. It wouldn't have been fair to me or to Nathaniel, although I suppose it'd make precious little difference to him."

"You never know."

"That's just it, Pat. He's very real to me, you know, although he passed away on May eighteenth or nineteenth in 'sixty-four. There's some question as to whether it was the eighteenth or the nineteenth. But he's very real to me. Very."

This gentle fanatic, quietly drinking himself into a stupor three nights a week, driven home in a taxi with a standing order, and reappearing punctually at eight-thirty after a night's absence, became Pat Collins's favorite companion among the brotherhood. George was in his early fifties, childless, with a full head of snowy white hair brushed down tight on one side. As he spoke he moved his hand slowly across his thatch, as though still training it. Whatever he said seemed to be in answer to a question, a studied reply on which he would be marked as in an examination, and he consequently presented the manner, looking straight ahead and far away, of a conscientious student who was sure of his facts but anxious to present them with care. To Pat Collins the mystery was how had George Shuttleworth come to discover whiskey, until well along in their friendship he learned that George had begun drinking at Yale and had never stopped. Alcohol had killed his wife in her middle forties—she was the same age as George—and Boylan's brotherhood had taken the place of the drinking bouts George had previously indulged in with her. "The Gibbsville Club is no place for me in the evening," said George. "Games, games, games. If it isn't bridge in the card room, it's pool in the billiard room. Why do men feel they have to be so strenuous—and I include bridge. The veins stand out in their foreheads, and when they finish a hand there's always one of them to heave a great sigh of relief. That's what I mean by strenuous. And the worst of it is that with two or possibly three exceptions, I used to beat them all consistently, and I never had any veins stand out in *my* forehead."

As the unlikely friendship flourished, the older man, by the strength of his passivity, subtly influenced and then dominated Pat Collins's own behavior. George Shuttleworth never tried to advise or instruct his younger friend or anyone else; but he had made a life for himself that seemed attractive to the confused, disillusioned younger man. Ambition, aggressiveness seemed worthless to Pat Collins. They had got him nowhere; they had in fact tricked him as his wife and his most admired friend had tricked him, as though Madge and Whit had given him a garage to get him out of the way. He was in no condition for violent action, and George Shuttleworth, the least violent of men, became his guide in this latter-day acceptance of defeat. In spite of the friendship, George Shuttleworth remained on an impersonal basis with Pat Collins; they never discussed Madge at all, never mentioned her name, and as a consequence Pat's meetings with his friend did not become an opportunity for self-pity.

The time then came—no day, no night, no month, no dramatic moment but only a time—when George Shuttleworth had taken Whit's place in Pat Collins's need of a man to admire. And soon thereafter another time came when Pat Collins was healed, no longer harassed by the wish or the fear that he would encounter Whit. It was a small town, but the routines of lives in small towns can be restrictive. A woman can say, "I haven't been downtown since last month," although downtown may be no more than four or five blocks away. And there were dozens of men and women who had been born in the town, Pat's early acquaintances in the town, who never in their lives had seen the street in the northeastern section where Pat and Madge now lived. ("Broad Street? I never knew we had a Broad Street in Gibbsville.") There were men and women from Broad Street liberated by the cheap automobile, who would take a ride out Lantenengo Street on a Sunday afternoon, stare at the houses of the rich, but who could not say with certainty that one house belonged to a brewer and another to a coal operator. Who has to know the town as a whole? A physician. The driver of a meat-market delivery truck. A police officer. The fire chief. A newspaper reporter. A taxi driver. A town large enough to be called a town is a complex of neighborhoods, invariably within well-defined limits of economic character; and the men of the neighborhoods, freer to move outside, create or follow the boundaries of their working activities—and return to their neighborhoods for the nights of delight and anguish with their own. Nothing strange, then, but only abrupt, when Pat Collins ceased to see Whit Hofman; and nothing remarkable, either, that three years could be added to the life of Pat Collins, hiding all afternoon in a poolroom, clinging night after night to a glass.

"What did you want to tell me this for?" he had said.

"Because I thought it was right," she had said.

"Right, you say?"

"To tell you, yes," she said.

He stood up and pulled off his belt and folded it double.

"Is that what you're gonna do, Pat?"

"Something to show him the next time," he said.

"There'll be no next time. You're the only one'll see what you did to me."

"That's not what I'm doing it for."

"What for, then?"

"It's what you deserve. They used to stone women like you, stone them to death."

"Do that, then. Kill me, but not the strap. Really kill me, but don't do that, Pat. That's ugly. Have the courage to kill me, and I'll die. But don't do that with the strap, please."

"What a faker, what a bluffer you are."

"No," she said. She went to the bureau drawer and took out his revolver and handed it to him. "I made an act of contrition."

"An act of contrition."

"Yes, and there was enough talk, enough gossip. You'll get off," she said.

"Put the gun away," he said.

She dropped the revolver on a chair cushion. "You put it

away. Put it in your pocket, Pat. I'll use it on you if you start beating me with the strap."

"Keep your voice down, the children'll hear," he said.

"They'll hear if you beat me."

"You and your act of contrition. Take off your clothes."

"You hit me with that strap and I'll scream."

"Take your clothes off, I said."

She removed her dress and slip, and stood in brassiere and girdle.

"Everything," he said.

She watched his eyes, took off the remaining garments, and folded her arms against her breasts.

He went to her, bent down, and spat on her belly.

"You're dirty," he said. "You're a dirty woman. Somebody spit on you, you dirty woman. The spit's rolling down your belly. No, I won't hit you."

She slowly reached down, picked up the slip and covered herself with it. "Are you through with me?"

He laughed. "Am I through with you? Am *I* through with you."

He left the house and was gone a week before she again heard from him. He stayed in town, but he ate only breakfast at home. "Is this the way it's going to be?" she said. "I have to make up a story for the children."

"You ought to be good at that."

"Just so I know," she said. "Do you want to see their report cards?"

"No."

"It's no use taking it out on them. What you do to me, I don't care, but they're not in this. They think you're cross with them."

"Don't tell me what to do. The children. You down here, with them sleeping upstairs. Don't you tell me what to do."

"All right, I won't," she said. "I'll tell them you're working nights, you can't come home for dinner. They'll see through it, but I have to give them some story."

"You'll make it a good one, of that I'm sure."

In calmer days he had maintained a balance between strict parenthood and good humor toward the children, but now he could not overcome the guilt of loathing their mother that plagued him whenever he saw the question behind their eyes. They were waiting to be told something, and all he could tell them was that it was time for them to be off to school, to be off to Mass, always time for them to go away and take their unanswerable, unphrased questions with them. Their mother told them that he was very busy at the garage, that he had things on his mind, but in a year he had lost them. There was more finality to the loss than would have been so if he had always treated them with indifference, and he hated Madge the more because she could not and he could not absolve him of his guilt.

One night in Boylan's speakeasy George Shuttleworth, out of a momentary silence, said: "What are you going to do now, Pat?"

"Nothing. I have no place to go."

"Oh, you misunderstood me. I'm sorry. I meant now that Overton's has closed."

"That was over a month ago. I don't know, George. I haven't found anything, but I guess something will turn up. I was thinking of going on the road again. I used to be a pretty good hat salesman, wholesale, and when I was with Overton I told the traveling men to let me know if they heard of anything."

"But you don't care anything about hats."

"Well, I don't, but I can't pick and choose. I can't support a family shooting pool."

"Isn't there something in the automobile line? A man ought to work at the job he likes best. We have only the one life, Pat. The one time in this vale of tears."

"Right now the automobile business is a vale of tears. I hear Herb Michaels isn't having it any too easy, and I could only move four new Cadillacs in fourteen months."

"Suppose you had your own garage today. Could you make money, knowing as much as you do?"

"Well, they say prosperity is just around the corner."

"I don't believe it for a minute."

"I don't either, not in the coal regions. A man to make a living in the automobile business today, in this part of the country, he'd be better off without a dealer's franchise. Second-hand cars, and service and repairs. New rubber. Accessories. Batteries. All that. The people that own cars have to get them serviced, but the people that need cars in their jobs, they're not buying new cars. Who is?"

"I don't know. I've never owned a car. Never learned to drive one."

"You ought to. Then when you go looking for material for your book, you'd save a lot of steps."

"Heavens no," said George Shuttleworth. "You're referring to trips to Salem? New England? Why it takes me two or three days of walking before I achieve the proper Nineteenth Century mood. My late lamented owned a car and employed a chauffeur. A huge, lumbering Pierce-Arrow she kept for twelve years. I got rid of it after she died. It had twelve thousand miles on the speedometer, a thousand miles for each year."

"Oh, they were lovely cars. Was it a limousine?"

"Yes, a limousine, although I believe they called it a Berliner. The driver was well protected. Windows on the front doors. I got rid of him, too. I got rid of him *first*. Good pay. Apartment over the garage. Free meals. New livery every second year. And a hundred dollars at Christmas. But my wife's gasoline bills, I happened to compare them with bills for the hospital ambulance when I was on the board. Just curiosity. Well, sir, if those bills were any indication, my wife's car used up more gasoline than the ambulance, although I don't suppose it all found its way into our tank. But she defended him. Said he always kept the car looking so nice. He did, at that. He had precious little else to occupy his time. I believe he's gone back to Belgium. He was the only Belgian in town, and my wife was very sympathetic toward the Belgians."

"Took his savings and—"

"His plunder," said George Shuttleworth. "Let's not waste any more time talking about him, Pat. You know, of course, that I'm quite rich."

"Yes, that wouldn't be hard to guess. That house and all."

"The house, yes, the house. Spotless, not a speck of dust anywhere. It's like a museum. I have a housekeeper, Mrs. Frazier. Scotch. Conscientious to a degree, but she's made a whole career of keeping my house antiseptically clean, like an operating surgery. So much so, that she makes me feel that

I'm in the way. So I'm getting out of the way for a while. I'm going away."

"Going down South?"

"No, I'm not going South. I'm going abroad, Pat. I haven't been since before the War, and I'm not really running away from Mrs. Frazier and her feather dusters. I have a serious purpose in taking this trip. It has to do with my book. You knew that Nathaniel spent seven years abroad. Perhaps you didn't. Seven years, from 1853 to 1860."

"You want to see what inspired him," said Pat.

"No, no! Quite the contrary. He'd done all his best work by then. I want to see how it spoiled him, living abroad. There were other distractions. The Civil War. His daughter's illness. But I must find out for myself whether European life spoiled Nathaniel *or* did he flee to Europe when he'd exhausted his talent. That may turn out to be my greatest contribution to the study of Hawthorne. I can see quite clearly how my discoveries might cause me to scrap everything I've done so far and have to start all over again. I've already written to a great many scholars, and they've expressed keen interest."

"Well, I'll be sorry to see you go, George. I'll miss our evenings. When do you leave?"

"In the *Mauretania*, the seventh of next month. Oh, when I decide to act, nothing stops me," said George Shuttleworth. "I want to give you a going-away present, Pat."

"It should be the other way around. You're the one that's leaving."

"If you wish to give me some memento, that's very kind of you. But what I have in mind, I've been thinking about it for some time. Not an impulse of the moment. How much would it cost to set you up in a business such as you describe?"

"Are you serious, George?"

"Dead serious."

"A small garage, repairing all makes. No dealership. Gas, oil, tires, accessories. There's an old stable near where I live. A neighbor of mine uses it to garage his car in. You want to go on my note, is that it?"

"No, I don't want to go on your note. I'll lend you the money myself, without interest."

"Using mostly second-hand equipment, which I know where to buy here and there, that kind of a setup would run anywhere from five to ten thousand dollars. Atlantic, Gulf, one of those companies put in the pump and help with the tank. Oil. Tools I'd have to buy myself. Air pump. Plumbing would be a big item, and I'd need a pit to work in. Anywhere between five and ten thousand. You can always pick up a light truck cheap and turn it into a tow-car."

George Shuttleworth was smiling. "That's the way I like to hear you talk, Pat. Show some enthusiasm for something. What's your bank?"

"The Citizens, it was. I don't have any at the moment."

"Tomorrow, sometime before three o'clock, I'll deposit ten thousand dollars in your name, and you can begin to draw on it immediately."

"There ought to be some papers drawn up."

"My cheque is all the papers we'll need."

"George?"

"Now, now! No speech, none of that. I spend that much every year, just to have a house with sparkling chandeliers."

"Well then, two words. Thank you."

"You're very welcome."

"George?"

"Yes, Pat."

"I'm sorry, but you'll have to excuse me. I—I can't sit here, George. You see why? Please excuse me."

"You go take a good long walk, Pat. That's what you do."

He walked through the two crowds of men and women leaving the movie houses at the end of the first show. He spoke to no one.

"You're home early," said Madge. "Are you all right?"

"I'm all right."

"You look sort of peak-ed."

"Where are the children?"

"They're out Halloweening. They finished their home work."

"I'm starting a new business."

"You are? What?"

"I'm opening a new garage."

"Where?"

"In the neighborhood."

"Well—that's good, I guess. Takes money, but it'd be a waste of time to ask you where you got it."

"It'd be a waste of time."

"Did you have your supper?"

"I ate something. I'm going to bed. I have to get up early. I have to go around and look for a lot of stuff."

"Can I do anything?"

"No. Just wake me up when the children get up."

"All right. Goodnight."

"Goodnight."

"And good luck, Pat."

"No. No, Madge. Don't, don't—"

"All right. I'm sorry," she said quietly. Then, uncontrolled, "Pat, for God's sake! Please?"

"No, Madge. I ask you."

She covered her face with her hands. "Please, please, please, please, please."

But he went upstairs without her. He could not let her spoil this, he could not let her spoil George Shuttleworth even by knowing about him.

"Hello, Pat."

"Hyuh, Whit."

Never more than that, but never less.

Agatha

Both dogs had been out. She could tell by the languid way they greeted her and by the fact that Jimmy, the elevator operator, had taken his twenty-five-cent piece off the hall table. Or was it Jimmy? Yes, Jimmy was on mornings this week; Ray was on afternoons and evenings. Jimmy liked dogs, Ray did not. The day was off to a better start when Jimmy took the dogs for their morning walk; it was nicer to start the day with the thought that Jimmy, who liked dogs, had exercised them, and not Ray, who made no attempt to conceal his distaste for the chore. Ray was paid a quarter, just the same as Jimmy, for taking the dogs down to the corner, but Mrs. Child had very good reason to believe that that was *all* he did—take them to the corner, and hurry right back without letting them stop at the curb.

"Good morning, boys," she said, addressing the dogs. They shook their tails without getting up. "Oh, you're such spoiled boys, you two. You won't even rise when a lady enters the room. Muggsy, don't you *know* that a gentleman *always* stands up when a lady comes in? You *do* know it, too, and you're not a very good example to your adopted brother, are you? How can I expect Percy to have good manners if you don't show him how? Percy, don't you pay a bit of attention to Muggsy and his bad manners." The dogs raised their heads at the sound of their names, but when she finished speaking they slowly put their heads back on their paws. "Oh, you're hopeless, the two of you. Really hopeless. I don't see why I put up with two such uncouth rascals."

She proceeded to the kitchen door and pushed it open. "Good morning, Mary," she said.

"Good morning, Mrs. Child," said the maid. "I heard you running your tub. Will you have toast this morning?"

"Just one slice, please. Maybe two slices, but bring me my coffee first, will you?"

"Yes ma'am."

"I didn't see any mail. Was there any?"

"Got it here on the tray. Which'll you have? Marmalade, or the blackberry jam?"

"Mary, you're not cooperating at all. You know perfectly well if you mention marmalade or jam, I'll *have* marmalade or jam, and I'm trying not to."

"Oh, if I don't mention it you'll ask for it."

"I'm such a weak, spineless creature. All right, you mean old Mary Moran, you. You know me much too well. I'll have the blackberry jam. Were there any packages?"

"None so far, but United Parcel don't usually get here before noontime. That's the way it works out. Some neighborhoods they only deliver in the afternoon, some in the morning. I guess they have a system."

"And speaking of other neighborhoods, when am I going to be able to lure you away from Mrs. Brown?"

"Oh—I don't know about that, Mrs. Child," said Mary Moran. "Will you have your first cup standing up?"

"No, I'll wait. I'll be in the livingroom," said Mrs. Child.

Mary Moran would have been expensive, and there really wasn't enough work to keep her busy, but Mrs. Child knew that Mary's other employer, Mrs. Brown, had been trying to persuade her to give up Mrs. Child and work full-time for her. It did no harm, every once in a while, to remind Mary that she had a full-time job waiting for her with Mrs. Child—and subtly to remind Mary that she had been with Mrs. Child a good two years longer than she had been with Mrs. Brown. There were a lot of things Mary could not do, but in what she could do, or would do, she was flawless. Mrs. Child did not need Mary Moran at all, when you came right down to it. The building provided maid service of a-lick-and-a-promise sort, and you could have all your meals sent up and served by the room-service waiters. But Mary Moran was acquainted with every article of clothing that Mrs. Child possessed; she was a superb laundress of things like lingerie; a quick and careful presser; very handy with needle and thread. She could put together a light meal of soup and salad, and she could do tiny sandwiches and a cheese dip for a small cocktail group. But she would not serve luncheon or pass a tray among cocktail guests; not that she was ever there at cocktail time, but as a matter of principle she had made it one of her rules that serving was not to be expected of her. She was not very good about taking telephone messages, either; it had taken Mrs. Child two years to discover that Mary was ashamed of her handwriting and spelling. Nevertheless she would have been an excellent personal maid, and Agatha Child never gave up hoping that she could lure—lure was the word—Mary away from the Browns, whoever *they* were beyond the fact that they had a small apartment on Seventy-ninth Street and were away a good deal of the time. It would have been worth the money to have Mary Moran on a full-time basis, not only for the work she did, but because her coming to work full-time would have been an expression of the approval that Agatha Child suspected that Mary withheld.

"We haven't talked about that for quite some time," said Agatha Child.

Mary Moran had just brought in the breakfast tray. "What's that, Mrs. Child?"

"About your coming to work for me full-time."

Mary Moran smiled. "Well, it suits me, the way it is," she said.

"You'd make just as much money. And don't you find it a nuisance, to finish up here and then have to take the bus to Seventy-ninth Street?"

"I usually walk. I enjoy the walk. I get a breath of fresh air."

"Do you know what I think? I think you have a gentleman friend that you have lunch with. You almost never have lunch here."

"Well, there may be some truth to that. We have a bite to eat. It's on the way."

"Oh, my guess was right? How fascinating. Tell me about him."

"No, I don't think I'll do that."

"Of course not. It's none of my business, and I don't want to appear inquisitive. But of course I'm dying of curiosity. You've been with me eight years and this is really the first time we ever got on that subject."

"Well, you made a good guess for your first try."

"Is he Catholic?"

"No ma'am."

"You'd rather not say any more."

"Rather not. It's him and I."

"Yes. Well, I won't badger you any more. I just want to say that I hope he appreciates you, and if you ever feel the need to talk to someone about it—about him."

"Thank you, ma'am."

"Remember, I've been married three times."

"I know that, yes."

"And I'm a lot older than you. Probably fifteen years."

"Not quite. I'll be forty-one."

"Well, almost fifteen years. How did you know my age? Did you see it on my passport?"

"No ma'am. Your scrapbook, where you have that newspaper cutting of when you eloped and all. The big green scrapbook."

"Oh, yes. That's a dead giveaway, isn't it? Well, what difference does it make? Anybody can find out my age if they want to take the trouble. All they have to do is go to the Public Library, and there it is in big headlines, seventeen-year-old heiress and all that tommyrot. Never lived it down. But that's where I can be of help to you, Mary, in case you ever *need* any help."

"They'd never put *me* in the headlines, whatever I did."

"You can be thankful for that," said Agatha Child.

"Will you want me to—changing the subject—will I send the black suit to the dry cleaner's, or do you want to give it another wear?"

"I guess it could stand a cleaning. Whatever you think," said Agatha Child.

"I had a look at it this morning. It's about ready to go."

The day's mail was fattened up by the usual bills and appeals. She put a rubber band around the unopened bills, for forwarding to Mr. Jentzen, who would scrutinize them, make out the appropriate cheques, and send her the cheques for signature. She saw Mr. Jentzen just once a year, at income tax time, when he would deliver his little lecture on her finances, show her where to sign the returns, and have one glass of sherry with her. On these occasions Mr. Jentzen could almost make her feel that he was paying for the sherry and for everything else. Bald, conscientious Mr. Jentzen, who looked like a dark-haired version of the farmer in Grant Wood's "American Gothic," and who in some respects knew her better than any husband or lover she had ever had, but who politely declined her suggestion that he call her Agatha. "Not even if I call you Eric? It's such a nice name, Eric." And so unlike Mr. Jentzen, she did not add. She could have gone right ahead and called him Eric; she was, after all, at least five years older than he, but she knew that he was afraid of even so slight an intimacy because he was the kind of man who would be afraid to get entangled with a woman who had had three husbands and an undetermined number of gentlemen friends.

It occurred to her now, as she doubled the rubber band about the bills, that her life was full of small defeats at the hands of people who rightfully should have obeyed her automatically. Mary Moran, Eric Jentzen, and Ray the bellboy were three she could name offhand who refused to yield to her wishes. With Ray the bellboy it was a case of attitude rather than outright disobedience; he did what she asked, but so churlishly that his obedience became an act of defiance. Mary Moran, crafty little Irishwoman that she was, was practically an illiterate but she was adroit enough to avoid a showdown on the question of giving up the Browns. And Eric Jentzen used his sexual timidity to keep from losing the arrogated privilege of lecturing her on her extravagances. (It was quite possible that Mr. Jentzen got some sort of mild kick out of that safe intimacy.)

The dogs were now sitting up. "One little piece of toast is all you're going to get," she said. "No, Percy, you must wait till your older stepbrother has his. See there, Muggsy? If you'd taught him better manners he wouldn't be so grabby. One piece is all you're going to get, so don't bother to look at me that way. Down, boys. I said down. *Down*, God damn it! Percy, you scratched me, you son of a bitch. You could cause me all sorts of trouble, explaining a scratch like that. *If* there was anybody I had to explain to." She lit a cigarette and blew smoke in the dogs' muzzles. "Now stay down, and don't interrupt me while I see whose sucker list I'm on today."

Two of the appeals were for theatrical previews at twenty-five dollars a crack. By an amusing coincidence both contained similarly worded personal touches. "Do try to come" was written across the top of the announcements; one was signed with initials, identifiable by going down the list of patronesses; the other was signed "Mary," and didn't mean a damned thing.

Mary. What a crust a woman had, to sign just Mary and expect people to know who Mary was. Agatha Child went through the list and discovered three Marys behind the married names and one Mary who was a Miss. "I'll tell you what you can do, Mary dear. You can invite me to dinner and the benefit and shell out fifty dollars for me and some likely gentleman, and I *will* do-try-to-come." She dropped the announcements in the wastebasket. She immediately retrieved them and went over one of the lists again. Yes, there it was: Mrs. W. B. Harris, the wife of her second husband. What a comedown that would be for Wally, if he should ever learn that she had seen that name, which once she bore, and it had failed to register. True, she had always given the name the full treatment: Wallace Boyd Harris. True, too, there were so many Harrises. One too many, or two too many, if it came to that, which was how she happened to become Agatha Child. For the second time she dropped the announcements in the wastebasket, but at least they had given her some amusement. Wally Harris, afraid of his own shadow—more accurately, afraid of the shadow of her first husband. Well, it hadn't been a mere shadow; more like a London peasouper that lasted four years. Four dark, miserable years that she could recall in every detail and had succeeded in suspending from her active memory, by sandwiching the whole period in between her first marriage and her third, so that it was worthless even as a wasted segment of her time on earth to cry over. He was an intimate man, Wally, wanting to know everything about everything she did, until there was nothing left to learn except all the things she felt and could not tell him, that no one can tell anyone unless she is asked the right questions, at the right moment, in the right tone of voice, and for the right reason which is love. Finally he had learned just about every fact of her marriage to her first husband and had accidentally discovered a few facts about the man who was to be her third. All that time that he had consumed in pumping her about Johnny Johns, in contemning Johnny Johns, in emulating Johnny Johns—a little of that time, only a little, Wally could more profitably have devoted to the ma-neuverings of his friend Stanley Child. When the blow fell and there was that tiresome scene that Wally had insisted upon ("I want you to hear everything I say to Stanley"), the thought kept running through her mind that Wally hated Johnny much more than he did Stanley. Despite the fact that she had been having her affair with Stanley right under his nose, Wally managed to bring up Johnny Johns, whom she had not seen or heard from in five years. "I thought you were all through with that kind of thing when you got rid of that Johns fellow," said Wally.

"I was—to marry you," she said. "Johnny could have been very unpleasant about *you*, don't forget."

"That lightweight," said Wally, unmistakably implying that Johnny was incapable of sustained indignation. Two years later Wally married the present Mrs. Harris, the lady of the patroness list, and immediately started having lunch with Stanley again. By Wally's lights it was all right to resume the friendship with Stanley Child as soon as he remarried, but not before. The friendship in its second phase was stronger than it had ever been, and it did not include the wives. "Wally and I are going over to play Pine Valley . . . Wally got me an invitation to Thomasville. Will you be all right?" At first she was not all right, at all; it was not her idea of fun to sit in a New York apartment while the two big boys, her husband and her ex, went off to play. She was not worried about what they would say about her; Stanley Child was simply not the kind of man who would discuss his wife with another man on any terms, and insensitive though he may have been about many things, Wally Harris would know better than to mention Agatha except when it was unavoidable. No, it was not the fear of their talking about her that annoyed her; it was her growing conviction that she could be the wife of two men and yet remain completely outside their lives, one after the other and the two together. In olden days they might well have fought a duel over her; in the fifth decade of the twentieth century they played golf together and tacitly denied her existence.

It was a dismal record for a girl who had only wanted to be liked, who had only tried to be pleasant to people. She loved Johnny Johns now, today, so many years later, but she had not even believed at the time that she was marrying Johnny for love. He was a screwy boy who would come charging into Canoe Place late Saturday nights, arriving alone and always leaving with some other boy's girl. Nothing vicious about him; he made no phony promises, and he nursed no hard feelings against the girls who refused to ditch the boys they had come with. To such steadfast types he would say, "Okay, but you don't know what you're missing," and it was as close as he ever came to the surliness of some of the other wolf types. At this point in her reminiscing she smiled.

Canoe Place, a Saturday night after a dance at the Meadow Club. He came and sat down beside her—actually in back of her—pulling up a chair from the next table. "Aggie Todd, I've a bone to pick with you. I hear you said I wasn't a wolf."

"You heard I said you *weren't* a wolf? Were not? Why is that a bone to pick with me?"

"You trying to ruin my reputation?"

"You're getting me all confused," she said.

"Did you or did you not say I was not a wolf?"

"I said you were not," she said.

"That's what I heard. What right have you got to go around saying nice things about me?"

"Huh?"

"The first thing you know, all the mothers and fathers will start approving of me. Then where will I be?"

She was young, and not very quick. "Oh, now I get it," she said. "You glory in a bad reputation, is that it?"

"I sure as hell don't want to turn into a Henny Ramsdell."

"You won't, never fear." This was fun because Henny Ramsdell at that very moment was seated on her left.

"Or a Bucky Clayton." Bucky Clayton was sitting across the table, looking at them and straining an ear to hear what they were saying. "Take a gander at Bucky, trying to read our lips."

"I know," she said.

"Why did you rush to my defense, Aggie?"

"Because I think—well I *don't* think you're a *wolf.*"

"Well, one of these days maybe I'll say something nice about you." He was a little more serious, and started to rise.

"Why not now?"

"All right," he said. Then, "No, I guess not. I don't want to turn your head."

"Ah, come on, turn my head, Johnny."

"You really want me to?"

"Yes."

"All right, but you asked for it, Aggie. I think you're the only girl in this whole damn bunch that I give a hoot in hell about."

"Is that true?" she said.

"It's true."

"Scout's honor?"

"Now don't push it. Yes, scout's honor. Come on, let's dance. Mr. Ramsdell, boy, I'm taking your girl away."

"The hell you are," said Henny Ramsdell.

"The hell I'm not," said Johnny. "Come on, Aggie, while you have the chance."

A week later they eloped, and during the next four years all the predictable mishaps of their kind of marriage came to pass. There was, in addition, a handicap that the pessimists had not counted on and the optimists had not foreseen: she was too young for companionship with most of the young wives in her set, and as a wife she was no longer compatible with the unmarried girls who were her contemporaries. It came down to a problem of often not knowing whom to have lunch with, and Johnny, working downtown, was impatiently lacking in an understanding of the problem. "You would never think," she said to Wallace Harris, "that a thing like that would make so much difference, but it does."

Wallace Harris was a bachelor, a few years older than Johnny. "Do you mean to say you're lonely?"

"That's *just* what I'm saying."

"Why don't you have a child?"

"We did. I never saw it."

"Sorry."

She had not been very bright about Wallace Harris. She had had no curiosity about him, and when she drifted into an affair with him she was all but shocked to discover that he had always been promiscuous, that women by the dozen had succumbed, if that was the word, to his availability. It was difficult to believe him as he told her the number and kinds of women who had slept with him, but she could not wholly doubt him since she was now one of that list herself. What made it difficult to believe him was her unthinking acceptance of the notion that roués had fun, and inevitably were gay; but for Wally there seemed to have been no fun, only a succession of women who used him as much as he used them. As for gaiety, one of his outstanding characteristics was a total lack of it. In this respect, however, she came to understand his success with women: he was so lacking in gaiety that a woman would automatically credit him with discretion and reliability. But poor Wally was essentially nothing more than a well-scrubbed male, who never needed a haircut or a manicure, and would have been far happier without women if the men he liked had been able to do without them too. He would never have been clinically curious about her life with Stanley Child as he had been about Johnny Johns; without asking, he would guess that Stanley's demands on a woman were much like his own—and he would have been right. He understood Stanley, but Johnny Johns was a lightweight . . .

Agatha Child heard herself say, "What? What?"

Mary Moran was standing in the doorway, with the jacket of the black suit over her arm and holding up the skirt. "I didn't mean to startle you, ma'am."

"Oh—I was off somewhere," said Agatha Child. "What is it, Mary?"

"Well, I was wondering if maybe there's a little hole in the skirt we should have rewoven."

"A hole in it? Let me see."

"Right here, ma'am, just back of the knee. You musta caught it on something."

"Yes. I wonder if it'd be worth it. Reweaving is awfully expensive."

"Now if it was a country suit, you wouldn't care so much. But you don't want to go around with a hole in your skirt in the city."

"I forget how much they charged the last time I had something rewoven. I paid four hundred dollars for that suit, when was it, three years ago?"

"You had this three years, that's right. It's a beautiful suit, no doubt about that. I think it's worth getting it rewoven."

"It's too bad you can't wear my clothes. I'd give it to you, then I'd have an excuse to buy myself a new one."

"No, I could never get into this. I was always too big an eater."

"You *could* have a nice figure, if you'd take off about fifteen pounds. You really ought to be ashamed of yourself, Mary. That's all since you've come to work for me."

"Aach, and if they don't like me this way it's too late for me to change."

"Too late? Nonsense. Forty-one. If I gave you a course at Elizabeth Arden, would you go through with it?"

"Me at Elizabeth Arden's? Huh."

"Well, any place."

"Thanks just the same. I got the determination, if I want to starve off the fifteen pounds, but I'd only put it back on again."

"Do as you please," said Agatha Child.

"And what about the suit, ma'am?"

"Have it rewoven, of course. And tell them not to take so long. The last time I think they took over a month."

"That was a big cigarette burn, in your gray."

"You don't have to make excuses for them, Mary. Just tell them what I said."

Mary Moran left, saying no more. If she had stayed longer, said any more, Agatha Child would have fired her. The woman had snubbed her twice within the hour, less than an hour, actually. Agatha, at the thought of time, glanced at the little gold and enamel clock at her side. It was twelve-twenty-two, according to the clock—which obviously had stopped during the night. She reached for the clock to wind it, but it had *not* stopped; the winder took only one full turn. She held the clock to her ear, and it was steadily ticking away. Was it possible that she had been sitting here for an hour and ten minutes? Had she fallen asleep after her coffee and cigarette? She looked for her cigarette. It was not in the ash tray, and yet she remembered having a cigarette, blowing the smoke at the dogs.

Casually, so that Mary Moran would not come in and catch her in the act of looking for the cigarette butt, she bent over to the right and then to the left of her chair. The cigarette was on neither side. She leaned forward, and there it was, having burnt itself out and formed a small crater in the carpet. She *had* been asleep, and once again she had gone to sleep with a cigarette burning, just as she had done while wearing the gray suit, which Mary Moran knew about, and one other time that the maid did not know about, all within a space of six or eight weeks.

She picked up the cigarette butt and put it in the ash tray. Then she dipped a napkin in the glass of icewater and tried to rub the blackened crater in the carpet so that the burn would not show. This was only partially successful. The crater remained, and some of the piling was permanently blackened.

It was no time to panic; it was a time to face facts, to look at things calmly. She would begin by admitting that this was the fourth, not only the third, time that a cigarette had given her some kind of trouble recently. The third time, fortunately, was in a taxicab. The fourth time—a week ago—was here in the apartment, when she went to the bathroom and found a merry little fire in the tin wastebasket. She extinguished that fire easily by putting the basket under the bathtub tap and letting the water run. The contents of the basket she flushed down the toilet; the scorched basket itself presented a bit of a problem, which she solved by wrapping it in newspapers and taking it down to Madison Avenue and dropping it in the city basket. Mary Moran noticed that the bathroom basket was missing. She noticed everything. "I got tired of it," Agatha Child told her. "I threw it out with the trash last night."

"It was kind of pretty," said Mary Moran.

"Cheap," said Agatha Child. "I saw a nicer one at Hammacher's."

"Oh, one of them with the mirrors all around it?" said Mary. "Mrs. Brown has two of them."

"Yes. The other basket was here when I took this apartment, and I don't know why I kept it so long. But yesterday I decided I couldn't look at it one more day."

It was the kind of explanation that would satisfy Mary Moran, with her unspoken but unmistakable opinion of Agatha Child as a frivolous woman. The same opinion had made credible the explanation for the burn in the gray suit. "I'm almost sure that it was some awful woman at the cocktail party I went to yesterday. She carried a long cigarette holder, and I noticed her waving it around."

Explanations were imperative. Agatha Child had heard of some woman who had been asked to leave some apartment-hotel because she was a fire hazard, falling asleep and setting fire to her bedclothes. It would not do, it would not do at all, to let Mary Moran know that Agatha Child had had any such experiences.

Agatha Child rose and sauntered to the livingroom door, listened, heard Mary Moran humming a tune, which she did when she was busy. Now quickly Agatha Child got a bottle of ink and a fountain pen and went back to her chair. She carefully poured ink on the crater in the carpet, watched it soak in, then sharp and loud she exclaimed, "God damn it! Oh, God damn it."

Mary Moran appeared in the doorway. "Something the matter?"

"Look at the mess I've made. Trying to fill my pen."

"They can get that out."

"I wonder. I know they can get the stain out, but look how deep this is. One of those places where the dogs have chewed the carpet. Boys, you really do try my patience sometimes. Oh, well this was my fault, no use trying to blame the dogs."

Brilliant. Inspired. At the moment of pouring the ink she had not even thought of the dogs and their, or Muggsy's, habit of digging holes in the carpet. It was the kind of inspiration she would not have had if she had not refused to panic. Face facts, look at things calmly.

"Will I phone the rug man?" said Mary Moran.

"Yes, will you, before you leave? And I won't be here this afternoon, Mary. I've just decided to blow myself to a new suit."

"Another black, ma'am?"

"Anything but. This is something for spring," said Agatha Child. "Do you think I'm mad, Mary? I *am* a little mad, aren't I?"

Exterior: with Figure

As the years, the decades, go by, it is not so remarkable that the most interesting member of the Armour family should turn out to be Harry Armour, Mr. Henry W. Armour, himself. His wife and his children all had a shot at being interesting, and they all did behave or misbehave in ways that had one or another member of the family always being talked about. If it wasn't Kevin, it was Mary Margaret; if it wasn't Mary Margaret, it was Rose Ann; and if it wasn't either of the children, it was Mrs. Armour, one of the first women in town to have her own car, and the first woman in the county to be involved in a fatal motor accident. It is strange, then, for me to say now that in my younger days my principal recollection of Harry Armour was of a man who was always going for walks, but whom I seldom saw walking. He would stand in front of someone's house, apparently admiring the rose bushes, or I would see him watching the telephone linemen at work, his hands clasped behind his back while he stood at a non-conversational distance from the workmen. As it happens, I often rode horseback with Harry Armour, but I do not think of him as a riding companion. I think of him as a man who could stand and look at nothing by the hour, and that, of course, is a visual record that I wish to correct.

I say it is not so remarkable that this man should turn out to be interesting. And why do I say that about a man who seemed almost lifeless? Well, in view of what has happened to his family, he becomes interesting either because of his influence on their lives—or because he had no influence whatever. One's first guess, and the once prevalent one, would be that Harry Armour had no influence.

He looked like a butler, or at least like a non-comic butler in a serious play. He was, of course, smooth-shaven, *clean*-shaven at all times. His skin had a polish rather than a shine, and though he was not a thin man, the skin was tight over the cheekbones and the bridge of his nose and the jaw-line. His lower lip protruded slightly because the upper lip was pulled in and down. He was fairly tall, perhaps five foot ten, and broad-shouldered, but he had the appearance of solidity rather than of muscular strength. His clothes were exquisitely tailored, of sombre materials, and you could be sure that he was not a man who put on his jacket and waistcoat in a single operation, and that he made sure his pocket flaps and lapels were lying flat before he put on his overcoat. He would have his gloves on before he left the house, and his hat on in the vestibule. He wore a starched linen collar that was called, I think, a Dorset; it was a turn-over, perhaps two inches high, showing none of the knot of the necktie. He went on wearing Dorsets long after even the oldest men gave them up.

Dressed for the street, he would go for one of those walks of his, but I cannot remember how he walked—short steps or long, fast or slow. The logical conclusion is that he walked very slowly, since I never saw him on foot more than five or six blocks from his house, and whenever I saw him he was standing still and *maybe* admiring a rose bush, *maybe* fascinated by the digging of a sewer, but more likely, I thought, totally unaware of the beauties of the petals or the efficiency of the laborers.

It is a curious thing about the old-fashioned small town, where everyone was supposed to know all about everyone else, that there were so many people whose privacy was impenetrable. It was known about Harry Armour, for instance, that he and a brother had owned some mineral rights which they sold to the big coal company for a great deal of money. Mrs. Armour, with money of her own, also got her money from coal mining. But having established themselves in their large new house on Lantenengo Street, the Armours made no further effort to get into society, and in my generation there were those who believed that the Armours got their money from meat-packing. Such was not the case, as I knew because my father was an usher at Harry Armour's wedding, had known Harry Armour all their lives, and hardly ever spoke to him. If I had had a little active curiosity I might have found out a lot of things about Harry Armour, but my father died when I was nineteen, and I never knew what went on between the two extremely reticent men. We were Catholics, and so were the Armours, and I guess that when Harry Armour was choosing his ushers, he picked my father because he was a doctor,

handsome, a bit of a dude, a member of the Gibbsville Club
and of the Gibbsville Assembly, and a North-of-the-Mountain
boy like Armour himself. I do not believe that there was ever
any feeling of friendship between the two; on the other hand,
Mrs. Armour had a younger brother, who died before I was
born, for whom my father expressed what amounted to affection. "Ray Reilly was the best of *that* lot," he said.

One day, when I was about twelve or thirteen, I was told
that I was wanted on the telephone. I naturally expected that
the call was from one of my contemporaries, but when I said
"Hello," the voice at the other end of the wire said, "James,
this is Mr. Armour. Would you like to go riding with me?"

The Armour son, Kevin, had a high-pitched, through-the-
nose voice. His father had bought him a good saddle horse,
but Kevin was afraid of horses and I knew it was not he calling.
Nor was it the kind of practical joke that my friends would
think up. "What did you say, Mr. Armour?" I said.

"Riding. Would you care to go riding with me tomorrow?"
said Harry Armour. "You could stop for me at our house, four
o'clock, after school."

"Yes, thank you," I said.

"Fine, fine. Goodbye," he said.

To my surprise, my father was not at all surprised. "You be
polite to Mr. Armour," my father said. "He's not a very good
rider. Don't show off."

"Why does he want *me* to ride with him?"

"Because his horse needs the exercise," was my father's
oblique answer.

"And Kevin is afraid of horses," said my mother. "He dreads
it."

The next day I arrived at the Armours' house around four
o'clock. They had a combination stable and garage; one box
stall, an open stall, and room for three cars. It was a handsome
brick building, a simpler version of the main house, with a
cupola and a golden horse for a weathervane. Mr. Armour,
smoking a cigar, was looking up at the weathervane when I
rode up the driveway. "Hello, James," he said. He turned and
spoke to the chauffeur-groom. "Jerry, bring my horse out."

Jerry led the chestnut, already saddled, and stood at the
horse's head while Mr. Armour mounted. He did two or three

wrong things that revealed his lack of experience with horses, but once he was in the saddle he smiled, and I had never seen him smile. "All right, where shall we go?" he said.

"Anywhere," I said. "I don't care."

"Out to The Run?" he said.

"All right," I said.

"Where do you usually ride to?"

"Oh—all over," I said. "Sometimes out to The Run. But you haven't been riding much, have you, Mr. Armour?"

"Not lately, not since I used to ride with your father."

"Then maybe we'd better not go all the way to The Run," I said. "There and back is pretty far for the first day. You'll get sore."

"Sore? Oh, you mean in the seat," he said.

I was slightly embarrassed to be making any kind of reference to the rear end of a man who was the father of one of my contemporaries. "Maybe halfway would be better," I said.

"Yes, I think you're right," he said. "Thanks for reminding me."

He was not a good rider and never would be one. He asked me, on our rides during that winter and spring, to correct him when he did things wrong, and I made a lot of suggestions that he adopted. But you cannot be taught to ride well any more than you can be taught to dance well. It has to be there. Someone must have told him that a rider should fix his sight between the horse's ears, and it is true that when you are learning to jump horses, that is one of the things they tell you. But we were not jumping our horses—thank God!—and yet Mr. Armour always rode with his eyes staring at that point between his horse's ears. As soon as he was in the saddle he always tightened up and stayed that way throughout the ride. I never suspected that he was afraid of the horse; it was not the tension of fear. It was determination to stay on the horse's back for five or ten miles while he and the animal got their exercise. I taught him, for instance, to post to the trot, and watching him do it I was reminded of the pistons in an automobile engine. In the six or seven months that we rode together we never galloped and we seldom cantered, although the chestnut had a nice, free canter. I will say this for Mr. Armour: although he held a tight rein, he was not cruel with the curb or with his spurs. In the beginning he carried a bone-handle crop with a silver ferrule. It was brand-new, like his tweed jacket and checked breeches and boots and derby, all from Wanamaker's London Shop in Philadelphia, expensive and faultless. I knew to the dollar what he had paid for everything, because I had priced them all, hopefully. He wore a stock—so did I—which on him was a continuance of his Dorset collars. I tried to think of some way to get him to stop carrying the crop; four reins were enough in the hands of a man who rode so tight. Then one afternoon he dropped it and I rode back and picked it off the ground without dismounting. "It sure is a nice-looking crop," I said, overacting a little.

"Would you like to have it, James? I'll give it to you. It's yours."

"Honestly? You mean it?" I said.

"Make you a present of it," he said. "I don't see why I carry it anyway, I'd never use it."

"Well, thanks. Thank you very much," I said.

Our conversations, such as they were, always took place on the way home. My mare had a good fast walk, faster than the Armour chestnut, and sometimes Armour would have to go into a slow trot to keep up with me, a fact which did not help conversation. In the winter months we usually were riding in the dark on the homeward half and were safer riding single file, and that, too, was a conversation deterrent. But in the spring months we did a little talking. As a matter of loyalty we refrained from any mention of his son, the obvious person to talk about. The next logical person was my father, but what can a boy say about his father to a man whom the father sometimes cut dead, sometimes merely nodded to? But in the only conversation that I remember clearly we touched upon both his son and my father. "Are you going to study medicine?" said Mr. Armour.

"I don't know," I said. "I don't think so."

"But you ought to. Think how proud your father would be," he said. "He wants you to, doesn't he?"

"Oh, sure. But I'd rather be something else."

"What?"

"A writer," I said.

"A writer? Of what? Of stories? Books?"

"Yes."

"Well, I suppose there's good money in that, if you make the grade. But nobody in your family was ever a writer."

"Not that I know of."

"Then why do you think you could be one? How would you go about it?"

"Don't ask *me*," I said.

"Well, you'll probably change your mind."

"What does Kevin want to be?"

"Kevin? He never told me. He may turn out to be a gentleman of leisure, but I hope not. It's better to be doing something."

That was one of our last rides together. The Armours went away for the summer, to their cottage in Ventnor, and when the fall came I went away to school. So many new things entered my life, things and people, that I scarcely ever thought of Mr. Armour. It certainly never occurred to me to ask about him. I may have seen him at the late Mass when I was home on vacation, but we had no conversation. In fact it was two or maybe three years later, when the Armours had a birthday party for Kevin, that I next visited their house and learned that they had sold the chestnut. After I finished prep school, and my father died and I went to work on a newspaper, I would sometimes see Mr. Armour on one of his walks, and by that time he had become, to our crowd, somewhat of a character.

We had various characters. The drinking judge. The drinking mother of one of the girls in our crowd. The lecherous father of a boy and girl. A retired army colonel who wrote unprintable—though not obscene—insulting letters to the newspapers. A retired Navy commander, another drinker, who suddenly appeared at my house one day to give me all his old tennis balls, which were stamped with a fouled anchor. A man who was related to quite a few of our crowd, who had locomotor ataxia and was half blind, but attended most of the club dances. An awesomely respectable lawyer, married, and his schoolteacher lady friend. Among our group the first names or titles or our nicknames for the characters became synonymous with special weaknesses, such as alcoholism and lechery or physical handicaps. The commander, for instance, never knew this, but when we began to have drinking parties we always, at some point during the evening, recited: "Here's to the commander, he's true blue/he's a drunkard, through and through/ so fill him up a bumper and celebrate the day/if he doesn't go to heaven, he'll go the other way/so it's drink, chucka-chuck chucka-chuck, so it's drink, chucka-chuck, chucka-chuck." He had taught us the toast, and if we saw him on the street one of us was sure to say, "Chucka-chuck." I don't think there was any meanness in these criticisms of our elders, although there was plenty of scorn in our laughter at the lecherous father of the boy and girl, and a Goddard—the name of the pious lawyer—was in our code language a hypocrite. Sometime during this period Mr. Armour became a character, but his name did not become symbolic of anything. In an extremely dull way he was unique.

Things were happening to members of his family. Mrs. Armour had her automobile accident, skidding into a man on a motorcycle. No charge was preferred against her, but it was generally believed that some money changed hands. Then Kevin, practically in secret, developed into an expert shot and from the age of sixteen he was high gun at county and state matches. He had never displayed any other signs of coordination, and this accomplishment astonished us. He was sought after by older men, and he spent so much time in their company that he grew bored with us, his contemporaries. He was winning a lot of money on bets, and at eighteen he was a heavy drinker. He managed to get admitted to the University of Virginia, and there, with his guns and his Wills–Ste. Claire, he remained for two full—very full, as we used to say—years. His family had no control over him, although they did not try very hard or very long. They threatened, but only threatened, to stop his allowance, and his reply was to win fifteen hundred dollars in a live bird match. If he had not been so stupid, so totally lacking in a sense of humor, he would have been insufferable; but when Bob Reynolds, the kidder in our group, asked Kevin who was buried in Grant's Tomb, Kevin thought a moment and caught on. "You trying to razz me?" he said. He was not easily distracted, and he therefore played a competent game of bridge and a safe game of poker. One of the girls in our crowd was madly in love with him and made no bones about it, but when Kevin was away on a shooting trip she would call the rest of us until she found someone to take her out. She was much higher than he in the social scheme, but he would not marry her because she was not a Catholic. I doubt that Kevin could have explained what was meant by the Immaculate Conception, but he was a staunch Catholic. At Mass he would take out his beads and I know he was saying his Hail Mary's because I could see his lips moving, but I do not think he prayed. He thought he was praying.

The praying one in the Armour family was Rose Ann, three years younger than Kevin and a colleen specimen; creamy white skin, blue eyes, black hair, a voluptuous little figure. She was ebullient, a laugher, at parties, but in church she read her Missal and was acutely attentive to the ritual on the altar, oblivious of the people in her pew and of the other worshipers. There could be no doubt that she was devout. Still it came as almost as big a surprise to me as to our Protestant friends when Rose Ann became a novice in a convent in upstate New York. Mrs. Armour wept on my mother's shoulder and I gathered that they were not tears of joy. Apparently Mrs. Armour would have been willing to donate her other daughter, Mary Margaret, who had the misfortune to look exactly like Mr. Armour, to the service of the Lord. Mary Margaret already had the appearance of a young mother superior, but Rose Ann was *pretty*. It was a scandal in reverse, so to speak, and the only really amusing thing about it for me was to listen to several of the Protestant girls who said they wished they could become nuns. "They cut off all your hair," I told them, thereby discouraging some vocations.

Then one day Mr. and Mrs. Armour quietly left town and nothing was heard from them for three or four weeks. Neither Mary Margaret nor Kevin volunteered any information, but it was reported that Mr. and Mrs. Armour had gone abroad and that they were accompanied by Rose Ann. My mother was in on the secret and I suppose my father was too, but not until the whole town had the story did my mother reveal any of it to me. Something—I was not told what—had occurred at the convent, a couple of weeks before Rose Ann was to take the veil. Mr. and Mrs. Armour were sent for, and they made their sudden arrangements to have Rose Ann go abroad with them.

Mr. Armour stayed in Europe a couple of months, then returned home alone. Mrs. Armour remained with Rose Ann for about a year, then she too returned alone. Meanwhile no one had had a word from Rose Ann, not even a post card to indicate her whereabouts. Meanwhile, too, Mr. Armour had resumed his walks, his starings at nothing, which for him were so normal that in this unusual situation he seemed to be hastening the restoration of usual, normal conditions. He had returned, and because of his unapproachability and the neighbors' tact during a delicate period, he had considerably reduced the inquisitiveness of the neighbors when Mrs. Armour came home. They had gotten used to seeing Mr. Armour around, and some of their curiosity was dispelled or simply evaporated.

Betty Allen, a friend of Rose Ann's, telephoned Mrs. Armour to say she was going abroad and would like to have Rose Ann's European address. It was a bold move, but Mrs. Armour gave her the address. "I'm sure she'd love to see you," said Mrs. Armour. "She had a nervous breakdown a year ago, you know, but she's fine now. Living with this French family about forty kilometres outside of Paris. Her appearance has changed. She's put on much too much weight, but there'll be time to do something about that after she gets her health back. I'll tell her to expect to hear from you."

Betty went to see Rose Ann, and her report was contained in a long letter which I read. Betty was genuinely fond of Rose Ann, and the accuracy and incompleteness of her account of her visit had to be judged on a basis of friendship. Nevertheless it was, I recall, a sad letter. Rose Ann had indeed changed in more ways than in her appearance. She was stout, said Betty, and during the three days of Betty's visit Rose Ann ate enormous meals and drank a great deal of wine—without, Betty added, getting tight. Rose Ann wanted to know all about the boys and girls in the old crowd, and she surprised Betty by recalling things that had happened to us when we were small children. But she was hazy or completely wrong on things that had happened more recently, even where they concerned members of her own family. She had Kevin, for instance, in love with a Philadelphia girl whom Kevin had never had a date with. Then when Rose Ann calmly spoke of Mary Margaret as her dead sister, Betty had to fight back the tears. On the last day of Betty's visit they went for a walk together, and at one point Rose Ann led Betty to a barn. "I didn't want to frighten you," said Rose Ann. "But we were being followed. It's all right now. He's gone."

Betty spoke good French and was able to form a judgment of the middle-aged couple at whose house Rose Ann was a paying guest. They were childless. The husband owned a garage, the wife had been a trained nurse, and Rose Ann was not the first paying guest that had been sent to them by Rose Ann's doctor. The doctor came out from Paris once a fortnight and had a meal with Rose Ann and the couple, then he would chat with Rose Ann while the couple were doing the dishes. They were a decent, hard-working couple, frankly pleased to have the extra money from their p.g., equally frank about their personal attitude toward Rose Ann as a commercial proposition. It was not for them, they told Betty, to provide anything but peace and quiet, a clean room, and good plain food. They referred to Rose Ann as a *malade à domicile*.

When Betty returned home she went to see Mrs. Armour, and I learned about their conversation from Betty herself. "You may have thought I should have told you about Rose Ann," said Mrs. Armour. "I didn't, for a reason. I wanted her to see you just as you are, and I didn't want you to go there all self-conscious, making forced conversation. I wanted you to be your natural self, or she'd have noticed the difference right away."

"It was a shock, though, Mrs. Armour."

"Yes, I'm sorry," said Mrs. Armour. "But I wouldn't have given her address to anyone but you."

"I hope my visit did some good."

Mrs. Armour shook her head. "Who knows? She never even mentioned your visit the next time the doctor went to see her."

"I met Dr. Claverie, you know," said Betty. "He was awfully nice."

"I know you did, and he said the same thing about you."

"It was amazing how much he knew. I mean, the questions he asked me, you might have thought he was there all the time I was with Rose Ann."

"Like her thinking she was being followed?"

"And the kind of things she remembered and didn't remember."

"He is an amazing man," said Mrs. Armour. "I just hope he's the right man. She never goes to church, and I should have thought he'd encourage her to go. Such a deeply religious girl. I know I always turn to the church when I have something troubling me."

Betty changed the subject. "When are you going to see Rose Ann again?"

"When Dr. Claverie lets me. Whenever he sends for me. I have no idea when that will be."

It was about a year later that the French psychiatrist sent for Mr. and Mrs. Armour. Rose Ann was dead, drowned in a canoeing accident in one of those narrow, swift, deep little streams that the French call rivers. They brought her body home for burial, and my mother and I were kept busy explaining to our Protestant friends that the Church was satisfied that Rose Ann had not committed suicide, otherwise there would have been no requiem Mass. I was not exactly telling a lie, but I did not believe what I was saying. The church, which was large, was nearly half filled with the young and the no-longer young. What is sadder than the death of an unhappy young girl? I did not go along with those of my friends who said that Rose Ann was better off. Why, there is some hope even for a girl whose lungs are filled with water. I was an honorary pallbearer, and I cried all through the Mass and the blessing of the body. At our house, after the burial, my mother said to me, "Were you in love with Rose Ann?"

"No! God damn it, *no*!" I shouted.

There was something in my profane outburst that my mother took personally, and she slapped my face. Well, she was right. I was protesting against her lack of understanding. My mother was old enough to forget that Rose Ann was us, the young. "Don't you *dare* speak to me that way," said my mother.

"I'm sorry for swearing," I said.

I have no recollection of even *seeing* Mr. Armour at the church, at the cemetery, or at lunch at his house after the funeral. He was there, of course; it is just that I have no recollection of him, although I must have shaken hands with him at least once and probably muttered some words of condolence.

This failure of my memory was not caused by my grief, but rather by his failure to say or do or look anything that would make me remember him. On the other hand, I do remember that on the very next afternoon I saw him standing at a street corner three blocks past his house. He appeared to be reading the collection sign on a mailbox—a box that he must have passed a thousand times. He was wearing overcoat and scarf, and he had no letter in his gloved hand.

Mary Margaret Armour, whom we sometimes referred to as Horse Face, kept her sister's death alive much too long. I, we, wanted to have Rose Ann as a secret sorrow. We would not forget her, but we did not want to be reminded of her whenever three or more of us got together. Mary Margaret refused to cooperate. At a bridge party, two months after Rose Ann's funeral, Mary Margaret announced that she had had the nicest letter from some teacher of Rose Ann's and wanted to read it to us all. "Very nice," a few of us said, when she finished reading it.

"Well, *I* thought so," said Mary Margaret, implying that we had failed to appreciate the letter. A few weeks later, at another party, she announced that she had had another letter, from someone else.

"Oh, for God's sake, Mary Margaret," said Betty Allen.

"What?" said Mary Margaret.

"Do you *have* to?"

"No, I don't have to. And I don't have to stay here, either. *You*, Betty Allen, I know all the horrible things you said about Rose Ann."

No one said a word. Sixteen young people at four bridge tables sat in indignant silence. It was a lot of silence. Mary Margaret looked around, saw no relief or assistance, and again turned on Betty Allen. "I could kill you."

The hostess, Nan Brown, stood up. "Mary Margaret, I'm terribly sorry, but I'm going to have to ask you to leave. You're being very unfair to Betty, and—"

"Ask me to leave? That's a laugh. I wouldn't stay in this house another minute. Kevin Armour, are you coming with me?"

"Nan, do you want me to go, too?" said Kevin.

"No, of course not," said Nan Brown.

"That's the kind of brother I have. Lily-livered son of a bitch. *Stay!*"

Betty Allen stood up. "I started this, Nan, and I'm very sorry. I'll apologize to Mary Margaret if she'll apologize to me. Then we can forget the whole damn—"

"I don't want your apology and I'm not going to forget one single word," said Mary Margaret. She left.

"I'm sorry, everybody," said Nan Brown. "Maybe I could get Mother to take her hand."

"Whoever is dummy at the other tables can sit in for Mary Margaret," someone suggested. "It'll slow things up, but . . ."

Play was resumed, and for the rest of the evening the score was kept for Mary Margaret, in her name, and on the final count it turned out that she had won second prize, a small silver ash tray with the figure of a Scottie in the center. I don't know if anyone else thought of it, but I wanted to inquire if the dog was supposed to be a bitch. However, I kept quiet.

"Will you give this to Mary Margaret?" said Nan Brown to Kevin.

"I will not. Give it to the third. Who was third?"

"Third? Why, third was none other than Mr. James Malloy," said Nan.

"I'll take it," I said. "I always wanted a Scottie."

"You knew it all along," someone said. "When you were my partner you got set four tricks, doubled and redoubled, and that's part of Mary Margaret's score."

"Well, I wanted that Scottie," I said. "Not to mention the fact that you, you dumb bastard, you left me in that bid and never even mentioned your hearts."

Some rough kidding always took place in our bridge games, but on this occasion it was urgent and nervous; we all knew that Mary Margaret Armour could be extremely unpleasant, in the best of circumstances.

She stayed away from the country club and declined all invitations—which I must say were extended half-heartedly after her behavior at Nan Brown's. Through political pull she got a very minor job in the Court House, and I would occasionally see her in the speakeasies and roadhouses, drinking with politicians and county detectives, and semi-pro athletes, all men who considered two fifty-dollar bills a fortune. More than once, when she spoke to me, I caught her making a face at me and whispering something to her companions. She would have started trouble for me, but her companions happened to be men who liked to see their names in print, favorably, and my job had me covering some politics, some sports, and general assignments. Often, very late at night, I would see her driving her Chrysler convertible home alone, going like hell and un-mistakably stewed. She was sore at the world, and nobody liked her much either.

The Armours, mother and children, took turns in getting talked about, but I moved to New York and the doings of Mrs. Armour and Kevin and Mary Margaret were of no interest to me at that distance. Mrs. Armour had an operation for cata-racts. Mary Margaret eloped with a county detective, then had the marriage annulled. Kevin was sued for breach of promise by a switchboard operator in a Reading hotel. The case was settled out of court for five hundred, a thousand, maybe two thousand dollars. Such items were conveyed to me from time to time, and between times I heard nothing. It became a custom, very nearly a tradition, that the only information concerning the Armours that was passed on to the Gibbsville colony in New York was bad news. To break the monotony I once asked how Kevin was getting along with his shooting; had he won the State championship? Oh? I hadn't heard about that? Hadn't anyone told me that Kevin had had to give up shooting because of an abscess in his ear? And that the real rea-son was not an abscess in his ear, but that he had been barred from competition because he had grown careless with guns? At a match near Allentown he had accidentally blown a hole in the ground with a 16-gauge pump gun that had one live shell left in the magazine; at another match he accidentally killed a valuable pointer.

If there was any good news of Mary Margaret it was not made known to me.

There are, most definitely, such things as hard-luck people, hard-luck families; at least it is a working thesis that misfortune is repeatedly attracted to certain families like the Armours. At first the incidence of misfortune is looked upon as a phenom-enon; then it becomes a wry joke; and then, self-protectively, we hesitate to bring up the family name for fear of hearing one more bit of evidence that bad luck begets bad luck, that we too, once started on a run of bad luck, may have to endure not only a single disaster but a lifetime of it. As something of a mystic and very much of an overprotesting enemy of superstition, I deliberately deprived myself of information about the Armours, and years went by, twenty years, thirty years, during which I created a practical non-curiosity about them. I did not know which of them were alive, which dead.

Then one day last winter I read a small item in a newspaper that I bought on the train from New York to Washington. It stated that Kevin Armour had been sentenced to prison for defrauding some woman who had entrusted him with fifteen thousand dollars' worth of securities. In Washington I was meeting a boyhood friend, and by this time I was so insulated against the Armour bad luck that I mentioned the newspaper article. "Yes, they finally caught up with Kevin," said my friend. "This time they really nailed him."

"Have they any money left?" I said.

"Who?"

"The Armours," I said.

"The Armours? There aren't any more Armours. Kevin's the last. Mrs. Armour died ten or fifteen years ago. Mary Margaret not long after. The sauce did it to her, although I will say it took a lot of it."

"And old Henry W.?" I said.

"Lived to be eighty-four. He died last year in a veterans' home."

"Veteran of what?"

"The Spanish-American War, I think. Yes, it must have been. Anyway, that's where he died."

My friend in those few sentences had wiped out the Armour family, and if I had once been afraid of them and their bad luck, I was afraid no longer. My friend and I talked a little about them, their individual personalities, their money, their scale of living, and we exchanged the usual commonplaces about the evanescence of wealth. I did not want to spend much time talking about the Armours; I wanted to think about them, and I have done so.

I had not seen any of them in more than thirty years,

consequently had only an out-of-date recollection of the physical appearance of Mr. and Mrs. Armour and Kevin and Mary Margaret. They had traveled many miles—no matter where—and lived through three decades, more or less, and I had to invent the grossness that would have come into the faces of Kevin and Mary Margaret when youth was gone, the ravages to the faces of Harry Armour and his wife when old age set in. It was not much of a pastime; they refused to hold still for my fanciful portraits of them, kept returning to the mental photographs I retained from the days when I had known them well.

I discovered that I had learned, by 1930, all that I wanted to know about the Armours, perhaps all of value that there was to know. Mrs. Armour, a flighty, silly woman who had killed a man with her motor car, was no less flighty for having had bad eyesight. Mary Margaret, trying to trade on the tragic death of her pretty sister, was not much different from the self-indulgent lush that she made herself into. Kevin, submissive to a faith that his lazy mind would not accord the respect of curiosity, would at twenty-five have stolen from a woman if he had needed the money. And even poor Rose Ann, for whom I had once wept ("Weep not for me, but for yourselves and for your children"?), had got only as far as laughter would take her.

And Harry Armour. Henry W. Armour himself. Harry Armour. Henry W. Armour. Mr. Armour. He was—what? A man who stood and looked at nothing? I do not know. I wish I knew. I want to know, and I never can know. I wish, I wish I knew.

The Flatted Saxophone

SOMETHING HAPPENS to the tone of a tenor saxophone when it is played out-of-doors; they always sound flat, especially at wedding receptions, when the guests are queued up for the exchange of mutterings with the bridal party. The dancing has not begun, and the orchestra seems neglected and lonely and the tenor saxophone is expressing the musicians' self-pity. Later, when the bride and groom have done their turn (to a two-tune medley of "I Love You Truly" and "Get Me to the Church on Time"), and general dancing is under way, the flatness of the tenor sax is not so noticeable. It gets lost in the babble of human voices, especially the women's voices, and the musicians have stopped feeling sorry for themselves, the tenor sax therefore has nothing to express, the orchestra plays "From This Moment On" at the cadence of the Society Bounce, and if the tenor sax is flat, so too may be the champagne, but it does not matter much.

"The way I look at it," said George Cushman, "if I want good champagne, I've got some at home. And if I want to hear good saxophone, I'll find out where Bud Freeman's working."

"I didn't hear a word you said," said Marjorie Cushman.

"That's perfectly all right," said her husband. "I'll repeat it, word for word, but if I do you're going to say it wasn't worth repeating—and you'll be right."

"Oh, we're in *that* mood," said Marjorie Cushman. A man came to their table and asked her to dance. "Now don't let anyone grab my chair."

"I'll put my feet up on it," said George Cushman.

"You don't have to do *that*," she said. "Just keep an eye on it."

"I'll keep an eye on you, too," he said, but she did not hear him.

He was now alone at a table for six, and a man and a woman separately asked if all the chairs were taken. "Sorry, all spoken for," he said. A third person, a young man in a cutaway, simply put his hands on the backs of two chairs and started to walk away with them.

"Hold on, sonny boy," said George Cushman. "Bring them back. Just put them right back where you found them."

"Sorry," said the young man, and replaced the chairs.

"And try asking, next time," said George Cushman.

"Why should I?" said the young man, and went away.

"Yeah, why should you, you little jerk," said George Cushman. "With your soft collar and your A. T. Harris cutaway."

A woman seated herself in the chair next to him. "You look lonesome all by yourself, Georgie," she said.

"Oh, hello, Becky," he said. "Yeah, I'm just sitting here eating my heart out, thinking of my lost youth."

"Our lost youth," said Becky Addison.

"No, I wasn't thinking about your lost youth. Just mine. If you want to think about yours, okay. Do you miss it?"

"Not terribly," she said.

"You know, neither do I. Mine, I mean. Not yours. How many weddings have you and I been at? The same weddings, I mean."

"You and I? Oh, dear," she said. "Well, we started going to the same weddings over forty years ago."

"Right."

"And those first years, there were a lot of weddings," she said.

"A powerful lot. Everybody got married, everybody."

"Just about," she said.

"Excuse me, Becky," he said. "Waiter, you wouldn't want to do us a special favor and bring us four Scotches and water, would you?"

"Hello, Mr. Cushman. Yes, sure. I'll bring you a whole tray full. You don't remember me, but I worked at your daughter's wedding."

"Good for you, glad to see you again," said George Cushman. The waiter interrupted his passing of champagne to go to the bar.

"You must have done very well by the waiters at Sue's wedding," said Becky Addison. "Most of them, if you ask them to get you a Scotch, they'll say yes and that's the last you ever see of them."

"It's funny, I don't remember this fellow at all. They were paid by the caterer, but then I gave each of them a five-dollar tip. So now we can have Scotch. That's called bread cast on the waters, Becky. I know you never read the Bible, so I'm explaining it to you. Where is the great man?"

"Charles? My lord and master?"

"Well, who else?"

"He's in Mexico City," she said. "I see Marjorie. Looks lovely."

"She *is* lovely, and she's my wife, and I am devoted to her, and I am not good enough for her, and nobody knows what she sees in me."

"You don't have to lay it on that thick, not with me," said Becky Addison.

"No, I guess not," said George Cushman. "Have a cigarette?"

"I've quit," she said.

"No special reason, I hope," he said.

"No, not really. That is, I haven't been forbidden to smoke. Combination of hysteria from reading all those things in the magazines, *and* I *was* smoking too *much*. Sixty cigarettes a day. So I quit, and I've gained ten unnecessary pounds."

"In how long?"

"Nine weeks tomorrow," she said.

"Nine weeks. Speaking of which, we never did finish guessing how many weddings we'd been to."

"No. Well, the weddings we went to and were in, including our own. Those years there were a lot of big weddings. And lately, the last few years, our children's weddings and our friends' children. An average of five a year, do you think?"

"Times forty. Two hundred. It somehow seems more than that," he said.

"But I don't think you and I have been to two hundred of the same weddings, have we? Maybe we have," she said.

"Pretty close to it," he said. "And the funny thing is, we nearly always sit together, at least for a little while. Did you come alone?"

"Yes," she said. "I didn't go to the church. Did you? I suppose you did."

"Try and keep Marjorie from missing any part of it. Yes, we were there. Marjorie burning up because we didn't have any special pew to go to. To *think* that Ann Bartholomew, her own second cousin, didn't have us sitting with family. Well, maybe

Marjorie has a point. There were plenty of people there I never saw before."

"*Weren't* there? I mean, *aren't* there? Looking around here I don't know half the people our age," she said.

"Why don't you and I get married, Becky? Would you like to toy with that idea?"

"I did, once," she said.

"Oh, that was when we were in love. Christ, that was that greasy kid stuff."

"Mm-hmm."

"It doesn't take any real imagination to think about getting married when you're twenty years old."

"Eighteen and twenty-one, I think we were," she said.

"At that age, and especially you and I, we didn't know what you did next except get married. God, how long would we have lasted? Two years, do you think?"

"Two or three," she said. "Or as soon as we found out we didn't love each other. Thank God we found it out without getting married."

"I know, and that makes it so much better now," he said. "Would you leave Charley now?"

"No, I don't think so," she said.

"Well, you don't have to ask me if I'd leave Marjorie. Like a shot, would be the answer."

"Then why haven't you?" she said.

"I don't know. I could give you plenty of reasons. *She* gave me plenty of reasons."

"But they were never good enough reasons, were they? You wanted to stay married to her, so you did."

"Yes, that's true," he said. "But I'd leave her now, like a shot. To marry you, that is."

"Georgie, I know what's behind this," she said.

"You do? What?"

"It's a very romantic notion," she said. "It's not young-romantic. It isn't that. But it's as desperate as young love."

"It's more so," he said.

"Yes," she said. "The feeling that we'd be happy together with what time we have left."

"You guessed it," he said. "And we would be, Becky."

"We might be. We probably could be," she said. "If we could

get up right now and walk out together, if that's all there was to it. But two old crows like us, Georgie. All that time we'd have to spend with lawyers. Your lawyers, my lawyers. Marjorie's. Charles's. Who gets what? Charles would want the Andrew Wyeth, but I'd want it too. By the time we got through all that we'd both be exhausted, you and I. And we'd start asking ourselves, what the hell *for*?"

"Jesus, you're practical," he said.

"I am now. You would be later," she said. "Neither one of us is strong enough to go through all that. Or what we feel isn't strong enough, this loving each other dearly. And that's what it is, Georgie. Loving each other dearly. The dear, wonderful love of two old friends."

He nodded. "You're right," he said.

She put her hand on his. "Come on, dance with me," she said.

"Good," he said, and got to his feet. Then, "Let's wait. I promised Marjorie I'd guard these chairs."

"All right," she said. "Oh, look. Our friend, with there-must-be-sixteen Scotches. I've never *seen* so many Scotches."

"I told you, bread cast on the waters," said George Cushman.

"One, two, three, four, five, six, seven, eight, nine, ten, eleven, twelve, thirteen, fourteen, fifteen, *sixteen*, seventeen, eighteen, nineteen. Nineteen Scotches," she said. "You didn't really want to dance, did you, Georgie?"

The Man on the Tractor

THEY WERE the fabulous Denisons, Pammie and George. There was a time when Booth Tarkington and Louis Bromfield, who had never met the Denisons, were called upon to admit or deny that they had used the Denison family in certain novels. By letter and in person the novelists tried to make it clear that they had relied on invention, and though coming so close to the facts of the Denison family, they had not been assisted by a knowledge of the Denison history, past or present. A letter from a Gibbsville lady to F. Scott Fitzgerald went unanswered, and the lady and her friends agreed that Fitzgerald did not dare deny that the automobile accident in *This Side of Paradise* was right out of life. Why, even the car was the same as George Denison's old Locomobile. True, George Denison had run over a man on the Boston Post Road, but obviously Fitzgerald had made that change to confuse people. And if Daisy in *The Great Gatsby* was not patterned after Pammie Stribling Denison, the lady from Gibbsville would eat your hat. For instance, Pammie Stribling, as everyone knew, had been madly infatuated with Johnny Gruber, the qualified assistant pharmacist at Hudson's drug store. Same initials as Jay Gatsby's; and wasn't Gatsby somehow mixed up in patent medicines or something? Fitzgerald would not have had a leg to stand on, and he was pretty smart not to answer those letters. He wouldn't have had a leg to stand on. How absurd of Booth Tarkington to pretend he had not patterned the Ambersons after the Denisons; how ridiculous of Louis Bromfield to protest that the Shaynes were not more or less based on the Denisons.

Regardless of the denials and the non-denial, the legend of the Denisons as literary source material went into the Gibbsville lore, along with the firmly held belief that Lichtenwalner's ice cream was famous the world over and that the town was the richest per capita of all third-class cities east of the Mississippi. As it happens, Lichtenwalner's has gone out of business, and little is said these days of per capita wealth in Gibbsville; but due in part to the Fitzgerald revival the Denison legend has persisted. Men and women of a certain age have told their children that not only Fitzgerald, but Booth Tarkington and Louis Bromfield too, wrote stories about the Denisons. It has been denied that Scott and Zelda ever visited Gibbsville, but the denials have grown weaker, and it is certainly true that Pammie and George did once have as house guests a screwy couple with an Irish name who could very well have been the Fitzgeralds. The man was short and good-looking and insisted on playing the drums at a club dance; the woman stayed in her room all the time she was at the Denisons'. Walter Spiker, the Denisons' best friend, would have been able to say for sure whether it had been the Fitzgeralds, but Walter, alas, was dead. Long dead, and during the last five years of his life had lost the power of speech. If Walter had had any literary ability *he* could have written about the Denisons—and how! He knew more about the Denisons than the Tarkingtons and Bromfields and Fitzgeralds all put together, and he would have got it right.

Pammie and George were in town not long ago, stopping at the John Gibb Hotel, but they saw only a very few people. Their reservation at the hotel was handled by a clerk who wrote out a slip for M & M Geo. Dennison; the name meant nothing to him, but the request for the reservation had come from a reputable travel agency in New York. When Mr. and Mrs. Denison arrived at the hotel the clerk saw only a man and woman who were pretty sure of themselves in a hotel lobby, with four pieces of expensive foreign luggage; the woman in a tweed suit with a little cape on the shoulders, the man in a striped gray flannel suit and a reversible tweed-and-gab topcoat over his arm. "Check-out time is three P.M.," said the clerk.

"Is it indeed?" said the man, signing the registration card.

"But an extra hour, I guess we won't charge you a full day," said the clerk.

"I'm sure of it," said Denison. "Maybe even two hours."

"I don't know about *two* hours. It's our—"

"*I* do," said Denison. "Will you see that my car's washed and serviced, high-test gas, and back here in an hour, please? It's the green Bentley. The bellboy knows. But I want *you* to see that I have it back in an hour."

"I'll try," said the clerk.

"You do a little better than try, won't you?" said Denison.

"Let's find out if there's a hairdresser in the hotel," said his wife.

"Is there?" said Denison.

"No sir, not in the hotel. There's one around the corner to the right, three doors to the right. Our switchboard will connect you."

"Dear, it's twenty of three," said Denison to his wife. "You go on upstairs. I'm going over and see Andy Stokes before the bank closes. I'll only be a few minutes, but I don't want to miss him."

The mention of the name Stokes had as much impact on the clerk as the name Bentley. "If there's anything I can do, sir."

"There is. Will you send up a bottle of Scotch, any good Scotch that you have, and a bottle of sherry. Bristol Cream. And the Gibbsville papers."

"There's only the one paper in the afternoon."

A man had come up behind Denison during the exchange with the clerk. The man fully recognized Denison, but he allowed himself the protection of a feigned uncertainty. "Isn't this George Denison?" said the man.

Denison turned. "Yes it is," said Denison.

"George, you don't remember me, it's such a long time and all," said the man. "Karl Isaminger? Used to drive for your Aunt Augusta, Mrs. Hamilton?"

"Why, I *didn't* recognize you, Karl," said Denison.

"Hello, Karl," said Pammie Denison.

"Hello, Mrs. Denison."

"What are you doing now, Karl?" said Denison.

"Oh, I'm the night man at Coleman's Garage."

"Coleman's? I don't know that name."

"Used to be Jimmy Brady's that had the Studebaker agency."

"Uh-huh. Aren't you up rather early for a night watchman?"

"Oh—I can't stay in bed more'n six hours at the most. I had this operation three years ago the twentieth of May. You remember Doc Robbins, or was he since you left town?"

"Must have been after my time. You living here at the hotel, Karl?"

"Ah, you, George. Living *here*? No, I come in here to buy a magazine. Gives me something to read at work, and when I get finished with it the wife likes to look through it. The print's a little small for her, but she says her glasses gives her a headache. Won't *wear* glasses. I said to her—"

"Dear, if you're going to get to the bank before it closes, I hate to interrupt but—" said Pammie Denison.

"Oh, ixcuse me, I didn't—"

"That's all right, Karl," said George Denison. "You can walk to the bank with me, if you like."

"No, I wouldn't do that, George. I just wanted to come up and say hello to you and Mrs. You're both looking fine. I'd of known you anywhere. Remember the old Pierce-Arrow, Mrs. Denison? 'Karl, go fetch Pammie Stribling,' Mrs. Hamilton used to say. Remember when you used to come and play the piano for the old lady? Rainy days, she used to like you to come play the piano for her."

"Oh, do I? Shades of 'Country Gardens.' Dum-dum tee dum-dum, dum-dum tee dum. But always followed by hot chocolate and *sand* tarts."

"*I* remember them sand tarts," said Karl Isaminger.

"So do I," said George Denison. "Mrs. Hamilton used to send them to me at school. But this isn't getting to the bank. Karl, nice to see you. Remember me to your wife. Dear, I'll see you in about an hour or less."

"Don't hurry, George," said Pammie.

"The sand tarts had little pieces of citron in the middle," said George Denison. "Some had pecans, but I preferred the citron." He left them.

Andy Stokes was expecting him. They had had correspondence over the years, and Andy Stokes was one of the few Gibbsville citizens who occasionally saw the Denisons. When the pleasantries were over Stokes rang for his secretary. "Miss Arbogast, will you bring me the papers on the Denison sale?" said Stokes.

"Certainly," said Miss Arbogast. She smiled at George Denison, who had already greeted her in the outer office.

Andy Stokes sat back in his chair. "It's kind of sad, George," he said. "I don't mean how little you're getting for the property. I guess your tax man has that all figured out for you. But this land is your last link with Gibbsville."

"Except for my stock in this bank," said George Denison.

"Well, that, of course. I hope you never part with that," said

Stokes. "But that's not the same as actual land. That land's been in the Denison family close to a hundred years. I had a look at the title search, naturally, but I hadn't realized how long you'd held it. Do you know what I wish?"

"What do you wish, Andy?"

"Well, I wish you and your tax man could figure out some way to donate the land for a playground, a park, something on that order. And continue the Denison name."

"My tax man would much rather have me take the money," said George Denison.

Miss Arbogast came in with the papers, laid them on Stokes's desk, smiled again at Denison without looking at him, and departed.

"Yes, I suppose he would. That was just a sentimental thought I had," said Stokes. "Considering how little you're getting for the land. If it was a big deal I never would have thought of it, but what's eighteen thousand to you?"

"I don't know, but my tax man does. He said to unload it, and I'm unloading it."

"Well, I wouldn't give *him* an argument. From the correspondence I've had with him, I'd say he was as smart as a tack. Doesn't miss a trick."

"He's kept me out of prison, that's as much as *I* know," said George Denison.

"Okay, George. All you have to do now is sign your name on these papers, where you see the check-mark. Miss Arbogast will notarize them and have one of our people witness them. Here's your cheque. It's made out to the Denison Land Company. Want me to forward that to Longstreet?"

"Yes, will you please?" said Denison, busy with Stokes's desk pen.

"The last transaction of the Denison Land Company," said Stokes. "In the old days an occasion like this would call for some kind of a celebration."

"Well, we're not exactly celebrating, Pammie and I, but we decided to make the trip. They sure have done a lot of things to the roads around here. The town is practically by-passed. What ever happened to South Main Street? We never did get on South Main. And these God damn one-way streets. I almost got a ticket. If I hadn't had a Connecticut license, the cop at Main and Scandinavian was going to slap me with a summons."

"That was Paul Keppler. He's tough."

"Oh, God, is that who that was? The big fat baby-faced guy? That would have been appropriate. His father arrested me back in 1920 or thereabouts. But he took a look at my driver's license and let me go. He never said who he was, or pretended to know me. 'Just watch the signs,' he said, and waved me on."

"You can be damn sure he knew who you were, though. We think he's the best cop on the force. He graduated from the FBI school, and he's the only one the kids pay any attention to."

"There," said George Denison, laying down the pen. "I guess that does it." He picked up the cheque, read it, and put it back on Andy Stokes's blotter. He found that Stokes was looking at him, half smiling, trying to read his mind. George Denison smiled back and shook his head. "No, Andy, I'm not going to cry," said George Denison.

"Maybe not, but for just a few seconds it hit you," said Andy Stokes.

"I suppose so," said George Denison.

"I'll tell you who we're having tonight," said Stokes. "Out of deference to your wishes we kept it small. We couldn't get Joe and Verna. Joe's in Philadelphia, having a big operation. Cancer. It doesn't sound so good, either. Verna told Alice that we might as well be prepared for the worst. So they're out. But we did get Stubby and Jean."

"That's good."

"Stubby and Jean. Bob Rothermel and Cynthia. That's two, four, six, eight. And Henry and Ad. There won't be much drinking with that group. Stubby's been on the wagon five or six years. Henry is AA, very active in it. Bob still likes to put it away, but Cynthia only drinks a little wine at dinner. Alice never did drink, as you know, and I limit myself to two before dinner, usually a bourbon on the rocks."

"What about Ad, and what about Jean?"

"Ad is AA, too. Jean is unpredictable. She's on and off the wagon from one month to the next. She may arrive tonight with the blind staggers. On the other hand, she may not take a drink. It all depends. You knew their daughter had to be put away?"

"No, I didn't. Was that Barbara?"

"Barbara, yes. Bobbie. Oh, yeah. It was a tragic thing. She cut her wrists, and another time an overdose of sleeping pills. Some guy in Wilkes-Barre she was crazy about, so they said. Stubby went on the wagon, but Jean still ties one on. They sold their house, and then Stub was out of a job for over a year. He's got something now, Henry gave him a job at the brewery as a sort of a coordinator with the advertising agency."

"Stubby? He's a civil engineer."

"He's not the only guy with a Lehigh degree that's doing something altogether different. Do you remember Chuck Rainsford?"

"Sure. General superintendent of the Dilworth Collieries. I used to play golf with Chuck."

"Not any more. I'm afraid he's come down in the world. He gives a course in geology at the adult education setup we have here. Two nights a week. They pay him something like a hundred and fifty dollars a term, and he tells me he's glad to get the money."

"I've seen him bet that much on a single putt," said George Denison. "Haven't you any *good* news, Andy?"

"Well, you know how it is. The good news is always less spectacular. Let me think. Of those coming tonight? Henry and Ad's oldest grandson ran for the state legislature and nosed out the Democrat."

"That's always good to hear," said George Denison.

"Well, it's a start," said Stokes. "Let me think, now. Cynthia's taken up painting, but I don't know whether you'd classify that as good news, exactly. It's what she calls non-representational. In other words, not supposed to represent anything—and believe me, as far as I'm concerned, it doesn't. Both their kids have moved away. Young Bobby is a test pilot for one of the big aviation companies in California. The daughter married a fellow from Chicago and they're living out there. The husband is with Continental, the bank. There's no money here, George. Not the way we knew it. We're losing population, a thousand a year. The town is back to where it was in the 1910 census, and no new industries coming in. These people that are buying your land, they'll put up a supermarket and a big parking lot, but sure as hell that's going to be the end of some more of the smaller stores. And if they lease the rest of the land to a drive-in movie, which is what I understand, that'll close down one of our movie theaters. Banking isn't much fun any more, the hard luck stories I have to listen to. When I first started working here I used to hear a lot of crazy schemes that we had to turn down, but at least there was some imagination at work. Not any more. It's the fast buck, the quick turnover, build as cheaply as possible, take your profits and get out. Some of our people drive as much as fifty miles to work and fifty back. Car pools. Our biggest cash depositor, week to week, used to be the old Stewart department store. Now do you know what it is? The numbers racket. A few of our old friends have made some money in the stock market, but that's not here. That's New York and Philadelphia, and representing industries as far away as California."

"That's enough good news for one day," said George Denison.

"I know, and I have to live with it three hundred and sixty-five days a year. If there was only some way we could reduce the population and become a small town, with enough work for everybody. I wouldn't mind being a small town again. But I'm a banker, and I have to keep up this pretense, like a booster. Well, in three more years I retire. A banquet at the hotel, a silver cigarette box, and the responsibility passes on to one of those young fellows you see out there. He's welcome to it."

"I've been away too long, you've stayed here too long," said George Denison.

"That's about the size of it, I guess," said Stokes. "Yes, I guess that's just about the size of it."

"I must be going, Andy. I'll see you a little later."

"Mike will let you out. You remember Mike Kelly? If you don't, he'll remember you. Used to pitch in the Twilight League, and was on the police force. About our age. He'll appreciate it if you remember him—and so will I."

Mike Kelly was waiting to unlock the heavy plate-glass door. His eagerness to be recognized was almost a supplication.

"Hello, Mike," said George Denison.

Mike Kelly put the door key in his left hand and shook hands with George Denison. "George, it's mighty good to see you. You're looking great, George. Great."

"Well, you might be able to go nine innings yourself," said George Denison.

"You remember those days? You used to play under the name of—what was the name?"

"George Denny."

"George Denny," said Mike Kelly. "So you wouldn't lose your amateur standing. You could hit. You were a good hitter, George. There was a couple times there where you threw to the wrong base—"

"Never. I never threw to the wrong base in my life."

"Now you know you did, George. But when it come to hitting that apple, you had the power. There was only one pitcher could get you out. Marty Boxmyer, pitched for the Knights of Pythias. Marty was such a little guy and he had so much steam that you never knew where the ball was coming from. But outside of Marty, you could hit any pitcher in our league."

"Yes, I could even hit you, Mike."

"I'll admit it. I wasn't the greatest pitcher in the league. But there was very few could get a long ball off of me, when my sinker was going right. How long you gonna be in town, George?"

"Just overnight."

"Living in Connecticut, I hear. How's your missus?"

"Fine thank you. And yours?"

"Passed away, George. I buried her two years ago the sixth day of May. But I have eight grandchildren. Five boys to carry on the name. One of them at Villanova was scouted by a couple of major league clubs. He has three one-hitters to his credit, one of them against your old college alma mater. A two-to-one win against a good Princeton team. Pardon my ignorance, George, but you didn't have a son if I recollect."

"Two daughters, but one of the grandsons is on the Harvard crew."

"Well, that's good, George. You could of been a great athlete if it wasn't for that one thing. You know what I mean. I don't have to say it."

"I guess you must be referring to the suds," said George Denison.

"Not the suds. It was the hard stuff."

"I don't think it made much difference, Mike. I wouldn't have been much better, and I wouldn't have had as much fun."

"I used to try to lecture you," said Mike Kelly.

"Yes you did. Mike, it's nice to see you, and maybe I'll see you again before I leave. If not—keep the faith."

"You remember that, huh? Keep the faith. So long, George. Glad we run into one another."

Back at the hotel George Denison found his wife standing at the window, looking down at the traffic on Main Street. "I was watching you," she said. "You came all the way from the bank without being recognized. I was trying to remember the stores between here and Scandinavian Street. Do you realize there's not a one that used to be here that's still here? Not a one, in the same place. There may be some that moved."

"They didn't move. They closed. At least that's what I gather from Andy. Did you get an appointment with the hairdresser?"

"No. They wouldn't take me before tomorrow."

"Then let's go for a ride," said George Denison.

"Where to?"

"Oh—wherever old Dobbin takes us. I'll just wrap the reins around the buggy-whip."

"What's this quaintness, all of a sudden? Old Dobbin? Did you ever know anyone that had a horse called Dobbin?"

"I knew a girl that had a dog called Dobbin," said George Denison.

"She must have been terribly affected. I suppose she had a horse called Rover."

"Towser," said George Denison.

"Frankly, I don't believe it," said Pammie Denison.

"Come on, put your coat on while there's still daylight," he said.

She put on her coat and hat. "Did you really know a girl that had a dog called Dobbin?" she said in the elevator.

"I really did," he said.

"When?"

"During what we sometimes refer to as the Tommy Williams Period."

"Oh," she said, and in the presence of the elevator boy said no more.

The green car was at the door. They got in and he drove south on Main Street. "Who *was* the girl that had—"

"With a dog called Dobbin? What difference does that make now? She was never as important to me as Tommy Williams was to you."

"All right. I was just wondering whether she was one that I knew about or one that you never mentioned. Where are we headed for?"

"You'll soon see," he said.

"Oh, then I guess I know," she said.

"Right," he said.

After a while he drove off the main highway and up into the hills, and presently he stopped the car on a township road, midway between two farmhouses. "Are you going to kiss me?" she said.

"Don't you think I ought to?"

"Yes I do," she said.

He kissed her on the lips, and when he drew away she was looking down at the floor, vaguely smiling. "That was very nice of you," she said.

"I feel rather self-conscious about it," he said. "But it's just about the only chance we'll get."

"Do you know something, George?"

"What?"

"After twenty-five years, twenty-seven, whatever it is, this is the first time I've really felt that you've forgiven me for Tommy Williams."

"Really? Well, maybe it is the first time. I don't know."

"I forgave myself a long time ago," she said.

He laughed. "I'm sure you did."

"Oh, it wasn't as easy as all that. A girl that's made a damn fool of herself—first she has to justify herself. Then she has to forget all about that and start being honest with herself—if she can. And I did. And that was when I was harder on myself than you ever were. It was at least a year before I could forgive myself for what I did to you and to myself."

"I didn't realize it'd taken you that long," he said.

"I know you didn't. That's why today, just now, is the first time I feel that you've really forgiven me. All those years in between, you took me back and we've been nice to each other, but there's always been something missing. Why is that?"

"I don't know," he said. "I've had it in my mind that I wanted to come here, to this very spot where I first kissed you over forty years ago. And I planned to kiss you. Then on the way to Gibbsville I more or less gave up the idea. Oversentimental. Forced. Awkward. But then I saw old Karl Isaminger. Then I had a long talk with Andy and heard what's happened to people we used to love. To this town. Life has been awful to them, Pam, the town and the people, and it hasn't been nearly as bad to you and me. Not yet, anyway. But our luck will start running out. We're getting there. And I wanted to bring you here and tell you that I've always loved you. Here, where I told you the first time."

"Then what I felt was right," she said.

"Yes," he said.

"From now on I guess we have to be ready for anything," she said.

"Yes," he said. With the tips of his fingers he caressed the back of her neck. "And don't be depressed by what we see tonight, at Alice and Andy's."

"Thank you," she said. "I won't. Now."

"Here comes a man on a tractor," he said. "He thinks we're lost."

At the Window

THE FIRST thing to go was the gilded-horse weathervane on top of the barn. From an upstairs window Moore had been watching it as it spun crazily, clockwise and counter-clockwise, resisting the wind and going with it. The ornament was a rather ugly thing, resembling—unintentionally, Moore was sure—one of those quarter horses that are raced in the Southwest, with a body that was too long and legs that were too short. Nevertheless Moore was sorry to see it go. In the last fifteen minutes he had come to forgive it its ugliness and admire its spirit, as though it were a real animal and putting up a struggle against the gale. Then the rod snapped, and the whole weathervane was carried away.

"There goes our horse," said Moore.

"What horse?" said Helen Moore.

"The weathervane," he said.

"Is *that* what you've been watching?" she said. "I thought you were sitting here brooding about the trees."

"I am. But I got fascinated by the weathervane," he said. "I wonder how old it was."

"It was here when we came," she said.

"I know it was. And that'll give you an idea of how it's blowing out there."

"I don't need that to tell me," she said. "All I have to do is listen."

"All the storms we've had since we moved here, but this is the one that finally blew away the weathervane. I hope we'll be able to find it."

"*I* hope we'll still *be* here," she said. "There's no electricity. The stuff in the refrigerator's going bad, and everything in the deep freeze. The water pump. I've been filling pots and pans with water, while you've been up here watching a weathervane. I just hope the wind doesn't come along and blow away our bottled gas."

"The wind isn't coming from that direction," he said. "I'm afraid we can expect to lose some trees, though."

"Yes, and the radio said to expect possibly four inches of snow."

"Are you worried?"

"Well, not yet," she said. "I mean, we have plenty of food in the house, and we can cook it. And there's lots of firewood down in the cellar."

"If it snows we'll have plenty of drinking water."

"Don't worry, it's going to snow. The phone is on the blink, and our only communication with the outside world is the radio."

"One-way communication, at that," said Moore. "There! The first snowflakes. God, they're big. Look, you can hardly see the Williamses'."

"I notice they've lit a fire."

"Oh, an hour ago," said Moore. "They must have lit theirs as soon as the electricity went off."

"Well, they have to have a warm room for old Mr. Williams. Now you can hardly see their house. I don't think I've ever seen so much snow come all at once."

"Every year I talk about getting a Delco and one of those little tractors."

"What's a Delco?"

"An electric power plant."

"Oh, that's a Delco?"

"There are different makes. The first one I ever knew of was a Delco and I call them all that. Isaac Hostetter. He was a farmer in our valley when I was a boy. He was the first one to have a tractor, too. The other farmers thought he was out of his mind. He was, a little, I guess. He went into deep debt to buy all sorts of modern equipment. The most modern thing most of them had was a De Laval. A cream separator, operated by hand. We had one. I used to crank it, sort of like winding the dasher when my mother made ice cream. Didn't I ever tell you about old Isaac Hostetter?"

"Maybe you did, I don't know. I guess there won't be any mail today."

"Oh, I doubt it now," said Moore. "I doubt if they'd start out in this weather. Last year we didn't get any mail for two days, remember?"

"Twice. Once for two days and another for three. No, I guess that was the year before when we didn't have mail for three days."

"Well, there's no use of their starting out and then getting stuck somewhere. How would you like to have Mr. Andrews as our house guest for two or three days?"

"The postman Mr. Andrews? Not very much," she said. "Why?"

"Well, if he got stuck in the road anywhere near our house, what else could we do but invite him to stay?"

"Oh, in that case of course we'd have to have him. We couldn't turn him away," she said.

"Actually, of course, he's not a bad fellow. Just a bit of a bore to talk to. And he's a talker."

"Now you can just about make out our barn."

"Imagine if we had cows?" said Moore.

"And you had to feed them?"

"Not only feed them. *Milk* them. If you were a real farmer's wife you'd have to do the milking twice a day."

"No thank you," she said.

"That's the way it used to be, when I was a boy."

"Your mother didn't have to milk cows."

"No, but the farmer's wife did. Mrs. Stroub. Pretty soon we won't be able to see our fence," he said.

"I hope it'll be there to see when this is over," she said.

"Isn't it strange what the wind does? It'll blow down a tree that's stood fifty years, a deeply rooted tree. But a tin mailbox stays right there. And a big thing that you'd think would make a good target, the tool shed, it hardly seems to shake. But my little weathervane with the horse on it, away it goes."

"Oh, I guess it's a lot like life. When your time comes, you go too."

"Uh-huh," he muttered. "I never get tired watching the snowflakes. Do you ever try to pick out one snowflake and watch it all the way to the ground?"

"Yes, I have," she said.

"Really? We've been married thirty-three years and that's something we never knew about each other."

"You can't expect to know everything about a person, no

matter how long you live with them. I wouldn't want to know everything about a person. And anyway, how could I? Every day you live you add something new to yourself."

"And lose something, too, I suppose," he said. "Think of the things we forget about ourselves. Mentioning old Isaac Hostetter, I remember something that happened fifty years ago, at least, and I haven't thought about it in all that time, till just now."

"I don't think you ever mentioned him to me before," she said.

"Oh, I must have mentioned him, years ago, but not lately."

"It's an unusual name. I'd have remembered it," she said.

"Yes, but there were a lot of unusual names, unusual to you when we were first married. Hostetter. Hochgertel. Fenstermacher. Womelsdorf. Wynkoop. Zinsendorf. Just thinking of names in our valley."

"How did a Moore get in there?"

"I must have told you that story," he said. "A farmer by the name of Billy Poffenberger. He ran up a big bill at my grandfather's store and for two years he didn't pay anything on account. He finally told my grandfather that he could have the farm for a receipted bill and a thousand dollars cash. It was a good farm, only Poffenberger'd let it go to hell, so my grandfather made the deal. He left it to my father in his will."

"I knew your father inherited it," said Helen Moore.

"To show you what neglect will do, it took my grandfather most of five years to get the property back in shape. I guess he must have spent quite a little money on it, but it was worth it. When my father died my mother sold the farm for forty thousand dollars, that's with everything on it. The livestock, the implements, and so forth. She had the house all fixed up nicely. Our house, that is. Jake Stroub, our farmer, he'd never spend any of his own money on their house. They had another house on the other side of the barn, he and his family. They kept it clean, but they didn't even have a picture on the wall. All the walls were bare. They used to have a calendar in the kitchen, and that was all. A farmer has a hard time getting along without a calendar. I don't remember their ever having a clock, but they always had a calendar. The Swedish Haven

Bank gave out calendars every year, and every farm in the valley had one. The one thing you'd see in every kitchen. We had one in our kitchen, too, but that was natural because my father was a director of the Swedish Haven Bank. A funny thing was, we were never there much in the wintertime. We didn't usually open up our house till around Easter. My mother said it was too gloomy during the real dead of winter, and of course we kids had to be in school in town. But as soon as we opened up the house around the first of April, one of the first things my father always did was to hang the bank calendar in the kitchen. I can remember him tearing off January, February, and March, and every year he always said the same thing. 'Well, that winter passed quickly,' he'd say."

"Yes, he had a good sense of humor," said Helen Moore.

"I guess he had to have, to put up with me," said Moore.

"And I guess your mother wasn't too easy to get along with," said Helen Moore.

"No, I guess she was pretty neurotic. That's what they'd say about her today. Neurotic. I suppose they would have called me a juvenile delinquent."

"Well, that's what you were, weren't you?" said Helen Moore.

"Oh, I don't deny it," he said.

"No, don't deny it to me," she said.

"I never have, have I? You can't say I ever pretended to be any better than I was, Helen. That's one thing I never did."

"No, I guess if you'd have tried to be a hypocrite I never would have married you," she said.

"I never had any use for a hypocrite," he said. "I had one or two friends of mine, and I don't have to tell you who they were. But they were getting away with murder, only because they never got caught. But no matter what I did, I always got caught at it sooner or later. You take now for instance, Johnny Grattan. The night I had my accident, Johnny'd been driving the car and he almost went off the road a couple of times, so I made him change places with me. The result? When the truck hit us, he was sound asleep, dead drunk, in the back seat, and *I* was the one that was pinned behind the steering. But it could have been Johnny that lost his arm instead of me."

"I don't see how that makes him a hypocrite," said Helen Moore.

"Well, it doesn't make him a hypocrite exactly. But in a way it does. I mean, he pretended he was sober enough to drive, but he wasn't. That's the way he was, you know. He was always putting up a big bluff. Always bluffing. Oh, sure. He could drive the car. A whole bunch of people on the porch of the Sigma Nu house, and I started to get in behind the steering, but no. Johnny had to show everybody how he could drink twice as much as everybody else and still drive. He lasted to the other side of Allentown, and then I had to take the wheel."

"Well, which is worse? For forty years he's blamed himself for what happened to you," she said.

"Now that's what I call being a hypocrite. He blames himself, but he has both arms. And I wonder how much sleep he lost over me."

"He never took another drink," said Helen Moore.

"So he says," said Moore.

"Well, you *know* he didn't, Frank."

"Sure. Sure. Good for him," said Moore. "Let's move back to Swedish Haven so we can see more of John L. Grattan, the non-drinker."

She suppressed her reply. "Well, this isn't getting my work done," she said. "Do you want anything?"

"Do I want anything? What, for instance?"

"Well, I thought I'd spend the rest of the morning in the attic, sorting out things for the rummage sale."

"The attic? Do you know what it'll be like up there? You'll freeze to death."

"Oh, I have my big thick sweater. I won't be cold. And if it does get too cold, I'll stop. But I promised the committee I'd be ready when they sent the truck."

"This snowstorm will put everything back at least three days," he said.

"Well, I'm more than three days late. I should have done this a week ago. There's coffee in the glass pot. You may want to heat it. I put the milk and cream out on the windowsill. It'll keep just as well there as in the refrigerator."

"We used to have a box to keep things in during the winter.

It was just outside the kitchen window, and you could keep meat and vegetables there. It opened from inside the kitchen. We ought to have one of those."

"Yes, that'd be a good idea. I suppose we could get a carpenter to make one."

"You know damn well I couldn't," he said. "You need two hands for that."

"All right, we'll ask Mr. Rosetti. But first let's find out how much he's going to charge us. Not like the last time, when he charged us eighty-five dollars just to fix a few feet of fence."

"Well, he knows I can't do it."

"Oh, Frank, will you stop?" she said. She left the room, got her sweater and retired to the attic.

She did not remain there long. It was a hard cold in the attic, with the sound of the wind beating against the roofing, and the power failure keeping the room in just enough darkness to make her chore difficult. She gave up and descended through trapdoor to ladder to the second-story guest room where her husband was still sitting at the window.

"I couldn't get anything done," she said. "No light, and my hands got cold. Would you want an early lunch?"

"I don't know what came over me," he said. "How long is it since I bellyached about my arm? I don't do that often, do I?"

"No," she said.

"One thing leads to another," he said. "I got on the subject of Johnny Grattan and before I knew it I was back there forty years ago. Forty years, that's a good solid block of years."

"Well, let's hope it's out of your system," she said.

"It'll never be out of my system altogether. It gave me a good excuse for being a bum."

"Oh, you're not a bum, Frank. That's silly," she said. "They should have made you get an artificial arm, then you could have done certain things and you'd have gotten used to it, so that when those new ones came along, the World War Two arms, you'd have been ready. I don't know, maybe you could still learn to use one of the new ones. They say they're marvelous."

"No, I couldn't learn to use one now. I'd only get discouraged, and I'm bad enough as it is."

"Only when you're feeling sorry for yourself. Then you can

work yourself into such a state that you can be a disagreeable son of a bitch."

"Well, I don't enjoy it when I'm that way."

"I should hope not," she said. "How would you like some soup and a sliced chicken sandwich for lunch? I have the last of that chicken. Or I could fix you some cold cuts with a hot soup? I have some ham and liverwurst."

"The cold cuts," he said.

"I'm going to give you a steak tonight. We had three left in the deep freeze. If they get the electricity back on soon—but I'm not counting on that."

"No," he said. "I guess they'll try to have it on for tonight, but I wouldn't count on it much before dark."

"Old Mr. Williams must be miserable."

"Do you know what the Eskimos do with their old people? They put them out in a storm and they just fall asleep and never wake up. It seems to me a very sensible way."

"Are you suggesting that that's what they ought to do with Mr. Williams?"

"Not seriously, no," he said. "But this would be their chance, wouldn't it? And the Lord knows, Mr. Williams isn't getting much enjoyment out of life. He's over ninety."

"His mind is all right, though," she said.

"For a man over ninety. But he hasn't got much control over himself. He's practically helpless, and he's nothing much to look at. One of the funny sights is to see that old man, born right after the Civil War, shaving himself with an electric razor."

"Well, he won't be able to use it today."

"Oh, he probably doesn't have to shave more than once or twice a week. I'm thirty years younger than he is, but I notice a shave lasts me longer than it used to."

"He must be a problem in weather like this," said Helen Moore.

"Yes. Well, he's clinging to that last spark of life," he said. "And I guess they have enough firewood to keep him warm. I imagine they have him in their livingroom."

"Yes, I would think so. He doesn't sleep upstairs any more. They more or less turned their diningroom into a bedroom for him."

"I didn't know that," said Moore.

"Oh, last year," she said. "They had that lavatory in the hall, so all they had to do was bring down a bed from upstairs. Once a week they take him upstairs and give him a bath. That's the part I wouldn't like, giving an old man his bath. But Rachel doesn't complain. She's very fond of the old man."

"Well, that was the understanding, you know. He put up the money for the farm, on condition they'd give him a home. I guess they never expected him to last *this* long, though. That was twenty years ago."

"Yes, he got his money's worth. But Rachel doesn't look at it that way."

"It's still coming down," he said. "I think the wind has let up a little. Slanting. I noticed one little spot behind the tool shed, no snow on the ground at all. Just that one little spot. But I'll bet you there'll be two feet of snow there tomorrow, if not before."

"Well, let's hope it fills up all the reservoirs. We don't want any more water shortages next summer."

"No. Just think if we farmed this place," he said. "I mean if we had to depend on it for a living. Tom Williams told me last fall, I forget how much he said he lost last year. He about broke even on the dairy end, but he lost on the sweet corn and his potatoes. And Tom's a pretty good farmer. He uses all modern methods and reads up on all the latest information. But if you don't get rain at the right time and in the right amount, you can be the smartest farmer in the country and for all the good it does you you might as well stay drunk."

"Tom doesn't drink," she said.

"I didn't mean *he* might as well stay drunk. Anybody. Although you're wrong about Tom not drinking. Once or twice a year Tom ties one on that lasts four or five days."

"Oh, he used to, but not any more," said Helen Moore.

"Have it your way, but I happen to know better. The difference is, now he goes away, and I know where he goes. He and his brother, from Wilkes-Barre, and one or two friends of theirs go up to a shack they have in the Poconos. To go deer-hunting, they say. But last year Tom took a case of bourbon with him and it was all gone when he came back. Figure it out for yourself. Twelve bottles of whiskey. Four men. Four days. That's pretty good drinking for a man that doesn't drink. I could have gone with them. He invited me. Just bring some money, he told me. They play poker. I almost went."

"What stopped you?" she said.

"Well, if you think back, that was when you just got back from the clinic that time. You were waiting to hear from the doctor."

"Oh," she said. "Well, I'm glad you didn't go. Thank you."

"What the hell? I knew you were worried."

"You didn't say anything," she said.

"Neither did you. But it was a natural thing to be worried. And I probably wouldn't have had any fun. I don't like to be around a bunch of men when they're drinking and they have a lot of guns around."

"Why do you have to spoil it? You do something nice, and then it's as if you were ashamed of it," she said.

"Well, I don't know," he said. "Maybe I would have gone, and maybe I wouldn't. I don't know."

"You *would* have," she said.

"Well, I usually win at five-card stud," he said. "But then somebody gets a little drunk and they start all those fancy variations. Seven-card high-low, wild cards. Takes all the pleasure out of it for me."

She kissed him.

The Answer Depends

THEY WONDER how we can sit and watch ourselves in those old movies on television. Doesn't it embarrass us to be reminded of the awfulness of the bad pictures, and embarrass us in a different way to see the inferior quality of our pictures that were supposed to be good? Our makeup was so awful, the lighting was so unprofessional, the cutting so jumpy, the direction so unimaginative when it was not artily intrusive, the dialog so dated, the stories so untrue to life. They laugh, the younger ones, and kid the clichés and ask us why we don't buy up those old pictures and burn the negatives. One of them said to me last week, "Come on, Bobby, you have enough money stashed away. You can afford to buy back a thing like *MacKenzie of the Royal Rifles*." Well, I have not got enough money to buy back *MacKenzie*, but even if I had, I wouldn't buy it. Yes, I am momentarily uncomfortable when my grandson sees me as a gallant young subaltern—wearing too much lipstick and too much eye-shadow. Only too well do I know what he is thinking: his grandfather must have been a swish. His manners are just good enough to keep him from coming out and saying so, but he looks at me on the TV screen and then at me, there in my den, and in his mind are serious doubts of my virility. I, on the other hand, cannot banish those thoughts by revealing to him that at the time I was making *MacKenzie of the Royal Rifles*, his grandmother was sulking in our North Canon Drive mansion because I was away on location with Doris Arlington. I cannot tell the boy that his grandmother had every good reason to sulk. I would not tell him that I very nearly did not go back to his grandmother, that Doris Arlington and I went from the High Sierras location to a cruise in a borrowed yacht that had nothing to do with the making of *MacKenzie of the Royal Rifles*. "My boy," I could but cannot say to him, "if Doris Arlington had been a better sailor, you would not be alive today, and neither would your father."

We don't see what *they* see in those old movies. The news and sports and the weather are finished, and the night's movie comes on. Sometimes it is a picture I never heard of, sometimes it is a picture in which I had the male lead. Most often it is a film that stars men and women I used to know, and frequently I am able to recall the giant première at the Chinese or the Egyptian or the Carthay Circle. The pra-meer, they pronounced it. That was the year I had my first Duesenberg. That was the year I had my first Rolls. That was the opening that Lowell Sherman came to in a broken-down flivver—but there I am confusing fact with scenario. Lowell Sherman did that in a film called *What Price Hollywood?* Someone else did it in real life. Who was it, who *was* it that came to a world pra-meer in a broken-down flivver? I remember Connie Bennett in *What Price Hollywood?*, the Brown Derby waitress in a starched, ballooning-out skirt. It was a good, good picture. Gutsy, with a suicide ending. But who actually did drive the flivver to a grande luxe opening? I can remember Connie singing "Parlez moi d'amour" in the film, but why can't I recall the actual driver of the actual flivver? I make a note to telephone Bill Powell in Palm Springs. He'll remember. But by the time the night's picture is finished I forget to telephone Bill.

Oh, we would never do anything to keep those old films off TV. It would be like burning a diary. It would be worse than burning a diary. I did burn a diary before I went to the hospital a few years ago. No one else knew that I had kept the diary, no one in the world. It contained no written-out names, but there were a few people who would have been able to make pretty good guesses as to identities and events, and their guesses would not have made anyone happy. The doctor said my operation would be merely exploratory, which is what it turned out to be, but he was quite pleased that I seemed to be so calm. "Most men your age put on a good act, but you're not a bit worried," he said. I told him I had great confidence in him and let it go at that. I didn't want to tell him that I had prepared for the operation by burning a diary. Surgeons are such hams, every bit as bad as we are, every bit as hungry for a little applause. And at my age my doctor is almost a companion, if not exactly a friend. I have no friends who are also companions. Bill Powell is in Palm Springs, Dick Barthelmess was until recently in Southampton, Ned Revere has his farm in upstate New York, Jack Paisley has returned to England. They are all far removed from my little ranch in the San Fernando

Valley. But I don't really miss them. I could move to New York and join the actors' clubs, take up bridge and pool, and sit in the club bars with men who would do to me what I would do to them—interrupt my reminiscences with questions of fact or because I had been talking too long. I know those clubs, I used to belong to them in my movie-star days because membership in them spruced up my biography in *Who's Who*; but I seldom went near them, and when I did I always came away depressed and re-determined never to end my days in them. I don't need clubs, and I certainly don't want my recollections to be interrupted by other retired actors who think their memory is more accurate than mine.

I get very good reception on my TV set at my ranch. Day or night I can go to my little den and sit alone. My family and my neighbors know that my doctor has told me to stay out of the sun, and they think I am "making the best of it." Well, I am, but not in the way they believe. I am having a very good time. Every old movie, whether it was a super production or what we used to call a program picture, takes me right back to the exciting days when I was on my way up, or to those later days when (according to one magazine writer) my face was on some screen in some part of the world every hour of every day, when I was making fifteen thousand a week and spending at least half that. I bought suits twenty at a time, ordering them from swatches, and many of them I gave away without having worn them a single time. I once owned a speedboat that I never even saw because I was too busy to go to Catalina. Now, of course, I am limited to a stationwagon and a black sedan, neither of them in the five-thousand class, but a couple of weeks ago I was watching an old film about a monarch in a mythical kingdom, played by Jack Paisley. There was a scene in which Jack is riding through a village in the royal town car. The car runs over a child, and a revolution starts. I had forgotten about that film, but I recognized the car. It was my car, a Rolls with a Barker body, and I had lent it to Sidney Gainsborough, of Gainsborough Pictures, as a personal favor, for that picture. I think he paid me a thousand dollars a day, although I had not asked him for any money. They kept the car on the Gainsborough lot for three or four weeks while making the picture, and I recall that the money they paid me was more than the car had cost me new. That was how we did things in those days, too. The strange thing was that it made sense, according to Sidney, to rent my car instead of waiting a whole year while the Rolls and the Barker people built a car new. That was how we thought in those days, too. We who remember those days are not mystified by the cost of making pictures, even forty-million-dollar pictures. I was never paid a million to make a picture, but I made a million a year for six or seven straight years, and Tom Mix made much more than I did. This Taylor girl, by the time she gets through paying her taxes, will wind up with a lot less than Mary Pickford put away, and don't you forget it. In fact, I wouldn't be surprised if when she reaches my age, she has less than I have now. I spent it freely, but I didn't spend it all. Ronnie Colman, Warner Baxter, Bill Powell, Dick Barthelmess, Jack Paisley, Ned Revere and I held on to enough to give us security. Even Ned Revere, with five ex-wives, won't die broke on that farm of his up near Cooperstown, N. Y.

Good old Ned, the rascal. This present wife of his was an acquisition of his post-Hollywood days, and I don't know very much about her, but she must be a pretty good sort. Ned had that automobile accident ten years ago that left him rather badly crippled just when he seemed about to be embarking on a new career on Broadway. He got those excellent notices in one play that folded after three weeks, and some young fellow who had never seen him in those comedy movies wrote a play especially for Ned. I would never have thought that Ned would strike anyone as the type to play a broken-down old politician in a Southern town. I had known Ned so well that the ravages of time had not been particularly noticeable; to me he was a good light comedian who was getting older, as I was getting older. But to the young playwright, seeing him for the first time, he was the perfect actor to play an unprincipled old buzzard who had always been able to get by on his charm. To some extent that was true of Ned himself, in real life, but it had never occurred to me that anyone would get that impression of Ned so strongly as to want to write a play about it. Ned understood it, though, and he told me when he went into rehearsal that it was going to be very difficult to overcome the temptation to play himself instead of the character as written. It was especially difficult, he said, because he was a native Southerner and after all those years of stifling his accent, he was being encouraged to lay it on thick. He was genuinely apprehensive, and for the first time in his life he was thinking of someone else, in this case, the young playwright who had such confidence in him. He wanted to be good for the playwright's sake. Well, as everyone knows, he was. The notices were unanimously favorable and there was praise for all concerned; for Ned, for the playwright, for the supporting cast, the director. Then Ned was injured in that smash-up of his taxi and a mail truck, and the only luck Ned had was that he came out of it alive, plus the fact that he met the lady who eventually became Number 6. She was in the hospital at the same time, and they would meet in their wheelchairs in the sun room. She was a widow, fully aware of Ned's matrimonial record, and inclined to be moralistic about it. But besides being moralistic she was sympathetic toward the afflicted, as moralistic people are sometimes apt to be, and Ned was at his lowest ebb. He had a good deal of pain during a series of operations, and was pessimistic as to his future. His old ebullience was gone, and she began to think of him more as a discouraged invalid than as a much-married movie actor. He in turn began to realize that she never said a word about her own illness, which was cancer, and that she was giving him a lesson in courage. She invited him to visit her at her farm near Cooperstown, repeated the invitation when she was leaving the hospital, and he found after she left that he missed her companionship so much that when it came time for him to leave the hospital, he went to Cooperstown and stayed.

I hear from him once in a while. He has one of those golf carts that enables him to get around in good weather. I have a standing invitation to visit him, but it is one I shall never accept. It isn't only that Cooperstown is too far away. In fact, in a manner of speaking it is much too near. Ned Revere, dependent on a golf cart to get him around, is not Ned Revere in a Stutz Bearcat or a Mercer Raceabout, as he always was when we were making silent films. When the talkies came in we bought the newer cars; Ned persuaded me to buy my first Duesenberg. He doesn't even remember that, and I will not go all the way to Cooperstown to get into an argument over it. He wrote to me a couple of months ago, and I saved his letter, although I don't know why I did. It is so full of misinformation that it is practically a classic.

Dear Bobby [he wrote]: I suppose you saw in the papers that Dick Barthelmess has passed on. The ranks are getting thin. I had not seen Dick in recent years. He spent most of his time on Long Island. Am told he had seven operations and was down to 110 lbs when he died. Was always fond of Dick in the old days. Sent me a wire on opening night of *The Blighted Magnolia* & had tickets for the night after I had my accident with the taxi and the mail truck. He was one of the first to send me flowers to the hospital. Dear old Dick, a real gentleman & a fine actor.

I caught you on TV the other night, the late show. It was *Lord of the Forest* the one in which you played a civil engineer who wants to build a big dam & the girl threatens to shoot you when she sees you surveying the timberland. If they show it in California don't look at it. You will want to cut your throat. It wouldn't be hard, either, as you go around in all kinds of weather with your collar open and your chest showing as if you were a sweater girl. It is not the worst picture I ever saw but it will do till a worse one comes along. All I could think of watching that picture was you and Edna Blaine, who played the girl. My wife was watching the picture with me & she said you seemed to be really in love with the heroine. "I'll say he was," I said to her. I told her about how you and Edna sneaked away after the shooting was finished and went off on a cruise in Sid Gainsborough's yacht. But you were seasick from the minute the yacht left the dock and Edna got so fed up that she made the captain turn back after you were only gone two days. Still, you were quite a chaser as long as you stayed on dry land. I saw another of your pictures *MacGregor of the Royal Rifles* with you and Doris Arlington. She was just a kid at the time, everybody was after her, including yours truly, but she was really stuck on you. I was always surprised you didn't marry Doris. I guess you would have if you had to. Then some new kid came along & you palmed Doris off on Jack Paisley, a lousy trick to pull on any girl. I don't watch TV very much. They are always reviving our old pictures & there ought to be some kind of a law like invasion of privacy to keep them from digging into our past. I guess one good thing is that the young people today think we are all dead. The young fellow who manages our farm, a young Cornell graduate, worked for us two years before he discovered that Edward J. Revere was the Ned Revere he saw on the late show. I guess if the truth be told I always hated Hollywood. They kept me doing those damn comedies till I could never get a decent part in anything serious. I was in my late fifties before I ever got a chance to show I could act & then it was Broadway, not Hollywood, that gave me the chance. I was never cut out to be a comedian. I should of left Hollywood thirty years ago and concentrated on the legitimate stage, maybe doing a comedy now & then like Alfred Lunt but mostly sticking to dramatic roles. Well, it is too late now and there is no use being bitter . . .

No use being bitter, he says. Poor Ned. I see him on the late movies, and it is true that those comedies were not worth remembering (although they made money for everyone connected with them). But I pay so little attention to the dramatic content of our old pictures. I don't try to follow the plot lines of Ned Revere's films. In a few minutes after one of his pictures has begun to roll, I am in a daze of recollection, of remembering Ned as a gay companion; irresponsible, Quixotic, romantic, attractive to men as well as to women, and with no illusions then as to his stature as an artist. He himself often said that his pictures were all the same picture, based on the foolproof formula of boy meets girl, boy loses girl, boy gets girl. I confess that I may have envied him a little in those days. I had to work so hard to create a new character in every new picture, whereas Ned, with his perennially youthful countenance and those sure-fire parts, could show up at the studio with absolutely no preparation and let the director do the thinking when any was necessary. I remember a discussion with Jack Quinlan, who directed so many of Ned's films, silents and talkies. Ned's mind, Jack said, was like an old-fashioned schoolboy's slate. You wrote something on it, then you rubbed it out and wrote something else. Ned was never bothered by subtleties or nuances, and I don't suppose he had ever read a book in his life. He had a perfect light-comedy face, as Jack pointed out to me. Regular features, a small straight nose, a fine head of hair with a widow's peak, and an awkward grace that was natural and could not be copied by anyone else in the business. There was absolutely no difference between Ned on-screen and off, and the smart directors like Jack Quinlan never tried to make Ned do anything or say anything that required discipline or invention on Ned's part. It was his naïveté that got him into so many marriages. He might just as reasonably have married five other girls instead of the five he did marry. He merely happened to have proposed to five girls who accepted his proposals. He had a daughter by his second wife, his only child, but she grew up with her stepfather, took her stepfather's name, and probably has not heard from Ned in more than thirty years. I doubt if Ned ever gives her a thought. Certainly he never used to mention her to any of us. Come to think of it, I can't recall his ever mentioning his mother either. I suppose you would call him a man with no emotional ties, who never inflicted his problems on us because he had none. His lack of them, of course, made him an ideal companion for the rest of us, who may have had a tendency to exaggerate our emotional involvements. You could tell him anything, he would listen, nod at the right places, and forget what you said. I told him, for instance, that Doris Arlington had been seasick on Morris Spitzer's yacht, but he will believe to his dying day that I was with Edna Blaine on Sid Gainsborough's yacht. Sid never had a yacht, but he did have Edna Blaine. I don't know who is better off: me at my TV, with memories as fresh as the news in the morning paper; or Ned, scornful of those pleasant and profitable days, and with the lingering bitter taste of that one success on Broadway. Who is better off? Why I am, of course, unless you put the same question to Ned Revere.

Can I Stay Here?

THE FAMOUS actress went to the window and gazed down at the snow-covered Park. The morning radio had said there would be snow, and there it was, an inch of it settled on trees and ground, and making her warm apartment so comfortable and secure. She would not have to go out all day. John Blackwell's twenty-one-year-old daughter was coming for lunch, and would probably stay an hour and a half; then there would be nothing to do until Alfredo Pastorelli's cocktail party, and the weather had provided an excuse for ducking that. As for dinner at Maude Long's, any minute now there would be a telephone call from Maude. Any minute—and this was the minute.

"Mrs. Long on the phone, ma'am," said the maid.

"I'll take it in here, Irene."

"Yes ma'am," said the maid.

"Hello, Maudie. I'll bet I know what you're calling about."

"Oh, Terry, have you taken a look outside? I just don't think it's fair to ask George and Marian to go out in weather like this. I could send my car for them, but that'd mean O'Brien wouldn't get home till after midnight. And he's been so good lately."

"So you've called off the party. Don't fret about it, Maudie," said Theresa Livingston.

"You sure you don't mind? I mean, if you'd like to come to me for dinner, just the two of us. We could play canasta. Or gin."

"Maudie, wouldn't you just rather have a nice warm bath and dinner on a tray? That's what I plan to do, unless you're dying for company."

"Well, if you're sure you don't mind," said Maude Long.

"Not one single bit. This is the kind of day that makes me appreciate a nice warm apartment. Oh, the times I'd wake up on days like this and wish I could stay indoors. But would have to get up and play a matinee at the Nixon. That's in Pittsburgh, or was."

"Yes, it's nice to just putter, isn't it?" said Maude Long. "What are you going to wear?"

"Today?"

"Yes. I always like to know what you're wearing. What do *you* wear when you're just staying home doing nothing?"

"Well, today I'll be wearing my black net. That sounds dressy, but I'm having a guest for lunch. A young girl that I've never met, but her father was an old beau of mine and she's coming to see me."

"That could be amusing. Could be a bore, too."

"I can get rid of her, and don't think I won't if she turns out to be a bore."

"Trust you, Terry. Well, let's one of us call the other in a day or so, and I'm sorry about dinner."

Having committed herself to her black net, Terry Livingston reconsidered. In fairness to John Blackwell she could not give his daughter the impression that his actress girl friend had turned into a frump. Not that the black net was frumpish, but it *was* black net, and something brighter would be more considerate of John, and especially on a day like this. "I'm not going to keep this on, Irene. What have I got that's brighter?"

"Your blue silk knit, ma'am. With that you can start breaking in those blue pumps."

"I wonder what jewelry. This young lady that's coming for lunch, I've never seen her, but her father was one of my biggest admirers, back in the Spanish-American War days."

"Aw, now ma'am."

"Well, it wasn't World War Two, I can tell you," said Theresa Livingston. "And not too long after World War One."

"Try her with one good piece," said Irene. "I always like your diamond pin with the squiggly gold around it."

"With the blue silk knit, do you think?"

"If you wear it over to the one side, casual."

"All right. You've solved the problem. And I suppose I ought to start breaking in those pumps."

"They've been just sitting there ever since you bought them, and the old ones are pretty scuffed," said Irene. "Will you be offering her a cocktail, the young lady?"

"Oh, she's old enough for that. Yes. Let's put out some gin and vodka. They drink a lot of vodka, the young people."

"And I'll send down for a waiter at one o'clock."

"A little earlier. Have him here to take our order at one sharp."

"I won't promise he'll be here. That's their busiest time, but I'll try. In case you may want to get rid of her, what?"

"The usual signal," said Theresa Livingston. "At two-fifteen I'll ask you if you've seen my cigarette holder. You pretend to look for it. You find it and bring it in and remind me that I have to change for my appointment."

"Where is the appointment supposed to be?"

"Three o'clock, downtown in my lawyer's office."

"Just so I make sure," said Irene. "I made a botch of it the last time Mrs. Long was here."

"Oh, well, with Mrs. Long it didn't matter. I wonder if I ought to have some little present for Miss Blackwell. Her father was very generous to me. Some little spur-of-the-moment gift that I won't miss."

"You have any number of cigarette lighters that you don't hardly ever use."

"Have I got any silver ones? A gold one would be a little too much, but a silver one might be nice."

"You've one or two silver, and a couple in snakeskin."

"The snakeskin. Fill one of the snakeskins and put a flint in it if it needs it. I'll have it in my hand. A spontaneous gesture that I'm sure she'll appreciate, just before she's leaving. 'I want you to take this. A little memento of our first meeting.'"

"I'll pick out a nice one. Snakeskin or lizard, either one."

"And you'll see about the drinks? Tomato juice, in case she asks for a Bloody Mary. Now what else? We'll have the table in the center of the room. I'll take the chair with my back to the light. At this hour of the day it doesn't make a great deal of difference, but she's young and she might as well get the glare. You listen to what I order and be sure the waiter puts my melon or whatever on that side of the table."

"Yes ma'am."

"When she gets here I'll be in my bedroom. They'll announce her from downstairs and I'll wait in my bedroom. You let her in. She'll naturally turn right, I imagine, and you tell her I'll be right with her. I don't like that picture of President Eisenhower where it is. Let's take it off the piano and put it more where she can see it. I don't suppose she'd recognize

Moss Hart, so we'll leave that there. Dwight Wiman? No, she wouldn't know who he was. She might recognize Noël Coward's picture, so we won't disturb that. That's a wonderful picture of Gary Cooper and I. I must remember to have that enlarged. Gary. Dolores Del Rio. A writer, his name I forget. Fay Wray. That's Cedric Gibbons. He was married to Dolores Del Rio. Frances Goldwyn. Mrs. Samuel. Dear Bill Powell and Carole Lombard. There we all are, my first year in Hollywood. My second, actually, but I have no pictures of the first time. That was a Sunday luncheon party at Malibu. Look at Gary, isn't he darling? He wasn't a bit interested in me, actually. That was when he and the little Mexican girl, Lupe Velez, they were quite a thing at that time. You know, I haven't really looked at that picture in ages. Certainly dates me, doesn't it? And this one. Do you know who that is? I must have told you."

"I never remember his name."

"That's H. G. *Wells*. One of our *great* writers. Not one of ours in the American sense. But British. I think he was out there visiting Charlie Chaplin or somebody. They all went to Hollywood sometime or other. Never mind. I made a lot of money in pictures, and people heard of me that never would have if I'd confined myself to the theater. Well, this isn't getting into my blue knit."

"You have over a half an hour," said the maid.

They went to the bedroom. Irene laid out the blue dress, and produced three cigarette lighters. "You don't want to give her the one with the watch in it," said Irene. "I took notice, the watch is from Cartier's."

"No, I'll take this little thing. I think it must be lizard. Quite gay, don't you think? And doesn't go at all badly with my dress. I haven't the faintest idea who gave me this one."

"Just so it wasn't the young lady's father."

"Oh, no. Not John Blackwell. Downstairs, in the safe, that's where I keep his presents. Or at least I've had most of them reset, but he never gave me any cigarette lighters. He's president of the United States Casualty and Indemnity Company, and his father was, before him. One of those firms that you don't hear much about, but I wish I had their money. Baltimore. Did you ever hear of a horse called One No Trump? A *famous* horse. I'm not sure he didn't win the Kentucky Derby.

This girl's father owned him. I'll tell you another little secret to add to your collection. For when you write your memoirs. Mr. Blackwell, John, always wanted to name a horse after me, but of course he was married and I was too, at the time, and we were both being *very* discreet. I just wonder how much this girl today knows about me. Anyway, John knew he couldn't actually call a horse by my name, but he had a very promising filly that he thought would win the Kentucky Derby. Only one filly ever won the Derby, you know. A horse with the unfortunate name of Regret. So John wanted to name this filly after me, but instead of giving it my name, he gave it my initials. He called it Till Later. T.L. That was our secret. *One* of them, I might add. Oh, dear, I think of all the little lies we told to protect other people. Including this girl that's coming today. *There.* How do I look?"

"Let me just smooth the skirt down over the hips," said Irene.

"It has a tendency to crawl up. I wonder if I ought to put on another slip?"

"You'll be sitting down most of the time. It's not very noticeable. Here's your pin," said Irene.

"Right about here, do you think?"

"Yes. Maybe about an inch lower."

"Here?" said Theresa Livingston.

"Just right."

"There. Now we're ready for Miss Evelyn Blackwell."

"She ought to be here in another five minutes."

"I hope she's prompt."

"She will be, if she knows what's good for her," said Irene.

"Well, if she's anything like her father. He had the best manners of any man I ever knew." Theresa Livingston lit a cigarette, had a couple of looks at herself in the full-length triplicate mirrors. She was alone now; Irene was in the kitchen. Being alone was not bad. Ever since she had rated her own dressing-room—and that was a good many years—Theresa had always insisted upon being alone for the last five minutes before going on for a performance. It gave her time to compose herself, to gather her strength, to be sick if she had to be, to slosh her mouth out with a sip of champagne which she did not swallow, to get ready for the stage manager's summons, to go out there and kill the sons of bitches with her charm and beauty and talent. Perceptive of Irene to have realized that this was just such a time, if only for an audience of one young girl. Too perceptive. All that prattle had deceived Theresa herself without for one minute deceiving Irene.

She wanted to remain standing so as not to give the blue silk knit a chance to crawl up, but after ten minutes she was weary. The buzzer sounded, and Theresa heard Irene going to the hall door. It was the waiter with the menus. Loyally Irene was annoyed by the young girl's lateness. "Why don't you just order for the both of you?" said Irene. "Or do you want me to?"

"I'm not terribly hungry," said Theresa. "You order, Irene."

"Yes. Well, the eggs Florentine. Start with the melon. The eggs Florentine. You won't want a salad, so we won't give *her* one. And finish up with the lemon sherbet. Light, but enough. And you'll want your Sanka. Coffee for her. How does that sound to you?"

"Perfect. And it'll take a half an hour before it gets here. She certainly ought to be here by then."

"If she isn't, I'm not going to let her come up."

"Oh, well, traffic. She'll have *some* good reason."

"What's wrong with the telephone? She could of let us know," said Irene. "I'll give him the order and then *you're* gonna have a glass of champagne."

"All right," said Theresa.

"We'll give her till ha' past one on the dot," said Irene.

It was ten minutes short of one-thirty when the girl arrived. "She's here," said Irene. "But you'll have to judge for yourself the condition she's in."

"You mean she's tight?" said Theresa.

"She's something, I don't know what."

"What is she like? Is she attractive?"

"Well, you don't see much of the face. You know, the hair hides the most of it."

"What makes you think she's tight?"

"'Hi,' she said. 'Hi. Is Miss Livingston at home? I'm ex-pected. Expec-ted.' I said yes, she was expected. Didn't they call up from downstairs? 'Oh, that's right,' she said. 'Oh, there's Ike,' she said. 'Isn't he cute?' Ike. Cute."

"Oh, dear. Well, let's get it over with," said Theresa. "Tell her I'll be right out."

"I'll tell her you're on the long distance," said Irene.

"It might be a good idea to stay with her. Keep an eye on her so she doesn't start helping herself to the vodka. Is she that type?"

"I wouldn't put it past her," said Irene. "I wouldn't put anything past this one. And remember, you're supposed to be going downtown and see your lawyer."

"Yes, we won't need the cigarette holder bit."

Theresa Livingston allowed a few minutes to pass, then made her brisk entrance, and saw immediately that Irene had not exaggerated. The girl stood up and behind her lazy grin was all manner of trouble. Theresa Livingston gave her the society dowager bit. "How do you do, my dear. Have you told Irene what you'd like to drink?"

"She didn't ask me, but I'll have a vodka martini. I might as well stick with it."

"Irene, will you, please?" said Theresa Livingston. "Nothing for me. I've ordered lunch for both of us. Save time that way, you know. The food is good here, but the service can be a little slow."

"I know."

"Oh, you've stopped here?"

"No, we always stay at the Vanderbilt, but I was with some friends in the What-You-Call-It-Room, downstairs."

"I see," said Theresa.

"I guess I was a little late, but I got here as soon as I could."

"Well, let's not talk about that," said Theresa. "Why don't you sit there and I'll sit here. I was so pleased to hear from your father. I hadn't realized he had a daughter your age. Did you come out, and all the rest of those things?"

"Oh, two years ago. The whole bit."

"And from your father's note I gather you've given up school. Are you serious about wanting to be an actress?"

Irene served the cocktail, and the girl drank some of it. "I don't know. I guess I am. I want to do something, and as soon as I mentioned the theater, Daddy said he knew you. I guess if you were a friend of Daddy's you know how he operates. If I said I wanted to be in the Peace Corps he'd fix it with President Johnson, or at least try."

"Well, I don't know about that, but your father was a very good friend of mine when we were younger. Not that I've seen him in—oh, dear, before you were born."

"Oh, I know that. It's been Mrs. Castleton ever since I can remember."

"What's been Mrs. Castleton?"

"Daddy's girl friend."

"But your father and mother are still married, aren't they?"

"Of course. Mummy's not giving up all that loot, and why should she? Could I have another one of these? I'll get it, don't you bother."

"Well, yes. You may have to finish it at the table."

"Do you want to bet?" The girl took her glass to the portable bar. "First Mummy said they'd stay married till after I came out, although why that's important even in Baltimore. But then I came out, and nothing more was heard about a divorce. If Aunt Dorothy wanted him to get a divorce he'd get it, but being Dorothy Castleton is still a little bit better socially than being Dorothy Blackwell. And they're all old."

"Yes, we are."

"I didn't mean that personally, Miss Livingston."

"I don't know how else you could mean it, considering that I'm the same age as your father and mother. I don't know about Mrs. Castleton, of course."

"Same age. All in their late fifties or early sixties, I guess. Anyway, not exactly the *jeunesse dorée*."

"No. Well, Baltimore doesn't seem to be very different from any place else, does it? And meanwhile, your father asked me to have a talk with you about the theater. Which I'm very glad to do. But *you. You* don't seem to have any burning, overwhelming desire to become an actress."

"I couldn't care less, frankly. It's Daddy that as soon as I mentioned the theater—"

"How did you happen to mention it, though?"

"How did I happen to mention it? Well, I guess I said I wanted to do *something*, but when it came down to what I could do, we exhausted all the possibilities except riding in horse shows and modeling."

"So naturally you thought of going on the stage."

"No, I didn't. That was Daddy's idea. This whole thing was his idea. I think he just wanted to name-drop that he knew you. I have no delusions about being an actress, for Christ's sake."

Irene went to the door to admit the waiter with the rolling table.

"You would have lost your bet," said the girl. "I won't have to finish my drink at the table."

"Well, then, it isn't a question of my using my influence to get you into the American Academy or anything like that," said Theresa. "I must say I'm relieved. I certainly wouldn't want to deprive a girl of a chance that really cared about the theater."

"Forget it. I'm sorry I wasted your time, but it wasn't all my fault. Daddy's a powerhouse, and when he gets an idea he keeps after you till you give in."

"Shall we sit down? Why don't you sit there, and I'll sit here," said Theresa.

They took their places at the table, but the girl obviously had no intention of touching her melon. "Would you rather have something else?" said Theresa. "Tomato juice, or something like that? We wouldn't have to send downstairs for it."

"No thanks."

"We're having eggs Benedict," said Theresa.

"Eggs Florentine, ma'am," said Irene.

"Don't worry about me," said the girl.

"Have you had any breakfast, other than a vodka martini?" said Theresa. "Why don't you have a cup of coffee?"

"Where's the bathroom?" said the girl.

"Will you show her the bathroom, Irene?"

"Yes, ma'am."

"Just tell me where it is, don't come with me," said the girl.

"Through that door, which leads to the bedroom. And the bathroom you can find," said Theresa.

"The eggs Florentine," said the girl. "Eggs anything." She left the room quickly.

"I hope she makes it," said Irene.

"Yes," said Theresa. "I think you'd better move this table out in the hall. Leave the coffee. I'll have some myself, now, and you might make some fresh, Irene."

"You're not gonna eat *any* lunch?"

"No."

"Nine dollars, right down the drain."

"I know, but I'm not hungry, so don't force me."

Theresa had two cups of coffee and several cigarettes. "I think I ought to go in and see how she is," she said.

"You want me to?" said Irene.

"No, I will," said Theresa.

She went to the bedroom, and the girl was lying on the bed, clad in her slip, staring at the ceiling. "Do you want anything, Evelyn?"

"Yes," said the girl.

"What?"

"Can I stay here a while?"

"Child, you can stay here as long as you like," said Theresa Livingston.

I Spend My Days in Longing

IT WAS bad enough to feel lousy when you knew what was wrong with you, knew that something was wrong with you, but none of the doctors he had seen could find anything wrong—organically, at least. The lungs, okay; the ticker, okay. Go easy on the cigarettes and coffee, they said. Be better if he did not drink so much brandy. But they were just whistling "Dixie," and they knew it and he knew it. He was a transient patient, a one-shot visitor to the offices of hotel doctors, mostly, from Boston to San Francisco. He would get an appointment, usually through the desk clerk, and half the time he would be the only patient in the reception room, the only *person* in the reception room, because hotel doctors did not have much of a setup. Two little rooms on the mezzanine, nobody in the reception room, a sign that said to push the button and be seated. The doc would open the door of his private office, come out and hand him a form to fill out which would provide his name and occupation, age, health record, married or single, by whom recommended. "I'll be with you in just a moment," the doc would say, and go back to his private office while Jimmy filled out the form. The form was all part of the act, like the doctor's pretending to be busy. You got inside the private office and the doc would give you a hard look. It was, it had become, a recognizable look, from coast to coast. As soon as they saw that his occupation was musician they would try to anticipate his request for heroin. Some of them were very quick about it. "Musician, eh? With a jazz band? Well, if you're sick, that's one thing, but if you came here hoping to get some dope you came to the wrong man." By the time they got through examining him they would know he was not a drug addict, but they were not all convinced that he had not been sent to get some dope for a friend. But they found nothing wrong with him, and they did not try to understand why a fairly healthy young man should want to spend ten dollars because he felt low all the time. "What you probably need more than anything I can prescribe is a night in bed with a woman," some of them had said. "How long since you've been laid?"

In reply he had once lied to the doc. "I guess it's close on to three years, Doctor."

"Three years? Why? Did you get burned?"

"No, I guess I just didn't find the right girl," Jimmy said.

"Listen, the right girl for you is the one that will get in bed with you. You're a good-looking young fellow, shouldn't have any trouble. Did you happen to notice the girl behind the cigar counter downstairs?"

"No."

"Well, instead of giving me ten dollars you should have given it to her. She'd be good for what ails you. If you want me to I'll give her a ring right now and introduce you to her over the phone. From then on it's up to you, but that's my advice. Take her out to dinner, get a few drinks in her. Straight gin is what she likes. And for the price of a good meal, a young fellow like you she'd most likely take you back to her apartment and she'd forget about the money."

"I have to work tonight. We're playing at some park and we have to be there at ha' past eight."

"Oh, all right. If you're afraid of women," said the doc.

"Yeah, I guess that's it, Doctor. But thanks anyway."

"You *have* had intercourse, haven't you?"

"Oh, sure. I was married four times. But that's all they want, women. They want to go to bed all the time, and it's all they ever talk about."

"Well, what do *you* want to talk about?"

"My hobby."

"What's your hobby?"

"Crocheting. I do beautiful work."

"Oh, you think you're funny. Well, let me tell you something, young fellow, you may not be as funny as you think."

"I am so, you old doctor you. So long, pal."

His musician friends blamed his depressions on his choice of instrument. A bass player, unless he happened to be a Steve Brown, never got any recognition outside the business. There were jokes about oboe players, that the instrument made them screwy. But the musicians had a theory that a man had to have a few screws missing to take up the bass fiddle in the first place. Steve Brown had recently gone from Goldkette to Whiteman, not only because he was a good musician but because he was a showman. The people who went to hear orchestras as much as to dance to them had begun to catch on to Steve Brown, and college boys were buying bull fiddles and imitating Steve's slap. But until Steve's new popularity a bass player might as well have been playing for his own amusement. He lugged that cumbersome instrument around and he and it were the butt of jokes about the doghouse. The more reliable he was, the less likely it would be that anyone but a musician would appreciate how good he was. The sound was there, the *music* was there, but if it was not unobtrusive it was disturbing. The arrangers for the big bands had got away from the Sousaphone and the tuba and were writing parts for the bass fiddle, but the bass player got no solo. "You're like a left fielder against a ball club that's all lefties," said Jimmy's friend Percy Ballard, the trumpet player. "You're just standing there, and nobody paying a God damn bit of attention. You used to play a little tenor sax, around the edges. Why don't you give up the box and take up the saxophone again? There's worse tenor players than you making a living."

"You don't understand, Percy," said Jimmy. "I don't like the tenor sax. I don't like what comes out of it. Anyway, not when I play it. And I do like the bass viol. I like what comes out of it. Voom. Voom-voom-voom. No noodling. I hate noodling. I'd sooner work in the post office than play saxophone. I'd sooner get a job with the National Biscuit Company."

"What doing?"

"At the National Biscuit Company? I don't know. Whatever they had for me."

"No, you don't wanta go there, Jim. You wouldn't be able to stand it for long. That would tell on you in no time. My brother had a job like that one time."

"What was he doing?"

"I don't know, but boy, he hated it. But you're down there all the time with the bass. You know? You don't get up."

"I get up as high as I want to. That's as high up as I want to get. You know who I don't like? I never knew her personally, but Lily Pons."

"Oh, yes."

"Or Harry Goldfield. Or Busse."

"What about me, Jim? I get up there."

"Well, what the hell? You're a friend of mine."

"Armstrong?"

"Singing. On the vocal I like him, but when he gets up there I want to go away."

"He's good, Jim. Honest he is."

"All right, but I don't like it when you guys get up there. Why do you have to? You know, they got a dog whistle that you and I can't hear. Only dogs can hear it."

"I heard about it. I was thinking of buying one."

"Yeah, but what if you learned to play it? Busse couldn't hear you. Goldfield couldn't hear you. I can tune my bass a little lower and play the bottom string open and that'd be the same idea as you playing that dog whistle, but you could *hear* me."

"Not if you tune it too low. The string'll be too loose, you won't get any sound."

"I could make the box bigger. I'd get a sound."

"Well, there's no use talking to you, Jim. Down there is where you like it."

"But I don't like to *be* there all the time," said Jimmy.

"Why don't you buy yourself a little tin flute at the dime store? Then when you're in the dumps maybe you could play yourself out of it on the flute?"

"Why don't I buy myself a kazoo and go to work with the Mound City Blue Blowers? I go around and see all these doctors and they all tell me there's nothing wrong with me. I guess I'm intended to be this way, but that don't say I have to like it."

"The broads go for it, I'll say that much," said Percy.

"That isn't much of a compliment, when you look at some of the guys broads go for. Who's the ugliest man you can think of, quick?"

"No doubt about it, Ernie Mundy."

"That's who I was thinking of. Who's the handsomest?"

"The handsomest? Hard to say. Smith Ballew. Or maybe a young guy from Yale, plays saxophone."

"You mean Vallee?"

"No, this is another fellow. I don't remember his name."

"Well, I'll bet he can't compare with Ernie Mundy when it comes to the broads."

"Nobody compares with Ernie. And a drummer, at that," said Percy.

"That's what I mean. He's ugly, and he isn't even a musician. But wherever he goes they line up for him. They follow him. There was two of them followed him from Mahanoy City, P A, to Cincinnati in a car. A red Jordan Playboy. He couldn't get rid of them. Or was it Dayton? No, Cincinnati."

"I remember one that followed you, Jim," said Percy.

"Yeah, but that was one. Two followed Ernie, both in the same car. You'd think they'd fight over him. Jealous. But they were the best of friends. Broads go for ugly trap drummers, they go for leaders that can't read a note. They go for singers that sit there with a prop guitar. And they go for me."

"Well, is that bad?"

"It's not bad. But it isn't good. I used to think when I was a young kid around sixteen, my idea of heaven would be a job with a name band and a Marmon, and a different broad every night."

"I remember that Marmon you had."

"I bought it for eighteen hundred dollars, a place up near Columbus Circle. It had a crack in the engine block, but I sold it to a fellow played trombone with Fletch. I got what I paid for it."

"It was a beautiful car. You had it that summer you were in Atlantic City."

"I had to put in four quarts of oil every time I took it out, but in those days I used to think you had to do that with every big car. I soon found out."

"It was a yellow roadster. I envied you that car. Do you remember that yellow Rolls-Royce George Mingo had in L.A.?"

"No."

"It belonged to some movie star, formerly. George paid six thousand for it."

"George Mingo never had six thousand dollars."

"Yes he did. He won it in a crap game—and he lost it in a crap game."

"How much was he shooting for?"

"I wasn't there, but I know that's how he lost it. He was cleaned, and the guy with the dice said, 'So much open,' and George threw in the keys of his Rolls-Royce. 'You're faded,' he said, and the guy rolled a natural."

"I wish I would of been there. George Mingo was the worst

guy to work for I ever saw. The union should have took away his card. He owed everybody. I was working for scale, but he still held out on me. The hell with George Mingo. I hope he croaks."

"He did."

"What? Croak?"

"Sure. Didn't you hear about George?"

"No."

"Do you want to hear about him?"

"If it's bad, I do," said Jimmy.

"Well, I guess it was bad enough," said Percy. "They operated on him for a brain tumor, and he never came to."

"Maybe that's what I have. How do they know if you have a brain tumor?"

"You got me. I guess you get dizzy or something."

"He was plenty dizzy all right."

"Compared to some we know he wasn't so dizzy."

"When did he check out?"

"You're asking me when he checked out, but I couldn't tell you that, Jim. I'm no good on dates. Last year, I guess it was. He had a band was playing in some hotel in Chicago."

"We're in Chicago," said Jimmy. "That's where we are now."

"You're right," said Percy. "When I get talking to you I always think we're back in New York."

"No. Chicago. You're at the Edgewater Beach, and I'm at the Drake."

"Oh, I know, once we get it straightened out that we're in Chicago I know where I'm working. Anyway, they operated on him and he never came to."

"Well then I guess I'll wait till we go to Kansas City. It'd be just my luck to draw the same doctor that operated on George."

"You don't have no brain tumor, Jimmy."

"How can you say that when I don't even know it myself?" He smoothed down the hair on the top of his head.

"What are you, feeling for a lump? It's inside. I know that much. It don't show up in a lump."

"Where's Janet living now?"

"George's wife? As far as I know she was in Chicago the last I heard, but that was last year sometime. The union would probably know. Or look up some of the band bookers if you want to get in touch with her. Al Rosen was booking George the last heard."

"Did he book him into the hospital? I know Al. He probably took his end off the doctor. Fifteen percent of what the doc charged for the operation."

"I wouldn't put it past him. He sure as hell didn't get any money when George checked out. George was in him for plenty."

"That's the best news I heard all day. Six for five."

"Huh?"

"Al. You could always put the arm on Al as long as you paid him his rate. Six dollars a week for five he loaned you. And you paid up or you got a broken arm. You think he had George insured?"

"How would I know that? I wouldn't want to know it. This is a town where I don't want to know anything. In New York the hoods don't bother us much, but here they're there to meet you when you get off the bus. Protection. Not only us. The big stars from show business, right down the line."

"Yeah, well that's why I always ask for more money when I'm booked into Chicago."

"Right down the line and every whichway. Even Al has to pay protection, or that's what I was told. Dog eat dog, here, boy."

"Did Janet get fat? She had a tendency to get fat. If she wasn't working she'd sit around all night, putting away the grog. A lot of those girls, they sing it off. As long as they're working they can keep the weight down, but as soon as they lay off they sit around all night, drinking drink for drink with the guys, and then they have a hard time getting rid of the lard. It affected her disposition, too. The fatter she got the worse dispositioned she was. As long as she could get up there and sing, she was all right. But when she married Mingo he made her quit her job, and I didn't want to be around her then."

"Mingo didn't want you around her, maybe."

"That's for sure."

"She oughtn't to married George. If she was gonna marry anybody she oughta married you, Jim."

"Why do you say that?"

"That's what everybody said."

"How could I marry Janet when I had a wife in New York?"

"Only you didn't have a wife in New York," said Percy.

"Well, she wasn't my wife but I was paying her alimony—when I paid it. That's why I had to stay out of New York nearly two years. Sophie wanted to put me in jail for back alimony."

"They always want to put you in jail. How can you make any money in jail? I had the same trouble."

"That's right. They always want to put you in jail."

"Getting even with you. Revenge," said Percy.

"Yeah, but not the money angle. They want to put you away where you can't get in the hay with another woman. It isn't the money angle, Percy. Sophie had plenty of money. Her first husband left her a bundle."

"I didn't know that."

"A bundle," said Jimmy. "You never knew Sophie. She was ten years older than me."

"I knew she was older. I didn't know that much."

"Ten years. And she watched me like a hawk. She wasn't so old. Thirty-four when I was twenty-four, but she was ten years older. If I wanted to step out I had to plan it like I was gonna hold up a bank. Then half the time she outsmarted me. She used to belt me all over the place."

"A big broad?"

"Not so big, but I was never a fighter. I never heard anybody say anything to me that made me want to fight them. If I got sore at somebody I'd hit him with a music stand, maybe, but you'd never catch me in any fist fight. Supposing I hit a guy with my left hand and broke a finger? Where would I be for the coffee and cakes? Up the creek is where I'd be. Sophie used to belt me around all over the place, and I always used to put my left hand under my right arm."

"Didn't you ever hit her back?"

"No. I'd just wait till she got tired. I will say this for her. Every time she gave me a thumping, the next day she'd go down to Cartier's and buy me some present."

"To remember it by?"

"Right. If I would have been a little smarter I would of cheated more and got caught, because she'd give me a beating and the next day buy me a present. You know when I finally

powdered out on her I had a boxful of stuff. I had one set of
studs and cuff links I got eight hundred dollars for, which'll
give you an idea how much they cost her new."

"Three or four gees, I imagine."

"Easily," said Jimmy. "It's all gone now, though. I don't have
any of it left. Now I understand the shoe is on the other foot.
She gets thumped around. She married her brother-in-law, the
brother of her first husband. He married her to get hold of
the stock in the family business. You wouldn't think a dame as
smart as that would be so stupid, but she was. She thought she
was gonna take him, but he took her, and when he don't like
something he works her over. She called me up one night in
St. Paul and talked long distance for three hours. She wanted
me to take her back. She said she was all covered with bruises.
What the hell would I want with a broad that was all covered
with bruises? That used to work me over and tried to get me
put in jail? You know what?"

"What?"

"She said she knew I really loved her, because she found out
she really loved me."

"What did you tell her?"

"I said I'd be in New York on the next train. Not the next
train, but to meet the Broadway Limited two days later. For all
I know she's still waiting."

"You never heard from her again?"

"No, but she'll show up someplace. I hope I see her first."

"Maybe she's why you got the miseries all the time."

"No, I had them before I ever knew her."

"When did you start getting them? When did you begin to
notice it first?"

"I don't know. They came on me gradually. You know there's
not many arrangements I have to read. Give me the key and I
don't care if it's a tune I never heard before, I can fake, because
what I fake is probably what they got written down anyway.
But when I was with Charley Van he had a piano player named
Augie Gunsel or something like that—"

"Augie Gundle. I know the guy. A bald-headed queen."

"That's the guy. Fancied himself as an arranger, and he wrote
an arrangement of 'Body and Soul' that Johnny Green would

have shot him dead. You know the release in 'Body and Soul,' ya da da dada, da dada, da dada, da dada, da da da da—"

"Ya da da dada, da *dada*, da dada, da dada, da dada, da da da da da. I know it, sure," said Percy. "Great."

"Yeah, but pretty tough. I mean, it's not 'Always,' or 'My Blue Heaven.' But to make it tougher, this Augie has a key change in the middle of the release."

"No! But yeah, I could see where he'd put it."

"Sure you can. But I'd always forget it, so the second part of the release I was playing one clinker after another. I stayed with the same key, and the guys in the brass section would hunch up their shoulders as if I was sticking pins in them. And I don't blame them. It sounded just as bad to me."

"But you had the miseries before that, Jim."

"Right, I did. But that was the first time I began to think I was slipping. I couldn't even play that arrangement if I had it in front of me. We got a lot of requests for the number, it was brand-new, but I told Charley, I said if he didn't want me to louse it up I had to be tacit. So you know Charley, good-natured and kind of sloppy, he said all right, I didn't have to play it. With four in the brass, four in the reeds, piano, guitar, and drums, he had enough volume. It was a small room, too. Maybe the size of the Roosevelt Grill."

"And that's when you began to think you were slipping?"

"As best I can remember. Oh, I was going to doctors before that, shelling out a sawbuck to be told there was nothing wrong with me. But I got plenty wrong with me, Perce. I got no life in me any more. I'm thirty-one years of age and I'm like I was eighty."

"You never tried muggles, or sniffed?"

"I'd be afraid to. I smoked a couple reefers when I was first getting started, but they scared me and I only got sick. I guess what scared me was seeing guys that had to have a drag after every set. Brandy don't seem to have much effect on me, but a couple of guys tell me that's when I better watch out. Maybe they're right. I don't know. You notice I never get stewed, but I wouldn't want to go to bed at night if I didn't have, oh, five or six of these."

"How about in the mornings, when you wake up?"

"One is enough. I only need the one, then I can go all day without it. I don't miss it till I'm through work."

"It's supposed to be very bad for the ticker, brandy," said Percy.

"No, the only time I notice it is if I'm somewhere and I have to go to bed without it. Boy, then the ticker is thumping away and I get these nightmares."

"Did you ever mention that to any of these doctors?"

"Why the hell should I? They'd only tell me to lay off the brandy, and what the hell do they care if I wake up with the sheet wrapped around my neck? You know, I made pretty good money since I was eighteen years of age. I been all over this country three or four times, and to Europe twice. Broads, I had the best in the world. All kinds, shapes, and colors. And the kind of work I like to do, the only kind of work I could do. Could you see me opening up a store every morning at eight A.M., and going around with a feather duster? My parents owned a shoe store, and that's what I was supposed to do, run a shoe store in North Philly, only I had an aunt that paid for my music lessons. Violin and piano. I took both."

"I didn't know you played piano."

"Well, if you heard me you wouldn't feel sorry for Phil Ohman or any of those, but I can play everything but trum-*bone*. My arms aren't long enough for trum*bone*. I can play your instrument, Percy. You never knew that, either."

"No, I never knew that."

"I don't have a lip any more, but I played cornet in high school. Hated it."

"You play guitar?"

"Guitar, tenor banjo. Dick McDonough recommended me for a job one time."

"And you stupid bastard, you end up a bass player."

"No, that's not how I end up. I end up playing nothing, not even the kazoo. One of these days I'm just gonna walk out after a set, and I'm not coming back. I give myself till about the sixteenth of August, 1935."

"And what'll you do then?"

"That'll be my thirty-fifth birthday. Number thirty-five in the old book."

"What are you going to do?"

"Well, I'll tell you, because you wouldn't try to stop me. I'm going to hire a rowboat and go out as far as I can and jump in. I can't swim."

"You figure thirty-five is all you ever want to be?"

"Thirty-one is all I want to be, but I'll give it four more years."

"Well, I don't know, Jim," said his friend. "I thought of it sometimes, too."

"Yeah, whenever you think about playing Mahanoy City again."

"Mealey's, in Allentown."

"Bach's, in Reading."

"That one I never played. Reading, I remember a park on top of a mountain. Revere Beach, in Boston."

"That island, in Harrisburg. Maybe I'll be playing Harrisburg. It would save me a lot of trouble. What the hell is that river? The Susquehanna."

"Thirty-five, eh? I'll be that before you will. I'm thirty-three right now. Am I supposed to forget this conversation, Jim?"

"No, if you want to remember it there's nothing wrong with that. But keep it to yourself."

"I won't blab," said Percy.

"I know you won't. And don't even talk about it to me. I'll be seeing you here, and probably New York. Nobody else knows about my intentions, and I don't know why I told you tonight, but somehow we got to talking."

"Yeah, I had a good time tonight," said Percy. "This town gets me down."

"You ever been down to the Stockyards, Perce?"

"No."

"Go down there sometime if you ever want to hear the high note."

"Oh, you mean the pigs?" said Percy.

"I sure as hell mean the pigs."

"My high note don't sound like that."

"All high notes sound like that to me."

"Well, that thing you play sounds like a grunt."

"To you I guess it does. Speaking of grunts, here comes the grunt." A waiter laid their bill on the table. "Let me get this, in honor of the occasion."

"All right, it's yours," said Percy.

They met again, several times in Chicago, frequently in musicians' hangouts in New York and Los Angeles, but they had had their final conversation and they knew it. Percy was therefore solemnly proud on the morning of August 17, 1935, when a telegram was delivered to him, which read, "Thanks for not blabbing." It was signed Jimmy, and it was sent from Cincinnati. Cincinnati, of course, is on the Ohio River.

I Can't Thank You Enough

ARTHUR FELZER stopped at the desk, and allowed the woman behind him to get ahead of him. She said whatever she had to say to the clerk and moved on.

"Yes, Mr. Felzer?" said the clerk.

"I'm gonna be checking out of 1214 and will you have my bill ready?" said Felzer.

"We'll send it to you, as usual," said the clerk.

"No, no. This one I want to pay cash," said Felzer.

"Cash? Well, I guess we're always glad to accept cash," said the clerk. "Your bill'll be ready whenever you come down. You have no extra charges since breakfast, Mr. Felzer?"

"No, I don't think so. Since breakfast. Maybe some phone calls. I tell you, Ray. Let me pay the bill now, and I'll give you a few bucks in case there was any charges since breakfast."

"You don't have to do that, Mr. Felzer. We'll bill you or carry it over, whatever you like."

"No, let's do it my way, Ray. I don't want this bill sent to my office. I'll give you, oh, say twenty dollars and you take care of any phone calls or anything since breakfast. What's left over, you can have that for yourself. Buy yourself a couple neckties, maybe. I don't want to have to stop here on my way out."

"I see," said the clerk. "Will I have them bring your car around?"

"Yeah, would you do that, Ray?" said Felzer. "And have the boy take the luggage out to the car."

"I'll send one right up. You be ready to go in about how long?"

"Oh, a half an hour, maybe less. How much do I owe you?"

The clerk stepped to the cashier's cage and asked her for the total charges on Room 1214. "Ninety-four sixty-two," she said.

"Ninety-four sixty-two, Mr. Felzer."

"Ninety-four sixty-two. Well, all right, here's a hundred and twenty, Ray. You take care of everything for me?"

"Yes indeed, and thank you very much, Mr. Felzer. Hurry back, as they say down South."

"Right," said Felzer. "Oh, I'll leave the key with the bellboy."

He went to his room and let himself in. She was sitting in the easy chair, reading a newspaper. She had on a skirt and shirtwaist, and the jacket that matched the skirt was hanging on the desk chair. "Hello," she said.

"Good, you're all ready," he said.

"Oh, sure. I've been ready for about a half an hour or so."

"I'm a little later than I said I'd be, but I got tied up," he said.

"That's perfectly all right," she said. "Gave me a chance to read the paper. I don't often read the paper at breakfast except on Sundays."

"No, I guess not. What time do you have to be at work?"

"Well, that depends. School starts at nine and we're supposed to be there at eight-thirty. But we take turns getting there at eight."

"Eight A.M., I guess that's pretty rough, eh?" he said.

"Yes, but fortunately it's only every ninth week. Did you get everything accomplished?"

"Yes, more or less."

"I was still asleep when you left. That's very unusual for me, to sleep past eight o'clock, even on Sunday. You must have had breakfast downstairs."

"A cup of coffee around the corner. I don't ordinarily eat a very big breakfast."

"Neither do I, but I did this morning. I had everything. A *big* glass of orange juice. Two poached eggs. Toast. Marmalade. And two cups of coffee. And I haven't got a hangover. I thought I might have one, but I didn't. Did you?"

"Well, maybe a little one. Nowadays when I get up in the morning I often have a hangover and I didn't do any drinking the night before. Are you all packed?"

"Just to put a few things in, hairbrush and things. I notice your bag is ready. I'll be ready in less than a minute. I won't hold you up."

"That's all right," he said.

She went to the bathroom and closed the door, and came out presently with a plastic toilet kit in her hand. She put the kit in her suitcase and closed it, and her fingers lingered on the bag.

"Trying to remember if you forgot something?" he said.

"No. Just thinking," she said.

"What?"

"Oh, I don't know," she said.

"Sure you do," he said.

"Yes. I was thinking as I closed the bag, I was closing a chapter in my life."

"Oh," he said.

"Wasn't a very long chapter, was it?" she said.

"Well, who said it was over?"

"Who had to? We both know it," she said. "Well, I'm ready whenever you are."

"Boy'll be here any minute."

"I guess we just have to wait for him," she said. She sat down and lit a cigarette. "I was wondering, Arthur. Don't you think it'd be better if I met you somewhere outside? I really don't want to stand in the lobby while you're paying the bill."

"That's all taken care of," he said. "I paid the bill on my way up, and we don't have to hang around. The car'll be waiting outside. Do you want to go down and wait in the car? I'll take care of the bags."

"Would you mind if I did that?"

"Hell, no. You know the car."

"You're very considerate. I can't thank you enough."

"You didn't expect it from Arthur Felzer, did you?"

"It isn't you, it's anybody. I don't think men *are* very considerate as a rule."

"Well, I don't know. Some are, and some aren't."

"Well, you happen to be one of those that are," she said.

"And you're surprised. You forget, Jane. I had a lot of experiences since I used to work for your father. Two years in college, an officer in the war. *I* stayed in some of the finest homes in England. And I made a bundle of dough."

"Papa said you would, too," she said.

"Well, he was all right, Mr. Campion. He sent me a copy of the letters he wrote when I used him for a reference. College *and* the Air Force. Maybe I wasn't as honest as he said I was, but I was neat and orderly. What else did he say I was? Energetic. *Diligent!* That's the word I was trying to think of. You know, some son of a bitch when we were in England, if you left anything lying around they'd go through your private papers. Letters and all. And some bastard came across the copy of the letter your father wrote, so for a while there the guys called me the diligent bombardier. The diligent bombardier. But that nickname didn't last very long. They didn't either, the guys that called me that. You know I was tempted to send your father my first Air Medal, but my mother would have killed me."

"Oh, he would have been so pleased," she said.

"Well, I figured the old lady was entitled to it. Then when we got the D.F.C. I *couldn't* send *that* to your father. That *had* to be for my old man. So I guess I never showed your father any appreciation."

"That's not why he helped you. He didn't expect anything in return."

"He sure as hell wouldn't think *this* was showing any appreciation," he said.

"Taking his innocent daughter to a hotel in Philadelphia? I don't think he had any illusions about me. I often caught him looking at me, trying to puzzle me out. He—"

"That's the boy for the bags," said Felzer. "You go on down and get in the car. I'll stall this guy."

She was sitting in the car when he showed up with the luggage. He tipped the doorman and they drove away. "We had a narrow escape," she said.

"How do you mean?" he said.

"I'd just got in the car and was lighting a cigarette when who do you suppose came out of the hotel and *stood* there, waiting for a taxi? Albert Stout."

"Yeah, he always stays there. Did he recognize you?"

"No, fortunately. I sat with my cigarette in my hand, over my face."

"Well, that'd be all over town by tomorrow night, if he recognized you."

"Do you think he could have seen us last night?"

"Not Albert," said Feltzer. "He doesn't hit the hot spots. He wouldn't spend a nickel if he could help it. Were you scared?"

"Well, startled," she said. "What would your wife do?"

"My wife? You know what she'd probably do? She'd probably go somewhere and buy herself a new fur coat."

"Oh. What if she knew it was me?" she said.

He smiled. "If she knew it was you? If she knew it was you I guess maybe she'd buy two fur coats. I don't know."

"And that's all? She wouldn't go see a lawyer?"

"No. I got her old man working for me, and her brother. She's got her own car, a nice home. She isn't giving all that up because I took a girl to Philly."

"A girl," she said. "You know how old I am, Arthur. But thanks for the compliment."

"Well, a woman. Any female."

They were silent until he got out of the midtown traffic.

"If you turned left up here," she said, "I could show you where I went to school."

"You want to do that?" he said.

"Oh, no. I was just thinking how this city's changed. All these new highways and boulevards. I just happened to recognize that bridge. I was there for four years, and I've never gone back."

"Do you want to have a look at it? We have plenty of time. I was thinking we'd get out of town and then stop some place for lunch."

"No, I have no feelings about the school. That's all past history, all of that."

"Yeah, I guess it is or you wouldn't be sitting here. You know, Jane, I got a confession to make. You know when I asked you if you'd go with me, on this trip, I didn't expect you to say yes."

"Well, I was a little surprised to hear myself saying yes, but I popped right out with it, didn't I?"

"Yes. Right away I thought, Jesus, I should have asked her ten-fifteen years ago, or more. Except then I guess you would have said no."

"Then I would have said no. I had someone else I was in love with."

"A married man?"

"Well, he *got* married. I guess he must have found out about my father's financial condition. That's a nasty thing to say, but I'm afraid it's true. A lot of things changed for us then. I certainly never thought I'd become an old-maid schoolteacher. I only took that job for a year, so I wouldn't have to take any money from my mother. And now I've been at it, this is my twenty-third year."

"And my kid went there. Boy, I was surprised when they let her in."

"You needn't have been. She was a perfectly nice little girl, and you have all that money."

"There's some things we're kept out of," he said.

"Well, maybe they're not worth getting into, Arthur. I hope you don't fret over them."

"I don't, but Leonia does."

"You're speaking of the Tuesday Club?" she said.

"Yeah, she never even heard about it till we joined the country club. Then she said well if we were good enough to join the country club, why didn't we get invited to the Tuesday? I said what did she want to get invited to the Tuesday Club for?"

"Actually, you know there is no such thing as the Tuesday Club any more. They stopped being a club a long time ago. It's just a group of people that have dinner together."

"Sure, but always the same people."

"Well, yes, but as long as they don't call themselves a club she doesn't have to feel that she's being kept out of anything."

"Who are you kidding? That makes it so much worse, for her."

"Well, *that's* too bad, because that's one group that will never change. They'll die off, maybe, but you have to be at least a cousin to get invited now."

"She hates them. I said to her, what did she want to have dinner with a lot of people she hated."

"And now she'd hate one of them more than ever, if she knew."

"Yes, she would."

"Did you ever hate us, Arthur?" she said.

"Did I ever hate you? Candidly, not till the first Christmas I came home from State. They had some dance and I got an invitation, but I didn't get invited any place for dinner. And I figured out I was one of the suckers. They invited us to pay ten dollars a head for the dance, so they could hire a name band. But all they cared about was our ten bucks. Glen Gray, or somebody, they got. But they didn't get me again. You were at that dance, Jane."

"Was I? I suppose I was. At the hotel?"

"At the hotel. I went over and cut in on you, and the guy you were dancing with said no cutting in. A God damn lie. Everybody was cutting in. But I was a meatball. No meatballs cutting in on your crowd. Ed Stokes, Junior. That was who was dancing with you. Was that who didn't marry you when your father went bust?"

"Yes," she said.

"Kind of figured it was," he said. "Well, the poor son of a bitch, I guess when you have one of those dinners you have to serve him milk."

"Yes, when he comes at all. They took out part of his stomach, you know."

"Yeah, I heard. The son of a bitch. No stomach, married the wrong girl, lost over eighty-five thousand dollars on that motel he put up. I said to him at the time, I said 'Ed, for Christ's sake, take a look around at some of the other motels.' I said you drive around at night and all you see is the neon signs, vacancy, vacancy, vacancy. So he blew over eighty-five thousand dollars. How I happen to know that, they asked me to come in for a one-quarter piece, the same as Ed. I said, 'Gentlemen, I'll wait two years and pick up the whole thing for eighty-five.' Oh, Christ, were they sore at me. But I got news for you. I could get it for sixty, and I don't want it. Fifty is all I'd give them. It's worth it to me. Not for the motel. Oh, no. But they got the land, all graded and all, and the water lines are in. Electricity. Black-top parking space. Filling station. I'll give them fifty, and then I'll go to town, with a supermarket *and* a bowling alley. That's why I was in Philly this time. Lining up some of the concessions for the supermarket. The fellow I talked to this morning, you think the women go to the supermarket to buy meat and vegetables. Canned goods. Well, sure they do. But this morning I was talking to the fellow that wants the drug and cosmetics concession. Once I got him signed, I'm going after some of the smaller ones. Like I got a guy, he won't use much more space than the front seat of this car, but I'm gonna sign him for the watch repair concession. Not big, you know, but it all adds up. When I was out in Vegas a couple years ago, you know if I could put in just penny and nickel slot machines I'd coin money, but I can't do that here. They got the slot machines next to the cashier's counter, and all the small change goes into the one-armed bandits. It breaks your heart to think how much money I have to pass up."

"How do you make your money now, Arthur? I know it's something to do with real estate."

"Jane, I got so many irons in the fire. Real estate, yes. But I don't limit myself to real estate. How much do you know about depreciation, tax-wise?"

"Nothing."

"Then I'd have a hard time explaining it to you. What it amounts to, I can own a property and over twenty years the depreciation works out so I can sell the property and it's all gravy. I'm not going to try to explain it to you."

"No, don't. It's too depressing."

"Yeah, but not to me. I own a record shop, where the beat-niks buy rock-and-roll. I got an interest in a drive-yourself car rental. This car we're in now, the registration isn't in my name. If Leonia wants to get even with me and hit me with two fur coats, I don't get them wholesale. I do better than that, or the furrier has to pay his rent on time. And they don't, you know. They're seasonal. The bill I just paid at the hotel, that's the first time I paid cash at a hotel since I was incorporated. They don't know what cash is at hotels any more. I got Leonia down for manager of the record shop and she never goes near the place. She took a trip to New York to hear those Beatles. Why not? She's in the record business. Rented one of my cars and drove to New York."

"I don't want to hear any more, Arthur. But thanks for paying cash for our bill."

"Oh, well."

"How much was it, may I ask? Do you mind telling me?"

"Ninety-four sixty-two."

"Good Lord! Where did it all go?"

"Well, the room was thirty-five. There's seventy right off. The rest was breakfast, around eight or nine dollars."

"But why did they charge you for two nights? We were only there one."

"I reserved the room for two, in case you could get away the night before last."

"And they made you pay?"

"I didn't make any fuss," he said.

"And it wasn't worth it," she said.

"Well, what the hell, Jane? Yes, it was worth it. Certain things, certain people. If it was just you and me maybe it would have been all right. But we had too many other people in that room with us. Your father. Your mother. I guess probably Ed Stokes."

"No, not Ed Stokes, Arthur."

"Well, I'm glad of that, anyway," he said. "Listen, you don't hear any beef out of me. Maybe if we would of stayed another night it would of been all right. I don't know, Jane. We're not kids."

"I know we're not, and that's what makes it a little worse. I behaved like one. How can a middle-aged spinster behave like a teenager?"

He smiled. "That's not what I hear about teenagers."

"I guess not," she said. "Something you said a minute ago, about depreciation."

He shook his head. "No, you have to own the property twenty years."

"Well, I'll tell you this, Arthur. You own me now more than any man I've ever known."

"No, you don't have to say that, Jane," he said. "Candidly, I'd just as soon we didn't talk about it any more."

"But I would, Arthur," she said. "Don't you see that—do you remember what I said about closing a chapter? In the room?"

"Oh, yes. I remember."

"What I'm afraid of is closing the whole book."

"Yeah, yeah. I see. You don't have to think of it that way."

"But I do. Couldn't we go away again sometime?"

"I'll tell you, Jane," he said. "It's kind of hard for you to get away. The school and your mother and all like that. And I got a kind of a you might call it a commitment. A girl, a young woman lives in Reading. I usually take her on trips once in a while. You know?"

"I know I don't believe you," she said. "I can always tell when my pupils aren't telling the truth, and you're making this up."

"Well, I could tell you her name, but you wouldn't know her."

"Ruth Miller," said Jane.

"I don't know any Ruth Miller."

"Neither do I, but I'm sure there are a lot of Ruth Millers in Reading. Probably a lot of them in Allentown. Lebanon. You've given up on me, haven't you, Arthur? There is no girl in Reading."

"No, there's no girl in Reading. I play the field."

"You don't know what my life is like, do you? You don't know what it is to have been attractive, to have had love affairs. Real love affairs. And then to have it all stop completely, while you teach first and second grade nine months of the year, and take care of a mother that's half dotty. And be a lady, and watch every penny while the Leonia Felzers drive around in fur coats and Cadillacs. Now do you know why I said yes when you asked me to go away with you? No one else had asked me in so long that I had no other answer. And now what? You'll drop me at home, and if anybody shows the slightest interest I can tell them that you gave me a lift from Philadelphia. And they'll believe me. That's all anyone cares. No one would think for a minute that I went away with you or anyone else. Jane Campion, the spinster schoolteacher. Didn't you *want* me to go with you, Arthur?"

"Sure. I asked you, didn't I?"

"Then ask me again," she said.

"No, I don't want to do that."

"All right," she said.

"Wuddia say, shall we see what's on the radio?" he said.

"Yes."

"Any particular station you like?" he said.

"No, I don't hear the radio very often. Mother likes the TV," she said. "And at this time of the day I'm usually in school."

"Is that window too much for you?"

"Not now, but it may be later on," she said. They would be stopping for lunch soon, and she could roll up the window then.

In the Mist

REX SINCLAIR eased the Sixty Special into the garage, put on the brakes, switched off the engine. "Well, you see we made it," he said.

"Yeah, I never thought we would," said Buddy Longden. "For a while there I wished I had my rosary beads."

"You a Catholic?" said Rex Sinclair.

"I used to be, but now I'm nothing."

"I wouldn't say you were nothing," said Rex. "Anybody that can play your kind of piano. I'd rather be able to do that than anything I can think of."

"I'll trade you," said Buddy.

They got out of the car and stood in the driveway. "Ordinarily this is one of the best views around," said Rex. "You can look down that way and you get the famous Los Angeles at night. The magic carpet of lights and so forth. Then over there all the little houses on the mountain. That's a view I like. The lights in the little houses."

"I have to take your word for it tonight," said Buddy.

"Yeah, well you get a fog like this and personally it gives me a wonderful feeling. It gives you a feeling of accomplishment, to be able to do something that there aren't many people can do."

"You mean driving your car home?" said Buddy.

"Don't make it sound like nothing. I'll bet you a thousand dollars to ten that you couldn't take my car and make it back to Hollywood the first try. I'll bet you five hundred to ten you couldn't make it the first try *in daylight*. Don't bet me. I had taxi drivers can't find this place even when they have directions. There's two or three places if you don't make the proper turn, you find yourself back on Franklin. Another place, if you don't make the right turn you find yourself in a dead end and if you're making any kind of speed, you could easily go through the fence and that'd be bye-bye."

"You like that, living so isolated," said Buddy.

"It's not isolated for me. I can be from here to Paramount in under fifteen minutes. I've done it. I can be at Columbia in twelve. I'm not isolated. Christ, I could live in Beverly if I wanted to, but this is what I like. What do you think is on top of that garage?"

"You got me."

"A tennis court. In Beverly if I had a tennis court I'd have to use up land that the taxes are murder. Here I have as big a garage as anybody in Beverly *and* a tennis court, and I'm paying taxes on the same amount of land. Two for the price of one, you might say. We do have one problem here."

"What's that?"

"Rattlesnakes. These mountains are full of them. So here, take a flashlight. I never saw one at night, the nine years I've been living here, but I don't take any chances."

"Jesus, you make me wish I didn't come."

"Don't worry. I always have this, too, and I know how to use it." Rex showed Buddy Longden a .38 caliber Banker's Special.

"How about if we go inside and get a drink?" said Buddy.

"Certainly. I'll lead the way," said Rex.

"You're damn right you will," said Buddy.

The livingroom was large and comfortably furnished. Before the fireplace were two low, deeply upholstered davenports facing each other and a circular table between them. At one end of the room was a card table, with decks of cards and bridge score pads and pencils on it. At the other end was a bar, professionally equipped. The floor was polished hardwood and on it lay rugs of varying dimensions as well as the skins of a white bear and a leopard. In all there were probably two dozen chairs scattered about. The walls were covered with pictures, running largely to blown-up photographs of movie actors and actresses, interspersed with seascapes and detailed paintings of sailboats. An oil portrait of Sinclair in the costume of a captain in the Army-in-India was the only picture with its own illumination. One corner of the room contained a Steinway concert grand, a studio piano, and a set of drums and traps which included a hi-hat and two bongo drums.

"Quite a layout," said Buddy.

"Yeah, when I got rid of Marcy I made this room into a place where I could sit down and relax. She had it all gussied up in case Noël Coward ever came here. But he didn't. She wouldn't have known what the hell to say to him if he had, but that was my life for six years. Waiting for Hollywood society to take us up. Big star, I ought to be in society. She could never understand that. She used to wonder why the hell Cesar Romero got invited to places and I didn't. I never had the answer for that. Pour yourself a drink, have a cigarette, and sit down and play me 'Washboard Blues.'"

"God, I don't know if I know it any more, it's so long since I got a request for it," said Buddy.

"You'll remember it. It'll come back. I heard you play it two years ago at a party at Hank Fonda's. Hell, play anything you like. If you want any help with the lyrics of 'Washboard,' I'm word-perfect in it. Then I'd like you to play 'Blue Lou.' Then 'Stop, Look and Listen.' Then I'll try you on some real oldies."

"That depends on how far back you go," said Buddy.

"'Helen Gone.' You remember that? 'She could dance all night until the dawn? I said dawn.'"

"Fletcher Henderson?"

"I'm not sure," said Rex Sinclair.

"You want to sing, that's it," said Buddy.

"I want to sing, I want to hear you play the piano. Mostly I want to hear you play the piano," said Rex. "Will it bother you if I go along on drums? Just the brushes."

"That depends."

"Oh, don't worry about the beat. I have a solid beat. I come home from the studio some days, have a snort, put on some records, and I can sit here for two hours, just beating it out with the brushes."

"Did you ever do it for a living?"

"High school, I used to play in a little band we had in high school. No union. Two, three dollars a night. Snare, bass, two cymbals, wood block, cowbell. Sixty dollars for the whole set. Ludwig. Maybe it wasn't even sixty dollars. My aunt gave it to me and my old lady wanted to have her put in the insane asylum. But oh, boy, when I got paid real money, two dollars, three dollars. Then the old lady changed her mind."

"With me it was just the opposite. My old lady had me taking lessons from the time I was six years of age," said Buddy. He went to the piano and played a few chords. "After what I'm used to, the action on this is a little stiff."

"But there's nothing the matter with the tone," said Rex.

"No, there sure as hell's nothing wrong with the tone," said Buddy. Out of nowhere he began to play, four repeated chords, some right hand, followed by four repeated chords higher on the scale.

"God damn it, man! I know what that is," said Rex. He sprang to the drums. "It's the verse, the *verse* of 'Stairway to Paradise.'"

Buddy nodded and smiled and went on playing. They played steadily for half an hour, mostly Gershwin, some Porter, some Berlin, some Kern, some Henderson, some Ellington. Rex would suspend the beat of the brushes between pieces until Buddy got into the next tune, then he would pick up the beat and they did not need to speak. At the end of a half hour Buddy lit a cigarette and opened and closed his fists.

"Not used to a good piano," he said.

"Take five, and I'll get you a drink. Take ten," said Rex. "As we used to say, I never had so much fun with clothes on." He poured drinks for Buddy and himself. "Where else have you been since I saw you at Fonda's?"

"Oh, I don't know. Ratting around."

"You don't want to talk?"

"I don't mind talking, but what the hell? I had a couple of club jobs. CBS for a while. Made a few cuts."

"What's that, cuts?"

"Recording dates."

"What's your trouble? The booze?"

"I guess that's what some people would say," said Buddy.

"The broads? *A* broad?"

"Now look, Mr. Sinclair, you promised me a hundred bucks to play piano for three hours, right?"

"In other words, don't get too inquisitive. All right. You ready to play again?"

Buddy took a long sip of his drink and a long drag of his cigarette and turned back to the keyboard. "I remembered 'Washboard,' but let me do it without the brushes, huh?"

"Sure," said Rex.

"I'll do it the way Hoagy did it, but he had a band behind him I think Beiderbecke was in that band if I'm not mistaken. Then I'll do 'In a Mist' for you. That's kind of logical, isn't it?"

"You're the maestro," said Rex.

Buddy did a faithful rendition of "Washboard Blues" and when he had finished the playing and singing he stopped.

"Now 'In a Mist,'" said Rex.

"No more. That's it," said Buddy. "You owe me thirty-three dollars."

"What's the matter, Buddy?"

"I don't know."

"Some kind of a sentimental association?"

"Christ, no. You mean on account of Beiderbecke? The great Bix? I never went for that stuff. That's for guys like you, Mr. Sinclair. Amateur trap drummers. How's for calling me a cab? I'll give you the concert for free."

"You get your hundred," said Rex. "But the cab is another story. Till the fog lifts, you're stuck. Call the taxi company and see what they tell you. I know from experience."

"I'd walk if I wasn't afraid of snakes. Will you lend me your gun?"

"No. You can have a flashlight and I'll give you a cane."

"Like a God damn blind man," said Buddy.

"You want to spend the night in the guest room? There's everything there. Pajamas. New toothbrush. You might as well."

"What are you gonna do? Play records?"

"Well, I was just thinking. I know somebody that can get here in the fog, if she isn't busy."

"Maybe she has a friend," said Buddy.

"Maybe she has, if you want me to ask her."

"How much would this set me back? I'll go for the hundred, but not any more."

"I'll take care of that," said Rex.

"You don't have to do that."

"I don't have to do anything, but I wanted company, so I guess I'm going to have company." Rex went to the telephone, dialed a Crestview number, and waited. "Sandra? Rex. Oh, come on, it isn't all that late. Well, how about getting into your car and—oh, listen, I have a friend of mine here spending the night. Can you persuade a friend of yours to make it a foursome? No, he's not in pictures. I doubt if you'd know him. I'd say he was in his middle thirties. He's a business man. In the piano business. Very important guy in the piano business. Well, if you must know, I met him several years ago at a party at Hank Fonda's. Why all the questions? Well, if she's a new girl she wants to meet all the right people, doesn't she? All right. But you'll have to bring her in your car. The fog is terrific. That's a good girl, Sandra. I'll remember you in my prayers." He hung up. "She has a friend, and they'll be here in about a half an hour. How about a sandwich or something?"

"Who's Sandra?"

"Well, I guess you could gather from the conversation, she's a high-class hooker. She makes more that way than she did in pictures, so that's how she makes it. And it has to be cash with Sandra. No cheques. She doesn't believe in the income tax, and I'm right with her there."

"Who's she getting for me?"

"Some new girl. Lives in the same building as Sandra. That's as much as I can tell you now. You afraid she's going to turn out to be your ex-wife or something?"

"I never said I had an ex-wife," said Buddy.

"No, but you figured to," said Rex.

"You're right. Not one, but two," said Buddy. "But I don't have to worry about them turning up as call girls. One's dead, and the other's married to a trombone player, NBC house band back in New York."

"Which one does 'Washboard' remind you of?"

"The dead one. She liked 'Lazybones,' and there's a part there in 'Washboard' that I'm positive Hoagy took out of 'Washboard' and made into part of the melody of 'Lazybones.'"

"Show me," said Rex.

Buddy looked at him. "You want to get me back to the piano. All right." He sat down and demonstrated his theory of the source of a segment of the "Lazybones" melody. "What else do you want me to play?"

"Nothing, if you don't feel like it."

Buddy turned around on the tufted stool. "You know, this is the first time I was ever in a movie star's home that there wasn't a party going on. I worked for Henry Fonda and Jimmy Stewart and some others, but there was always a lot of people. It's altogether different."

"How do you mean?"

"Well, you. You come into a joint and right away the boss comes over and says it's Rex Sinclair, as if we didn't know. And he says to play show tunes, that you always like show tunes.

Figures you to be good for a hundred bucks or so if you stay a while. So I play some show tunes and you come over and bring your drink over and you *know* it's a lousy piano, so you offer me a hundred bucks and I come up here. Just you and me. You, one of the biggest stars in the movie business. Me, a club piano player."

"Not one of the biggest stars. Not as big as Fonda or Stewart. But steadily employed. I'll work in pictures they wouldn't spit on."

"Well, I don't know about that part of it, but I consider you a big star. And then when I get here we have a session, me on piano and you on drums. Nice. You could never work in a good band, but in about a third-rate band you could get a job. Can you read?"

"Yes, I used to be able to read."

"Your kind of drumming you'd be better off if you couldn't read. Forget about your drum lessons and just fake. You'll loosen up. Get more enjoyment out of it."

"All right. So you were saying how different it is than you expected."

"Well, I wouldn't want to be you. I thought I might be willing to trade places, but you got damn near nothing. This house, and a tennis court on your garage, and three cars inside the garage. But you got damn near nothing. At ha' past four in the morning, you have to call a hooker."

"That's right. That's the story. Half past four in the morning I have to call a hooker."

"So where are you better off than I am?"

"Well, I guess except for the fact that *I* can pay *you* a hundred dollars to play piano for *me*, and another hundred dollars for a hooker, I guess I'm no better off. Does that make you feel better?"

"It sure does. Temporarily," said Buddy. "I got one room down on Melrose. A Chevy coop. At the end of the week I got my bar bill to take out of my pay, so I'm lucky to go home with fifty or sixty dollars. But I don't have to dress up or any of that, and once you're asleep the cotton sheets are just as good as silk."

"Keep talking, if it makes you feel any better. Have a drink," said Rex.

Buddy looked at him with a dead resentment. He suddenly

swung around and played four bars of the fast instrumental part of "Washboard," then abruptly stopped. "*You* can't do that."

"No, and you didn't do it so good then, either," said Rex. "You hit a couple of clinkers. Have a drink, Buddy, and quit trying to make me feel sorry for myself. I'm going out and make a sandwich. You want a sandwich? Come on out and help yourself."

"I'll drink my sandwich," said Buddy.

"You do that," said Rex. He went to the kitchen and made himself a cold roast beef sandwich on rye bread. He sat eating it in the breakfast nook, washing it down with a glass of Dutch beer, and had been gone about ten minutes when the quiet and the calm, a quiet and a calm which seemed to *come from* the livingroom, to emanate from the livingroom, made him wonder what his guest was doing. On a strong impulse he got up, half a sandwich in one hand, beer shell in the other, and went back to the livingroom, making as little sound as possible.

Buddy was standing in front of the portrait, the illuminated one of Rex in a turban and gauntlets and tunic and breeches. Buddy had in his right hand a large pair of library shears.

"What the hell would you want to do that for?" said Rex.

"I don't know. I was just debating whether I ought to," said Buddy. He put the shears back on a table.

"It cost me twenty-five hundred dollars, that picture," said Rex.

"That didn't worry me," said Buddy. He returned to the tufted stool, the only place where he had actually sat since coming to the house.

"It's supposed to be a pretty good portrait. I don't mean of me. But it was a good artist. He died last year up in Carmel. He was supposed to be pretty good. He didn't usually paint portraits of people."

"So you gave him a hundred dollars to play the piano for you," said Buddy.

"I see what you mean," said Rex. "Yes, as a matter of fact. It was something like that. I heard he was on his duff, financially, so I gave him the job. Commissioned him. And I paid for it myself. The studio didn't pay for it. And it's supposed to be pretty good, according to some people in art. But you weren't going to cut it up because you didn't think it was artistic. You wanted to cut *me* up. Why?"

"Because you're a phony. Having your picture painted in that uniform."

"I was pretty good in that picture. That's the closest I ever came to an Academy nomination. The picture got nominated. If it'd been directed by John Ford it probably would have got the Oscar."

"The hell with that. You just wanted to have your portrait painted in that uniform," said Buddy.

"Partly that. But I only got the idea through meeting Ben Leisenring, the artist that painted it."

"You took pity on him," said Buddy.

"Partly that, too. But when he started coming here to do the actual painting, I didn't pity him any more. He was as good in his line as you are in yours. Better, in fact. And he wasn't a sorehead cry-baby. Also he could drink better. He put away a bottle of Martel's every time he came here, and he always left sober. And he knew he was dying. He was here five days a week for almost two months."

"I suppose you gave him two bottles of Martel's for the other two days," said Buddy.

"I guess it amounted to that. I sent him a case of it."

"Another whore. Just like me, or the two broads you got coming tonight."

"Don't put yourself in the same class with Ben Leisenring."

"As a whore, you mean?" said Buddy.

"As a man, as an artist."

"Where would *you* put me? About the same class as you?"

Rex smiled. "Yeah, just about. You're far from a Joe Sullivan, Buddy. And I think I know why you didn't want to play 'In a Mist.' Bix didn't only play it. He *wrote* it. Did you ever hear of Charley Dawes?"

"Yes. He was with Whiteman. He played tenor saxophone."

"Now who's the phony? He was the vice-president of the United States."

"I'm thinking of somebody else. Charley Somebody."

"You had to pretend you knew. You were faking. Charles G.

Dawes, vice-president of the United States. Do you recognize this?" Rex went to the piano and with one finger played thirteen notes.

"'All in the Game,' Tommy Dorsey made a cut of it," said Buddy.

"Yes he did. But the melody was written by Charles G. Dawes, vice-president of the United States."

"Well good for him, and so what? To me it sounds like Rube Bloom. *You* heard of Rube Bloom."

"The way you say it, you expect me to say no. Well, if you're talking about the Rube Bloom that wrote 'Sapphire' and 'Soliloquy,' yes, I heard of him. Buddy, you're just an argumentative, disagreeable sorehead."

"I know I am, and I was supposed to be here as an entertainer. You sure made a bad deal tonight."

"Oh, I don't know. I had about a half an hour's pleasure that first set."

"'That first set.' Greetings, Gate, let's syncopate. You like to talk musician talk. You're hep to the jive, man. Yeah, man. Hep to the jive."

"I'm going to put the lights on for the girls. And you better start getting into a better mood," said Rex. He went to the front hall and switched on the driveway floodlights. "It doesn't help much, but it helps some."

"What's the name of this dame you got for me?"

"I have no idea."

"What if I don't like her?"

"Then you can play gin rummy with her."

"What if I don't like her but I do like this Sandra?"

"Then you can still play gin with the other one. You don't get Sandra. Sandra's a money proposition but I also happen to like her."

"Now I understand you, Mr. Sinclair. If you can buy it, it's fine. A hooker, an oil painter, or a musician."

"No, Buddy, it just happens to work out that way," said Rex. "You're close, but that's not the whole story. *There*, that's Sandra's horn." Rex picked up a flashlight and went out to greet the girls.

He came back with his arms around both girls' shoulders.

"Ladies, this is my friend Mr. Longden, very big in the piano business. This is Sandra, and this young lady is Karen."

"Do you manufacture them, or sell them?" said Sandra.

"I'm in the sales end," said Buddy.

"That makes you a piano salesman. Well, I know a joke about a piano salesman, but maybe I better not tell it," said Sandra.

"Save it for later," said Rex. "Ladies, how about a little libation. Sandra, I know what you want. Karen?"

"Never touch it," said Karen.

"Are you serious?" said Rex.

"She's leveling, she doesn't drink," said Sandra.

"I could tell that right away," said Buddy.

"You could? How?" said Sandra.

"Karen knows I could tell it," said Buddy.

"Did you know each other before?" said Rex.

"I never saw her before in my life, did I, Karen?"

"No," said Karen.

"Can you always tell if a person doesn't drink?" said Sandra.

"No, but I could tell with Karen, couldn't I, Karen?"

"Oh, shut up," said Karen.

"Well, now that the ice is broken," said Rex. "Sandra, brandy and ginger ale, the Sandra special."

"He likes people that drink brandy, I notice," said Buddy.

"Who else? Nobody else is drinking brandy that I see," said Sandra.

"Oil painters, hookers."

"Watch it, Buddy," said Sandra. "You're just liable to get a bottle of it cracked right over your skull. And by me, if you want to know who by."

"You wouldn't want a thing like that to get in the papers," said Buddy. "Drunken brawl at home of big movie star. And Karen wouldn't like to be locked up overnight."

"Give me your keys, Sandra. I want to get away from this fellow."

"Don't be afraid of him, he's just a jerk," said Sandra.

"She's not afraid of me," said Buddy. "She just doesn't want to be locked up. She has claustrophobia. Claustrophobia of the needle."

"Oh," said Sandra. "Is that what he meant, Karen?"

"Yes."

"Oh," said Sandra. "You didn't tell me that."

"I don't go around bragging about it."

"How did *he* know?" said Rex.

"He knew," said Karen. "He looks like he was a user, too, but I wasn't sure. Kicked it, maybe. But he pegged me, and I knew he did. There's a certain look. This guy is trouble and I want out. Give me your keys, Sandra."

"You'd have a hell of a time in this fog," said Rex.

"It's murder, and *I* know the way, Karen," said Sandra.

"That's right," said Rex. "So Buddy, I guess you're elected."

"To what?" said Buddy.

"To take a walk in the fog."

"Not me, I won't go out there with them snakes."

"Oh, they wouldn't hurt *you*. They'd know you were one of the gang," said Rex. "I'll let you have a flashlight."

"You can't make me go," said Buddy.

"Oh, but that's where you're so wrong."

"You mean you got a gun," said Buddy.

"No, I didn't mean that. Do you want me to throw you out? If you make me do that, I won't give you the flashlight. Then you *could* be in trouble. Take the flashlight and start walking. Make plenty of noise and keep walking, and maybe in an hour or two the fog'll clear. Then you can ask the milkman for directions. About an hour they start delivering. So which is it? I throw you out on your can, or be a nice boy and I let you have the flashlight?"

"Throw him out," said Sandra.

"No, I invited him here. He's my guest. But now I'm asking him to leave. Oh, forgetting something." Rex reached in his pocket and took two fifty-dollar bills out of his money clip. He tossed the money on the bar.

Buddy picked up the money. "Gimme the flashlight," he said.

"First I'll go with you to the end of my driveway. *Then* I'll give you the flashlight. I want to be sure you left. Not that I don't trust you, Buddy. I'll be back in a minute, girls."

Rex followed Buddy to the front door, opened it, and told Buddy to go out. "The floodlights are on, as you see," said Rex. "But once you're on your way I'm turning them off. And

I want to tell you something, Buddy boy. Don't come back. Honestly, don't come back, because then you won't be invited."

"What'll you do? Shoot me?"

"No, I'll just call the cops. If they want to shoot you, that's their business. But if I were you, on a night like this, I'd take my chances with the snakes. You know, the cops get irritable, and you're kind of an unpredictable son of a bitch. I'll give you a tip. Not that you deserved it, but take the first two turns to your right, and the next left, and stay on that till you get to Vista del Monte. From there on it's downhill all the way."

"How can I trust you?"

"That's the funny part of it. You can't," said Rex. "But you'll have plenty of time to figure that out. *I* don't trust *you*, so I'll put the flashlight on the ground and you can pick it up yourself. I want both hands free in case you try to slug me."

"Cheap actor," said Buddy.

"All right, but you learn these things playing cops and robbers," said Rex.

Buddy picked up the flashlight and started walking. "First two turns to your right, next left, and stay on that road till Vista del Monte," Rex called to him. Then he ran to the house and switched off the floodlights.

"What happened?" said Sandra.

"Nothing, so far. But a lot could, to a guy that's afraid of snakes and has enough imagination," said Rex. "You know what he almost did? You see those big scissors?"

Afternoon Waltz

IN MANY American towns it often happened that on the main residential street there would be one or two blocks that for one reason or another gave an impression of retiring. Sometimes it was because the leafage of the trees in those blocks darkened the sidewalks. Sometimes the character of the dwellings was uniformly conservative, as if an early house or two had set a style that succeeding builders felt compelled to follow. Whatever the reasons, it was certainly true that when such a block had remained intact for a full generation, it attracted (or held) the kind of people who belonged in that particular neighborhood. The block, the houses, seemed to be occupied by grandparents and the unmarried sisters and brothers of grandparents.

Between Tenth and Eleventh on Lantenengo Street all the houses on the north side were porchless and none was set back from the building line. Most of them had vestibules. A few were constructed to have the front parlor half a story above the street level, so that not even a very tall passer-by could see in the parlor windows. Where the front parlor was on street level, the passer-by's curiosity was frustrated by curtains of heavy lace and lowered window-shades. But the residents of the ten-hundred block were their own best protection against casual peering-in on the part of men on their way to work and women on their way to market. What was there to see in the front parlor or anywhere else in the John Wesley Evans house at 1008?

In point of fact, if an accurate count had been kept of the persons who had set foot in the Evans house since its construction in the 1890's, the total number would not have exceeded a thousand, and that would have included invited visitors, physicians, clergymen, tradesmen and craftsmen. Wesley John Evans, the father of John Wesley Evans, had built to stay, and as there never had been any small children or careless servants in the house, the wear and tear had been kept at a minimum. Wesley Evans and his wife got sick and died, but only in their terminal illnesses had they required doctors and nurses. Their social life was so severely restricted that they had never served a meal to a non-relative on a purely social occasion. When John Wesley Evans entered the house for the first time, he was a college senior on Christmas vacation, and it would never have occurred to him to invite a friend to be his house guest.

As the only child of his parents to reach maturity, John Wesley Evans was brought up in an atmosphere that was compounded of desperate affection and conscientious discipline. He rebelled against neither. He was, in fact, a good boy; obedient, honest, and clean. When in senior year he told his father and mother that he was not yet ready to study for the ministry, they deferred to his wish. It was just as well, since his father died the next summer and his mother would have passed the remaining two years of her life alone in the house at 1008. In the thirty years of her marriage to Wesley John Evans she had never been separated from him for more than three days at a time, and the continual presence of her son was her only comfort against pain and terror. She could not have stood her last ordeal without him. Then too, if he had gone to a seminary and become more imbued with religious doctrine, he might have refused to place within her reach the medicine that enabled her to put an end to her agony. "An accidental overdose," said Dr. Phillips. "But she didn't have long anyway, so if you don't say anything about it, I won't say anything about it."

"I won't say anything about it, Dr. Phillips," said John Wesley Evans.

"No, I was sure you wouldn't," said Dr. Phillips. "If you're ever asked what your mother died of, tell them it was a complication of diseases."

"Is that what my father died of, too? A complication of diseases?"

"Oh, no. He died of quinsy. I was *here* when *he* died," said the doctor. "Nobody was here when your mother died."

"I was in the next room," said John Wesley Evans.

"Yes, I know," said the doctor. "Best we don't carry on any more conversation now, John. We'll just let her rest in peace, as they say." The doctor smiled. "I hope my son'll be as considerate when my time comes. Maybe I might have to send for you."

"If you send for me, I'll come," said John Wesley Evans.

"Well, it'd be only fair. I brought you into the world," said the doctor. "But now let's stop talking. I'll most likely see you at the service."

Thus at age twenty-five John Wesley Evans found himself virtually alone in the world, with capital amounting to $160,000 and a rather large, comfortable house to live in. It surprised him to discover that the freedom he now enjoyed could so quickly become so much of his life that it was all of it. He had not been conscious of being contained by his mother and father, but now that they were no longer there to say or do anything, anything at all, he began to understand that what he wanted most was the release that had come to him through their deaths.

Every morning almost his first thought, which carried through breakfast and beyond, was of a new day in which he could do as he pleased. The small things of major importance gave him opportunities to indulge himself. He never, for instance, had been permitted to lie abed past the hour of eight; now he sometimes appeared in the diningroom at nine. Like all children of his day, he ate what was put before him, a habit which he continued during his four years in college. Now, at twenty-five, he broke the habit, broke it and abandoned it. Sarah Lundy, who did the cooking and general housework, never knew what he was going to want for breakfast. She would bring him his first cup of tea and stand in the doorway while he considered the meal that was to follow. "Today I'll have liver and bacon. Corn bread. Apple butter," he would say. Whatever he ordered, it was never quite like the breakfast that other people ate, and there had to be a lot of it. Breakfast was his big meal. Everybody else ate a big dinner at noon and a light supper, but John Wesley Evans would often eat nothing but fruit, cheese, and bread for the noon meal; then in the evening, at six o'clock, he liked a thick soup and hot apple pie with heavy cream. Throughout the day he might eat a bunch of grapes, some Seckel pears, or whatever else Sarah Lundy had put on the sideboard. Where all the food went she did not know; he remained, as he had always been, all skin and bones; the kind of child and young man that parents feared would die of consumption. Also, he was unusually tall, six foot one, and tall, thin people were often said to have a tapeworm. But if John Wesley Evans had a tapeworm it did not affect his disposition, and people with a tapeworm were generally cranky. John Wesley Evans was generally cheerful, so that Sarah Lundy did not mind much if he put her to a lot of extra work with his unpredictable menus. Until her final illness his mother had done the cooking in the Evans household, and Sarah Lundy was agreeably shocked when John Wesley Evans told her that she was a much better cook than his mother had been. It was the kind of thing he often said to her, the unexpected kind of thing that he had never said while his parents were alive. Sarah Lundy was the first person to realize that John Wesley Evans was an altogether different person from the shy young scarecrow who had always come straight home from school every afternoon and done his sums on the diningroom table. In those days you would hardly know he was in the house. Many times she had entered a room to do her dusting and would be startled to discover him, lying on the floor and reading a book. Thick books, they were, from the glassed-in bookcase in the front parlor, which had a key in the lock. The boy's father and mother did not read the books, and Sarah Lundy was not at all sure that the boy had permission to remove the books from the case. The books, which did not fill all the shelves, were for show, and had been there throughout Sarah Lundy's employment in the Evans household—at the old house on Second Street and the house at 1008 Lantenengo. Sixteen years she had put in with the Evans family; watched two Evans children pass on before either of them reached the age of seven; helped carry W. J. Evans to his bedroom when he had his second stroke; been kept awake at night by Mrs. Evans's moaning and groaning; and now she was being witness to changes in the household that she would have liked better if she understood them better.

There was no doubt about it; her own lot had improved. She did not have to be washed and dressed and downstairs by six-thirty in the morning. As long as the house looked neat and clean she could do her chores on her own schedule. She was practically her own boss, and once John had had his breakfast and his bedroom tended to, she could leave the house to do the marketing three or four days a week, which gave her an opportunity to chat with outsiders and gossip with friends along the way. The walk back up the Tenth Street hill was a little tiring, but the exercise of authority at the grocer's and butcher's and the pleasant conversations made it worth it. Before Mrs. took sick Sarah Lundy had never done the marketing; now she made decisions. "How is your lamb chops today? . . . Do you have any turnips fresh? . . . Let me have a basket of them peaches . . . What are your sweet potatoes selling at?" She had not yet been designated housekeeper by John, but she so considered herself. She could not quite get up the nerve to enter the house by the front door, but that would come. John had voluntarily raised her pay to $35 a month, which was a good sign, especially as he had not raised the pay of the woman who came in on Monday and Tuesday to do the washing and ironing. The week's wash was not as big as it had been, and there were plenty of women only too glad to work for a dollar a day and dinner. (You had to keep an eye on them or they'd walk home with a pound of sugar under their cloaks.) No doubt about it; for both occupants of 1008 Lantenengo Street an era of ease and comfort had begun with the passing of John Wesley Evans's mother.

On the other hand Sarah Lundy, who was Irish and a Roman Catholic, had never been *un*comfortable in a household that was Welsh and Methodist. There were no blacker Protestants than the Welsh Methodists, and they were actively and deeply hated by Sarah Lundy's Irish Catholic friends, particularly those whose menfolk worked in the coal mines. Of very recent memory was the execution of the Mollie Maguires, and the feeling persisted that the Mollies had been hanged because they were less powerful than the Welsh bosses. In theory the Mollie Maguire organization had been broken up by the hangings, by the threats of excommunication by the higher clergy, and by the public indignation over the Mollies' crimes. In fact the organization continued to meet in greater secrecy, necessarily in smaller numbers, keeping their hatred alive and making absurd plans for the future. For the time being murder was ruled out, and violence took the form of beatings administered to non-Mollies by Mollies. No one had to distinguish between one and the other; all the Irish knew which was which. In spite of the division, the non-Mollies were loosely united with the Mollies by the common enemy, the Welsh Protestants, and when Sarah Lundy first went to work for the Evans family neither party could guess how the arrangement would turn out. Sarah, with her distrust of Welsh Protestants, correspondingly was distrusted by Wesley and Gladys Evans. Sarah had come highly recommended by her previous employers, but as it happened she was the first servant ever employed by the Evanses, who had just begun to make money. Gladys Evans was not a lady, and her treatment of Sarah Lundy was unsure, varying from unreasonable demands to spurts of kindness, until Sarah Lundy subtly and patiently established a reasonable relationship. Thereafter she fitted into the household. The Evanses were not a family to inspire affection, but their Methodist morality matched in many ways the aversion to sin that had been drummed into Sarah Lundy by her own people. Liquor, beer, tobacco, snuff, card-playing, dancing, breaking the Sabbath, and free intermingling of the sexes were forbidden in the Evans household. So had they been at the Lundys'. When Patrick Lundy came home drunk, he had the choice of sleeping in the woodshed or the privy, but not in the house, and Rose Lundy was a strong enough woman to enforce her rule. Life as the Evanses' hired girl was thus not much different from Sarah's life at home, except that she got paid and the food was better and there was more of it. Gladys Evans did not like Sarah's having a crucifix over her bed and holy pictures on her bureau, but as it was unlikely that Wesley Evans would ever enter Sarah's bedroom, the tokens of Sarah's papist affiliation were allowed to remain. It was well known, of course, that churchgoing Catholics never stole, and Gladys Evans never refused Sarah permission to go to church.

Sarah Lundy was not critical of John Wesley Evans and his ways. Compared to other women in her position in the ten-hundred block she had it soft, and she knew it. Nevertheless she was bothered by a superstitious feeling that things were going too well. Life was not that easy. For a little while a person might go along unplagued by trouble and sorrow and pain, but Sarah had been taught that God had not intended that the life here below was to be anything but preparation for the life hereafter. The godless, the sinful, who took their pleasures on earth, would all too soon learn that they had paid for them at the price of eternal bliss. God had given man a free will, and he could make his choice between earthly satisfactions and heavenly salvation. Sarah Lundy believed that Wesley and Gladys Evans, who presumably had been baptized Christians, were quite possibly in purgatory, expiating their venial sins. That was what could happen to Protestants if they lived good lives. The worst that could happen to them would be to spend eternity in limbo because they had not been baptized. The important thing about Wesley and Gladys Evans was that they had served God as well as they knew how, avoiding sin and the occasions of sin, and God would take into consideration the circumstances that kept them from becoming Catholics. Sarah Lundy did not for one minute forget that bad Catholics could be condemned to eternal damnation. God would be more severe in His judgment of Catholics, because they were supposed to know better. It was a very complicated subject if you got into it too deeply, and it was not a subject to discuss with non-Catholics, who asked ignorant questions. But it was a subject that Sarah Lundy occupied her mind with much of the time, and most of the time she was thinking not of just anyone but of John Wesley Evans.

There was no harm in him, no evil. True, he did not have a job, he did not work. Indeed, he seldom went out of the house. But she could not judge him guilty of sloth, one of the seven deadly sins. Some men were meant to work with their hands, some were meant to work with their brains. John Wesley Evans escaped the charge of sloth because he was doing something with his brains. Bit by bit he was converting the sitting-room back of the parlor into a workroom. "It sounds a little fancy, Sarah, but from now on we'll call this the library," he announced one day.

"The liberry," she said. "All right. I'll get used to it."

"I'm going to build some bookshelves, and some day both these walls will be lined with books from top to bottom."

"Covering the wallpaper?"

"Covering the wallpaper. You'll be able to say you remember this room when it didn't have a single book in it."

"What would I want to say that for?"

"Well, if you don't want to say it there's no reason why you should. But the time will come when you'll be *able* to say it. And the time may not be too far off. This was always the room

I liked best. Not the way Papa and Mama had it, but my way. The nicest thing about it is the bay window."

"Where the Mrs. would sit and do her sewing."

"It has the north light. I may take up painting as my hobby."

"Picture-painting?" said Sarah Lundy.

"Oh, I have no such intention, but if I had, this would be a very suitable room for a studio," he said. He paused. "I wonder if I have any talent in that direction. You never know till you try."

"You was always drawing pictures when you was little," said Sarah Lundy.

"When I was little," he said. "The trouble is, I wouldn't know how to start. I never knew anyone that painted pictures. No, it won't be painting I'll do here."

"What will it be?"

"Reading. Thinking."

"Just reading and thinking? What's that for a young man to be doing? You ought to be out on these nice days, making friends with people. Enjoying the sunshine. Here you're only twenty-five years of age and a body'd think you were up in your fifties. Reading and thinking. You'll be an old man soon enough, John Evans. The years go by before you know it, I can say that knows."

"Then you should be told that I intend to spend the rest of my life in this house and the greater part of it in this room," he said. "Reading, and thinking."

"Then you'll never live to your father's age, cooped up like that. Your father never would of seen sixty-two if he didn't move around and get the fresh air in his lungs."

"They went to a great deal of trouble to protect me from the fresh air."

"Only because they were terrified you'd get the consumption."

"Well, I didn't, so they must have been right. And since they seem to've been right, I'll continue their methods. Take a miner out of the mines and he dies in a year."

"Little do you know. And that's not saying how many die of the miner's asthma before they're forty."

"Sarah, I'm properly grateful for your concern, but I've made up my mind. I've already sent away for over a hundred books. At least a hundred."

"A—hundred—books?"

"Before I'm through there'll be at least a thousand in this room, and I'll be able to tell you what's in them."

"I wouldn't listen," said Sarah Lundy. "Nor neither would anyone else in their right senses."

"That I'm sure is true," said John Wesley Evans.

"There! Then what do you want to read a thousand books for? You say yourself nobody's going to listen to you tell what's in them. So what's the good of stuffing your brain with what's in them? I ask you that. Your brain won't hold all that. A thousand books. My Lord and Savior, that's a terrible, terrible thing, John. A terrible thing. I could read and write when I was seven years of age, not saying how long ago that was, and I read me prayerbook and the newspaper, and the leaflets we get after Mass. I could read more if I had to. But a thousand books!"

"I may go to two thousand."

"Your eyesight'll give out before that. There's another thing to worry about. Your eyesight."

"Yes," he said.

She had frightened him and she was sorry. "Not that your eyesight won't last forever if you don't strain it too hard. You understand that. It's the same as anything else. Too much of a good thing's as bad as none at all, and that goes for reading and thinking and fresh air and all."

Sarah Lundy's discovery that John was fearful of damage to his eyesight came as a surprise to her, with a surprising effect. For not only was it news that he worried about his eyes; it was news that he ever worried about anything. Until now she had thought of him as a skinny, bloodless individual; a vegetable of a boy, who lay on the floor and read books when he ought to be out climbing trees. She could not remember his ever crying at night, or coming home with a bloody nose, or threatening to run away, or being punished for sins with his own or the opposite sex. If he had been a pretty or a handsome child, or a remarkably ugly one, a troublesome or happy one, she would have been better prepared for the unmistakable admission contained in the single word "yes" and the way he uttered it. After saying it he left the room, and her female instinct, flabby from disuse, returned to life in a surge of compassion.

This aging virgin now knew that he could use her pity. He was afraid of something.

2

Two doors to the west of 1008 lived Mr. and Mrs. Percy B. Shields, and theirs was the first house in the block to have striped awnings over the front windows, upstairs and down. There was not much practical use for awnings in that block. The trees that stood on the edge of the brick sidewalk kept the sun from being too bothersome, and the other residents of the block found curtains and roller-shades and inside shutters very satisfactory. But Mrs. Percy Shields wanted striped awnings, upstairs and down, and it did not bother her that some of her neighbors said the awnings made her house look like a circus. In the first place, they did not make the house look like a circus or like anything else but a house with striped awnings. In the second place, they made the house cooler. She could open her windows, which her neighbors could not do if they insisted on keeping their shades lowered. In the third place, it was her house and as long as she was not breaking any law she could have striped awnings or blue awnings or yellow awnings or any other kind she wished. What her neighbors objected to, if they would only come out and say it, was any bright touch, anything unusual. They might object to her striped awnings, but it might interest them to learn that the most disgraceful houses on Railroad Avenue had exactly the same kind of lace curtains that her neighbors had in their windows. And no awnings. How did Mrs. Percy Shields know about houses on Railroad Avenue? Never mind, she knew. She had it on good authority.

Never for a moment was it suspected that the authority might be Percy Shields. For one thing, he was much too old. Age had kept him from going to the defense of the national capital in 1861, and he was now forty years older. It took him a good twenty minutes to go from his house to the Gibbsville Club, a seven-block downhill walk all the way, and in recent years he had had to depend on his carriage to bring him home. It was true, as they said, that on the way home he had to carry in his belly a quantity of Old Overholt, but he never could have got home if he relied on his legs. Even the downhill walk to the club took some courage; at his time of life a tumble could result in a broken hip, and he had never known any of his contemporaries to recover from that. He therefore walked with care; slowly, and never raising his feet higher than was necessary to keep them from scraping the ground. During the winter months, when there was ice and snow, he was compelled to suspend his walks. Arthur Hawkins, who was hostler, gardener and man-of-all-work for the Shieldses, would help Percy into the swan-type cutter, cover him up with a buffalo robe, and take him to the club. Percy would spend the same amount of time at the club as he did in kinder weather, but he would miss the exercise. Percy's need of Arthur and the horse also interfered with his wife's morning schedule, as it postponed her marketing. Consequently the wintry weather inconvenienced both Harriet and Percy Shields, and on the afternoons of extremely inclement days they could hardly bear to be in the same room with each other.

Harriet Shields observed the custom of afternoon tea, which was made possible by the fact that they had no children and could have their evening meal at a later hour than most households. Harriet served tea six days a week to a different woman friend every day. The amount of information she thus acquired was considerable and of a large variety. Her guests had been chosen for that purpose, and they represented the well-to-do, the genteel poor, the witty, the vicious, and ages from forty to sixty-five. Women past sixty-five, Harriet had found, did not hear much gossip, possibly for the reason that they had difficulty hearing anything at all, and worthwhile gossip could not be shouted to a deaf person. For one maiden lady and one widow Harriet's teas were an ample substitute for the evening meal; the four other regulars came because Harriet Shields had invited them to come, and no one wished to incur her displeasure. They all were, in a word, afraid of her. They had all heard her comments on other women and some men, and the faithful six preferred to remain on her good side. In the course of their weekly conversations with Harriet Shields they had entrusted her with personal confidences, which were safe only so long as her visitors were in good standing with her.

But if they were afraid of her, they also were addicted to the opportunity she provided for a free expression of their own observations and opinions. From week to week they saved up items of confidential and unprintable news for Harriet. Since there were never more than two women present, Harriet and her guest, it was possible to repeat intimate and slanderous details without reckoning with a third person. And while Harriet was duly appreciative of interesting items, she was never shocked and seldom surprised by anything. Another good thing about Harriet was that she did not interrupt; a friend who was emboldened to tell a lurid story did not lose her courage halfway through. If Harriet had heard the story before—as often she had—she would hear the new version all the way out, and then, but not until then, supply corrections and additions. It could be said of Harriet that she practiced scandalmongering as an art.

She, of course, was invulnerable. Such displays of eccentricity as her striped awnings and her taste in millinery were irritating, but not such stuff as gossip is made on. Harriet Shields was still pretty, healthy, and vigorous, but she was not in the least flirtatious or concupiscent. A glass of wine was all she ever drank. She had never taken laudanum. She paid her bills promptly. She did not lose her temper in public or have hysterics. She had a personal fortune, inherited from her father, which gave her a social and financial background that was very nearly the equal of any in the town, and made her immune to the charge that she married Percy Shields for his money. Indeed, it was the other way around: if anyone was vulnerable in that respect it was Percy, who had married a woman with much more money than he and who was a great deal younger. But Percy Shields had always been an affable mediocrity; everyone wished him well, and when Harriet consented to marry him there was universal sanction of the union. No one would have to worry about Percy any longer, and Harriet Stokes's share of the Stokes wealth would remain in Gibbsville. It was also said at the time that it was a real love match. Later this was amended to "ideal marriage." At sixty Percy Shields retired from the practice of the law, a formality which consisted only of his giving up his office in the second-floor rear of the Keystone Trust Company building and moving his law books to a hallway bookcase at 1012 Lantenengo Street. He never looked at them again. Not even once. Not even to notice that a couple of them had been put in upside down.

Harriet Shields's house had somewhat more grandeur inside than the other houses in the ten-hundred block. At the foot of the front stairway was a bronze statuette, mounted on the newel post, of a knight in dull armor holding a spear which supported a gas lamp. The gas line went through the hollow spear. One day Harriet detected a strong odor of gas leaking from the burner. Someone somehow had turned the valve half on. She immediately sent for the plumbers and had the pipeline sealed permanently. The statuette remained on the newel post for decorative purposes, but as a lighting fixture it was useless. "Why don't we get that lamp fixed?" Percy would say once or twice a year.

"Yes, I must remember to do that," Harriet would say. But she had developed a theory that Percy, after one of his long days at the club, had reached out for support on his way upstairs and inadvertently turned the key of the gas valve. Right or wrong, the theory covered a possibility, and the bronze knight provided no more light until he was electrified.

In her front parlor Harriet Shields had a crystal chandelier that was the largest in a private house in all Lantenengo County. Twice a year her maids unhooked each of the thousand and more bits of glass, washed and dried each one and replaced them. The task always took two days, and the entire operation was supervised by Harriet. It was not as simple as Percy Shields made it out to be, for not only was there the job of unhooking the bits of crystal and washing away the six months' collection of grime, but there was also the polishing with ammonia. Harriet and the maids would have to interrupt their work to get away from the smell of the ammonia. On the second day Harriet was at her efficient best, directing the rehanging of the bits of crystal, like stringing pearls. This she accomplished with the help of a detailed sketch of the chandelier, and when the task was completed and the gas turned on, even Percy admitted that there was beauty in the sparkling, subtle changes of color. "Louis Quatorze," he would say. "We must give a ball."

"You always say that, Percy," Harriet would say. "And you'd sooner die than have a ball."

"I'd rather die than arrange for one, is what you mean. But if you did all the work I'd enjoy it."

"We could never have a ball without inviting our neighbors, and who'd want to have *them*?"

"Not me, I'm sure. Consider the subject closed." It would be closed until it was reopened after the next cleaning of the chandelier.

Elegance, luxury, modern conveniences were not put in for the pleasure of Harriet's neighbors. When she added something to the interior of her house she did not even feel compelled to display it to her daily visitors. "Harriet, is it true that you've put in a laundry chute?" said Ellen Walker one day.

"Now where did you hear that?" said Harriet.

"I forget who told me, but I understand you have a new laundry chute that's lined with tin, all the way from the third floor to the basement."

"We have one, but it's been there for over a year. Think of attaching so much importance to a laundry chute."

"There aren't very many in town, you know," said Ellen.

"I'm sure I have no idea how many there are, Ellen. By the way, it's lined with copper, not tin. If I'd thought you'd be interested in a *laundry* chute, I'd have shown it to you a year ago. But good heavens, I'd never think of boring my friends with things like that."

"It would surprise you to know how curious people are, especially about your house."

"It wouldn't surprise me in the least. Not in the least."

"So many people have asked me if I've ever seen your wall safe. A wall safe with a combination lock?"

"Are you asking me if I have one? At least that's more interesting than a laundry chute. Yes, we've had one for a long time."

"Is it because you don't trust banks? That's the rumor I heard."

"Well, all I can say is it wasn't a rumor that started at the Keystone Trust Company. That's where I keep my money and Percy keeps his, and my father kept his and my brother Harry keeps his. That kind of a rumor could do a lot of harm. It *could* have been started by one of the other banks."

Ellen Walker's husband Louis was cashier of the Coal City Trust Company. Momentarily Ellen was on dangerous ground and having difficulty composing a suitable comment.

"I'm sure Louis'd scotch that rumor," said Harriet, who was positive that Ellen was repeating Louis Walker's very words. "Yes, we have a wall safe to keep our things in. My jewelry. Percy's good studs. Things I got from Mother. We're not worried about things being stolen, but the safe is fireproof. Fireproof, Ellen."

"Of course. I never thought of that."

"Well, I had to, you know," said Harriet Shields. "Some day all my things will go to my nieces and my nephews' wives. I can't expect to last forever."

"Looking at it that way, it's a responsibility," said Ellen.

"There's no other way to look at it. Those things increase in value every year. Mother's solitaire—well, it isn't polite to talk about such things, but it's worth three times what Papa paid for it. Tripled in twenty years, mind you."

"It's the largest diamond in town, I know that," said Ellen.

"No, there's one larger. But mine is better cut. It isn't only the size of a diamond, Ellen. For instance, yours I imagine is worth more than some I've seen, because it's newer, and the cutting methods are constantly improving."

That was another thing about Harriet Shields. She *knew* so many things. She never went away; a spring trip to Philadelphia to see the new styles, and another in November to do her Christmas shopping. But she did not like to leave Percy, and he could not travel in comfort. Nevertheless Harriet kept up to date on everything in the outside world as well as on matters pertaining to her own circle of acquaintances. She was the only woman on Lantenengo Street who had taken the trouble to find out all the reasons for the war with Spain, which she had done by writing to the district member of the House of Representatives. The name Harriet *Stokes* Shields and the Lantenengo Street, Gibbsville, address carried weight. She knew about Spain, and diamond-cutting, and the superiority of copper over tin, and how to rehang strands of crystal on a chandelier. She spoke French and had once taken lessons on the flute. There seemed to be no end to the variety of subjects that could claim her interest. Imagine writing to a Congress-man for information on a war that only lasted a few months!

One day she came out of her house and saw her neighbor, young John Evans, standing in front of his own house but staring at her striped awnings. "Well, Mr. John Wesley Evans. Are you trying to stare a hole through them?"

He removed his hat. "Good morning, Mrs. Shields. I didn't hear what you said."

"I *asked* you if you were trying to stare a hole through my awnings. They've been there, this is the third year. No, next year will be the third. But haven't you ever noticed them before?"

"I noticed them, but I never took a good look at them."

"I'd heard you didn't leave your house much, but even so."

"Well, I was thinking of getting some. I didn't know so much for the front of my house, but my bay window in the back. If it wouldn't be prying, would you mind telling me about how much they ask for an awning?"

"I couldn't say exactly, but if you want to come in I'll look it up. Come on," she said, and turned about, fully expecting that he would obey. He did.

It was his first visit to the Shields house, and he was the first Evans to visit the house. "I've never been in here before," he said.

"Is that so? Well, just sit down a minute and I know right where to find the receipt. Hillyard and Son. Hall. Hill. Hill-yard. Here it is. Goodness, I'd forgotten about that."

"What?" said John.

"How much they overcharged me. Eight windows. Two, three, and three. I thought it was going to be forty dollars for the whole thing, but he charged me three dollars extra for the windows on the top floor. He said he had to rent ladders from somebody. His ladders wouldn't go that high. Here, you can see on one receipt, 'Received $40 and no cents, part payment.' Then here's the second receipt, balance due on awnings, paid in full. That was Bert Hillyard. His father was a man of his word. If he said forty dollars, he meant forty dollars. No charging extra because his ladders wouldn't reach. Unfortunately, there's no one else in town that does that kind of work, so you'll have to go to Hillyards'. But if you deal with young Bert, get it all down in black and white first. Now that you're here, would you care for a glass of root beer? We have it on ice, so it should be nice and cool on such a warm day."

"Well, if it wouldn't be going to too much trouble," he said.

"Amy! Two glasses of root beer, and a plate of salty pretzels. Now, John, tell me what you do with yourself all day. I heard that you were writing a book. Is that *true?*"

"No, I'm not writing anything."

"That's what I said. I know you graduated from college, but I was sure they didn't teach you to write. What was the name of your college?"

"Wesleyan. Middletown, Connecticut."

"How far is that from New Haven?"

"Uh, let me think."

"Never mind. I only asked because you knew my brother went to Yale. Harry."

"Yes, I guess everybody in town knows that Mr. Stokes went to Yale."

"What was that again?"

He smiled, and said nothing.

She glared at him, but her glare changed to a smile. "Well, it *is* true that my brother's very proud of having gone to Yale."

"He spoke to my father about sending me there, but Yale was too stylish for us. That was when I was thinking of becoming a preacher."

"I take it you've given that up," said Harriet Shields.

"Yes, I've given it up."

"What do you plan to do instead?"

"Nothing. At least, not take a job, or learn a profession."

"Why, everybody does something in Gibbsville. At least till they're old enough to retire. But you're not old enough to retire."

"I don't have to retire. I never did anything to retire from."

"Then it's not going to be easy for you to find a wife. A man that sits around the house all day isn't what the modern girl is looking for."

"Probably not, but there are two sides to that question, too."

"Meaning, I suppose, that you're going to remain a bachelor."

"I guess that's what I am. A bachelor. I never thought of

myself as a bachelor. Just a fellow that wasn't planning to get married. But after you reach a certain age I guess they call you a bachelor."

"You're not a woman-hater, are you?"

"No, I like some. I never got to know many girls."

"What kind of girls do you like?"

"What kind do I like? My goodness, that's another thing I never thought of. I'd have to think."

"I should imagine that a girl would have to show how much she appreciated you before you'd take a fancy to her."

"Then I have a long while to wait."

"Not necessarily. If you gave them a chance. Girls are intelligent, too, you know. But you'll never meet the intelligent ones just sitting at home all the time. You have to get out once in a while. Otherwise you'll be an old bachelor before you know it. There are so many different ways to meet girls. Do you play cards?"

"In *our* house?"

"That's true. You're Methodist. They don't allow dancing, either, do they? Well, here's our root beer. I thought you were going to take all day, Amy."

"No ma'am," said the maid. "I had to move a big cake of ice. The iceman pushed everything in back of the box so there was fifty pounds of ice in front of the soft drinks. I told him a hundred times—"

"Thank you. We'll talk about it later," said Harriet. She sipped her root beer. "Yum! Go ahead, drink it while it's nice and cool."

"I was enjoying the smell of your cologne. Is that what you call it? Cologne?"

"Roger and Gallet's Eau de Cologne. Thank you, I'm glad you like it. You see, you're not a woman-hater at all, if you appreciate scent."

"I never said I was a woman-hater. I just don't know any, or hardly any."

"And those you've known haven't been the right kind. Would you like to join the Assembly, now that your parents are gone?"

"What for? You know I don't dance."

"The Assembly isn't only a ball, John. Mr. Shields doesn't dance any more, but we'd never miss an Assembly. Why, for some people in town it's the only opportunity they get all year to put on their best bib-and-tucker, display their party manners. It's a very nice occasion."

"I guess the women would enjoy it, but do the men?"

"Ah, indeed they do. As much as the ladies. I think there's a meeting in a week or two. Suppose I ask Mr. Shields to put your name up? If *he* puts you up, you'll get in, then you'll be a member for life. As long as you pay your ten dollars a year."

"Ten dollars?"

"Oh, now ten dollars won't send you to the almshouse, and some day you may be very glad you joined."

"I can't dance, I don't have a full-dress, and I hardly know any of those people."

"It's time you rectified all those things. A young bachelor who lives on Lantenengo Street has certain obligations. If you don't agree, then you ought to move to the other side of town, where such things don't matter."

"My father was never in the Assembly."

"No, and if he had wanted to be, he couldn't have been."

"Then why should I want to join it? What was the matter with my father?"

"Morally, or financially, nothing, I suppose. But socially, everything."

"I'm no better, socially."

"Oh, yes you are. You have more finish."

"Not so's you could notice it."

"You're wrong. I *have* noticed it. You haven't got *la politesse*, as the French say, but you have a manner. I don't quite know how to describe it, but it's there. Now I suggest that you arrange to take dancing lessons—privately, of course. Then by the time New Year's Eve is here, you'll be able to trip the light fantastic as well as any of them. And you have a great advantage over most of the men—you're tall."

"Dancing lessons?"

"Professor Long and his wife. They give private instruction in Union Hall, you know."

"I couldn't do that, Mrs. Shields. I'd feel foolish."

"Very well, then *I'll* teach you. Tomorrow afternoon you come here at two o'clock, and we'll start our lessons."

"Here?"

"Of course, here. Look at this floor. It was meant for danc-ing. Take up a few rugs, move a few chairs, and this is really a ballroom. From two o'clock to three. If you haven't got the proper shoes, go down to Schoffstal's and buy a pair. That's where Mr. Shields buys his and most of the other gentlemen. And don't let Bert Hillyard overcharge you the way he did me." She rose. "I'm sorry there isn't room for you in my buggy, or you could ride down to Schoffstal's with me. But the walk'll do you good."

He walked with her to her carriage, and even in the open air her perfume was inescapable.

3

During the rest of that summer and into the months of au-tumn John Wesley Evans was seen going in and out of the Shields house twice or three times a week, always early in the afternoon. At that time of day Percy Shields was invariably at the club, and his absence from home during John Evans's visits was duly noted, as was the fact that young Evans had departed before the tea-time arrival of Harriet Shields's daily callers. When the visits had occurred frequently enough and regularly enough, the curious advanced beyond mere speculation: they questioned Sarah Lundy when they encountered her at the meat-market, the grocery store, and on the slow climb up Tenth Street. Even a less subtle woman than Sarah Lundy could not have failed to notice the new friendliness of housewives who in the past had ignored her entirely or had thought nothing of preempting her place in the customers' lines. "Good morning, Sarah. No, you go right ahead, you were here first," they would say. Then they would manage to engage her in conversation which unfailingly included a reference to her young employer. "Busy as ever, with his French lessons," said one woman.

"What French lessons?" said Sarah Lundy.

"I understood he was taking French lessons from Mrs. Shields," said the woman.

"First I heard of it," said Sarah Lundy.

"Oh, yes. Three or four days a week he has a lesson. At least that's what I understood. Well, it's nice for him that he has someone so near."

"First I knew about any French lessons. He goes over there, but I didn't know that's what it was for."

"In connection with a book he's writing," said the woman.

"Ah, that I knew about. He's forever talking about books," said Sarah Lundy.

It was as exasperating to Sarah Lundy as to the curious that she had so little information to give. John Wesley Evans had never so much as told her that he was going to call on Mrs. Shields. At five minutes to two in the afternoon, three afternoons a week, he would leave the house, destination unannounced, and be gone till five or ten after three. Sarah Lundy soon knew that he went to call on Mrs. Percy Shields, but did not know why. When he got home he would close the door of his library, but she could hear him muttering, "*One* two-three, *one* two-three, *one* two-three," over and over again, and once when she made some excuse to enter the library he was doing some kind of exercise.

"You know I don't like to be disturbed when I'm working," he said. "What *is* it?"

"I thought I heard you call me," she said.

"You didn't think any such thing. Go on about your business."

"Either you called me or you're getting the habit of talking to yourself. Is that from one of your French lessons?"

"What French lessons?"

"The ones you're taking off of Mrs. Shields."

"*French* lessons? I see. Is that something you figured out for yourself, or someone else figured out for you? I hazard a guess that it was someone else. Well, you're both wrong. And I'm going to keep you in the dark as long as possible. Forever, if I can."

"I'm sure I care little enough what goes on with you and the old lady. Although she isn't that old that a young man's company—"

"Go on about your business, I said."

He weighed the matter, and after eating a banana and a whole bunch of grapes he came to the conclusion that he must report the conversation to Mrs. Shields.

"Well, I do declare," she said, when he had finished.

"You're not angry?" he said.

"Of course I'm angry," she said.

"Not at me, I hope," he said.

"Good gracious, no. Nor at your clumsy Sarah. But I am angry with whoever tried to pump her. I'll find out who that was, and make her pay for it. I love gossip, but I believe in certain rules."

"Certain rules about gossip?"

"Well, yes, in a way," she said. "A lady doesn't descend to gossip with a servant. It's mean and disloyal. They gossip about us, every chance they get, and that's to be expected. But when a woman of our station in life tries to extract juicy morsels from a servant, that's treacherous. Servants find out enough without any help from one of us. I'm going to punish that woman, whoever she was."

"How will you find out who she was?"

"I don't know, but I'll set a trap for her. It could be one of my own little toadies. I rather suspect it is."

"Your own little toadies? One of your servants?"

"Don't you pay attention to what I say? *Not* one of my servants. One of the ladies I have in for tea every day. Those are my toadies."

"Oh, I thought they were your friends," he said.

"I have no friends. If I had any, I lost them when I married Percy Shields. It was perfectly all right for him to marry me, but it was all wrong for me to marry him. You probably won't see the difference, but there was one."

"Why *did* you marry him?"

"Because he was ardent. You're too young to know about such things, but when you're thirty years older you'll know that a man in his fifties *can* be ardent. And he can seem especially so to an ignorant, inexperienced young woman. I adored him."

"But you don't any more?" he said.

"That doesn't last very long, even with two people of the same age. They have children, and that's what makes the marriage last."

"But you had no children, and your marriage has lasted."

"I had a child. A man in his sixties. A toothless baby that had to learn how to walk. Yes, and even had to have his bottle every day. Haven't you ever noticed that my husband walks as if he were afraid he was going to fall, like a little child?"

"I never thought of it that way," he said.

"That's why I love to dance with you, John. When I was a young girl I loved to dance. Not just round-dancing, but any kind. My mother used to tell me that I was getting too big to skip on my way home from school. But I wasn't skipping. I was dancing. Well, let's get to our lesson."

"I don't think you feel like it today," he said.

She looked at him and frowned. "No, I don't," she said. "But how did you know?"

"Oh—mental telepathy. Something like that," he said.

"Call it that, I suppose. It's not a term that has any sweetness, tenderness. But you're afraid of tenderness, aren't you?"

"I don't know," he said.

"You are. And so am I," she said. "I could show you what it can be, but then you'd never come back. Don't look at my neck, my chin, John. The rest of me is very nice."

"I want to see the rest of you," he said.

"Sometime I'll let you, but now you must go."

"Why not now? The door is closed," he said.

"Please go. But if you want to, you can come back tonight."

"How can I? Your husband will be here."

"Come at eleven o'clock. The front door will be unlocked, and I'll be here."

"Where will your husband be?"

"My baby will be sound asleep, snoring, and dead drunk. And nothing will wake him before five o'clock tomorrow morning. At eleven o'clock there won't be anyone on the street, and most of the leaves are still on the trees. I'll be waiting for you, I promise. And if you decide not to come, don't ever come again."

4

The great doctor in Philadelphia said there was nothing to be done. "This is a thing that started in your left eye, most likely when you were no more than ten or twelve years old," said the doctor. "That was when you started wearing glasses."

"Yes sir," said John Wesley Evans. "Fifth grade. I'm going by the teacher I had the first time I put them on."

"Your parents took you to a man in a jewelry store, and he gave you your first pair of glasses. But Dr Phillips tells me there was a good eye-ear-nose-and-throat man in your town. I don't understand it. Your family weren't poor."

"My mother bought my glasses at the same place where she bought hers," said John. "I guess she didn't know any better."

"That was it, I suppose," said the doctor. He studied his patient. "I can't say now how much difference it would have made, Mr. Evans. But a good eye-doctor would have looked at your left eye and noticed things that needed attention. By that time your right eye had started to go."

"Yes, I had to get new glasses every two years."

"Always from the man in the jewelry store?" said the doctor.

"Yes sir. He let me try on different glasses till I found the ones that were the most comfortable."

"And you'd wear them for two years?"

"Just about. Maybe a little longer. When I went away to college I got thicker ones. Stronger lenses."

"You used your eyes a lot, studying."

"I always did, not only studying but reading. I like to read."

"You haven't spent much time outdoors, have you?"

"No, I liked to read," said John.

"The sunlight bothered you?"

"Yes, I guess it did, thinking back."

"Dr. Phillips tells me you thought of studying for the ministry."

"I gave that up a long time ago. Why?" said John.

"I was thinking of your future," said the doctor. "You ought to plan for it, have something to do."

"It won't be the ministry. I don't believe in God, and I believe in Him less now than I ever did."

"That's understandable, but in the times I've seen you you impressed me as having quite a lot of courage."

"That's bluff," said John.

"Bluffing takes courage under the circumstances, Mr. Evans," said the doctor. "Now I'll be frank with you, because I've found out that I can be. There are probably some doctors who would perform an operation on your eyes. I won't put you through that, because in my opinion the operation would not be successful. However, if you feel that you owe it to yourself to have the operation, Dr. Phillips knows the names of other doctors in my field."

"That isn't giving me much choice, is it?"

"No, and that's why I put it that way. I'm usually the doctor that they come to as a last resort."

"Dr. Phillips said you were the best," said John.

"Well, I don't believe in false modesty, especially in a surgeon. If I knew of a better man, I'd send you to him myself. In about six years I'm going to have to stop doing surgery, and by that time we'll know more and there'll be new men coming along. But not in time to do you any good."

"How long is it going to be before I go completely blind?"

"You'll be able to see, to get around, for another eighteen months, I should say. But you're not going to be able to read more than four or five months. Reading is going to be more and more difficult for you. It is already. Have you done much traveling?"

"None at all," said John.

"Would you like to see the Parthenon? The Eiffel Tower? In other words, I'm suggesting that since you can afford it, now is the time to travel, to see things. And people. If *I* were in your position I'd spend part of that time looking at beautiful women, preferably in bed, and all sizes and colors. But my morals have never been my strong point, as anyone in Philadelphia will tell you."

"I have no morals, either," said John Wesley Evans, more to himself than to the doctor.

"I find that hard to believe," said the doctor.

"Oh, I've never disgraced my parents or anything like that, but *inside* I have no morals. I've never wanted to be a good man. I just wanted to be left alone. You go your way, and I'll go mine. That was my philosophy of life. You find it hard to believe that I have no morals, but I once killed a person."

"You did? How?"

"I didn't shoot them or anything like that. But I helped this person to commit suicide. The person could not have committed suicide without my help."

"Well, legally I suppose you could be held responsible for manslaughter. Not knowing the circumstances, I can't say. But right here on Walnut Street there are dozens of men of the medical profession who face that problem every day. Religious men, too. As an eye doctor I don't have to face the problem as much as a man who does abdominal surgery, for instance. But here on Walnut Street, and all over the country, all over the civilized world, surgeons operate on men and women, make the incision, and discover an absolutely hopeless condition. The patient is asleep, under chloroform. Why not let the poor man, or woman, stay asleep?"

"Why not?"

"Ah, but it's not that easy. There may be another doctor there, and there are always surgical nurses. Some of them know as much about surgical techniques as some doctors. That's the practical side, the chance of being reported and ruined professionally. On the ethical side, it's as bad or worse. Doctors discuss ethics while they're medical students, but after medical school you don't hear as much of that talk. We doctors tend to keep those thoughts to ourselves, the older we get and the more set in our ways. We confine our ethical discussions to something we call ethics, but is really no more than professional courtesy."

"What if I see a woman naked and fall in love with her? Isn't it going to be worse when I can't look at her any more?"

"I was wondering what you were thinking during my speech about ethics," said the doctor.

"Why did you think you had to make a speech?"

"That leaves two questions unanswered," said the doctor. "Well, I mentioned the Parthenon. I was in Athens a great many years ago, and I've never gone back. But I remember the beauty of the Parthenon, and always will. I'm very glad I saw it when I could. That should answer your first question, especially since you're not going to lose your sense of touch. I have often touched women in the dark, and so will you. As for your second question, I make these speeches to get you to talk. I want you to be stimulated to ask me questions. Remember, Mr. Evans, this has been my lifework, and I've had to tell other patients the same thing I've told you. If I can't help you in one way, I may be able to help you in others."

"Now I understand," said John Wesley Evans. "Will I ever stop being afraid?"

"You've already begun to stop," said the doctor. "But that's not saying you aren't going to have a difficult time later on. The fear will pass, but getting reconciled to your blindness may take time. Have you got a friend, a very close friend?"

"One, yes," said John.

"You're lucky," said the doctor. "Man, or woman?"

"A woman."

"She's older, and she's married. Am I right?"

"Yes."

"Does she know you've been to see me?"

"Yes."

"Could you ask her to come and see me?"

"What for?"

"To answer the questions she wants to ask me," said the doctor.

"You certainly do know a lot, Doctor," said John. "She's here in Philadelphia. She's staying at the Bellevue-Stratford Hotel."

"You might as well tell me her name. I'm very close-mouthed. I've had to be."

"Her name is Mrs. Percy B. Shields."

"I could ring up the hotel on the telephone."

"You don't have to. She's waiting outside in a hansom cab."

"Will you go out and ask her to come in?" said the doctor.

John Wesley Evans smiled. "She wanted to come in with me, but I wouldn't let her. She's always right."

5

There is nothing more that need be added to this small story. The reader can fill in for himself the assumption that the news of John Wesley Evans's blindness created genuine dismay. The devotion of Harriet Shields to her young neighbor was soon of a piece with her devotion to her aged husband. When Percy Shields died, the townsfolk were prepared to be tolerant of a marriage between Harriet and John Wesley Evans, but it did not take place. In a little while John Wesley Evans became truly if prematurely a typical resident of the ten-hundred block, one of the sequestered men and women who gave a character to the neighborhood that was as solemn as brownstone and brick.

But sometimes on a summer afternoon, on a favorable day in May, a warm day in September, there would be the sound of a waltz coming from Harriet Shields's talking-machine. It was not loud enough to disturb anyone.

The Assistant

THE ALARM clock went off, and she did not remember setting it. It was a small clock, brass-plated, with a dial that was less than two inches in diameter, and the noise-making apparatus of it was annoying but not powerful enough to be commanding. Without stirring from her pillow she looked at it and said the first defiant thing that came into her head—and let it ring itself down. Then, before closing her eyes again, she looked to see what time it was. It was half past five.

She closed her eyes and dozed off into an enjoyable half-sleep, rather delicious it was because it was stolen sleep. Half past five itself meant nothing to her, but half past six might mean something. Half past six, or more likely, seven o'clock. Seven o'clock. What was there that she had to do, where was there that she had to be, at seven o'clock that would cause her to set her alarm clock for half past five? Seven o'clock was the time, all right. It would take her at least an hour to dress, and another half hour to get anywhere. She was to meet someone at seven o'clock, or at seven o'clock someone was coming here to her apartment. The big question was not so much where as who.

Now she reached out and with the skill of a blind person she took a cigarette out of a china box, and with somewhat less confidence she groped around the night table until her fingers found a lighter. With her eyes still closed, to protect her eyes from the glare—sometimes that first flame lighting that first cigarette could be as blinding as the bomb on Nagasaki—she brought the lighter to the end of the cigarette and took in that first shallow drag. Now, to all intents and purposes, she had come awake, or as a friend of hers was fond of saying, had rejoined the human race. George Waller. As he took his first drink of the day, he would nearly always say that he was rejoining the human race. He had got it out of a book somewhere. She wished it was as easy to remember whom she had a date with as it was to remember George Waller—or to forget George Waller, for that matter.

Less tentatively she took a fuller drag on her cigarette and sat on the edge of the bed, scratching little itches with her free hand and rubbing the area of the right clavicle. It was a little too soon to know how she was going to feel when she got to her feet, but so far the day was not as bad as some had been lately. Bravely, she stood up and went to the kitchen and put the water on to boil. By the time she finished her first visit to the bathroom the water would be ready for the instant coffee. Certain things she did methodically, no matter what might be said about her life in general. She was not, for instance, going to rack her brain with her seven o'clock problem until she had had some coffee.

It was not necessary.

On the kitchen table, under a pepper-mill to keep it from being blown away, was a note: "Seven P.M. Jimmy R." It was in her handwriting, and now it all came back to her. She poured the hot water over the two teaspoonfuls of coffee powder, stirred it, put in a lump of sugar, took a sip, lit another cigarette, and slowly drank the strong hot brew. Jimmy Rhodes, who had brought her home last night, was coming for a drink at seven o'clock, and her entire future could depend on what happened then.

In all the years she had been in show business, all the parties she had gone to, the meals and drinks she had had at the old Romanoff's, the new Romanoff's, at 21 and Elmer's, the Copa and the Chez in Chicago, the This and the That in cities all over the country, the Savoy and the 400 in London, Maxim's and the Boeuf in Paris—she had never met Jimmy Rhodes until last night. He had said exactly the same thing. "You know, Maggie, we should of met before this. I been hearing about you since—well, I go back to when you were singing with the old Jack Hillyer band."

"Forget it," she said. "My God, you know my exact age."

"Within a year or two, most likely. Where you living now? Here, or on the Coast?"

"Oh, here," she said.

"Yeah, I guess the Coast is through," he said.

"Not for TV," she said.

"No, I guess not for TV, but who cares about TV?"

"I do. I go out there every so often to do a guest shot," she said.

"Well, I don't watch it much. What about Vegas?"

"They don't pay anything," she said.

"You know, I heard that, too," he said. "I heard some of those people supposed to be getting like twenty-five gees, I hear it's closer to two or three."

"If that, in a lot of cases," she said. "There's nothing there for me."

"Well, you don't have to work anyway, do you?"

"No, I don't have to. Unless I want to eat. Whose gag is it? I formed a bad habit when I was young. Eating."

"Come on, I thought you—"

"That's what everybody thinks," she said. "Do you think I'd take some of the jobs I take if I still had all that glue?"

"Well, it was over a million bucks, wasn't it?"

"It was nowhere near that," she said. "The papers called it a million-dollar settlement, but what it actually was was twenty-five thousand dollars a year. It'd take me forty years to get a million. So now you know. And I had lawyers to pay."

"Didn't you make Robinson pay the lawyers?"

"That was part of the settlement, yes. But it didn't end there. In other words, the money my lawyers got from the Robinsons didn't entitle me to a free ride for the rest of my life."

"What was the inside on that story, Maggie?"

"The inside? There wasn't any inside, unless you want me to tell you what Robinson was like in the hay, and there you'd be wasting your time, because I wouldn't tell you. Not because I want to protect him. He didn't care what people thought about him, but I just as soon forget about it. And I more or less have. That was a long time ago, and I've had to work for a living. I met worse than Robbie since then."

"Did he beat you?"

"Sure he beat me. That was all proved in court."

"And that caused you to lose the child?"

"Yes. The Robinsons' own doctor had to admit that," she said. "You got me talking about things I stopped talking about seventy-five years ago. Why?"

"Well, I always wanted to meet you. I was in the army when your case came to trial, but I followed it in the papers."

"I didn't know you were ever in the army," she said.

"The army, and then the air force. I was in air force public relations, mostly."

"Well, that figures," she said. "What were you?"

"I came out a major."

"No, I meant what did you do?"

"Oh—a little of this and a little of that. Public relations. I handled the war correspondents from the big papers and press associations. Fellows I knew in civilian life. And some of the big political brass."

"What did you do? Get girls for them?"

"Well, yes, I introduced them to a few girls. How did you happen to pick that out?"

"I didn't pick it out, exactly. You were kind of famous for that, weren't you?"

"At one time, maybe. But I don't have to do that any more."

"Now you're a big shot. Well, I know that, too. I mean, I see your name in the papers. Jimmy Rhodes, Rhodes Associates and all that jazz."

"Why do you want to put me on, Maggie? If I did a little pimping twenty years ago, are you gonna hold it against me now? You ought to come and have a look at my office. I have forty-two people working for me. Six Harvard graduates. Two Vassar girls. A Bryn Mawr girl. I got a half a dozen of my people that are in the Social Register. I got the daughter of a United States senator and I just took on a retired major general of the air force. I got offices in London, Paris, and Madrid."

"My, you're so important I'm surprised you'd even talk to me," she said.

"Well, there were some things I wanted and I never got," he said. "You were one of them."

"Maybe you should have tried a little harder. I was as they say available."

"Not always, and I had a wife a good deal of the time. Two kids. A daughter just graduated from Wellesley last June, and my son's a junior at Princeton."

"You said you had a wife. Past tense. What happened there?"

"Well, she's married again. Married a fellow he's now the managing editor of a paper out West. He was one of the guys I got a girl for in London, and then he came home and moved in on my wife. They were cheating on me for four or five years before I ever got wise to it."

"And all that time you were behaving like a model husband."

"No, I couldn't say that. But when they had me up before that Senate committee, that was when my wife and her boy friend hit me with the divorce suit, and I didn't stand a chance. She got the children, and a bundle of dough. I was practically fighting for my life with those senators. I very nearly went to the cooler. And one night during the hearings I dropped in the Statler and you were there."

"I remember that date. Ted Straeter's band. A two weeks' booking and they held me over another week."

"It was before you married Robinson. He had a table at ringside. I stood. I didn't have a table. And you sang 'More Than You Know,' which I'd never heard you sing before. And 'So in Love.' Those are two I remember. They were giving it to me but *good* in the Senate Office Building, and on top of that my wife's lawyer had got in touch with my lawyer. I had about seventy-five Scotches and I said to myself, this was the night to move in on Maggie Muldoon. So I said to the maître d', a friend of mine from the old days, how about fixing it up for me? He shook his head. 'Not a prayer, Jimmy,' he said. He pointed to Robinson. 'Een like Fleen,' he said. And he was right."

"Yes, I married Robbie two weeks later," she said.

"I know you did. That was as close as I ever came to meeting you."

"Well, where would we be now if you had?" she said.

"Sixteen years. Seventeen years," he said. "You lasted two years with Robinson, and then you married another fellow. How long did that last?"

"Four."

"What was his name again?" he said.

"Dick Hemmendinger. Guitar player. Ladies' man. Junkie. Crossword puzzle expert. And financial wizard—with my money. He died of pneumonia."

"Or froze to death? You ought to know, but didn't I read about him freezing to death?"

"Yes, you could have. They found him in an alleyway in Toronto, Canada. But it was pneumonia. Nobody ever knew what he was doing in Canada. I hadn't heard from him in over a year, and I have to admit I hoped he was gone for good.

Well, he was. He was very pretty when I first met him. Kind of on the order of Eddy Duchin. That kind of looks. *And* a good guitar player. But a bum, in spades."

"What did you, marry him on the rebound?"

"Oh, I don't know. He was with Hillyer when I first started out with the bands, but I was Hillyer's girl then. My God, I thought Jack Hillyer was all a girl could ask for. I would of no more thought of cheating on Hillyer, and he was paying me two hundred a week, except weeks when the horses weren't running so good. Most people used to complain about one-nighters, but I didn't. I liked the one-nighters. That meant I got paid. But when we got booked into a hotel or a club date, then Jack'd make a contact with the local bookmakers and I could never be sure if I was going to get paid that week. So a couple times I had to borrow money from the sidemen, like Dick Hemmendinger. For coffee and cakes. Lipstick. The hairdresser. I remember one night in Boston, I showed up with my hair all straggly and no makeup on and Hillyer took a look at me and blew his lid. 'That's what you get,' I said. After that he never held out the whole two hundred, but when he broke up the band he was still in me for over a thousand. And the price of one abortion. But imagine having a kid by that louse, what he probably would have been like. Anyway, that was how I first got to know Dick, and then he wrote me a very sympathetic letter when I was in court with Robbie. I saw Jack Hillyer about two weeks ago, standing at the corner of Fifty-second and Broadway. Over there near the Local 802 offices. You know, he was just standing there on the curbstone, not *with* anybody, and he looked about seventy-five years old. I could still recognize him, but he was old. He even had a cane. I went up and said hello to him. I said, 'Do you remember me, Jack?' And he looked at me, but I'm positive he's blind in one eye. 'Yes, hello there,' he said. But he didn't know me. 'It's the Muldoon,' I said, and he said, 'The Muldoon, oh, yes. The Muldoon.' Then when he said it a couple times he remembered me. I asked him what he was doing and he said he was around looking for musicians. He said he was starting up a new band. The big name bands were coming back, he said, and he'd been talking to—then he named off a half a dozen musicians, and at least half of them were dead. He said he was going out with an integrated band and he was getting Fletcher Henderson to do most of his arrangements. Well, how long is it since Fletch passed on? Is it ten years? It's at least five. He looked just awful, Hillyer. Clean, but an old polo coat and a Tyrolean hat with a feather in it. This man I'd been to bed with a hundred times or more, and there he was all wrapped up in an old polo coat that was too big for him. So was his hat. His hat was too big for him, it sort of rested on his ears. And his chin kind of kept moving up and down, even when he wasn't talking. You know, I was brought up a Catholic and I thought I got over all that a long time ago, but standing there talking to Jack Hillyer, this man I used to quiver when he touched me, I suddenly after all these years got a guilty conscience. Sin. I committed sin with this old man. I didn't, you know. I mean, I slept with him all those times, but then he was young and built like a lifeguard. Shoulders, and no waistline. I never thought of sin in those days. But here he looked like he could of been my own father, and that made me feel like I ought to tell the whole thing in confession. His neck. The back of his neck so thin and weak-looking. I didn't mind the lies he was telling. He was always a liar. In fact, that was all that was left of the original Jack, the lies. I don't know how to explain it, how he made me feel sinful. Anyway, I said to him I remembered I owed him twenty dollars from the old days, and I was glad I ran into him. He took the twenty dollars and looked at it, and I knew it would have killed him to part with it, but he said, 'Well, if you're sure you can spare it,' and I said yes, and he stuffed it in his coat pocket. Then something went through his mind and it slowly dawned on him that he actually had twenty dollars on him, and he said how would I like to go to Charlie's and have a drink, but I said I had to run. And he began to remember me. I mean, you could see that something was telling him that he used to sleep with me, and he said we ought to get together. In the voice of an old man, with his chin moving up and down. And I said to call me, I was in the phone book, which I'm not, and it wouldn't of made any difference because he'd already forgotten my name. So I said goodbye and left him standing there. I saw him put his hand in his pocket and feel the money, but he just kept standing there."

"Jack Hillyer," said Jimmy Rhodes.

She took a long sip of her drink.

"You thinking about Hillyer?" he said.

"I'm thinking about you. There's something you told me and it isn't quite kosher."

"No? What's that? What did I say?"

"Some things I remember and some things I don't, especially before and after I had seventy-five drinks. But I know this much, Mr. Jimmy Rhodes Associates. You're some kind of a liar."

"I'm a habitual liar," he said.

"You are? So am I. That is, I'll tell one to get out of something any time. Mind you, I don't like to be a liar, but in this rat-race that I been in for the past seventy-five years, I never knew anybody that wasn't a liar. Sooner or later, you catch them. But I caught you right away. You said you read about my divorce while you were in the army, but the war was over when I got my divorce. I didn't even marry Robbie till after the war, and if you think back a minute, you just proved it. By your touching little story about being in Washington when I was working at the Statler. That was a couple years after the war. I ought to know when I got married. You see this rock? Six carats. Robbie gave it to me the week we got married, and it's just about the last thing I got left of his presents. But if you wanted to take the trouble to look inside, if you had a magnifying glass, you'd find the date. April the fifth, 1948. So that makes you a liar."

"Well, it wasn't much of a lie. I got a little mixed up, that's all."

"Perfectly all right," she said. "I knew there was something wrong about your stories, because I made a record of 'So in Love,' and I had Robbie at the studio with me. It was the first time he ever saw a recording date, and that had to be at least a couple years after the war."

"Don't tell me you're still in love with Robinson," he said.

"Well, maybe I am. You know, I get these moments when I think back over some fellow. Sometimes it's Robbie. Sometimes it'll be Jack Hillyer. Dick Hemmendinger. George Waller."

"There's George Waller over there in front of the fireplace."

"I know. I came with him. We're nothing now, but we did

a little swinging a few years ago. Now I just call him up when I want somebody to take me to a party and I don't have an escort. George went fag a couple years ago."

"That's what I was wondering," he said.

"But every damn one of them—and I didn't give you the whole box-score—they all meant something to me at the time. You take like Hillyer, Jack Hillyer. I was a young kid singing with a band and I was naturally stuck on Hillyer. But if I didn't get stuck on Hillyer, I was the only girl traveling with fifteen musicians and every one of them more or less on the make. I knew one girl—well, never mind. She was with a bigger band than Hillyer's, and she went through them all. But lucky for me I liked Hillyer, and the guys working for him didn't try very hard. Then I went into a couple of shows, and radio, and I married Robbie. He was a dumb cluck, but he had all that glue. And I want to tell *you*, any time I hear anybody talking about the rich people and the way they live, they can ask me, because Robbie's family were really loaded. And I had close to four years of that. They didn't like me, but I was their son's wife, so I got the full treatment. My own personal maid, my own personal car with a chauffeur. I could go to the best restaurants in town and I didn't even have to sign the tab. They put the tips on. Twenty percent for the waiter, ten percent for the captain. I didn't even have to sign my initials. Of course when you have to level and be the man's wife, just you and him, that's the payoff. You're just the same as if you were married to a thirty-five-dollar-a-week guy like my father was, back in Hazleton, PA. Not that Robbie was so bad. But after Hillyer he was kind of a nothing and he knew it, and that's why he began using me for a punching-bag. Some day I knew I'd have to go back to work, and I didn't want him to ruin my looks, so one day I just walked out and didn't come back. There was no objections by his family, and they sent me all my jewelry and clothes. They kept the Cessna. I had a little Cessna I learned to fly, and I logged over two hundred hours in it, but it belonged to some corporation of Mr. Robinson's. It was the only real fun I had all the time I was married to Robbie, was flying that airplane. That, and getting gassed. My grandfather was a lush, and my old man was a strict temperance man, but I take after my grandfather. He used to hold up a glass of whiskey in front of him and smile at it and say, 'My assistant.' He always called it his assistant. So do I, but people don't know what I'm talking about. They think I'm saying my 'assistance,' but they're wrong. I consider it my assis-tant. I don't know what I'd do without my assistant."

"Would you care for another assistant?" said Rhodes.

"You don't call this an assistant, what's in my glass now. Sure."

She opened her purse and looked at herself in the mirror. Her makeup did not need refreshing, and Jimmy Rhodes had been sitting quite close to her for a good half hour. So long as she held up her chin it did not double up, and all things considered—as she looked around at the other women at the party—she did not have to apologize for her appearance. She had been a star, she had been the wife of the heir to a fairly famous fortune, and in the world in which she lived and even beyond it she did not need an introduction. Everyone knew who she was. Jimmy Rhodes certainly knew who she was; he had been having a ball. It was too bad that there was not more to him. He was masculine enough, with a clear and practically unwrinkled complexion. About half of his front hair was gone, but he had all his teeth and obviously he had used them on many good steaks. He was probably twenty-five pounds over-weight. His dinner jacket was not what Robbie would have worn—the lapels too narrow, and touches of satin piping at the pockets and on the sleeve. His shoes were funny; patent leather with tassels. And his shirt was frilled down the middle. The rims of his glasses were just a little thicker than they had to be and the lenses were larger than most. There was thought behind everything he had on, and behind the thought no taste. She had learned, in four years, to look at men's attire as Robbie's father or the Robinson butler would look at it, and Jimmy Rhodes was all wrong. Instinctively all wrong. With a great deal of care, all wrong. By the way he had pulled down the jacket when he got up to get her highball, she knew he thought he was all right. He had six Harvard graduates working for him, and nobody to tell him anything.

"Your assistant," he said, handing her the glass.

"Don't you drink?" she said.

"Never after dinner," he said. "I got no taste for it. The same way with smoking. I quit smoking right after I got outa the service. I like to be in good physical condition."

"What for?"

He laughed. "Well, I'm not a weight-lifter. But I can pick up say about a hundred and thirty pounds."

"Close," she said. "I'm a hundred and thirty-two."

"I judged you to be somewhere in there."

"Do you play the field, or do you go steady?" she said.

"Oh, the field. No more wedding bells for me."

"How do you get away with it?" she said.

"How do I get away with it? Well, for a while I used to tell them I was carrying the torch for Grace Kelly. I never even met Grace Kelly, but I owe her a debt of gratitude."

"Send her a planeload of Texas millionaires."

"They don't gamble," he said.

"They don't?"

"They spend it, some of them, but not foolishly, like you and I would. A Texan'll buy a cream-colored Rolls-Royce for $30,000, but don't forget he has the Rolls after he spent that money."

"Who'd want a cream-colored Rolls?"

"Me. I happen to have one downstairs. Wuddia say we take a ride in it? As soon as you're finished with your assistant. Don't hurry."

"Where is this ride going to take us?"

"Well, I have an apartment over on Park."

"Not far enough."

"All right, where is your apartment?"

"That's too far. Much too far," she said.

"Like how far?" he said.

"A lot farther than you're gonna get," she said.

"Do you wanta bet?"

"Not on a sure thing. I'm not a Texan. I don't mind betting but not on a sure thing."

"Why? Don't you like me?"

"The funny thing is, I do," she said.

"What's funny about it? A lot of dames like me."

"Well, I like you," she said.

"Then what's funny about it?"

"It's kind of hard to put into words," she said.

"You're a good talker. You know how to express yourself. Go ahead."

"Well, I like you, but you could never mean anything to me."

"Why not?"

"You don't give out enough. A man has to give out, and you don't. Didn't any other girl ever tell you that?"

"They not only didn't tell me that, but I never even heard about this giving out. You mean like an extrovert?"

"That's a word I never knew the definition of. Try something else."

"Well, a guy that's always giving out, I guess. I give out, but I always keep something in reserve."

"That's what I mean. You keep more in reserve than you give out."

"I guess that's true."

"See, that's where we differ. I give out. With a song, I always gave out. I couldn't belt one like The Merm, but in my own style I always gave out like I was never gonna sing another number the rest of my life. They used to tell me to modulate, but I couldn't modulate. My agents and the a. and r. men at the record companies used to pick numbers for me that I had to modulate, but I gave out anyway. It worked out pretty good on some recordings. Look what Peggy Lee did with 'Lover.' A sickly kind of a waltz that she took and just whaled the hell out of it into an exciting number. Peggy and Ella. This new kid, Eydie Gormé, she might make it. Although she isn't getting to be a kid any more. One more assistant and then I think I'll cut out of here."

"Have it with me, at my apartment."

"Now don't start to be a bore, Jimmy. If you want to take me home, all right. But if you got any ideas about tonight, forget it. I had about seventy-five drinks tonight, and if Richard Burton came knocking on my door I'd send him away. I don't take anybody to my apartment when I made the load. There's two things I don't do. I don't smoke in bed, and I don't take strange guys to my apartment when I get saturated. Those are my only two rules, for my own protection. If you would of come over and introduced yourself to me earlier, it might be a different story. But I got a little bell inside of me that says, 'Maggie, no strange men tonight.'"

"In other words, if I would of come over when you only had thirty-seven and a half drinks? That's half of seventy-five," he said.

"Maybe. But the little bell rang about two hours ago."

"How about if I catch you early tomorrow?"

"How early?"

"We have a couple drinks and go some place for dinner," he said.

"All right. Why not? You call for me at seven o'clock."

He had a cream-colored Rolls. She remembered that, but not much from then on. She got up from the kitchen table and made herself another cup of instant coffee. It was bringing her around. She lit another cigarette and sat down again and as she sipped the coffee she began making plans. Take a shower, and that would bring her to and she could have a vodka after her shower. She would wear her little black dress that actually did more for her figure than the new one with the deep décolletage. She had no idea where he would be taking her in the course of the evening, but she was determined to give him an altogether different impression from the one she had given him last night. The black dress would help there. She would space out her drinks, and if they saw any society people she would be sure to introduce him to them. Society people liked it when she spoke to them, even if they never invited her to their houses. She would show him that she knew how to order a meal—those little questions to the headwaiter, like "Is this hothouse asparagus, or fresh?" She would let him see any number of little things that she had picked up from the Robinsons' butler during those four years. She would come home sober and early, and if everything went as she planned, she soon would have nothing to worry about the rest of her life.

It was bad luck to sing before breakfast, but two coffees were all the breakfast she was going to have, and she hummed a tune as she rinsed out the cup and saucer. She went back to the bathroom and put on a rubber cap and took a shower. She toweled herself, put on her bra and panty-girdle and dressing-gown, and now she had earned her vodka.

The living room was still dark. She switched on the ceiling lights and went to the portable bar. And then she saw him, seated in one of the highback chairs. "How the hell did *you* get here?" she said. But even before she finished the question she knew she would never get an answer from him. He was in an attitude of sleep, an unattractive attitude. His mouth was open, and so were his eyes. The poor slob, in his frilly shirt and tasseled shoes. For all she knew, or would ever know, he had died while waiting for her to call him to her room. The worst was his eyes, seen through those thick lenses.

She had her vodka, her assistant, and went to the telephone in her bedroom. The logical person to call was her lawyer, and she did not have to look up his number. She knew it by heart.

Fatimas and Kisses

AROUND THE corner from where I used to live there was a little store run by a family named Lintz. If you wanted ice cream, by the quart or by the cone, you could get it at Lintzie's; you could buy cigarettes and the less expensive cigars, a loaf of bread, canned goods, meats that did not require the services of a butcher, penny candy and boxed bon-bons, writing tablets and pencils, and literally hundreds of articles on display-cards that novelty salesmen had persuaded Lintzie to put on his shelves, and which he never seemed to reorder. I doubt if there are many stores like Lintzie's around any more, but his place was a great convenience for the people in the neighborhood. When a housewife ran short of something she would tell her child to go down to Lintzie's for the bottle of milk or the half pound of butter or the twenty cents' worth of sliced ham. And Lintzie would charge it. He well knew that the housewives in the neighborhood preferred to deal with the downtown meat markets and grocery stores, and that his trade was at least partly on a semi-emergency basis. That, and the fact that he allowed people to charge things, gave him the excuse to maintain a mark-up on most of his stock, and the housewives called him a highway robber. They called him that to his face. But they were careful how they said it. O'Donnell's meat market was the best, and Gottlieb had the best grocery store, but they were downtown and they would not open up for you if you needed a can of soup or a quart of milk at half past eight in the evening. Lintzie and his wife and two children lived upstairs over the store, and someone would always come down and open up for a customer.

Lintzie was a thin man with a Charlie Chaplin moustache and hollow cheeks that were made hollower still by his habit of leaving out his upper plate. He was young to have false teeth; in his late twenties. He had been in the Marine Corps, although he had not gone overseas, and all his worldliness, all his travels, were by benefit of his having been a Gott damn chyrene. He was a Pennsylvania Dutch farm boy, from somewhere east of Reading, and it wondered me, as the Dutch say, how he had ever heard of the marines. So, being in my teens and curious, I asked him. "How I heart abaht the Marine Corps? I didn't never hear about them till once I seen one of them there posters in the post office. I seen a picture of a marine, all dressed up in his plues, his rifle at right shoulder arms, his bayonet in a white scabbard. He looked handsome to me, so I went home and said to my old man I was going to enlist. I won't tell you what the old man said. He said to go ahead, only he said other things besides. Glad to get rid of me. Him and my brother could run the farm without me. My brother was glad to get rid of me too. That way the old man would leave him the farm and me nothing. So I went to where it said on the poster and signed the papers. By Jesus if I knew what it was like them first three months I would of never enlisted. Son of a bitch sergeant with a swagger stick. Drill. Bivouac. Snakes. By Jesus nights I was too tired to cut my throat. That's no joke. But I guess it all done me good. I come out stronger than I went in, but minus the most of my teeth."

"How did that happen?"

"Oh, I got in a fight with a sailor, me and another Gott damn chyrene we were on duty in the Lackawanna Railroad Station in Hoboken, New Chersey. We took him in custody, he was drunk. But then all of a sudden from all over come them sailors. I had a .45 in my holster but it done me no good. They must of been ten of them chumped us all at once, and one of them hit me across the mouth with my own billy club. That was all the fighting I ever done in the Gott damn chyrenes. The Lackawanna Railroad Station in Hoboken, New Chersey. I got a discharge in October 1918, two weeks before the armistice. But I used to raise a lot of hell in Philly and New York City and Boston, Mass. I could tell *you* some stories if you was older. I was a pretty good-looking fellow till them sailors chumped me. But the son of a bitch that started it, he got something like thirty years' hard labor."

"You identified him?"

"I sure did. I picked him out of twenty of the bastards. I hope he rots. I would of got corporal if it wasn't for him. Maybe I would of stayed in and got gunnery sergeant. But they let me go and now I can't even chew a steak, not with the teeth I got now."

Lintzie's wife was a placid, rather slovenly woman whose hair was never in place. She had an extraordinarily lovely complexion and white little teeth and large breasts that swayed unencumbered by a brassiere. When he addressed her by name, which was seldom, he called her Lonnie. She called him Donald or Lintzie; Lintzie, if she was shouting to him from the back of the store or upstairs, and Donald if she was standing near him. He hardly ever looked at her unless her back was turned. In front of people my age and younger he would say to her, "Go fix yourself up decent, for Christ's sake."

"Aah, shut up," she would say.

But when older people were present they hid their animosity by paying no attention to each other. One day when I went to buy cigarettes, which he was not supposed to sell to me, I waited for Lintzie or Lonnie to appear and wait on me, but neither came. I went back and reopened and closed the door so that the bell would ring again, and she came running downstairs. "Oh, it's you," she said.

"Will you give me a pack of Camels and a pack of Fatimas," I said.

"Charge or pay?"

"*Pay*," I said.

"Who are the Fatimas for? Some girl?"

"For my uncle," I said.

"Yeah, your uncle standing out there with the bicycle. You better watch out, Malloy. Her old lady catches her smoking cigarettes, they'll tell your old man and you'll get hail-Columbia. Give me thirty-five cents."

"Where's Lintzie?" I said.

"To Reading. Why?"

"Just wondered," I said.

"Why?"

"Just wondered," I said. I looked out toward the sidewalk and at the half-ton panel truck parked at the curb, driverless. She put two packs of Camels and two packs of Fatimas on the counter.

"I'll treat you to the butts," she said. "Okay?"

"Thanks," I said.

"The next time her old lady comes in, I won't say anything about you buying her kid Fatimas. Okay?"

"All right," I said.

They never knew—older people—at just what age you started to notice things like a driverless truck and a husband's absence and a delayed appearance, and put them all together. But now Lonnie knew that I had put them all together, and I knew that I had put them together accurately. My discovery was too momentous and mature to confide in the girl who was waiting with her bike. It was too much the kind of thing that I wanted to protect her from, and was indeed eager to protect her from all her life. Those were things I already knew too much about, along with the sight of death and the ugliness of things I had seen in my father's office and in ambulances, hospitals, the homes of the poor, when my father was still trying to make a doctor of me. I could barely endure to see those things myself, but I was a boy. She was a girl, and in ten years or maybe less she was going to be my wife. *Then* I might tell her some of those things, but now Fatimas and kisses were as much as she was ready for.

The bell tinkled as I opened Lintzie's door and tinkled again as I closed it. I guess it was the sound of the bell as much as the Fatimas I flashed that made her giggle. "You got them?" she said. It was a throaty whisper.

"Sure," I said. "Fat-Emmas for you, humps for me. Where do you want to go?"

"Have you got matches?"

"We don't need them. I have my magnifying glass." Matches in a boy's pockets were prima facie evidence of the cigarette habit, like nicotine stains on the fingers. A magnifying glass only created the suspicion that he had been seeing too much of Craig Kennedy, the scientific detective, in his struggles to outwit The Clutching Hand.

I went away to school around that time, and during vacations my hangout was a downtown drug store. Lintzie's was not that kind of place; the neighborhood kids congregated on the sidewalk, drawn to the store by the candy and ice cream, but Lintzie and Lonnie discouraged them from remaining inside. "Get your fingers off them Easter eggs," Lonnie would say. "Stop fooling around with them searchlights. Do you want to wear out the battery?" Lintzie and Lonnie would threaten to put items on the kids' family bills, and sometimes they made good on the threats. Sometimes they billed the wrong family; a fair amount of pilfering went on in spite of the Lintzies' vigilance, and you would see a kid who had just been driven out of the store furtively but proudly displaying a mechanical pencil or a put-and-take top or a carton of fig newtons that he had stolen. One of my younger brothers never came out of Lintzie's empty-handed, even if all he got was a cucumber. I did once see him steal a cucumber. The custom was known locally as the five-finger-grab, and it contributed to the Lintzies' pedophobia, which did not exclude their own messy children. "Go on up and wipe your nose," Lintzie would say. "Tell your mother to sew them buttons on." As a young buck who had danced with Constance Bennett and visited the Pre Cat, I stayed away from Lintzie's as much as possible during that period.

But then my father died and I had to get a job as cub reporter on one of the town papers. Temporarily—and I never considered it anything but temporary—my sphere of activity was limited to my own county. We had almost no income, and my mother kept us going by converting her bonds to cash, a desperation measure that obviously could not last forever. It did not make economic sense—nothing did—but very soon we were steady customers at Lintzie's instead of at the cash-and-carry a block away, where everything was much cheaper. My mother ceased to be a customer at O'Donnell's and Gottlieb's; lamb chops and asparagus seldom appeared on our dinner table. We bought a loaf of bread at a time, a jar of peanut butter, a half dozen eggs, a quarter pound of butter, a half-pint of cream, because at Lintzie's prices nothing must go to waste, to turn stale or sour. "On your way home, stop in at Lintzes' and get a can of tomato soup," my mother would say. She had never referred to it as Lintzie's and she was not going to start now. I had always been able to tell that she did not like Lintzie or his wife, and she liked them less when she owed them money twenty-nine days out of every month. They were not overly fond of her, either; she was a better bookkeeper than they, and never hesitated to prove it.

I had become, among other things, quite a drinker, although I was not yet twenty years old. How I managed to drink so much on no money is still somewhat of a mystery to me, but cheap booze was cheap, and politicians and "members of the sporting fraternity" were expected to buy drinks for newspaper men. "Why not?" an old-timer said to me. "It's small recompense for the dubious pleasure of their company." Lintzie was neither politician nor prizefight promoter, but one afternoon, when I stopped in for a last-minute purchase, he invited me to have a drink with him at Schmelinger's, a neighborhood saloon that had never bothered to pretend to be a speakeasy. "I'm broke," I said.

"I'll buy," said Lintzie.

"That's a different story," I said.

Schmelinger had been a patient of my father's, and I therefore had never been a patron of Schmelinger's, but Lintzie was greeted with the gruff politeness of the barkeep toward the good customer. We sat at a table and had three or four whiskeys—straight, with water chasers—and spent a most enjoyable hour together. In that neighborhood nearly all the men were at work all day, and Lintzie had no men friends. I gathered that he would run over to Schmelinger's for a shot in the middle of the morning and along about three or four in the afternoon, before the housewives' and schoolkids' rush. That was on a Lincoln's birthday, a school holiday. I was rather sorry that I could not count on being fitted into Lintzie's schedule, but I need not have worried. He changed his schedule to fit mine.

At that stage of my life I took my charm for granted; I did not inquire into the possible reasons why a man who was ten years older than I would want to buy me four dollars' worth of expertly cut rye whiskey once or twice a week. But slowly I began to understand first that he had somehow become indifferent to the difference in our ages. From our conversation it appeared that during my time away at school I had somehow added ten, not four, years to my age. Secondly, like everyone else, he needed someone to talk to. And he talked. He had certain recollections of his Marine Corps days that he liked to dwell on repetitiously: practical jokes on comrades-in-arms, small revenges on young officers, standing two feet away from Woodrow Wilson, visits to a whorehouse on Race Street, Philadelphia. From his whorehouse reminiscences he would often proceed, with unconscious logic, to some revelations concerning Lonnie. Her people had intended her to be the wife of his brother, but when Lintzie came home on his first furlough he threw her on the ground and gave her what she'd been asking for. On his next furlough he married her despite the fact that his brother had meanwhile thrown her on the ground and given her what she'd been asking for. But Lintzie had been first, and the baby was almost surely his. Now that the kid was old enough to look like somebody, he did look more like Lintzie than like his brother, so Lintzie guessed he had not made any mistake in that respect. He was not so sure about the second kid, the daughter. She didn't look like anybody, like a Lintz *or* a Moyer (Lonnie having been a Moyer). But by the law of averages it was probably Lintzie's kid, and he had never been able to prove anything. Lonnie hardly ever went out of the house. Most of the time she waited on customers in her carpet slippers. When she had to go back home for her brother's funeral her shoes did not fit her, so she had to stop on the way to the station and buy a new pair. Two months later, when she was taking the kids to their first day at Sunday School, the new shoes were too small for her. It was hard to believe that she had ever been pretty, but when she was seventeen or eighteen she was as pretty as any girl in the Valley. Some girls didn't care what they looked like after they got married, and Lonnie was one of them. Well, which was worse: the ones who didn't care, or the ones who cared about nothing else and flirted with every son of a bitch with pants on? In another year or two you'd be able to leave her at a hose company picnic and she'd be as safe as if she stayed home. Lintzie had told her as much, and all she said was, "Aah, shut up." That was her answer for everything. Shut up. To Lintzie, to the kids, to her mother, but most of all to Lintzie, and she had said it so often that it sunk in, finally sunk in, and he *did* shut up.

After a while it sunk in on *her* that he had practically stopped talking to her, and she complained about it. He told her he was only doing what she had been telling him to do: she had been telling him for years to shut up, and that's what he did. If she didn't want to listen to anything he had to say, he would talk to her only when it was positively necessary. And her automatic reply to that statement was to tell him to shut up. He realized that she used the expression the way some people say "Go to hell" or "Aw, nuts" but "Aah, shut up" was actually what she said, and he took her at her word. To some extent it made life livable, not to have to talk to her. She was not very much of a talker, not what you'd call a chatterbox, a windbag, but half of what she said was complaints, bellyaching. If it wasn't about money, it was about her feet getting bigger, and if it wasn't about her feet it was why didn't he do more about raising the kids instead of sneaking off to Schmelinger's morning, noon, and night? The funny thing about her complaining was that it was never twice about the same thing. It was probably better than if she harped on the same thing all the time, which would soon drive a man crazy, but on the other hand, she would complain about something and if you paid enough attention to go and do something about the complaint, you damn soon found out that she didn't even remember complaining about it. Like the time he went out and paid $185 for a new Stromberg-Carlson and she asked what the hell did he want to have two radios for, entirely forgetting that she had complained about the old radio and had specifically mentioned the Stromberg-Carlson as the one she wanted next. One day, out of a blue sky, she said to him, "Why didn't you stay in the marines? If you stayed in the marines we'd be living in Hawaii instead of a dump like this." It was such an infuriatingly unreasonable complaint that he hauled off and gave her a kick in the behind. "What'd you kick me for?" she said. Sometimes he thought she didn't have any brains in her head, but she was no dumbbell. In some things she was pretty smart. He let her do the ordering when some of the salesmen came around. She didn't know that seven eights was fifty-six, but she never took the first price on anything, and every time she ordered something, say a gross of pencils, she made the salesman fork over something for nothing. Before she would even begin talking about a sale she would demand free samples—candy, chewing gum, novelties—and use them later to reward kids who went on errands for her.

In the strictest confidence and after more than the usual ration of rye and water, Lintzie told me one day that Lonnie had discovered that most housewives did not bother to keep tabs on what they bought. My mother did not let her get away with it, he said, but other women in the neighborhood did not seem to notice when Lonnie added items to the monthly bills. She was pretty good at it, too. It was hardly ever more than a dollar's worth of stuff per account, but if you added a dollar to every bill it came to around a hundred a month clear profit. At Christmas it was even more. Anyway, it was well over a thousand dollars a year, which was Gott damn good for a woman that couldn't multiply seven eights. Like picking it up off the floor. Thereafter I did not mind taking Lintzie's free drinks. I was, so to speak, the guest of the neighborhood housewives, among whom were a few who had failed to settle accounts with my father's estate.

It also occurred to me that I was receiving a bribe from Lonnie that supplemented the original four packs of cigarettes. It probably would have done her no good to complain, but she could have protested when Lintzie rang up a No Sale on the cash register and helped himself to the money to pay for his hospitality to me. No doubt she was glad to get him out of her sight. Nevertheless I became convinced that Lonnie was appreciative of my early silence, if possibly a little apprehensive that I might break it now that Lintzie and I were drinking companions. Ethically I was not standing on firm ground, but my ethics and my morals and my conscience were taking a continual beating in other areas as well. I was giving myself trouble over girls and women and love and theology and national politics and my uncontrollable temper. Not the easiest of my problems was my willingness to spend as much time with a man whom I regarded as a moron. It was true that I was the victim of circumstances back beyond my control, but I was unable thereby to justify my association with this loquacious lout. Since I could not justify it, I gave up trying to.

Downtown, in back of a second-rate commercial hotel, was another saloon that was as wide open as Schmelinger's and served the same grade of whiskey. Unlike Schmelinger's it catered to a considerable transient trade, principally the traveling salesmen who stopped at the hotel. It was a busy joint, and often half filled with strangers. I went there one night, alone, and sat at a table to drink beer, eat pretzels, and read the out-of-town papers. At the next table were two strangers drinking rye and ginger ale. Salesmen, most likely, and getting drunk. They did not bother me, but I began to pick up some of their conversation. One was telling the other about a customer of his, nothing much for looks, but a positive, guaranteed lay. Nothing novel about that conversation between salesmen, but the speaker gave his companion directions on how to find the accommodating customer, and the address was Lintzie's store. "I got put on to her a couple years ago," he said. "Don't look for any great beauty. This is for a quick jazz when you don't have a date. No money. You give her a dozen samples or shave your prices a little. And you gotta watch out for the husband. He's in and out of the place all day. A boozer. My last time in this town, I was upstairs with the broad and the husband came back from the saloon. I had to hide in a closet till he went out again. All he had to do was open that closet door and I'm cooked, but I been taking off her for a couple years and that's the first time we ever had a close one. Don't tell her I sent you. The first time, you gotta make it on your own, but I want to tell you something, that—ain't—hard. And buddy, she likes it."

I could easily have struck up a conversation with the traveling man and learned more about Lonnie's behavior, but a friend of mine joined me and we were town people against strangers. The salesman had confirmed my suspicions about Lonnie, dormant suspicions because I had not realized that Lonnie was quite so adventurous or quite so careless. Oddly enough, my immediate impulse was to warn Lonnie to use some caution, and my second, contradictory to the first, was no more than a feeling of pity for Lintzie. The practical effect of what I had overheard was to give up my pleasant enough drinking sessions with Lintzie. There was going to be trouble there, I knew it, and I had a very positive wish to stay away from it. I did not want to be drinking with Lintzie while Lonnie was using his absence to entertain a gabby salesman.

In later years I came to believe that Lintzie's first suspicions of Lonnie dated from my withdrawal from our sessions at Schmelinger's. My excuse to him was flimsy, although based partly on fact: that the paper had promoted me to columnist, an extra job that had to be done on my own time. It was flimsy because Lintzie did not believe me. Whenever I saw him he gave me the special look of small dignity offended, the look of small people who do not feel entitled to anger. My subsequent theory about Lintzie's suspicions of Lonnie was that without me (or anyone else) to talk to, he was left entirely with his thoughts, and his world was very small. He had a wife, two kids who gave him no pleasure, and the clientele of his store for whom he had no respect. And of course he had the memories of his ten months as a private in the Marine Corps, patrolling railway stations and piers and being sneered at by sailors and petty officers; occasional visits to whorehouses along the Eastern Seaboard; the time he stood frozen at attention when the President of the whole Gott damn United States passed within two feet of him at the Union Depot in Washington. His brother had never been as far as New York, his father had never been as far as Philadelphia, his mother had never even been to Reading before she was thirty. For a Berks County farm boy Lintzie had seen a lot of the world, but he had not been seeing much of it lately. Schmelinger ran a very sober saloon; the only decoration in the place was a pre-Prohibition framed brewery advertisement, depicting a goat in Bavarian costume raising a beer stein. Schmelinger himself was a strict Roman Catholic who had a daughter a nun and a son studying for priesthood. It was in these surroundings that Lintzie was spending a great deal of his time, probably as much of it as in his own store.

A full year and a little more passed during which I did not have a drink with Lintzie and actually did not set foot in his store. (My mother could send one of my brothers for those last-minute quarts of milk.) I was getting twenty dollars a week on the paper, and the owner, in his benevolence, allowed me to fill the tank of my four-cylinder Buick at the paper's expense. So I was coming up in the world, and I loved my column, which was one of the numerous imitations of F.P.A.'s Conning Tower. One afternoon, after the paper had gone to press and the other reporters had gone home, the phone rang on the city editor's desk and I went to answer it. "Malloy speaking," I said.

"Oh, it's you, Malloy. This is Christine Fultz."

"Hello, Chris, what have you got?" I said. She was a "correspondent" who picked up a few dollars a week for news tips and unreadable (and usually outdated) accounts of church suppers.

"Well, I'll tell you, there's something very funny going on out here."

"Is it funny enough to go in my column?"

"What column is that?" said Chris.

"Never mind. What have you got? Spill it."

"I want the credit for the tip, mind you."

"I'll see that you get the credit for the tip, but first you have to tell me what tip on what," I said.

"It's at Lintzie's. There's a whole crowd of people standing outside there."

"Maybe they're having a bargain sale."

"Be *serious*. Somebody said he shot her."

"Lintzie shot Lonnie?"

"That's what I said, didn't I? But I don't know if it's true or not. I couldn't get very near, there's such a crowd. There was another story circulating that he shot her and the two children, but I don't know that either."

"Are the police there?" I said.

"If they are, they're inside. I didn't see no police."

"When did this happen, do you know?"

"Well, it couldn't of happened very long ago, because I went past Lintzie's an hour ago and there was nobody there. But when I came back you should of seen the crowd. So it must of happened between the time I went past there an hour ago and when I was on my way home."

"Now you're using the old noodle, Chris. What else?"

"*Somebody* said he shot a *man*."

"Lintzie shot a man?"

"Don't go blaming me if that's just a rumor, but that's what one person told me. There's supposed to be a dead man in there, and Lonnie and the two kids."

"But Lintzie? Where is Lintzie?"

"I don't know. He's either inside or he got away. Or maybe he's dead too."

"That's the old noodle again, Chris. Well, thanks very much. You'll get credit for the tip."

"Are you coming out?"

"Try and stop me," I said.

In less than ten minutes I parked my car across the street from Lintzie's. It was my neighborhood, and everyone knew that I was working on the paper, so they made way for me. A cop, the newest on the force, got between me and the door. "No newspaper reporters," he said.

"Who said so? *You*, for Christ's sake? Get out of my way. If you'll turn your thick head around you'll see your boss waving to me to come in." Inside the store Joe Dorelli, a sergeant and detective—all detectives were sergeants—was signaling to me. "You see?" I said to the rookie cop. "I was covering murders when you were playing high school football." It was a lie, but rookie cops were our natural enemies. I went inside.

"What the hell is this, Joe?"

"Lintzie, the Dutch bastard. He come home and caught her in bed with a guy and he shot them. Then the kids come running in from the yard and he shot them too. You want to see the gun? Here's the gun." On the counter was a holster stamped USMC and in it was a Colt .45 automatic pistol.

"Where is Lintzie?" I said.

"Back in the kitchen, talking to the chief. You'd think he just got elected mayor, honest. He phoned in. Me and the chief come right out and the first thing he done was offer us a cigar. Then he took us upstairs and showed us the wife and the boy friend. Wait'll you see *them*. We're waiting for the fellow to come and take their pictures. Then Lintzie took us down in the cellar and showed us the two kids."

"He shot them down in the cellar?"

"No, on the stairway, between this floor and the bedroom. Then he carried them down in the cellar. I don't know why, and he doesn't either. I said to him why didn't he shoot himself while he was at it? That's what they often do. But he was surprised at such a question. Why should he shoot himself? He looked at me like I wasn't all there."

"Is he drunk?"

"You can smell it on him, but he don't act it. He asked were you here."

"He did?"

"By name," said Dorelli "That's what I wanted to talk to you. Did you know this was gonna happen? Nobody knows who the guy is. Well, we know his name and he was some kind of a salesman. His wallet was in his pants pocket, hanging on the back of a chair. From Wilkes-Barre, he is, but working for a company over in Allentown. Sidney M. Pollock, thirty-two years of age. But did you know about him and the Lintz woman?"

"No, but I might recognize him."

"We'll get him identified all right."

"I'd like to take a look at him."

"From the front you would. You know what a .45 slug'll do. The right-hand cheekbone it went in. She got it in the heart. Two. He gave her one for good measure. The kids he gave one apiece. Five shots, four dead. But he was a marine, and they teach them to shoot in the marines. I took notice there was a picture of him in the bedroom. Marksman and expert rifleman. Well, do you want to take a look at them?"

I only wanted to see the dead man, and I did recognize him. He was the companion of the traveling salesman who had talked so seductively of Lonnie Lintz. Even after a year there was no mistaking that nose and that hairless skull. I could not have recognized the big-mouth salesman; he had been sitting on my right; but Pollock had been facing him, and me. It was perhaps too much to say that if I had struck up a conversation with them that night, Pollock would not now be lying dead in his underwear on a messy bed in a strange town, in disgrace. I thought of Pollock's wife, if any, and his probably orthodox mother and father in Wilkes-Barre.

"Now you got another treat in store for you," said Dorelli. "Down in the cellar."

"No thanks," I said.

"Me either," said Dorelli. "I had to, but if I didn't have to I wouldn't have. Two kids, for Christ's sake, around the same age as two of mine. This guy is crazy, but don't you write that. That's what he'll claim—and maybe he had a right to kill her and the Jew, but not the kids. He can't pull that unwritten law on the kids. For that he deserves to fry."

"I didn't know you were such a family man, Joe."

"Listen, what you don't know about me would fill a book," he said. "You had enough, we'll go down and see if the chief'll let you talk to Lintz."

I waited in the store while Joe conferred with the chief. A cop named Lundy came in while I was there. "That's something you don't often hear in this town," he said.

"What's that?" I said.

"Them women out there, they want to lynch him."

"We've never had a lynching in this town," I said.

"We never will. It's just talk, but you don't often hear that kind of talk in Lantenengo County. Just talk, but all the same I'm gonna tell the chief to get him outa here."

"You mean you're thinking of *suggesting* to the chief," I said.

"Aah, smart guy," said Lundy. "I hear Lintz and you was great buddies."

"Doing some detective work at Schmelinger's, eh, Lundy? Do you think you'll solve this case?"

"I'll solve you one right in the puss, Malloy," said Lundy.

"Then you'll be right back on the garbage truck. We supported *this* mayor," I said.

Dorelli, at the rear of the store, beckoned to me.

"Any message you wish me to convey to the chief, Lundy?" I said.

"No, you wouldn't get it right, just like that rag you work for," said Lundy. He laughed and I laughed. Lundy was a good cop and he knew I thought so.

"I'll put in a good word for you, then," I said.

"Jesus, don't do that. That'd be the ruination of me, a good word from you."

I joined Dorelli. "You can talk to him, but one of us has to be there."

"Oh, come on, Joe. There's no mystery about this case. Let me talk to him alone."

"We'll do it our way or not at all," said Dorelli.

"Then we'll do it your way," I said.

Dorelli led me to the kitchen. A uniformed cop was standing outside the kitchen door; the chief was sitting across the table from Lintzie, his chin on his chest, staring at him in silence. Obviously the chief had momentarily run out of questions to ask Lintzie. Lintzie turned when I entered. "Oh, there's my buddy. Hyuh, Malloy."

"Hello, Lintzie," I said.

"Say, Chief, let me send over to Schmelinger's for a pint," said Lintzie. "I'll pay for it."

"Pay for it? You got a lot to pay for, you son of a bitch," said the chief.

"I'll be down in the cellar," said Dorelli, and left.

"Well, I guess I went and done it," said Lintzie.

"How did you happen to pick today?" I said.

"I don't know," said Lintzie. "I was over at Schmelinger's and I guess I started to thinking to myself. There was a whole truckload of stuff piled up on the kitchen porch, waiting to be unpacked. I knowed Gott damn well Lonnie wouldn't start unpacking it. It had to be unpacked and put down in the cellar out of the way. So I said to myself if I got it all unpacked I could make the kids take it down in the cellar when they got home. It was a truckload of stuff from the wholesaler. Canned goods. Heavy. In wooden boxes. All I needed was my claw-hammer and I could unpack the stuff and the kids could take it down the cellar a couple cans at a time. Ten or fifteen minutes' work for me and I could be back at Schmelinger's. So I said to Gus I'd see him later and I come home."

"What time was that, Lintzie?" I said.

"Search me. I lost track of time," said Lintzie.

"About quarter of three," said the chief. "Between half past two and three, according to Schmelinger."

"I come in the store door, and I took notice to the salesman's car outside. But I went inside and no Lonnie, and no salesman. The chief don't believe me, but I caught her once before with a salesman, only it wasn't the same one."

"Why don't you believe him, Chief?"

"Because this was a deliberate murder. All this stuff about the packages on the back porch, that's the bunk."

"Look outside, the boxes are there right now in plain sight," said Lintzie.

"He pretended he was going to spend a couple hours at Schmelinger's, the way he usually did. But he only went there long enough to give his wife and the salesman time to go up-stairs," said the chief. "He admitted himself he usually kept the .45 upstairs but today he had it hanging on a peg in the cellar stairway. This was a planned first-degree murder."

"How about that, Lintzie?" I said.

"The chief don't have to be right all the time."

"But why was the gun hanging in the stairway?"

"To get it out of the way of the kids. Lonnie said she caught the boy playing with it and I was to get it out of the way. So I took and hung it on a peg in the cellar stairway, where he couldn't reach it. That was two-three days ago. Lonnie could—I was just gonna say Lonnie could back me up on that, but I guess not now."

"No," I said. "So then what?"

"Yes, listen to this part, Malloy," said the chief.

"Then what? Then I went upstairs and caught them in bed."

"Wait a minute, Lintzie. You're skipping a lot. Did you get the gun and then go upstairs?" I said.

"Me? No. I went upstairs and caught them and then I got the gun."

"Did you, before you went upstairs, did you call Lonnie to see where she was? Upstairs or down-cellar?"

"Well, she could hear the bell when I come in the store."

"But you could have been a customer. You didn't call her, or did you?"

"He didn't call her, and he *didn't* come in the front door," said the chief. "He told Dorelli one story and me another, and now he's an altogether different one. He told Dorelli he went around the back way and got his claw-hammer and started opening the boxes. There's no mark of a claw-hammer on any of the boxes, and anyway you make a certain amount of noise opening a wooden box with a claw-hammer. You know, you put the claws under the slats and you start using leverage and it makes a peculiar kind of a noise. But that would have warned the people upstairs. No, he came in the back door, where there is no bell, and he got the .45 and sneaked upstairs and took careful aim and killed the salesman. One shot. Then he let her have two slugs right in the heart. I had a look at the .45 and I'll tell you this much, Malloy. If all my men kept their guns in as good a condition I'd be satisfied. I know something about guns. If you leave a gun in a holster for any length of time, the oil gets gummy, but not this gun. This gun was cleaned and oiled I'd say in the last twenty-four, forty-eight hours."

"I always kept my gun in good condition," said Lintzie.

"Yes. For just such an occasion," said the chief.

"Tell me what you did, Lintzie," I said.

"I shot them, for Christ's sake. And then the Gott damn kids come yelling and screaming and I shot them, too. I ain't denying it. Go ahead and arrest me."

"Oh, we'll arrest you, Mr. Lintz," said the chief. "You *were* arrested, nearly an hour ago. Sergeant Dorelli placed you under arrest, but you don't have a very good memory."

"You shot the kids on the stairway, and then you told Dorelli that you carried them down to the cellar."

"That's what I done. Yeah."

"But I understand that a bullet from a .45 has a terrific impact, that it'll knock a grown man back several feet. So I was wondering, maybe when you shot the kids the impact knocked them down the stairs, and then you picked them up and carried them to the cellar. Is that about right, Lintzie?"

"No," he said.

"What did happen?"

"I held the kids, one at a time, and shot them," said Lintzie.

"Jesus," I said, and looked at the chief.

"They wouldn't hold still," he said.

"Jesus Christ," I said.

"Oh, this is quite a fellow," said the chief. "It takes a real man to grab hold of a kid with one hand and shoot him with the other. And do the same thing all over again with another kid."

"Which did you shoot first, Lintzie? The girl or the boy?"

"Her. Then he come at me. I don't remember holding him."

"The boy tried to defend his sister," said the chief.

"He didn't try to defend nobody, that kid. He was getting ready to shoot me. Him and Lonnie."

"But I thought Lonnie told you to hide the gun," I said.

"Till he got older, that's all. She was gonna wait a couple years till we had more money saved up."

"Oh, and then she was going to let him shoot you?" I said.

"You got the idea," said Lintzie. He grinned at me and sneered at the chief. "She thought I was dumb, but I wasn't so dumb."

"You said something about catching her with another man once before," I said. "You never told me about that."

"Yes, I did. Didn't I?"

"No, you never told me that. When did you catch her? Was it like today, you came home and found her with another man?"

"Night," he said.

"Oh, you came home one night and found her?"

"No! I was home. Upstairs. The night bell rang and she went down to see who it was."

"You thought it was a late customer," I said.

"I thought it was, but it was a foreigner. He had whiskers and he wore those funny clothes. You know. He had whiskers on his chin, all the girls were stuck on him."

"Oh, yes. Once I had a billygoat, he was old enough to vote. He had whiskers on his chin. I remember the song."

"This was *him*, though. Not a song."

"Oh, really? And he came in the store and made passes at Lonnie?"

"*She* made passes at *him*. She made passes at everybody except you. She didn't like you, or your mother, or any of you. Boy, oh, boy, the things she used to say about your old man."

"She never knew my old man, but what did she say about him?"

"How he used to operate on people when they didn't have nothing wrong with them. Any time your old lady wanted a new dress, your old man would operate on somebody."

"Oh, well that was true, of course," I said.

"Stop humoring him," said the chief.

"And that's why Lonnie never made passes at me, because she didn't like us. But what about this foreigner with the beard, Lintzie? Did you ever see him any place else? Did you ever see him at Schmelinger's?"

"He used to come in there but I never talked to him."

"He did come in there, though?"

"I seen him there," said Lintzie.

"He had whiskers. Did he wear a kind of a coat with little straps across the front?"

"Such a coat, yes," said Lintzie. "But I never seen him when you were there."

"No, but I think I knew the fellow you mean."

The chief looked at his gold hunting-case watch. "You had long enough, Malloy. I'm taking this fellow down to the squire's office."

"Charging him with first-degree murder?" I said.

"We sure are. An open-and-shut case, like this watch."

"I'll make you a small bet he never goes to Bellefonte," I said.

"I wouldn't take your money," said the chief.

"Bellefonte? Where the electric chair is?" said Lintzie. "Huh. Not me."

"See? He doesn't think so either," I said.

"Who did I used to guard during the war? Tell him, Malloy," said Lintzie.

"Woodrow Wilson, the President of the whole Gott damn United States," I said.

"Can I go upstairs a minute, Chief?" said Lintzie.

"No. You mean you want to go to the toilet?"

"No, I want to get something for Malloy."

"Call Lundy, tell him what it is and he'll get it," said the chief.

"My picture of me, upstairs on the bureau," said Lintzie.

"Oh, for Christ's sake. All right," said the chief.

Lundy went upstairs and brought down the photograph, which I had never seen before, of Private Donald Lintz, U.S.M.C., in his greens and the old-style cap that sat squarely on the top of his head, two badges for shooting pinned to the blouse.

"Put that in the paper, Malloy," said Lintzie.

"That I promise you," I said. "And how about pictures of Lonnie and the kids?"

"You want them too?" said Lintzie. "What do you want them for? I don't want them in the paper."

"Are there any more up there, Lundy?" I said.

"Sure," said Lundy. "Plenty. Her before she got fat, and the two kids."

"No, you can't have them," said Lintzie.

"Get them, Lundy," said the chief.

"You son of a bitch, Malloy," said Lintzie. "You want to make people feel sorry for them."

"Maybe he doesn't, but I do," said the chief. "Malloy, why do you think this fellow has a Chinaman's chance? You can tell me. The D.A. prosecutes, I don't."

"Can you spare five minutes?" I said.

"What for?"

"Will you come with me? It'll only take five minutes at the most," I said.

The chief called Dorelli, told him to keep an eye on Lintzie, and accompanied me to Schmelinger's. I pointed to the old-time beer ad on the wall. "There's Lonnie's other boy friend," I said. "Any fifty-dollar alienist will keep Lintzie out of the chair."

"Maybe you're right," said the chief.

"Something on the house, gentlemen?" said Schmelinger.

"Maybe you're right," said the chief.

"You, Malloy?"

"Not on the house," I said. "You've just lost your best cash customer."

"I won't miss him," said Schmelinger.

"He was good for fifty bucks a week and he never gave you any trouble," I said.

"I won't miss him," said Schmelinger. He ignored me and addressed the chief. "After this fellow stopped coming in with him he just sat there and stared at the Bock beer picture. And I bet you he don't even know it was there."

"Is that so? Well, thanks, Gus. Next time I'm out this way I'll have one with you," said the chief.

We walked in silence halfway to Lintzie's, then the chief spoke. "I thought a great deal of your father. What's a young fellow with your education throwing it all away when you could be doing some good in the world?"

"What education? I had four years of high school," I said.

"You were away to college," he said.

"Away, but not to college."

"Oh, then you're not much better than the rest of us," he said.

"I never said I was, Chief."

"You never said it, but you act it. Your father *was* better than most of us, but he didn't act it."

"No, he didn't have to," I said.

Natica Jackson

O NE AFTERNOON on her way home from the studio in her cream-yellow Packard 120 convertible coupe Natica Jackson took a wrong turn, deliberately. Every working day for the three years that she had been under contract at Metro she had followed the same route between Culver City and her house in Bel-Air: Motor Avenue, Pico Boulevard, Beverly Glen, Sunset Boulevard, Bel-Air. In the morning it was Bel-Air, Sunset Boulevard, Beverly Glen, Pico Boulevard, Motor Avenue, Culver City, the studio. She was fond of saying that she knew the way in her sleep, because many mornings she might as well have been asleep as the way she was. In the afternoons and early evenings, tired though she was, it was not quite the same. The reason it was not the same was that when she got through working it was like being let out of school. In those days she was still close enough to high school to have that feeling. It had not been so long since a Warner talent scout saw her in a school play in Santa Ana and wafted her the fifty thousand miles from Santa Ana to Hollywood. They gave her a seven-year contract beginning at $75 a week, and in six months she was released, just before they would have had to pay her $125 a week. Then she got an agent who helped someone at Metro discover that she could sing and dance; and pretty soon the public discovered that there was something in the spacing between her eyes and the width of her upper lip that made her stand out, made them want to know who she was. Among beautiful women and cute girls she was the one that the public liked. She became everybody's favorite niece, and she also looked extremely well in black opera-lengths. The studio teamed her up with Eddie Driscoll in two dreadful musicals, the second so dreadful that it was scrapped halfway through, but Jerry B. Lockman saw enough of it to want her for a straight, non-musical comedy he was doing, and she walked away with the picture. Walked away with it. In the executives' diningroom they could not agree that Natica Jackson had star quality, but no one could deny that she was ready for stardom. Not Garbo stardom, not Myrna Loy stardom, but sure as hell Joan Blondell stardom, and maybe, in the right pictures she would develop into another Jean Arthur. The God damn public liked her. She couldn't carry a picture by herself, but whenever she was in a picture the people would come out of the theater saying how wonderful she was.

She bought the house in Bel-Air with money she had not yet earned, but her agent knew what he was doing when he helped her finance it. "I don't want you rattling around some apartment on Franklin," he said. "I'm thinking of ten years from now, when you ought to be making easily a couple hundred thousand dollars a year. Move your mother in with you and stay out of the night spots."

"And have no fun," said Natica.

"Depends on what you mean by fun. You have Jerry Lockman."

"He can't take me out anywhere," she said.

"I'll take you anywhere you ought to go. Anywhere I can't take you, you shouldn't be there."

"Don't try to make me into something I'm not," said Natica.

"How do you know what you're not? You know Marie Dressler?"

"Tugboat Annie, you mean?"

"You know who she pals around with? Vanderbilts and Morgans, those kind of people. And you should make a year what she makes."

"Well, I hope she has more fun than I do."

"I hope you have as much fun when you're her age. Over sixty and making what she makes. Well loved throughout the entire civilized world. If all is not well with you and Jerry, get yourself a younger fellow. Only don't go for some trap drummer in a cheap night club. I'll look around and see if I find the right kind of a fellow for you. I coulda told you a few things about Jerry, but you didn't take me into your confidence till it was too late. But we can get rid of Jerry. You *graduated* from his type pictures. I got great confidence in your future, Natica. Not just next week or the week after. I'm talking about 1940, 1950, 1960!"

Natica had already been around Hollywood long enough to have respect for her agent, and she obeyed him in all things. Morris King was a rich man, an agent by choice, and not one of the artists' representatives who waited hopefully for a permanent connection with one of the studios. Morris had turned down offers of producer jobs. "I'll take L. B. Mayer's job, should they offer it to me, but not Eddie Mannix's or Benny Thau's," he would say. He had a big house in Beverly Hills, a 16-cylinder Cadillac limousine with a Negro chauffeur who wore breeches and puttees, and he had Ernestine, his wife, who according to other agents was the real brains of the Morris King Office. Ernestine would sit with Morris at the Beverly Derby, the Vine Street Derby, Al Levey's Tavern, the Vendome, Lyman's downtown, with her fat forearms resting flat on the table and her hands clasped, her eyes sparkling as she followed the men's conversation. She would wait, she would always wait, until Morris or one of the other men asked her what *she* thought, and her opinions were always so clever or so completely destructive that the men would nod silently even when they did not agree. She had opinions on everything; who was going to be the boss at Universal, who was going to win the main event at the Legion Stadium, why was Natica Jackson worth Morris King's personal attention. "Ernestine thinks like a man," said one rival agent. "I was having a discussion with her and Morris the other night. We happen to be talking about something, and in the midst of it I pulled a couple cigars outa my pocket and accidentally I offered one to Ernestine. I didn't mean anything by it. It was just like I said, she thinks like a man, and I done it like you offer a coupla men a cigar. Did she get sore? No, she didn't get sore. You know what she said? She said, 'The supreme compliment.' I don't say she's *all* the brains, but when it comes to thinking I give her credit for fifty-one percent. I give her the edge. Incidentally, she *took* the cigar. She don't smoke, but she wanted the cigar for a souvenir, a memento."

The Kings had no children, and at forty-four Ernestine was as reconciled to childlessness as at twenty-two she had been fearful of pregnancy. They loved Morris's business, going out every night, and each other. But Morris thought he saw through Ernestine's interest in Natica Jackson. "She's a little like you, Teeny," he said. "If you had a daughter that's what she'd be like. She even resembles you facially."

"You think you're smart, don't you?" said Ernestine.

"Maybe not smart, but not dumb either," said Morris. "It's all right if you don't want to tell me. I got my own two eyes."

"I know you have, honey," she said. "But I was never as pretty as Natica Jackson. That I can't claim."

"I only said she resembles you facially. I didn't say she was the exact duplicate."

"What if she was the exact duplicate? Would you go for her?"

He rubbed his chin as though he were stroking a Vandyke. "You know what I think? I think you're trying to find out if I *do* go for her. Like I saw the facial resemblance back there two-three years ago, and said to myself here was a modern-day version of Ernestine Schluter. Well, if that's what you're thinking, you're all wrong. The first time I saw her I took notice she had a pair of legs like Ruby Keeler and a kind of a face on the order of Claudette Colbert, only not as pretty."

"Claudette has a pair of legs on her."

"I'm telling you what *I* thought, not what you're thinking now, if you'll let me continue," said Morris. "So I did a little selling job at Metro. Then *you* liked her and the public liked her, and you more or less took her under your wing. As to me going for her like Jerry Lockman went for her, you got no cause to be suspicious."

"I know, Morris, I know. I was just kind of putting you on the pan," said Ernestine.

"Sure. But you got something on your mind, whatever it is," he said.

"It isn't much. The way some of you men buy a prizefighter and have him for a hobby, that's my interest in Natica."

"You wanta buy her from me? I'll sell you her contract and let you service her?"

"Not me. If there's anything I don't want to be it's a woman agent. But I'd like to have the say in her career, just for a hobby."

"All right."

"Starting with getting rid of Jerry Lockman."

"That's easy. She's fed up to here with Jerry."

"So am I, and she's been with him long enough. Everybody in town knows about Jerry and how he's peculiar, but if Natica keeps on being his girl they'll think the same of her. Get her a new fellow. An Englishman, or a writer, or I don't care if you get her an out-and-out pansy. But somebody that can be her escort."

"You want me to find a new girl for Jerry?"

"That shouldn't be hard. They're a dime a dozen in this town. The next new girl comes into your office, send her out to Jerry."

"Well, I guess I can do that," said Morris. "But you find a guy for Natica."

"All right," said Ernestine.

She found an Englishman who was also a writer and an out-and-out bisexual, who was more than willing to act as Natica's escort and lover. It was not the ideal arrangement for Natica, but they kept her busy at the studio, gave her bonuses for waiving vacations, and sent her home at night too tired to think. Alan Hildred, her English beau, sold the studio two original stories for Natica Jackson pictures, and one of them, *Uncles Are People*, was actually produced and did well. Twenty-five thousand dollars, less Morris King's ten percent, more than made up for the times when Natica did not wish to see him—or for the times when she did wish to see him. It became an understood thing that Alan Hildred was to make *some* money, as author of the original or collaborator on the screenplay, on every Natica Jackson picture. Natica's mother, who would have liked being a dress extra, was persuaded to take a job as saleslady in a florist's shop owned by Ernestine King. Natica's father, a brakeman on the Southern Pacific, went right on being a brakeman, but he had been separated from his wife for a good ten years. No one knew where Natica's brother was. Last heard from as a deckhand on one of the Dollar Line ships. But he was bound to turn up sometime and when he did he would have to be taken care of. Natica's maternal uncle, who had moved into the Jackson household when Natica's father left, was employed as a gardener at Warner Brothers. He had expected to move into the Bel-Air house, but there Natica put her foot down. "That dirty old son of a bitch can stay away from here," said Natica.

"That's no way to talk about your own flesh and blood," said her mother.

"Listen, Mom, there's no law says *you* have to live here either," said Natica. "You're making seventy-five a week."

"Yes, but for how long? My arthritis."

"Don't kid me, with your arthritis. If you have the arthritis I'll send you to the desert. Go see the doctor, and if he says you have the arthritis I'll get you a place to stay. But if Uncle Will thinks he's moving in here, you just tell Uncle Will it was Mr. King got him the job at Warners', and the same Mr. King can get him kicked out on his big fat can."

"I don't see why Mr. King can't get me a job as a dress extra. Then I wouldn't have to be in and out of that refrigerator all day."

"Well, I'll tell you why," said Natica. "They don't want you on the lot is why. And another reason is because they give those jobs to people that can act. Professionals. The only acting you ever do is putting on this act with the arthritis. Don't you exhaust my patience, Mom. Just don't you exhaust my patience."

"Sometimes I wish we never left Santa Ana."

"Here's fifty bucks," said Natica. "Go on back."

"Yes, you'd like to get rid of me, wouldn't you?"

"Oh, cut it out. I'm tired," said Natica. "I get up at five o'clock in the morning and get pushed around all day, and when I get home evenings I have to listen to your bellyaching."

It was a day or two later that Natica Jackson, on her way home from the studio in her little Packard, deviated from her customary route. There was a point on Motor Avenue where the road bore to the right. At the left there was a street—she didn't know its name—that formed the other arm of a Y. She had wondered sometimes what would happen if she turned in at that street. Not that anything would happen except that she would be a little later getting home and she would have seen a Southern California real estate development that she had never seen before. But at least she would have gone home by a different way. And so she turned left into a street called Marshall Place.

She had to slow down. Marshall Place was a winding road, S-shaped and only three-car width and a tight squeeze at that. The houses were quite close together and English-looking, and Natica wondered if the street had been named after Herbert Marshall, the English actor. The cars that were parked in Marshall Place were cars that were suitable to the neighborhood: Buicks, Oldsmobiles, a Packard 120 like Natica's, a LaSalle coupe, an oldish foreign car with a name something like Delancey. It was a far superior neighborhood to the section of Santa Ana where Natica had lived, but she had so quickly become accustomed to Bel-Air that Marshall Place seemed almost dingy. She came to another turn in the road and now she could see Motor Avenue again, and she was not sorry to see it. Marshall Place was certainly nothing much, and whatever curiosity she had had about it was completely satisfied. Just another street where people who worked in offices lived. Fifty yards from Motor Avenue and farewell to Marshall Place—and then her car banged into a Pontiac.

The Pontiac was pulling out from the curb and she hit it almost broadside. It was a noisy collision in the quiet street. The driver of the Pontiac shouted, "What the hell?" and other things that she did not hear. She backed her car away and he reversed to the curbstone and got out. "What do you think you were doing?" he said. "Didn't you see my hand? I had my hand out, you know."

"I'm sorry," she said. "I didn't see your hand. It's kind of dark. I'm covered with every kind of insurance." She was wearing a silk scarf over her head and tied under her chin.

"Aren't you Natica Jackson, the actress?" he said.

"Yes," she said.

"I thought so," he said. "Well, my name is H. T. Graham, and I live in there, Number 8 Marshall Place. I suppose you have your driver's license and so forth? You'd better pull up to the curb or you'll be in the way of any cars that want to get through."

"Listen, Mr. Graham, don't start bossing me around like you were taking charge here. You say you had your hand out, but I don't have to take your word for it. The insurance company will pay for your damages, only don't start bossing me around. Here. Here's my driver's license and you can look on the steering if you want to copy down the registration."

"Don't pull any movie actress stuff on me," he said. "You were completely in the wrong and the condition of the two cars proves it. I didn't smack into you. You smacked into me." He took out a fountain pen and wrote down her name and address and various numbers in an appointment book. "Have you got a pencil?"

"No," she said.

"All right. Then I'll copy it all down for you." He did so, and tore a sheet out of his appointment book and handed it to her. "Some people would get a whole new car out of this, a crackup with a movie actress," he said. "But all I want is what I'm entitled to."

"Big-hearted Otis," she said.

"You movie people, you wonder why you're so unpopular with real people, but I'll tell you why. It's the way you're be-having now. Like a spoiled brat. You think a cheque from the insurance company is all that's necessary. This time you can drive your car home and tomorrow you can buy a new one. But the next time you may kill somebody. This is a narrow street, residential, small children. Luckily they're all home having their supper now, but a half an hour earlier this street would have been full of children. I read all about that drunken director that killed three people down in Santa Monica. He should have been put in the gas chamber."

"Listen, Mr. Graham, all I did was wrinkle your fender and put a few dents in your door."

"But if the window'd been up you could have blinded me with flying glass. Stop trying to make this seem like nothing."

"You stop trying to make it seem like a train wreck."

"Oh, go on home," he said. "And try and get home without killing anybody. Go on, beat it."

"I can't," she said.

"Naturally, your motor isn't running. Step on the starter."

"It isn't that," she said.

"Are you hurt?"

"No, not that either. I just don't want to drive. Would you mind going in your house and calling a taxi? Suddenly I lost my nerve or something. I don't know what it is."

"Are you sure you didn't bang your head on the windshield?" He looked at her closely.

"I'm not hurt. Please, will you just call me a taxi and I'll send somebody to pick up my car."

"No, no, I'll drive you home. You feeling faint or anything? Come on in and I'll get you a glass of water. Or maybe a brandy is what you need."

"Honestly, all I want is if you'll get me a taxi and I'll be all right. I'm doing a delayed take, I guess, but I positively couldn't drive home if you paid me."

He got in her car and drove it to Bel-Air. She spoke only to give him directions in the final stage of the ride. "Now I'll get *you* a taxi," she said, when they reached her house. "Can I offer you a drink?"

"No thanks," he said.

"I guess you expected me to have a big car with a chauffeur."

"It'd go with this house, all right," he said.

"It's too big for just my mother and I."

"Aren't you married?"

"No." She telephoned the taxi company. "There'll be a cab in five minutes," she said. "I'm sorry I was such a jerk back there."

"I was pretty rough on you."

"Oughtn't you to tell your wife where you are?"

"She's away. She and the kids are down at Newport."

"Oh, then I guess you were on your way out to dinner when I bumped into you."

"I was going over to Ralphs in Westwood. I usually go there when I'm batching it."

"How about a steak here? I have dinner by myself and go to bed around nine. My mother doesn't wait for me. She eats early and then goes to the show."

"So I'm all alone with a movie star. This is the first time that ever happened to me. I have a confession to make, though. I've never seen you on the screen. I recognized you from the ads, I guess. I don't go to the movies very much."

"Well, what do *you* do for a living? Maybe I don't buy what you sell, either."

"No, I don't guess you do. I'm a chemist with the Signal Oil Company."

"I buy oil," she said.

"Well, my job isn't the kind of oil you use. I'm supposed to be developing certain by-products."

"Whatever that means. Wouldn't you like to make a pass at me?"

"You mean it?" he said.

"Yes. If you don't, I'm liable to make a pass at you," she said. "Come on over and sit next to me."

"I don't get it," he said.

"Neither do I, but I don't care. I don't even care what you think of me. I'll never see you again, so it won't matter. But when the taxi comes, here, you give him this five-dollar bill and tell him you won't need him. That's him now. They're very prompt."

"You sure you want to go through with this?"

"Well, not if we start talking about it. Will you send the cab away?"

"Sure," he said. He went to the door and dismissed the taxi. "What about your mother?"

"My room's in a different part of the house. We can go back there now." She stood up and he embraced her, and they knew quite simply that they wanted each other. "See? You did want to make a pass at me."

"Sure I did, but I wouldn't have," he said.

"Well, I would have," she said. "Come on."

They went to her room and he stayed until eleven o'clock. "I wish you didn't have to go, but I have to be up at five o'clock. And I guess you'll probably want to phone your wife. Do you phone her every night?"

"Just about."

"Well, tell her you didn't phone her earlier because you were in bed with a movie star."

"Shall I say who?"

"No, maybe you better not. You're going to have to tell her about the accident, and that's the first thing she'll think of, is what happened after the accident. Do you realize something?"

"What?"

"You're never going to be able to mention my name again without her thinking you did go to bed with me. That's always going to be in the back of her mind."

"No."

"Yes. Believe me. That's what I'd think, and that's what she's going to think. That maybe, *maybe* that night you had the accident and didn't phone her, *maybe* you spent the night with that Natica Jackson."

"I don't know but that you could be right," he said. "You

have her figured out pretty well, for somebody that never saw her."

"That's because I think I know the kind of a girl you'd be married to. Did she ever know you were untrue to her?"

"Well, there was only one other time and that was in Houston, Texas."

"But I'll bet she watches you like a hawk."

"Yes, she's inclined to be jealous."

"And so are you."

"Yes, I guess I am," he said.

"Well, Hal Graham, I guess it's time you went home," she said. "I'll call you another cab." She did so.

"Where is your mother now?" he said.

"My mother? I guess she's in her room. Why?"

"I just wondered," he said. "You know, she'd think it was strange if she was sitting out there in the livingroom and I walked by."

"Well, she might," said Natica. "It doesn't happen all the time."

"That's what I meant."

"Don't get me wrong. It does happen. But not all the time," said Natica. "That is, I don't have a strange man here every night."

"I could tell that," he said.

"How?"

"Oh—it's hard to say. But you know these things. This house is so quiet, I got the impression that it's always quiet, and you're lonesome. Lonely, I guess is the better word. I get an altogether different impression than I had before."

"Of how a movie star lives?"

"Yes."

"Yes. Well, of course some of them are married. Most of them are," she said. "But I never got that lonely, that I wanted to marry the kind of a guy that wanted to marry me. I wouldn't marry an actor, even if I was in love with him. But if I didn't marry an actor, who else would I marry? Regular people don't understand the way we have to live. The only person for me to marry is a director. Then I wouldn't be always wondering whether he married me because I was a movie star, because I made a lot of money. I'd be willing to marry a big director, but they all have somebody. A wife or a girl friend. Or both. Or they're queer."

"You wouldn't marry a queer," he said.

"No, I guess not. Of course some of them are double-gaited, and some of the double-gaited ones are just as masculine as anybody."

"Do you speak from experience? You sound it," he said.

"Don't start asking me about my experiences. By tomorrow morning you'll be one of my experiences. And I'll be one of yours."

"The big one. Practically the only one. I don't know whether I'll be able to take it so casually."

"Yes you will. You will because you have to. Maybe not casually, offhand. But don't look at the dark side. Look on the bright side. From now on you'll be able to say to yourself, these movie stars are just like anyone else."

"The only trouble with that argument is I didn't think of you as a movie star. I never would have made a play for a movie star."

"You didn't have to. The movie star made a play for you."

"I had other girls make a play for me."

"But you didn't go to bed with them."

"Before I was married I did, but not after I was married. Except for the girl in Houston, Texas."

"And she was a whore," said Natica.

"No. She was the wife of a friend of mine."

"Oh, I thought she was some girl you met at one of those conventions."

"It was a convention, but I knew her before. She and her husband live there in Houston. He's another chemist. I went to Cal with him, and she was there at the same time, a couple classes behind us."

"Was she your girl at Cal?"

"No. I didn't have a girl at Cal, till senior year. The girl I married."

"Oh, so the one in Houston—"

"Was never my girl. But when I showed up at the convention and we all had a lot of drinks, that's all it was. Her husband passed out completely, and she said we ought to make up for lost time."

"Was he your best friend?" said Natica.

"No, just a friend. A fraternity brother. He was never my best friend. I don't have a *best* friend. I have guys I like to go fishing with, and others I work with at the lab, and there's two or three of us that play tennis together. But for instance I don't have anybody that I could tell what happened tonight, even if I thought they'd believe me. You're the first person I ever told about the girl in Houston."

"Then maybe I'm your best friend," she said.

He smiled. "Well, at least temporarily," he said.

"Did you ever stop to think that maybe we're both kidding ourselves?"

"How so?"

"About never seeing each other again," she said.

"Well, we oughtn't to," he said.

"You're weakening," she said.

He stared at the empty fireplace. "Possibly," he said.

"I've weakened already," she said. "I go by your house every day, twice a day, only a half a block away. Today I just happened to feel like turning off Motor Avenue into Marshall Road."

"Place. Marshall Place. Yes, you told me," he said.

"Why?" she said.

"Because you were tired of taking the same route every day. You told me."

"But I didn't say why, because I don't *know* why," she said. "Why did I turn off today instead of last week, when your wife was home? Why did I happen to be starting your car just at the same exact moment that I came along? Why did you feel like going to Ralphs at just that exact moment? If you stopped to tie your shoe or change your necktie, you wouldn't have been in your car when I hit it. It would have been sitting there at the curbstone, and I would have driven right by your house."

"The laws of probability."

"I don't know what that means," she said.

"Oh, I was just thinking of probability and chance, in mathematics. There wouldn't be any way to work it out mathematically, that I know of. So it comes down to luck, which is beyond our comprehension. Good luck or bad luck, or a little of both."

"Mathe-*matics*?"

"I use mathematics in my work, quite a lot."

"I thought you were a chemist, with test tubes full of oil."

"Actually I'm a chemical engineer, in research. It saves time to say I'm a chemist, since nobody knows or cares what kind of work I'm doing. Not even my wife. She was an English major, and if I told her what I did at the lab on any given day, she wouldn't understand it any more than you would. Plus the fact that it's a team operation, with five other men working on it."

"You have five men working under you?"

"As a matter of fact, I have," he said. "But how did you know I was in charge?"

"Just guessed," she said. "Then you must be pretty important."

"I'll be pretty important if I get the right results."

"And rich?"

"Rich? Well, no, not rich, but I'll be set for life. I probably am anyway. That is, I'll always make a pretty good living."

"What do they pay you now?"

He laughed. "Well, if you must know, eighteen thousand a year."

"I guess that's a lot in your business," she said.

"It's a lot in any business except yours, and I don't consider movies a business."

"Money is money," she said. "They don't look at a ten-dollar bill and say, 'Oh, this is Signal Oil Company money. That's worth twice as much as Metro money.'"

"No, they don't. But what will you be earning twenty years from now?"

"Two hundred thousand dollars a year," she said.

"What?"

"That's what Morris King says."

"Who the hell is Morris King?"

"My agent, and a multye-millionaire."

"Well, I hope he's right, for your sake," he said.

"He usually is. He advanced my career from seventy-five a week to seventy-five thousand a year, and next year I get more, and the year after that and the year after that."

"A young girl like you making that much money."

"Shirley Temple makes more, and she's a lot younger," said Natica. "But I'm getting started, according to Morris."

"Is that what you want most? Money?"

"I know God damn well I never want to be without it," she said.

"What about love? A home? Children?"

"Yeah, what *about* love? And a home and children. You picked a fine time to ask."

"Yes, I did, didn't I?"

"You have a home and children, and I suppose you love your wife, but you're still not satisfied."

"No, I guess I'm not," he said.

"Well? What do *you* want most?" she said. "Not money."

"No, not money for its own sake. I want to do certain things in my work, and I guess that's uppermost. And have a nice home and educate my children."

"And every once in a while somebody like me," said Natica.

"Yes."

"But not too often," she said. "You'd like to have your home and children and someone like me, off to one side, and your work uppermost. That's funny, me in the same category with your wife and kids. That would get a laugh in Culver City. But I guess that's the way most men would like to have it, and that's why I don't get married. I'm too independent, I guess."

"Maybe," he said.

"But I'm not independent," she said. "I have to get up at five o'clock in the morning and drive to Culver City. I'll toot my horn when I'm passing your house."

"You'd better have them check your alignment. You hit my car just hard enough to knock yours out of line."

"No, I think I'll just trade mine in on a new LaSalle. So the next time I run into you I'll have a new car. How early do you have to get up?"

"Oh, generally around seven," he said.

"You'll sleep soundly tonight," she said.

"I'll say I will."

"So will I," she said. "Be funny if all we got out of this experience was a good night's sleep for both of us. But don't count on it."

"I won't. What you started to say about if I stopped to tie my shoe, or put on a different necktie. We got sidetracked, but there's something in it."

She scribbled on a piece of paper. "Here. This is the number of my dressing-room. It's private, doesn't go through the Metro switchboard. If I don't answer it'll be my maid, but don't tell her anything. She gossips plenty about other girls she worked for, so she's sure to gossip about me. Tell her Mr. Marshall called, and I'll know who it was."

"I'll give you my number at the office," he said.

"No, I don't want to know it. You think it over, and if you want to see me again, call me up. But think it over first. You have the most to lose. Besides, *I* may not want to see *you*. But don't count on that, either."

"What's a good time to phone you?" he said.

"You have to keep trying. I never know when I'll be in my dressing-room or on the set." She looked at him, standing with his hand on the doorknob.

"What are you thinking?" he said.

"Wondering," she said. "But not really wondering. I know."

"So do I," he said.

"Left, and then straight down the hall," she said.

She heard the taxi pulling away. She reached out her hand to the table beside her bed and picked up a typescript, opened it to the next day's scene. "No," she said aloud and replaced the script and turned out the light.

At half past five the next morning she left her house, went down Sunset Boulevard, turned in at Beverly Glen and across to Pico and from Pico to Motor Avenue. She slowed down when she came to Marshall Place. She turned right and moved along in second gear. His car was at the curb. The left door and the running board had been given quite a banging. She looked up at the second-story windows. Two of them were wide open. His bedroom, without a doubt. He was sleeping there, and without a doubt he was sleeping heavily. If she tooted her horn she would wake up the whole neighborhood. She did not mind waking up the whole neighborhood, but it would be cruel mean to wake him. And so she kept going, through Marshall Place to the other end where it led into Motor Avenue, and ten minutes later she was on the Metro lot.

The early workers were already at their tasks and Natica Jackson was soon at hers, which began with the arrival of the young man from Makeup. "Somebody didn't get enough sleep last night," he said.

"You're so clever," said Natica.

"Oh, it's not bad," he said. "Not hopelessly bad. You're young. Not like some of these hags I have to bring to life again. Actually I love to work on you, Miss Jackson, especially around your eyes. But get your eight hours, always try to get your eight hours. And here's some of those drops for when you start shooting. Remember now, don't put them in your eyes till you're ready to shoot, and use them sparingly. They're very strong, and I don't want you to get used to them." He prattled on, and his prattling and professional ministrations returned her to her movie-actress world, and she stayed there all day. Lunch was brought to her in her dressing-room. She read the gossip columns in the newspapers and the trade papers. She was visited by a man who owned a chain of theaters in New England, who was being given a tour of the studio. He wanted her *personal* autograph and not just one of those printed things that meant nothing. She asked him if he would care for a sandwich or something, but he thanked her and said he was having lunch with William Powell and Myrna Loy. She resumed eating her lunch and was interrupted by a girl from Publicity who wanted her to give an interview to the Hollywood correspondent of some paper in Madrid. "Don't do it if you don't feel like it," said the publicity girl. "But if you do, make sure you don't get alone with him. He's a knee-grabber." A stout man with a cigar tapped twice on her screendoor and pushed it open. "May I come in? Jason Margold, from New York City. I see you're eating your lunch," he said. "Would you rather I came back in ten-fifteen minutes?"

"Who did you say you were?"

"Jason Margold, from New York City. But I don' wanna disturb you while you're— I see you got a preference for cottage cheese. You know what's good with cottage cheese? Try a little Major Grey's chutney."

"What's this all about? Who are you?"

"My card," he said. "My business card."

She read it aloud. "Jason Margold, vice-president, Novelty Creations, New York, London, Paris. So what?"

He removed the day's newspapers from a folding chair, placed them on the floor, and seated himself. "You mind the cigah?"

"Quit stalling around, will you?" she said.

"I won't take but a minute of your time, Miss Jackson," he said "It jus' happened I said to Jerry Lockman, I said who in his opinion was the real coming star on the Metro-Goldwyn lot."

"Oh, you know Jerry Lockman?"

"Jerry jus' happens to be my brother-in-law, once-removed. His sister, the former Sylvia Lockman, is married to George Stern. George used to be married to my sister Evie till she passed away of heart trouble several years ago."

"And?"

"So I asked Jerry, who was the young star that they were banking on the most here at Metro-Goldwyn. And without a moment's hesitation he named you. Miss Natica Jackson. So I said right away I wanted to have this talk with you for the purpose of sounding you out on this excellent proposition whereby, whereby we could work this out to our mutual advantage and profit."

"Is this a tie-in?"

"Well, you might call it a tie-in, but tie-in usually means a product gets tied in to a certain motion picture and like they run your picture in the ads and the actress never gets a nickel out of it, only the publicity for the motion picture. We'd be willing to pay you a royalty on every item we sold bearing your name."

"What is the item? A pessary?"

"Huh?"

"You're so God damn mysterious, I thought you didn't want to come out and say what it was."

"Well, it isn't anything like what you mentioned, Miss Jackson. It's an item of hand luggage that we expect to sell up in the millions."

"If I got five cents on every pessary I'd make a lot of money, too. The Natica Jackson pessary."

"You got a sense of humor, I'll give you that," he said.

"I need it, in this business," said Natica. "Just a sec." She dialed a number on the intra-studio telephone. "Me speak to Mr. Lockman. It's Natica Jackson."

"You checking on me?" said Margold.

"Hello, Jerry? This is my lunch-hour and I'm supposed to get some rest. What the hell do you mean sending some jerk relation of yours to my dressing-room? Come and get him out of here before I call the studio cops. That's *all*." She hung up daintily.

"Now*way*da minute. Why did you have to go and do that?" said Margold.

"Miss Garbo's dressing-room is down the way. Try *her*," said Natica Jackson.

"You din even listen to my proposition," said Margold.

"Screw, bum," she said. "Take a powder."

Margold left. It was fun to have Jerry Lockman in such an embarrassed position. She could imagine how he was stewing now, for fear that she would tell other executives about his brother-in-law once-removed. Let him stew. Let him roast in hell.

"The car's downstairs," said her maid.

It was an elderly Cadillac limousine, to take her to the back lot. "You ready to go? You got everything?" said Natica.

"I think I got everything," said the maid. "Two packs of Philip Morris, makeup box, your mules, two packs of Beech-Nut gum."

"Do you have the eye drops?"

"In the makeup box."

"We're off," said Natica. She was in a bathing suit and a bath robe, ready for the scene on the back lot, in which she was to drive a motorboat a distance of forty feet. The scene had originally been written to take place in a diner, but it had been changed to give her an opportunity to wear the bathing suit. They had shot the scene five times that morning and it had never been right. They were afraid to expose her to the sun for more than a few minutes at a time. The last thing they wanted was for her to acquire a natural sunburn that would not match her body makeup. The shooting schedule called for a ballroom scene the next day, and two hundred extras had been hired for it, but if the fair skin of Natica Jackson was reddened by the sun in the motorboat scene, they would have to shoot around her. Moreover, the natural light changed at three o'clock in the afternoon, and if they didn't get the motorboat scene right before three they would have to come back and shoot it again sometime. The complications had nothing to do with acting, but Natica was used to that. Acting was the last thing you did after everything else was ready, and you did that for two minutes at a time. Then they glued those two minuteses together until they had eighty minutes that made sense—and then they put you in another picture. She could not understand how people got an impression of you from this collection of two-minute, one-minute, thirty-second snatches, but they did, and if they liked you that was all that mattered. Of all the girls she had known in Santa Ana she was the only one who could say, "I'm going to get a new LaSalle," at eleven o'clock at night and be sure that it would be delivered to her the next afternoon. She was certainly the only Santa Ana girl who had been kissed by Robert Taylor, and Garbo had smiled at her. Life was funny.

They did the motorboat scene three times while the light was still right. The director rode back to Natica's dressing-room with her. "I think the second take'll be the one, but I won't know till I see the dailies," said the director. "Let me have a look at your nose."

"It feels all right," said Natica.

"Yeah, it looks all right," said the director. His name was Reggie Broderick and he had grown up in the business. He spoke the jargons of the camera and lighting crews, he knew or could improvise sight gags that were not in the script, and he loved to direct motion pictures. He was not quite an artist, but his pictures always displayed ironic touches that other directors admired. "You got a new fellow, Natica?" he said.

"Maybe," she said. "Why?"

"Maybe, meaning you're not sure he's going to be your fellow?" said Reggie Broderick.

"Something like that," she said.

"Well, that's all right," said Reggie. "But send him home early, in time to get your eight hours. It's a good thing we didn't have any close-ups today, or you'd have been a total loss."

"I'm sorry," she said.

"No harm done, but tonight go to bed early."

"Was it my eyes?" she said.

"It wasn't only your eyes. You went around all day with your buttons showing."

"My buttons? In a bathing suit?"

"Your nipples, dear," he said. "You were a woman fulfilled, today. You can hardly wait to get back to this guy, whoever he is. Which is all right, as long as you get your sleep."

"I never even thought about him, all day," she said.

"Subconsciously you never thought of anything else," he said.

"Well, maybe you have something there," she said.

"We only have twelve more days on this picture, kid. As a favor to me will you postpone any emotional crisis? Only twelve more days."

"You know what I said to him last night?" she said.

"No, I can't even *guess* what you said to him last night."

"We were talking about marriage—he's married. And I said the only kind of a guy that I ought to marry is a director. I wouldn't think of marrying an actor, and the only person I could think of marrying was a director."

"Well, I tell you what you do. You finish this picture for me and I'll marry you. Unless you had some other director in mind."

"I didn't even have *you* in mind," she said.

"I must be losing my grip," he said.

"You never showed any interest, that way," she said.

"That's because this is our first picture together," he said. "The next time we do one, I'll see to it that we have a couple weeks on location. Where would you like to go? Don't say Catalina. That's too near. How about the High Sierras?"

"Why does it have to be on location?"

"Because I have to go home at night otherwise," he said.

"Oh, this wasn't going to be marriage," she said.

"I thought we got away from marriage," he said.

"I'm back to it," she said. "I think you ought to marry me and see that I get to bed early."

"Or vice versa. But meanwhile what about this guy that kept you up last night? What do we do about him?"

"That's going to be a problem," she said.

"Who is he? Can you tell me? I'm not butting in, but you went serious on me all of a sudden. How is he going to be a problem?"

"I guess I *was* thinking about him all day, subconsciously. I expected him to phone me, and he didn't," she said.

"He might have phoned while there was nobody here," he said.

She shook her head. "I expected him to keep trying. I was here all during the lunch break, and my phone never rang. And we've been sitting here over half an hour."

"And there's some reason why you can't phone him," he said.

"I told him I wouldn't. That he had to phone me. I don't even know his number. I know where to reach him, but I told him I wasn't going to try, that it was up to him."

"Are you going to sit here all evening in case he does phone? I don't think that's such a good idea."

"No, if he hasn't phoned me by this time, he isn't going to," she said.

"How would you like to come home and take pot-luck with the Brodericks? Mona's a great fan of yours. If you don't mind eating dinner with two small boys, aged seven and ten."

"I can't figure you, Reggie," she said. "Are you a family man or aren't you?"

"I'm a family man," he said.

"And a Catholic, I guess, with that name."

"A family man and a Catholic," he said. "But I've had some things to tell in confession. And not just eating meat on Friday."

"Then why didn't you go for me?"

"I don't always go for the girls in my pictures. Not even most of the time. Very seldom, in fact. It interferes with the work, and this is my job."

"But you like me. I can tell that. You've been nicer to me than any director I ever worked with," she said.

"Yes, I like you. I asked to do this picture, you know. They had me down for something else, but I wanted to work with you."

"Who was in the other picture?" she said.

"A prima donna. Somebody I never worked with, but I heard all about her from another director. And *she* wanted *me*. The studio got a little tough when I said I wanted to do this picture and not hers. They would have put me on suspension if they hadn't been afraid of the bad publicity. Not the bad publicity for me. They didn't give a damn about that. But it would have got out that I preferred working with you, and that would have given her a black eye. So they told her I was off on one of my benders and wouldn't be in shape by the starting date of her picture."

"Were you off on a bender?"

"No, but I'd have gone on one," he said.

"Why did you want to work with me?"

"Because so far all they've done is photograph you. I looked at every picture you ever made, including one dog you made at Warner's."

"And was that ever a dog!" she said.

"Then I saw you in a dumb musical they made here, and a comedy Jerry Lockman produced. You used to be his girl."

"Yes."

"I can well understand why you gave him the air. They've never known what to do with you around here. This picture we're doing now. It isn't the greatest thing in the world for you, but I've made a good try with it. It's a common-ordinary program picture that'll make some money, but the pleasure I get out of it is what it'll do for you, and therefore for me. You're going to be surprised when you see this picture. How much have you seen?"

"Most of the footage that I'm in, but that's all," she said.

"Well, there's a lot more to the picture than that. By this time I can pretty well visualize the whole thing, the final cut. From now on you can figure to be in pictures the rest of your life. You have a career."

"I thought I *had* a career," she said.

"Two years? Three years? You'd be surprised how many women had two or three years at a big studio, and then disappeared. I don't mean disappeared to Republic. I mean disappeared entirely. And you never quite know why. They brought a girl out from New York. She was beautiful, she could act. She'd been a hit in two big plays on Broadway, and they signed her to a contract that was something fantastic. Five thousand a week. They gave her a deal that was absolutely unheard of for somebody that'd never been before a camera, but they wanted her. Do you know where she is now? She's back in New York, living in a hotel and waiting for Hollywood to come to their senses. She was in exactly two pictures. The first one was one of the most expensive pictures they ever made here. The story costs alone amounted to over two hundred thousand dollars.

A top director. An expensive cast. The works. And it wasn't bad. It really wasn't a bad picture. But nobody went to see it. The people didn't care whether this girl had a Broadway reputation, or how many writers worked on the picture. They couldn't knock her looks. She photographed beautifully, and she had a good voice. *I* couldn't figure out why the picture laid such an egg. Then I happened to be in New York about a year ago and I was having lunch at the Algonquin and this girl came in. I never knew her when she was in pictures, and I asked the guy I was having lunch with what she was doing. The guy was a playwright, knew all the Broadway crowd, and when I asked him about this dame he said—as if I was supposed to know—he said she had a new girl friend. She was a Lez. I'd never known that, and I don't think most people in Hollywood knew it. But do you know who did know it? Those people that pay to go to see movies. Most of them have never heard of the word Lesbian. Wouldn't know what I was talking about if I said some actress was a Lez. But they knew something was wrong, something was missing. Some warmth that wasn't there. As soon as I got back to the Coast I ran that picture, and there it was. But only after I'd been told. I called up the director, a friend of mine, and asked him about this dame. I put it to him straight. Did he know she was a Lez when he was working with her? He said no, never suspected it for one minute. He knew there was something lacking, but he blamed himself. He never knew about her till after she washed up in pictures, and then some New York actress told him."

"You should have asked me," said Natica.

"You know who I'm talking about?"

"Sure. Elysia Tisbury."

"Now how did you know? A high school kid from Santa Ana?"

"My feminine instinct," said Natica.

"No, I won't buy that. No."

"Well, I was given a hint," said Natica. "She used to go out with Alan Hildred."

"Oh, your English boy friend. So she did. So she did."

"But that doesn't mean I'm that way," said Natica.

"You know, if I ever found out that you were, I think I'd

start wondering about myself," he said. "You're about the last person in the world I'd ever think that about."

"Ooh, but when I get to be a big star," she said.

"You're planning to turn Lez?"

"I'm thinking of it," she said. "Alan says I'm terribly unsophisticated."

"Well, he's not."

"I know. He tries to sophisticate me."

"A guy like that could sophisticate you right out of pictures. Or would, if you didn't have so much common sense."

"Well, I'll say this for Alan. He's fun to *be* with. Not all the time. But I never knew anybody like him in Santa Ana. There *isn't* anybody like him in Santa Ana."

"There aren't very many like him in Hollywood," he said.

"You don't like him, but you're not a woman. If I was just one of those girls I went to high school with, I never would have understood a person like Alan. All they ever wanted was to marry a boy that had a father that owned a bank or something. That wasn't what I wanted. I wasn't even sure what I did want till I got this offer from Hollywood. Then I knew what I wanted, all right."

"What?"

"To have every big star know who I was," she said. "Not for me to know every big star. But every big star to know me."

"Well, they just about do," he said.

"G.G. spoke to me one day. Not exactly spoke to me, but nodded her head and smiled. I think she knows me now."

"All right. What's next?"

"To have my name in lights on the Statue of Liberty."

"That seems reasonable enough," he said. "Then what?"

"After that? Well, maybe a statue of me there."

"That'll probably happen. The Goddess of Liberty doesn't look very American, and you do. After that, what?"

"You know Joan of Arc?"

"Not personally."

"I'd like to be something like her," she said.

"You don't want to be barbecued."

"No, I guess I wouldn't go for that part. Who were some of the other famous women?"

"Cleopatra, but she got a snake to bite her right on the teat."

"No. Who else? Queen Elizabeth."

"Too late. She was known as the virgin queen."

"Do you think she really was? How old was she?"

"You can forget her. She wasn't very pretty. Mata Hari, but she got shot."

"It'd be fun to be a spy, but if I was famous I couldn't be a very good spy. They all seem to get in some jam. Martha Washington, but they only know about her through George."

"And Lincoln's wife went off her rocker," he said.

"My big trouble is, I'm not very glamorous. You can be famous without being glamorous. I'm pretty famous now, I guess, but people think they know all about me. America's niece, is what Alan calls me."

"You'll be more than that when we finish this picture."

"But not glamorous."

"No, but not all sweetness and light, for a change. The sexiest shot of you, you're wearing that housedress. I hope it gets by."

"I know which one that is. That was what you had the wind-machine for. Where I'm standing on the roof."

"That's the one. Better than a skin-tight bathing suit. You should have heard them in the projection room when they saw that shot."

"What did they say?"

"They said, 'Wow!' And they meant every word of it," he said. "Tomorrow they'll see you in a bathing suit and it won't mean a thing. But in that housedress, with the wind against you, you might as well have been soaking wet. But at the Hays Office they watch out for dames in soaking-wet dresses. This way I may sneak it by them."

"Was Jerry Lockman at the rushes?"

"Jerry Lockman? Jerry Lockman, the way he stands now, couldn't get in a projection room if he paid admission. You don't keep up with your old boy friends. I hear they offered him the job of producing travelogs, and if he's smart he'll take it. They've gone sour on him."

"Oh, dear. Why?"

"You never know the real reason."

"Maybe the public found out that he's a Lez," she said.

"You may be kidding, but the things that turn the big shots against a man make just about as much sense. You and I, what they call the talent people, we tend to overlook the fact that our jealousies are nothing compared to what goes on among the big shots. Now Jerry Lockman, for instance. He more or less discovered you, with a little help from Morris King. So Jerry was instrumental in helping your career. Fine. But there are fifteen other supervisors on the lot that *didn't* discover you. Every single one of them thinks that's a black mark against *him*. So there are fifteen supervisors, or associate producers, or whatever they want to call themselves, that automatically hate Jerry. One of them happens to be Joe Gelber, the man that's producing our picture. He particularly hates Jerry because you were Jerry's discovery, so Joe has to go after Jerry hammer and tongs. Joe absolutely has to see to it that Jerry gets none of the credit if our picture turns out well. Which it will, don't worry about that. It'll make nice money. But Jerry Lockman mustn't be able to claim that he had even a tiny pinch of the credit for you. For the last sit months, ever since Joe Gelber was assigned to this picture, he's had to put the knock on Jerry Lockman. Not only where you're concerned, but in every direction you can think of. I've heard him. He'll make fun of his clothes. Drops little jokes about his sex life. I heard him say it was very odd, very strange that Jerry went abroad on the *Europa* a couple years ago."

"What's wrong with that? I remember that," said Natica.

"The *Europa*? That's one of Hitler's boats. In case you're thinking of taking a trip abroad, young lady, don't book passage on the *Europa* or the *Bremen*. Not while you're under contract here. Hitler isn't very popular in Hollywood."

"Oh, *Hitler*. He's against the Jews," said Natica.

"Hitler's against the Jews, that's right."

"But Jerry's a Jew," she said.

"Sure he is. But what kind of a Jew will travel in a boat owned by Hitler? Every opportunity Joe gets, he puts the rap on Jerry. And when a guy like Joe Gelber goes to work on somebody, he never loses his temper or says things that aren't true. He'll point out a hundred little faults that nobody ever noticed before, or that never bothered anybody. Jerry Lockman's neckties are no worse than L. B. Mayer's. But if you keep hammering away, calling attention to any man's shortcomings, you can finally get somewhere. And Joe Gelber has finally done a job on Jerry Lockman."

"Isn't it childish?"

"Yes. Childish and vicious. And it's exactly what Jerry would have done to Joe Gelber if he'd had the chance."

"You bet he would," said Natica. "A phony intellectual is what Jerry used to call him."

"If there's anything intellectual about Joe Gelber, it sure is phony."

"I wouldn't know," she said. "He has all those books in his office. I wondered when he got time to read them, but I didn't say anything."

"Well, he's on my side now. And yours. By the way, why did you ask me if Jerry was at the rushes?"

"I was wondering what he'd say when they all said 'Wow.' He would have been the only one that knew what was underneath that dress."

"Would you care what he said?"

She hesitated. "I guess I wouldn't," she said. "Not any more. A few years ago I would have. But you know I discovered something. When a man and a woman have something peculiar about their sex life, people always laugh at the man. They make fun of the man, but not of the woman. Have you ever noticed that?"

"I never thought of it before, but you may be right."

"Do you know why that is?" she said.

"No. I'd have to think about it."

"It's because men aren't supposed to be that much interested in sex. They should be more busy with their work and stuff. Sex is all right for women, but men ought to have it and forget about it."

"To rise supremely above it?" he said.

"I'm serious! A man that thinks about sex all the time, like Jerry, or Alan Hildred, I think he ought to have something else to think about."

"You're just restating an old poetic theory. 'Man's love is of his life a thing apart, 'tis woman's whole existence.'"

"Yes, we had that in high school," she said. "But look at

the way a woman is constructed. She's built for sex. And a man—well, a man only partly. You never saw anybody put a brazeer on a man. Except at a drag. And even a drag! What do they do at a drag? They dress up like women."

"Do you really like sex, Natica?"

"I love it, but I'm a woman. I don't think men ought to like it so much. And yet every man I ever slept with does. Except that son of a bitch that didn't call me all day. Never gave me a jingle. And I know why. I was the one that made the first pass."

"Make a pass at *me*, dear heart, and *I'll* phone you tomorrow," he said.

"You know, I almost would. If we were at my house I would, but not here. Even in Jerry's office, when he'd lock the door and shut off the phone, I never felt right about it." She looked around her dressing-room, and shook her head. "Just a lousy chaise-lounge."

"For purity," he said. "Well, how about coming home and having dinner with us?"

"I just remembered. I'm supposed to have a brand-new LaSalle waiting for me." She dialed a studio number. "This is Miss Jackson. Natica Jackson. Do you have a car there for me? You have? How does it look? Does it have white-walls? Fine. Thank you. Okey-doke." She hung up.

"It's there?" he said.

"It's been there since early this afternoon. I'm glad. I loved my Packard, but I'm glad I don't have to see it again. Once I make up my mind to get rid of a thing, I don't care to see it any more. I wish I could be the same way about people."

"Who says you're not?" he said.

"It's not as easy with people," she said. "I'll give you the first ride in my new car."

"And have dinner with us?"

"I'd love to," she said.

"Let me call Transportation and I'll have somebody drive my car home, and maybe I ought to tell Mona you're coming. She won't want to have her hair up in curlers when you arrive."

"I won't mind."

"A figure of speech. I've never seen her hair up in curlers."

On the walk to the parking lot she was always half a step

ahead of him. They admired the new car from all sides, and the parking attendant showed her the starting and lighting controls.

"Well, off we go," she said. Darkness had come.

She was a good driver and was taking pleasure in her new car. "Your new pony cart," he said.

"I never had one," she said.

"Hey! Straight ahead," he said. "Pico is straight ahead."

"This is Marshall Place, where I had my accident yesterday," she said. She had slowed down.

"Oh."

"He lives at Number 88. There, on the right. And there's his car. See the door, where I hit him? House all lit up. Maybe his wife came home unexpectedly. And maybe I'm just making excuses for him." She blew her horn, held her hand on the button, and drove away. "Well, so long to you, Mr. Hal Graham."

"He isn't one of our people," said Reggie Broderick. "Don't lose any sleep over him."

"Oh, you just don't want me to lose any sleep," she said.

They went to Broderick's house in Beverly Hills, and she was affable. The Broderick sons were delighted with her, the Broderick wife—after one hard look—was friendly. Natica gave the boys a ride in her new car (they chose to sit in the rumble seat), and when she brought them home again she did not get out of the car. She said goodnight to all the Brodericks and went home to Bel-Air. She lay in her warm, perfumed bath and wondered what the hell.

They finished the picture a day ahead of schedule, and Natica went away with Alan Hildred, to a borrowed cottage at a place called San Juan Capistrano. The water was too cold for her to swim in but Alan went in three or four times a day. They observed silences. He would take a pipe and a book and be self-sufficient until mealtime, sitting in the sand close enough to hear her if she called him. She slept late every morning, had breakfast of orange juice, toast and coffee; read the newspapers until lunchtime. After lunch she would read magazines and detective stories until sleep overtook her. She would nap for an hour, have coffee, and do some telephoning and letter-writing, and then it would be time for cocktails. He would have five, she would have two Martinis, and then dinner. The owners of the house, California friends of Alan's, had left behind an assortment of phonograph records as heterogeneous as the books on the shelves. Some good, some bad, and some cracked. At eleven o'clock, never later, she would go to bed and Alan would come in and make love to her, and for her it was a combination of sensation and detached remote observation. So it went for four days, as pleasant a stretch of time as she had ever known. On the fifth afternoon she went out and lay, belly-down, on the sand beside him. "Do you want to go home?" she said.

He took the pipe out of his mouth. "I suppose it's time we were thinking about it. Are you getting restless?"

"I could stay here forever, just like this," she said.

"Oh, really? I know *I* couldn't. I've got to think about making some money. So have you, for that matter. Don't they expect you for fittings next week?"

"Tuesday," she said. "Oh, I'm not kidding myself. I'm not rich enough to stop working, and wouldn't want to anyhow. But I've been so relaxed, Alan. That was you. I never knew anybody that was so relaxing. You can just sit and read, and smoke your pipe, off by yourself, and be perfectly content."

"You didn't know that side of me," he said.

"How would I? I guess I never knew you till now," she said. "Were you ever married, Alan?"

"Oh, yes."

"You never mentioned your wife. I just took for granted you were always a bachelor."

"Oh, no, I had a wife. Would you like to hear about it?"

"I'm dying to," she said.

"Well, it isn't much of a story, actually," he said. He sat cross-legged, tailor-fashion, and ran sand through his hands. "I'm older than you think."

"I was sure you were older than you look."

"Mm, thanks. I'm thirty-seven."

"You had to be, to've been to all the places you've been to," she said.

"Well, in some of them I didn't stop very long." He laughed. "In one place they wouldn't even let me land. Apparently my reputation had preceded me."

"What were you then? Were you a writer then, too?"

"Not, uh, recognized as such. I'd written a very bad novel, but I believe it stopped selling at two hundred copies. It was reviewed in a Yorkshire paper, and a pal of mine mentioned it in *Sketch*. No, I wasn't a writer. Various other things, but not a writer. Odd jobs, some of them very odd indeed."

"How did you meet your wife?"

"That was just after the war. I'd been in it, and I was still wearing His Majesty's uniform. I had a week or two to go before I was required to get back into cits, and I took every advantage of that situation. There were a great many parties in London, and crashing them wasn't at all difficult. I was, let me see, twenty-two. Been to a *fairly* good public school. Had two pips on my shoulder straps, and I'd acquired the M.C., the Military Cross. By purchase. It made all the difference, you know. No one asked how I got it, but they'd look at the ribbon and nod approvingly and *compel* me to drink some more champagne. It was too good to last, and I was only too well aware of that fact. Consequently, when I was introduced to Miss Nellie Ridgeway, the soubrette, who'd just been divorced from one of our more solvent bookmakers, I confessed to an undying devotion to her. There was some truth to that. I'd seen her in one or two shows, and I remembered one of her best songs. 'You and I in Love,' it was called. She was forty. Or she may have been forty-two. Perhaps a trifle thick through the middle, and not too firm up above, but the legs were good. Well, she consented to be my bride. Her money was unfortunately tied up in real estate holdings, not easily converted to cash, and I had one hell of a time getting my hands on any of it. She gave me ten quid a week, pocket money, but out of that I had to pay her cab fares and odds and ends, and she was extremely disagreeable because she didn't have a show that season and was having to spend her non-theatrical income. Actually, she was quite a chiseler, as so many actresses are apt to be. Always economizing on food and drink unless it was for show. A great one for professional discounts, too, and my tailor didn't give professional discounts."

"Was she good in the hay?"

"In a word, no. But insatiable. Stingy women are apt to be, I've found."

"So you divorced her."

"I left her. I took a few things. Her best gewgaws were locked up in a safe to which I didn't have the combination, but I realized about a thousand pounds on cigarette cases and vanities and that sort of thing, and off I went. I left a note, saying I was going to Scotland to try to think things out and do some writing, and she'd hear from me soon. That gave me time to board a rusty old tub that was bound for South Africa. Very astute of me. Naturally she didn't quite believe the Scotland story, but expected me to head straight for the French Riviera. I wasn't the tramp steamer type, and certainly not the South Africa type. I was one of the Mayfair boys, or so she thought. I'd never given her any reason to think otherwise."

"How long were you married?"

"How long did we live together? Less than a year. We were never divorced. She died while I was on tour with the Miller Brothers–101 Ranch Circus. I read about it in the newspapers."

"What were you doing with the circus?"

"I was a Cossack."

"Could you ride?"

"Of course I could ride. I could do all those things. My father was a very keen sportsman, and as I was the only son amongst five daughters, I had a vigorous boyhood. Riding. Boxing. Shooting. Fishing. Not to mention the defense of my chastity against the onslaughts of the elder sisters. A nasty pair, they were. The English public school has a lot to answer for, but the upper middle-class English home such as mine, with five daughters and one rather pretty son—between the two I'll take the public school. It's possible to buy off an older boy with money or sweets, but two predatory older sisters are unbribable."

"Oh, well that's not just England. There was a girl on our street that had her little brother a nervous wreck, and her parents never caught on. Did you ever get married again?"

"No. The other side of me, that you've seen these past few days, has kept me from marriage or any similar involvement. I must have my privacy."

"Is that the way you pronounce it? You make it sound like an outdoor toilet. A Chic Sales. I say pry-vacy."

"Very well."

"What would you think of marrying me?" she said.

"Is that a proposal of marriage? I'd like you to state it more unequivocally."

"You mean lay it on the line? All right. Would you marry me?"

"Thank you very much, but no," he said. "I only wanted you to say it so it could go in my memoirs. October the some-thingth, 1934. Received proposal of a marriage from lovely young movie star. Why would you want to marry me, Natica? You know I've pimped and buggered my way around the world all these years. I know you're a lonesome kid, dissatisfied. But don't for heaven's sake get yourself into anything like that."

"If I didn't like it, I could get out of it," she said.

He lit a cigarette. "May I offer two bits' worth of advice?"

"Sure," she said.

"Don't marry before you're fifty," he said.

"*Fifty*?"

"Take lovers, and make a lot of money, but don't marry. It'll only complicate your life, and it isn't as if you had to prove something by getting a husband. That presents no problem."

"You're wrong. No one ever asked me to marry him."

"Well, that's a quibble, isn't it? You could have a husband if you liked. These few days down here have been very pleasant for both of us. But they're only a holiday, and you can take a holiday when you feel like. Not always in such charming company, it's true, but the charming company can also be very difficult." He looked away. "I might bring a friend home with me. And he might be hard to get rid of. That *has* happened, you know."

"Oh."

"I can't help it, Natica," he said. "I seem to have a limited capacity for feminine companionship, and then I turn to some-one of my own sex. Isn't that putting it delicately?"

"You get tired of girls, and then you go for the boys," she said.

"I was afraid you might have put it more crudely, but I should have known better," he said. "You don't seem to mind."

"I never said I didn't mind, but it was sort of none of my business."

"Well, of course it wasn't, was it?" he said. "The Kings, or at least Ernestine King, made it worth my while to officiate as your gentleman-in-waiting. Unhappily, as I made more money, I spent more. Old friends turned up that I hadn't seen in years. One of them came to stay, or so he thought."

"How did you get rid of him? How do you get rid of people like that?"

"In this case, I took him for a ride. A modification of the Chicago gangster method. We drove up beyond Oxnard and I stopped the car on the roadside. It was late evening, and I daresay I'd given him the impression that I had romantic notions. But I got out of the car and pulled him out, and my old boxing lessons stood me in good stead."

"You beat him?"

"Unmercifully," he said. "A boy for whom I'd once had a feeling of real tenderness. I couldn't stop punishing him. When he could no longer stand up, I gave him my boot. I left him there. What ugliness."

"Well, I guess he asked for it," she said.

"Oh, yes," he said. "He was no rose."

"That's another side of you I never saw," she said.

"And I hope you never do." He got to his feet and peeled off his sweatshirt. He was a slender man, with overdeveloped biceps and forearms that seemed to have been attached to the wrong torso. He walked slowly to the water and stood at knee depth, and when he was good and ready he dived in and swam out a long distance. She had seen him do that before, and the first time she was frightened, but when he returned, and she told him he had scared her, he had only smiled and said, "That's one thing I *can* do, my dear." Now she could see him, doing the dead man's float, and she was not worried about his ability to get back. But she knew with sudden clarity that one day—and it could be soon—he would not want to come back. He was—what was he? Thirty-seven—and ageless. He got older, because we all get older by the day, but he already spoke of his life, the events of his life, as though they had no relation to the present. An end had been put to his life, and the thing that had put an end to it was not an occurrence, a nasty event or a tragic occurrence, but simply the exhaustion of his will to live. She had never known anyone who caused her to think such thoughts. Everyone else spoke of things to come, for them, for her. But for Alan Hildred she had always been dimly aware that it was all over, and that she had forced or demanded the continuation of his existence. She had often put him aside, but she had always picked up with him again, and during this stretch of peace she had reached a state that she wanted to prolong by a marriage that could only be prolonged under precisely the conditions of these five days. If, this minute, he came out of the water and said he would marry her, she would go through with it. But the man floating in the troughs of the waves was going to stay there. He had tried to tell her that he was empty of desire for her, and it did not really matter now where he went next. She would let him go, and she would not ask him to come back.

She rose from the sand and returned to the house and took a bath. She put on a suit of lounging pajamas and went to the sitting-room, and presently he appeared, dressed in his blue blazer and slacks and rope-soled espadrilles. He had a scarf at his neck.

"Martini time?" he said.

"Sure," she said.

"It's a bit early, but the gin may warm me up," he said. "Besides, I have a rather important announcement to make."

"What's that?" she said.

"I'm leaving Hollywood," he said. He stirred the drinks and poured them.

"For good?"

"If you mean permanently, yes." He sipped his drink and obviously he was in a good mood. "I arrived here, in Hollywood, with something under two hundred dollars. I'm leaving with just under twenty thousand. I call that a successful sojourn, especially as the money was paid me for services rendered. Nothing illegal about it. They gave me twenty-five thousand apiece for the stories they bought for you, and they paid me to work on the scenarios. But it isn't going to last forever, is it? I imagine I could find someone a great deal less attractive than you to squire about, but you've spoiled me for the Nellie Ridgeway types. And I'm afraid the time has come when you're ready to give me my walking papers."

"What made you think that?"

"Your proposal of marriage, oddly enough. As I was lying out there in the deep blue sea, I asked myself what was behind your proposal. The good time we've had this week, obviously. But you've got to be back in town Tuesday next, and this relationship will never again seem as pleasant to you as it's been here. You had a premonition of that, too. I'm very happy to've made you at all happy, Natica, and in these four or five days I have given you some happiness, if that's not too big a word."

"Yes, you have," she said.

"Then forgive me if I desert you before you give me the air," he said.

"All right," she said. "You're under no obligations to me."

"Sensible girl," he said. "Extraordinarily sensible girl."

"Where will you go?"

"Sensible girl, asks the sensible question, too. I'm going home to England. I've been naughty, but my peccadillos have been committed in far-off lands. There's no one back home who's apt to turn me in for stealing Miss Ridgeway's gold lighters and ivory cigarette holders."

"And what will you do there?"

"Oh, we have a film industry in England, too, you know. And I have several imposing screen credits on Natica Jackson pictures. I shouldn't have too much trouble finding gainful, legitimate employment. And it's fifteen years since I've been home."

"Have you missed it?"

"Not in the beginning. But I don't want to die out here."

"Are you planning to die in England?" she said.

"Yes," he said. "And planning to is the word. My father cut me off when I married Miss Ridgeway, and all I'll have is the money I take back with me. I can live on that reasonably comfortably for four years without working in the films, without doing a tap. But I'm not going home to scrounge around or work as a dustman. I shall live at a certain scale, and when my money runs out, I'll shoot myself. Nothing terribly dramatic about that. Life isn't very dear to me anyhow. Look at mine. Look at me. Look what it's always been, and now I'm thirty-seven. Life has had its chance to be attractive to me, and I say it's failed dismally."

"I don't know whether you're joking or not," she said.

"I believe you know I'm *not* joking," he said. "I wish I could make love to you now, Natica, and have it mean much more than it ever has. But unfortunately all passion's spent. Will you accept that rather tired bouquet?"

"I accept it," she said.

"Will you also forgive me if I nip off first thing in the morning?"

"In whose car? You can't have mine."

"I'll hire one."

"I guess I might as well go too," she said. "I wouldn't want to stay here by myself."

"Splendid. Then let's get an early start, shall we?"

"Okay by me," she said.

They had dinner, and he drank more than usual. He finished the batch of Martinis, had sherry with his soup, and a Mexican red wine with his steak. He put a bottle of cognac at his side while he had coffee, and she saw that he was determined to get drunk. "I'm going to bed if we're getting up early," she said. "Did you tell Manuel we were leaving in the morning?"

"He's heartbroken," said Alan. "Rita's heartbroken, too, but not as much so as Manuel. He hopes we will come back many times and stay longer."

"Will you tip them in the morning?"

"Whatever you wish, my dear. I suggest twenty dollars, ten apiece."

"I'll give it to you in the morning," she said. "Goodnight."

In the morning her car was gone. Alan was gone, but his clothes had not been packed. She telephoned Morris King and had him send a Tanner Cadillac for her. When she arrived at Bel-Air her brand-new LaSalle was parked in her driveway, without a scratch on it. But she never knew what Alan did with her car in the meanwhile. She never heard another word from him, ever, and neither did anyone else in picture business.

"I could fix it so he'd never get work at Gaumont-British," said Morris King.

"Why would you want to do that?" said Natica.

"I thought maybe you'd want me to," said Morris.

"What did he do to me? I wouldn't want to keep anyone out of a job."

"Well, he sort of humiliated you," said Morris.

"I think you got that idea from Ernestine," said Natica. "He sort of humiliated her, because he didn't turn out right. But I have nothing against him."

"Then okay, we'll forget about him," said Morris. "You go in Tuesday for fittings, right?"

"Right," she said.

"I worked them for a $5000 bonus," said Morris.

"You did? Good for you, Morris."

"And it's all yours. No commission. That make you feel better?"

"Five hundred dollars better," she said.

"Buy yourself something nice with it, with my compliments. You can consider it my bonus for being a good girl. However, Natica, you gotta be ready to go on suspension after the next picture."

"I do? Why?"

"Because when this one's in the can, then I'm going after a new ticket. Tear up the present contract and write a new one for you. This they will not do without some cries of anguish, including they'll put you on suspension. They gotta do that, Natica. The suspension gimmick is something a studio gotta do to keep people in line. Not you, so much as other people. They'll make it look like it's costing you a lot of money to turn down your next picture, but you'll get the money back in the long grun. That'll be taken care of. But I'm just forewarning gyou now, that this picture you work as hard as you ever worked in your whole life. Give them no cause for complaint, you see what I mean. Then they come around with a picture to follow this one and down we turn it. Flat. They turn around and say you don't work anywheres else, and so forth. Well, *we* know that. You're under contract to Metro, and you'll still owe them a couple more pictures under that contract. You can't work anywheres else. We know that. But in this business you strike while the iron is hot. I'm not waiting till they offer you a new contract, two pictures from now. I'm hitting them as soon as you finish this next one. They moan and wail, and they hit you with a suspension. But when they get done crying and threatening, I go in and talk to them and say who's the loser? And they know who's the loser. They are. You lose a few thousand dollars' salary on suspension, but it's big money if your suspension holds up a picture, and that's when New York starts calling gup. Straighten out that Jackson contract and quit futzing around, New York says."

"Well, I hope you're right," she said.

"Natalie, you're on the verge of—"

"Natica."

"Yeah, Natica. A slip of the tongue, when I get all enthused. Anyway, dear, we're gonna get you a contract that frankly you're not entitled to yet. Frankly, you're not. But we're only getting you what you'll be entitled to two or three years from now. I'm gonna fight to get you the kind of money they pay bigger stars than you are, but I'm doing git for a reason. You want to know what that reason is?"

"Sure."

"That reason is because your whole life is gonna be in pictures. Don't ever come to me and say get you out of a contract so you can do a Broadway play. If you do, you're gonna have to look for representation elsewhere. To me you are motion pictures and no place else. I don't want you to as much as walk on a Broadway stage. I don't want you monking around with Broadway."

"I'm not a stage actress. I know that," she said.

"You know it now, but these Broadway managers come out here and put the con on picture people. Art. The Theater. And all they do is stir up trouble. I got clients I *want* to go back and do a Broadway play every once in a while. *Let* them go back and take fifteen hundred a week or less. But that's for the actors and actresses that started on Broadway. I got all the confidence in the world in you, Natica, but I never want to see some Broadway critic take a crack at you because you're a movie star. You know why? Because I'll tell you why. Because I been going through the reviews of all your pictures since you were at Metro, and I never came across one single review that was a rap. Here and there they rap the picture, but never you. Everybody likes you. You. But some hundred-a-week guy on a New York paper is just liable to rap you because he don't like picture people."

"Well, that wouldn't kill me."

"Kill you, no. But out here they never saw a bad notice for you. They never *saw* one. And I don't want them to ever see one. But if some hundred-and-a-quarter critic on a New York paper raps you, the spell is broken, Natica. And we got a fortune at stake. Human nature is human nature, and once somebody takes a rap at you, others will follow suit. It's human nature, and I won't allow it. I got actors on my list that they go back to Broadway, and if they get one good notice in some New York paper, it keeps them alive for a year. They come back here and work in pictures, make some money, and they start itching for Broadway again. So all right. They're not picture stars. They're Broadway people. You are a film star, and you stay that way."

"Morris?"

"What?"

"Is somebody trying to get me for Broadway?"

"Huh? What makes you ask that question at this particular time?"

"Are they?"

"Hell, there's always some manager wishing to capitalize on a picture reputation."

"What is it? A musical comedy, or a play without music?"

"You know, for a young girl that was never outside of the State of California, I have to hand it to you," he said. "Ernestine often said to me, she said one of these days you'd surprise me with how sharp you were."

"I learned it all from you, and Ernestine. You still haven't said what the offer was."

"A musical comedy," he said. "I told them to get lost. They wanted to pay you a thousand a week and no guarantee of any kind whatsoever. They wouldn't even guarantee me they'd open in New York. You could spend all that time in rehearsal, anywheres from three weeks to a couple months out of town, and they could close the show in Baltimore. I told them to get lost. Imagine you coming back here after closing a show on the road, and I go into L. B. Mayer's office and start telling him why you ought to have a new contract. It makes me positively sick to think of it."

"What did Ernestine say?"

"She was positively nauseous, the gall they have coming out here and making an offer like that. The guy said it was a chance to prove what you could really do. And Ernestine said to him right to his face, 'Fifty million people go to the movies every week, and they're all that much farther ahead of you, Mister.'"

"Mr. What?" said Natica.

"You want to know his name? It's a fellow named Jay Chase. If that name don't appeal to you he used to have another one when I knew him in the old days. But what the hell, I had a different name then myself, and Natica Jackson used to be Anna Jacobs if I'm not mistaken."

"Getting me off the subject of Jay Chase, Morris," she said.

"Yeah, I was. But I'll get you back on the subject I wanted to talk about. You and pictures. Natica, I see you—do you know what I see you as? I see you as like Garbo. Gable. Lionel Barrymore. Crawford. I see you as much a part of the Metro organization as Mr. Schenck. L. B. Mayer. The lion. Wally Beery. Them. Some of my clients I can never hope for such an arrangement, whereby they got a home lot and it's a regular second home to them. You think of Metro and automatically you think of Natica Jackson. You think of Natica Jackson and automatically you think of Metro. That's the way I want it to be, because that way you're set for life. I want that for you before you start getting married and maybe you marry a fellow that gets you all discontented. But if you got a permanent home lot, that much of your life is all taken care of."

"You want me to marry Metro."

"Exactly. Or Metro to marry you. I don't care how you put it."

"Some people say a star is better off independent," she said.

"Yeah, that's what they say. You hear that all the time, from actors that it don't look so good for their next option. You hear it from actors that the studio only wants them for one picture. You hear it from agents that can't land a contract for more than one picture. Yeah, a star is better off independent, once he got about two million stashed away and don't care if he never works. But that won't be you for another ten years or so. You're a working girl, Natica."

"That's the only thing you said so far that makes any sense to me. I'm a working girl," she said. "Morris, you and Ernestine stop filling me up with big talk. All of a sudden I'm not a kid any more. I was eighteen and got into pictures, and almost got out. Then you and Jerry Lockman and Joe Gelber and a half a dozen pictures, and this guy and that guy. And my folks sponging off of me, and I get overcharged in the stores. And nearly all the girls I went to high school with are married and started a family. And I'm nearly twenty-four years old. A woman. Not a girl any more. Sixty million girls would like to trade places with me, and I'd be one of them if I wasn't Natica Jackson. I'm lucky, and I know it. But one of these days don't be surprised if I blow my lid."

"You're entitled," he said.

"Just don't be surprised, that's all," she said.

"What are you thinking of doing?"

"I've been thinking of going after something *I* wanted, for a change."

"A fellow?"

"What else? I can buy nearly anything else," she said. "This one I couldn't buy."

"Oh, you got him picked out. Well, you talk to Ernestine and next week we'll take him to the fights. Is he—"

"Oh, no, Morris. You and Ernestine have to stay out of this."

"Who is the fellow? How did you conceal him from us?"

"You put your finger right on it," she said. "You and Ernestine and the studio have to know everything I do. But this was one time I got away with something. Imagine. I slept with a fellow, and you and Ernestine didn't know about it."

"When did you have time to?" he said.

"I get a kick out of this," she said. "I got you puzzled."

"Just don't get yourself into any trouble."

"I know. A fortune's at stake."

"And you want to be sure he's worth it. Don't do nothing you'll be sorry for."

"I sure will," she said. "I am already, but I didn't know how good that can feel. The only thing I *have* felt, these last couple of years."

"Married, this fellow?"

"The works. Married. A good job. Respectable."

"What does he get out of it? What good's it gonna do him?"

"Him? It may not do him any good at all," she said.

The new picture went into production and Natica Jackson was a dream to work with. Everybody said she was a dream to work with: the director, the other actors and actresses, the

producer, the unit man from the publicity department, the
script girl, the assistant director, the little people from Wardrobe and Makeup, the little people from Central Casting, the
little people from Transportation. She had always been easy
to work with, but now she was a dream. She was cooperative,
tractable, patient, and cheerful; and she was punctual and always knew her lines. She was also good. There is in Hollywood
a legendary tribute to a scene well played. It is that moment
when a performer finishes a scene and the grips and the juicers
burst out in spontaneous applause. It is a phony. It does not
happen. But there is the real thing, which happens no more
than once or twice in a dozen pictures. It is that moment when
a performer has finished playing a scene, and for perhaps a
count of three seconds no one on the set speaks. There is complete silence on the part of everyone who has been watching
the scene. The silence is usually broken by the director, who
says—and does not need to say—"We'll print that." Then all
the people on the set go about their business once again, the
better for having witnessed a minute-and-a-half of unrecaptur-
able artistry. Natica had two such moments in the new picture.
One was during the scene in which she hears shots that she
knows will kill her brother. The other was in a church pew,
kneeling beside the gangster who she knows has killed him.
In the one she blinks her eyes as though she were receiving
the shots in her own body. In the other she is full of fear and
loathing of her brother's murderer. Both were routine bits
of screen writing, but they were redeemed by her potentially
explosive underplaying. "This girl can go," said the director.
"She can really go."

"Oh, she can go, all right," said Joe Gelber.

"Reggie Broderick told me she could go," said the director.
"But you know how it is, Joe. One director can get it out of an
actor, and the next director can't."

"You're getting it out of her, Andy," said Gelber.

"I know I am, but it had to be there in the first place," said
Andrew Shipman. "What was she doing with that English fag?"

Gelber shrugged his shoulders. "What was she doing with
Jerry Lockman?"

"That's true," said Shipman. "And who else did she have?"

"I don't know. Reggie Broderick, maybe."

"No, he said no," said Shipman. "He said she'll talk about it, but that's about as far as it gets."

"Well, you have over a month to find out."

"She may be what I call a cucumber," said Shipman. "Show business is full of cucumbers, but particularly in our business. They look good as hell, the answer to all your wildest dreams. But you get in bed with them and that's when you discover the cucumber. No steam. No blood. It's all an accident of how they photograph. Either that, or they save it for their acting. This girl may be a cucumber, but I hate to think so."

"She may be. Jerry Lockman, and the English fag. That's all we got to go on."

"Pending further investigation," said Shipman. "You're sure you never looked into the matter, Joe?"

"Listen, I'd tell you in a minute," said Gelber.

"Yes, I guess you would," said Shipman.

"I'd tell you quicker than you'd tell me. You held out on me before this."

"Only temporarily," said Shipman.

"Well, you want to know the truth, Andy," said Gelber. "I like them prettier than her. Either they gotta be prettier or so God damn perverted I don't want to be seen in public with them."

"You're as bad as Jerry Lockman," said Shipman.

"Maybe worse, but everybody found out about Jerry. I operate different. One big-mouthed dame spread it around about Jerry, because she was a star. Who would of listened to her if she wasn't a star? My motto is—well, I don't know. I guess I don't have any motto."

"I have. My motto is, if at first you don't succeed, you're wasting your time. I'll give you a report on Miss Jackson later on. But meanwhile, the kind of report the studio's interested in is all good. She can really go."

Every shooting day the girl who could really go drove her LaSalle past the Marshall Place intersections of Motor Avenue and was pleased with herself. Now the temptation to reenter Marshall Place and Hal Graham's life was completely controlled. Her mind was made up, she would call the shots. Early in the morning, on her way to the studio, as she came to the Marshall Place entrance she would call out, "Sleep well, get your beauty sleep, Mr. Graham. I'll be with you in a little while." First she must finish this picture, working hard and well and cheerfully. Then Morris King would make his demands, suspension would follow, and her time would be free. Homeward bound in the evenings, she would call out, as she came to Marshall Place, "Another day, another dollar, Mr. Graham. See you soon, Mr. Graham." She was happy. They were wonderful to her at the studio, they let her know they were pleased with her, and Morris King confided to her that he was planning to adjust his demands upward, so that her suspension might be longer than his original guesses of four to six weeks.

"The things I been hearing about your performance," said Morris. "If they were just a little smarter, the studio, they'd come to me and they'd offer to voluntarily tear up your contract. Imagine how good that would make them look? But the studio mind ain't constituted that way, so what'll happen is naturally I'll go in some day and they'll be able to tell by the look on my face that I didn't come in for any social call. But wouldn't they be so much smarter if they anticipated me?"

"And you say to them, you have all your other clients that will never work for Metro unless they give me a new contract," said Natica.

"You *think* it, and you get the thought across so *they* think it. But with Metro you don't threaten. RKO you can threaten. Universal you can threaten. Republic you don't even answer your phone. But Metro, the lion is the king of beasts, you know. You threaten without saying ganything. Jack Warner you can threaten, Harry Warner you don't. Harry Cohn threatens you first, and bars you from the lot. Sam Goldwyn don't use enough people, so when he wants somebody you let him come to you. He'll scream at your price, irregardless of what it is, but when he wants somebody he wants them, so you wait till he calms down and you knock off a few dollars and you got a deal. Agenting is a great business as long as they can't bully you. Nobody can bully me any more, and even Metro knows it, but all the same I'm careful who I threaten. None of these guys are using their own money, and I am."

"You're using my money if I get put on suspension," she said. "I'm the one that's not getting paid."

"You'll get it all back in the long grun. Just don't lose your confidence in yourself. And don't lose your confidence in me."

"I'm kidding," she said. "I've never been so confident in my whole life."

"Yeah, and it makes me wonder," said Morris. "Also it worries Ernestine. If you got one real friend in this business, it's Ernestine. So don't go antagonizing her too far. Everybody has to have one real friend in this business."

"Morris, you handle the studio, and let me ruin my own life," she said.

"I'll let you run your own life, but it sounded as if you said *ruin* your own life, by accident."

"Ruin is what I said," she said.

"All right, have it your own way," he said.

She invented, and rejected, a dozen ruses which would bring about her next encounter with Hal Graham. Some of them were neat and logical, and some relied on sloppy coincidence. They were all pleasant time-killers, anticipating the actual event, which she was willing to postpone because the postponement was in her hands. She was on the final week of the picture and beginning seriously to consider her plans for Graham and herself, and one afternoon Andrew Shipman told her she might as well go home early, that there was nothing more for her to do that day. "I'll need you in the morning," said the director. "Made up and on the set at eight-thirty."

"Eight-thirty? That's practically the afternoon," she said.

"Well, this won't take long. It's a retake of the long shots in front of the church. You might as well get used to loafing again."

"Thanks," she said. She did not point out to him that it would be close to five-thirty by the time she left the studio. Five-thirty was still better than seven-thirty.

She took off her makeup and changed into her slack suit and left the studio. It was still daylight as she drove up Motor Avenue, and as she proceeded she noticed that a pest was following her in a black Buick convertible. She was familiar with the type. They hung around the studio parking lots until they saw an actress leaving by herself. Sometimes they were impossible to shake until she got to the gate at Bel-Air, but once there she could stop and ask the watchman to intervene.

This one was the playful type. He began blowing his horn, and made no pretense whatever of not following her. She stepped on the gas, hoping to lose him, but he kept the same distance, and at Pico he even drove through the stop signal to keep up with her. Instead of turning in at Beverly Glen she kept on to Westwood Boulevard, hoping that the added distance would enable her to lose him in the Pico traffic. The strategy did not work. She was driving through the university campus, with Sunset Boulevard in sight, when he drew up beside her and maintained her speed.

"Do you want me to call a cop?" she shouted at him.

"No," he said.

Then she recognized him. He was grinning. "How do you like my new car?" he called to her.

She pulled over and stopped her car, and he did likewise. He got out and came to her car. "So it was you," she said. "I thought it was some high school goon."

He put one foot on her running board and his elbows on the right-hand door. "How've you been?" he said.

"Oh, eating my heart out because you never called," she said. "You know, I've forgotten your name."

"Hal Graham," he said. "I've been reading a lot of compliments about you."

"You have? I thought you didn't like picture people."

"I don't, but you're the one I knew," he said. "This is *your* new car, eh?"

"Not so new. I got it the day after you ran into me."

"I ran into you," he said. "Well, we'll skip that. How do you like my chariot? I just took delivery on it last week. I almost got a LaSalle, but the resale value is better on a Buick. Of course you don't have to worry about that angle."

"Do you want to get in and sit down, or would you rather follow me home?"

"Whatever you want me to do."

"If we stay here the autograph hounds will start collecting," she said.

"Yeah, these kids are UCLA. Up at Cal we have more sense."

"If you're going to be unpleasant—"

"No, just joking." He went back to his car, and when she pulled away his followed her to her house.

"Is your mother home?" he said.

"Why?"

"I don't know. I just asked," he said.

"No. She's down at Santa Ana at some funeral. Would you like a drink?"

"Are you having one?"

"No."

"Then I won't."

"The last time you were here, your wife was down in Balboa or some place. Did she ever get back?"

"The next day. One of the kids took sick and she came home."

"And that's why you decided not to call me?" she said.

"Partly. Not entirely," he said.

"You were ashamed of yourself."

"Yes, I guess so. There was no percentage for you or me."

"Then why did you follow me today, blowing your horn like a God damn idiot kid? Going through that light at Pico. All those people from the Fox lot. You could have killed a dozen."

"I just wanted to see you, that's all. To talk to you," he said.

"What about, for God's sake?"

"Listen, don't be so stupid. In the first place, you're not that stupid. As soon as I saw you I would have followed you to Santa Barbara."

"Why not make it San Francisco? Santa Barbara isn't very far. Well, what shall we talk about, Mr. Graham?"

"Nothing, if you're not more friendly."

"Don't expect me to be as friendly as the last time. I learned *my* lesson. You should have learned yours, too."

"Well, I didn't. I thought I did, but I didn't," he said.

"I guess not. Not if you were willing to follow me all the way to Santa Barbara. That must be a hundred miles. You *are* romantic."

"No, it isn't a hundred miles," he said. "It's closer to sixty."

"I have no sense of distance," she said.

"You're sore at me because I didn't phone you that time. I'll make it worse. The kid didn't get sick. I made that up. The fact of the matter is, if I would have seen you the next day I never would have stopped seeing you."

"Is that so?"

"Well, as far as I was concerned."

"So you went back and worked on your invention," she said. "You had some kind of an invention you were working on. How did it come out?"

"It's coming along. It isn't an invention. It's a process."

"Tell me all about it, but some other time. So you went back to your process, and the wife and kiddies. Have you had any more kiddies?"

He hesitated.

"Don't *tell* me," she said.

"There's one on the way," he said. "I got a raise, and my wife decided we could afford another child."

"Oh, it wasn't that you were so ashamed of yourself that you had a guilty conscience, and became attentive to her?" she said.

"I wonder."

"You're stupid, aren't you?" she said.

"In some things, I guess I am," he said. "I don't pretend to be very good about people. I remember telling you I didn't have any close friends. My wife says I'm too wrapped up in my work, but why shouldn't I be? I know I'm good and I'm headed for somewhere. They gave me a raise, and next year the company's doubled my appropriation. My work is showing results two years ahead of time."

"Why, it's just like bringing a picture in ahead of schedule," she said. "You're stupid enough to be an actor, and you're almost good-looking enough to rate a screen test. You know you're good-looking, don't you?"

"So I've been told."

"Well, you are."

"Looks don't mean anything in my job. I never think about my looks, one way or the other. And it sure as hell wasn't my looks that you went for. You're with those movie actors all day."

"I want to ask you something. Is your wife pretty?"

"Oh, yes."

"Has she got a good shape?"

"Terrific. Beginning to get big now, with the kid on the way, but she has a great figure."

"Then why don't you get in your new Buick and dash home and jump right in the hay with her?"

"Because I don't feel like it."

"And why don't you feel like it?"

"Because I never got over you," he said.

"Oh, nuts," she said.

"That's true. And you never got over me. I told you, maybe you forgot, but I remember telling you I had plenty of girls before I was married."

"And then you quit, except for one girl in Dallas."

"Well, it was Houston, but I see you remember," he said. "I remember everything, too. I can tell you every word you said to me. I could draw you a sketch of the headboard on your bed. I am stupid about some things, because I don't care. But I remember everything about you."

"Well, do you want to refresh your memory?"

"If I do, Natica, this time we're starting something that may be hard to finish. I'm not going to just think about you all the time. So send me home now if you don't believe me."

"I believe you," she said.

"My wife's going to catch on, and she's going to make trouble."

"I know that. She would."

"Bad trouble, for you *and* me."

"Oh, stop talking about it. *Bad* trouble. What other kind is there?"

"Well, if I didn't love you it wouldn't be so bad. But I do."

"Do you? I never even thought about that," she said. "Well, maybe I did. Maybe I never thought about anything else."

"Why are you smiling?"

"Something a director said. It was about my buttons," she said. "I'll tell you later."

"Order me the hamburger and baked potato," said Morris King. "I want to go over and talk to Leo McCarey a minute."

"It'll get cold," said Ernestine.

"Well, order me one anyway and tell the girl to save it for me," he said.

"All right," said Ernestine. She turned to Natica. "What do you feel like having, Natica?"

"I think I'll have the avocado with the Russian dressing, to start with. Then I'll have the hamburger too."

Ernestine shook her head. "Where does it all go to? If I had the avocado—well, I'll have it anyhow." She waved the menu to summon the waitress.

"Good evening, Mrs. King. You decided?"

"Hello, Maxine. Yes, there'll be two avocados with the Russian dressing, and two hamburgers with the baked potato. Then also I want you to hold a hamburger and baked potato for my husband. He's over with Mr. McCarey."

"And coffee with?" said Maxine.

"Yes, I'll have coffee," said Natica. "How are you, Maxine?"

"I'm fine, thanks. I was home last Tuesday. They were all asking me did I ever see you. I said you come in once in a while."

"I didn't know you two knew one another," said Ernestine.

"We went to high school together," said Natica.

"Yeah, but what a difference," said Maxine. "I end up in a balloon skirt and look where she is today. Well, we're all proud of her. Nobody begrudges her success."

"Thank you," said Natica.

Maxine left. "She's cute," said Ernestine.

"Yes. She took a fellow away from me or maybe I would have married him."

"How could she take a fellow away from *you?*"

"By being cute. She married him, too, but I guess it only lasted a little while. Joe Boalsby. As dumb as they come, but awful pretty. Blond curly hair and built like a Greek god."

Ernestine put her elbows on the table, and looked at Natica. "I had a visit from your mother, Natica. She's fit to be tied."

"Well, get a rope and tie her."

"Is it true what she said? She said you put her out of the house."

"It's true," said Natica. "I got her an apartment on Spaulding. Eighty-five a month, furnished, and a colored woman to come in five days a week."

"Yes, well, Morris and I are kind of worried about that. You remember when we helped you with the house in Bel-Air, it was the understanding that your mother was to live there."

"I know," said Natica. "And I owe money on the house. But if my mother stays, I go. I'll take the apartment on Spaulding."

"She's in the way. Is that it?"

"That's part of it. I don't care where I live, but it's got to be alone. No member of my family is going to live with me. I can be out of the Bel-Air house tomorrow. Morris can sell it, and give me what I put into it."

"You're too big a star now to have a dingy little apartment on Spaulding."

"It isn't a dingy little apartment. It's a duplex with plenty of room, and the furniture is better than what my mother bought for the Bel-Air house. Listen, Ernestine. Let's quit beating about the bush. I have a new fellow. He's married, and has a job and all like that. He has no intention of marrying me, and I have no intention of marrying him. So far his wife hasn't gotten wise to it, but she will sooner or later, and then I don't know what'll happen. But the way I feel now, I'll trade places with Maxine if necessary. You can take Metro-Goldwyn-Mayer and stick it. I'm crazy mad for this fellow, and I never was that way for anybody. You have Morris, that you were married to for twenty years, but all I ever had was Joe Boalsby, that ditched me for Maxine, and Jerry Lockman, and Alan Hildred, and this one and that one in between. Do you want me to shock you? Or maybe it won't. Maybe it won't shock you at all. But to show you how hard up you can get, I asked Alan Hildred to marry me. I think that's what frightened him off, the poor bastard."

"Yes, it would," said Ernestine. "Not because he's a fag. But because he's a snob. You knew he married that English actress, older than he was."

"He finally told me, but I had to ask him," said Natica.

"He was ashamed of it. He's ashamed of his whole life, because he's a snob. Everything about his life he's ashamed of. You know who seduced him, don't you? His older sisters. And he turned fairy when he went away to prep school."

"You had the same conversation with him I had."

"Uh-huh."

"You're not trying to tell me he was *your* boy friend," said Natica.

"The only one," said Ernestine.

"Why? Did Morris cheat on you?"

"Not that I know of. Maybe he did. But that wasn't my excuse. I didn't have any excuse, except that I wanted to have a lover, and Alan showed up at the right time. Maybe I would have gone for him no matter when he showed up. I know for a while there I had Alan Hildred on the brain. Brain, nothing. I was like any silly middle-aged dame that gets stuck on a younger man."

"How did you get to know him?" said Natica.

"Oh, he came in the office one day, trying to get Morris to handle him. About four years ago, this was. He had a copy of some book he wrote, and he gave it to Morris and said he didn't think there was a picture sale in it, but he understood the movies were looking for new writers. Morris never reads anything, so he took the book and said he'd have someone in the office look at it. Meaning me, of course, only he didn't say so. Well, you know how Alan could be, when he wasn't having one of his homo spells. Charming. And I was having a hard time keeping from making passes at elevator boys. So we walked out of the office together and we went to a speakeasy, and he began sizing me up, and the first thing I knew I was lending him a hundred dollars. Me! I never lend anybody a nickel, without a promissory note, but here I was giving this total stranger a hundred dollars that I knew I'd never get back. But it wasn't only the hundred dollars. Morris and I were worth well over a million and I could afford it. But that Alan, he knew my psychology. 'Wouldn't you like to see where I live? It's only a few steps from here,' he said. And I went. One room in a little bungalow just off Vine. So I had my lover. He never asked for too much. I told Morris to get him a job polishing English dialog. They were doing a lot of English plays that they got American writers to adapt, but the dialog was too American. So that's how Alan got in pictures. Two hundred a week. Three hundred. Never any screen credit, but a living, and learning a little about writing for pictures."

"And then you palmed him off on me," said Natica.

"Well, later. I got a little afraid that he'd tell one of his boy friends about Mrs. Morris King. I wasn't afraid of Alan. I always trusted him. He was a gentleman. But some of his boy friends were real scum. Male whores. And I was afraid I might get a disease, and give it to Morris. That frightened me as much as blackmail, so I gave him up."

"I could have got a disease," said Natica.

"You were old enough to look out for yourself," said Ernestine.

"Then *let* me look out for myself," said Natica. "If I was old enough then, I'm that much older now."

"You're right, you are," said Ernestine. "Well, I had to talk to you, though. Morris wanted me to, and I'll always do what he says. Tomorrow's the day he goes to Metro and hits them for a new contract, and he wanted me to talk to you."

"And you did," said Natica.

"And I didn't get you to change your mind."

"You didn't want me to, did you?"

"I'd like to been able to tell Morris I got you to change your mind. But in a thing like this, one woman trying to change another woman's mind is only wasting her breath. I just hope you come out of this no worse off than I did with Alan Hildred. I could of got myself into a lot of bad trouble, but instead of that I only made a fool of myself in my own eyes."

"Bad trouble. That's what he says we have to be ready for," said Natica.

"Well, if he knows that maybe he'll have some sense, or at least be a little more careful," said Ernestine. She patted the back of Natica's hand. "I'm with you, if you need anybody."

"Thanks, Ernestine. I guess all you can do is pacify my mother. Keep her out of my way."

"If it was all as easy as that," said Ernestine. "Three days' work as a dress extra and she'll be glad to go back to the flower shop. Your mother is one of the dumbest dumbbells I ever knew."

"And one of the meanest."

"Yes, I'll bet she is," said Ernestine. "There's Bing Crosby sitting down at McCarey's table. I better get Morris away from there or he won't have sense enough to leave them alone. *Maxine, will you tell my husband we want him back?*"

They sneak-previewed the new picture in Long Beach and Van Nuys and the comments were so good that the studio was in an awkward position, torn between the urgency to spread the word in the industry and the wisdom of postponing the happy news until Natica's contract was renegotiated. "They're playing it very smart," said Morris. "They can't suspend you till you turn down the next picture, so they don't seem like they're gonna show you a script. So you're still on salary. They may keep you on salary a long time without sending you a script. They can afford that. But on the other hand they want to be able to announce you in a new picture for next season. Sometimes they're smarter than I give them credit for."

"Well, what do you want me to do?"

"Keep out of trouble," he said. He was firmer, closer to anger, than she had ever seen him. "Get yourself in a scandal and all my work goes for nought. This fellow you're sleeping with, he's just about the perfect example of what a movie actress should lay off of. A young professional man, with a wife and kids and an excellent reputation. The All-American ideal husband, with the All-American ideal home. Broken up by a movie actress."

"Oh, you found out who he is," she said.

"You wouldn't tell me yourself, so I got someone else to find out for me. Yeah, a detective. The license number of his car, parked in your driveway. I got his credit rating, how much he earns, what he's working on. I guess you knew his father-in-law is a Presbyterian minister in Oakland."

"No, I didn't know that," she said.

"His uncle that he's named after, the same identical name, is the superintendent of schools in Whittier. Oh, I got it all, believe me. Your boy friend Graham, as far as I've been able to find out, there isn't a member of his family on either side that got so much as a parking ticket."

"Well, you don't want me getting mixed up with some saxophone player."

"You can lay off the sarcasm, too," said Morris. "You ever meet his wife?"

"No."

"Well, I got pictures of her when they were married and a trip they took the year before last. You know what type woman she is? The Irene Dunne type. In other words, he don't have the excuse of being married to some homely broad. This is a good-looking woman, and to cap the climax, she's having another kid. Oh, you picked good this time. What ever made you give up that English fag?"

"Graham."

"Well, what'll make you give up Graham?"

"Nothing. Nothing except Graham," she said.

"I wonder what'd make him give you up?"

"Right now, nothing. I don't say it's going to last, but we want it to."

"You just won't listen to anybody, will you?"

"I'll listen. I'm listening now," she said.

"This guy has a clean record, Natica. I spent over two thousand dollars checking, and outside of some college-boy dates, the only woman he ever got mixed up with was his wife."

"That may be," she said.

"You can count on it. Also, her record is even cleaner. She was a studious type and didn't have dates till she started going out with him. She wrote poems. She got some prize for writing a poem. People like that, you know, they're not like people in our business. They take things big. I'm trying to warn you."

"I've been warned. By Graham. I'll take the consequences."

"Big talk. What consequences? How much sleep are you gonna lose if you break up a home with three children?"

"Don't try that argument, Morris. I had to grow up without both my parents. I'm in love with this guy, and I don't want to think about anything else."

"All right. I give up."

"That's good. Don't try any fast ones," she said.

"When the roof falls in, I'll get you a good lawyer. That's all I can do now."

Beryl Graham's poetry prize was a certificate, eight inches by ten, made of a simulated parchment stock, and matted and framed. It rested, rather out of sight, on top of the built-in bookshelves of the den at 88 Marshall Place. The text of the document stated that the eighth annual first prize for poetry of the San Luis Obispo County Poetry Society was awarded to Miss Beryl Judson Yawkey for her sonnet, "If I at Dawning." The certificate shared space atop the bookshelves with Beryl's Bachelor of Arts degree, Hal Graham's Bachelor of Science degree, his commission as second lieutenant in the Army Reserve, and the Grahams' high school diplomas.

It should have been a comfortable room. The chairs were chosen for comfort; well cushioned and with pillows. An effort had been made, too, to create a comfortable relaxed atmosphere, with a sampler that said "God Bless Our Home," and the coats of arms of the Sigma Nu fraternity and the Pi Beta Phi sorority on the walls; a portable phonograph, a small radio, a portable typewriter, a magazine rack filled with recent copies of *Time* and *The Saturday Evening Post*, three silver-plated tennis trophies, half a dozen framed photographs of the Graham family. But everything in the room had been given its carefully selected place, and once given its place had never been put anywhere else. The room had acquired a stiffness that was the opposite of the intended effect. It was just like all the other rooms in the house, from kitchen to bedroom. The nubbly counterpanes had to be where they belonged at ten o'clock every morning, and at one P.M. the Venetian blinds on the west windows were closed against the strong afternoon sun.

Beryl Graham could not have lived any other way, no more than she could have permitted herself the fifteenth line of a sonnet. Sometime in the first year of her marriage she had arrived at a personal ritual of lovemaking, with limits beyond which she would not go, and the ritual remained constant throughout the succeeding years. She did not wish to hear of other women's and other men's variations. She accepted Hal's admiration of her body as a proper compliment not only to herself but to all womankind, and she would speak generously of another woman's "lovely" figure without going into detail that might cause her husband to dwell upon the individual woman as an individual. Beryl made herself the guardian of all women's mysteries. Being a woman was something that no man could ever understand, and he must be prevented from violating women's secrets. It was quite enough for him to be a partner to her climax. He must be satisfied with that intimacy, and he must then go to sleep, gratefully.

She was happiest in the company of other women. It was always a clouding conclusion to a pleasant afternoon when a husband would appear to call for his wife after a bridge game. It was a male intrusion into a feminine world, an end for that day to the pleasing gentleness of women's voices and the pretty sight of feminine things. Beryl loved her kitchen and her bathroom, the tapestries in her hall, the chinaware in her diningroom, and the husband and children that so admirably completed her establishment, *her* establishment among the establishments of other women. She had a son as well as a daughter, but a son was a boy and a boy was a child that was not a girl and children belonged to the mother, a woman. A boy was not a man, and even when he became a man he would become the husband of a woman. It would be nice if her boy went into the ministry. There was still time to direct his steps. He worshiped her, even if he did understand the terms of his father's profession. Howard in a pulpit was an inspiring dream. The Reverend Howard Yawkey Graham. She could see his name in white letters under glass on the sign on a church lawn up North. Sacramento. Fresno. Oakland. San Francisco. The Reverend Howard Yawkey Graham will preach on "Woman's Role Today."

Jean, of course, was already so much like her mother that Hal sometimes would jokingly refer to her as little Beryl. He could just as well have referred to Beryl as big Jean, for with the exception of the overt sexual relationship there was little difference in his treatment of the one and the other. Correspondingly, their treatment of him was tolerantly maternal. The daughter had learned fast.

Howard was nine years old, Jean was seven, and they had been told to expect a new little brother or sister. The age gap between Jean and the unborn child worried Beryl not at all. She fully expected the older children to assume a proper responsibility toward the child that she had tentatively named Emily, after Emily Dickinson. The difference in ages between Emily and the older children was perfectly calculated, she felt. One of the women in her group (whom she did not like very much) had introduced her to the term, sibling jealousy, which turned out to be a name for the hitherto nameless concern that Beryl had disposed of before undertaking her third pregnancy. She disposed of it by deciding firmly that Howard and Jean must learn to love "Emily" before she was born. In this she was succeeding nicely, and for a little while she had no unnecessary worries. In spite of the obstetrician's reassurances Beryl discontinued conventional lovemaking with Hal and they went back to the "heavy necking" that was as much as she would allow in the weeks before the formal announcement of their engagement and the wedding ceremony. Hal's protests were mild, and then he told her that he had decided to stay away from her until after the baby was born. He would sleep in the guest room.

It was such a sensible idea that she playfully accused Hal of suddenly acquiring the ability to read her mind. No man on earth could read her mind, she was certain, but she had so strongly wished that Hal would come to just that decision that she wondered if she did not possess some extra-sensory powers that could be as effective as the spoken word. In many marriages the husband and wife often found themselves thinking the same thought simultaneously, and Hal's decision might only be an extension of this common coincidence. The power of her wish had been undeniable, and if it had not been such an intimate matter, she would have mentioned it to her father as bearing a close relation to the power of prayer. It was too bad, in a way, that she had never discussed those things with her father. But then she had never discussed them with her mother either. She had never really discussed them with anyone, not excepting Hal. She was much too proud of being a woman to relax her own reserve. The same pride had often served her well when Hal made love to her; it was unthinkable that she would ever let him know that *he* could leave *her* unsatisfied. No woman should be that dependent on a man.

But nearly seven years had intervened since Hal had slept in the guest room, and in all those years not a single week had gone by without his getting in bed with her. It was healthy for him. Five years ago, when she had her appendix out, he had slept alone for five or six weeks, but that did not count. She remembered it, though, because he had been so nervous and irritable in spite of himself and his good intentions; and there had been a remarkable demonstration of men's dependence on sex when the doctor said it was completely safe for her to allow Hal to make love to her again. Overnight he became cheerful and relaxed and his old sweet self. Now that he had once again betaken himself to the guest room she began to look for indications of a return of his nervous irritability. At the end of the second week of his celibacy—a fair test—she could see no bad effects, physically or spiritually. He was neither constipated nor petulant. She kept track of his bowel movements and she watched his manner with herself and the children. He was normal. And then she knew, for a fact beyond the suspicion stage, that Hal Graham was having sexual relations with another woman.

She did not need proof. She did not want proof, in the usual sense of the word. Hal Graham was all the proof she needed. She knew him like a book, a man who did complicated equations in a laboratory and could speak for an hour on problems so abstruse that not a hundred men in the entire State of California could follow him for five minutes. That was all there was to him, really, all that set him apart from the race of men. Otherwise he was a vapid, uninspiring person who drove a certain kind of car, played certain games, wore certain clothes, said certain things, and was now indulging certain animal instincts with a certain inferior type of female. Beryl Graham's contempt for her husband had never had occasion to be expressed. The feminine woman, to avoid being a freak, required a husband, a male to fertilize her and to signify his responsibility to her by giving her his name. The inconveniences attendant upon this convention were bearable so long as the relationship was not cheapened by disrespect. But sexual infidelity was disrespect of the most grievous kind. It placed the wife on equal terms of messy intimacy with the husband's mistress. The unfaithful husband sought in his mistress the thrilling shudder that was the proud woman's weakest moment. The cheap and traitorous woman gave him what he sought, and while she was a pitiable and contemptible person, she must be punished for her disloyalty to her sex.

The punishment, however, must be carefully thought out. It need not be visited directly upon the traitorous woman. It should unquestionably be administered indirectly through the offending, disrespectful man. And under no circumstances should it be of a character that would further lower the dignity of the offended wife. Beryl Graham almost automatically discarded the notion of divorce. There was no dignity in becoming the self-proclaimed victim of Hal Graham's disrespect. She next ruled out financial punishment. She could impose upon him a financial burden that he would carry all his life, but two factors decided her against that: fundamentally he cared very little about money, and, secondly, he was so indispensable to his company that they would make some arrangement to help him. It was quite possible, too, that the woman, whoever she was, had money of her own. She was certainly not costing Hal any money now. Beryl knew where every penny went.

No, the usual forms of punishment and revenge were not acceptable to Beryl Graham. They were insufficient, inadequate to the offense, and they were *unsubtle, unfeminine*. They were the thinking of men, the thinking of lawyers, and most lawyers were men.

In her present condition Beryl had plenty of opportunity for calm reflection. Her pregnancy gave her an excuse to give up tennis with the women of Marshall Place, and now that she was convinced of Hal's disrespect to her she used her pregnancy as an excuse to give up the enjoyment of her afternoon bridge games. After she sent the children off to school in the mornings she did her housework and was left with the entire day in which to be alone with her thoughts. When Marshall Place neighbors dropped in she would let them stay only a little while, and she soon discouraged their casual visits. It was not long before she had almost the whole day to herself, and she went through her household duties mechanically while occupying her mind with the problem of dealing with Hal and his unknown woman. It was not a problem that could be solved as he would solve one of his chemical formulae, if he solved chemical formulae. It was not a mathematical thing or a test tube thing; it was not a materialistic matter. It was a problem for a poet.

"How are you getting along?" he said to her one night, when the dishes were put away and the children had been put to bed.

"Me? Fine, thanks. Why?" said Beryl.

"I just wondered," he said. "You have any trouble with little Emily?"

"Not a bit," said Beryl.

"Do you feel life?"

"Of course I feel life," she said. "Men don't understand those things."

"I guess not," he said. "Well, I guess I'll say goodnight."

"Goodnight," she said. She gave him her cheek to kiss.

"Are you sure everything's all right?" he said.

"Why shouldn't it be?"

"I don't know," he said.

"If there's something bothering you, for heaven's sake tell me."

"Well, something is," he said.

"Oh? What?"

"The children. Well, not both children. But Howard said he hoped you'd have the baby soon."

"Why?" said Beryl.

"Because you're acting strangely. He didn't say that, but he thinks it."

"What *did* he say?"

"He said you talk to the baby as if it was alive."

"Well, it is alive."

"I know, but he doesn't understand that."

"And what did you tell him?"

"Well, I tried to explain that the baby's alive, and that it had to grow a little more before it was ready to be born."

"He knows that. I've told them that."

"But he doesn't understand why you'd talk to it now."

"Well, do *you*?"

"I do, because you used to talk to *him* before he was born, and Jean, too."

"I suppose I did," said Beryl. "I believe mothers *should* talk to their babies."

"They don't usually, before they're born," he said.

"Don't they? How would you know? There we are again, you see. A man is so different from a woman that it's just hopeless for him to try to understand us."

"All the same, Beryl, you have to admit it's kind of confusing to a young boy Howard's age, to overhear his mother talking to someone and you can't even see who she's talking to."

"I don't admit anything of the kind. It may be confusing to Howard, because he's a boy. But I'm sure it isn't confusing to Jean."

"I don't know," he said. "She hasn't mentioned it, but she wouldn't anyway. She doesn't confide in me, and never has."

"Naturally. If she had anything to say, she'd say it to me."

"I guess so," he said.

"Oh, I know so," said Beryl. "And there's nothing else on your mind?"

"No."

"Nothing out of the ordinary at the lab?"

"Not a thing," he said. "The usual slow progress. We try one thing, and if it doesn't work, we start all over again and try something else. But we know we're in the right direction."

"That must be such a great satisfaction, knowing you're at least in the right direction," she said. "But what if you found out some day that you were going in the wrong direction?"

"What do you mean by that?"

"Just what I say. Suppose you discovered that these last five years' work was all wasted? That you were completely wrong?"

He smiled. "That would be impossible, now. This is scientific work, you know. Every step is experimental, yes, but when we've proved something by one experiment, that's scientific fact. Then we take up the next experiment. Step by stop, experiment by experiment, we accumulate our scientific facts. Those are things you can't deny. Certain elements behave certain ways under certain conditions. Those aren't laws that man made. Man only discovers them."

"But what if something new comes along and proves you were wrong?" she said.

"Nothing new comes along. It was always there, but we hadn't discovered it. Where we can go wrong is through ignorance. But the things we've proved, scientifically, are never wrong."

"You're all so conceited. So sure you're right."

"Not for one minute," he said. "We're sure that the laws are right. The laws of physics, I mean. But the man that's sure *he's* right, disregarding those laws, doesn't belong in the lab. He *is* conceited, and we don't want him around."

"How interesting," she said.

"You're getting bored. I'll let you go to bed," he said. "Goodnight."

"Goodnight," she said.

He closed the door of her bedroom and she sat with the pillows propped up behind her and a limp-leather volume of Wordsworth's poems lying open at her side. She had a feeling that she was getting closer to the solution of her problem. Whatever it was, it would certainly involve his destruction. This blindly conceited man, with his prattle about laws, must be rendered harmless. There must be a castration of his egotism, so that he could never again take that superior tone. How he had gloated over her and her unconscious, innocent habit of talking to the child in her womb! Did *he—he*—presume to judge her strange?

On the morning of the second Friday after the preceding conversation Beryl waited until Hal had left the house and then announced to the children that she had a surprise for them. They were not to go to school that day, but instead she was taking them to Newport a day early. Daddy, she said, would join them the next day.

She drove them to their cottage, had them get into their bathing suits, and informed them that as a special treat she was taking them for a ride in a motorboat. They went to Red Barry's pier, where the Grahams customarily hired boats, and Red gave them a new Chris-Craft because he trusted Beryl's ability to handle it.

They took off into the San Pedro Channel, which was calm, and when they were about five miles from shore, Beryl stopped the boat and told Howard he could go for a swim. The boy dived in, and Beryl then told Jean that she could go in too. The girl was somewhat reluctant, but she lowered herself into the water. Beryl then started the motor and pulled away. She made a wide circle until she saw first the boy and then the girl disappear beneath the surface. She circled again several times before turning back to shore.

In the words of Red Barry: "She brought the boat in all right, and tied it up herself. And then I thought to myself, 'Hey, wait a minute,' and I asked her. I said where were the two kids? And she looked at me like I was asking some kind of a dumb question, and said, 'They're out there somewhere.' And I said to her what did she mean by out there somewhere, and did she mean she had some kind of an accident? You know, I thought she was out of her mind from shock. But she was just as calm as if nothing happened, and I took notice her dress wasn't wet. Her hair was dry. In other words, she hadn't been in the water. And I thought, Jesus Christ, what *is* this? So I right away went to my shack and phoned the police. I didn't know what the hell else to do. Now there's a woman I been dealing with, her and Graham, five or six years at least. I would of trusted her with my own kids. And it isn't as if she wasn't a great swimmer. Pregnant, yes, but maybe that's the cause of it. You know, when a woman's expecting, and it's six or seven years since she had a child, it's hard to say. In fact, if you ask me, it's hard to tell about them anyway. Like I thought, well the first thing I better do is repaint that boat a different color, but I'm a son of a bitch if there wasn't a party of four wanted to take it out the following Sunday. They asked specially for it. I couldn't let them have it, though. The police impounded it. And how would you like to be Graham the rest of your life? He wasn't even here, but how do you live that down? Because right away people began saying he must of had something to do with it. A guy is married to a crazy woman, a real monster, but they try to shift the blame on him. Well, I guess if I didn't know him I'd probably think the same thing."

Morris and Ernestine King came out of the Beverly Derby, the one-legged newsboy handed Morris the folded morning papers and was handed a fifty-cent piece. "You want to go to the Troc for a little while?" said Morris.

"I don't know. For a little while," said Ernestine.

"Yeah, we might as well go for a little while. It's early."

Their car was crossing from the parking lot.

"What's the headline? There's a big headline," said Ernestine.

"There's always a big headline," said Morris. "'Mother Held in Tots' Drowning.' Now that's nice. To practically accuse a mother of drowning her kids."

"Let me see it," said Ernestine.

He handed her the *Examiner*, and she read the big story. "If I live to be a hundred, I'll never get used to Newport being in California. To me, Newport—wait a minute. Oh, *wait a minute*. Morris. What's the name of Natica's boy friend?"

"The name of Natica Jackson's boy friend? Some name like Hamilton. One of those names. Why?"

"Hamilton," said Ernestine. "You're sure it isn't Graham?"

"Graham is what it is," said Morris King.

"Harold T. Graham?"

"Yeah, why?" said Morris.

"Get in the car," said Ernestine. She spoke to the chauffeur. "Eddie, take us out to Miss Jackson's house."

"Natica Jackson, in Bel-Air?" said the chauffeur.

"Yes, and I'm sorry, Eddie, but don't figure on getting home at a decent hour tonight," she said.

"That's all right, ma'am, as long as I can have tomorrow off," said Eddie.

"Don't even count on that," she said.

Morris was reading the newspaper under the dome light of the town car as they proceeded out Wilshire Boulevard. He finished the *Examiner* and read the *Times*. Before they had got as far as Beverly Glen he refolded both papers and put out the light. "You got any ideas?" he said.

"First we have to find Natica," said Ernestine.

"Yeah, first we find her, then what?"

"What's the use of ideas till we had a chance to talk to her?"

"I guess so," said Morris. "I was thinking we ought to se-crete her someplace. I hope we can secrete her before she finds out about this."

"We don't know anything, where she is or what she knows. Have a cigar to steady your nerves."

"A good stiff hooker of brandy is what my soul cries out for at this particular moment," said Morris.

"You're behaving admirably, Morris," said Ernestine. "Con-sidering what's going on inside. When the chips are down, I have to hand it to you."

"And a hell of a lot of chips are down right now. A matter of two hundred thousand dollars, our end. A million-eight for Miss Natica Jackson. And from the studio's point of view, *you* guess. Now when we get there, I'm gonna let you handle the situation. One woman to another, till we find out where we are. But I want to be in the room all the time."

"If she's there," said Ernestine.

"If she ain't there, I want to go somewhere and get pissy-assed drunk."

"No, you don't want to do that," said Ernestine.

"There you're wrong. I won't do it, but I'll want to. I want to now. If I wasn't afraid of you thinking I was a kyoodle, I'd quit the business tonight."

"Never would I think that, Morris," she said.

The car halted at Natica's door and they got out. Morris pushed the doorbell button, and after a pause the door was swung open by Natica, who closed it quickly behind them. "I had to be sure who it was," she said. "I apologize for making you wait."

"You got a peephole?" said Morris.

"Yes. It isn't in the door. It's off to one side so it won't show the light. It's in the lavatory."

"Oh, good idea," said Morris. "You had any other visitors?"

"No," said Natica. "I phoned you, but they said you were out for the evening."

"We came out of the Beverly Derby and Ernestine happen to take a glance at the morning papers."

"Oh, you found out that way," said Natica. "Can I get you both a drink?"

"You wouldn't have any celery tonic?" said Morris.

"What's that?" said Natica.

"If you have a Coke or some ginger ale," said Ernestine. "Morris'll get it. Dearie, bring me a ginger ale with maybe a little twist of lemon peel."

"What do you want, Natica?" said Morris.

"A big slug of brandy, but I guess I better stick to Coke," said Natica. "Thanks, both of you, for showing up like this."

"Yeah. Well, you two talk while I get the drinks," said Morris.

Natica sat down and lit a cigarette. They were in a small room which contained a portable bar, and ordinary conversational tones sufficed. "He was supposed to come here around five," she said.

"This is Graham, you're talking about?" said Morris.

"Uh-huh. I had a hair appointment for three o'clock, but I decided the hell with it and lucky I did or I wouldn't of been here when he phoned. He was phoning from some gas station on the way to Newport. The police down there notified him what happened and told him he better get there right away. That was after he got back from lunch. He usually has lunch with some fellows on La Cienega every Friday, and then he goes back to the lab. The laboratory. So the police finally got in touch with him around ha' past two. He told me what they told him. That the two children met with an accident and his wife was at the police station. He asked them to put her on, but they said she was in custody. The poor guy, he asked them what they meant by that and all they'd say was he better get down there as soon as he could. They wouldn't even tell him if the kids were alive or dead. They said they didn't know for sure. And he started to tell them he thought his wife and the kids were still home. They weren't supposed to leave till tomorrow. But the cop said he didn't want to talk any more on the phone, and for Hal to get there as soon as possible. The rest I got by listening to the radio."

"We have the morning papers," said Ernestine. Morris served the drinks and took a chair. "And naturally you haven't heard any more from Graham?" said Ernestine.

"No. And he said for me not to try and get in touch with him. He said it looked very bad, and he didn't want me to get mixed up in it. God, I don't want to get mixed up in it either, but I'd like to help him."

"And the way to help him is to stay the hell out of it," said Morris. "The only way."

"Oh, sure. I know that," said Natica. "There isn't any doubt about it, is there? I mean, she did drown the two kids?"

"Wait till you read the papers and you'll be convinced of that," said Morris. "They're holding her on an open charge, but the whole thing is there for anybody to read. They got him quoted saying he didn't know why she'd do it. The grief-stricken husband and father, it says. The pregnant mother showed no signs of remorse or even awareness of the tragedy. The father went out on a Coast Guard boat to join in the search, which already attracted more than fifty small craft containing volunteers and curiosity-seekers. The *Times* has an aerial photograph of the boats, and there's a statement here from a veteran fishing captain who says it may be days before the children's bodies are found. A man named Barry rented her the boat and he's the one that reported it to the police. He refused to talk to reporters, but it was learned that he observed her return to his pier and questioned her as to the whereabouts of the children, and she is alleged to have told Barry that he would find the children 'out there.' He then telephoned the police. Mrs. Graham was taken into custody while returning on foot to the attractive cottage which the family had rented annually for the past five years. And so forth. I'd say the woman was what they call criminally insane."

"She talked to herself," said Natica.

"She did?" said Ernestine.

"And not to herself, really. She talked to the baby in her womb. She worried the poor kids, according to Hal. But he wasn't as worried as they were, because he remembered she did the same thing when she was carrying the boy *and* the girl."

"She'll get off," said Morris.

"They'll put her away somewhere," said Ernestine. "It's too bad they didn't a long time ago."

"Yes, you're right," said Morris. "But now let's talk about you, Natica. First, who knows you were sleeping with Graham?"

"Well, you two do. She didn't. That I know for a fact. She never accused Hal of sleeping with anybody. Not once, and she wasn't the kind that would let him get away with it."

"She wasn't the kind that would murder her two children, either. That's how well Graham knew her," said Morris. "So we don't know what she knew. Who else?"

"Nobody, unless Hal told some friend of his, and he said he didn't."

"It'd be pretty hard for a guy like that to not brag about getting in the hay with Natica Jackson," said Morris.

"He wasn't the bragging kind," said Natica.

"And he had something to lose," said Ernestine. "How about you? Who did *you* tell?"

"A long time ago, Reggie Broderick, but I never told him who the guy was," said Natica.

"What about your servants? Your mother?" said Ernestine.

"My mother doesn't know a damn thing about him. The cook and the maid, if he gets his picture in the paper—"

"Which you can be damn sure he will, tomorrow," said Morris.

"Let me finish. The cook never saw him. The maid could have, if she hid somewhere and watched him leave, a long time ago. Lately he never came in the front door, or left by it. I have a door in my bedroom that opens out into the garden and then through the back gate. I'm not worried about the maid. And if he had to phone me he used the name of Mr. Marshall. There's one person that does know, Morris."

"Who's that?"

"Your detective," said Natica.

"God damn it, that's the thing that's been plaguing me. I knew there was somebody. I knew it, God damn it."

"He has his name. License number. Address. Every damn thing about him and his wife," said Natica. "So, it's up to you, I guess."

"It's absolutely up to me," said Morris.

"Who was it? Rosoff?" said Ernestine.

"Yeah."

"Well, how much can you trust him? He never popped off before."

"No, but he never had anything as big as this," said Morris.

"How much do you think he'd settle for?" said Ernestine.

Morris shook his head. "Who knows? A pension, the rest of his life."

"Well, he wouldn't be the first in this town to get that kind of a pension," said Ernestine. "Do you have his number?"

"Yes, I guess so. You mean with me? Yes. Why?"

"I have an idea," said Ernestine. "Get him on the phone, tonight. Right away. Tell him you have a big job for him, but don't say right away what it is. Find out if he connects up this Graham with the one he investigated."

"He will."

"All right, suppose he does. I have to think a minute," said Ernestine. They were all three silent, until Ernestine tapped her kneecap. "This is what you do. The minute he thinks you're buying him off, you're in for it. He'll bleed you, he'll bleed Natica. I wouldn't even be surprised if he tried to take the studio."

"That he better not try, if he wants to walk around on two legs," said Morris. "Me and Natica he can take, but the studio won't fool around with a small-time operator like Rosoff."

"So you don't want him thinking you're buying him off. Instead of that, you want him thinking you want him to do a little dirty work. You're in it together. You pretend you're taking him into your confidence. 'Rosie,' you say—now let me think." She paused. "I got it. You tell him you're worried about Natica getting mixed up in this thing. Be frank, like. And you say you got a tip that Mrs. Graham, Beryl, went to Europe several years ago and had a child by somebody that wasn't her husband. You aren't sure whether it was Paris, London, or Monte Carlo. But you want him to go abroad right away, as quick as he can, and check the hospital records of all the private hospitals in Paris and London. You'll pay all expenses and fifty dollars a day, or whatever he charges. But he has to do it right away or you'll have to get someone else."

"It won't work," said Morris.

"I guarantee you it will, Morris. Fifty dollars a day and all expenses? I know Rosie well enough to know he won't pass up a chance like that. That's, uh, for two months that's three thousand dollars plus his living, plus a little larceny on the expense account. And a nice de luxe trip to Europe."

"You're spending my money, Teeny, but what for? What do I get out of it?"

"Jesus Christ! The one thing you want right now. Time. *Time.* You get this goniff out of the way for the next five, six, seven weeks. He won't find anything, but he won't be around here making trouble. By the time he gets back to L.A., Mrs. Graham will be put away somewhere. And by that time there'll be five other scandals for the newspapers to occupy their attention. If Rosie wants to blackmail us then, we laugh in his face. But I wouldn't laugh in his face tonight, or next week. Tonight I'm afraid of him. Tomorrow I'm afraid of him. I'm afraid of him till he gets on board The Chief and I'm still afraid of him till he gets on board the *Ile de France.* Then I begin to rest easy."

"It'll work," said Morris. "It'll positively work. Natica, where's your phone?"

"Right there where you're sitting," said Natica.

Within an hour Morris had tracked down Rosoff at a gambling house on the Sunset Strip. "Rosie? You winning, gor losing? Well, can you meet me at the Vine Street Derby in three-quarters of an hour? I need your very urgent help in a matter, and it won't keep till tomorrow. Right, Rosie. If you get there first you tell Chilios I'm on my way, and if I'm there first I'll wait there. But be a good boy now, Rosie, and don't you keep me waiting." Morris hung up. "He says he's winning. I say he's losing or he wouldn't answer the phone. You couldn't get him away from that blackjack game if he was winning. I seen him on two or three occasions blow a couple months' pay inside of an hour. So did you, Teeny."

"Yes I did," said Ernestine. "He's a chump from the word go. You want me to come with you?"

"This time, no. If you were there, he'd smell a rat. No offense, sweetheart. But you know. He'd be looking for an angle. With just me there, he don't get suspicious. You ladies wish to sit and talk, keep one another company till I phone you?"

"If Natica wants my company," said Ernestine.

"Of course I do, you silly," said Natica.

"All right. Then get going, Morris. And good luck," said Ernestine.

"Too bad Natica's not a hunchback. I could rub it for luck. Why wouldn't it be just as lucky to give you a little rub in front?" said Morris. "Wuddia say, Natica?"

"Get out of here," said Ernestine.

"Ah, she knows I'm only kidding."

"Yeah, but do *you* know it?" said Ernestine.

He left.

"There goes a nice little fellow," said Ernestine. "Tough. Shrewd. He'll murder you in a business deal. He'll have the gold out of your teeth before you open your mouth. But if he likes you, once he gets to liking you, you never saw such real, genuine loyalty. And he likes you, Natica."

"I'm positive of that," said Natica.

"How do you feel?" said Ernestine.

"I feel all right. I felt panicky till you and Morris got here. I couldn't think who to turn to. The only person I could think of was Reggie Broderick. All the people I know in Hollywood, and the only ones I had to turn to were you and Morris and Reggie. I would of phoned Alan Hildred if I knew where he was."

"Yes, in a spot like this you could count on Alan. A no-good English fag, but you could count on him in this kind of a situation. Well, that's four people. That's not so bad."

"I ought to feel worse about those two little children, but I don't. He was crazy about them, Hal. But the mother never let him get very close to them."

"What do you know about her?" said Ernestine.

"Hardly anything, it turns out. I thought I knew a lot, mostly from knowing him. But he didn't know much about her either. Married all that time and that's as well as they ever got to know each other. You'd think a married couple would know each other better, but they didn't. I know one thing about her he told me."

"What?"

"She never wanted to look at his private parts. He could look at her, but she wouldn't look at him. She wasn't modest about herself, but he always had to keep covered up till they turned out the lights. She wasn't a Lez, but she hated men."

"She was a Lez," said Ernestine.

"That's what I said, but he said no. She liked to be laid, but she didn't care what happened to him. It was all for her. I don't know, Ernestine. I often felt the same way with Alan. Maybe I'm like her."

"I doubt that," said Ernestine.

"I was with Alan."

"But not with Graham," said Ernestine.

"No, not with Graham."

"Well, you see I was just the opposite with Alan," said Ernestine. "If he told me to—one time he did tell me to do something terrible in front of one of his boy friends, and I did. That was the last time I had anything to do with him, but he had that power over me. That was why I had to stop seeing him. But he had no power over you, and Graham did."

"I would have done anything Graham wanted me to, anywhere, any time. And I would now."

"Well, with me it was Alan. Starting with the first time I ever met him, when I lent him a hundred dollars."

"How did you have the strength to break it off?" said Natica.

"I don't know. Fear, I guess. Not strength. If he could make me do that in front of his boy friend, what next? Those kind of people, people like Alan, that have that much power over a person, maybe the good Lord only gives them so much power. If they had a little more power—but they don't. And that's how the good Lord protects us. You see what I mean?"

"Yes, but how do we protect ourselves from ourselves?"

"Search me. I guess we don't, till we get frightened."

"You think I'm gonna get frightened?"

"Yes, I do," said Ernestine.

"You're right. I am frightened. I'm frightened of that crazy woman with the child in her womb."

"Of what she'll do, or what she'll say?"

"Neither one. I don't think she can do anything, locked up

in an institution. And nobody'll pay much attention to what she says."

"Then what are you frightened of?" said Ernestine.

"Her. I never even saw her, and I probably never will. But I'll be afraid of her for the rest of my life, like she was some kind of a ghost. Her and those two children, but mostly her. I want to talk to Reggie Broderick."

"What the hell for, Natica?"

"He's a Catholic."

"I'm Jewish. You can talk to me."

"No, I remember those Catholic girls I grew up with. They'd get into trouble—not just knocked up, but other kinds of trouble—and they weren't as afraid as the rest of us."

"It only seemed that way. They were just as afraid, if not more so. And anyway, is Reggie Broderick going to get rid of your ghost? I doubt that, Natica. Him *or* his religion. Think it over before you start spilling everything to Reggie."

"Well, maybe you're right," said Natica. "Right now I don't know my ass from first base. I wish to hell I could get drunk. I wish Hal Graham would walk in this room. Only I don't. A terrible thing is I don't want to see him and maybe I never will want to again, with that damn crazy murderess looking over his shoulder at me. That's my ghost, Ernestine."

"Yes, I see what you mean," said Ernestine.

"What happens to her baby when it's born?"

"I don't know what the law says about that."

"I wasn't thinking about the law. I was wondering about the child's future."

"I imagine the father will be given custody, and I suppose he'll move away. Maybe change his name. Get a new job and so forth."

"Do you know something, Ernestine? As sure as we're sitting here, he's never going to see me again. He'll want to, maybe, but the kind of man he is, he'll have a ghost, too. Not only his wife locked up in an institution, but a child to raise. And he'll never try to see me. And all of a sudden I'm beginning to realize that that crazy woman knew what she was doing."

"What?"

"Just as if she called me on the phone and told me. Maybe

she doesn't know my name, even, but I get it inside me, Ernestine. She's telling me."

"Telling you what, dear?" said Ernestine.

"She's saying, 'This is what you have to live with. Ann Jacobs or Natica Jackson, or whatever you call yourself, this is what you have to look forward to.'"

"I wish I didn't believe that," said Ernestine.

"But you do," said Natica.

"I won't lie to you. It's the only thing to believe that makes any sense," said Ernestine.

They were silent for a moment, then Natica spoke. "I told him once, if he hadn't stopped to put on a necktie I never would have smacked into his car."

"I don't get it," said Ernestine.

"Oh, I'll tell you sometime, but not now," said Natica.

"We ought to be hearing from Morris," said Ernestine.

"No hurry. I can wait," said Natica. "I have complete confidence in Morris."

How Old, How Young

Y<small>OU DID</small> not often see a woman crying on the street. You sometimes saw one in the neighborhood where the doctors had their offices, coming out of an office with another woman or a man and crying from pain. Sometimes they would be coming from a dentist's office, but they would be holding bloodstained handkerchiefs to their mouths. Doctor's office or dentist's office, they would usually get in a waiting car or a taxi and not be on the street very long, and anyway their crying was easily explained. You just about never were walking along the street and saw a young woman crying out of emotional anguish, weeping tears that were tears of sorrow and not caring that she might be making a spectacle of herself. But on this particular afternoon a long while ago James H. Choate, who had a summer job as runner for the family bank, was on an errand to a law office and coming toward him he saw this young woman and if he had not known her he would have said she was plastered. She was wearing white shoes with brown wing tips and medium high heels, and yet she walked as if she had on ski boots. She was wearing a simple dark blue linen one-piece dress with a thin black belt and a white collar, and a straw hat that was varnished black—pretty much of a uniform among certain types of girls in those days. But she was walking like a drunken tart. Then when she got closer he saw that it was Nancy Liggett and that she was weeping without any self-restraint and leaving her misery naked for people to stare at. Jamie Choate wanted to cover her, as though her nakedness were the real thing. He stopped and stood in her uncertain path, but she walked around him. "Nancy!" he said. She kept on going and he watched her indecisively until she reached her car. She got in, and he was glad that it was a coupe; it offered her some shelter from the mystified stares of people, including himself. It was twenty minutes of three, and he had to get to the lawyers' office and back to the bank before closing time. He had not been told the nature of the envelope he was to pick up, but he had been ordered to get it back before three, without fail. He was very unimportant at the bank; they did not think much of him there. He made a special effort on this errand. He got back in plenty of time—five minutes to spare—as much because he wanted to see if Nancy's car was still in the block as to make a good impression at the bank. The car was gone.

There was a swimming-party-picnic that night that Nancy Liggett should have been at but wasn't. Some people had a boathouse at a dam in the woods about fifteen miles out of town. The water was always very cold and so was the air, and even though the bank thermometer that day had registered above ninety degrees, people at the picnic were drinking straight rye to keep off the chill. Quite a few people got tight. It was a Friday, the beginning of the weekend for most of the people, but Saturday morning was a very busy time at the bank, and Jamie Choate stayed sober. His cousin, Walker Choate, was at the picnic to remind him, in case he forgot. Walker was an assistant paying teller and a regular member of the staff. Very patronizing toward Jamie. "Remember, you have all those blotters to change in the morning," said Walker. "Need a steady hand and a clear mind for that."

"Oh, go to hell," said Jamie. "I wonder why Nancy Liggett isn't here tonight."

"Why the sudden interest in Nancy?" said Walker.

"Because I've fallen in love with her," said Jamie.

"Then why didn't you bring her?"

"I don't know. I was hoping you would and then I'd take her away from you."

"If I ever brought Nancy to anything it wouldn't be hard to take her away from me. Even you could. Why don't you go take a look in the woods. Maybe she's here and forgot to check in with you."

"Walker, you *are* a wet smack," said Jamie.

"Yeah, and you're not dry behind the ears," said Walker.

It was a fairly large party and included people who were still in prep school and people who had children of their own, and a greater number of those in between. It would have been possible for Nancy to have arrived at the boathouse, stayed there a few minutes, and vanished in the woods without Jamie's having seen her. To make sure she hadn't, he went to the hostess-chaperone, Gwen Lloyd, and said, "I've been looking all over for Nancy Liggett."

"She isn't here," said Gwen. "She called up and said she wasn't coming. Offered no excuse, and she was supposed to help out with the food."

"Oh, you spoke to her? How did she seem?" said Jamie.

"How did she seem? She seemed rude and inconsiderate," said Gwen. "She was supposed to bring three dozen ears of corn for corn on the cob, and when I started to ask her about them, she just hung up."

"Not like her," said Jamie.

"Well, it'll be a long time before I count on *her* again. I don't know what's got into her lately. Don't tell me you have a sneaker for her, Jamie."

"What if I did?" said Jamie.

"Well, that's your business, but you'd do better with someone your own age."

"Nancy's the same age. Exactly the same age. We were both born in 1904."

"Girls mature earlier," said Gwen. "You're still in college, and she's been home two or three years."

"What are you not saying that you're kind of hinting at?"

"Just that she's older than you, even if you were born the same year."

"Well, at least she called up and said she wasn't coming," said Jamie.

"Yes, you do have a sneaker for her," said Gwen.

"I'm not as naïve as you'd make me out to be," he said.

"You're away most of the time. I just hope you don't fall for Nancy Liggett," said Gwen.

"I think maybe I have."

"Then forget everything I've said," said Gwen. "Heaven knows she needs someone she can depend on. And that's *all* I'm going to *say.*"

"You married people! You'd think you had some monopoly on how people react."

"In certain things we have more experience," said Gwen.

"I'll say you have," said Jamie. "Who's going to chaperone the chaperones, that's what we always say."

"Uncalled for, that remark," said Gwen. "If you're not having a good time, nobody's asking you to stay."

"Then I bid you a fond adieu," said Jamie. It was close to

eleven o'clock and from his point of view the party had been a frost. Some of the people had paired off and vanished; the singers were going through their repertory; two tables of bridge had settled down in the boathouse; Walker Choate was trying to persuade an out-of-town girl to go canoeing with him. It was all very much like every other swimming-party-picnic the Lloyds had given, except that on this one Jamie had had no fun, no fun at all.

On his way home he slowed down as he passed the Liggetts' house. There was a light on in the room that he knew to be Nancy's bedroom, but Mr. and Mrs. Liggett were not the kind of people who sanctioned midnight visitors. At home Jamie went to the icebox and got a glass of milk, to the cakebox and got a couple of brownies. He sat on the kitchen table with his feet resting on a chair and pondered the newest mystery in his life: why had he never fallen in love with Nancy Liggett until he had seen her good looks washed away by tears, her face made plain by misery? Ah, well, it was not much of a mystery, really. Her good looks had always kept him away, and now she was just like anyone else—except that he was in love with her. And he would never be the same again. A new organ had come to life, somewhere in his chest, and it was pumping something warm and sweet through the rest of him. Nancy Liggett, who needed someone she could depend on.

He had a ladder match to play the next afternoon, and he thought of defaulting, but his best chance of seeing Nancy would be at the club pool. He played the match and won, had a ginger ale with the kid he had beaten, took a shower and put on his bathing suit and went to the pool. She was there, sitting by herself with her chin on her knees and her arms clasping her legs. She looked up at him as he dropped his towel and sat beside her. "Hello," she said.

"Do you mind?" he said.

"I'm not being very conversational," she said.

"Well, that makes two of us," he said. "You didn't go to the Lloyds'?"

"No," she said.

"I left fairly early. It was still going strong, but the only person I wanted to talk to wasn't there."

"No?"

"No," he said.

"I warned you I wasn't being very conversational," she said. She picked up her bathing cap and pulled it on, tucking in wisps of her blonde hair, cocking her head as she did and unconsciously being extremely feminine and attractive. She stood up and went to the edge of the pool, hesitated, and dived in. He waited to see her when she got out, with her wet bathing suit sticking to her body, but he also wanted to see if she would return to their place. He had quite a while to wait. She swam very slowly up and down the length of the pool, floated a bit, and finally climbed out.

"You weren't going to get rid of me that way," he said.

"It was worth a try," she said. She took off her cap and dried the back of her neck and ran her fingers through her hair. She lit a cigarette and lowered herself to the concrete.

"How's the water?" he said.

"Very damp," she said. "You ought to investigate it."

"All right. Will you be here when I get back?"

"Why not? I was here first," she said.

He dived in and repeated her slow swim and float, and climbed out. "Can I have one of your butts?"

She pushed the pack and matches toward him. He lit one and took a couple of drags. "Don't be sore at me, Nancy. I didn't do anything. I just happened to *be* there, coming out of the bank."

"I'm not sore at you—just as long as you don't ask any questions," she said.

"I want to know, though. And it isn't just idle curiosity."

"What else is it?"

"Do you really want to know?" he said.

She turned and faced him. "Yes."

"It's love," he said.

"Oh, for Jesus' sake," she said.

"You said you wanted to know, and I told you," he said.

"I certainly didn't want to know that," she said.

"It doesn't put you under any obligation."

"I'll say it doesn't," she said.

"I just found out myself, last night."

"Because you saw me blubbering on the public street, you came to the conclusion that you're in love with me. You'd change your mind pretty quickly if you knew *why* I was crying," she said. "And you'll know soon enough. Everybody will. All of you. Everybody at this pool. Old Mr. Griffiths down there on the eighth tee. Johnny Wells, Mr. Charlton, Stanley Griffiths. The fussy foursome. You'd better get away before they all see you with me."

"What's the matter, Nancy?"

"Oh, for God's sake leave me alone," she said. She pulled up her knees again and rested her chin on them, and wept.

"What *is* it? I *love* you, Nancy."

"Oh, Christ almighty, Jamie. I want to die. I want to *die*."

"Let's go someplace. Get dressed and we'll go for a ride," he said. She looked at him and she was not pretty, but there was the beginning of trust in her eyes.

"Where will you take me?" she said.

"Anywhere you say."

She put her towel to her face and sniffled. "Where's your car?"

"In the second row, halfway down the hill."

"I'll be there in ten minutes," she said. "Don't you come with me. I'll meet you in your car."

It took them longer than ten minutes, but she was there waiting when he got to his car. She was pretty again, in a flowery print sleeveless dress and a necklace of tiny Tecla pearls.

"Any place you want to go?"

She shook her head, and with her fingers only she waved to the clubhouse. "Goodbye, club," she said. "Nice to have known you."

They passed through two towns before either of them said anything. "Are you thirsty? I am," he said.

"Very," she said.

He stopped the car at a roadside stand and got a couple of mugs of root beer. "This is all they had," he said. "Out of everything else."

"I love root beer," she said. "Remember those picnics when we were very little? At the Griffiths farm? I got stung by yellowjackets one year."

"I was there. You were certainly a mess. All puffed up."

"And Mrs. Griffiths put clay all over me, supposed to take the sting out but it didn't."

"The wrong kind of clay, I guess."

"I minded that worse than the sting, that mud all over my face and arms," she said. "Well, I should have gotten used to it. The mud's going to fly thick and fast."

"You don't have to talk about it, Nance," he said.

"Oh, I can now. We're not even in the same county, so I can talk, and I want to." She handed him her mug, and he returned it to the refreshment stand. They drove away.

"Do you think I'm pregnant, Jamie? Is that what you think it is?"

"The possibility occurred to me."

"Well, it might be a possibility but it doesn't happen to be what I was crying about," she said. "It's my father."

"Your father?"

"They came and arrested him this morning. It'll be in the paper this afternoon. Judge McDermott released him on bail, but he's going to have to go to prison."

"For what?"

"Misappropriation of funds. Daddy is a thief. He stole over sixty thousand dollars in three years."

"At the Trust Company?"

"Yes. When you saw me yesterday he had just signed a confession. I was there when he signed it. I went to his office to ask him for some money. Poor Daddy. He hated to refuse me anything, and didn't very often. But there I was, and some lawyers and a detective—although I didn't know that that's what they were. 'Gentlemen, my daughter is here to ask me for some money. Shall I tell her what my excuse is for turning her down?' One of the men said no, it would be cruel. But Daddy said I had to find out sometime. Sixty thousand dollars, and he doesn't know where it all went. He told me to go home and be with Mother when she got the bad news. Today I went to the club for the last time ever. Monday I start looking for a job."

"Your mother has some money, hasn't she?"

"Some. Enough for her to live on, I guess, but not in our house."

"I wondered why you said 'Goodbye, club.' I had a feeling it meant something."

"And you were right," she said. "About *that*. You weren't right in suspecting I was pregnant. I'm much too careful for that."

"I wouldn't know," he said.

"No, and the only person that would know—I don't expect to see *him* any more. Not after he hears about Daddy. So I guess I'm going to start being virtuous, for a change."

"Oh, stop trying to be so sophisticated. You make me sick. Whoever the guy is—and I'll bet I could guess—you don't know *what* he's going to do."

"Don't I? He's quaking in his boots right now, terrified that he'd somehow get mixed up in this."

"If that's your opinion of him, why did you have an affair with him?"

"Oh, Jamie, what a question. I knew what I was letting myself in for, but that didn't stop me."

"Well, at least his wife doesn't know. Although she is sore at you."

"How do you know?"

"Because you were supposed to bring three dozen ears of corn to her picnic last night," he said.

"Oh," she said.

"Who else could it be? As soon as I knew I was in love with you, I spent all last night figuring out all the possibilities. I finally narrowed it down to two."

"Who was the other?" said Nancy.

"That wet-smack cousin of mine, Walker," he said.

"No. Not Walker."

"I'm glad of that, anyway," he said.

"He is a wet smack, isn't he? And his wife is so unattractive. At least Gwen is pretty. A bitch, but pretty. At least I never felt that I was taking candy from a baby."

"Gwen thinks you ought to have someone you can depend on," he said.

"How touching."

"I think so, too," he said.

"And so do I. That makes three of us."

"Why don't you marry me?" he said.

"Let me find a job first," she said. "What do they pay you at the bank?"

"Fifteen dollars a week."

"Which is probably what I'll get, if I'm lucky. We could be gloriously happy on thirty a week, you and I."

"I'll have some money when I'm twenty-five."

"Yes, but what do we do in the meantime? Thanks for the offer, Jamie. But you have another year in college, and then I suppose they'll pack you off to the Harvard Business School, and then you ought to have a year or two in Wall Street. You and I are exactly the same age, but do you see how young you are? And how old I am?"

"I didn't like the sound of that when I heard it from Gwen," he said.

"Ask me again four years from now," she said.

"I don't want to have to wait that long," he said.

"We don't have to wait, for everything," she said.

The Farmer

Aᴛ ᴛʜᴇ sight of a young woman sitting on a tree stump at the side of the road Kramer might ordinarily have slowed down, but he would not have stopped. This young woman, however, was wearing riding breeches and boots, was smoking a cigarette, was such a picture of dejection, that curiosity and the instinct to be helpful made him stop. "Can I do anything for you?" said Kramer.

She looked at him with hostility, impatience, and it was obviously against her will that she made the effort to be civil. "Yes, if you'll get me to a telephone," she said.

"We have one, the second farm down the road. Get in," said Kramer. He opened the door of the half-ton and she stood up. As she approached the truck she limped. She got in beside him and he put the car in low gear. "You get thrown off your horse?" he said.

"Wasn't *my* horse," she said. "I never would have been thrown off my horse."

"What'd he do? Shy up at something?"

"A snake. A nasty little snake went slithering across the road."

"Yes, we had a lot of copperheads around. The dry weather brings them out. I killed one this morning, right in my barnyard. Near the water trough."

"I wish you'd have killed that one."

"I noticed you limping. Where were you hurt?"

"At the base of my spine," she said.

"Oh," he said.

"He reared up and back I went."

"And ran away," said Kramer. "Well, he most likely headed for home. Where are you staying? Dr. Jones's?"

"Yes, how did you know?"

"They're the only ones still keep any saddle horses in the Valley. I can take you there, it isn't much farther."

"All right, if it isn't too much trouble," she said.

"I guess you're a friend of Martita's. You're about her age."

"Yes, I'm staying there."

"Are you from town?"

718

"What town?"

"Gibbsville," he said.

"Yes," she said. "My name is Sheffield. Barbara Sheffield."

"Oh, Sheffield-that-has-the-lumber-company's daughter. Out there on Twelfth Street."

"Yes."

"I bought all the lumber for my tractor barn from Sheffield."

"That's nice," she said.

"My name is Kramer. Irwin Kramer. Your father wouldn't know me, but I know Gus Bohmer pretty well."

"Oh, yes. The foreman."

"Gus is related to my wife's people."

"Is that so?"

"Here's my farm, on your right. I'm on both sides of the road, but those are the farm buildings on the right."

"My, it's quite impressive. Quite an establishment," she said.

"It belonged to my father *and* my grandfather. I wasn't going to farm it, but I had my older brother was killed in the war in France, so I was the only one left. Two older sisters, but both married. One living in Reading and the other in Swedish Haven."

"What were *you* going to do instead of farming?"

"Well, I guess if I had my way I'd have finished my college education and maybe gone to law school."

"Oh, you did go to college?"

"For a year to Muhlenberg. But then Paul got killed with Company C, the 103rd Engineers. You know, mostly from Gibbsville."

"Yes. I had two cousins in that company."

"Sheffield?"

"No. One was a Hofman and the other was a Davis."

"Yes, I didn't remember any Sheffield in Company C. There was a Dayton Sheffield in Company D."

"He was another cousin," she said.

"I had my cousin Walter Kloster in Company D. I guess you saw my brother Paul's name on the roll of honor they put up at the armory."

"Yes, I must have," she said.

"Corporal Paul M. Kramer, under the killed in action," he said. "I guess you're a college girl?"

"No. I didn't go. I should have been a sophomore now, but I wouldn't have got anything out of it. I'm a non-producer."

"A what?"

"That's what a friend of mine calls me. He says I'm a non-producer. Anybody that doesn't work or do something he calls a non-producer. He's certainly right about me."

"Well, you have plenty of time, and I guess if your father owns the Sheffield Lumber Company you don't need the money. In other words, you don't have to go to work. I wouldn't work if I didn't have to."

"Not even as a lawyer?"

"No. I didn't take any special liking to being a lawyer. I just wanted to get away from the farm. But I never will now."

"Sell it," she said.

"Ho-ho. Sell it! Did you ever try to sell a farm? You never get what you put into it. Sure, I could sell it to my neighbor, for five thousand dollars. Take a mortgage and all that. Did you ever go to a farm auction? See those prices? Five dollars for a cultivator. Six dollars for a lime spreader. Fifty cents for a set of harness. Two dollars for a DeLaval. They come around like chicken hawks, looking for the bargains. Maybe you think your farm is worth twenty, twenty-five thousand, but wait till you go and put it up for sale. Georgie Laubenstein over in the next valley. Four hundred acres, thirty-two head of Holstein, a practically brand-new tractor, a house with running water, a new Delco. You know what Elsie Laubenstein got when she sold? Fifteen thousand dollars. Fif-teen thousand dollars. If you don't have a son that's ready to take over, and run your farm, your widow is lucky to get a quarter of the value for a quick sale. I bet you Dr. Jones put in thirty, forty thousand dollars since he bought the Snyder farm, but I'll bet you they don't get any thirty thousand for it when he dies. Not that he's a regular farmer. He's what they call a gentleman farmer, uses it for a hobby. Any time you see a saddle horse on a farm around here, that means a rich man that farms for a hobby. Do you have a horse at home, in town?"

"Yes. I hope I don't have to give him to Dr. Jones for losing his horse."

"Don't worry. The doctor's horse'll be in the barn when we get there."

"Would you mind stopping a minute?" she said.

"No. Is your back hurting you? This half-ton don't ride too easy."

"It isn't my back. I'd just like to smoke another cigarette before I have to face Dr. Jones and Martita. Will you have a cigarette?"

"I don't mind," he said. "I don't very often smoke a cigarette. In the house I smoke a pipe or an occasional cigar, but I never smoke anything around the barn. And I never took up chewing. Most farmers chew, but not me." He drew the truck over to the side of the road. "I don't even carry matches, so you have to light your own."

"What if that damn horse didn't go back to the barn?"

"He will. But even if he didn't they'd find him. Which one was it? The chestnut?"

"No, the white one. The white gelding. You seem to know the Jones horses," she said.

"Farming, you get so you know all the stock everybody has. There's not so many people to know, so the next thing is you know the stock. The cattle. The horses. Dogs. All the animals that last a few years. Not the poultry or the pigs. They don't last long enough. But there's not a farmer in the two valleys that wouldn't know Dr. Jones's white horse."

"I suppose not," she said.

"We're all used to him. The doctor comes down here all year round, not just the summers. And he'll go for rides on that white horse in all kinds of weather."

"Yes, I know," she said.

"Soaking wet I've seen him, the doctor. He must enjoy it."

"He loves his farm," she said.

"He can buy mine any time he wants to, providing he offers me a decent price. But his place is too far from mine. He wouldn't want to buy mine. Did your father ever think of buying a farm?"

"Not that I know of. His relaxation is playing golf. And he likes to go fishing, in the Poconos. As far as I know, he never showed the slightest interest in farming."

"I thought maybe if he knew my farm is for sale, he could come and have a look at it."

"I don't think there's much chance of that," she said. "You really want to get rid of it, don't you?"

"As quick as you say Jack Robinson, if I was offered a decent price. But that'll never be, and I know it. I'm tied down to it. Trapped."

"Maybe if you did sell it and went away, you'd miss it."

"Not me. I only had the one year away from it, one year in Allentown, at Muhlenberg. But my goodness, I made friends there with a Chinaman. A boy from China, a freshman with me. You'd never meet anybody from that far away living on a farm all your life. It's only by accident I met you."

"Aren't you married?" she said. "You are. Our foreman is related to your wife's people."

"I'm married," he said.

"Doesn't your wife like living on a farm?"

"She was never anywheres else. Not even to Philly, except when we passed through it on our way to Atlantic, on our honeymoon. She didn't like it. The farm she came from, over in the other valley, her parents didn't have any of the modern conveniences. They had to pump water by hand. Coal-oil lamps. No such thing as the telephone."

"So your farm is luxury to her."

"Luxury is right. Her mother brings her ironing over every Tuesday, because we have the electricity. The last baby, her mother stayed with us a week and she never went to bed till two o'clock in the morning, listening to the radio. I have such an Atwater-Kent set I bought last year. The old lady won't believe it that the music comes from Chicago, through the air. She thinks it comes over the electric power line, or like the telephone."

"Well, I don't understand it either."

"But you know it doesn't come over the telephone line," he said.

"I know it because that's what I was told. Understanding it is something else again," she said.

"Well, I guess if you're talking about the scientific part, I don't understand it either. You'd have to know more about electricity than I know."

"I don't want to hold you up," she said. "You were on your way home."

"No hurry. I don't so often have an interesting conversation," he said. "A person doesn't get to talk much to his neighbors. Like I'm out plowing or something like that, in the field, and I see my neighbor plowing in his field. 'Hyuh, Kramer,' he says to me, and I say hello to him. But we don't always stop and talk. When we do stop and talk, maybe he wants to borrow something off of me. I want to borrow something off of him. Or maybe they're going to vote on spending some money on the road. The road needs it, but nobody wants to spend the money. Every spring the road is so bad we have to spend the money, but it's township money, and township money is our money. The county won't help, the state won't help. It's all right if county people want to use the road, but they won't give us the money. That's why the road's in such bad condition. Look at the condition of this road."

"It's pretty awful," she said.

"They fill in with a wagonload of traprock, but that only lasts a little while. We ought to have a whole new road. You'd be surprised how long it takes to wear out a set of tires on this road, and tires cost money. They had this meeting of the township supervisors last Feb'uary and I went to it and I told them, I said let's do something about the road this year. Let's everybody vote to spend the price of a new set of tires, around forty dollars apiece, and get a halfway decent road. You would have thought I was a crazy man, the hollering and yelling that went up. So along comes April and they fill in the holes with some traprock, the same as ever. It's enough to make you sick. Next year it'll be the same, but I won't say anything. I said my say. It's hard to get a farmer to part with his cash, the little he has. But what they're afraid of most of all is raising the assessments. They figure if the road gets better, the assessments will go up. And they will, too. But we'll be getting something for our money."

"I never thought of farmers having these problems, but I suppose they do," she said.

"People are dumb, and there's nobody dumber than a dumb farmer. I'm the only farmer in the Valley that gets the paper in the mail. The only farmer in the Valley. It's two days old, but it's still news. Those that have a radio set can listen to what's going on in Pittsburgh, KDKA. But they don't know what's going on in Gibbsville, eleven miles away."

"There's not much going on there," she said.

"Oh, I don't know. My wife only reads the ads, but I like to read about what's happening. There's always something new."

"I wish I thought so," she said.

"I see your father and mother's name in the paper every so often."

"Always with the same people. Mr. and Mrs. Joseph Chapin entertained friends at dinner at their home on North Frederick Street. Among those present were."

"Well, yes, but they're not just sitting home every night."

"Nearly every night."

"Here it's *every* night," he said. "Three hundred and sixty-five nights a year. Up at six o'clock every morning, or earlier. Even when it's a heavy rain you have your chores to do."

"Well, my father gets up at seven."

"But he wouldn't have to."

"He's at the lumber yard every morning at half past eight."

"I'd trade places with him," he said.

"I hope you don't. He wouldn't make much of a farmer."

"Neither do I. I do what I have to do, and I earn a living, but by Jesus I hate it. Pardon the French."

"How many children have you got?" she said.

"Two, and one on the way."

"What are you going to do with them?"

"Well, the boy is three and a half. The girl is two. It's too soon to say, but I hope the boy finishes college and goes away. By that time I'll be about fifty, I guess. Maybe I could sell the farm and get work in town. Twenty years from now, who can tell?"

"Maybe the boy will want to be a farmer."

"If he listens to his mother he will, but not if he listens to me."

"She likes the farm."

"She likes it better than town. She doesn't know any better. I guess I oughtn't to said that, but it came out."

"Is she pretty? Your wife?"

"I guess you could call her pretty. She was only sixteen when we got married, and she put on some weight since. She's a farm girl. She's so Dutchy you'd have a hard time understanding her talk. She only went to the eighth grade. That's as far as most farm girls go. They don't need more than that. They're better off without it, I guess. She cooks, bakes, sews, all those things. And when she was living home she did the milking and all that. Butchered."

"Butchered?"

"Sure. Butchered. Made soap. She says she could shoe a horse, but I never saw her."

"You ought to be proud of her. She sounds like a very remarkable person."

"In some things."

"In a lot of things, it seems to me."

"You don't have to take her side against me," he said. "I appreciate her, and I'm good to her. Get that straight. I'm good to her. But I know what you're thinking. You're thinking I don't appreciate her."

"That's exactly what I was thinking," she said. "You have some idea that she's not good enough for you."

"She is now, because I turned into a dumb farmer and that's all I'll ever be any more. But what I should have done when my brother was killed in the war, I should have been smart enough to say I only had the one life to live. I should have stood up to my mother and said I wasn't going to run the farm."

"What could you have done? You were a freshman in college."

"What difference does that make? A man ought to be able to decide for himself. If he doesn't, then he has to blame himself for what comes after. I don't know where I'd be now, but I wouldn't be tied down to the farm, stuck away for the rest of my life, working from morning to night at work I don't like. Raising kids. Talking to myself. I used to hear about China, and I wanted to go there. I wanted to go everywhere, see everything while I was still young, not be like my father and my grandfather, stuck away on this God damn farm. Last summer one day I was so disgusted, I was out in the field getting in the hay, a thunderstorm was coming. I said to myself, what was the use of it all? And I stood there with a pitchfork in my hand and I held it up in the air for the lightning to strike. But it didn't. It hit a tree on my neighbor's farm, but not me. If I took my shotgun and blew my head off, they wouldn't get the insurance. But if I got hit by lightning they would. They'd have been all right, and so would I. Are you ready to face Dr. Jones?"

"I guess so," she said.

"O.K.," he said. He put the car in gear and they moved on. He was a man of about medium height, wearing overalls and faded blue shirt and a straw hat that was frayed at the brim. His face below the forehead and his hands below the wristbone were burned by the sun. A leather thong attached to a button on the bib of his overalls led to the watchpocket, and a blue bandanna handkerchief was tied about his neck. He looked like any ordinary farmer who would be driving a half-ton on a country road, who would come to the assistance of a pretty girl in riding breeches.

We'll Have Fun

IT WAS often said of Tony Costello that there was nothing he did not know about horses. No matter whom he happened to be working for—as coachman, as hostler, as blacksmith—he would stop whatever he was doing and have a look at an ailing horse and give advice to the owner who had brought the horse to Tony. His various employers did not object; they had probably sometime in the past gotten Tony's advice when he was working for someone else, and they would do so again sometime in the future. A year was a long time for Tony to stay at a job; he would quit or he would get the sack, find something else to do, and stay at that job until it was time to move on. He had worked for some employers three or four times. They would rehire him in spite of their experience with his habits, and if they did not happen to have a job open for him, they would at least let him bed down in their haylofts. He did not always ask their permission for this privilege, but since he knew his way around just about every stable in town—private and livery—he never had any trouble finding a place to sleep. He smoked a pipe, but everybody knew he was careful about matches and emptying the pipe and the kerosene heaters that were in most stables. And even when he was not actually in the service of the owner of a stable, he more than earned his sleeping privilege. An owner would go out to the stable in the morning and find that the chores had been done. "Oh, hello, Tony," the owner would say. "Since when have you been back?"

"I come in last night."

"I don't have a job for you," the owner would say.

"That's all right. Just a roof over me head temporarily. You're giving that animal too much oats again. Don't give him no oats at night, I told you."

"Oh, all right. Go in the kitchen and the missus will give you some breakfast. That is, if you want any breakfast. You smell like a saloon."

"Yes, this was a bad one, a real bad one. All I want's a cup of coffee, if that's all right?"

"One of these nights you'll walk in front of a yard engine."

"If I do I hope I'll have the common sense to get out of the way. And if I don't it'll be over pretty quick."

"Uh-huh. Well, do whatever needs to be done and I'll pay you two dollars when I get back this evening."

The owner could be sure that by the end of the day Tony would have done a good cleaning job throughout the stable, and would be waiting in patient agony for the money that would buy the whiskey that cured the rams. "I got the rams so bad I come near taking a swig of the kerosene," he would say. He would take the two dollars and half-walk, half-run to the nearest saloon, but he would be back in time to feed and bed down the owner's horse.

It would take a couple of days for him to get back to good enough shape to go looking for a steady job. If he had the right kind of luck, the best of luck, he would hear about a job as coachman. The work was not hard, and the pay was all his, not to be spent on room and board. The hardest work, though good pay, was in a blacksmith's shop. He was not young any more, and it took longer for his muscles to get reaccustomed to the work. Worst of all, as the newest blacksmith he was always given the job of shoeing mules, which were as treacherous as a rattlesnake and as frightening. He hated to shoe a mule or a Shetland pony. There were two shops in town where a mule could be tied up in the stocks, the apparatus that held the animal so securely that it could not kick; but a newly shod mule, released from the stocks, was likely to go crazy and kill a man. If he was going to die that way, Tony wanted his executioner to be a horse, not a God damn mule. And if he was going to lose a finger or a chunk of his backside, let it be a horse that bit him and not a nasty little bastard ten hands high. Blacksmithing paid the best and was the job he cared the least for, and on his fiftieth birthday Tony renounced it forever. "Not for fifty dollars a week will I take another job in a blacksmith's," he swore.

"You're getting pretty choosy, if you ask me," said his friend Murphy. "Soon there won't be no jobs for you of any kind, shape or form. The ottomobile is putting an end to the horse. Did you ever hear tell of the Squadron A in New York City?"

"For the love of Jesus, did I ever hear tell of it? Is that what you're asking me? Well, if I was in New York City I could lead you to it blindfolded, Ninety-something-or-other and Madison Avenue, it is, on the right-hand side going up. And before I come to this miserable town the man I worked for's son belonged to it. Did I ever hear tell of the Squadron A!"

"All right. What is it now?" said Murphy.

"It's the same as it always was—a massive brick building on the right-hand side—"

"The organ-i-zation, I'm speaking of," said Murphy.

"Well, the last I seen in the papers, yesterday or the day before, this country was ingaged in mortal combat with Kaiser Wilhelm the Second. I therefore hazard the guess that the organ-i-zation is fighting on our side against the man with the withered arm."

"Fighting how?"

"Bravely, I'm sure."

"With what for weapons?"

"For weapons? Well, being a cavalry regiment I hazard the guess that they're equipped with sabre and pistol."

"There, you see? You're not keeping up to date with current happenings. Your Squadron A that you know so much about don't have a horse to their name. They're a machine-gun outfit."

"Well, that of course is a God damn lie, Murphy."

"A lie, is it? Well how much would you care to bet me—in cash?"

"Let me take a look and see how much I have on me?" said Tony. He placed his money on the bar. "Eighteen dollars and ninety-four cents. Is this even money, or do I have to give you odds?"

Murphy placed nineteen dollars on the bar. "Even money'll be good enough for me, bein's it's like taking the money off a blind man."

"And how are we to settle who's right?" said Tony.

"We'll call up the newspaper on the telephone."

"What newspaper? There's no newspaper here open after six P.M."

"We'll call the New York *World*," said Murphy.

"By long distance, you mean? Who's to pay for the call?"

"The winner of the bet," said Murphy.

"The winner of the bet? Oh, all right. I'll be magnanimous. How do you go about it? You can't put that many nickels in the slot."

"We'll go over to the hotel and get the operator at the switchboard, Mary McFadden. She's used to these long-distance calls."

"Will she be on duty at this hour?"

"Are you trying to back out? It's only a little after eight," said Murphy.

"Me back out? I wished I could get the loan of a hundred dollars and I'd show you who's backing out," said Tony.

In silence they marched to the hotel, and explained their purpose to Mary McFadden. Within fifteen minutes they were connected with the office of the *World*, then to the newspaper library. "Good evening, sir," said Murphy. "This is a long-distance call from Gibbsville, Pennsylvania. I wish to request the information as to whether the Squadron A is in the cavalry or a machine-gun organ-i-zation." He repeated the question and waited. "He says to hold the line a minute."

"Costing us a fortune," said Tony.

"Hello? Yes, I'm still here. Yes? Uh-huh. Would you kindly repeat that information?" Murphy quickly handed the receiver to Tony Costello, who listened, nodded, said "Thank you," and hung up.

"How much do we owe you for the call, Mary?" said Murphy.

"Just a minute," said the operator. "That'll be nine dollars and fifty-five cents."

"Jesus," said Tony. "Well, one consolation. It's out of your profit, Murphy."

"But the profit is out of your pocket," said Murphy. "Come on, we'll go back and I'll treat you. Generous in victory, that's me. Like Ulysses S. Grant. He give all them Confederates their horses back, did you ever know that, Costello?"

"I did not, and what's more I don't believe it."

"Well, maybe you'd care to bet on that, too? Not this evening, however, bein's you're out of cash. But now will you believe that the ottomobile is putting an end to the horse?"

"Where does the ottomobile come into it? The machine gun is no ottomobile."

"No, and I didn't say it was, but if they have no use for the cavalry in a war, they'll soon have no use for them anywhere."

"If you weren't such a pinch of snuff I'd give you a puck in the mouth. But don't try my patience too far, Mr. Murphy. I'll take just so much of your impudence and no more. With me one hand tied behind me I could put you in hospital."

"You're kind of a hard loser, Tony. You oughtn't to be that way. There's more ottomobiles in town now than horses. The fire companies are all motorizing. The breweries. And the rich, you don't see them buying a new pair of cobs no more. It's the Pierce-Arrow now. Flannagan the undertaker is getting rid of his blacks, he told me so himself. Ordered a Cunningham 8."

"We'll see where Flannagan and his Cunningham 8 ends up next winter, the first time he has to bring a dead one down from the top of Fairview Street. Or go up it, for that matter. There's hills in this town no Cunningham 8 will negotiate, but Flannagan's team of blacks never had the least trouble. Flannagan'll be out of business the first winter, and it'll serve him right."

"And here I thought he was a friend of yours. Many's the time you used his stable for a boudoir, not to mention the funerals you drove for him. Two or three dollars for a half a day's work."

"There never was no friendship between him and I. You never saw me stand up to a bar and have a drink with him. You never saw me set foot inside his house, nor even his kitchen for a cup of coffee. The rare occasions that I slept in his barn, he was never the loser, let me tell you. Those blacks that he's getting rid of, I mind the time I saved the off one's life from the colic. Too tight-fisted to send for Doc McNary, the vet, and he'd have lost the animal for sure if I wasn't there. Do you know what he give me for saving the horse? Guess what he give me."

"Search me," said Murphy.

"A pair of gloves. A pair of gauntlets so old that the lining was all wore away. Supposed to be fleece-lined, but the fleece was long since gone. 'Here, you take these, Tony,' said Mr. Generous Flannagan. I wanted to say 'Take them and do what with them?' But I was so dead tired from being up all night with the black, all I wanted to do was go up in his hayloft and lie down exhausted. Which I did for a couple of hours, and when I come down again there was the black, standing on his four feet and give me a whinny. A horse don't have much brains, but they could teach Flannagan gratitude."

After the war the abandonment of horses became so general that even Tony Costello was compelled to give in to it. The small merchants of the town, who had kept a single horse and delivery wagon (and a carriage for Sunday), were won over to Ford and Dodge trucks. The three-horse hitches of the breweries disappeared and in their place were big Macks and Garfords. The fire companies bought American LaFrances and Whites. The physicians bought Franklins and Fords, Buicks and Dodges. (The Franklin was air-cooled; the Buick was supposed to be a great hill-climber.) And private citizens who had never felt they could afford a horse and buggy, now went into debt to purchase flivvers. Of the three leading harness shops in the town, two became luggage shops and one went out of business entirely. Only two of the seven blacksmith shops remained. Gone were the Fleischmann's Yeast and Grand Union Tea Company wagons, the sorrels and greys of the big express companies. The smooth-surface paving caused a high mortality rate among horses, who slipped and broke legs and had to be shot and carried away to the fertilizer plant. The horse was retained only by the rich and the poor; saddle horses for the rich, and swaybacked old nags for the junk men and fruit peddlers. For Tony Costello it was not so easy as it once had been to find a place to sleep. The last livery stable closed in 1922, was converted into a public garage, and neither the rats nor Tony Costello had a home to go to, he said. "No decent, self-respecting rat will live in a garridge," he said. "It's an inhuman smell, them gazzoline fumes. And the rats don't have any more to eat there than I do meself."

The odd jobs that he lived on made no demands on his skill with horses, but all his life he had known how to take proper care of the varnish and the brightwork of a Brewster brougham, the leather and the bits and buckles of all kinds of tack. He therefore made himself useful at washing cars and polishing shoes. Nobody wanted to give him a steady job, but it was more sensible to pay Tony a few dollars than to waste a good mechanic on a car wash. He had a flexible arrangement with the cooks at two Greek restaurants who, on their own and without consulting the owners, would give him a meal in exchange for his washing dishes. "There ain't a man in the town has hands any cleaner than mine. Me hands are in soapy water morning, noon, and night," he said.

"It's too bad the rest of you don't get in with your hands," said Murphy. "How long since you had a real bath, Tony?"

"Oh, I don't know."

"As the fellow says, you take a bath once a year whether you need it or not," said Murphy. "And yet I never seen you need a shave, barring the times you were on a three-day toot."

"Even then I don't often let her grow more'n a couple days. As long as I can hold me hand steady enough so's I don't cut me throat. That's a temptation, too, I'll tell you. There's days I just as soon take the razor in me hand and let nature take its course."

"What stops you?" said Murphy.

"That I wonder. Mind you, I don't wonder too much or the logical conclusion would be you-know-what. My mother wasn't sure who my father was. She didn't keep count. She put me out on the streets when I was eight or nine years of age. 'You can read and write,' she said, which was more than she could do. With my fine education I was able to tell one paper from another, so I sold them."

"You mean she put you out with no place to sleep?"

"Oh, no. She let me sleep there, providing she didn't have a customer. If I come home and she had a customer I had to wait outside."

"I remember you telling me one time your father worked for a man that had a son belonged to the Squadron A. That time we had the bet."

"That was a prevarication. A harmless prevarication that I thought up on the spur of the moment. I ought to know better by this time. Every time I prevaricate I get punished for it. That time I lost the bet. I should have said I knew about the Squadron A and let it go at that, but I had to embellish it. I always knew about the Squadron A. From selling newspapers in the Tenderloin I got a job walking hots at the race track, and I was a jock till I got too big. I couldn't make the weight any more, my bones were too heavy regardless of how much I starved myself and dried out. That done something to me, those times I tried to make a hundred and fifteen pounds and my bones weighed more than that. As soon as I quit trying to be a jock my weight jumped up to a hundred and fifty, and that's about what I am now."

"What do you mean it done something to you?" said Murphy.

"Be hard for you to understand, Murphy. It's a medical fact."

"Oh, go ahead, Doctor Costello."

"Well, if you don't get enough to eat, the blood thins out and the brain don't get fed properly. That changes your whole outlook on life, and if the brain goes too long without nourishment, you get so's you don't care any more."

"Where did you get that piece of information?"

"I trained for a doctor that owned a couple trotters over near Lancaster. Him and I had many's the conversation on the subject."

"I never know whether to believe you or call you a liar. Did you get so's you didn't care any more?"

"That's what I'm trying to get through your thick skull, Murphy. That's why I never amounted to anything. That's why poor people stay poor. The brain don't get enough nourishment from the blood. Fortunately I know that, you see. I don't waste my strength trying to be something I ain't."

"Do you know what I think, Tony? I think you were just looking for an excuse to be a bum."

"Naturally! I wasn't looking for an excuse, but I was looking for some reason why a fellow as smart as I am never amounted to anything. If I cared more what happened to me, I'd have cut my throat years ago. Jesus! The most I ever had in my life was eight hundred dollars one time a long shot came in, but I don't care. You know, I'm fifty-five or -six years of age, one or the other. I had my first woman when I was fifteen, and I guess a couple hundred since then. But I never saw one yet that I'd lose any sleep over. Not a single one, out of maybe a couple hundred. One is just like the other, to me. Get what you want out of them, and so long. So long till you want another. And I used to be a pretty handsome fellow when I was young. Not all whores, either. Once when I was wintering down in

Latonia—well, what the hell. It don't bother me as much as it used to do. I couldn't go a week without it, but these days I just as soon spend the money on the grog. I'll be just as content when I can do without them altogether."

. . . One day Tony was washing a brand-new Chrysler, which was itself a recent make of car. He was standing off, hose in hand, contemplating the design and colors of the car, when a young woman got out of a plain black Ford coupe. She was wearing black and white saddle shoes, bruised and spotted, and not liable to be seriously damaged by the puddles of dirty water on the garage floor, but Tony cautioned her. "Mind where you're walking, young lady," he said.

"Oh, it won't hurt these shoes," she said. "I'm looking for Tony Costello. I was told he worked here."

"Feast your eyes, Miss. You're looking right at him," he said.

"You're Tony Costello? I somehow pictured an older man," she said.

"Well, maybe I'm older than I look. What is there I can do for you?"

She was a sturdily built young woman, past the middle twenties, handsome if she had been a man, but it was no man inside the grey pullover. "I was told that you were the best man in town to take care of a sick horse," she said.

"You were told right," said Tony Costello. "And I take it you have a sick horse? What's the matter with him, if it's a him, or her if it's a her?"

"It's a mare named Daisy. By the way, my name is Esther Wayman."

"Wayman? You're new here in town," said Tony.

"Just this year. My father is the manager of the bus company."

"I see. And your mare Daisy, how old?"

"Five, I think, or maybe six," said Esther Wayman.

"And sick in what way? What are the symptoms?"

"She's all swollen up around the mouth. I thought I had the curb chain on too tight, but that wasn't it. I kept her in the stable for several days, with a halter on, and instead of going away the swelling got worse."

"Mm. The swelling, is it accompanied by, uh, a great deal of saliva?"

"Yes, it is."

"You say the animal is six years old. How long did you own her, Miss Wayman?"

"Only about a month. I bought her from a place in Philadelphia."

"Mm-hmm. Out Market Street, one of them horse bazaars?"

"Yes."

"Is this your first horse? In other words, you're not familiar with horses?"

"No, we've always lived in the city—Philadelphia, Cleveland Ohio, Denver Colorado. I learned to ride in college, but I never owned a horse before we came here."

"You wouldn't know a case of glanders if you saw it, would you?"

"No. Is that a disease?" she said.

"Unless I'm very much mistaken, it's the disease that ails your mare Daisy. I'll be done washing this car in two shakes, and then you can take me out to see your mare. Where do you stable her?"

"We have our own stable. My father bought the Henderson house."

"Oh, to be sure, and I know it well. Slept in that stable many's the night."

"I don't want to take you away from your work," she said.

"Young woman, you're taking me *to* work. You're not taking me away from anything."

He finished with the Chrysler, got out of his gum boots, and put on his shoes. He called to the garage foreman, "Back sometime in the morning," and did not wait for an answer. None came.

On the way out to the Wayman-Henderson house he let the young woman do all the talking. She had the flat accent of the Middle West and she spoke from deep inside her mouth. She told him how she had got interested in riding at cawlidge, and was so pleased to find that the house her father bought included a garage that was not really a garage but a real stable. Her father permitted her to have a horse on condition that she took complete care of it herself. She had seen the ad in a Philadelphia paper, gone to one of the weekly sales, and paid $300 for Daisy. She had not even looked at any other horse. The bidding for Daisy had started at $100; Esther raised it to

$150; someone else went to $200; Esther jumped it to $300 and the mare was hers.

"Uh-huh," said Tony. "Well, maybe you got a bargain, and maybe not."

"You seem doubtful," she said.

"We learn by experience, and you got the animal you wanted. You'll be buying other horses as you get older. This is only your first one."

They left the car at the stable door. "I guess she's lying down," said Esther.

Tony opened the door of the box stall. "She is that, and I'm sorry to tell you, she's never getting up."

"She's dead? How could she be? I only saw her a few hours ago."

"Let me go in and have a look at her. You stay where you are," he said. He had taken command and she obeyed him. In a few minutes, three or four, he came out of the stall and closed the door behind him.

"Glanders, it was. Glanders and old age. Daisy was more like eleven than five or six."

"But how could it happen so quickly?"

"It didn't, exactly. I'm not saying the animal had glanders when you bought her. I do say they falsified her age, which they all do. Maybe they'll give you your money back, maybe they won't. In any case, Miss Wayman, you're not to go in there. Glanders is contagious to man and animal. If you want me to, I'll see to the removal of the animal. A telephone call to the fertilizer plant, and they know me there. Then I'll burn the bedding for you and fumigate the stable. You might as well leave the halter on. It wouldn't be fair to put it on a well horse."

The young woman took out a pack of cigarettes and offered him one. He took it, lit hers and his. "I'm glad to see you take it so calmly. I seen women go into hysterics under these circumstances," he said.

"I don't get hysterics," she said. "But that's not to say I'm not in a turmoil. If I'd had her a little while longer I *might* have gotten hysterical."

"Then be thankful that you didn't have her that much longer. To tell you the truth, you didn't get a bargain. There was other things wrong with her that we needn't go into. I wouldn't be surprised if she was blind, but that's not what I was thinking of. No, you didn't get a bargain this time, but keep trying. Only, next time take somebody with you that had some experience with horses and horse-dealers."

"I'll take you, if you'll come," she said. "Meanwhile, will you do those other things you said you would?"

"I will indeed."

"And how much do I owe you?" she said.

He smiled. "I don't have a regular fee for telling people that a dead horse is dead," he said. "A couple dollars for my time."

"How about ten dollars?"

"Whatever you feel is right, I'll take," he said. "The state of my finances is on the wrong side of affluence."

"Is the garage where I can always reach you?" she said.

"I don't work there steady."

"At home, then? Can you give me your telephone number?" she said.

"I move around from place to place."

"Oh. Well, would you like to have a steady job? I could introduce you to my father."

"I couldn't drive a bus, if that's what you had in mind. I don't have a license, for one thing, and even if I did they have to maintain a schedule. That I've never done, not that strict kind of a schedule. But thanks for the offer."

"He might have a job for you washing buses. I don't know how well it would pay, but I think they wash and clean those buses every night, so it would be steady work. Unless you're not interested in steady work. Is that it?"

"Steady pay without the steady work, that's about the size of it," he said.

She shook her head. "Then I don't think you and my father would get along. He lives by the clock."

"Well, I guess he'd have to, running a bus line," said Tony. He looked about him. "The Hendersons used to hang their cutters up there. They had two cutters and a bob. They were great ones for sleighing parties. Two-three times a winter they'd load up the bob and the two cutters and take their friends down to their farm for a chicken-and-waffle supper. They had four horses then. A pair of sorrels, Prince and Duke. Trixie, a bay mare, broke to saddle. And a black gelding named Satan, Mr. Henderson drove himself to work in. They were pretty near the last to give up horses, Mr. and Mrs. Henderson."

"Did you work for them?"

"Twice I worked for them. Sacked both times. But he knew I used to come here and sleep. They had four big buffalo robes, two for the bob and one each for the cutters. That was the lap of luxury for me. Sleep on two and cover up with one. Then he died and she moved away, and the son Jasper only had cars. There wasn't a horse stabled in here since Mrs. moved away, and Jasper wouldn't let me sleep here. He put in that gazzoline pump and he said it wasn't safe to let me stop here for the night. It wasn't me he was worried about. It was them ottomobiles. Well, this isn't getting to the telephone."

During the night he fumigated the stable. The truck from the fertilizer plant arrived at nine o'clock and he helped the two men load the dead mare, after which he lit the fumigating tablets in the stalls and closed the doors and windows. Esther Wayman came up from the house at ten o'clock or so, just as he was closing the doors of the carriage house. "They took her away?" she said.

"About an hour ago. Then I lit candles for her," he said.

"You what?"

"That's my little joke, not in the best of taste perhaps. I don't know that this fumigating does any good, but on the other hand it can't do much harm. It's a precaution you take, glanders being contagious and all that. You have to think of the next animal that'll be occupying that stall, so you take every precaution—as much for your own peace of mind as anything else, I guess."

"Where did you get the fumigating stuff?"

"I went down to the drug store, Schlicter's Pharmacy, Sixteenth and Market. I told them to charge it to your father. They know me there."

"They know you everywhere in this town, don't they?"

"Yes, I guess they do, now that I stop to think of it."

"Can I take you home in my car?"

"Oh, I guess I can walk it."

"Why should you when I have my car? Where do you live?"

"I got a room on Canal Street. That's not much of a neighborhood for you to be driving around in after dark."

"I'm sure I've been in worse, or just as bad," she said.

"That would surprise me," he said.

"I'm not a sheltered hothouse plant," she said. "I can take care of myself. Let's go. I'd like to see that part of town."

When they got to Canal Street she said, "It isn't eleven o'clock yet. Is there a place where we can go for a drink?"

"Oh, there's places aplenty. But I doubt if your Dad would approve of them for you."

"Nobody will know me," she said. "I hardly know anybody in this town. I don't get to know people very easily. Where shall we go?"

"Well, there's a pretty decent place that goes by the name of the Bucket of Blood. Don't let the name frighten you. It's just a common ordinary saloon. I'm not saying you'll encounter the Ladies' Aid Society there, but if it didn't have that name attached to it—well, you'll see the kind of place it is."

It was a quiet night in the saloon. They sat at a table in the back room. A man and woman were at another table, drinking whiskey by the shot and washing it down with beer chasers. They were a solemn couple, both about fifty, with no need to converse and seemingly no concern beyond the immediate appreciation of the alcohol. Presently the man stood up and headed for the street door, followed by the woman. As she went out she slapped Tony Costello lightly on the shoulder. "Goodnight, Tony," she said.

"Goodnight, Marie," said Tony Costello.

When they were gone Esther Wayman said, "She knew you, but all she said was goodnight. She never said hello."

"Him and I don't speak to one another," said Tony. "We had some kind of a dispute there a long while back."

"Are they husband and wife?"

"No, but they been going together ever since I can remember."

"She's a prostitute, isn't she?"

"That's correct," said Tony.

"And what does he do? Live off her?"

"Oh, no. No, he's a trackwalker for the Pennsy. One of the few around that ain't an I-talian. But she's an I-talian."

"Are you an Italian? You're not, are you?"

"Good Lord, no. I'm as Irish as they come."

"You have an Italian name, though."

"It may sound I-talian to you, but my mother was straight from County Cork. My father could be anybody, but most likely he was an Irishman, the neighborhood I come from. I'm pretty certain he wasn't John Jacob Astor or J. Pierpont Morgan. My old lady was engaged in the same occupation as Marie that just went out."

"Doesn't your church—I mean, in France and Italy I suppose the prostitutes must be Catholic, but I never thought of Irish prostitutes."

"There's prostitutes wherever a woman needs a dollar and doesn't have to care too much how she gets it. It don't even have to be a dollar. If they're young enough they'll do it for a stick of candy, and the dollar comes later. This is an elevating conversation for a young woman like yourself."

"You don't know anything about myself, Mr. Costello," she said.

"I do, and I don't," he said. "But what I don't know I'm learning. I'll make a guess that you were disappointed in love."

She laughed. "Very."

"What happened? The young man give you the go-by?"

"There was no young man," she said. "I have never been interested in young men or they in me."

"I see," he said.

"Do you?"

"Well, to be honest with you, no. I don't. I'd of thought you'd have yourself a husband by this time. You're not at all bad-looking, you know, and you always knew where your next meal was coming from."

"This conversation *is* beginning to embarrass me a little," she said. "Sometime I may tell you all about myself. In fact, I have a feeling I will. But not now, not tonight."

"Anytime you say," said Tony. "And one of these days we'll go looking for a horse for you."

"We'll have fun," she said.

The Sun Room

THE BUTLER who came to the door was English and correct, down to the black four-in-hand tie and gold watch-chain. "Good afternoon, sir," he said. "Mr. and Mrs. Barlow?"

"Yes, we're expected," said Henry Barlow.

"Yes, if you'll just follow me, please," said the butler.

"We're a little early," said Barlow. "We thought we'd have more trouble finding it."

"Very good, sir. If you'll just have a seat in here," said the butler, and bowed in the direction of a small room. Henry and Wilma Barlow sat down and the butler disappeared.

"A butler, yet," said Wilma Barlow.

"Yes," said her husband. "His name is Kenneth Kingsley. Didn't you recognize him?"

"Why should I?" said Wilma Barlow.

"Well, maybe you shouldn't. He's been in seventy-five thousand pictures."

"You know him?" said Wilma.

"No, but I recognized him," said Henry. "He never got to be a Leo G. Carroll or Arthur Treacher, but he worked."

"I guess I didn't notice butlers," said Wilma.

"That's why he worked. He wasn't supposed to be noticed. But he probably went right on year after year, making his fifteen or twenty thousand—and saving it. He probably owns some nice real estate."

"Then why would he be doing this?" said Wilma.

"Because Eileen asked him to, and because he couldn't say no to the money she offered him. How the hell should I know?"

"Funny he didn't recognize you," said Wilma.

"Why should he? He probably never saw me before, and believe me, movie butlers were never impressed by movie writers. I just happen to have an extraordinarily good memory for bit players and dress extras. I should have had a job at Central Casting."

"It worked out better this way," said Wilma.

"The pay was better this way," said Henry.

The butler returned. "Miss Elliott will see you in the sun room," he said. "This way, please." He now led the Barlows through corridors on varying levels and finally to a large, glass-inclosed porch. "Mr. and Mrs. Barlow," he announced.

"Of course, Henry and Wilma, you're so prompt," said Eileen Elliott. She gave them both hands and presented her cheek to be kissed. "What delicious intoxicant can I offer you?"

"A very light Scotch and water for me," said Henry Barlow.

"Oh—a vodka and tonic, if I may," said his wife.

"You may anything," said Eileen. "Let me bartend, I *want* to." She thus dismissed the butler, who bowed and vanished.

"Didn't he used to work for someone else?" said Henry.

"Some very old families named Fox and Goldwyn and Warner. Also the Paramounts and the Metros, and no doubt the Republics. His name is Kenneth Kingsley, and he's an old dear. I've been in any number of pictures with him. He won't come if I'm having a director friend or one of the old-time stars. It would embarrass him and embarrass them. But a writer is different. Didn't you recognize him, Henry?"

"Well, as a matter of fact, I did," said Henry.

"It was nice of you not to let on. He comes because he adores me. He doesn't need the money, the old fox. He owns a motel out in the Valley. He's as queer as a jaybird, but there was always a certain type of pansy that watched every single penny. If you were nice to them, you could always go to them for money, if they had any reason to think you'd pay them back. Kenneth lent me the money for my first abortion, that's how long I've known him. I couldn't go to the father, because he was a star and I was very much on the make for him, and he'd have dropped me like the proverbial hotcake. He did anyway, the stupid bastard. Why stupid? Because I kept him out of a picture when *I* became a star. And there you have the story of my first three years in Hollywood. I'm dying to know why you wanted to come to see me."

"I said in my note, I wanted Wilma to meet some of the real people," said Henry.

"That's subject to several interpretations," said Eileen. "I'm sure you know, Mrs. Barlow, that your husband and I had a torrid romance lasting two months."

"Three," said Henry.

"Was it three?" said Eileen.

"Yes, I knew," said Wilma.

"We were both very young, of course," said Eileen. "I was practically a virgin, having had only one abortion. And Henry was an innocent young writer who tried to lay every girl in Hollywood, and very nearly succeeded."

"I missed out on a few," said Henry.

"But we always stayed friends," said Eileen. "You could, you know. More than once, as I've gotten older, I've found myself admiring some middle-aged man and had to remind myself that there was a *time*, there was a *time*. We were so full of sex, and so active, that it left no impression whatever. Anyway, you'd go out of your mind re-living all your old romances. If a man wasn't an out-and-out fairy, and you weren't too tired, you'd say, 'All right, come on over,' and who cared whether you went to bed with him or didn't? If you didn't, he was almost sure to say you did. And if he was a big enough star, *you'd* say you did. I was married four times. I had a son by my first marriage, and he's over forty. He and his father live in my home town back in Ohio. Both married, have families of their own, and the only time I ever hear from them is when some friends of theirs want to visit a studio. My son was brought up by his stepmother, and she and his father have managed to convince him that I abandoned him for a career in pictures. The fact is that my first husband used to beat hell out of me whenever he got tight, and I did run off to Detroit with a band leader. My husband kidnaped my son and left me with the band leader, and I came to Hollywood with him. I could sing a little, but what made the difference was that I had a shape. A lot of girls had shapes, but that was during the flat-chested look, the tight bras. Not for me. I had them, and I showed them, and boy did the women hate me! But not the younger ones, and they were the ones that were going to the movies. In droves. The men liked me, and the young girls liked me, and I got paid ten thousand dollars a week. Five for the right one, and five for the left one."

"Oh, the face helped a little," said Henry.

"Thank you, dear," said Eileen. "You see why we had our mad romance, lasting three months? He remembered that I had a face too."

"It was a nice face. It had real sweetness," said Wilma.

"You must have been one of the younger ones," said Eileen.

"Well, not much younger."

"Did you belong to one of my fan clubs?"

"No. But I was a fan," said Wilma.

"You never wrote me for a picture, enclosing twenty-five cents to cover cost of mailing?"

"No, I didn't."

"The odd thing was that girls used to send me pictures of themselves, to prove that their bust development was as good as mine. Needless to say, I never rushed into a producer's office with one of those pictures. Right into the wastebasket they went. And the better the bosom the quicker the wastebasket. What kind of a damn fool did they think I was? Ten thousand a week. I wonder what ever happened to it—as if I didn't know."

"Are you broke, Eileen?"

"Make me an offer. No, I'm not broke. I have a nice income. It's no ten thousand a week, and it isn't as much as they pay the President of the United States. But Honest Andy Anderson— do you remember Honest Andy?"

"Sure. The agent," said Henry Barlow.

"Honest Andy made me go into the studio retirement plan, and it's paying off now. Also, I go back every summer and do the straw hat circuit for ten weeks, and that pays very well. And once a year I go to Vegas for two or three weeks. I'm not filthy rich any more, but I live nicely and I pay the taxes on this house. One of these days this house is going to make a lot of money for Eileen."

"It's beautiful, isn't it?" said Wilma.

"And I'd sell it at the drop of a hat, but I have to get my price. Would you like to buy it?"

"No, we're settled in Vermont," said Henry Barlow. "Wilma writes, too."

"Not really. I'm a teacher," said Wilma.

"She teaches creative writing, and so do I."

"And your books make money, don't they?"

"They do pretty well. We don't need much," said Henry. "I never got up to ten thousand a week."

"But you got two," said Eileen.

"No, fifteen hundred was my top. But I used to get as much

as twenty-five for an original, and a six-weeks' guarantee for working on the screen play. For a man of limited talent I did all right."

"Are you and Wilma going to write about me?"

"I hadn't thought of it," said Henry.

"Oh, what a liar," said Eileen. "Every writer that comes here goes away and writes something."

"Some of them have, there's no doubt about that," said Henry. "That's why I wanted Wilma to see for herself. But we're not going to write about you, so relax."

"Well, why *don't* you write about me? What you don't know, I'd be willing to tell you. And I wouldn't sue."

"I don't think people care that much any more," said Henry.

"Maybe you're right. There's practically nothing left to the imagination on the screen, so why should they want to read about it? Do you remember when we used to look at dirty movies at parties?"

"Yes," said Henry.

"I used to love them, frankly. But I saw a feature picture a week ago, two big present-day stars that got a half a million apiece for this picture. In our day they'd have got fifty dollars for just about the same thing. I mean, what they left out of this picture the other night I'm sure is on film. Because what they started, they had to finish, you know? We did one on 16-millimetre at Malibu. The works. It was practically suicidal to let that get around. The studio sent for me and I went to J.B.'s office and of course denied everything. The only trouble was, he had a print right there, and it was a dirty movie all right. So I broke down and admitted it, and waited for the ax to fall. The morals clause. Well, it was the morals clause that saved us. How the hell were they going to tell the American public that they were firing four of their biggest stars for being in a dirty movie?"

"What finally happened?" said Wilma.

"They got rid of one girl that they were going to get rid of anyway. They simply didn't renew her option. The rest of us got away with it, although it cost the studio a fortune to buy up the prints and the negative. I understand they're planning a remake of the picture."

"Oh, come on," said Henry.

"Oh, not with the original cast," said Eileen. "Actually, when I was in England shortly after the war I met a duke, who told me he had seen me in a film that not many people had seen. It was the dirty movie we made in Malibu, and the studio had shown it to a select few V.I.P.'s in New York. 'How was my makeup?' I said. I wasn't going to take any crap from him, duke or no duke."

"How *was* your makeup?" said Henry.

"'Outdoor Number 7,' I think I used," said Eileen. "Not taking any crap from you either, Henry."

"I'd forgotten Outdoor Number 7," said Henry. "There's so much I don't remember about picture business. But I did remember Kenneth Kingsley. Why did you have him here today? Not to impress us."

"Not exactly impress you, but yes, to impress you if you were going to be condescending."

"We're not in the least condescending, and anyway, how could we be? You're still Eileen Elliott."

"You can bet your sweet ass I am. Anybody that thinks they can tear that up and thereby make me into nobody—they soon find out. They can laugh at the scrapbooks and the souvenirs, but I have them. Some little jerk pretends to pity me, with my memories and my mementoes, but I can always say, 'And how many kings did you know, mister? How many presidents did *you* have *your* picture taken with?' And I'm not talking about college presidents. I'm talking about presidents of the United States. Coolidge, Hoover, F.D.R., Truman. Eisenhower, when he was a general but not when he was President. By that time I wasn't getting top billing, a hundred percent of the main title. I had some pushy little woman come and ask me to donate some money to some charity she was heading up out here. She said Mr. Eisenhower was honorary chairman and gave a strong hint that the major contributors would get an autographed picture. 'You mean *this* Eisenhower?' I said, and showed her a picture of Eisenhower and me during the war. Any autograph I don't have, I don't want. How many Lyndon B. Johnsons will you trade me for my Wallace Reid?"

"Wasn't he a little before your time?" said Henry.

"In his heyday, he was, but the poor junkie, I asked him for one anyway," said Eileen. "Tell me about your job, teaching at the University of Vermont."

"Anticlimax department," said Henry. "Well, it isn't the University of Vermont. It's a smaller college called Whitefield, privately endowed."

"That sounds rich," said Eileen. "Or are you here to put the bite on me?"

"We didn't have that in mind, but I'm sure a large donation would be gratefully accepted," said Henry. "No, it was started a few years ago by the Whitefield Foundation, mostly the heirs of the late Benjamin Whitefield and his brothers. They were in the textile business, and the Foundation started with twenty million but became worth a lot more. We have about five hundred and fifty students. Small, by present-day standards, but our entrance requirements are fairly high."

"You mean they don't let in any Jews, Henry?"

"I wouldn't say that. No restrictions based on race, creed, color, or national origin. Only on the individual's potential."

"I was wondering," said Eileen. "And Wilma teaches creative writing there?"

"I give a course in creative writing," said Wilma. "I don't like to say I *teach* creative writing."

"I guess if it's creative, it can't be taught. Is that what you mean?" said Eileen.

"Exactly," said Wilma.

"They wanted me to give a course in acting at one of the local universities. I thought about it. One week I'd lecture on bust development, which was such a great help in my career. The next week I'd demonstrate the technique of the casting couch, which was also a great help in my career. I could spend several weeks on that. Then of course the art of reading contracts. The man that came to see me about it was inclined to think I wasn't taking the thing seriously enough, but I assured him that I was. If he was talking about acting for the movies, it was a damned sight more important to know how to handle producers than it was to give out with the pear-shaped tones. But he wasn't talking about movies. He was talking about *films*. He called them films, and I called them movies. I never learned to call them anything else, try as I might. Always movies. Never films.

And never, never cinema. Those people that call them films, and cinema, they're the kind of people that talk about the art of some little broad that makes a sexy mouth and every man, woman and child in the world gets the message. That's art? Who's kidding who? The poor little broad begins to believe it, and the next thing you know she's late on the set, and fighting with the director, and coming out against poverty. She ought to be in favor of poverty. If it wasn't for poverty, who'd want to go to the movies? They used to say it was Mr. DeMille that popularized the bathtub. Nuts. It was the ordinary set dressers with ordinary tubs, not Mr. DeMille and a pool full of slaves. You might as well say Mr. DeMille popularized slavery. People who worked for him wouldn't give you an argument there. But I don't know that that was more true of Mr. DeMille than a lot of other directors. Give anybody too much authority and you have a slave-driver. I'll bet you can be a son of a bitch with your pupils, Henry."

"Students. I don't call them pupils," said Henry.

"*I* don't call them *students*," said Wilma.

"Well, you have to have some name for them," said Henry.

"Enrollees," said Wilma. "Time-passers. Excuse-makers."

"You gather she hates her work," said Henry.

"I really do," said Wilma. "But I'd never say so in Vermont."

"All work is disgusting," said Eileen. "Ten thousand dollars a week doesn't make it any the less so. But it's nicer to be paid ten thousand a week for doing something you don't like than fifty dollars a week for something you don't like. My idea of heaven was getting full salary for doing nothing. The home office used to call from New York and raise hell. 'When is that Eileen Elliott picture starting shooting?' And the supervisor, as we used to call them then, would say we were having script trouble. It almost never occurred to them to have the script ready ahead of time. And as far as I was concerned, it didn't make any difference. I was getting paid anyway. *Then*. When I began to slip a little and wasn't getting ten thousand fifty-two weeks a year, I began to feel the pinch. Only the pinch didn't come from the big producers. The pinch, or the feel, came from elderly English actors. I could always tell when I was beginning to slip. That was when the English actors began to make up for lost time. They wanted to be able to put it in their memoirs that they had put it in me. And I may say that one or two of them did. They weren't much different from the cloak-and-suiters, but they could make adultery seem high class. Adultery! What a word! What a fancy word! I don't think I ever stopped to think that I was committing adultery. The only time I was conscious of committing adultery was when I ran away with the band leader, and I wouldn't have thought of it then if my husband's lawyer hadn't reminded me. Legal language can take the fun out of anything. I'm still not sure what sodomy is. Is that when—well, never mind. I'd rather not know."

"Oh, you know, Eileen," said Henry.

"As a matter of fact I do," said Eileen. "But I have to stop and think. When I was a girl back in Ohio I thought it was one thing, and then I found out it was something else. Sodom and gonorrhea was the way I associated them. Does this remind you two of your conversations back on the old campus?"

"You should hear the conversations back at the old campus," said Wilma. "Those kids all know what sodomy is."

"Well, I should hope so," said Eileen. "They're supposed to be educated, aren't they? My son is a college graduate, and if he doesn't know what sodomy is, I wasted a lot of money. Oh, yes, I was allowed to pay for his education. His stepmother and his father didn't want me to abandon him *that* much. They thought it would embarrass me to come to his graduation, but I wouldn't have been a bit embarrassed. I could have brought the bills along to show I had a right to be there. Do I sound bitter? I don't mean to. If you want to know the truth, I'm confused. I haven't been able to figure out why you came to see me. Why did you?"

"No angle, no hidden motive," said Henry. "As I said before, I wanted Wilma to meet one of the real ones."

"The real what, Henry?" said Eileen. "The old-time movie star, waiting for the phone to ring? The broken-down glamor girl with a pansy actor for a butler? You have plenty of curiosity, or you wouldn't be here. So I'm entitled to some curiosity of my own. You say no angle, no hidden motive, but that's only what you *say*. Wilma, did you think it would be sort of fun to make love to me, or me to make love to you? That would be a good one to tell back in Vermont."

"I never thought of it," said Wilma. "Why did you?"

"Why did I? Because I always think that women that dress like you, those black blouses and tan cotton skirts, and those ballet slippers—they all look as if they spent a lot of time with the head-shrinker."

"I was in analysis," said Wilma.

"I was sure of it," said Eileen.

"Weren't you ever?"

"Of course I was, when it was the thing to do," said Eileen. "You either bought a Picasso, or you were psychoanalyzed. Sometimes both, but if you were making two thousand a week you did at least one. You *had* to. You were nothing if you didn't. I didn't know anything about art, so I settled for the couch. Well, now, I want to tell you, I went to that guy for two months, and what I didn't know about him at the end of two months simply wasn't worth knowing. But then we all got interested in the Hollywood Canteen, war work. Have your picture taken washing dishes and doing the Lambeth Walk with the service men. Loddy da-da loddy da, loddy da-da loddy da. I was just getting around to the interesting part, how I fell in love with the iceman's horse when I was ten years old, and I had to tell the head-shrinker that they wanted me in the war effort. So he slapped me with a nice fat bill for professional services and I guess no one will ever know about me and the iceman's horse. I go back to the day when there *were* icemen and they had *horses*. I cover a lot of American history. My father-in-law had a Haynes. Do you know what a Haynes is? Or was? It was a big car that people bought in Ohio. My father-in-law had one that he drove us to church in on Sunday. My husband washed it every Saturday so it'd be nice and shiny on Sunday, for church, and it was just about the only God damn time we ever got a ride in the God damn thing. My father-in-law was the meanest old bastard in the State of Ohio, and the only thing he ever loved was that Haynes car. He'd sit there on the side porch and watch my husband washing it. 'Don't get any water on the upholstery. It's bad for the leather,' he used to say. He was Presbyterian and I was brought up Lutheran, on top of which my father worked with his hands, and wore overalls. No trade, no steady job. Anything he could get. He played the cornet in the town band, and that was his way of getting free beer. Hard liquor he liked better, but beer was free for the men in the band. You see I had a musical background, what with my father and the man I ran away with. He also preferred hard liquor. In fact I never saw him take a glass of beer, not even to be sociable. But he was sweet. He really was. When he got tired of me and wanted to get rid of me for good and all, he did his best to pass me on to his tenor sax player, the highest paid man in the band. That's what I call sweet, don't you? If you don't, you don't know musicians."

"You were never much of a drinker, were you?" said Henry.

"Not then, and not now," said Eileen. "You'll see me put away a few scoops of vodka, or gin, or tequila as the day wears on. But it has very little effect on me except it makes me drunk. No, I wouldn't call myself a drinker. What the hell do you mean, I was never much of a drinker? I started hitting it when I was in my early twenties, and the only reason I'm alive now is because I never stopped. Some women, most women put on weight when they drink. It just so happens that I don't. We all have a different chemistry, and I don't put on weight. I may get disagreeable, or I may wake up and wonder who that is I'm in bed with, but I don't get fat. I weigh now just about what I weighed when they were paying me ten thousand a week, a hundred and twenty-eight pounds. I never diet, I never go on the wagon, I've never given up smoking, I don't take any exercise. They ask me what the secret is, and I tell them. Do what you please, and keep out of jail. I said that in an interview once and the studio had a hemorrhage. I was denounced from every pulpit, a man made a speech in Congress, and the women's clubs threatened to march on Hollywood. I was going to be boycotted all over the world. But it had the opposite effect. The grosses on my next picture were bigger than ever and it was a lousy picture, but my little announcement of my personal philosophy saved it. It isn't the public that cares whether a movie actress is having an affair with a married man. It's the studios. They have some idea that if they put the pressure on you morally, they can keep putting it on when option time comes up. As far as morals are concerned, I'd still be making ten thousand a week. But the one thing you can't beat is youth. Not age. Youth. Youth is another word for new faces. Not new figures. New faces. We all know how a woman is constructed, and why. But about once a year a new face comes along, and there's no way to fight it, and I can prove it. I could go out now and round up a dozen car-hops with figures as good as mine ever was. But I can't turn them into movie stars by just photographing their shapes. The kisser, the face is what counts. But they get hired for their shapes, the way I was. Why? Because they're hired by men, and men see the shape first. I've come to the conclusion that every studio should have a committee of Lesbians and fairies to pass judgment on the new talent, because they actually look at the faces. The only trouble with my idea is that the committee would be hiring all their little chums, and the queers go for some very strange mutts. The queers only go for people they can feel sorry for, feel superior to, masculine, feminine, or neuter. They can spot a weakness right away, and that makes *them* feel good. If you want to be popular with the queers, you'd better have a weakness. In my case, they liked me because they could make jokes about my shape, which they turned into a kind of a weakness. Fortunately, the normals didn't see it that way, and I became a big star. But I stayed popular with the queers because my morals were bad and I was always getting into trouble with the studio. You want to know, if I was popular with the queers, were the queers popular with me? Well, if you mean was I one of them—no. Did I play around with them? Maybe a little around the edges. A little. You go through phases in this town, and I guess I went through most of them, but my queer phase didn't last very long. A jealous man I can understand, but a jealous Lez is sort of ridiculous, as if she were carrying the masculine bit too far. At least that was what happened to me. I had a Lesbian girlfriend—and believe me, when they take over, they take over. She ran my house for me, and gave me financial advice, and got rid of some of the people that were sponging off of me. She was the same as a husband, except of course in the one department. And that was the whole trouble. I like an occasional man—a habit I got into when I was about fifteen and was never able to break myself of. Nature invented the male sex, and I refused to deprive myself of them. But my girl friend was very jealous and she finally said it was either them or her. Out of politeness I gave the matter some serious thought, like counting up to two, and came to my decision. She spread some nice stories about me, but how can you top the fact that for about a year she was living here with me and everybody knew it? How do you ruin a reputation like mine?"

"I never thought of your reputation as being especially notorious," said Henry.

"You take that back or I'll sue you!" said Eileen. "The only thing I was never accused of was murder, and I came pretty close to that. Not that I ever killed anybody, but I was on a party where a silly broad shot herself and everybody there was questioned. Do you remember Dolly Duval?"

"I do, but I don't think Wilma would," said Henry.

"She was—let's face it—one of those dime-a-dozen not-quite stars that had to shoot herself to get publicity. That may sound heartless and cruel, but it's the truth, and she'd have shot someone else, anyone else, if it would have done her any good. There've always been girls in picture business that would do anything for the publicity, but no matter what they'd do, the newspaper people wouldn't print it. Dolly was one of those. Another thing about them, they're always publicly in love with guys that aren't in love with *them*. They're what used to be called professional torch-carriers. Some guys would go to bed with them, thinking it was a one-night stand, and a couple of days later she'd be on the phone to the columnists saying that this was it, this was the only guy she ever loved, et cetera. Meanwhile the poor chump was in blissful ignorance of any romance, and the first thing he'd know about it was if one of the columnists called up to check. 'What's this about you and Dolly Duval?' they'd say. 'Dolly *Duval*?' he'd say. 'Come on, pal, you've got to do better than that.' But you'd be surprised at some of the big names that she got mixed up with. It finally got so that guys avoided her like Typhoid Mary, although she wasn't bad-looking and she had a nice little shape. She'd come to press parties alone, uninvited, and usually she'd go home with one of those correspondents for the foreign papers, the great free-loaders of all time. Even they were wise to her, but she was buying the dinner, also providing the other entertainment, and some of those creeps were hard to please."

"She was pretty. I remember her," said Henry.

"How well?" said his wife.

"Not *that* well," he said.

"No, Henry wasn't a star, and he was never one of those free-loaders. Dolly Duval wouldn't have gone for Henry— lucky for Henry," said Eileen. "This one night, there was a big opening, a world pre-meer at the Carthay Circle. Searchlights. Radio interviews. All the hired limousines. The bleacher seats for the fans. This one Dolly was invited to, because she had a small part in the picture, and her studio saw to it that she had an escort. He was a creature named Rod Something. Rod was a New York actor who usually played gangster parts, and hung around the Vine Street Derby. Rod Rainsford, he called himself, and he also had a part in the picture. Well, what do you know but he damn near stole the picture, and on the way out they were all talking about a new Cagney, a new Tracy, a new George Raft. And nobody was talking about Dolly Duval. Nobody. In those days everybody went to the Troc after every opening, and Dolly had reserved a table to make sure she got one. But when she and Rainsford arrived at the Troc he was whisked away by the studio big shots, and given a seat at their table between the head of the studio and Marlene Dietrich. I've never known anyone for being there at the right time like Marlene, and of course she was a bigger star than Dolly Duval. And where was Dolly? Dolly was at her own table, with a couple of bit players. In fact, one of them was Kenneth Kingsley, my temporary butler today. Kenneth looked well in tails, and he never got drunk, but he wasn't the lion of the hour. The lion of the hour was at the big shots' table with Marlene. After the Troc there was a party at somebody's house in Beverly, to which all the cast were invited, and Dolly couldn't keep away. She arrived alone, having sent Kenneth and the other person home, and she then proceeded to drink it up. Up to that time she'd stayed sober and on her good conduct, but she had a few things to say to Mr. Rainsford and she was going to get them off her pretty little chest."

"I remember. It was a pretty little chest," said Henry.

"It seems to me you remember too well," said Wilma.

"Go on with your story, Eileen," said Henry.

"Try and stop me," said Eileen. "One thing about our Mr. Rainsford, some of the people he hung out with at the Vine Street Derby were genuine hoods, and one of them was called Al Cummings. He was a gambler, a bookmaker, mixed

up in the rackets, and altogether a very bad boy. I imagine
Rainsford owed him money, because Rainsford was the kind
of guy that owed everybody money, including hoods. It was
easier to borrow money from hoods, because they charged
high interest, and they liked to have people like Rainsford in
hock to them. Cummings always carried a large bankroll, and
he always carried a medium-large revolver. They were sitting
there when Dolly arrived, and she had a big double bourbon
and went over and sat beside Cummings. 'Hello, Al,' she said.
'What are you doing wasting your time with this small-time
hambo? I thought you had better taste.' Something like that.
She was really burned up at Rainsford, and began making
passes at Cummings, in the course of which she came across his
revolver. 'What's this?' she said, and took it out of his pocket.
'Give it back,' said Cummings. 'No, let her play with it,' said
Rainsford. 'Let her blow her silly brains out.' And now I want
to tell you something, because I was there, and only about
from here to you away from them. That girl put the revolver to
her ear and did just that. She pulled the trigger and blew her
brains out. Ugh. Ugh. The whole half of her head, the whole
left side was scattered all over. The yelling and screaming that
went on, and at the same time the laughing, because the room
was half full of people that didn't realize what had happened."

"She just put the gun to her head and shot herself?" said
Henry. "Because Rainsford told her to? That seems incredible.
Why would she want to do that?"

"There you start going into something that there's no real
answer to," said Eileen. "How did she get into that state of
mind? It goes 'way back, I guess. She didn't do it because
Rainsford told her to, but that's exactly why she did it. Rainsford was nothing to her, but who was? It came out later that
Al Cummings was one of her many boy friends, but only one
of many, and never anything big. The procession of guys that
had to go to the district attorney's office was a parade of actors
and agents and cheating husbands and chiselers and wolves
and some nice guys that happened to be in Dolly's little book.
Girls like Dolly Duval always keep a little book. Never fail.
Alongside of some guy she's been sleeping with will be the
name of the Japanese gardener or her foot doctor, but they're

all in there. It would save a lot of trouble if they said who was what. I used to keep a diary, pretty hot stuff it was, too. But that was separate from the names of my foot doctor and the man that cleaned out my swimming-pool. Although one fellow that repaired my pool filter was in both. *There's* one I haven't thought of in years. He was absolutely beautiful, so consequently I was always having something the matter with my filter. You can take that any way you like, I don't care. You can knock California and I won't object, but where else could you call up the swimming-pool repairman at ten o'clock in the morning and at half past ten a beautiful blond Swede arrives to spend the day? He was an Olympic swimmer, or maybe a diver. Olympic I'm sure of. He's probably nothing now, but I suddenly remember him with great tenderness. He took my mind off Dolly Duval, and Kenneth Kingsley was never able to do that."

"Probably not," said Henry.

"They're always saying we had too much sex in Hollywood. But on the contrary, we never had enough," said Eileen.

"Do you mean on the screen, or off?" said Henry.

"Either. Both. On the screen the best they could do was once in a while in a mob scene they could sneak in a long shot of a man and a woman going at it, but that was always in some Roman orgy and you couldn't even be sure unless you had them rerun the footage. Even then you couldn't be positive. What they should have done back in the Thirties was show a couple of big stars going to bed together, the whole works. Close-ups. Two-shots. They'd have got a lot better acting, I can tell you, because it was all some of them could do. As a matter of fact they did get some good acting out of some of the men, who had no more desire to kiss a woman than I have to kiss a pig. Some of those male stars were so queer they'd come off the set after a love scene and be shaking with fright, afraid they were going to murder the girl. One of them told me once, 'Eileen, it isn't against *you* personally. It's because I can't stand to have a woman touch me.' But the director knew that, and he made us do our love scenes over and over again because he'd get one scene that he could print, and the actor would look like the most passionate lover in the history of the world. Why? Because real hate and real love are hard to tell apart. Dolly Duval loved herself and hated herself, which is why she blew her silly brains out. Or why any of us would. I never reached that stage, but I may yet. I'd hate to think my feelings weren't as deep as Dolly Duval's, but maybe that's why I'm still alive. If I were more sensitive, and more passionate, I could give myself a pretty good argument for knocking myself off. But I was never really passionate. Hot, but not passionate. You're my witness, Henry. Was I really passionate?"

"I thought you were, but maybe you were only hot," said Henry.

"I'm passionate, and not very hot," said Wilma.

"I was hoping you'd say that," said Eileen. "It was the way I had you figured. Henry wouldn't know the difference."

"There isn't any difference," said Henry. "You two just like to think there is."

"That's how much you know," said Eileen. "You've stayed married to a passionate woman, whereas the hot number that *I* was lasted a couple of months. Henry, you were more passionate than hot."

"That's not the way I remember it," he said. "But I could argue either way."

"And would, just for the sake of argument," said his wife. "The blond that came to fix your swimming pool—what was he?"

"Passionate," said Eileen.

"Because he'd stay all day?" said Henry.

"You're damn right," said Eileen.

"That wasn't passion, that was vitality, or virility," said Henry.

"You're damn right it was," said Eileen. "He could have stayed a week. Wilma, it was a pity you and he never got together, two passionate people."

"I probably would have taken an instant dislike to him. He probably looked too Nordic for me," said Wilma.

"He looked Nordic, all right. But you wouldn't have been the first Jewess I knew to go for a Nazi," said Eileen.

"Oh, he *was* a Nazi?" said Wilma.

"I don't know what the hell he was. Nordic, Nazi. When you say one you mean both, don't you?" said Eileen.

"Pretty much, I guess," said Wilma.

"Wilma could never have fallen in love with a Nazi," said Henry.

"Who said anything about love?" said Eileen.

"Have you got a picture of him anywhere around?" said Wilma.

"A *picture* of him?" said Eileen. "The man that took care of my swimming pool?"

"It wasn't all he took care of," said Henry.

"Why, I haven't even got a picture of *you*," said Eileen.

"That doesn't surprise me," said Henry. "But I was never Olympic, at anything."

"Don't be *too* modest, Henry. I don't want to have to boast about you in front of your own wife."

"Go right ahead. I might learn something," said Wilma.

"So might I," said Henry.

"Yes, we all might," said Eileen. "I could put myself into some kind of a trance and remember every man I ever had any kind of relations with. And sometimes I do. But I'm probably wrong half the time. Did you ever have your appendix out, Henry?"

"Yes, when I was in high school."

"Did I?" said Eileen.

"Well, I don't remember," said Henry.

"You see?" said Eileen.

"Yes, but we weren't looking for appendectomy scars," said Henry.

"I remember some," said Eileen. "My swimming pool man had a beaut."

"Yes, I guess there's not much about him you don't remember," said Henry.

"You sound just a trifle jealous. How nice," said Eileen. "But don't be. He was all body. Tight blond curls. Big shoulders. No hips. Wilma, you really should have seen him. I'd have lent him to you. I was never stingy about that, and you must have had a nice little figure."

"Would that have made any difference?" said Wilma. "He sounds like he'd have done anything you told him to."

"That was more or less true," said Eileen. "More or less."

"I wish you wouldn't try to get my wife all steamed up about some stud horse you had an affair with thirty years ago," said Henry. "It isn't good for her."

"I've really taken a tremendous dislike to this man," said Wilma. "In fact, I'm not even sure he ever existed. Are you sure he isn't all your fantasies rolled into one?"

"I never had much time for fantasies, Wilma," said Eileen. "I was much too busy with action."

"A fantasy doesn't take long. You can have one while the action is going on," said Wilma.

"You shouldn't have said that," said Eileen. "I know it, and you know it, but Henry won't like it."

"Men have fantasies," said Henry.

"We know that too, but you don't like us to have them," said Eileen.

"How old-fashioned can you get?" said Henry. "Wilma has been having an affair with Benjamin Disraeli since she was in high school."

"George Arliss must have spoiled it for her," said Eileen. "If there was ever a stuffed shirt it was George Arliss. I used to see him on the Warner lot. But I don't know who I'd have gone for in history. I can't think of anybody. Daniel Boone. He was a sort of Tarzan if you stop to think of it. Lafayette might have been fun, but I don't know much about him. Franklin—wasn't he quite a chaser?"

"I loved Disraeli, and he would have loved me," said Wilma.

"She really means that, too," said Henry.

"Arliss. That's all he is to me," said Eileen.

"Do you ever talk about anything but sex?" said Wilma.

"I guess I never get very far off the subject," said Eileen. "Maybe you'd rather talk about politics, but how long would it be before you got back on sex? Was Hitler a fairy, or wasn't he? He always seemed to be having a good time with that doll he was shacked up with but out here everybody insisted he was a queen. On the other hand, if it was so bad for him to be a fag, what about Marcel Proust?"

"Marcel *Proust*?" said Wilma.

"Yes, I heard of him, Wilma."

"You don't speak of him in the same breath," said Wilma.

"I do. I just did. I'm sitting right here with the first person that ever tried to get me to read Marcel Proust. Your husband."

"You tried to make her read Proust?" said Wilma.

"Yes, I tried," said Henry.

"And what's more, I did," said Eileen.

"And how did you like him?" said Wilma.

"Don't look down your schnoz at me, pal," said Eileen. "I didn't like him, but I didn't say so till after I read him. I know plenty of people that said they liked him, and hadn't read as much of him as I did. Don't look down your schnoz at me. Did you read him in French?"

"No, did you?"

"No, but I made ten thousand dollars a week. What did your father do for a living?"

"My father? He was in the textile business. And he *didn't* make ten thousand a week," said Wilma.

"Why not? That's what he was in it for, wasn't he? He wasn't in it because he liked the feel of cotton ginghams, was he? Or maybe he liked the feel of a size-ten model. Maybe we'd better get back on sex."

"Were we ever off it?" said Wilma.

"Not while I'm around," said Eileen. "I'm trying to be a good hostess, because I know damn well you and Henry came to see a sex freak. You came to the right place, all right. Now I think it's time you went back to Vermont and talked about Marcel Proust. But don't forget how I got my introduction to him. In a triple-size bed, with Mr. Henry Barlow, who wanted to improve my mind."

"We're being asked to leave, Henry," said Wilma.

"Oh, Henry can stay if he wants to," said Eileen.

"You bitch," said Wilma.

A Man To Be Trusted

WHEN I was growing up there was one house I always liked to go to. It was in a town about fourteen miles away by the country roads, and though there were two ways to get there, neither way totally avoided the crossing of a mountain. Consequently I had never been to the town before my father bought his first automobile, in 1914. It is hard to believe now that a town only fourteen miles away was so remote or inaccessible and yet in the same county as the town where I lived, but that was how things were when I was a boy, before we had a car and roads were paved. We lived in Gibbsville, which was the county seat, but people in Batavia who had business in the court house mostly had to take a railroad train to a station in the next county, change trains, and in effect double back to get to Gibbsville. There was no direct rail communication between Gibbsville and Batavia, and as Batavia was a good five miles to the west of the river and the canal, the two towns might just as well have been in different counties. It just happened that Batavia was in Lantenengo County instead of Berks County, and Batavia people found it easier to go to Reading, the next big town, than to Gibbsville. I would be inclined to guess that Batavia people felt that they had much more in common with Reading than with Gibbsville, and not only because of the fact that it was easier for them to get to Reading. Traditionally Reading was a Pennsylvania Dutch town, while Gibbsville was a mixture of Yankee, English, Welsh, and Irish that together outnumbered the Pennsylvania Dutch. And on court days the Batavia people would also be encountering the Poles and Lithuanians and Italians who worked in the coal mines and the mills and car shops, whom Batavia people called foreigners. There were no foreigners in Batavia, although Pennsylvania Dutch was their second language and in the case of some of the older people, their only one.

To this town, late in the nineteenth century, had come a man named Philip Haddon and his wife Martha. She was the daughter of old Mike Murphy, who had come up the hard way in the steel business in Ohio and had made enough money to send Martha to school in the East and then to Switzerland. The Murphys owned a big house in Cleveland, but Martha and her mother and sister preferred to live in New York, in a house that was less ostentatious but more elegant than the one in Cleveland. Martha Murphy was a handsome brunette, tall enough to wear her hair in a pompadour, and rich enough to attract titled Europeans who were her co-religionists and some American Protestants who could supply her with Knickerbocker names. But she fell in love with Philip Haddon and he with her, and he turned Catholic and married her. To the delighted surprise of Mike Murphy his new son-in-law went to work for Wexford Iron & Steel, which was named after Mike's home county in Ireland, and Philip was put in charge of a Wexford subsidiary in the town of Batavia, Pennsylvania. "It's nothing big now, mind you," said Mike Murphy. "But it's twice as big as when I bought it and there's over fifty second-generation puddlers on the payroll. It's got a future, Philip."

Martha would have lived anywhere with Philip, and Batavia looked nothing like a steel town. Indeed, it was not a steel town. It was a town on the edge of the Pennsylvania Dutch farming country that happened to have an iron foundry at one end of it. The foundry, as it continued to be called, filled special orders; deck plates and turrets for the Navy, parts for the independent manufacturers of automobiles and trucks; jobs that were too small to engage the facilities of the big mill at Wexford, Ohio. Philip Haddon ran the Batavia foundry efficiently and profitably, and was rewarded by his father-in-law's decision to promote him to an important post in the Wexford mill. Now Mike Murphy got his second surprise from Philip Haddon: Haddon told Murphy that he preferred to remain in Batavia, that he had no desire to move to Ohio, and furthermore had no ambition to be Murphy's successor as the chairman of the board of Wexford Iron & Steel. To a man like Murphy, who had fought his way up, Haddon's lack of enterprise was incomprehensible, and he did not hide his disappointment. He had a talk with his daughter Martha, hoping to persuade her to influence Philip to change his mind, only to discover that Martha was in agreement with Philip and was herself content to stay in Batavia. "Well, if that's the way you want it," said Murphy to his daughter.

"It's the way we want it, Daddy," said Martha.

"You're not saying why. In ten years Philip could be a rich man. In twenty years he could be as rich as me."

"Yes, he probably could," said Martha.

"He's not a lazy man. It's just that he don't have the ambition," said her father. "Maybe instead of a gentleman you'd have done better to marry one of my lads in the oil shanty, a fellow with more get-up-and-go."

"But I didn't. I married Philip, and you should be proud of him for making a success of Batavia."

"Batavia wasn't all his doing. He took over a going concern. He got no test of his abilities there. But if that's as far as he wants to go, he's not the man I thought he was. What I don't understand is why the two of you are content with Batavia. I gave you a million when you were twenty-one. He wouldn't have to work at all. How much of this is your doing, Martha?"

"Half of it, maybe a little less, maybe a little more," she said.

"I give up, I give up," said Mike Murphy.

"If you want Philip to resign from Batavia, he will. But if he does, you'll never see *me* again," said Martha.

"There's things you're not telling me, there's more to this than meets the eye."

"There always is, Daddy," she said. "There always has been."

"Now what do you mean by that remark? You're not resurrecting that old trouble between your mother and I."

"I'm not resurrecting anything, am I? You've always had someone else, and the whole world knew it."

"Your mother had a better understanding of that than you'll ever have."

"Acceptance of it, not understanding," said Martha.

"Ah, you're afraid that Philip'll get too big for you. Is that it, girl?"

"No, that's not it, Daddy."

"If he got as rich as me, you'd lose him. Is that it?"

"No. I'll never lose him. Or he me," she said.

"Well, that's something to be thankful for, isn't it now? To be so certain of everything the future holds for you. No temptations and deviations and allegations and fascinations and affiliations. Not to mention some other -ations I could think of."

"Yes, you left out fornications," she said.

"So I did, didn't I?" said her father. "Well, my girl, being's you have your future all worked out for yourselves, as your loving father I can only hope and pray that the good Lord concurs with your plans. It'd be a pity if ten or twenty years from now your husband belatedly suffered an attack of ambition. Belated ambition could be as bad in one thing as another for a man, whether it be business or pleasure. The time to pull a heat is neither too soon or too late."

"I'm sorry you're disappointed in Philip, Daddy. Maybe what I ought to be sorry about was that I had a sister instead of a brother. Then you'd have had a son and you wouldn't have counted on my husband."

"At that Margaret is more of a man than he is," said Murphy.

"Don't you believe it," said Martha. "Margaret's as feminine as I am."

The old man was too malleable to become misshapen by one defeat, and he sought and found a man of Philip Haddon's age whom he could train to succeed him at Wexford. The man he found was not a gentleman, and Mike Murphy lured him away from Pittsburgh and married him off to his other daughter, Margaret. It apparently made little difference to Margaret, who was unhappily married to a concert violinist of limited talent and strange ways. I was never sure what money changed hands in the process of Margaret's obtaining an annulment of her musical marriage and her union with her father's hand-picked successor. I was too young to know about such matters, and besides I never laid eyes on Margaret. In fact I was quite grown before I knew or cared that Martha Murphy Haddon had a sister. As far as I was concerned, Martha Haddon was the beautiful wife of Philip Haddon, and they lived in Batavia, fourteen miles from my home town, and I always liked to visit their house.

The Haddons had visited my house twice before we owned a car and paid our visit to Batavia. I must explain here—and especially now, in the seventh decade of the century—that the first meeting of the Haddons and my parents came about because my mother had gone to a Sacred Heart school. The Sacred Heart nuns are an order whose influence is world-wide, often compared to the Jesuits, but smaller in number and far subtler as a power elite. The children of the poor do not go to Sacred Heart schools, in Paris, in London, in Montreal, in New York, in Philadelphia, in Mexico City, in Madrid, in Vienna, and money alone was not an automatic qualification for admission to one of their schools, nor was membership in the Roman Catholic Church. What I might ironically call a freemasonry existed among Sacred Heart alumnae, and when Martha Haddon settled in Batavia, Pennsylvania, she got a letter from a Madame Duval, of the Sacred Heart order, who told her that my mother lived in Gibbsville. My mother likewise got a letter from Madame Duval, saying that one of her girls, Martha Murphy Haddon, had recently moved to Batavia. In due course my mother invited Martha to a ladies' luncheon at our house, and the ice was broken. My mother was older than Martha, and they had not been to the same Sacred Heart school, but they had friends in common among Sacred Heart alumnae in various parts of the world, and I suppose the two women looked each other over like two old Etonians who are thrown together on a rubber plantation in the Straits Settlements. Philip Haddon owned a green Locomobile phaeton, which was driven by a chauffeur without livery. We were accustomed to seeing Locomobiles and Pierce-Arrows and Packards, owned by mining superintendents and driven by men in business suits, and so I guessed that the Haddon car went with his job. I was about nine years old, impressed but not overawed.

A few months later my father bought his first Ford, and he and my mother and my sister and I returned the Haddons' visit. Batavia was a pretty town, much more countrified than I had expected, with great walnuts and chestnuts and elms on the principal streets. The foundry was at the southern end of the town, not noticeable from the Haddons' house except for a tall stack from which issued a thin trickle of smoke, the day being Sunday. "We usually go to Mass in Reading," I heard Mr. Haddon say to my father. "There's a priest that says Mass here every fourth Sunday, but the rest of the time we drive down to Reading."

"Oh, are you a Catholic too?" said my father.

"Yes, I became one when we announced our engagement."

"Well, I'd better be careful what I say. Converts are stricter than we are," said my father. The two men then talked about guns and shooting, and Haddon invited my father to spend the night when the season opened. Quail, and some pheasant, and always a good bag of rabbit.

"This young man isn't quite ready for that, is he?" said Philip Haddon, putting his hand on my shoulder.

"He's getting a .22 for Christmas, if he's a good boy," said my father.

"Well, would you like to go down in the cellar with me after dinner? I have a couple of .22's you might like to try," said Haddon.

"Me?" I said.

"I believe your father thinks you've been a good boy, don't you, Doctor Malloy?"

"Sometimes," said my father.

"Splendid. Dinner'll be ready in a few minutes," said Haddon.

"Oh, boy, thanks," I said.

"Not *thanks*. Thank *you*, Mr. Haddon," said my father.

"Thank you, Mr. Haddon," I said.

We had not finished dinner when the telephone rang. "It's for you, Doctor Malloy," said Haddon.

"Who could that be?" said my mother.

"I can guess," said my father. "Excuse me."

He came back from the sitting-room. "It's the hospital."

"Oh, dear," said Martha Haddon.

"Mr. MacNamara?" said my mother.

My father nodded.

"Won't you even have time to finish dessert?" said Martha Haddon.

"I hate to say it, but we have to go right away," said my father. "I apologize for this interruption—"

"Oh, not at all, Doctor Malloy," said Philip Haddon.

"Isn't that always the way, though?" said my mother. She was already standing, and my sister and I were rising.

"May I offer a suggestion?" said Haddon. "Why can't Mrs. Malloy and the children stay, and I'll drive them back to Gibbsville in my car?"

"In your Locomobile?" I said.

"Well, Katharine, it's up to you. I'm going to have to go straight to the hospital."

"Oh, no. That wouldn't be right. No, we'll go with you," said my mother.

"It's no distance at all, and the doctor's going to be busy all afternoon, I can see that," said Haddon.

"Well, you're right about that. I'm going to have to operate," said my father. "If it wouldn't be too much trouble, but I have to leave this minute. Katharine, you and the children finish your dinner and come home with Mr. Haddon."

"Good. Good work, Doctor Malloy. I can see that your mind is on more important things already. You just leave it all up to me," said Philip Haddon.

He was the first person I had ever known to make audible comment on my father's habit of distracting himself. We might not know which patient or which operation he was thinking of, but we knew the signs that his attention was elsewhere. Philip Haddon had recognized the signs, and what's more he had made so bold as to be frank about it. It was a rare thing when anyone made a personal remark to my father. Most people were afraid of him, in awe of him, but Philip Haddon was not. To a boy of nine it was an instructive experience to see someone unhesitatingly change my father's plans, and my father's submission. The moment my father left for the hospital a party-like atmosphere prevailed. We finished our dessert, the two women and my sister went upstairs, and Philip Haddon took me down-cellar to his rifle range. It was a gun room as well as a shooting gallery, with rugs on the concrete floor, glass-paned closets for his rifles, shotguns, and handguns, and framed pictures on the panelled walls. That room was my first real introduction to Philip Haddon, and for the rest of the afternoon I kept learning things about him that added to my information and respect.

I remember that that day he was wearing a brown tweed suit and brown spats over wing-tip brogues. My father went in for tweeds but not for matching spats. Philip Haddon had an American face and gold-rimmed glasses, no moustache, smoothed-down light brown hair parted not quite in the middle. He was taller than my father, probably about six-feet-one, and built like an end. He had been to West Point. "Is that where you learned to shoot?" I said.

"Well, that's where I learned the army way, but I've always

been fond of shooting," he said. "I must have been about your age when I started. What are you, ten?"

"My next birthday I'll be ten," I said.

"Good. Then you started earlier than I did," he said.

I was an inquisitive boy, especially if given the encouragement of sensible answers. "Why did you go to West Point? Did you want to be a soldier?"

"I didn't have much to say in the matter," he said. "My father and four of my uncles went there. But no, I didn't want to be a soldier. I wanted to be a painter."

"That paints pictures? An artist?"

"Yes. Do you want to be a doctor?"

"No," I said.

"What *do* you want to be?" said Philip Haddon. "Have you decided?"

"A state policeman," I said. "Or maybe own the circus."

"Yes, owning a circus would be fun," said Philip Haddon. "I'm not so sure about being a state policeman. Most of them were in the army, and I've *been* in the army."

"Why didn't you like it?" I said.

"Well, I suppose because I'm not very good at taking orders. As far as that goes, I didn't like giving them either. But that's something you can't avoid."

"You could run away," I said.

"Not really. You can't really run away."

"I'm going to. When I get bigger. When I'm twelve," I said.

"You're going to run away when you're twelve? Where to?"

"Out West. Wyoming, maybe. I can work on a ranch. Have you ever been there, to Wyoming?"

"Yes, I have, in the army. Twelve is a little young to be working on a ranch. Not that I want to discourage you, but I think you ought to wait a bit longer. Fifteen or sixteen. They have blizzards in Wyoming, and it gets awfully hot in summer. Much colder and much hotter than it gets here. Why a ranch? Do you like horses?"

"I'm a good rider," I said.

"Have you got a pony?"

"No, I have a horse. My sister has a pony but she doesn't know how to ride. She's too little, and she's scared."

"Well, she may get over that," said Philip Haddon. He

opened one of the gun closets and handed me a Winchester .22 with a nickeled octagonal barrel. "Let me see you handle it."

"Can I fire it?" I said.

"You're on your own," he said. He was watching me carefully. I took it off safety, aimed at the target, and pressed the trigger. "Good. You proved the piece. You've handled guns before."

"You bet. Since I was little," I said. He handed me a box of ammunition. "I know how to load it, too."

"It's all yours," he said.

I fired fifteen shots, the full load, uninterrupted by him. "Very good," he said. "Your grouping was good, once you got the feel of it."

"I never got a bull's eye," I said.

"No, but you got some 5's and 4's, and only two worse than a 3," he said. "Naturally you have a lot to learn, such as breathing, but you have the makings of a good shot. If it weren't Sunday we could try a revolver, but they make too much noise. Now I think it's time we joined the ladies."

"Thank you very much," I said.

He ran a cleaning rod through the rifle barrel, and I picked the empty shells off the floor and put them in a wastebasket, in imitation of his neatness. We smiled at each other. "We're going to get along fine," he said.

"Do you have a little boy?" I said.

"We did have, but he died. Diphtheria. Your father's a doctor, so you've heard of diphtheria."

"Yes, my brother had it. They had to put a silver tube in his throat," I said.

"But he got well. That's good."

"I had anti-toxin. That *hurt*," I said. "A needle in my back. But I didn't cry. My sister cried, but I didn't. All the kids in our neighborhood had anti-toxin, and I was the only one that didn't cry."

"You must be very brave," he said.

"My father said I had to set a good example. But it hurt that night and I cried then. It hurt as bad as the needle, only different. But I didn't have to set an example then, so I cried."

"It's very important to have to set an example," he said.

His wife called from the top of the cellar stairs. "Philip, Mrs. Malloy thinks it's time to go."

I wanted to stay, but the immediate prospect of riding in the Haddons' Locomobile was attractive. "Can I sit up front with you?" I said.

"Well, of course. Ladies in the back, gentlemen up front," he said. "Come with me while I get the car."

I accompanied him to the stable, where the green Locomobile, spotless and facing outward, occupied space on the ground floor. The car had Westinghouse shock absorbers, twin spotlights bracketed to the windshield, and a double cowl in the tonneau. Right there as it stood was one of the most beautiful cars in the world, and I was about to go for a ride in it. "*Some . . . car!*" I said.

"You approve?" said Philip Haddon.

Then I saw the box stalls at the other end of the barn. "Look! A white one and a sorrel," I said.

"Mrs. Haddon rides the white one, I ride the sorrel," said Philip Haddon.

Everything was so neat and orderly; each horse's halter hung outside his stall, half a dozen bridles and saddles—English and McClellan—were on pegs against the wall; brooms and buckets, curry combs and brushes, soap and harness oil and sponges were where they ought to be according to someone's plan. "The sorrel wants to go out but he ought to know better. We never ride on Sunday," said Philip Haddon.

"I do," I said.

"Yes, but you don't live in Batavia," said Philip Haddon. "Well, off we go." He started the motor, let it turn over for a minute or so, and we moved down the slag driveway to the porte-cochère. In the half hour that it took us to drive to our house I said not a word. Philip Haddon and his wife and my mother carried on a conversation that did not concern me, and besides I had things to occupy my mind: the location of electric switches and buttons and dials and meters, and an enameled-brass St. Christopher medal that said something in French, and a small brass plate that was marked "Built for Philip Haddon, Esquire."

My first day with Philip Haddon came to an end, and I had

so many things to tell my friends that I did not know where to begin. The next clay, at school and after school, I decided I would not tell anyone anything. Mr. Haddon and Mrs. Haddon—she was pretty and nice—were not to be shared with my friends.

Months passed before I saw them again, and the next time I saw him he was in the hospital, where my father had operated on him for appendicitis. "I'm taking you over to see Mr. Haddon," said my father. "He said he'd like to see you, I suppose he was only being polite. Anyway, you can only stay a few minutes. He had a close call."

Mrs. Haddon was sitting in a white iron chair. "I brought you a visitor," said my father.

"Oh, it's my friend," said Philip Haddon. He was weak and not wearing his gold-rimmed glasses, which made him look weaker and older. He put them on.

"I brought you some flowers," I said.

"Oh, are they from your garden?" said Philip Haddon.

"No, *they're* all *dead*," I said.

"Well, I almost joined them," he said. "I can thank your father that I didn't."

"I'll be back in a jiffy," said my father, and left us.

"Does it hurt?" I said.

"No, not really," said Philip Haddon. "But it did."

"We were very lucky that your father was here," said Mrs. Haddon. "He was just getting ready to leave the hospital when I called. Dr. Schmeck and I drove Mr. Haddon to the hospital, and they had the operating room ready when we got here."

"Oh, yes. Peritonitis," I said.

"You know about peritonitis?" said Mrs. Haddon.

"I know that's what happens with appendicitis," I said.

"I notice you and your father pronounce it *eetis* instead of *eyetis*," said Philip Haddon.

"That's the way they pronounced it when he was in medical school. Appendi*ceetis*, periton*eetis*."

"It must be the correct way, but I'll never get used to it," said Philip Haddon. "Well, how is school?"

"Oh—school. All right, I guess," I said.

"When I get out of here you must come down and see us

again," said Philip Haddon. "I won't be able to ride for a while. I'm going to have to wear a big belt."

"I know," I said.

"But we can shoot," he said. "Your father and I were going gunning together when the season opens, but I don't think he'd approve of that now. So you come instead."

"All right," I said.

"As far as that goes, you could ride with me," said Mrs. Haddon. "You could ride the sorrel. That is, if you don't mind riding with a lady."

"Don't let that fool you," said Mr. Haddon. "She rides as well as any man."

Well, the upshot of that conversation was that the Haddons remembered their invitation, and many times in the next couple of years I went to their house and rode with them and shot with him. It did not matter that at first I was aware I was taking the place of their dead son. I would board the morning train and get off at the main line station where Philip Haddon or his wife would meet me and take me to their house for the day. In the mornings I would ride with one of them, and after lunch he and I would shoot. I would arrive dressed in breeches and puttees, and she or he would be in boots or breeches; but nearly always it was she who rode with me. After his operation he had never regained his interest in riding, and if it had not been for me they would have sold the sorrel, and Mrs. Haddon would have had no one to ride with. My visits were fortnightly, seldom oftener than that, and always arranged by the Haddons in advance. I came to look forward to seeing her as much as I did him, and I reached the age where I became more and more conscious of her figure. She got into my dreams.

One day she met me at the train and immediately announced that there would be no shooting that day. Mr. Haddon had been called to Philadelphia on business. He was very sorry— but I was not. She said that instead of shooting that afternoon she would, if I liked, take me to the foundry and I could see the sights, have a ride on the dinkey engine and the traveling crane. Mr. Haddon said I might enjoy that. And so she and I rode the white and the sorrel, and she said she was going to have to change her clothes because Mr. Haddon did not like her to appear before the foundry workmen in riding breeches. "I'll only be a few minutes," she said. "A quick tub and change." I waited downstairs until I heard the water running in the tub, and then I went upstairs and entered the bathroom without knocking. She was standing naked, feeling the water in the tub. "What are you *doing* here?" she said.

"I wanted to look at you," I said.

She reached for a towel to cover herself. "But you mustn't," she said.

"I only wanted to look," I said.

"Well, I should think so, at thirteen," she said. "Now you've seen me, you must go."

"I want to kiss you," I said.

"Yes, well I knew that," she said.

"I love you," I said.

"That's not love, Jimmy. That's something else," she said. "Can't you see that you're embarrassing me. All right, you can kiss me here." She lowered the towel and put back her shoulders so that her breasts stood out. I kissed each of them. "That's enough now," she said. "Go on downstairs and we'll pretend this never happened. Never." But I put my arms around her and was rough with her and she struggled. "Stop it," she said.

"You wanted me to. You did. I could tell."

"Wanted you to what? Thirteen years old, you must be insane."

"What he does, Mr. Haddon," I said.

"Huh. What you think he does," she said. "You could be wrong about that, too. All right, open your trousers." She got down on the floor and I got on top of her, but I could not control myself and she lay there, wanting what I could not give her. "Now let me have my bath, and you go make yourself presentable."

She came downstairs in about half an hour. "We can dispense with the visit to the foundry," she said. "I can take you to the station, there's an earlier train. We can't talk about it any more till after lunch."

"I don't want any lunch," I said.

"Well, you'll damn well sit here while I have mine," she said. "I have the maid to consider." She chattered while the maid came and went.

"He ain't eating," said the maid.

"He lost his appetite," said Mrs. Haddon.

"He always stuffs," said the maid.

"Well, not today," said Mrs. Haddon.

"Maybe because the Mister ain't here," said the maid.

"Very likely," said Mrs. Haddon.

Later, in the sitting-room, I said, "Are you going to tell Mr. Haddon?"

"No. It wasn't all your fault," she said. "I must have been leading you on, without knowing it. I've seen you look at me, so I should have been forewarned. Have I ever looked at you that way?"

"No."

"Have you ever thought I was flirting with you?"

"No."

"Well, if it's any consolation to you, my husband thought I was flirting with you."

"Me?"

"You, and not only you," she said.

"I never thought so," I said.

"I never did either," she said. "But my husband does. There are some women who give that impression."

"Not you, though," I said.

"Do other women flirt with you? Not girls, but women."

"I don't know."

"Oh, you'd know," she said.

"Some, maybe."

"And what do you do?" she said.

"I don't do anything. With girls I do, but not women. You're the only one."

"Failing the opportunity, I suppose," she said. "Well, I'll be more careful in the future. I'll lock my bathroom door."

"You're not cross at me?"

"More with myself than with you. This could have had serious consequences, you know. The maid. My husband. Your father. Nothing like this must ever happen again. If my husband gave you a good beating, your father'd give you one too. Not to mention the fact that I'd also get a good beating from my husband."

"I'd kill him if he did," I said.

"Mm. How chivalrous, and what a mess. Hereafter confine your attentions to girls your own age."

"I don't like girls my own age," I said.

"Well, a little older, when their busts develop. Thirteen is too young for you to *think* of older women. I'm old enough to be your mother, you know. I am, you know. I'm ashamed of myself. I gave in to you. No matter what happened, I gave in to you. You'll always remember that—and so will I. I have a husband that I love dearly, and he loves me. But a thirteen-year-old boy could make me forget that. Do you realize how much that's going to make me hate myself? Are you mature enough to understand that? You could lose all respect for women after today. It could have a bad effect on the rest of your life. Giving in, that was the worst thing that happened today. That was a terrible sin."

"Don't think that, Mrs. Haddon," I said.

"Do you deny that it was a sin? I can't. I've heard of women like that. When I was at school abroad there was a girl's mother that had a weakness for young boys. It was such a scandal that the girl was asked to leave school. A highly respected family. The girl's life was made miserable by the weakness of the mother, but am I any better?"

The flow of her self-castigation would not stop, and it began to frighten me. I wanted to comfort her, but I did not know how without touching her, and an instinct told me that she wanted to be touched and that that would lead to what she called giving in. She wanted to weep and would not weep. My instinct to comfort her was confused with the sight of the rise and fall of her bosom, and whatever was going on inside her was happening to the woman on the bathroom floor. I could not stand it any longer and I kissed her on the mouth. Her response was complete and eager, but then as suddenly she pushed me away. "God, what am I doing?" she said. "What am I *doing?*" She put her hands to her cheeks. "He's right about me," she said, and I knew she was talking about her husband.

"Get your cap, and we'll get some fresh air," she said. She stood up, only barely discernibly unsteady. "I'll drive you to the station." She had her own car now, a Scripps-Booth roadster, a three-seater with the driver's seat forward of the other two.

"You don't have to do that," I said.

"You're wrong, I do have to. I want the cold air on my face, to bring me back to my senses. And you need it too, young man."

Because of the odd seating arrangement I had to lean forward in the noisy, windswept, little car, and she had to repeat half of what she said. But our conversation did not touch upon our intimacies. The cool, cold air was having its effect on her—and on me. The newness, the uniqueness of our experience lay for me in the fact that I was learning for the first time in my life that a woman could actively desire a man. I had kissed girls and sometimes found them responsive, but I had never known, never even heard, that a woman was more than submissive to a man. Now I was learning that it was in the nature of a woman to have a hunger for a man or a boy of thirteen who had the functions of a man. This revelation, this discovery was so violent that I needed someone to discuss it with me, but my inexperienced contemporaries were out of the question; already in experience I was so far ahead of them that none of them would believe me. The superlative irony was in the circumstance that the only man, woman, or boy or girl in whom I had the confidence for confiding was Philip Haddon. On my visits to his house I had told him many things about myself and my family and enemies and friends, and he had always listened with more than perfunctory interest. I almost laughed at the thought of telling him what had happened with his wife that day. Well, at least I was sure that she was not going to tell him either.

Just before we reached the station she said, "I'm never going to say any more about today, to you or anyone else. And don't you."

"I won't," I said.

"The next time you go to confession—do you ever go to an Italian priest?"

"No," I said. "Why?"

"Because Italian priests aren't as easily shocked," she said. "I'd always much rather go to an Italian priest. Whenever I have something naughty to confess, I go to the Italian parish in Reading."

"That's not a true confession, if he doesn't understand what you're saying," I said.

"I don't hold anything back. I tell him everything," she said.

"You're not confessing to a man. You're confessing to God."

"I know all that," she said. "All the same, I'd rather say those things to an Italian. And another thing, don't turn pious on me."

I wasn't ready—but is one ever?—for the physical and spiritual revolution that began for me that day. I had yielded to strong impulse, I had seen her naked body and made an incomplete attempt to commit adultery with her, and I was entertaining doubts about the sanctity of the confessional. She became the most fascinating, evil, ignorant, cynical woman the world had ever known. I wanted to escape from her and sin, but I knew that I would have to go back to her and sin and her secret delights and godless thoughts and infinite pleasures.

"I'm not pious," I said.

"No, I know you're not," she said. "In fact, you're very wicked to know as much as you do." With that she won me over to the side of wickedness, completely. I could not say to her that I was ready to abandon the pleasures of wickedness; I could not say it to myself when the opposite attraction was so powerful. As she drove me to the station I was aware that I was being chastised for improper conduct, the misbehavior of a boy of thirteen with a woman of whatever age she was. It was as much as I could expect, and it was the right thing for her to do. But already I had been matured by the day's experiences to the extent that my childhood was in the past and I knew it. That was all I knew at the moment, but that much was certain.

We sat in the car, waiting for the northbound train, and she seemed fully to have regained her self-possession, her own place in the world, so that she was protected by her dignity and her tweed skirt and her accustomed manner toward me. She offered me a cigarette and I took it, although her husband had never offered me a cigarette because he respected my father's rule against them. In a strange, conspiratorial way she had somehow managed to join with me in an alliance that supported the smoking of cigarettes while, in the time remaining, totally ignoring our sins of thought, word, and deed. The camelback engine came heaving up the track and I got out of the roadster, took off my cap, and looked at her with what must have been apprehension and longing.

"No, don't try to say anything," she said, and smiled reassuringly.

2.

I went away to boarding school that year where I did not know a soul. In the new life I made the new friends and enemies and the associations with the new things that came out of old books. It was impossible for me to risk the scornful disbelief of other boys with the story of my experience with Mrs. Haddon, and I kept it to myself. With girls my reticence was just as strong. They would let me kiss them, but some of them, most of them, would fight or cry if I put my hand on their growing breasts. They would threaten to tell their big brothers, although they never did. During that phase of my adolescence I had dreams about Mrs. Haddon's body, but they were so secret that she as a living person did not exist. When I went home on school vacations I did not see her, and the friendship between my parents and the Haddons was never meant to flourish. Two or three years went by, and Philip Haddon continued to be a patient of my father's; once or twice a year the Haddons and my parents would meet halfway for Sunday lunch at the Lantenengo Country Club; at Christmas they exchanged suitable presents. But Martha Haddon, if it was deliberate, managed to stay out of my sight, and of course I was falling in and out of love with girls closer to my own age. I had guessed her age to be about sixteen or seventeen years older than I, so that by the time I got out of prep school and went to work on a Gibbsville newspaper, she was in her late thirties. My father died, and my mother had a letter from the Haddons, who were traveling abroad and did not hear about his death until a month later. The letter was written by Martha Haddon and Philip Haddon was only formally included in it. "Mr. Haddon must not be well," said my mother. "Otherwise I think he'd have written. He and your father were closer than Mrs. Haddon and I."

"Well, some men hate to write letters," I said.

"Yes, but not Mr. Haddon," said my mother. As was often the case, she was right, for the next time I visited the neighborhood of Batavia I was on an assignment to cover a fatal stabbing, and because I was in the neighborhood I paid a call on the Haddons. From my paper's point of view it was not much of a story. Some Negroes living in a tent and working as day laborers on a highway construction had a drunken brawl in which one man was killed and the others immediately fled. The state police were not even sure of the names, and I was sure that my paper had no interest in the story. But my curiosity about the Haddons was active, and I had the paper's Oakland coupe and time to spare.

It was a hot August day, toward noon. The smoke from the foundry stacks hung thick and low, as though waiting for any light breeze to take it away. At the Haddons' house on the other end of town the awnings and the wire screens seemed to darken the rooms, and there was no sign of life in the yard. But as I got out of the Oakland the porch screendoor opened and Martha Haddon descended. "Are you from the Light Company?" she called.

"No, ma'am," I said. "I'm from the dark company." It was a feeble enough joke, but I would explain it to her later.

"Don't tell me! It isn't who I think it is," she said, and called back to the man on the porch. "Philip, we have a visitor. James Malloy."

"Oh, good," I heard him say. "Dr. Malloy's boy?"

"What on earth are you doing here on this sticky, hot day?" said Martha Haddon. "Come in out of the sun and have a glass of iced tea."

Philip Haddon rose slowly and rested his palm fan and newspaper on a wicker table. He was wearing a pongee suit, striped blue shirt, white canvas oxfords. We shook hands and I explained my presence in the neighborhood and my little joke. "Well, you'll stay to lunch," said Philip Haddon. "You might even have a swim. I think the pool is new since you were here last."

"It is," she said. "This is only our third summer with the pool."

"Has it really been that long since we used to shoot? But then it must be. You're not a boy any more. You're quite a young man. Newspaper work, and watching people carve each other up."

"Yes, I remember when my father carved you up," I said.

"And you came to see me in the hospital," he said. "Well,

damn it all, it is nice to see you again. Isn't it awful that we can live so near and never see each other? We've never even been to see your mother since your father died."

"Well, *you've* had some excuse," said Martha Haddon. "Mr. Haddon caught some kind of a stomach ailment in Italy."

"Say no more about it," said Philip Haddon. "I think it was nothing more than a recurrence of malaria. Everybody that was ever in the army got *some* malaria. Unfortunately, I've had to retire from the foundry, and we may have to move away."

"We *own* the *house*," said Martha Haddon.

"Yes, but the new superintendent may not like to have me looking over his shoulder," said Philip Haddon.

"As you've probably guessed, this is a frequent topic of conversation," said Martha Haddon. "But we don't really want to leave Batavia. Where to? Good heavens, we came here as bride and groom, and this has been our home, our only one."

"I'm sure Mr. Malloy'd much rather go for a swim than participate in our discussion," said Philip Haddon.

"No, I always liked this house," I said. "I hope you keep it."

"Then that settles it," said Philip Haddon. "You promise to visit us often when they finish the new highway."

For the first time ever I suspected that Philip Haddon was capable of subtlety. "I promise," I said.

"All right, fine, we'll hold you to that," he said. "Now if you'd like to have a dip before lunch, I'll get you a pair of trunks."

"Aren't you coming?" I said.

"No, if I get a chill I'm through for the day, maybe longer," he said. "But Martha will go with you."

"All right, we haven't much time," said Martha Haddon.

We put on our bathing suits and left him on the porch. The pool was in a corner of the yard, protected on four sides by a tall hedge, and on the way to the pool she and I wore bathrobes. "It's our one concession to Batavia," she said. "They wouldn't approve of a grown woman walking around in a bathing suit."

"Do you really like it in Batavia?" I said.

"I like it better than any place else," she said. "It keeps me on my good behavior—*most of the time*."

"Oh, you remember," I said.

"Of course I do. It's not something you forget."

"Well, what about him, Mr. Haddon? Did he ever know about me?"

"I didn't tell him," she said.

"That isn't answering my question," I said. "Something a minute ago made me think he knew *something*."

"You're a young man now," she said. "Yes, he guessed, but he never really wanted to know anything like that."

"Was there a lot to know?"

"You must think I'm very unattractive," she said.

"Far from it," I said.

"You must, if the best I could do was a thirteen-year-old boy," she said. "A twenty-year-old boy is better, but do you think there's been no one in between?"

"Well—*him*."

"Oh, he's happy now. He likes being an invalid."

"He wasn't always an invalid," I said.

"Most of the time," she said. "Do you know why he liked being a Catholic? It was because he thought it'd make me behave. But it didn't turn out that way. It made him behave, but not me."

"I thought you were deeply in love with him," I said.

"I am. But you have a lot to learn about love."

"I guess I've learned more from you than from anyone else," I said.

"It doesn't really matter who you learn it from, as long as you learn it. I even learned some from you."

I laughed. "From me? A hot-pants kid?"

"An inexperienced kid. You're not that inexperienced any more," she said.

"No," I said.

"You didn't teach me anything, but I learned from you. It was about myself. That I could want someone whether he was thirteen or thirty, provided he wanted me enough, and showed it. You have always been someone who wanted me."

"Today?"

"Of course today," she said. "Look at you. Just look at you."

"Then why don't we?"

"Because you're not thirteen now, and we can wait," she said. "He knows every move we can make, and he's sitting on the porch imagining it. So don't be surprised if he comes down here at just the wrong time."

"What would he do if he caught us?"

"That's a chance we're not going to take," she said.

"What would he *do*?" I said.

"I said we're not going to take the chance, and we're not. Anyway, not today."

"Oh, all right," I said. "He likes to think about it, and you like to talk about it. Which one's worse?"

"Take your swim, and be more respectful to your elders," she said.

I stood on the diving-board and turned my back on her.

"Go ahead, it'll do you good," she said.

I plunged in and the water was a shock but I took a few strokes to get used to the temperature, and when I climbed out Philip Haddon was standing above her at the side of the pool. "You see what I mean about the chill," he said. "It's water that comes from a spring."

"I'll say it does," I said.

"Say, by the way, I brought something to show you," he said. From his jacket pocket he took out an automatic pistol. "Ever seen one like it?"

"No," I said.

"It's a Browning automatic," he said. He handed it to me, and I hefted it.

"It's loaded, isn't it?" I said.

"Oh, yes," he said. "But I know I can trust you with firearms."

"Philip always remembered that he could trust you with firearms," said Martha Haddon.

The Journey to Mount Clemens

WE FINISHED up at Number 4 in time for supper. The dining-room closed at seven o'clock and we just made it. There were five in our party and we all sat at the same table. The food was good; the hotel had a reputation for good food, and we all knew that the next place where we would be stopping had no such reputation. Nevertheless we were not sorry to be on our way. Nothing had gone right during the two weeks we had been at Number 4, on a job that should have taken much longer. Carmichael, the chief of our party, had been putting the pressure on us because he wanted to get back to the main office in New York. He would have two days in New York and then he would be off to another assignment in the Sudan, where the Company was building a dam. Carmichael was known as a slave-driver anyway, but during the two weeks at Number 4 he had outdone himself. Breakfast every morning at seven, lunches packed so that we could eat on the job, supper at the hotel, and then night work, and no time off on Saturday or Sunday. Carmichael wanted to have the Number 4 job all cleaned up before he went abroad, and he thus had an incentive that we had not had. It was characteristic of him that he had not a word of praise or thanks for extra work we had been putting in, that made him look good but that did nothing for us.

Our work was not easy to explain. We were a valuation crew, which meant that we were putting a valuation on the entire physical property of an electric power corporation. Every item, from a box of paper clips to a steam turbine, had to be inspected and a price put on it. The purpose of the valuation was to enable the financial people in the main office to show what was being done with the corporation's capital. This information was doubly important: it was helpful when the corporation asked the power commissions for an increase in rates; and it showed the public that the corporation was a substantial enterprise when a new stock issue was offered. I was the only member of our party who did not hold an engineering degree, but even I had learned to identify such unusual items as a mercury arc rectifier and a Coxe traveling grate and a continuous rail joint. I was eighteen years old, knew nothing about electricity, had just been kicked out of prep school, and had got the job because Carmichael had been a patient of my father's. I was paid seventy-five dollars a month, but I was living on an expense account a good deal of the time, and I could count on at least five dollars a week from shooting pool with the other members of the party. They were not very good, and I was just enough better to win. But during the two weeks at Number 4 we had shot no pool, drunk no whiskey, chased after no girls. We had been working twelve-hour days, seven-day weeks; and we hated Carmichael, he knew it, and seemed to enjoy it.

Our bags were packed and waiting in the lobby as we ate our last supper at Dugan's Hotel. "Well, gentlemen, this time next Saturday I should be passing through the Strait of Gibraltar. No, not quite. I'll still be in the Atlantic a week from tonight. King, you've been to that part of the world. How long before I get to Gibraltar?"

"Depends on the boat. Eight or nine days. You stop at the Azores, more than likely, but I doubt if you go ashore. I didn't."

"I have no particular curiosity about the Azores, but I would like to see Gibraltar."

"See it is all you will do. You won't be going ashore there either, according to my recollection. You keep right on till you get to Naples. You can go ashore there."

"I've been to Naples," said Carmichael.

"Yes, I was a lot younger then," said King. "You can have a high old time in Napoli. Is your wife going with you?"

"Oh, no. Not on this trip. I'm afraid she's had her share of the tropics."

"Well, not me. One more winter in the North Temperate Zone and I'll be ready for the Sudan. Keep me in mind when you're out there, Carmichael."

"I'll do that," said Carmichael.

We all knew that King had once been Carmichael's boss, and that their positions had been altered by Carmichael's ambition and King's fondness for the booze.

"I'd go there in a minute," said King. "I don't suppose you know that I was the first man the company sent out there."

"I didn't know you were the first," said Carmichael.

"Well, I had another fellow with me. Ken Stewart. But he died while we were out there. Got one of those tropical bugs. But the original survey was done by me. I learned to speak Swahili. It's not hard."

"I didn't realize they spoke Swahili in the Sudan."

"I didn't say they did. I just said I learned to speak it. There's no damn use learning to speak those other languages. There's fifty of them, from one tribe to another. But if you learn Swahili you can get along. It's like French. You go anywhere in the world and if you speak French you'll find somebody to understand you."

"Swahili is like French? Come now, King."

"For Christ's sake, Carmichael. The French language isn't like the Swahili dialect. But if you speak Swahili in that part of Africa, it's like speaking French in the rest of the world. Now have I made myself clear?"

"Now you have, yes," said Carmichael.

King was the only member of our party who ever spoke that way to Carmichael. Indeed, I doubted that anyone else in the entire organization, regardless of rank, would be so disrespectful. The man was so austere, so inseparable from the tradition of efficiency and hard work, that no matter how much he was hated, his personal dignity was inviolate. We could share King's dislike of Carmichael, but I think we all felt that his behavior toward him was foolishness. But then there was a great deal of foolishness to be tolerated from King. To me, working at my first real job, one of the most fascinating things about the Company was that it could include and retain a Carmichael and a King in the same organization. Could it be that there was someone back there in an office on Lower Broadway who remembered that King had once learned to speak Swahili and remembered also that Carmichael had not always been King's boss? Reluctantly, inexplicably I was discovering that my pity for King could be changed into pity for Carmichael. The Company had got all it could out of King, and was now getting all it could out of Carmichael. I, eighteen years old, could see that Carmichael would some day be another King, bled dry, burnt out, and kept on the payroll in some minor job where former underlings would be disrespectful to him. In those days, on that job, I was fascinated by many things, but most of all by the subtleties and complexities of the relations among my superiors—and they were all my superiors. They were all anywhere from five to thirty-five years older than I; educated, experienced men who had, among them, been in just about every country on earth. Working with them, living with them, was rather like being a very junior officer in the regular army. As it happened, I was in home territory, never more than seventy-five miles from the place where I was born, but for the others in our crew Eastern Pennsylvania was only less strange than Shanghai or the Sudan or Ecuador. Indeed, they were more at home in the distant places, where they had spent more time, than in the mountains where I lived. One night before Carmichael arrived to deprive us of our free time, I had sat with them in the lobby of Dugan's Hotel and listened to King and Edmunds trying to carry on a conversation in Chinese, but they had made no sense to each other because King spoke one kind of Chinese and Edmunds another, and a word that meant duenna in King's dialect meant prostitute in Edmunds's. Then they had turned to me and asked me to spell shoo-fly as in shoo-fly pie, which we had had for supper. Then we all went down the street and I beat them at pool. It was a great job, just great.

Now it was time to get in the two Company cars and drive the twenty-eight miles to Mount Clemens, where there was a new sub-station. When we got outside the ground was covered with new snow. "Oh, dear," said Carmichael to the driver of his car. "How long has this been coming down?"

"A good two hours or more, ever since you was in the hotel," said the driver. "It's all right, though. I got the chains on."

"The chains? Will we need chains?"

"We'll need chains all right," said the driver. "We'd of needed them anyway, without this extra snow. Once you get off the main highway the road to Mount Clemens'll be slow going."

"Well, it's only about thirty miles," said Carmichael.

"*Only*," said the driver.

"What?"

"You said it was only thirty miles, but I'm glad it ain't any more."

"How long do you think it'll take us?"

"Well, we better allow about an hour and a half."

"To go thirty miles?"

"I seen it take six hours, when there was big drifts. If I was you, Mr. Carmichael, I'd bundle up warmer than that. Don't you have a pair of arctics?"

"Not with me," said Carmichael. He was wearing a topcoat, fedora, and low shoes. "I've put away all my winter clothes. I'm on my way to Africa."

"Try Dugan. Maybe he has a pair somebody left behind. And maybe you could get him to give you the loan of his fur coat. He has a big fur coat he wears. You ought to have a muffler to go around your ears. And warm gloves. You want *me* to ask Dugan?"

Carmichael hesitated.

"Mr. Carmichael, I know you only think it's thirty miles, but it's liable to be five below zero by the time we get to Mount Clemens. And if anything happens to the car we could be out there all night."

"It's been nowhere near that cold here," said Carmichael. "I haven't needed anything heavier than this coat."

"Yeah, but your office was only two-three doors away from the hotel."

"Well, I don't want to hold up the parade," said Carmichael. He returned to the hotel, having paid no attention to the rest of us who had stood waiting for him to assign us to the cars.

"Pig-headed son of a bitch," said King. "While we stand here freezing." He turned to me. "You and Edmunds might just as well get in the Studebaker. He'll want me and probably Thompson with him in the Paige."

Carmichael came back wearing a bearskin coat, arctics, and sealskin cap. He was accompanied by Dugan bearing three Thermos lunch kits. Dugan gave one to Edmunds and me. "Don't know how long the coffee'll stay hot, but it's better than nothing," said Dugan.

"You don't happen to have a couple of pints of whiskey," said Edmunds.

"You know I don't handle it," said Dugan. "But you know where you can get it. There's two ham sandwiches in there for you."

"What about our driver? Doesn't he rate anything?" said Edmunds.

"Mr. Carmichael didn't say anything," said Dugan.

"I'll be all right," said our driver. He held up a pint of whiskey. But thanks for askin'."

In a few minutes we were under way, and the moment we left the town we were in almost total darkness, broken only by the dashlight and the beam from the Studebaker's headlights. We lost sight of the Paige. "Carney must be in a hurry," said our driver.

"Carmichael," said Edmunds.

"No, I mean Carney. That's the other driver. But I ain't gonna try and keep up with him. I don't want to break a cross-link. The hell with that. You warm enough back there?"

"Fine, so far," said Edmunds.

"The secret is get one blanket under you and one over you. The best thing is if you have a dame with you. That keeps the old circulation going."

"The best thing is to stay home and have the dame in bed with you," said Edmunds.

"Well, you won't have a hard time finding them once we get to Mount Clemens. Lithuanian. Polish. Irish. But this being a Saturday night, some of them went to confession. Some of them won't go out with you Saturday night, or if they do it's a waste of time. They won't even have a beer with you after twelve o'clock midnight. Sunday night, that's an altogether different story. Talk about your hypocrites, them Catholics."

"You're talking to one right now," I said.

"Oh. Well, if you want to offer me out when we get to Mount Clemens."

"I will," I said. My stomach fell at the thought of having a fist fight at the end of our journey, but I had not learned to keep my mouth shut.

"I don't have anything against all Catholics. Carney's my best friend."

"Ah, shut up," I said.

"Both of you shut up," said Edmunds.

Conversation was suspended, but the absence of talk did not produce quiet. Now we listened to and thought about every sound, and most of the sounds were ominous, beginning with the rising and falling of the wind and the frequent changing down to second gear as we left the main highway. The side curtains were secure, we were not uncomfortable, but any minute we could expect the isinglass in the curtains to crack, and when that happened the wind and snow would rush in. Edmunds and I were dressed warmly in sheepskin-lined reefers, woolen helmets that rolled down over our ears and throats, and six-buckle arctics, the cold-weather clothes we had brought with us to Number 4. Our driver wore a plaid mackinaw and a helmet like ours. If the car broke down we would not freeze to death so long as we stayed inside—and the wind did not tear the curtains to shreds. We were moving slowly, very slowly. We came to a mining patch called Valley View—every county in Pennsylvania, I suppose, has a Valley View—which I knew to be less than ten miles from Number 4, and it had taken us half an hour to get that far. And the worst was yet to come. I had been over that road many times, in summer and winter, and one thing I remembered about it now was that between Valley View and Mount Clemens the road cut through practically virgin forest. There was no settlement large enough to be called a hamlet. My superiors, who had lived in jungles and spoke Swahili and Cantonese, probably had no idea how close they were to a wilderness. The bear and the rattlesnake were hibernating, but there were other hazards and the worst of them now was the cold. Every winter, in that part of the country, we would hear of men who had been found frozen to death and of others who had lost a foot by frostbite.

"You're not very talkative," said Edmunds.

"You told me to shut up," I said.

He laughed. "Well, I give you permission to talk now," he said. "I want to stay awake. I learned that in Wyoming and Montana. Don't fall asleep in this kind of weather, or you may not wake up."

"We'll be all right as long as we keep going."

"How much longer have we got to go?" he said.

"A little over half way," I said.

"We got about twenty miles to go," said the driver. "If we don't get to Mount Clemens by ha' past ten Carney said he'd come back and look for us."

"Well, at least we won't be stuck out here all night," said Edmunds.

"That's providing Carney gets through all right. If Carney gets stuck, we're stuck too."

"That's a pleasant thought," said Edmunds.

"Well, it's not so bad," said our driver. "If Carney don't get there by ten they'll send a Company truck out after us. We got nothing to worry about."

I was not so sure. "How big a truck?" I said.

"It's about a two-ton Dodge. One of them they got for the maintenance crews. They got them fixed up so they can stay out here all night if they have to. For when they have to repair a high tension line. I seen them go out when it was ten below. I wouldn't have that job if they paid me a hundred dollars a week. Sixty-six thousand volts. You don't even have to *touch* the God damn line. You get too close and the juice jumps out at you. I seen a guy got too close and it pops a hole right through the top of his skull. That's what sixty-six thousand volts'll do to you. Right through the top of your skull, a hole about the size of a silver dollar. I wouldn't work around that stuff if they paid me *two* hundred dollars a week."

"Well, it's better than freezing to death," said Edmunds.

"Maybe you're right at that," said the driver. "I never thought of it that way. Uh-oh."

Up ahead, in the middle of the road, stood Carney, waving both arms, flagging us down. The first thing I noticed was that the smoke was coming out of the exhaust pipe, which at least indicated that the Paige had not stalled.

"Get in," said our driver. "What's wrong, Carney?"

Carney got in the front seat, turned and addressed Edmunds. "You got another passenger. Mr. King is riding the rest of the way with you."

"How does that happen?" said Edmunds.

"Well, I guess that's not for me to say, but they had a little argument and Mr. King wants to ride with you."

"That's all right with us. Tell him to bring his blanket and come on back," said Edmunds. "Are you all right otherwise?"

"Yes, I guess so," said Carney.

"You don't seem too sure," said Edmunds.

"Well, I guess I ought to tell you. King took a poke at him."

"At Carmichael, I suppose?" said Edmunds.

"He gave him a bloody nose."

"A little argument. So Carmichael ordered him to ride with us."

"No. I did," said Carney.

"*You* did?"

"I told them, I said one of them had to change cars. They were swingin' away at one another back there, and I stopped the car. As far as I know they're still at it. They're acting like a couple of God damn kids."

"So you took charge. Well, good for you, Carney."

"I guess it'll mean my job, but those two bastards, rassling around back there, they could send me into a ditch."

"Sergeant Carney, of the 103d Engineers," said our driver. "You tell 'em, Carney."

"Supposed to be gentlemen, but acting like a couple of God damn hoodlums. I'll get another job."

"Don't worry about that now," said Edmunds. "Tell King to come on back here."

We watched King, being pulled out of the Paige by Carney and dragging a blanket along the snow, staggering toward us. He was talking to himself; you could see him.

Our driver switched his headlight off and on to signal to Carney that King was safely with us, and the Paige got under way again. King climbed in with Edmunds and me, and the Studebaker began to move.

"At your age you ought to have more sense," said Edmunds.

"Sense? If I'd had more sense, you're right. I'd have given him a *good* beating twenty years ago. I don't know why I didn't. He gave me plenty of cause to. In Quito, twenty years ago, I found out he was going over my head, sending back his confidential reports to the home office. That's when I should have given it to him, when I could have wiped up the floor with him. But I got in a couple of good punches tonight."

"Yes, and you've cooked your goose," said Edmunds.

"Have I? We'll see. And what if I have? They can retire me on half-pay and I'll open up a gas station in Florida. Maybe I'll let you come down and join me there, Edmunds. You're not getting any younger either."

"*You're* reverting to second childhood."

"Well, I hope it'll be better than my first," said King. "I grew up in a Methodist parsonage and that wasn't much fun." He took a deep sigh and turned over on his side. He was sitting in the left corner, Edmunds was in the middle, I was in the right corner. Now the going got really rough, and instead of being excited, as I had been, I was afraid. Up ahead the Paige, a heavier low-built car, was breaking the path for us, otherwise we could not have gone on. Several times we dropped down into low gear and our driver was zig-zagging to gain traction and keep moving. He was a good snow driver, I had to say that for him; he knew how to use the momentum of the car to keep from getting wedged in. Our undercarriage was higher off the ground than that of the Paige, but even so I could feel the transmission scraping the false crown in the center of the road. There was, of course, only one path. At best, in summer conditions, the road was narrow, not wide enough for two big trucks to pass. Now, if a third car had come from the direction of Mount Clemens we would have had to get out and shovel snow to make the path wide—and I knew who would be swinging the shovels: the two drivers and I. Maybe Thompson would have helped out; he was younger than the others of our party. But I was sure that Carmichael would have ordered me, as the low-ranking member of the party, to pitch in. I hoped that if another car came from Mount Clemens it would contain five hard-muscled Lithuanians.

As the Studebaker zig-zagged we in the back seat were jounced and jostled. "I'm lucky Gaston—in the middle again," said Edmunds.

"Do you want me to change places with you?" I said.

"No, stay where you are. You two keep me warm."

"Is King asleep?" I said.

"Yes, and I'm going to let him sleep. We must be more than half way," said Edmunds.

"We got about twelve miles," said the driver. "The last four miles is the worst, all uphill. We'll make it."

"You're doing very well. What's your name?"

"Stone. Ed Stone. They call me Stoney."

"Well, I'm going to give you a good report," said Edmunds.

"That'll help, in case they fire Carney," said Stone. "I ought to be due for a promotion, but there's no job for me as long as Carney's there."

"Don't raise your hopes on that score. Knowing Mr. Carmichael, I doubt if Carney'll be fired."

"Well, maybe you could see I got some overtime," said Stone.

"That's not my business, but I'll give you a good report," said Edmunds. The car lurched, and I could not guess whether

Stone was taking out his disappointment by mistreating the car or was making an honest zig-zag. In any case, King was thrown across Edmunds's chest and Edmunds impatiently pushed him back in his corner. I laughed.

"Lucky Gaston," I said.

"Don't get fresh," said Edmunds. "We've had enough for one evening, without a fresh kid to boot."

On the uphill climb I could almost literally follow each revolution of the wheels by the sound. The windshield wiper, operated by hand, gave Stone a view of the road ahead, but I could no longer tell where we were except to estimate by the steepness of the grade how far up the mountain we were. I had also lost track of time, and I was not sufficiently curious to take off my gauntlets and look at my watch. Over and over again I resigned myself to my fate, but the pessimistic composure did not last; the slightest change in the speed of the revolutions of the wheels put my imagination to work again. I had the disadvantage over Edmunds of knowing that the last mile or so was dangerous in daylight in any season; a car could drop three or four hundred feet before being stopped by timber, and here, of course, the wind was at its worst. I very nearly prayed, and my refusal to pray probably was prayer of a kind.

Then we were there. Out of the black darkness of the valley and the mountain road, and on the summit of Mount Clemens. Even through the isinglass and iced-over windshield we could discern the lights of the town, and we could feel the level progress of the car.

"Well, we made it," said Stone.

"Good work," said Edmunds. He reached over and shook King. "Wake up, fellow. We're almost there."

"You want to go right to the hotel?" said Stone.

"I sure do," said Edmunds. "Do you realize we never thought about the coffee? I'll bet it's still warm. But I'm going to have a drink."

"That's why I asked you," said Stone. "There's a couple places open where you can get booze. You can't at the hotel."

"No thanks, I have a quart in my suitcase," said Edmunds. "Come on, King. Wake up. I'm surprised he didn't wake up when I said I had a quart. King!"

But King was dead.

Christmas Poem

BILLY WARDEN had dinner with his father and mother and sister. "I suppose this is the last we'll see of you this vacation," said his father.

"Oh, I'll be in and out to change my shirt," said Billy.

"My, we're quick on the repartee," said Barbara Warden. "The gay young sophomore."

"What are *you*, Bobby dear? A drunken junior?" said Billy.

"Now, I don't think that was called for," said their mother.

"Decidedly *un*-called for," said their father. "What *are* your plans?"

"Well, I was hoping I could borrow the chariot," said Billy.

"Yes, we anticipated that," said his father. "What I meant was, are you planning to go away anywhere? Out of town?"

"Well, that depends. There's a dance in Reading on the twenty-seventh I'd like to go to, and I've been invited to go skiing in Montrose."

"Skiing? Can you ski?" said his mother.

"All Dartmouth boys ski, or pretend they can," said his sister.

"Isn't that dangerous? I suppose if you were a Canadian, but I've never known anyone to go skiing around here. I thought they had to have those big—I don't know—scaffolds, I guess you'd call them."

"You do, for jumping, Mother. But skiing isn't all jumping," said Billy.

"Oh, it isn't? I've only seen it done in the newsreels. I never really saw the point of it, although I suppose if you did it well it would be the same sensation as flying. I often dream about flying."

"I haven't done much jumping," said Billy.

"Then I take it you'll want to borrow the car on the twenty-seventh, and what about this trip to Montrose?" said his father.

"I don't exactly know where Montrose is," said Mrs. Warden.

"It's up beyond Scranton," said her husband. "That would mean taking the car overnight. I'm just trying to arrange some kind of a schedule. Your mother and I've been invited to one or two things, but I imagine we can ask our friends to take us there and bring us back. However, we only have the one car, and Bobby's entitled to her share."

"Of course she is. Of course I more or less counted on her to, uh, to spend most of her time in Mr. Roger Taylor's Dort."

"It isn't a Dort. It's a brand new Marmon, something I doubt you'll ever be able to afford."

"Something I doubt Roger'd ever be able to afford if it took any brains to afford one. So he got rid of the old Dort, did he?"

"He never had a Dort, and you know it," said Bobby.

"Must we be so disagreeable, the first night home?" said Mrs. Warden. "I know there's no meanness in it, but it doesn't *sound* nice."

"When would you be going to Montrose?" said Mr. Warden. "What date?"

"Well, if I go it would be a sort of a house party," said Billy.

"In other words, not just overnight?" said his father. "Very well, suppose you tell us how many nights?"

"I'm invited for the twenty-eighth, twenty-ninth, and thirtieth," said Billy. "That would get me back in time to go to the Assembly on New Year's Eve."

"What that amounts to, you realize, is having possession of the car from the twenty-seventh to the thirtieth or thirty-first," said his father.

"Yes, I realize that," said Billy.

"Do you still want it, to keep the car that long, all for yourself?" said his father.

"Well, I didn't have it much last summer, when I was working. And I save you a lot of money on repairs. I ground the valves, cleaned the spark plugs. A lot of things I did. I oiled and greased it myself."

"Yes, I have to admit you do your share of that," said his father. "But if you keep the car that long, out of town, it just means we are without a car for four days, at the least."

There was a silence.

"I really won't need the car very much after Christmas," said Bobby. "After I've done my shopping and delivered my presents."

"Thank you," said Billy.

"Well, of course not driving myself, I never use it," said Mrs. Warden.

"That puts it up to me," said Mr. Warden. "If I were Roger Taylor's father I'd give you two nice big Marmons for Christmas, but I'm not Mr. Taylor. Not by about seven hundred thousand dollars, from what I hear. Is there anyone else from around here that's going to Montrose?"

"No."

"Then it isn't one of your Dartmouth friends?" said Mr. Warden. "Who will you be visiting?"

"It's a girl named Henrietta Cooper. She goes to Russell Sage. I met her at Dartmouth, but that's all. I mean, she has no other connection with it."

"Russell Sage," said his mother. "We know somebody that has a daughter there. I know who it was. That couple we met at the Blakes'. Remember, the Blakes entertained for them last winter? The husband was with one of the big electrical companies."

"General Electric, in Schenectady," said Mr. Warden. "Montrose ought to be on the Lehigh Valley, or the Lackawanna, if I'm not mistaken."

"The train connections are very poor," said Billy. "If I don't go by car, Henrietta's going to meet me in Scranton, but heck, I don't want to ask her to do that. I'd rather not go if I have to take the train."

"Well, I guess we can get along without the car for that long. But your mother and I are positively going to have to have it New Year's Eve. We're going to the Assembly, too."

"Thank you very much," said Billy.

"It does seem strange. Reading one night, and then the next day you're off in the opposite direction. You'd better make sure the chains are in good condition. Going over those mountains this time of year."

"A house party. Now what will you do on a house party in Montrose? Besides ski, that is?" said Mrs. Warden. "It sounds like a big house, to accommodate a lot of young people."

"I guess it probably is," said Billy. "I know they have quite a few horses. Henny rides in the Horse Show at Madison Square Garden."

"Oh, my. Then they must be very well-to-do," said his mother. "I always wanted to ride when I was a girl. To me there's nothing prettier than a young woman in a black riding habit, riding side-saddle. Something so elegant about it."

"I wouldn't think she rode side-saddle, but maybe she does," said Billy.

"Did you say you wanted to use the car tonight, too?" said his father.

"If nobody else is going to," said Billy.

"Barbara?" said Mr. Warden.

"No. Roger is calling for me at nine o'clock," said Barbara. "But I would like it tomorrow, all day if possible. I have a ton of shopping to do."

"I *still* haven't finished wrapping all *my* presents," said Mrs. Warden.

"I haven't even *bought* half of mine," said Barbara.

"You shouldn't leave everything to the last minute," said her mother. "I bought most of mine at sales, as far back as last January. Things are much cheaper after Christmas."

"Well, I guess I'm off to the races," said Billy. "Dad, could you spare a little cash?"

"How much?" said Mr. Warden.

"Well—ten bucks?"

"I'll take it off your Christmas present," said Mr. Warden.

"Oh, no, don't do that? I have ten dollars if you'll reach me my purse. It's on the sideboard," said Mrs. Warden.

"You must be flush," said Mr. Warden.

"Well, no, but I don't like to see you take it off Billy's Christmas present. That's as bad as opening presents ahead of time," said Mrs. Warden.

"Which certain people in this house do every year," said Barbara.

"Who could she possibly mean?" said Billy. "I opened one present, because it came from Brooks Brothers and I thought it might be something I could wear right away."

"And was it?" said his mother.

"Yes. Some socks. These I have on, as a matter of fact," said Billy. "They're a little big, but they'll shrink."

"Very snappy," said Barbara.

"Yes, and I don't know who they came from. There was no card."

"I'll tell you who they were from. They were from me," said Barbara.

"They were? Well, thanks. Just what I wanted," said Billy.

"Just what you asked me for, last summer," said Barbara.

"Did I? I guess I did. Thank you for remembering. Well, goodnight, all. Don't wait up. I'll be home before breakfast."

They muttered their goodnights and he left. He wanted to—almost wanted to—stay; to tell his father that he did not want a Marmon for Christmas, which would have been a falsehood; to tell his mother he loved her in spite of her being a nitwit; to talk to Bobby about Roger Taylor, who was not good enough for her. But this was his first night home and he had his friends to see. Bobby had Roger, his father and mother had each other; thus far he had no one. But it did not detract from his feeling for his family that he now preferred the livelier company of his friends. *They* all had families, too, and *they* would be at the drug store tonight. You didn't come home just to see the members of your family. As far as that goes, you got a Christmas vacation to celebrate the birth of the Christ child, but except for a few Catholics, who would go anywhere near a church? And besides, he could not talk to his family en masse. He would like to have a talk with his father, a talk with his sister, and he would enjoy a half hour of his mother's prattling. Those conversations would be personal if there were only two present, but with more than two present everyone had to get his say in and nobody said anything much. Oh, what was the use of making a lot of excuses? What was wrong with wanting to see your friends?

The starter in the Dodge seemed to be whining, "No . . . no . . . no . . ." before the engine caught. It reminded him of a girl, a girl who protested every bit of the way, and she was not just an imaginary girl. She was the girl he would telephone as soon as he got to the drug store, and he probably would be too late, thanks to the conversation with his family. Irma Hipple, her name was, and she was known as Miss Nipple. She lived up the hill in back of the Court House. The boys from the best families in town made a beeline for Irma as soon as they got home from school. Hopefully the boys who got a date with her would make a small but important purchase at the drug store, because you never knew when Irma might change her mind. A great many lies had been told about Irma, and the worst liars were the boys who claimed nothing but looked wise. Someone must have gotten all the way with Irma sometime, but Billy did not know who. It simply stood to reason that a girl who allowed so many boys to neck the hell out of her had delivered the goods sometime. She was twenty-one or -two and already she was beginning to lose her prettiness, probably because she could hold her liquor as well as any boy, and better than some. In her way she was a terrible snob. "That Roger Taylor got soaked to the gills," she would say. "That Teddy Choate thinks he's a cave man," or "I'm never going out with that Doctor Boyd again. Imagine a doctor snapping his cookies in the Stagecoach bar." Irma probably delivered the goods to the older men. Someone who went to Penn had seen her at the L'Aiglon supper club in Philadelphia with George W. Josling, who was manager of one of the new stock brokerage branches in town. There was a story around town that she had bitten Jerome Kuhn, the optometrist, who was old enough to be her father. It was hard to say what was true about Irma and what wasn't. She was a saleswoman in one of the department stores; she lived with her older sister and their father, who had one leg and was a crossing watchman for the Pennsy; she was always well dressed; she was pretty and full of pep. That much was true about her, and it was certainly true that she attracted men of all ages.

The telephone booth in the drug store was occupied, and two or three boys were queued up beside it. Billy Warden shook hands with his friends and with Russell Covington, the head soda jerk. He ordered a lemon phosphate and lit a cigarette and kept an eye on the telephone booth. The door of the booth buckled open and out came Teddy Choate, nodding. "All set," he said to someone. "Everything is copacetic. I'm fixed up with the Nipple. She thinks she can get Patsy Lurio for you."

Billy Warden wanted to hit him.

"Hello, there, Billy. When'd you get in?" said Teddy.

"Hello, Teddy. I got in on the two-eighteen," said Billy.

"I hear you're going to be at Henny Cooper's house party," said Teddy.

"Jesus, you're a busybody. How did you hear that?"

"From Henny, naturally. Christ, I've known her since we were five years old. She invited me, but I have to go to these parties in New York."

"Funny, she told me she didn't know anybody in Gibbsville," said Billy.

"She's a congenital liar. Everybody knows that. I saw her Friday in New York. She was at a tea dance I went to. You ever been to that place in Montrose?"

"No."

"They've got everything there. A six-car garage. Swimming pool. Four-hole golf course, but they have the tees arranged so you can play nine holes. God knows how many horses. The old boy made his money in railroad stocks, and he sure did spend it up there. Very hard to get to know, Mr. Cooper. But he was in Dad's class at New Haven and we've known the Coopers since the Year One. I guess it was really Henny's grandfather that made the first big pile. Yes, Darius L. Cooper. You come across his name in American History courses. I suppose he was an old crook. But Henny's father is altogether different. Very conservative. You won't see much of him at the house party, if he's there at all. They have an apartment at the Plaza, just the right size, their own furniture. I've been there many times, too."

"Then you do know them?" said Billy.

"Goodness, haven't I been telling you? We've known the Cooper family since the Year *One*," said Teddy. "Well, you have to excuse me. I have to whisper something to Russ Covington. Delicate matter. Got a date with the Nipple."

"You're excused," said Billy. He finished his phosphate and joined a group at the curbstone.

"What say, boy? I'll give you fifty to forty," said Andy Phillips.

"For how much?" said Billy.

"A dollar?"

"You're on," said Billy. They went down the block and upstairs to the poolroom. All the tables were busy save one, which was covered with black oilcloth. "What about the end table?" said Billy.

"Saving it," said Phil, the house man. "Getting up a crap game."

"How soon?"

"Right away. You want to get in?"

"I don't know. I guess so. What do you think, Andy?"

"I'd rather shoot pool," said Andy.

"You're gonna have a hell of a wait for a table," said Phil. "There's one, two, three, four—four Harrigan games going. And the first table just started shooting a hundred points for a fifty-dollar bet. You're not gonna hurry *them*."

"Let's go someplace else," said Andy.

"They'll all be crowded tonight. I think I'll get in the crap game," said Billy.

Phil removed the cover from the idle pool table and turned on the overhead lights, and immediately half a dozen young men gathered around it. "Who has the dice?" someone asked.

"I have," said Phil, shaking them in his half-open hand.

"Oh, great," said someone.

"You want to have a look at them?" said Phil. "You wouldn't know the difference anyway, but you can have a look. No? All right, I'm shooting a dollar. A dollar open."

"You're faded," said someone.

"Anybody else want a dollar?" said Phil.

"I'll take a dollar," said Billy Warden.

"A dollar to you, and a dollar to you. Anyone else? No? Okay. Here we go, and it's a nine. A niner, a niner, what could be finer. No drinks to a minor. And it's a five. Come on, dice, let's see that six-three for Phil. And it's a four? Come on, dice. Be nice. And it's a—a nine it is. Four dollars open. Billy, you want to bet the deuce?"

"You're covered," said Billy.

"You're covered," said the other bettor.

"Anybody else wish to participate? No? All right, eight dollars on the table, and—oh, what do I see there? A natural. The big six and the little one. Bet the four, Billy?"

"I'm with you," said Billy.

"I'm out," said the other bettor.

"I'm in," said a newcomer.

"Four dollars to you, four dollars to Mr. Warden. And here we go, and for little old Phil a—oh, my. The eyes of a snake. Back where you started from, Billy. House bets five dollars. Nobody wants the five? All right, any part of it."

"Two dollars," said Billy.

When it came his turn to take the dice he passed it up and chose instead to make bets on the side. Thus he nursed his stake until at one time he had thirty-eight or -nine dollars in his hands. The number of players was increasing, and all pretty much for the same reason: most of the boys had not yet got their Christmas money, and a crap game offered the best chance to add to the pre-Christmas bankroll.

"Why don't you drag?" said Andy Phillips. "Get out while you're ahead?"

"As soon as I have fifty dollars," said Billy.

The next time the shooter with the dice announced five dollars open, Billy covered it himself, won, and got the dice. In less than ten minutes he was cleaned, no paper money, nothing but the small change in his pants pocket. He looked around among the players, but there was no one whom he cared to borrow from. "Don't look at me," said Andy. "I have six bucks to last me till Christmas."

"Well, I have eighty-seven cents," said Billy. "Do you still want to spot me fifty to forty?"

"Sure. But not for a buck. You haven't got a buck," said Andy. "And I'm going to beat you."

They waited until a table was free, and played their fifty points, which Andy won, fifty to thirty-two. "I'll be big-hearted," said Andy. "I'll pay for the table."

"No, no. Thirty cents won't break me," said Billy. "Or do you want to play another? Give me fifty to thirty-five."

"No, I don't like this table. It's too high," said Andy.

"Well, what shall we do?" said Billy.

"The movies ought to be letting out pretty soon. Shall we go down and see if we can pick anything up?"

"Me with fifty-seven cents? And you with six bucks?"

"Well, you have the Dodge, and we could get a couple of pints on credit," said Andy.

"All right, we can try," said Billy. They left the poolroom and went down to the street and re-parked the Warden Dodge where they could observe the movie crowd on its way out. Attendance that night was slim, and passable girls in pairs nowhere to be seen. The movie theater lights went out. "Well, so much for that," said Billy. "Five after eleven."

"Let's get a pint," said Andy.

"I honestly don't feel like it, Andy," said Billy.

"I didn't mean you were to buy it. I'll split it with you."

"I understood that part," said Billy. "Just don't feel like drinking."

"Do you have to *feel* like drinking at Dartmouth? Up at State we just drink."

"Oh, sure. Big hell-raisers," said Billy. "Kappa Betes and T.N.E.'s. 'Let's go over to Lock Haven and get slopped.' I heard all about State while I was at Mercersburg. That's why I didn't go there—one of the reasons."

"Is that so?" said Andy. "Well, if all you're gonna do is sit here and razz State, I think I'll go down to Mulhearn's and have a couple beers. You should have had sense enough to quit when you were thirty-some bucks ahead."

"Darius L. Cooper didn't quit when he was thirty bucks ahead."

"Who? You mean the fellow with the cake-eater suit? His name wasn't Cooper. His name is Minzer or something like that. Well, the beers are a quarter at Mulhearn's. We could have six fours are twenty-four. We could have twelve beers apiece. I'll lend you three bucks."

"No thanks," said Billy. "I'll take you down to Mulhearn's and then I think I'll go home and get some shut-eye. I didn't get any sleep on the train last night."

"That's what's the matter with you? All right, disagreeable. Safe at last in your trundle bed."

"How do you know that? That's a Dartmouth song," said Billy.

"I don't know, I guess I heard *you* sing it," said Andy. "Not tonight, though. I'll walk to Mulhearn's. I'll see you tomorrow."

"All right, Andy. See you tomorrow," said Billy. He watched his friend, with his felt hat turned up too much in front and back, his thick-soled Whitehouse & Hardy's clicking on the sidewalk, his joe-college swagger, his older brother's leather coat. Life was simple for Andy and always would be. In two more years he would finish at State, a college graduate, and he would come home and take a job in Phillips Brothers Lumber Yard, marry a local girl, join the Lions or Rotary, and play volleyball at the Y.M.C.A. His older brother had already done all those things, and Andy was Fred Phillips all over again.

The Dodge, still warm, did not repeat the whining protest of a few hours earlier in the evening. He put it in gear and headed for home. He hoped his father and mother would have gone to bed. "What the hell's the matter with me?" he said. "Nothing's right tonight."

He put the car in the garage and entered the house by the kitchen door. He opened the refrigerator door, and heard his father's voice. "Is that you, son?"

"Yes, it's me. I'm getting a glass of milk."

His father was in the sitting-room and made no answer. Billy drank a glass of milk and turned out the kitchen lights. He went to the sitting-room. His father, in shirtsleeves and smoking a pipe, was at the desk. "You doing your bookkeeping?" said Billy.

"No."

"What *are* you doing?"

"Well, if you must know, I was writing a poem. I was trying to express my appreciation to your mother."

"Can I see it?"

"Not in a hundred years," said Mr. Warden. "Nobody will ever see this but her—if she ever does."

"I never knew you wrote poetry."

"Once a year, for the past twenty-six years, starting with the first Christmas we were engaged. So far I haven't missed a year, but it doesn't get any easier. But by God, the first thing Christmas morning she'll say to me, 'Where's my poem?' Never speaks about it the rest of the year, but it's always the first thing she asks me the twenty-fifth of December."

"Has she kept them all?" said Billy.

"That I never asked her, but I suppose she has."

"Does she write you one?" said Billy.

"Nope. Well, what did you do tonight? You're home early, for you."

"Kind of tired. I didn't get much sleep last night. We got on the train at White River Junction and nobody could sleep."

"Well, get to bed and sleep till noon. That ought to restore your energy."

"Okay. Goodnight, Dad."

"Goodnight, son," said his father. "Oh, say. You had a long distance call. You're to call the Scranton operator, no matter what time you get in."

"Thanks," said Billy. "Goodnight."

"Well, aren't you going to put the call in? I'll wait in the kitchen."

"No, I know who it is. I'll phone them tomorrow."

"That's up to you," said Mr. Warden. "Well, goodnight again."

"Goodnight," said Billy. He went to his room and took off his clothes, to the bathroom and brushed his teeth. He put out the light beside his bed and lay there. He wondered if Henrietta Cooper's father had ever written a poem to her mother. But he knew the answer to that.

EDITOR'S NOTE

CHRONOLOGY

NOTE ON THE TEXTS

NOTES

Editor's Note

John O'Hara never tired of complaining about how underestimated he was, and he had a point, even if he made it far too often. He was a gifted and sensitive writer, with talents quite different from his those of his more highly regarded contemporaries: Hemingway, Faulkner, Fitzgerald. His strength and his limitation was that he was stubbornly earthbound. There are no similes in his work, no flights of lyricism or fancy writing, no hints of a deeper meaning beyond the moment. Nothing in O'Hara is "like" anything else. Things are vibrant and valuable for their own sake, and he described them—the make of a car, the cut of a suit, the song on the radio, the brand of cigarette, the sound of a broken tire chain on a snowy morning—with a scrupulousness that bordered on devotion.

O'Hara was also a remarkably prolific writer. He published fourteen novels in his lifetime, and hundreds of short stories, almost too many to count. The sixty stories in this volume amount to just a small fraction. In deciding what to reprint here, I worried less about choosing stories that were representative of O'Hara's vast and varied body of work than about singling out the ones that seemed to me the best, least dated, most accessible—stories that demonstrate why O'Hara is still worth reading. Without my quite intending it, though, the final selection also offers a pretty fair picture of O'Hara's range and variety. There are stories that run barely a page or so and stories that are novella-length; stories from the thirties, forties, fifties, and sixties; stories set in New York, in Hollywood, and in Gibbsville, Pennsylvania, O'Hara's fictional version of Pottsville, the town where he grew up and which in many ways he never really left. Missing here are some early, sketchlike pieces O'Hara wrote for *The New Yorker*, and the ones he wrote about the nightclub emcee Pal Joey, which eventually became the source for the Broadway musical. (Those will be included in a future Library of America volume.)

Pottsville, when O'Hara was born, in 1905, was the prosperous commercial center of Pennsylvania's anthracite region. His father was a successful and respected physician there, and the family belonged to the country-club, horse-riding gentry. Yet because he was Irish and Catholic, O'Hara felt himself to be an outsider, and all his life, even after he had become wealthy and famous, he retained an outsider's neediness and sullen defensiveness. His face was pressed against a glass that sometimes wasn't there. But the way outsiders do, he also became an uncanny observer of the world around him, someone who noticed everything. His father's early death, in 1925—together with Dr. O'Hara's history, it turned out, of living far beyond his means— ended O'Hara's dream of going to Yale, which would have been for him, he fantasized, what Princeton was for Fitzgerald. Instead, he got a more practical and—for his kind of writer—more useful education knocking around, spending marathon hours in speakeasies and working at a series of small-town newspaper jobs. He became, among other things, one of the great listeners of American fiction, able to write dialogue that sounded the way people really talk, and he also learned the eavesdropper's secret—how often people leave unsaid what is really on their minds.

In the late twenties O'Hara began publishing in *The New Yorker*, beginning an association that, with time out for feuds and hurt feelings, lasted some forty years, to the immense benefit of both parties. For O'Hara the magazine became a place where he could develop his talent almost experimentally—without the pressures and expectations that went with novel-writing—and he, in turn, became one of the magazine's most frequent and valued contributors. He helped invent what eventually became known as "the *New Yorker* story," one in which nothing necessarily "happens," in the old-fashioned sense, but in which some crucial loss or discovery is revealed just by implication. In lesser hands this kind of story-writing eventually became formulaic, a caricature of itself, but O'Hara brought to it a Chekhovian rigor, delicacy, and openness to possibility.

O'Hara's earliest efforts for *The New Yorker*, like most of what the magazine was publishing then, were virtually plotless little sketches— often snatches of overheard dialogue: a lonely man in a diner, for example, reminiscing about an old girlfriend. He also worked on three ongoing series: stories recounting the proceedings of the Orange County Afternoon Delphian Society, a New Jersey ladies' club; stories about a company called Hagedorn & Brown, a New York manufacturer of paint and varnish; and some stories that take the form of reports from the greens committee of a suburban country club. These stories are all satirical, making fun of Babbitry, small-town hypocrisy, and narrow-mindedness, but the humor is mostly as fond as it is pointed and the characters are never caricatures. Similarly, O'Hara's slice-of-life sketches are never condescending, and, perhaps because he continued writing from outsiderdom, a habit of affection and generosity toward his people, even the meanest and most disagreeable, went on to become an O'Hara hallmark.

The first of his *New Yorker* stories that O'Hara thought worthy of book publication was "On His Hands," the first story included here, a monologue in which a callow young man reveals more about himself than he intends to. It was republished in 1935 in O'Hara's first collection, *The Doctor's Son and Other Stories,* a volume that catches O'Hara in the process of becoming the writer we know. There, among the sketches, are a handful of stories as good as anything O'Hara ever wrote, including the long autobiographical title story, O'Hara's earliest account of his fraught relationship with his formidable father—a love story, really, if a frustrated, unrequited one—and "Over the River and Through the Wood," a formally daring story remarkable (especially for a writer still in his twenties) in its ability to evoke the mind of a sixty-five-year-old who has just ruined his life. O'Hara's talent didn't evolve, exactly—for a while he went on writing sketches, doing finger exercises, so to speak—but suddenly it found its proper scope. There are traces of Hemingway here, a hint of Fitzgerald, but the voice is unmistakably his own, brisk with the confidence of a young man who already knows his way around in the world.

All the pieces in O'Hara's next collection, *Files on Parade,* published in 1939, are full-fledged stories, and yet they retain, as do most of the stories published over the next decade, a sketchlike lightness and brevity—they grab your attention before you know where they're going. O'Hara later boasted that he wrote most of them in just a single sitting, and at *The New Yorker* he became famous for refusing to revise them afterward if the editors thought some clarification was needed. Yet a sense of speed and of economy is just what makes the best of these stories so thrilling. They seem to skim over the surface before allowing the reader to plunge into moments of unexpected depth and feeling.

In 1949 O'Hara pretty much quit writing stories and he didn't resume for more than a decade. He had been quarreling with *The New Yorker,* because he felt, among other things, that the stories he wrote for the magazine were so specialized he couldn't sell them elsewhere, and so he should be paid a kill fee for those that didn't work out. *The New Yorker*'s very negative review of his novel *A Rage to Live* was the last straw. He poured his energy into writing novels, which, as he never tired of pointing out, had become far more profitable. O'Hara returned to the fold in 1960, allowing *The New Yorker* to publish his novella "Imagine Kissing Pete" (the title is one of O'Hara's most provocative and inspired), and a flood of stories followed, close to a hundred in just the next three years. "I discovered I could begin again and do it better," O'Hara wrote. "I had an apparently inexhaustible urge to express an unlimited supply of short story ideas. No writing has ever come more easily to me."

Many of these new stories were longer and plottier than those that preceded them. Several of them are narrated by a successful writer named James Malloy, an O'Hara alter ego, and take the form of reminiscence. O'Hara had by then made a very happy third marriage, to Katharine Bryan, and, for decades a notoriously angry drinker, had given up alcohol entirely. He was easier in his own skin, and it shows a little in the writing: there are fewer stories about loneliness, isolation, or exclusion. Many of these later stories are set in the present—Lyndon Johnson is president, and people who used to go to bars or speakeasies are staying home and watching television—but some of the best revisit the tone and setting of the Gibbsville stories of the thirties and forties: "How Old, How Young," for example, a story of mismatched lovers, with an ending made thrillingly sensuous for not being spelled out, and "Christmas Poem," a story of late-adolescent unhappiness and frustration that ends on a note of piercing sweetness.

O'Hara wrote not about what he imagined but about what he knew, which was a lot—more than most writers. He knew about lowlife and high society, nightclubs and newsrooms, Broadway and Hollywood, politicians, bootleggers, and call girls. He knew, firsthand, all about drinking and hangovers, and understood the way Prohibition both corroded middle-class morality, lending even a country-club cocktail a faint tang of corruption, and bound men and women together in an aura of libidinous intimacy. He knew, probably better than any other American writer, about social class in this country: about all the subtle markers and distinctions used to indicate rungs in the hierarchy, and about how rigid and how fragile the system is, a maze of envy, snobbery, and insecurity.

O'Hara also knew a great deal about sex, and even became a little tiresome about it, reminding us, long after we needed reminding, of how helplessly carnal we are. But he wrote honestly and unabashedly about desire, male and female, at a time when other writers were more circumspect. He also wrote a lot about love (not always the same thing) and the many forms it takes. He was especially interested in the suddenness with which love can strike and then leave, or else the way it lingers and reignites, and, as with his affection for his father, the pain of love that's not returned at all. It's not uncommon in O'Hara for people to be in love without being lovers, and a number of his better stories present love recollected in something like tranquility, which makes it seem even more fleeting and precious. Seldom hazy or sentimental, O'Hara believed in emotional truth as much as in factual accuracy. The last thing he would have said about his work is that it was filled with a hidden sweetness, and yet it's there beneath the toughness and the frankness—a steady pulse of sympathy and lively affection.

Charles McGrath
March 2016

Chronology

1905   Born John Henry O'Hara on January 31, in Pottsville, Pennsylvania, first of seven children of Dr. Patrick Henry O'Hara and Katherine Delaney O'Hara. Named after John Henry Swaving, a Pottsville physician and friend of Dr. O'Hara's. (Patrick, b. 1867, was the son of Major Michael J. O'Hara, a Civil War veteran born in Ballina, County Mayo, Ireland, and Mary Franey, born in Shenandoah, Pennsylvania. He was a Catholic, a staunch teetotaler, and an amateur boxer. Attended Niagara College and medical school at the University of Pennsylvania; practiced medicine in Shenandoah and New Orleans before setting up practice in Pottsville in the early 1890s and becoming a surgeon renowned for trepanning, a frequent operation because of many mining accidents in the region. Katherine, b. 1880, was the daughter of Joseph Israel Delaney, owner of a prosperous general store in Lykens, Pennsylvania, and Alice Roark Delaney, formerly of Swatara, Pennsylvania; born to Quaker parents and orphaned at a young age, Joseph Delaney converted to Catholicism at age fourteen. Katherine attended a Sacred Heart finishing school outside Philadelphia, spoke French, and played tennis and the piano. She and Patrick were married on November 18, 1903, and at the time of their first son's birth they are living at 125 Mahantongo Street, in a building owned by Dr. O'Hara, whose office is downstairs. Pottsville is then a prosperous town of about 25,000 in the heart of Pennsylvania's anthracite country, known locally as "The Region." Mahantongo—which becomes Lantenengo in O'Hara's novels and stories set in fictional "Gibbsville," based on Pottsville—is the town's best address.)

1907   Sister Mary is born.

1909   Brother Joseph is born. O'Hara teaches himself to read.

1910   As he will throughout his childhood, spends part of the summer at his maternal grandparents' home in Lykens, about thirty miles from Pottsville. He grows particularly close to his grandfather.

1911   Brother Martin is born.

1912   O'Hara is enrolled in Miss Katie Carpenter's private
           school.

1913–17   Dr. O'Hara purchases home at 606 Mahantongo Street,
           an Italianate townhouse formerly owned by the Yuengling
           family, owners of Pottsville's largest and most famous
           brewery, and moves his family there but retains his office
           at 125 Mahantongo. He also owns the 160-acre Oakland
           Farm, six miles southwest of Pottsville, where he raises
           Jersey cattle and plays gentleman farmer. The family, well-
           to-do and respected, owns five automobiles and keeps
           several horses; young O'Hara becomes an accomplished
           horseman and takes weekly instruction at the Misses
           Linder's School of Dance. Dr. O'Hara belongs to the
           town's best clubs, and he and his wife are invited annually
           to the Pottsville Assembly, the town's grandest social occa-
           sion. O'Hara attends St. Patrick's School, a Catholic
           school across the street from the family's home. Brother
           Thomas is born in 1914 and brother James in 1916.

1917   O'Hara begins serving as an altar boy at St. Patrick's
           Church in Pottsville. Continues for about two years, then
           gradually drifts away from the church.

1918   Wins his first public recognition for writing talent, first
           prize for the best composition in his class at St. Patrick's
           School.

1919   Brother Eugene is born. By now O'Hara is chauffeuring
           his father around the Pottsville area on house calls, a task
           he will later fictionalize in the long story "The Doctor's
           Son," and is a precocious smoker and drinker, already
           coming home drunk on occasion. Relationship with father
           begins to sour; when he refuses father's offer to deposit
           $10,000 in a savings account for him if he agrees to
           become a doctor, father's disappointment in him becomes
           more or less permanent.

1920   Sister Kathleen is born. In February, enrolls at Fordham
           Preparatory School in the Bronx, New York. Some week-
           ends he stays with his maternal aunt and uncle, Mary and
           John McKee, in their home at 538 Central Avenue in East
           Orange, New Jersey. Also spends time visiting Manhattan
           and discovering the nightlife there. Works in summer for
           the Pennsylvania Railroad as a callboy, making sure that

train crews are notified of their working hours. He returns in the fall to Fordham Prep, where his unruly ways come into conflict with Jesuit discipline.

1921   Expelled from Fordham Prep in June. Father, as punishment for poor performance at school, has him work as manual laborer on the railroad, greasing locomotives and loading baggage. Enrolls in the fall in the Keystone State Normal School in Kutztown, Pennsylvania, a coeducational boarding school lacking the prestige of the elite schools that routinely send their students to Ivy League colleges. (By this point, O'Hara has become fixated on going to Yale, an ambition it takes him decades to shed.) But O'Hara finds having girls around him a compensation. Kutztown, he later recalled, "was a candy store, and I had a very sweet tooth."

1922   Refuses the principal's order to stop dating a daughter of one of Keystone's trustees, and is dismissed in June. (The principal's last name, Rothermel, will turn up in *From the Terrace* [1959], attached to one of the more despicable characters in O'Hara's fiction.) In Pottsville, spends a year working at various jobs: soda jerk, surveyor, and "evaluating engineer" for a local firm, traveling the region and taking inventory of mines and power plants.

1923   Begins dating twenty-two-year-old Margaretta Archbald, an elegant young woman whose wealthy Protestant family disapproves of O'Hara on numerous grounds, not limited to his age, lack of clear career plans, and religious background; relationship lasts fitfully for more than seven years. In fall, enrolls in the Niagara University Preparatory School, in Niagara, New York, on the grounds of his father's alma mater.

1924   Chosen as Niagara's valedictorian and class poet in June, but fails to graduate because of his drunken celebration the night before the ceremony. In the autumn, hired by Harry Silliman, the publisher of the Pottsville *Journal,* to work as a cub reporter, at first without pay but soon at a salary of six dollars per week. Reports on local crime.

1925   On March 18, father, afflicted with Bright's disease, dies of kidney failure at the age of fifty-seven. His last words to his son are said to be "Poor John!" Funeral has cortège of forty cars, but the family is plunged into financial ruin:

Dr. O'Hara left no will, so under Pennsylvania law the state claims one-third of his estate, which is in any case encumbered by debts and mortgages. The farm, cars, and horses all have to be sold, and O'Hara abandons his dream of attending Yale. Invited in May to celebrate the Pottsville *Journal*'s one hundredth anniversary by writing an account of his eight months there as a reporter.

1926 Fails to get a job with a local bootlegger, who tells him, "You're too good for this." In low spirits, becomes a familiar figure at Pottsville's roadhouses and speakeasies, where he develops a reputation for being an unpleasant drunk. Fired from the *Journal*.

1927 Hired in January as a reporter for the Tamaqua *Courier*, newspaper based not far from Pottsville, and works there until March, when he is let go. Begins contributing several items to "The Conning Tower," the syndicated column of "F.P.A." (Franklin Pierce Adams). In summer, gets a job as a waiter on the passenger liner *George Washington*, which takes him to Germany and back. Leaves Pottsville in October in an unsuccessful search for a newspaper job somewhere in the Midwest; gets as far as Chicago, where he stays briefly before returning home in November, deeply depressed.

1928 Decides to look for work in New York City, and lives at first with his maternal aunt Mary in East Orange. Hired in March as a reporter and rewrite man on the New York *Herald Tribune*, having been recommended by Franklin Pierce Adams to city editor Stanley Walker. Sells his first bylined piece to *The New Yorker*: "The Alumnae Bulletin" by John H. O'Hara, published May 5. "Overheard: In a Telephone Booth" two weeks later also bears that byline, the last time O'Hara uses the middle initial. Dismissed in August from the *Herald Tribune* for repeated lateness and drunkenness on the job. Rents various short-term apartments in the city. Through Britt Haddon, one of *Time* magazine's founders, is hired by that magazine in November and is listed on its masthead as a "weekly contributor"; at various other times he is listed as its "religion editor" and "sports editor." By the year's end, he has published in *The New Yorker* a dozen short pieces and is beginning what proves to be a forty-year relationship with the magazine, during which—with time out for feuds and quarrels—he becomes one of its most valuable contributors. In all, O'Hara publishes more than four hundred pieces in *The New Yorker*, a record unlikely ever to be broken. He does not particularly get along with Harold Ross, the magazine's founder and first editor, but finds an ally in Katharine White, the head of the fiction department, who becomes his editor. Most of the dozens of stories he publishes in *The New Yorker* over the next two years belong to the "Orange Country Afternoon Delphian Society" series, about the club meetings of a group of upper-class ladies similar to those his mother attended and told him about in detail, and then the "Hagedorn and Brownmiller Paint and Varnish Company" series, about a small business in Manhattan. Both series are influenced by satirists like Ring Lardner and Sinclair Lewis, capturing the ironically revealing speech of American types.

1929　Fired by *Time* in February soon after the death of Britt Haddon. Gets a job writing for *Editor & Publisher* magazine, then in July is hired as rewrite man for the *Daily Mirror*, an evening tabloid whose hours conflict with his socializing. Becomes an habitué of speakeasies and nightclubs, such as the Pre-Catalan, known as the "Pre Cat," on West 39th Street, where he indulges in jazz, women, and drink, often to excess. Becomes friends with the writer and *New Yorker* editor Wolcott Gibbs, after whom he will rename Pottsville as "Gibbsville" in many of his future novels and stories. In the fall, works at the New York *World* as an assistant to Heywood Broun, whom he admires professionally and personally. Other friends during these early years in Manhattan include the writers Robert Benchley and Dorothy Parker, whose work influences his early fiction, and the reporter John McClain.

1930　Begins correspondence with F. Scott Fitzgerald, who eventually becomes a friend and literary mentor. *The New Yorker* publishes story "On His Hands" on March 22; though this is the forty-third piece of O'Hara's short fiction published in the magazine, it is the first one he will consider of sufficient quality later to include in his first story collection, *The Doctor's Son and Other Stories* (1935). In the spring, gets job writing for the *Morning Telegraph*, a broadsheet newspaper that covers sports and entertainment, mainly horseracing and theater. Assigned to write a column covering radio, one of the first in the country, then asked to review films as well. Fired by *Morning*

Telegraph in the early autumn. At a dance late in the year, meets Helen Ritchie Petit, a graduate of Wellesley College who has an MA from Columbia University. At Christmas, out of money and job prospects, returns to live in Pottsville with his mother and siblings. This is the week, and Pottsville (as "Gibbsville") is the place, in which his first novel, *Appointment in Samarra*, is set—about a wealthy young man who self-destructs and commits suicide. He later describes 1930 as "the worst year in my life."

1931   In Pottsville, profoundly depressed, works on freelance articles and stories for submission to *The New Yorker*, *Scribner's*, and other magazines. Returns to New York in late February, and marries Helen Petit on February 28 in a civil ceremony. Her mother does not approve of the marriage, or of him. The O'Haras move into an apartment at 41 West 52nd Street, and O'Hara works as a publicity agent for Warner Brothers until June, when, flush with some money that Helen's uncle has given the couple, he quits his job and goes with Helen for a summer-long honeymoon in Bermuda. There he writes several fictional pieces, including the short story "Alone," which is bought by *Scribner's* magazine and is his first piece of short fiction not published by *The New Yorker*. Enters a novella entitled "The Hofman Estate," presumably about the wealthy Hofman family he will describe in many later Gibbsville stories, in a contest sponsored by *Scribner's*, but it fails to win and is now lost. When the couple returns from Bermuda in September they live briefly with O'Hara's mother-in-law in Brooklyn Heights before moving to a rented apartment in Manhattan. In the fall, is hired as a staff writer by *The New Yorker*, contributing short, unbylined pieces to the "Talk of the Town," but is let go after a month for insufficient production. Works at various short-term public relations jobs for Benjamin Sonnenberg's agency.

1932   In January, submits long story "The Doctor's Son" to *Scribner's* fiction contest; revises "The Hofman Estate." Works for the publicity department of RKO Studios, but loses job after missing too many working days because of hangovers. Continues publishing short pieces in *The New Yorker*, some of them genuine short stories. By the year's end, financial and other troubles strain his marriage to the breaking point, and O'Hara starts looking for work outside of New York City.

1933   "Early Afternoon" is selected for *Best Short Stories of 1932.* Helen becomes pregnant and has an abortion; the couple separate in the spring. In May, O'Hara accepts a salaried position as managing editor of a Pittsburgh magazine, the *Bulletin-Index,* which is trying to transform itself into a local facsimile of *The New Yorker.* Lives in Pittsburgh on the twelfth floor of the William Penn Hotel. Restructures the magazine along the lines of *The New Yorker* but soon regrets taking the job. Helen travels to Reno to obtain a divorce, which becomes final on August 15. O'Hara quits the *Bulletin-Index* in August and returns to New York City, where he lives in the Pickwick Arms Club Residence at 230 East 51st Street. Works late at night on his novel about Pottsville, using the working title "The Infernal Grove." Accepts suggestion by Dorothy Parker that he call it *Appointment in Samarra,* after the retelling of an ancient folktale by Somerset Maugham.

1934   In January, after submitting *Appointment in Samarra* to Viking, Morrow, and Harcourt, Brace, signs contract with Harcourt, which offers him $400 in weekly payments. While completing *Appointment,* fills in for his friend John McClain as editor of the daily newsletter published aboard the cruise ship *Kungsholm* during a three-week tour of the Caribbean. In April, submits the typescript of the completed novel to Harcourt, Brace, and accepts a three-month contract from Paramount Studios in Hollywood to work on film scripts. Moves to Los Angeles in June and lives at the Ravenswood Apartments at 570 North Rossmore Avenue. *Appointment in Samarra* is published on August 16 and, mostly well received by critics, sells well enough to soon require a second printing. Returns to New York in September. Selects short stories that will appear in *The Doctor's Son and Other Stories.*

1935   Publication of the first of O'Hara's books in Britain when Faber & Faber brings out edition of *Appointment in Samarra* on February 14. *The Doctor's Son and Other Stories,* volume of thirty-seven stories stretching back to 1930, is published by Harcourt, Brace on February 21. That month, travels to Miami to work on his second novel, *BUtterfield 8,* based on the sensational and mysterious drowning of Starr Faithfull, a twenty-five-year-old demimondaine found off Far Rockaway in 1931. Returns to New York, then spends a month in Cape Cod, still working on his novel. While in the Berkshires in April, meets

Barbara Kibler, a nineteen-year-old Wellesley undergraduate, with whom he falls in love and becomes engaged. Drives to Ohio to meet her parents, who are unimpressed with O'Hara and object to his career, age, and Catholic background. In July, leaves New York to travel in Italy and France, where he continues making progress on *BUtterfield 8*, finishing it on August 5 in Paris. The novel is published on October 17 and sells well, but the reviews, many complaining about the book's salaciousness, are disappointing. Particularly wounding is Clifton Fadiman's review in *The New Yorker*, where O'Hara had hoped for a friendlier response. Back in New York, he shares a large apartment at 103 East 55th Street with John McClain, with whom he drives around the southern U.S. as far as New Orleans. Visits Ohio again to stay with the Kiblers, who are dismayed by the novelist's growing reputation for writing disreputable books.

1936 Early in the year, Barbara Kibler breaks off her engagement to O'Hara, and he seeks solace in work, drafting the beginnings of *Hope of Heaven*, a novel set in Hollywood. He is in Los Angeles by February, living on the $300 per month that Harcourt, Brace is giving him as an advance on *Hope of Heaven*. Makes cameo appearance as a newspaper reporter in the film *The General Died at Dawn*, starring Gary Cooper. Resuming the heavy drinking he had curtailed while working on *BUtterfield 8*, he enjoys an active nightlife, playing tennis during the day with movie stars and other celebrities, and other writers. Dates a bookstore clerk named Betty Anderson, who as "Peggy Henderson" will be a major character in *Hope of Heaven*. Late in the year, he meets Belle Mulford Wylie, a twenty-three-year-old woman from New York City. When she flies back east, he travels to see her, stopping in Pottsville, where his mother and siblings are hard-pressed for money; pays a few of their overdue household bills. Moves back to New York City after Christmas.

1937 Continues to see Belle Wylie, trying to overcome his reputation for bad behavior. The Wylies are more socially respectable than either the Petits or the Kiblers, both in Manhattan and in the Long Island town of Quogue, which O'Hara will later describe as "the only real family place–cum–Social Register [town] on the eastern seaboard." Rents a cottage on Dune Road near the Wylies' house in Quogue, and spends time with Belle and her family that summer. Finishes writing *Hope of Heaven* in a Philadelphia hotel room. On December 3, he and Belle elope and are married in Elkton, Maryland; they honeymoon in Hobe Sound, Florida, staying at the winter home of their friends Adele and Robert Lovett.

1938   On March 17, Harcourt, Brace publishes *Hope of Heaven*, narrated by its protagonist Jim Malloy, the "doctor's son" of his 1935 story of that title. O'Hara believes it is his best book up to that point, but most critics compare it unfavorably with his two previous novels; sales disappoint the publishers and O'Hara, who feels that it did not receive adequate publicity. In April, the O'Haras leave for Europe aboard the *Paris*, where they unexpectedly find that O'Hara's first wife, Helen Petit, is a fellow passenger. They visit Paris and spend three months in London, where O'Hara meets the English bibliographer, critic, and editor John Davy Hayward, who becomes a good friend. After sailing back to New York, they spend time with the Wylies in Quogue, then stay in the Wylies' apartment on Fifth Avenue in Manhattan, until O'Hara decides to check into a hotel to write short fiction for submission to *The The New Yorker*. In October, publishes his first story about the colorfully unscrupulous nightclub emcee Pal Joey. The idea for the character comes to him after a three-day bender, when he awakes and decides he must be the worst heel in the world. Then it dawns on him: there must be someone even worse. Pal Joey was "the only good thing I ever got out of booze," he said later. Over the next two years, O'Hara will respond to the enthusiastic requests of *New Yorker* editor-in-chief Harold Ross for Pal Joey stories by writing eleven more of them for the magazine. By now, O'Hara's main editor at the magazine has become William Maxwell, whom he respects and with whom he begins a long, friendly correspondence. In September the O'Haras move to Hollywood, where O'Hara accepts a screenwriting job for RKO Studios and then for Twentieth Century-Fox, mainly polishing the dialogue of previous scriptwriters.

1939   On September 21, story collection *Files on Parade* is published by Harcourt, Brace, including four Pal Joey stories. Reception of this volume is positive, and O'Hara is beginning to be praised as a contemporary master of the short story form.

1940 Early in the year, at the suggestion of the screenwriter George Oppenheimer, O'Hara writes to composer Richard Rodgers asking whether he and lyricist Lorenz Hart would be interested in writing songs for a musical version of the Pal Joey stories; Rodgers agrees, and they collaborate on the project throughout the year, while the O'Haras live on Dune Road in Quogue and in a rented apartment on East 79th Street. In July, begins writing a column, "Entertainment Week," for *Newsweek*, adopting a blustering, name-dropping tone more irritating than entertaining, but he is paid handsomely, $1,000 weekly, and provides copy without putting in much time or effort. *Pal Joey*, collection of fourteen stories (twelve previously published in *The New Yorker*, plus two stories appearing for the first time), is published by O'Hara's new publisher Duell, Sloan and Pearce on October 23. The musical *Pal Joey* opens on Broadway on December 25, starring Gene Kelly in the title role and directed by George Abbott. It is a hit, running for 374 performances on Broadway despite its risqué content and antihero, and its success makes O'Hara a wealthy man.

1941 By January, the O'Haras have taken a duplex apartment at 8 East 52nd Street, just off Fifth Avenue. Back in Hollywood from March to July, writes the screenplay for *Moontide* for Fox, the only sole screenwriting credit of his career.

1942 In February, after eighty-four weeks, "Entertainment Week" column for *Newsweek* comes to an end. Using connections to his friends Robert Lovell, assistant secretary of war for air, and James Forrestal, undersecretary of the Navy, tries to get a commission as a naval officer, but his poor general health, and particularly his teeth, prevent his acceptance. Has most of his teeth extracted in April. Recuperates over the summer in Quogue, now subject to wartime blackout orders and other restrictions, and takes flying lessons, hoping perhaps to join the Civil Air Patrol. Serves as chief story officer for the film section of the Office of the Coordinator of Inter-American Affairs, supervising anti-Nazi propaganda to be distributed through South America, but is soon forced to resign for health reasons. Spends most of the war years depressed and unable to write anything much longer than a short story; later recalls that he was "drinking a quart of whisky a day and that takes time—not just to drink, but to have your hangover and get better."

1943   By October, the O'Haras' home address is 27 East 79th Street. Attempts to enlist in the Army but health is deemed too poor to perform even restricted duties; considers joining the merchant marine or the Red Cross. Is accepted by the Office of Strategic Services and reports to its training camp in November. Begins learning skills related to espionage and grows a beard, but he is not up to the physical demands of the training and in December either washes out or quits.

1944   Accepts assignment as a war correspondent for *Liberty* magazine in the Pacific, including for two months aboard the aircraft carrier *Intrepid*. Returns to the U.S. in October. Belle becomes pregnant.

1945   With a preface by Wolcott Gibbs, the collection *Pipe Night* is published in March by Duell, Sloan and Pearce, going through six printings. It receives a respectful review on the front page of the *New York Times Book Review* by Lionel Trilling, who praises O'Hara's command of detail and withering social analysis. The collection propels O'Hara, at the age of forty, to the top ranks of American short story writers. Daughter Wylie Delaney O'Hara is born on June 14. O'Hara inscribes copy of his latest book to his newborn: "Your old man will be remembered as a short story writer, if at all." Hired by M-G-M and travels to Hollywood to adapt Sinclair Lewis's novel *Cass Timber-laine* for the screen, but writing is eventually handed over to Donald Ogden Stewart and Sonya Levien, who are the two screenwriters credited when movie is released in 1947.

1946   Spends the year, with no books (and only twelve *New Yorker* stories) published, writing for movie studios and trying to write plays. Works on *A Miracle Can Happen*, a series of interrelated vignettes about the effect of a child on various people's lives, including characters played by James Stewart and Henry Fonda. (After a limited opening run as *A Miracle Can Happen* in 1948, the film was re-released later that year as *On Our Merry Way*; O'Hara is credited with writing only the material involving Stewart and Fonda.) Back in Manhattan, the O'Haras move to 55 East 86th Street. Unhappy with Duell, Sloane and Pearce and feeling that his career has stalled, O'Hara has lunch with Bennett Cerf, cofounder of Random House, and agrees to become a Random House author. He and Cerf begin an occasionally quarrelsome but mostly amiable relationship, and Random House remains O'Hara's publisher for the rest of his life—to the profit of both parties.

1947 Collection *Hellbox* is published on August 9 by Random House. It contains the first appearance of O'Hara's alter ego Jim Malloy since *Hope of Heaven* nine years earlier; Malloy will narrate several more O'Hara stories and novellas.

1948 Works on novel *A Rage to Live*, and only two stories are published the entire year. Enrolls briefly in Columbia University's School of General Studies to take its American History, 1865–1945 course, a period that coincides with the scope of *A Rage to Live*, O'Hara's first novel to take place over a character's lifetime. In June, writes a letter to *New Yorker* editor-in-chief Harold Ross, vigorously protesting the magazine's payment policies for short stories, particularly Ross's refusal to pay him a kill fee for stories rejected by the magazine, which O'Hara feels won't sell elsewhere. To research *A Rage to Live*, drives in the autumn through Pennsylvania with his friend Joseph Bryan to reacquaint himself with the geography, people, and farms of the region around Harrisburg.

1949 In January, completes *A Rage to Live*, which is published on August 16, the fifteenth anniversary of *Appointment in Samarra*'s publication. Reviews are generally good, and the book breaks a Random House record—8,000 copies in a single day, among the 100,000 sold in its first two months—but Brendan Gill, reviewing it for *The New Yorker* on August 20, calls it "sprawling" and "discursive" and compares it to the Kinsey Report. Gill had been a friend who resembled O'Hara in many ways (also Irish, also Catholic, and also a doctor's son, but he had made it to Yale, where he was even a member of the secret society Skull and Bones), and O'Hara feels doubly betrayed, not just by the reviewer but by Harold Ross. Continuing also to feel that the magazine's payment policies do not reflect his importance to its success, he angrily breaks with *The New Yorker* and submits nothing there until 1960. This break changes the course of O'Hara's career: while it lasts, he will write almost no short fiction, concentrating on longer novels, most of which sell very well but do little to raise his standing among critics. In September, the O'Haras rent a house at 18 College Road in Princeton, New Jersey.

1950   In February and March, O'Hara covers a medical-euthanasia trial for the International News Service extensively (and very sympathetically to the doctor on trial). The *Princeton Tiger*, the undergraduate humor magazine, makes O'Hara an honorary member, which is among the few honors he will receive from any academic institution. In September, reviews Ernest Hemingway's new novel, *Across the River and Into the Trees*, for *The New York Times*, and claims that Hemingway is "the most important author living today, the outstanding author since the death of Shakespeare"; he also uses the occasion to attack *The New Yorker*, calling its recent piece on Hemingway a "new low in something." O'Hara's friends in Princeton include the editor and critic Wilder Hobson, the businessman Joseph Outerbridge, and Princeton faculty members Hamilton Cottier and Rensselaer Lee. Also socializes with writers John Hersey and William Faulkner, sometimes contentiously. During the summers now always spent on Long Island, where O'Hara eventually buys his own beach cottage on Dune Road in Quogue, the O'Haras are friendly with cartoonist Charles Addams and his wife, who summer in nearby Westhampton.

1951   Moves to house next door in Princeton at 20 College Road. On November 8, Random House publishes the novella *The Farmers Hotel*, a reworking of one of the plays he wrote in 1946 and 1947. An account of travelers stranded in a country inn during a sudden storm, it is intended to be an allegory about international politics (though the public and critics seem not to notice) and enjoys a generally warm reception. In December, Harold Ross dies, making possible a rapprochement with *The New Yorker*, but O'Hara's current plans are to work on plays and novels.

1952   *Pal Joey* is successfully revived on Broadway, a financial boon for O'Hara; book with libretto and lyrics is published by Random House. Continues writing plays, one of which, *The Searching Sun*, opens for a ten-day run at Princeton's Murray Theater in May and receives poor reviews. At the urging of its editor, John McPhee, allows the *Princeton Tiger* to publish his story "The Favor."

1953   Collapses in August in Manhattan and is treated for a perforated ulcer at Columbia-Presbyterian Hospital. Accepts doctors' counsel to give up drinking. First wife, Helen Petit, dies on October 16. At year's end, begins writing weekly and often autobiographical "Sweet and Sour" column for the Sunday edition of the *Trenton Times-Advertiser*; its tone is argumentative, sometimes abrasive, and will help to foster view that O'Hara is a hypersensitive, difficult author, desirous of honors from institutions that he will never receive.

1954   On January 9, Belle O'Hara dies of a congenital heart weakness, aged forty-one. When a doctor advises him to take some whisky to cope with the shock of her death, O'Hara responds by pouring the whisky down the kitchen sink. He will be sober for the rest of his life. In February, begins publishing biweekly column in *Collier's* magazine, "Appointment with O'Hara," about the entertainment world; "Sweet and Sour" column ends in June. Becomes involved in summer with Katharine Barnes Bryan, known as "Sister," soon to be divorced from his friend Joseph Bryan. *Sweet and Sour*, collection of *Times-Advertiser* columns, is published in October, to poor sales. O'Hara refuses to work any longer with Saxe Commins, his editor at Random House, whom he regards as too intrusive, and Commins is replaced by Albert Erskine, with whom O'Hara works happily for the rest of his career.

1955   Marries Katharine Bryan on January 31, his fiftieth birthday, in New York City, and she moves into house at 20 College Road. In the spring, the couple moves to California temporarily with ten-year-old Wylie, whom Sister will later adopt, renting a house at 14300 Sunset Boulevard in Pacific Palisades while O'Hara works on the novel *Ten North Frederick* by night and by day on the movie script for Fox's *The Best Things in Life Are Free*. *Ten North Frederick* is published on November 24, 1955, Thanksgiving Day, which will become a tradition: ten more O'Hara titles will be published on subsequent Thanksgivings. Set in Gibbsville, the novel tells the life story of Joseph B. Chapin, a lawyer with political ambitions that are dashed by the deterioration of his marriage and the love affair that follows. It becomes a best seller and in 1958 is made into a movie starring Gary Cooper and Geraldine Fitzgerald.

1956 *Ten North Frederick* wins the National Book Award in February; while giving his acceptance speech at the ceremony, O'Hara breaks down, calling the award a vindication of his whole body of work. In March, publishes in *Collier's* "A Family Party," a long story brought out by Random House in book form on August 16; a sentimental monologue about a small-town doctor, it quickly sells out its initial print run of 8,000 copies and goes through three more printings by the end of the year. In Port Huron, Michigan, sale of *Ten North Frederick* is prohibited because of its inclusion on a list of books deemed objectionable by the National Organization of Decent Literature, a Catholic organization; censorship ends after a federal district court rules that the Port Huron prosecutor's office had exceeded its authority. Last "Appointment with O'Hara" column published in *Collier's* on September 28. *The Great Short Stories of John O'Hara*, drawn from his first two collections, is published by Bantam paperbacks, as is the Modern Library edition *Selected Short Stories of John O'Hara*, with an introduction by Lionel Trilling.

1957 In January, Bantam Books publishes *Ten North Frederick* in a 50-cent paperback edition; the police commissioner in Detroit, citing the paperback's inexpensive price, and Cleveland authorities ban its sale on the grounds that it is unfit for minors. In the spring, elected to the National Institute of Arts and Letters. Columbia Pictures releases film version of *Pal Joey* on October 25, starring Frank Sinatra, Rita Hayworth, and Kim Novak, changing the location from Chicago in the stage version to San Francisco; O'Hara is not consulted on this change or others in the screenplay. The O'Haras buy several acres of land three miles west of Princeton University and build a house on it, which they call "Linebrook," where O'Hara will live for the rest of his life. Works on novel *From the Terrace*, his longest and most ambitious book, which tells the story of Alfred Eaton, son of a Pennsylvania steel-mill owner, his rise to success in high finance and in government work, and his decline after a series of betrayals by those close to him. O'Hara and Bantam Books are indicted on December 13 in New York State for conspiring to distribute obscene literature in publishing *Ten North Frederick*.

1958 Obscenity charges against O'Hara in New York State are dismissed in July; bans elsewhere are also lifted. Friend

Wolcott Gibbs dies on August 16. *From the Terrace* is published on Thanksgiving, in a first printing of 100,000 copies. O'Hara considers it his masterpiece, but it receives mixed reviews and, typical of the reception he is by now accustomed to, is denounced for its sexual content.

1959 Invited by Rider College in nearby Lawrenceville, New Jersey, to deliver a series of lectures during spring term on the contemporary American novel, O'Hara summarizes his critical positions in three lectures that will be collected posthumously in *"An Artist Is His Own Fault"* (1977). Works on *Ourselves to Know*, another lengthy novel recounting the story of the main character's entire life. Unlike his previous long novels, which are told omnisciently, this one—about a man named Robert Millhauser, who eventually murders his young wife—is narrated by Gerald Higgins, a neighbor who pieces Millhauser's story together from a variety of sources. In September, the O'Haras sail to Great Britain aboard the *Queen Mary* and return in October aboard the *Queen Elizabeth*.

1960 In February, Random House publishes *Ourselves to Know*, which sells modestly and is generally not well received by critics. In the summer, at the urging of *The New Yorker* editor St. Clair McKelway, O'Hara ends his breach with the magazine, offering to submit fiction again but only if an editor will come out to Quogue and give him a decision on the spot whether to publish his work. An anxious William Maxwell spends the night with the O'Haras, and after reading the novellas that will be published in November as the three-volume edition *Sermons and Soda-Water*, is relieved to report that one of them, "Imagine Kissing Pete," is splendid and that the magazine will publish it in its entirety. The renewed relationship with *The New Yorker* is not without ups and downs, but O'Hara's friendship with Maxwell takes on new warmth and trust. He returns to short story writing in a burst of enthusiasm and over the next three years publishes almost thirty in *The New Yorker* alone. Film adaptation of *From the Terrace* is released in July.

1961 Quits National Institute of Arts and Letters, still simmering about its lack of protest at the censorship of *Ten North Frederick* and enraged that not he but Katherine Anne Porter and Kay Boyle were nominated for its Gold Medal for Fiction. Random House publishes *Assembly*, a story collection dedicated to the late Wolcott Gibbs; in introduction, O'Hara describes his joy at discovering that "I had an apparently inexhaustible urge to express and an unlimited supply of short story ideas."

1962 Complaining that Princeton winters make Sister stir-crazy, spends winter in Bermuda. Random House publishes *The Big Laugh*, his only novel about the movie business, in May, and story collection *The Cape Cod Lighter* on Thanksgiving. After John Steinbeck wins the Nobel Prize in Literature that year, begins openly campaigning for a Nobel of his own. "I want the Nobel Prize . . . so bad I can taste it," he writes. "And as long as I live and can be wheeled up to the typewriter, I'll try; by God, I'll try."

1963 In June, Random House publishes *Elizabeth Appleton*, a novel about a professor's wife in a western Pennsylvania college town. Awarded an honorary degree by American International College in Springfield, and is the subject of an admiring *Newsweek* cover story: "John O'Hara at 58: A Rage to Write." On Thanksgiving, *The Hat on the Bed*, story collection dedicated to William Maxwell, is published.

1964 Receives the Award of Merit for the Novel from the American Academy of Arts and Letters and weeps upon hearing the news. Asks to rejoin the National Institute, then a sub-branch of the Academy. (One honor that continues to elude him is an honorary degree from Yale, which he yearns for. On being asked why O'Hara was never awarded one, Yale's president, Kingman Brewster, replied: "Because he asked.") Begins writing a column for *Newsday*. The columns, which do not win O'Hara many new admirers, are truculent and conservative, mourning the closing of Peal's custom shoe workshop, decrying the rise of what he calls "Jerkism" in America, and endorsing Republican presidential candidate Barry Goldwater. (As late as 1956, he had written that he had always voted the "straight Democratic ticket.") Random House publishes *The Horse Knows the Way*, his fourth story collection in four years.

1965 Having promised himself a Rolls-Royce if he won the Nobel Prize, he now concludes that the prize is unlikely, and buys himself the company's Silver Cloud III model in April. In September, ships it over to England, where he travels with Sister and Wylie. Random House publishes *The Lockwood Concern*, the story of four generations of a

Pennsylvania family starting in the nineteenth century, which sells well enough to go through three hardback and four paperback printings.

1966 *My Turn*, a collection of his *Newsday* columns, is published in April. Wylie becomes engaged to Dennis Holahan, a Yalie of whom O'Hara thoroughly approves, and marries him in a lavish New York wedding on September 10. The reception, at the Colony Club, is the last big social occasion hosted by O'Hara; guest list includes Vanderbilts and Whitneys as well as Claude Rains and Truman Capote. Withdraws more and more to Princeton, but attends Capote's Black and White Ball at New York's Plaza Hotel, November 28. *Waiting for Winter*, a collection featuring many stories set in Hollywood, is published.

1967 Travels to England to be guest of honor at a luncheon given by Foyles Bookshop in London in May to celebrate paperback publication of *The Lockwood Concern*—the last formal recognition he will receive. Random House publishes *The Instrument*, a novel about a playwright who exploits women for material in his work; dismissed by the critics—about whom O'Hara has ceased to care much by now—it nevertheless sells well and becomes a Literary Guild Selection. In December, makes what turns out to be a farewell visit to Pottsville for a cocktail party given in his honor by a childhood friend. "For the first time since 1927, when I left Pottsville," he writes, "I had a good time there."

1968 Birth on October 26 of Wylie's first child, Nicholas Drew Holahan, whose arrival O'Hara greets enthusiastically. Travels to Palm Springs, where he spends an afternoon with former president Eisenhower, watching a golf tournament with the sound turned off. Though by now a Republican, gratefully accepts an invitation to a dinner at the Johnson White House, where he meets fellow Pennsylvanian John Updike. His health deteriorating, suffers bad fall in November and not long afterward, a mild stroke, which leaves him partially blind in his right eye. Story collection *And Other Stories* is published.

1969 Wylie's second child born September 30, named Belle after her mother, O'Hara's second wife. Hospitalized for eleven days and is diagnosed with diabetes; also suffers from a hiatal hernia. Travels with Sister to London in the fall as a birthday present for her, but needs to use a wheelchair at airports. Random House publishes short novel *Lovey Childs: A Philadelphian's Story*, about a Main Line woman who marries a playboy and for a while becomes a celebrity, which fails to attract much attention, critical or otherwise.

1970   In February, completes *The Ewings*, his last novel and the only one set in the Midwest, about the rise of an ambitious lawyer in the years after World War I. (Because of delays in settling his estate, it doesn't come out until 1972, along with *The Time Element and Other Stories*, a volume of previously uncollected stories put together by Albert Erskine. A second posthumous collection, *Good Samaritan and Other Stories*, follows in 1974.) On April 10, complains of chest pains while writing at his desk and goes to bed early. Found dead the next morning, April 11. Buried in the Princeton Cemetery. The inscription on his headstone, written by O'Hara himself, reads: "BETTER / THAN ANYONE ELSE / HE TOLD THE TRUTH / ABOUT HIS TIME / HE WAS / A PROFESSIONAL / HE WROTE / HONESTLY AND WELL."

Note on the Texts

This volume contains sixty stories written by John O'Hara from 1930 to his death in 1970.

O'Hara was a prolific writer of short stories, which he often completed very quickly. His earliest stories were published exclusively in *The New Yorker*, and throughout his career the magazine remained the primary venue for the first publication of his short fiction. Although he did publish in other magazines, he came to believe that the sort of stories he was writing was so closely aligned with *The New Yorker*'s preferred style of fiction that he would have difficulty publishing them elsewhere. "Every time I write a piece for *The New Yorker* I write it so that *The New Yorker* will buy it," he wrote to the magazine's editor William Maxwell in February 1939. "It won't go anywhere else." His relationship with its editors was by turns warm and contentious, and he often pugnaciously resisted when asked to make changes in his stories.

O'Hara gathered his stories into ten collections published during his lifetime, along with a three-volume edition of novellas entitled *Sermons and Soda-Water* (1960). After his death, Albert Erskine, his longtime editor at Random House (his publisher from 1947 onward), oversaw the publication of the posthumous volumes *The Time Element and Other Stories* (1972) and *Good Samaritan and Other Stories* (1974). The stories included in *The Time Element* were written in the 1940s, up to the period of O'Hara's quarrel with the editors of *The New Yorker* and his break with the magazine (see Chronology, 1948 and 1949), after which, according to his own account in the introduction to his collection *Assembly* (1961), he ceased writing stories for eleven years. The stories in *Good Samaritan*, many of them previously unpublished, were all written in the 1960s.

The texts of the stories printed here are taken from their first American book publications. (Many of his stories were published in England, but O'Hara's British editors took liberties with his spelling and usage. Recalling in 1966 the English edition of his novel *Appointment in Samarra*, O'Hara noted there had been "tinkering" with the text, adding, "Once I have read proof on the U.S. trade editions I have to trust to luck.") In the list that follows, the story's first magazine publication is given if it had been published before being included in one of O'Hara's collections.

From *The Doctor's Son and Other Stories* (New York: Harcourt, Brace, 1935): "On His Hands," *The New Yorker*, March 22, 1930; "Early Afternoon," *Scribner's*, July 1932; "It Must Have Been Spring," *The New Yorker*, April 21, 1934; "Over the River and Through the Wood," *The New Yorker*, December 15, 1934. "The Doctor's Son" was first published in this collection.

From *Files on Parade* (New York: Harcourt, Brace, 1939): "Price's Always Open," *The New Yorker*, August 14, 1937; "Are We Leaving Tomorrow?" *The New Yorker*, March 19, 1938; "The Cold House," *The New Yorker*, April 2, 1938; "Trouble in 1949," *Harper's Bazaar*, November 1938; "Do You Like It Here?" *The New Yorker*, April 1, 1939; "Too Young," *The New Yorker*, September 9, 1939.

From *Pipe Night* (New York: Duell, Sloan & Pearce, 1945): "Bread Alone," *The New Yorker*, September 23, 1939; "The King of the Desert," *The New Yorker*, November 30, 1940; "Summer's Day," *The New Yorker*, August 29, 1942; "Graven Image," *The New Yorker*, March 13, 1943; "The Next-to-Last Dance of the Season," *The New Yorker*, September 18, 1943; "The Pretty Daughters," *The New Yorker*, March 3, 1945.

From *Hellbox* (New York: Random House, 1947): "Common Sense Should Tell You," *The New Yorker*, February 9, 1946; "Ellie," *The New Yorker*, October 19, 1946; "The Moccasins," *The New Yorker*, January 25, 1947. "A Phase of Life" (submitted to *The New Yorker* but not published) and "Time to Go" were first published in this collection.

From *The Time Element and Other Stories* (New York: Random House, 1972): "The Heart of Lee W. Lee," *The New Yorker*, September 13, 1947; "Requiescat," *The New Yorker*, April 3, 1948. "Encounter: 1943," "The War," "The Time Element," and "Family Evening" were first published in this collection.

Imagine Kissing Pete: First published in *The New Yorker* on September 17, 1960, this novella was brought out as the second volume of O'Hara's three-volume collection *Sermons and Soda-Water* (New York: Random House, 1960).

From *Assembly* (New York: Random House, 1961): "Call Me, Call Me," *The New Yorker*, October 7, 1961. The other three stories printed here, "Mrs. Stratton of Oak Knoll," "You Can Always Tell

Newark," and "In the Silence," were first published in this collection.

The Cape Cod Lighter (New York: Random House, 1962): "Winter Dance," *The New Yorker*, September 22, 1962. There was no prior periodical publication for the other stories selected from this collection: "The Cape Cod Lighter," "Appearances," "Your Fah Neefah Neeface," "Justice," The Lesson," and "Pat Collins."

From *The Hat on the Bed* (New York: Random House, 1963): "Agatha," first published in this collection; "Exterior: With Figure," *Saturday Evening Post*, June 1, 1963; "The Flatted Saxophone," *The New Yorker*, June 1, 1963; "The Man on the Tractor," *The New Yorker*, June 22, 1963.

From *The Horse Knows the Way* (New York: Random House, 1964): "The Answer Depends," *Saturday Evening Post*, April 18, 1964; "At the Window," *The New Yorker*, February 22, 1964; "Can I Stay Here?" *Saturday Evening Post*, May 16, 1964; "I Spend My Days in Longing," *The New Yorker*, May 23, 1964. "I Can't Thank You Enough" and "In the Mist" were first published in this collection.

From *Waiting for Winter* (New York: Random House, 1966): "Afternoon Waltz," *Saturday Evening Post*, April 23, 1966; "The Assistant," *The New Yorker*, July 3, 1965; "Fatimas and Kisses," *The New Yorker*, May 21, 1966. "Natica Jackson, was first published in this collection.

From *And Other Stories* (New York: Random House, 1968): "How Old, How Young," *The New Yorker*, July 1, 1967. "The Farmer" and "We'll Have Fun" were first published in this collection.

From *Good Samaritan and Other Stories* (New York: Random House, 1974): "The Sun Room," *Saturday Evening Post*, February 8, 1969. "A Man To Be Trusted" and "The Journey to Mount Clemens" were not published during O'Hara's lifetime. "Christmas Poem," *The New Yorker*, December 19, 1964.

This volume presents the texts of the original printings chosen for inclusion here, but it does not attempt to reproduce nontextual features of their typographic design. The texts are presented without change, except for the correction of typographical errors. Spelling, punctuation, and capitalization are often expressive features and are not altered, even when inconsistent or irregular. The following is a list of typographical errors corrected, cited by page and line number: 29.11, expect; 56.20, Campbell's; 109.13, artists'; 164.15, 'You; 164.16, "NO.'; 176.2 (and *passim*), Ladies Aid; 189.5 and 189.9, Murial; 199.19, Sportsmen's; 203.24, gulf; 203.32 (and *passim*), aint; 256.37, *de*; 527.19, Charley; 625.23, mist of; 649.26, gyour; 649.32, Gray's; 694.7, along?'; 697.11, minute,"; 730.14, *The*; 755.4, Cathay; 779.32, he'd had; 798.21, that?" I.

Notes

In the notes below, the reference numbers denote page and line of this volume (the line count includes headings). No note is made for material included in standard desk-reference books. Biblical quotations are keyed to the King James Version. Quotations from Shakespeare are keyed to *The Riverside Shakespeare*, ed. G. Blakemore Evans (Boston: Houghton Mifflin, 1974). For references to other studies and further information than is included in the Chronology, see Matthew J. Bruccoli, *The O'Hara Concern* (Pittsburgh: University of Pittsburgh Press, 1975); *Selected Letters of John O'Hara*, ed. Matthew J. Bruccoli (New York: Random House, 1978); Finis Farr, *O'Hara* (Boston: Little, Brown, 1973); Frank MacShane, *The Life of John O'Hara* (New York: E. P. Dutton, 1980); and Geoffrey Wolff, *The Art of Burning Bridges: A Life of John O'Hara* (New York: Knopf, 2003).

1.21 Wetzel] Charles F. Wetzel, owner of a custom tailor shop on East 44th Street, just off Fifth Avenue.

2.30 Gauss] Christian Gauss (1878–1951), professor of modern languages at Princeton and one of the university's deans, 1925–46; he was a mentor to the Princeton undergraduates F. Scott Fitzgerald and Edmund Wilson.

2.35 a Cabot] Prominent Boston family going back to the early eighteenth century in America, whose members included George Cabot (1752–1823), Henry Cabot Lodge (1850–1924), and Henry Cabot Lodge Jr. (1902–1985), all of whom served as U.S. senators from Massachusetts.

3.21–22 Miss Comstock's music school.] Private day and boarding school emphasizing musical training founded and directed by pianist and educator Elinor Comstock (1856–1922), located on Manhattan's Upper East Side.

5.16–17 Northampton . . . Hanover.] Smith and Dartmouth Colleges, respectively.

5.34 the Fuller Brush man?"] Door-to-door salesman for the Fuller Brush Company, a manufacturer of household cleaning products.

6.22 dinched] Crushed out so as to be smoked later, said of cigarettes and cigars.

6.38 Twenty-One] "21," nightclub at 21 West 52nd Street in Manhattan, originally a speakeasy.

8.17 Golden Firefly] Show mare who won reserve world championship titles in the Fine Harness and Five-Gaited Divisions at the Kentucky State Fair World's Championship Horse Show in 1916.

8.37 Wanamaker's] Philadelphia department store, the city's first and largest at the time.

9.28 Melachrinos] Brand of Egyptian cigarettes.

10.20 trephine] Trepan, in a variant spelling.

11.1 *Over the River and Through the Wood*] Repeated line from "The New-England Boy's Song about Thanksgiving Day" (1844), children's poem by American writer Lydia Maria Child (1802–1880). A stanza from the poem was the epigraph for *The Doctor's Son and Other Stories* (1935), O'Hara's first story collection, in which "Over the River and Through the Wood" was first published in book form.

11.13 strapontin] A small folding seat, originally for a carriage but then carried over to early automobiles.

13.37 "*Pax tibi*,"] Latin: Peace be with you.

19.37 S. A. T. C.] Student Army Training Corps, program for military training instituted at colleges during World War I.

20.9–10 Hahnemann or Jefferson or Medico-Chi.] Philadelphia medical colleges; the Medico-Chirurgical College of Philadelphia became part of the University of Pennsylvania in 1916.

22.12 "500."] Popular card game in the United States in the first two decades of the twentieth century.

24.38 Wallace Reid] American silent film star (1891–1923), a matinee idol.

27.35 Hunkies] Central European immigrants.

33.24 USAAC] United States Army Air Corps.

33.34 Leavenworth] Military penitentiary at Fort Leavenworth, Kansas.

35.28 P. O. S. of A.] Patriotic Order Sons of America, a fraternal society.

37.32 hurrying to an "OBS."] Going to deliver a baby.

40.37 in the days of the King's Highway.] The King's Highway, a road running through Schuylkill County in Pennsylvania, dates from 1770.

48.30 Château-Thierry] In early June 1918, American troops helped stop a major German offensive in heavy fighting around Château-Thierry, a town on the Marne River forty miles east of Paris.

53.8 Walter Winchell] *New York Daily Mirror* gossip columnist (1897–1972).

53.39 Give another hoya and a choo-choo rah rah] From a fight song of the College of the Holy Cross in Worcester, Massachusetts.

64.23 H-Y-P] Harvard-Yale-Princeton Club.

66.4 "Chin up, mahst dress," he quoted from Bert Lahr.] From the sketch "Chin Up" from the Broadway revue *Life Begins at 8:40* (1934), in which American actor and comedian Bert Lahr (1895–1967) adopted an exaggerated upper-class English accent.

66.7–9 Maurice Chevalier . . . dey do."] From the popular song "You Brought a New Kind of Love to Me" (1930), written by Sammy Fain (1902–1989), Irving Kahal (1903–1942), and Pierre Norman (pseud. Joseph P. Connor, 1895–1952), sung by French actor and singer Maurice Chevalier (1888–1972) in the film *The Big Pond* (1930).

66.29 Junior League] Charitable aid organization of upper-class young women founded in 1901 by a railroad magnate's daughter, Mary Harriman (1881–1934).

66.38 at 21] See note 6.38.

82.1 *Bread Alone*] See Matthew 4:4, where Jesus quotes Deuteronomy 8:3: "It is written, Man shall not live by bread alone, but by every word that proceedeth out of the mouth of God."

86.2–3 old record of "You Go to My Head"] Popular song written in 1936 by J. Fred Coots (1897–1985) and Haven Gillespie (1888–1975), first a hit in 1938, when it was recorded by bands led by Teddy Wilson, Larry Clinton, and Glen Gray.

96.28 The Boss] President Franklin Delano Roosevelt.

97.34–35 the Clipper to London] One of the transatlantic flights of Pan-American Airways' Clipper service.

98.7 Union League or Junior League] Union League, elite private social club on East 37th Street in Manhattan; Junior League, see note 66.29.

99.8–9 chain . . . golden pig.] A sign of membership in Harvard University's Porcellian Club ("the Pork" at 99.17), an exclusive social club.

99.12–13 illustrious brethren . . . Ossining."] Richard Whitney (1888–1974), a four-term president of the New York Stock Exchange, embezzled funds from the exchange, the New York Yacht Club, and his father-in-law's estate. After his misconduct was exposed in 1938, he was convicted of grand larceny and served three years and four months of jail time in Sing Sing prison in Ossining, New York. At Harvard he had been a member of the Porcellian Club.

103.6–7 singing of D.K.E., the mother of jollity, whose children are gay and free] From the "Phi Marching Song" of the college fraternity Delta Kappa Epsilon.

103.28 Sonny Greer] Jazz drummer born William Greer (1903–1982), who played from the 1920s through 1951 in Duke Ellington's bands.

103.32 the late E. T. Stotesbury] Investment banker, financier, and executive Edward T. Stotesbury (1849–1938), a prominent Philadelphian.

103.33 Mercersburg] Mercersburg Academy, a college-preparatory boarding school in Mercersburg, Pennsylvania.

104.12–13 Stan Lomax] Sports broadcaster (1899–1987) for WOR radio in New York, whose nightly fifteen-minute roundup of the day's sports news was broadcast nationally on the Mutual network from the early 1930s through the mid-1970s.

106.31 a Jordan] Automobile manufactured by the Jordan Motor Car Company, based in Cleveland.

114.4 Eddie Schmidt] Tailor and clothes designer for Hollywood stars, based in Beverly Hills.

114.6 Asprey's] London luxury-goods store.

115.32 Arlen] Songwriter and composer Harold Arlen (1905–1986), who wrote the music for "Stormy Weather" (1933), "Over the Rainbow" (1939), and many other songs.

118.20 Upmann cigar] Cigar manufactured by H. Upmann, venerable brand of Cuban cigars founded in 1844.

119.15–16 "21" . . . Larue's] "21," see note 6.38; La Rue, restaurant at Park Avenue and 58th Street.

122.23 Randolph-Macon] Women's college in Lynchburg, Virginia, until 2007 when it was renamed Randolph College and became coeducational.

123.25 El Morocco] Fashionable New York nightclub, originally a speakeasy, at 154 East 54th Street.

124.18 the Dorsey brothers] American bandleaders Tommy Dorsey (1905–1956) and Jimmy Dorsey (1904–1957).

124.23 the tune, "Blue Lou,"] Jazz composition (1935) with words and music by Irving Mills (1894–1985) and Edgar M. Sampson (1907–1973).

125.9 late Hugo Bezdek or early Rockne era.] The 1920s, referring to the successful coaching careers of Prague-born football coach Hugo Bezdek (1884–1952) and Notre Dame coach Knute Rockne (1888–1931).

138.24 Delmonico glass] Tulip-shaped glass with a small stem holding about five ounces, also called a sour glass.

141.6 Willkie] Wendell Willkie (1892–1944), American politician, lawyer, and business executive who was the Republican candidate for president in 1940.

142.32 Victor Mature] American actor (1913–1999), whose films included *Kiss of Death* (1947), *Cry of the City* (1948), and *Samson and Delilah* (1949).

142.37–143.1 Herbert Marshall. Ronnie Colman.] Suave English actors Herbert Marshall (1890–1966), who starred in *Foreign Correspondent* (1940) and several adaptations of the fiction of W. Somerset Maugham, including *The Moon and Sixpence* (1942), and Ronald Colman (1891–1958), whose films included *A Tale of Two Cities* (1935) and *Lost Horizon* (1937).

143.33 the 21 and the El Morocco] See notes 6.38 and 123.25.

144.4 the Automat] A self-service restaurant chain founded in 1912; its flagship was located at Broadway and 45th Street.

144.30–33 Dewey . . . Al Smith] New York governor Thomas E. Dewey (1902–1971) was the Republican Party's presidential candidate in 1944 and 1948, and was defeated both times; New York governor Al Smith (1873–1944) ran unsuccessfully for president as the Democratic candidate in 1928.

145.1 Waac] Women's Army Auxiliary Corps.

147.4–5 Joe Lopez] Headwaiter at the Copacabana, restaurant and nightclub at 10 East 60th Street in Manhattan.

147.14 Tony Galento] Heavyweight boxer and entertainer (1910–1979), nick-named "Two-Ton."

147.25–27 Diamonds Brady . . . at the tain of the century.] American railroad tycoon James Buchanan Brady (1856–1917), known as Diamond Jim Brady, was famed for his gargantuan appetite.

147.37 Madelon Carroll with that picture. "The Steps."] English actor Made-leine Carroll (1906–1987), female lead in Alfred Hitchcock's film *The 39 Steps* (1935).

151.16–17 in high school it was Rudy Vallee's place, not the Copa] The restau-rant and nightclub at what was later the site of the Copacabana was called the Villa Vallee from 1929 to 1931, when it was owned by the singer and band-leader Rudy Vallée (1901–1986).

151.19 Evander] Evander Childs High School in the Bronx.

164.18–19 South Kent . . . Westover."] Connecticut boarding schools in South Kent and Middlebury, respectively.

166.22 the Brearley] The Brearley School, private girls' school on East 83rd Street in Manhattan.

167.9 "LaRue's,"] See note 119.15–16.

169.24–25 "Do It Again," a danceable number of 1922.] With music com-posed by George Gershwin (1898–1937), lyrics by Buddy DeSylva (1895–1950).

179.17 Ichabod] After Ichabod Crane, the tall and physically awkward protag-onist of Washington Irving's story "The Legend of Sleepy Hollow" (1820).

181.9–10 wearing a Delta Tau Delta pin . . . Psi U.] A woman wearing a fra-ternity pin indicated that she was in a committed relationship with one of its members.

181.23 gone to the Mexican Border in 1916] After supporters of Mexican revo-lutionary Pancho Villa (Doroteo Arango Arámbula, 1878–1923) killed twenty-four Americans during a raid on Columbus, New Mexico, on March 9, 1916, a punitive expedition commanded by Brigadier General John J. Pershing (1860–1948) entered Mexico on March 15. Tensions increased after twelve American cavalrymen were killed and twenty-three taken prisoner at Carrizal on June 21 while fighting troops loyal to President Carranza, but the prisoners were released on July 1 and war was averted. The last U.S. troops left Mexico on February 5, 1917, with Villa still at large.

181.26 Croix de Guerre with palm.] French military medal ("war cross") instituted in 1915, which could also be awarded to members of allied armed forces; the bronze palm on the medal's ribbon indicates a mention of valor in an army dispatch.

183.3–4 another generation called Cloud 90] O'Hara's biographer Matthew J. Bruccoli records the following exchange between O'Hara and his editor at Random House, Albert Erskine: "When Erskine queried the expression 'Cloud 90' in *Sermons and Soda-Water*, citing *The Dictionary of American Slang* as authority as the source for 'Cloud 7,' O'Hara's reaction was: 'Cloud 90. And don't cite dictionaries to me, on dialog of the vernacular. Dictionary people consult me, not I them.'" Bruccoli, *The O'Hara Concern*, p. 266.

191.11 "noble"] In his speech accepting the Republican nomination for president, August 11, 1928, Herbert Hoover referred to Prohibition as "a great social and economic experiment, noble in motive and far-reaching in purpose."

191.35 the losing, not the lost, generation.] Reference to Gertrude Stein's characterization of the generation who had come of age during World War I, quoted as the epigraph to Ernest Hemingway's *The Sun Also Rises* (1926): "You are all a lost generation."

199.19–20 Sportsman's Bracer chocolate] Sportsman's Chocolate Bracer, flat cakes of chocolate marketed as a sandwich filling for hunters and other outdoorsmen, manufactured by New York City's Knickerbocker Chocolate Company.

199.26 Blair Academy] Boarding school in Blairstown, New Jersey.

199.27 Pierce-Arrows] Luxury cars made by the Pierce-Arrow Motor Car Company from 1903 to 1938.

200.27 "Body and Soul"] Jazz standard (1930), music by Johnny Green (1908–1989), lyrics by Edward Heyman (1907–1981), Robert Sour (1905–1985), and Frank Eyton (1894–1962).

210.16 Jeeves] Valet to the gentleman Bertie Wooster in stories by the English comic novelist, playwright, and lyricist P. G. Wodehouse (1881–1975).

214.26 War Production Board] Government agency established in 1942 to administer the procurement of materials for the war effort and to direct war production.

215.8 Gershwin's "Do It Again"] See note 169.24–25.

215.19–20 a Romberg tune . . . personal anthem] Popular song "When Hearts Are Young," words by Cyrus Wood (1893–1942), music by Sigmund Romberg (1887–1951), from the musical *The Lady in Ermine* (1922).

224.18 Essengial industry!] Men of draft age working in an "essential indus-try" during World War II were eligible for draft deferments.

224.19 4-F] Draft-board designation for those deemed unfit for military ser-vice.

239.39 Paramounts] Automobiles manufactured by the British company Para-mount Cars in the 1950s.

241.3 another Fatty Arbuckle case] Roscoe "Fatty" Arbuckle (1887–1933), si-lent film comedian, was tried three times for manslaughter in the death of Vir-ginia Rappe (1895–1921), whom he was accused of raping at a party he hosted in 1921. The legal proceedings against Arbuckle were widely publicized. Al-though after two mistrials he was acquitted by the jury with an apology for what they considered a gross injustice given the entire lack of evidence against him, his career was destroyed.

241.30 *My Fair Lady*] Musical (1956) by Alan Jay Lerner (1918–1986) and Frederick Loewe (1901–1988), based on George Bernard Shaw's play *Pygma-lion* (1913).

243.14 Ralph Kramden] Husband in the popular television comedy *The Hon-eymooners* (1955–56), played by Jackie Gleason (1916–1987).

244.9–10 delusions of Laurette Taylor in *Menagerie.*] Stage actor Laurette Taylor (1884–1946) was critically acclaimed for her performance in the in-augural Broadway production of Tennessee Williams's *The Glass Menagerie* (1944) after an absence of several years from the stage.

244.11 Camp Fire-y"] Reference to the Camp Fire Girls of America, youth or-ganization established in 1910 as a companion group to the recently founded Boy Scouts of America.

247.11–12 Foxcroft . . . St. Mark's.] College preparatory schools: the Foxcroft School, school for girls near Middleburg, Virginia, and St. Mark's School, in Southborough, Massachusetts.

248.15 lovely British movie] *Laxdale Hall* (1953), also known as *Scotch on the Rocks*, British comedy directed by John Eldridge (1917–1960) and starring Ronald Squire (1886–1958) and Kathleen Ryan (1922–1985).

248.21 "Men of Harlech" in the Welsh] The popular war song "March of the Men of Harlech" celebrates Welsh military glory. Harlech Castle was the site of a long siege during the Wars of the Roses, in which Yorkists laid siege to the fortress for several years before its defenders were forced to capitulate because of starvation.

255.40–256.1 Jim Fisk and Dan Drew and Gould] American financiers James Fisk Jr. (1834–1872), Daniel Drew (1797–1879), and Jay Gould (1836–1892).

257.25 Tuxedo] Tuxedo Park, exclusive community north of New York City.

259.20 John Held's] John Held Jr. (1889–1958), American cartoonist who helped create the image of 1920s Jazz Age youth.

260.31 "Art Hickman, Ted Lewis, and Markel's orchestra."] The bandleaders Art Hickman (1886–1930) and Ted Lewis (1890–1971); band led by pianist Mike Markel.

260.37 Louis Sherry."] Restaurateur and caterer (1885–1926), whose business was patronized by New York's elite.

261.8 Rum Row] Prohibition-era name for areas just outside the limits of U.S. territorial waters where ships smuggling alcohol congregated because they could not be searched or seized by the Coast Guard; smaller, faster boats would deliver their illegal cargo to shore.

262.19 McGraw] Hall of Fame baseball player and manager John J. McGraw (1873–1934), who managed the New York Giants from 1902 to 1932.

262.30 International League, Binghamton] A slight anachronism: the Binghamton Bingoes in professional baseball's International League folded in 1919.

263.15 Frank Hague] Democratic Party boss Frank Hague (1876–1956), mayor of Jersey City, New Jersey, 1917–47.

267.12–13 Maxfield Parrish . . . Sheeler.] American artists Maxfield Parrish (1870–1966), George Luks (1867–1933), and Charles Sheeler (1883–1965).

268.14–15 Jules Bache] American financier and art collector (1861–1944).

271.31 Delco plant] An electric generator.

277.5 Zuleika Dobson] Novel (1911) by English novelist, essayist, and caricaturist Max Beerbohm (1872–1956).

288.21 Frank Kramer] Champion American cyclist (1880–1958).

304.7 Guadal] Guadalcanal, island in the Solomon Islands, site of a U.S. victory over the Japanese in February 1943 after six months of fighting.

304.18 Austin-Healey] British sports car manufacturer.

308.21 Quantico] Marine Corps base in northeastern Virginia.

318.13–14 in the Admiralties] Fighting to drive out Japanese forces on the Admiralty Islands in the western Pacific north of Papua New Guinea, February 29–March 18, 1944.

318.15 Seabees] Common name for the United States Naval Construction Battalions.

318.23 Groton] Private boarding school in Groton, Massachusetts.

319.13 Norfolk suit] A pleated tweed jacket worn with knickerbockers.

320.17 Morgan-Harjes Unit during the war] Ambulance corps of about two hundred Americans attached to the French Army during World War I.

320.33 U. P.] The United Press news agency.

327.3 Andover] Phillips Academy in Andover, Massachusetts.

328.26 Belleau Wood] World War I battle, June 1–26, 1918, near Château Thierry, France, an American victory won with heavy casualties.

329.1 Distinguished Service Cross] U.S. Army medal for valor.

330.31 Cunningham] The firm of James Cunningham, Son and Company, based in Rochester, New York, an early manufacturer of luxury automobiles.

332.2–3 like the rich on the North Shore, or maybe more like Aiken] The North Shore of Long Island, New York, and Aiken, South Carolina, site of a popular resort for wealthy visitors in wintertime.

332.5 Westbury] Town on the North Shore of Long Island.

337.2 big Packard Twin-Six] Luxury automobile manufactured by the Packard Motor Car Company, named for its V-12 engine.

341.9 "Rose of the Rio Grande,"] Song (1922) by Ross Gorman (c. 1890–1953), Edgar Leslie (1885–1976), and Harry Warren (1893–1981).

341.11–12 *was* about Chinese—"Limehouse Blues."] Song, words by Douglas Furber (1885–1961) and music by Philip Braham (1881–1934), originally popularized by Gertrude Lawrence (1898–1952) in the musical revue *A to Z* (1921).

London's Limehouse district bordering the Thames was home to a Chinese community, sung about in the song.

341.21 Terrible-Tempered Mr. Bangs.] Comic character created by the syndicated cartoonist Fontaine Fox (1884–1964).

342.38 "Stumbling"] Hit song (1922), words and music by composer, arranger, and pianist Zez Confrey (1895–1971), often performed as an instrumental, as in the version by Paul Whiteman and his orchestra.

347.15 M-G's] Sports car manufactured by the British automotive company MG.

347.27 Mr. McCaffery] Radio and television newscaster, quiz-show host, and author John K. M. McCaffrey (1913–1983), host from 1952 to 1963 of *11th Hour News* on New York's WNBC-TV, which opened with the phrase, "What kind of a day has it been?"

348.7–8 Mary Roberts Rinehart] American fiction writer and playwright (1876–1958), author of many mystery novels, including *The Circular Staircase* (1908), *Where There's a Will* (1912), and *The Case of Jennie Brice* (1913).

355.5 at Farmington."] Miss Porter's School, elite boarding school in Farmington, Connecticut.

362.19 Adele Astaire] American dancer and actor (1896–1981) who performed with her younger brother Fred as a child and as a vaudeville and stage performer.

362.22–23 'I lahv . . . neeface.'"] From "Funny Face," song with music by George Gershwin, lyrics by Ira Gershwin (1896–1983) from the musical (1927) of the same title. Fred and Adele Astaire starred in its opening Broadway run.

378.21 Kew Gardens] Neighborhood in Queens in New York City.

380.19 "the last call to the diner,"] Standard announcement that food service in a train's dining car would soon end.

380.19 *l'age dangereux*] The age of forty ("the dangerous age" in French); the title of a novel (1910), later adapted for the screen, by Danish writer Karin Michaëlis (1872–1950) about a divorced forty-year-old woman's relationship with a younger man.

392.36 Errol Flynn] Australian-born screen star (1909–1959), known for his roles as the swashbuckling heroes of films such as *Captain Blood* (1935) and *The Sea Hawk* (1940) and for the excesses of his personal life.

393.34–36 All-American?" . . . Walter Camp] In 1889, Yale football coach, promoter, writer, and rules reformer Walter Camp (1859–1925) originated the annual All-America Team for college football, a list of players deemed the best at their position in a given year, and for many years selected the team.

404.24 Pierce-Arrows] See note 199.27.

404.26 Marmons, Packards] Automobiles manufactured by Marmon Motor Car Company of Indianapolis, Indiana, which made luxury automobiles from 1902 to 1933, and by the Packard Motor Car Company, automobile manufacturer from 1899 through the 1950s.

405.13–14 Dario Resta and the brothers Chevrolet] Italian-born English champion auto racer Dario Resta (1884–1924), and the three Swiss immigrant brothers to the United States who were auto racers as well as automobile-company founders and executives: Louis (1878–1941), Arthur (1884–1946), and Gaston (1892–1920).

405.26 Simplexes] Luxury automobiles manufactured by the Simplex Automobile Company (after 1915, the Crane-Simplex Company) from 1904 to 1922.

405.28 Hispanos and Blitzen-Benzes.] Luxury automobiles made by the Spanish firm Hispano-Suiza; race cars manufactured by the Benz & Company in Germany.

406.15 Upper Darby] Suburb bordering Philadelphia to the west.

408.18 Mercer phaeton] Luxury car manufactured by the Mercer Automobile Company.

414.13–14 National Guard for Mexican Border service] See note 181.23.

414.15–16 Croix de Guerre with palm during his A.E.F. service.] See note 181.26. A.E.F.: American Expeditionary Force.

416.14 "Bambalina,"] Hit song (1923), music by Vincent Youmans (1898–1946), words by Herbert Stothart (1885–1949), Otto Harbach (1873–1963), and Oscar Hammerstein II (1895–1960), from the musical *Wildflower*.

419.10 Chrysler "70"] Six-cylinder automobile manufactured and sold by Chrysler, 1925–27.

419.38 'A stranger in a strange land,'] Exodus 2:22.

435.27 'Ukulele Lady'] Popular song (1925), words by Gus Kahn (1886–1941), music by Richard A. Whiting (1891–1938).

436.4 "Yaaka hula hickey dula,"] Popular song, words and music by E. Ray Goetz (1886–1954), Joe Young (1889–1939), and Pete Wendling (1888–1974) from the musical *Robinson Crusoe, Jr.* (1916), in which it was first performed by Al Jolson.

446.34 Hancock."] Fort Hancock, coastal army post and training area in Sandy Hook, New Jersey.

448.33 Triangle Club] Drama group at Princeton University.

448.35 Sheff] Yale University's Sheffield Scientific School.

457.13 His daughter's illness.] Hawthorne's daughter Una (1844–1877) contracted malaria in the winter of 1858 and was ill for several months.

466.18–19 Pine Valley . . . Thomasville.] Pine Valley Golf Club in southern New Jersey, generally considered among the best golf courses in America, with highly restricted access; the Glen Arven Country Club in the resort town of Thomasville, Georgia.

470.8–9 course at Elizabeth Arden] Health retreat of Canadian-born cosmetics and beauty entrepreneur Elizabeth Arden (pseud. Florence Graham, 1878–1966) on her Maine Chance Farm estate in Maine; there was also a branch in Arizona.

471.26 Hammacher's."] New York City hardware store Hammacher, Schlemmer & Co.

479.27 Wills-Ste. Claire] Luxury car manufactured by the C. H. Wills Co., 1921–26.

482.19 *malade à domicile*] French: someone confined to the house because of illness.

488.22 "Weep not . . . children"] Cf. Luke 23:28.

489.9 two-tune medley of "I Love You Truly"] Song originally part of *Seven Songs as Unpretentious as the Wild Rose* (c. 1901) by American songwriter Carrie Jacobs-Bond (1862–1946).

489.9–10 "Get Me to the Church on Time"] Song with words by Alan Jay Lerner and music by Frederick Loewe from the musical *My Fair Lady* (1956).

489.14–15 "From This Moment On"] Song (1950) by Cole Porter (1891–1964).

489.15 the cadence of the Society Bounce] Fast tempo known as "Society Tempo" or "Businessman's Bounce."

490.7 A. T. Harris cutaway."] Tuxedo from A. T. Harris Formalwear, high-end clothing store on East 44th Street near Fifth Avenue in Manhattan.

494.3–4 Booth Tarkington and Louis Bromfield] American novelist, story writer, and dramatist Booth Tarkington (1869–1946), whose novels included *The Magnificent Ambersons* (1918) and *Alice Adams* (1921); American novelist Louis Bromfield (1896–1956), author of *The Green Bay Tree* (1924; alluded to in the reference to the "Shaynes" at 494.28) and *Early Autumn* (1926).

494.14 Locomobile.] Luxury car manufactured by the Connecticut-based Locomobile Company of America.

497.10 Pierce-Arrow] See note 199.27.

497.15 'Country Gardens.'] English folk song best known in the arrangement (1918) of Australian-born composer Percy Grainger (1882–1961).

502.17–18 Knights of Pythias] Fraternal organization founded in 1864.

517.3–4 première at the Chinese or the Egyptian or the Carthay Circle.] Lavish Los Angeles movie theaters: Grauman's Chinese Theatre at 6925 Hollywood Boulevard, Grauman's Egyptian Theatre at 6706 Hollywood Boulevard, and the Carthay Circle Theatre at 6316 San Vicente Boulevard.

517.5 Duesenberg.] Luxury car manufactured by the Duesenberg Automobile & Motors Company, 1913–37.

517.9 *What Price Hollywood?*] Film (1934) directed by George Cukor (1899–1983) and starring Constance Bennett (1904–1965) and Lowell Sherman (1888–1934).

517.12 Brown Derby] Chain of Los Angeles restaurants of which the first opened on Wilshire Boulevard in 1926. Its Hollywood branch was located at 1628 North Vine Street, 1926–85.

517.15 "Parlez-moi d'amour"] Song (1930) by French composer and songwriter Jean Lenoir (1891–1976).

517.17 Bill Powell] American actor William Powell (1892–1984), star of *The Great Ziegfeld* (1936), *My Man Godfrey* (1936), and six movies in the Thin Man series (1934–47) playing Dashiell Hammett's detective Nick Charles.

517.37 Dick Barthelmess] American movie actor Richard Barthelmess (1895–1963), whose films included *Broken Blossoms* (1919), *Way Down East* (1920), *Tol'able David* (1921), and *Only Angels Have Wings* (1939).

518.28 Catalina] Catalina Island, off the Southern California coast.

518.35 Barker body] The British coachmaker Barker & Co. made the body and interior of many Rolls-Royce automobiles from 1905 to 1938, when it was taken over by Hooper & Co., one of its rivals.

518.36 Sidney Gainsborough] Fictional character of O'Hara's who had previously been a movie publicist in his 1932 short story "Sidney Gainsborough, Quality Pictures."

519.9 Tom Mix] American movie actor (1880–1940) who starred in Westerns mostly during the silent era.

519.10 This Taylor girl] American actor Elizabeth Taylor (1932–2011).

519.11 Mary Pickford] Canadian-born silent movie actor (1892–1979), known as "America's Sweetheart," star of *Rebecca of Sunnybrook Farm* (1917) and *Daddy Long-Legs* (1919).

519.14 Ronnie Colman] See note 142.37–143.1.

519.14–15 Warner Baxter] American movie actor (1889–1951) of the late silent and early sound eras, who played the Cisco Kid in the Western *In Old Arizona* (1929).

520.35 Stutz Bearcat or a Mercer Raceabout] Sports cars of the 1910s and 1920s, manufactured by the Stutz Motor Company and the Mercer Automobile Company, respectively.

522.12 Alfred Lunt] American stage actor (1892–1977), one half of a popular husband-and-wife duo with wife Lynn Fontanne (1887–1983).

527.1 Moss Hart] American playwright and director (1904–1961), whose hit plays included *You Can't Take It With You* (1936) and *The Man Who Came to Dinner* (1939), both coauthored with George S. Kaufman (1889–1961).

527.1 Dwight Wiman] Broadway producer (1895–1951), who had been an actor in the silent era.

527.5–6 Dolores del Rio . . . Cedric Gibbons.] Mexican actor Dolores del Río (1905–1983), glamorous film star of the late silent era, was married to

Hollywood art director Cedric Gibbons (1893–1960) from 1930 until their divorce in 1941.

527.6 Fay Wray.] American actor (1907–2004), best known for her starring role in *King Kong* (1933).

527.7 Mrs. Samuel.] Frances Goldwyn (née Howard, 1903–1976), second wife of movie producer Samuel Goldwyn (1882–1974).

527.7–8 Dear Bill Powell and Carole Lombard.] Bill Powell, see note 517.17. His wife from 1931 to 1933, American comic actor Carol Lombard (1908–1942), starred in films including *Twentieth Century* (1934) and *My Man Godfrey* (1936).

527.12–13 he and the little Mexican girl, Lupe Velez, they were quite a thing] Mexican actor Lupe Vélez (1908–1944) became involved with American actor Gary Cooper (1901–1961) after they met as costars of the film *Wolf Song* (1929).

528.8–10 one filly ever won the Derby . . . Regret.] Regret won the Kentucky Derby in 1915.

531.26 *jeunesse dorée.*"] French: gilded youth.

535.39 Steve Brown . . . recently gone from Goldkette to Whiteman] Bass player Steve Brown (born Theodore Brown, 1890–1965) left Jean Goldkette's band and joined the Paul Whiteman Orchestra in 1927.

536.37 Lily Pons."] French-born American coloratura soprano (1898–1976), a principal soprano at New York's Metropolitan Opera, 1931–60.

536.39 Harry Goldfield. Or Busse."] Russian-born trumpet player Harry Goldfield (c. 1898–1948), for many years a member of Paul Whiteman's orchestra; German-born Henry Busse (1894–1955), also a trumpet player for Whiteman's orchestra before forming his own band in 1928.

537.2 "Armstrong?"] Jazz trumpeter, singer, and composer Louis Armstrong (1901–1971).

537.24 Mound City Blue Blowers?] Novelty jazz group from St. Louis cofounded by Red McKenzie (1899–1948), who played comb and kazoo and sang.

537.33 Smith Ballew] Singer, bandleader, and movie actor (1902–1984).

537.35 Vallee?] Rudy Vallée (see note 151.16–17).

538.4 red Jordan Playboy] Sports car introduced in 1919 by the Jordan Motor Car Company.

538.15 Marmon] See note 404.26.

538.20 with Fletch.] In the jazz band led by pianist, arranger, and composer Fletcher Henderson (1897–1952).

542.39 'Body and Soul' . . . Johnny Green] See note 200.27.

543.5–6 'Always,' or 'My Blue Heaven.'] Popular songs "Always" (1925), music and lyrics by Irving Berlin (1888–1989); "My Blue Heaven," music by Walter Donaldson (1893–1947), lyrics by George A. Whiting (1884–1943), first a hit for singer Gene Austin in 1928.

543.23 Roosevelt Grill."] Restaurant and jazz club in New York's Hotel Roosevelt, on Madison Avenue at 45th Street.

543.30 muggles] Marijuana cigarettes.

544.22–23 Phil Ohman] Ragtime pianist, composer, and bandleader (1896–1954), member of a popular piano duo with Victor Arden (born Lewis John Fuiks, 1893–1962), 1922–32.

544.30 Dick McDonough] Jazz guitarist and banjo player (1904–1938).

550.7 Air Medal] U.S. military award instituted in 1942 for heroism while participating in aerial flight, though "not of a degree that would justify an award of the Distinguished Flying Cross," the most prestigious medal given for heroism in flight.

550.10 D.F.C.] Distinguished Flying Cross.

552.36 Glen Gray] Bandleader and saxophonist (1906–1963) who led the popular jazz dance band the Glen Gray Casa Loma Orchestra, 1927–63.

557.2 Sixty Special] Luxury car introduced by Cadillac in 1938.

559.3–4 Cesar Romero] American stage, movie, and television actor (1907–1994) who played the Cisco Kid in a series of Westerns, 1939–41, and starred in films such as *Wee Willie Winkie* (1937) and *Captain from Castile* (1947).

559.6 'Washboard Blues.'] Jazz song (1926) by Hoagy Carmichael (1899–1981), Fred Callahan (1893–1959), and Irving Mills, a hit recording for the Paul Whiteman Orchestra.

559.12 'Blue Lou.'] See note 124.23.

559.13 'Stop, Look and Listen.'] Jazz song (1936) by Ralph Freed (1907–1973) and George Van Eps (1913–1998), recorded by the bands of Tommy Dorsey and Paul Whiteman, among others.

559.15 'Helen Gone.'] Song recorded by Vincent Rose and His Montmartre Orchestra in 1924, with words by Harry Owen, music by Vincent Rose (1880–1944) and Buster Johnson.

560.6–7 'Stairway to Paradise.'] "I'll Build a Stairway to Paradise" (1922), music by George Gershwin, words by Buddy DeSylva and Ira Gershwin (writing under the pseudonym Arthur Francis), first featured in the revue *George White's Scandals* of 1922.

560.37–38 Hoagy . . . Beiderbecke] American composer, pianist, singer, and entertainer Hoagy Carmichael; jazz cornetist and composer Bix Beiderbecke (1903–1931).

560.39 'In a Mist,'] Composition (1927) by Bix Beiderbecke.

562.24 'Lazybones,'] Song (1934), music by Hoagy Carmichael, words by Johnny Mercer (1909–1976).

565.31 Joe Sullivan] Jazz pianist (1906–1971) who played with Louis Armstrong, Benny Goodman, and as accompanist for Bing Crosby, among others.

566.4 "'All in the Game,' Tommy Dorsey made a cut of it,"] An arrangement of the instrumental "Melody in A Major" (1911), written by Charles G. Dawes (1865–1951), later vice president in the Coolidge administration, was recorded by Tommy Dorsey and His Orchestra in 1943; a 1951 version entitled "It's All in the Game" with lyrics by Carl Sigman (1909–2000) has been frequently recorded.

566.8–9 Rube Bloom] American songwriter, pianist, and bandleader (1902–1976) whose compositions included "Sapphire (A Musical Gem)" (1927) and "Soliloquy (A Musical Thought)" (1927).

574.27 the execution of the Mollie Maguires] Twenty members of the "Molly Maguires," a secret society of Irish coal miners who engaged in violence against mine owners and operators, were hanged in 1877–79 after being convicted of ten murders committed between 1862 and 1875.

599.22–23 the old Romanoff's, the new Romanoff's] Romanoff's, Beverly Hills restaurant located at 362 Rodeo Drive from 1941 to 1951, when it opened in a new location nearby at 240 North Rodeo Drive.

599.23 at 21 and Elmer's, the Copa] "21," see note 6.38; Elmer's, nickname for El Morocco (see note 123.25); the Copa, see note 147.4–5.

599.24 the Chez in Chicago] Chez Paree, popular cabaret and nightclub of the 1930s, '40s, and '50s at 610 North Fairbanks Court.

599.25–26 the Savoy and the 400 in London, Maxim's and the Boeuf in Paris] The Savoy Hotel in London's West End, and the exclusive 400 Club in Leicester Square; Maxim's restaurant and the cabaret Le Boeuf sur le Toit (The Ox on the Roof), both in the eighth arrondissement in Paris.

602.6–7 the Statler] Bar at the Statler Hotel, at 1001 16th Street NW in Washington, D.C.

602.8 Ted Straeter's band.] Big band led by American pianist Ted Straeter (1914–1963).

602.11–12 'More Than You Know,'] Song (1929), music by Vincent Youmans (1898–1946), words by Billy Rose (1899–1966) and Edward Eliscu (1902–1998).

602.13 'So in Love.'] Song by Cole Porter from the musical *Kiss Me, Kate* (1948).

602.20 'Een like Fleen,'] "In like Flynn," phrase said to have originated as a reference to the Democratic Party machine's political dominance of the Bronx under the leadership of "Boss" Ed Flynn (1891–1953); it is also associated with actor Errol Flynn (see note 392.36).

603.2 Eddy Duchin] Jazz pianist and bandleader (1909–1951).

604.2–3 Fletcher Henderson] See note 538.20.

609.19 belt one like the Merm] Singer and stage actor Ethel Merman (1908–1984), star of *Annie Get Your Gun* (1946), *Gypsy* (1959), and other musicals, was known for her vigorous, exuberant singing.

609.22 a. and r. men] Artist-and-repertoire men, record-company employees who signed and worked with musicians and produced their recordings.

609.25 Peggy Lee did with 'Lover.'] Jazz singer Peggy Lee (1920–2002) had a hit song in 1952 with her version of "Lover" (1932), music by Richard Rodgers (1902–1979), words by Lorenz Hart (1895–1943).

609.27 Ella] Jazz singer Ella Fitzgerald (1917–1996), who recorded a version of "Lover" in 1956.

609.28 Eydie Gormé] Jazz and popular-music singer Eydie Gormé (1928–2013), who had hits as a solo artist as well as in a duo with her husband Steve Lawrence (b. 1935).

615.30–31 Craig Kennedy, the scientific detective . . . Hand.] Craig Kennedy was the detective hero of many stories and novels written by Arthur B. Reeve (1880–1936) starting in 1910; his nemesis was a master criminal known as "The Clutching Hand."

616.12–13 danced with Constance Bennett . . . Pre Cat] Constance Bennett (1904–1965), socialite and movie star whose films included *Born to Love* (1931) and *What Price Hollywood?* (1932); the Pre Catalan, New York nightclub on West 39th Street.

622.26–27 F.P.A.'s Conning Tower] Syndicated column by journalist and humorist Franklin P. Adams (1881–1960).

630.33–36 Bellefonte . . . Where the electric chair is?] Facility now called the State Correctional Institution Rockview, site where Pennsylvania's executions are carried out, located six miles south of Bellefonte in the center of the state.

633.29 opera-lengths.] Evening gloves.

633.37–634.2 Myrna Loy . . . Joan Blondell . . . Jean Arthur.] Movie actors Myrna Loy (1905–1993), most famous for her portrayal of Nora Charles in the Thin Man movies of the 1930s; Joan Blondell (1906–1979), who had roles in *Night Nurse* (1931), *Three on a Match* (1932), and other films; and Jean Arthur (c. 1905–1991), whose films included *The Whole Town's Talking* (1935), *Mr. Deeds Goes to Town* (1936), and *The More the Merrier* (1943).

634.20–21 Marie Dressler] Popular comic actor of vaudeville, stage, and screen (1868–1934) who starred in the title role of Tugboat Annie (1933).

635.3–5 producer jobs . . . Benny Thau's,"] Louis B. Mayer (1884–1957), American movie mogul, cofounder and head of MGM Studios, 1924–51; MGM executives Eddie Mannix (1891–1963) and Benny Thau (1898–1983).

635.9–11 Beverly Derby . . . downtown] Branches of the Brown Derby restaurant chain, see note 517.12; the Hollywood restaurant Al Levy's Tavern, at 1623 North Vine Street; the Vendome, nightclub at 6666 Sunset Boulevard; Mike Lyman's Grill at 751 South Hill Street in downtown Los Angeles.

635.19 Legion Stadium] Venue for boxing and wrestling matches at 1628 El Centro Avenue, 1919–59.

636.14–15 Ruby Keeler . . . Claudette Colbert] Ruby Keeler (1909–1993), a featured dancer in the 1928 Ziegfeld Follies and later a film actor; French-born movie actor Claudette Colbert (1903–1996), star of *The Smiling Lieutenant* (1931), *It Happened One Night* (1934), and other films.

638.37–38 Herbert Marshall, the English actor.] See note 142.37–143.1.

640.7 "Big-hearted Otis"] Name of comic strip (1927–28) created by writer and artist Fred Fox (1903–1981), referring to its central character, Otis Galahad Gay.

640.16–17 that drunken director that killed three people down in Santa Monica] On the night of September 8, 1935, choreographer and film director Busby Berkeley (1895–1976) caused a three-car collision while driving erratically on the Roosevelt Highway in Santa Monica. One woman was killed instantly, and two others died later of injuries sustained in the crash. Several other people, including Berkeley, were seriously injured. Charged with second-degree murder, Berkeley was acquitted in September 1936 after two mistrials. Witnesses in the trial testified that he had been intoxicated at the time of the accident.

649.19 William Powell and Myrna Loy] Stars of several films in the Thin Man series (see notes 517.17 and 633.36–634.2).

652.12 Robert Taylor] American actor (1911–1969), whose films included *Camille* (1936), *Waterloo Bridge* (1940), and *Undercurrent* (1946).

656.8 the Algonquin] Restaurant at the Algonquin Hotel, at 59 West 44th Street in New York City.

658.29–30 Hays Office] The Motion Picture Producers and Distributors of America, often called the "Hays Office" after its head from 1922 to 1945, Will H. Hays (1879–1954). In 1930 it adopted a production code regulating the moral content of movies, which remained in effect until 1966.

659.40 L. B. Mayer's.] See note 635.3–5.

660.37–38 'Man's love . . . woman's whole existence.'] Cf. Byron, *Don Juan* (1819), canto I, st. 194–95.

664.4 *Sketch*] *The Sketch* (1893–1959), English illustrated weekly of upper-class life and leisure.

664.13 the M.C., the Military Cross] British military award for officers and warrant officers instituted in 1914.

665.11 Mayfair boys] The Mayfair Playboys, English gang of thieves that included several upper-class young men.

665.15–16 Miller Brothers-101 Ranch Circus] Traveling Wild West show organized by Joseph Miller (d. 1927) and his brothers Zachary (1878–1952) and George Lee (d. 1929), first presented in 1907. Since 1893 the Miller family had operated its 101 Ranch in Oklahoma.

665.38 A Chic Sales.] An outhouse. American actor and vaudevillian Charles "Chic" Sale (1885–1936) was the author of *The Specialist* (1929), a play about an outhouse builder.

670.32 Gaumont-British] British film production and distribution company.

674.12–13 Lionel Barrymore] American stage and movie actor and director (1878–1954) whose films included *A Free Soul* (1931), *Young Dr. Kildare* (1938), and *It's a Wonderful Life* (1946).

674.14 Mr. Schenck] Russian-born movie executive Nicholas Schenck (1881–1969).

674.14–15 Wally Beery] American actor Wallace Beery (1885–1949) with starring roles in films such as *Min and Bill* (1930) and *The Champ* (1931).

683.38 Leo McCarey] American director, screenwriter, and producer (1898–1969), whose films included the Marx Brothers' movie *Duck Soup* (1933), *The Awful Truth* (1937), and *An Affair to Remember* (1957).

698.23 the Troc] Cafe Trocadero, glamorous nightclub at 8610 Sunset Boulevard from 1934 to 1946.

704.12 goniff] Yiddish: thief.

720.20 a DeLaval.] Hand-operated cream separator.

731.11 Pierce-Arrow] See note 199.27.

731.12 Cunningham 8] Eight-cylinder car manufactured by James Cunningham, Son and Company. See note 330.31.

732.12 Garfords] Trucks manufactured by the Garford Motor Truck Company, founded in Ohio in 1909.

732.12–13 American LaFrances and Whites] Firefighting vehicles produced by the American LaFrance Fire Engine Company and the White Motor Company.

732.13 Franklins] Luxury cars manufactured by the Franklin Automobile Company, based in Syracuse.

732.36–37 Brewster brougham] Carriage made by the American coach builder Brewster & Company.

742.20 Leo G. Carroll or Arthur Treacher] English movie and television actors Leo G. Carroll (1886–1972), who played roles in several films by Alfred Hitchcock, and Arthur Treacher (1894–1975), whose film characters included the valet Jeeves (see note 210.16).

747.38 Wallace Reid?] See note 24.38.

749.9–11 Mr. DeMille . . . slaves.] Director Cecil B. DeMille (1881–1959) was known for his lavish film epics set in biblical or classical antiquity.

751.17 the Hollywood Canteen] Restaurant and nightclub at 1451 Cahuenga Boulevard in Hollywood, 1942–45, that offered free food and entertainment for soldiers heading overseas and was staffed by film-industry volunteers, including many movie stars.

751.18 Lambeth Walk] English dance popularized in 1938 through the song of the same name, music by Noel Gay (1898–1954), words by Douglas Furber (1885–1961).

754.31 Typhoid Mary] Mary Mallon (1869–1938), Irish immigrant cook who carried the organism causing typhoid fever without manifesting symptoms of the disease. Vehemently denying that she was infected, Mallon spread the disease to at least fifty-three people (three fatally) while working in New York City and Long Island. After spending 1907–10 in quarantine, she continued to work as a cook and to transmit the disease. In 1915 she was returned to quarantine, where she remained for the rest of her life.

755.4 pre-meer at the Carthay Circle.] See note 517.3–4.

755.10 Vine Street Derby.] See note 517.12.

755.13–14 new Cagney, a new Tracy, a new George Raft.] American film actors often cast in tough-guy roles in the 1930s: James Cagney (1899–1986), Spencer Tracy (1900–1967), and George Raft (1895–1980).

760.17–19 Benjamin Disraeli . . . Arliss.] Among the best-known vehicles of English actor George Arliss (1868–1946) was *Disraeli*, based loosely on the life of Benjamin Disraeli (1804–1881), English novelist and Conservative prime minister. Arliss first played the role in the play's premiere in 1911, then starred in film versions of 1921 and 1929.

766.19–20 Straits Settlements] Geographically separate British colonies in Southeast Asia, 1826–46, including Penang, Dinding, Singapore, and Malacca.

766.20 Locomobile] See note 494.14.

768.38 built like an end.] Large and muscular, like a player on the offensive or defensive line in football.

771.36 St. Christopher medal] Devotional medal depicting St. Christopher, patron saint of travelers, often placed in cars.

776.38 Scripps-Booth roadster] Luxury car produced by Scripps-Booth, a Detroit-based company founded in 1913 and taken over by Chevrolet in 1917; automobiles under its name were made until 1923.

780.7–8 Oakland coupe] Automobile manufactured by the Oakland Motor Car Company, which became part of Pontiac in 1931.

788.28 the Paige] Luxury car manufactured by the Paige-Detroit Motor Car Company, 1909–27.

794.5 "Lucky Gaston,"] Reference to an old joke (usually involving someone known as Lucky Pierre) about the middle man in a sexual threesome.

796.5 Dort."] Mid-level car built by the Dort Motor Company in Flint, Michigan, 1915–24.

797.9–10 Russell Sage] Women's college in Troy, New York.

802.2 Harrigan games] A billiards game, also known as Kelly pool.

804.6–7 Kappa Betes and T.N.E.'s.] The secret societies Kappa Beta Phi and Tau Nu Epsilon, with reputations for excessive drinking.

804.7 Lock Haven] Lock Haven State Teachers College, now Lock Haven University in Lock Haven, Pennsylvania.

804.8 Mercersburg.] See note 103.33.

804.25 Safe at last in your trundle bed."] From the Dartmouth College song "Where, Oh Where Are the Pea-Green Freshmen."

804.33 Whitehouse & Hardy's] Shoes from the eponymous chain of shoe and clothing stores.

*This book is set in 10 point ITC Galliard, a face
designed for digital composition by Matthew Carter and based
on the sixteenth-century face Granjon. The paper is acid-free
lightweight opaque that will not turn yellow or brittle with age.
The binding is sewn, which allows the book to open easily and lie flat.
The binding board is covered in Brillianta, a woven rayon cloth
made by Van Heek–Scholco Textielfabrieken, Holland.
Composition by Gopa & Ted2, Inc.
Printing and binding by Edwards Brothers Malloy, Ann Arbor.
Designed by Bruce Campbell.*

THE LIBRARY OF AMERICA SERIES

The Library of America fosters appreciation of America's literary heritage by publishing, and keeping permanently in print, authoritative editions of America's best and most significant writing. An independent nonprofit organization, it was founded in 1979 with seed funding from the National Endowment for the Humanities and the Ford Foundation.

1. Herman Melville: Typee, Omoo, Mardi
2. Nathaniel Hawthorne: Tales & Sketches
3. Walt Whitman: Poetry & Prose
4. Harriet Beecher Stowe: Three Novels
5. Mark Twain: Mississippi Writings
6. Jack London: Novels & Stories
7. Jack London: Novels & Social Writings
8. William Dean Howells: Novels 1875–1886
9. Herman Melville: Redburn, White-Jacket, Moby-Dick
10. Nathaniel Hawthorne: Collected Novels
11 & 12. Francis Parkman: France and England in North America
13. Henry James: Novels 1871–1880
14. Henry Adams: Novels, Mont Saint Michel, The Education
15. Ralph Waldo Emerson: Essays & Lectures
16. Washington Irving: History, Tales & Sketches
17. Thomas Jefferson: Writings
18. Stephen Crane: Prose & Poetry
19. Edgar Allan Poe: Poetry & Tales
20. Edgar Allan Poe: Essays & Reviews
21. Mark Twain: The Innocents Abroad, Roughing It
22 & 23. Henry James: Literary Criticism
24. Herman Melville: Pierre, Israel Potter, The Confidence-Man, Tales & Billy Budd
25. William Faulkner: Novels 1930–1935
26 & 27. James Fenimore Cooper: The Leatherstocking Tales
28. Henry David Thoreau: A Week, Walden, The Maine Woods, Cape Cod
29. Henry James: Novels 1881–1886
30. Edith Wharton: Novels
31 & 32. Henry Adams: History of the U.S. during the Administrations of Jefferson & Madison
33. Frank Norris: Novels & Essays
34. W.E.B. Du Bois: Writings
35. Willa Cather: Early Novels & Stories
36. Theodore Dreiser: Sister Carrie, Jennie Gerhardt, Twelve Men

37. Benjamin Franklin: Writings (2 vols.)
38. William James: Writings 1902–1910
39. Flannery O'Connor: Collected Works
40, 41, & 42. Eugene O'Neill: Complete Plays
43. Henry James: Novels 1886–1890
44. William Dean Howells: Novels 1886–1888
45 & 46. Abraham Lincoln: Speeches & Writings
47. Edith Wharton: Novellas & Other Writings
48. William Faulkner: Novels 1936–1940
49. Willa Cather: Later Novels
50. Ulysses S. Grant: Memoirs & Selected Letters
51. William Tecumseh Sherman: Memoirs
52. Washington Irving: Bracebridge Hall, Tales of a Traveller, The Alhambra
53. Francis Parkman: The Oregon Trail, The Conspiracy of Pontiac
54. James Fenimore Cooper: Sea Tales
55 & 56. Richard Wright: Works
57. Willa Cather: Stories, Poems, & Other Writings
58. William James: Writings 1878–1899
59. Sinclair Lewis: Main Street & Babbitt
60 & 61. Mark Twain: Collected Tales, Sketches, Speeches, & Essays
62 & 63. The Debate on the Constitution
64 & 65. Henry James: Collected Travel Writings
66 & 67. American Poetry: The Nineteenth Century
68. Frederick Douglass: Autobiographies
69. Sarah Orne Jewett: Novels & Stories
70. Ralph Waldo Emerson: Collected Poems & Translations
71. Mark Twain: Historical Romances
72. John Steinbeck: Novels & Stories 1932–1937
73. William Faulkner: Novels 1942–1954
74 & 75. Zora Neale Hurston: Novels, Stories, & Other Writings
76. Thomas Paine: Collected Writings
77 & 78. Reporting World War II: American Journalism
79 & 80. Raymond Chandler: Novels, Stories, & Other Writings

81. Robert Frost: Collected Poems, Prose, & Plays

82 & 83. Henry James: Complete Stories 1892–1910

84. William Bartram: Travels & Other Writings

85. John Dos Passos: U.S.A.

86. John Steinbeck: The Grapes of Wrath & Other Writings 1936–1941

87, 88, & 89. Vladimir Nabokov: Novels & Other Writings

90. James Thurber: Writings & Drawings

91. George Washington: Writings

92. John Muir: Nature Writings

93. Nathanael West: Novels & Other Writings

94 & 95. Crime Novels: American Noir of the 1930s, 40s, & 50s

96. Wallace Stevens: Collected Poetry & Prose

97. James Baldwin: Early Novels & Stories

98. James Baldwin: Collected Essays

99 & 100. Gertrude Stein: Writings

101 & 102. Eudora Welty: Novels, Stories, & Other Writings

103. Charles Brockden Brown: Three Gothic Novels

104 & 105. Reporting Vietnam: American Journalism

106 & 107. Henry James: Complete Stories 1874–1891

108. American Sermons

109. James Madison: Writings

110. Dashiell Hammett: Complete Novels

111. Henry James: Complete Stories 1864–1874

112. William Faulkner: Novels 1957–1962

113. John James Audubon: Writings & Drawings

114. Slave Narratives

115 & 116. American Poetry: The Twentieth Century

117. F. Scott Fitzgerald: Novels & Stories 1920–1922

118. Henry Wadsworth Longfellow: Poems & Other Writings

119 & 120. Tennessee Williams: Collected Plays

121 & 122. Edith Wharton: Collected Stories

123. The American Revolution: Writings from the War of Independence

124. Henry David Thoreau: Collected Essays & Poems

125. Dashiell Hammett: Crime Stories & Other Writings

126 & 127. Dawn Powell: Novels

128. Carson McCullers: Complete Novels

129. Alexander Hamilton: Writings

130. Mark Twain: The Gilded Age & Later Novels

131. Charles W. Chesnutt: Stories, Novels, & Essays

132. John Steinbeck: Novels 1942–1952

133. Sinclair Lewis: Arrowsmith, Elmer Gantry, Dodsworth

134 & 135. Paul Bowles: Novels, Stories, & Other Writings

136. Kate Chopin: Complete Novels & Stories

137 & 138. Reporting Civil Rights: American Journalism

139. Henry James: Novels 1896–1899

140. Theodore Dreiser: An American Tragedy

141. Saul Bellow: Novels 1944–1953

142. John Dos Passos: Novels 1920–1925

143. John Dos Passos: Travel Books & Other Writings

144. Ezra Pound: Poems & Translations

145. James Weldon Johnson: Writings

146. Washington Irving: Three Western Narratives

147. Alexis de Tocqueville: Democracy in America

148. James T. Farrell: Studs Lonigan Trilogy

149, 150, & 151. Isaac Bashevis Singer: Collected Stories

152. Kaufman & Co.: Broadway Comedies

153. Theodore Roosevelt: Rough Riders, An Autobiography

154. Theodore Roosevelt: Letters & Speeches

155. H. P. Lovecraft: Tales

156. Louisa May Alcott: Little Women, Little Men, Jo's Boys

157. Philip Roth: Novels & Stories 1959–1962

158. Philip Roth: Novels 1967–1972

159. James Agee: Let Us Now Praise Famous Men, A Death in the Family, Shorter Fiction

160. James Agee: Film Writing & Selected Journalism

161. Richard Henry Dana Jr.: Two Years Before the Mast & Other Voyages

162. Henry James: Novels 1901–1902

163. Arthur Miller: Plays 1944–1961

164. William Faulkner: Novels 1926–1929

165. Philip Roth: Novels 1973–1977

166 & 167. American Speeches: Political Oratory
168. Hart Crane: Complete Poems & Selected Letters
169. Saul Bellow: Novels 1956–1964
170. John Steinbeck: Travels with Charley & Later Novels
171. Capt. John Smith: Writings with Other Narratives
172. Thornton Wilder: Collected Plays & Writings on Theater
173. Philip K. Dick: Four Novels of the 1960s
174. Jack Kerouac: Road Novels 1957–1960
175. Philip Roth: Zuckerman Bound
176 & 177. Edmund Wilson: Literary Essays & Reviews
178. American Poetry: The 17th & 18th Centuries
179. William Maxwell: Early Novels & Stories
180. Elizabeth Bishop: Poems, Prose, & Letters
181. A. J. Liebling: World War II Writings
182. American Earth: Environmental Writing Since Thoreau
183. Philip K. Dick: Five Novels of the 1960s & 70s
184. William Maxwell: Later Novels & Stories
185. Philip Roth: Novels & Other Narratives 1986–1991
186. Katherine Anne Porter: Collected Stories & Other Writings
187. John Ashbery: Collected Poems 1956–1987
188 & 189. John Cheever: Complete Novels & Collected Stories
190. Lafcadio Hearn: American Writings
191. A. J. Liebling: The Sweet Science & Other Writings
192. The Lincoln Anthology
193. Philip K. Dick: VALIS & Later Novels
194. Thornton Wilder: The Bridge of San Luis Rey & Other Novels 1926–1948
195. Raymond Carver: Collected Stories
196 & 197. American Fantastic Tales
198. John Marshall: Writings
199. The Mark Twain Anthology
200. Mark Twain: A Tramp Abroad, Following the Equator, Other Travels
201 & 202. Ralph Waldo Emerson: Selected Journals
203. The American Stage: Writing on Theater

204. Shirley Jackson: Novels & Stories
205. Philip Roth: Novels 1993–1995
206 & 207. H. L. Mencken: Prejudices
208. John Kenneth Galbraith: The Affluent Society & Other Writings 1952–1967
209. Saul Bellow: Novels 1970–1982
210 & 211. Lynd Ward: Six Novels in Woodcuts
212. The Civil War: The First Year
213 & 214. John Adams: Revolutionary Writings
215. Henry James: Novels 1903–1911
216. Kurt Vonnegut: Novels & Stories 1963–1973
217 & 218. Harlem Renaissance Novels
219. Ambrose Bierce: The Devil's Dictionary, Tales, & Memoirs
220. Philip Roth: The American Trilogy 1997–2000
221. The Civil War: The Second Year
222. Barbara W. Tuchman: The Guns of August, The Proud Tower
223. Arthur Miller: Plays 1964–1982
224. Thornton Wilder: The Eighth Day, Theophilus North, Autobiographical Writings
225. David Goodis: Five Noir Novels of the 1940s & 50s
226. Kurt Vonnegut: Novels & Stories 1950–1962
227 & 228. American Science Fiction: Nine Novels of the 1950s
229 & 230. Laura Ingalls Wilder: The Little House Books
231. Jack Kerouac: Collected Poems
232. The War of 1812
233. American Antislavery Writings
234. The Civil War: The Third Year
235. Sherwood Anderson: Collected Stories
236. Philip Roth: Novels 2001–2007
237. Philip Roth: Nemeses
238. Aldo Leopold: A Sand County Almanac & Other Writings
239. May Swenson: Collected Poems
240 & 241. W. S. Merwin: Collected Poems
242 & 243. John Updike: Collected Stories
244. Ring Lardner: Stories & Other Writings
245. Jonathan Edwards: Writings from the Great Awakening
246. Susan Sontag: Essays of the 1960s & 70s

247. William Wells Brown: Clotel & Other Writings

248 & 249. Bernard Malamud: Novels & Stories of the 1940s, 50s, & 60s

250. The Civil War: The Final Year

251. Shakespeare in America

252. Kurt Vonnegut: Novels 1976–1985

253 & 254. American Musicals 1927–1969

255. Elmore Leonard: Four Novels of the 1970s

256. Louisa May Alcott: Work, Eight Cousins, Rose in Bloom, Stories & Other Writings

257. H. L. Mencken: The Days Trilogy

258. Virgil Thomson: Music Chronicles 1940–1954

259. Art in America 1945–1970

260. Saul Bellow: Novels 1984–2000

261. Arthur Miller: Plays 1987–2004

262. Jack Kerouac: Visions of Cody, Visions of Gerard, Big Sur

263. Reinhold Niebuhr: Major Works on Religion & Politics

264. Ross Macdonald: Four Novels of the 1950s

265 & 266. The American Revolution: Writings from the Pamphlet Debate

267. Elmore Leonard: Four Novels of the 1980s

268 & 269. Women Crime Writers: Suspense Novels of the 1940s & 50s

270. Frederick Law Olmsted: Writings on Landscape, Culture, & Society

271. Edith Wharton: Four Novels of the 1920s

272. James Baldwin: Later Novels

273. Kurt Vonnegut: Novels 1987–1997

274. Henry James: Autobiographies

275. Abigail Adams: Letters

276. John Adams: Writings from the New Nation 1784–1826

277. Virgil Thomson: The State of Music & Other Writings

278. War No More: American Antiwar & Peace Writing

279. Ross Macdonald: Three Novels of the Early 1960s

280. Elmore Leonard: Four Later Novels

281. Ursula K. Le Guin: The Complete Orsinia

282. John O'Hara: Stories

283. The Unknown Kerouac: Rare, Unpublished & Newly Translated Writings

284. Albert Murray: Collect Essays & Memoirs

285 & 286. Loren Eiseley: Collected Writings on Evolution, Nature, & the Cosmos

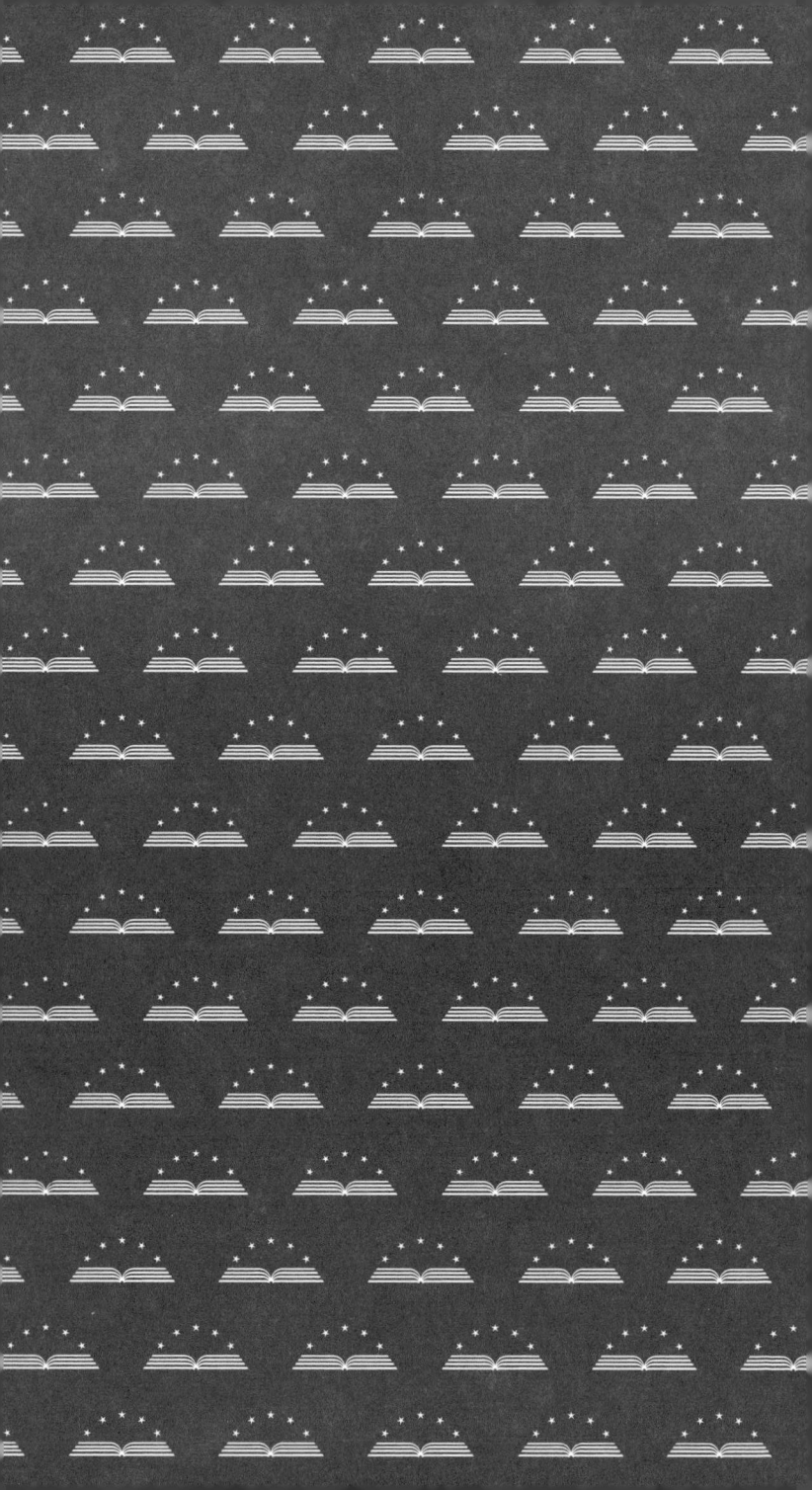